PENGUIN BOOKS

Memoirs of Hadrian

Marguerite Yourcenar was born Marguerite de Crayencour in Brussels in 1903; her mother was Belgian and her father was French. Her mother died shortly after her birth and she was brought up and educated by her father. She was reading Racine and Aristophanes by the age of eight and her father taught her Latin at ten, and Greek at twelve. When she was eighteen he paid for the publication of her first book of poetry and together they worked out her pen name – an inexact anagram of Crayencour. After her father's death when she was twenty-four, she continued to travel throughout Europe.

Her first novel *Alexis* was published in 1929; several essays and collections of stories followed and by 1939 her reputation as a writer was established. Later her great friend, the translator Grace Frick, invited her to America. There she lectured in comparative literature at Sarah Lawrence College in New York, and translated in her spare time. She also began again on *Memoirs of Hadrian* (she had burned an earlier version of the manuscript) and when the book was published in France in 1951 it was an immediate success and met with great critical acclaim.

Marguerite Yourcenar won several literary honours but in 1981 she entered the ranks of the 'Immortals' when she was elected – the first woman ever to be so – to the Académie Française. One of the most respected writers in the French language, she published many novels, several plays, critical essays, and poetry, as well as three volumes of memoirs. Her letters and journals, including her correspondence with Grace Frick, have been deposited with Harvard University, where they will remain sealed until fifty years after her death. She died in December 1988.

MARGUERITE YOURCENAR

MEMOIRS

OF

HADRIAN

AND REFLECTIONS
ON THE COMPOSITION OF
MEMOIRS OF HADRIAN

TRANSLATED FROM THE FRENCH
BY GRACE FRICK
IN COLLABORATION WITH THE AUTHOR

WITH AN INTRODUCTION BY PAUL BAILEY

PENGUIN BOOKS

PENGUIN BOOKS

Published by the Penguin Group
Penguin Books Ltd, 80 Strand, London WC2R 0RL, England
Penguin Putnam Inc., 375 Hudson Street, New York, New York 10014, USA
Penguin Books Australia Ltd, 250 Camberwell Road, Camberwell, Victoria 3124, Australia
Penguin Books Canada Ltd, 10 Alcorn Avenue, Toronto, Ontario, Canada M4V 3B2
Penguin Books India (P) Ltd, 11 Community Centre, Panchsheel Park, New Delhi – 110 017, India
Penguin Books (NZ) Ltd, Cnr Rosedale and Airborne Roads, Albany, Auckland, New Zealand
Penguin Books (South Africa) (Pty) Ltd, 24 Sturdee Avenue, Rosebank 2196, South Africa

Penguin Books Ltd, Registered Offices: 80 Strand, London WC2R 0RL, England

www.penguin.com

Mémoires d'Hadrien first published 1951
First published in the United States by Farrar, Strauss & Giroux 1954
First published in Great Britain by Martin Secker & Warburg Ltd 1955
Published in Penguin Books 1959
This edition published 1986
Reprinted in Penguin Classics 2000

031

Printed and bound in Great Britain by Clays Ltd, Elcograf S.p.A.
Typeset in 10/12pt Linotron 202 Bembo

ISBN-13: 978-0-141-18496-8
ISBN-10: 0-141-18496-5

www.greenpenguin.co.uk

CONTENTS

INTRODUCTION BY PAUL BAILEY   7

ANIMULA VAGULA BLANDULA   13

VARIUS MULTIPLEX MULTIFORMIS   35

TELLUS STABILITA   87

SAECULUM AUREUM   133

DISCIPLINA AUGUSTA   181

PATIENTIA   229

BIBLIOGRAPHICAL NOTE   249

REFLECTIONS ON THE COMPOSITION OF
MEMOIRS OF HADRIAN   267

INTRODUCTION

'The melancholy of the antique world seems to me more profound than that of the moderns, all of whom more or less imply
that beyond the dark void lies immortality. But for the ancients
that "black hole" is infinity itself; their dreams loom and vanish
against a background of immutable ebony. No crying out, no
convulsions – nothing but the fixity of a pensive gaze. Just when
the gods had ceased to be and the Christ had not yet come, there
was a unique moment in history, between Cicero and Marcus
Aurelius, when man stood alone. Nowhere else do I find that
particular grandeur.' Thus Flaubert, in an undated letter to his
friend Madame Roger des Genettes, the graceful lady who
was known as La Sylphide. It is a letter of which Marguerite
Yourcenar is especially fond. In 1927, some three years after she
first had the idea of writing about the Emperor Hadrian, she
chanced on it while leafing through a volume of Flaubert's
correspondence. She was struck by his notion of that 'unique
moment . . . when man stood alone'. 'A great part of my life was
going to be spent in trying to define, and then to portray, that man
existing alone and yet closely bound with all being,' she observes
in her 'Reflections on the Composition of *Memoirs of Hadrian*',
which are reprinted here. It was not until 1948 that she found the
assurance to move at ease in Hadrian's empire, to capture the
'fixity of a pensive gaze', to write as he might have written. The
result of that late-flowering assurance is a timeless masterpiece.

It is timeless precisely because it captures a past age – the second
century – through the mind of an extraordinary human being.
Since the lasting achievements of that age are mostly Hadrian's, it
is apposite that he should recount them. In *Memoirs of Hadrian*,
Marguerite Yourcenar rigorously eschews the piling-on of period
detail to be encountered, and endured, in the majority of historical
novels. It is the living spirit of Hadrian that concerns her; not the

pomp and pageanty of Ancient Rome. That is not to say that the pomp and pageantry are missing, rather that they are seen from a discreet perspective. Mme Yourcenar lets us know what clothes Hadrian wore, and on which occasions; what food he ate and what wine he drank; what sports and games he pursued. These, and other, necessary facts are introduced effortlessly into the flowing narrative – not highlighted; not slung in to remind the reader that the author has done her homework.

Which she has, of course. Every page of *Memoirs of Hadrian* is informed by her profound scholarship. Marguerite Yourcenar has been a classicist from childhood, and her admiration for Hadrian dates back to an early reading of Spartianus's biography of the emperor in the *Historia Augusta*. But scholarship alone does not a novel make, and all Yourcenar's efforts to create the character of Hadrian would have been in vain if she had not been possessed of a rare talent for storytelling. To remark that her fiction is French is in no way to diminish it. I cannot imagine an English novelist, of either sex, writing with a similar elegant gravity. Yourcenar herself has suggested that had she been alive in the seventeenth century she would have made her Hadrian the hero of a Racinian drama. A hundred years later, he would have been the subject of a lengthy essay. She is, in a curious sense, a traditionalist, despite the nonconformity of her homosexual heroes – Alexis, in the novel of that name; Zeno in *L'Oeuvre au Noir* (translated as *The Abyss*), and the mighty Hadrian himself. These free individuals are accounted for in prose that is exquisitely disciplined, refined to the last comma. She treasures the skeletal beauty of the French language and is angry when it is debased or misused. According to Mavis Gallant, in a most perceptive article on Yourcenar's art published in a recent edition of the *New York Review of Books*, the young in France are put off by her linguistic conservatism, which smacks to them of a rigid literariness unsuited to the contemporary world.

Yet it is that very rigidity that makes for the tension and excitement of her narrative style. I used the word 'flowing' earlier, and that is appropriate, for her spare way with words speeds the attentive reader along. Colloquialisms, especially of the 'Gadzooks' and 'Prithee, my liege' kind, are not for her. Something of that flowing spareness has been caught in the translation of *Memoirs of Hadrian* by Mme Yourcenar's friend and companion, Grace Frick, which she did in collaboration with the author. In other words, it has a Gallic flavour to it even though it has been rendered into exact and recognizable English. That awful non-language – part-American, part-English, cliché-clinkered and jargon-ridden – into which most books from Europe are translated these days is not to be met with in this loving version.

As I implied at the beginning, *Memoirs of Hadrian* is a book that took a long time to write. For many years, Marguerite Yourcenar felt inadequate to the task. Perhaps she realized that great figures from history lose their vitality, become stuffed dummies mouthing eternal platitudes, when converted into fictional characters. To try to enter the mind of a genius takes daring, or – as is the case with Irving (*The Agony and the Ecstasy*) Stone – sheer bloody cheek. In an abandoned draft of 1934, she set down the sentence that was to give her the point of view from which to have Hadrian tell his story: 'I begin to discern the profile of my death.'

A humanist herself, a sceptic by nature, Marguerite Yourcenar presents us in these memoirs with one of mankind's best friends, an architect of peace and justice as well as buildings. Written in the form of an extended letter to his successor, Marcus Aurelius, the book is Hadrian's valediction to a world that has pleased him. It opens with premonitions of his imminent decease and closes with his drifting quietly away from life, surrounded by adoring friends and servants. It is, in fact, the preparation for death, the ultimate acceptance of it, that lends to these imagined memoirs their incomparable authority, particularly in a culture like ours, where the biggest taboo is our own mortality, not sex. In *Memoirs of Hadrian*, we are reminded of the transience of human existence, and what that transcience, if properly acknowledged and re-spected, affords us. Yourcenar's Hadrian becomes strong through doubt, through his keen appreciation that truth is often partial, through his ability for self-examination. Everything is seen through Hadrian's generally unclouded eyes, the eyes that are discerning the profile of his own death. His military triumphs, his love of music and poetry, his passion for the boy Antinous, his supporters and his enemies are all remembered from the perspec-tive of death, 'against a background of immutable ebony'. What

Flaubert calls 'the melancholy of the antique world' is captured for ever in *Memoirs of Hadrian*. It is a sane, not a morbid, melancholy; a melancholy that Marguerite Yourcenar believes Western civilization is the poorer for having lost.

PAUL BAILEY

ANIMULA VAGULA, BLANDULA,
HOSPES COMESQUE CORPORIS,
QUAE NUNC ABIBIS IN LOCA
PALLIDULA, RIGIDA, NUDULA,
NEC, UT SOLES, DABIS IOCOS. . . .

P. AELIUS HADRIANUS, IMP.

ANIMULA VAGULA BLANDULA

My dear Mark,

Today I went to see my physician Hermogenes, who has just returned to the Villa from a rather long journey in Asia. No food could be taken before the examination, so we had made the appointment for the early morning hours. I took off my cloak and tunic and lay down on a couch. I spare you details which would be as disagreeable to you as to me, the description of the body of a man who is growing old, and is about to die of a dropsical heart. Let us say only that I coughed, inhaled, and held my breath according to Hermogenes' directions. He was alarmed, in spite of himself, by the rapid progress of the disease, and was inclined to throw the blame on young Iollas, who has attended me during his absence. It is difficult to remain an emperor in presence of a physician, and difficult even to keep one's essential quality as man. The professional eye saw in me only a mass of humors, a sorry mixture of blood and lymph. This morning it occurred to me for the first time that my body, my faithful companion and friend, truer and better known to me than my own soul, may be after all only a sly beast who will end by devouring his master. But enough . . . I like my body; it has served me well, and in every way, and I do not begrudge it the care it now needs. I have no faith, however, as Hermogenes still claims to have, in the miraculous virtues of herbs, or the specific mixture of mineral salts which he went to the Orient to get. Subtle though he is, he has nevertheless offered me vague formulas of reassurance too trite to deceive anyone; he knows how I hate this kind of pretense, but a man does not practice medicine for more than thirty years without some falsehood. I forgive this good servitor his endeavor to hide my death from me. Hermogenes is learned; he is even wise, and his integrity is well above that of the ordinary court physician. It will fall to my lot as a sick man to have the best of care. But no one can go beyond prescribed limits: my swollen limbs no longer sustain me through the long Roman ceremonies; I fight for breath; and I am now sixty.

Do not mistake me; I am not yet weak enough to yield to fearful imaginings, which are almost as absurd as illusions of hope, and are certainly harder to bear. If I must deceive myself, I should prefer to stay on the side of confidence, for I shall lose no more there and shall suffer less. This approaching end is not necessarily immediate; I still retire each night with hope to see the morning. Within those absolute limits of which I was just now speaking I can defend my position step by step, and even regain a few inches of lost ground. I have nevertheless reached the age where life, for every man, is accepted defeat. To say that my days are numbered signifies nothing; they always were, and are so for us all. But uncertainty as to the place, the time, and the manner, which keeps us from distinguishing the goal toward which we continually advance, diminishes for me with the progress of my fatal malady. A man may die at any hour, but a sick man knows that he will no longer be alive in ten years' time. My margin of doubt is a matter of months, not years. The chances of ending by a dagger thrust in the heart or by a fall from a horse are slight indeed; plague seems unlikely, and leprosy or cancer appear definitely left behind. I no longer run the risk of falling on the frontiers, struck down by a Caledonian axe or pierced by an arrow of the Parths; storms and tempests have failed to seize the occasions offered, and the soothsayer who told me that I should not drown seems to have been right. I shall die at Tibur or in Rome, or in Naples at the farthest, and a moment's suffocation will settle the matter. Shall I be carried off by the tenth of these crises, or the hundredth? That is the only question. Like a traveler sailing the Archipelago who sees the luminous mists lift toward evening, and little by little makes out the shore, I begin to discern the profile of my death.

Already certain portions of my life are like dismantled rooms of a palace too vast for an impoverished owner to occupy in its entirety. I can hunt no longer: if there were no one but me to disturb them in their ruminations and their play the deer in the Etrurian mountains would be at peace. With the Diana of the

forests I have always maintained the swift-changing and passionate relations which are those of a man with the object of his love:
the boar hunt gave me my first chance, as a boy, for command
and for encounter with danger; I fairly threw myself into the
sport, and my excesses in it brought reprimands from Trajan.
The kill in a Spanish forest was my earliest acquaintance with
death and with courage, with pity for living creatures and the
tragic pleasure of seeing them suffer. Grown to manhood, I
found in hunting release from many a secret struggle with adversaries too subtle or too stupid in turn, too weak or too strong
for me; this evenly matched battle between human intelligence
and the wisdom of wild beasts seemed strangely clean compared
to the snares set by men for men. My hunts in Tuscany have
helped me as emperor to judge the courage or the resources of
high officials; I have chosen or eliminated more than one statesman in this way. In later years, in Bithynia and Cappadocia, I
made the great drives for game a pretext for festival, a kind of
autumnal triumph in the woods of Asia. But the companion of
my last hunts died young, and my taste for these violent pleasures
has greatly abated since his departure. Even here in Tibur,
however, the sudden bark of a stag in the brush is enough to set
trembling within me an impulse deeper than all the rest, and by
virtue of which I feel myself leopard as well as emperor. Who
knows? Possibly I have been so sparing of human blood only
because I have shed so much of the blood of wild beasts,
even if sometimes, privately, I have preferred beasts to mankind. However that may be, they are more in my thoughts,
and it is hard not to let myself go into interminable tales of
the chase which would try the patience of my supper guests.
Surely the recollection of the day of my adoption has its
charm, but the memory of lions killed in Mauretania is not bad
either.

To give up riding is a greater sacrifice still: a wild beast is first
of all an adversary, but my horse was a friend. If the choice of
my condition had been left to me I would have decided for that
of centaur. Between Borysthenes and me relations were of almost
mathematical precision; he obeyed me as if I were his own brain,
not his master. Have I ever obtained as much from a man? Such
total authority comprises, as does any other power, its risk

of error for the possessor, but the pleasure of attempting the impossible in jumping an obstacle was too strong for me to regret a dislocated shoulder or a broken rib. My horse knew me not by the thousand approximate notions of title, function, and name which complicate human friendship, but solely by my just weight as a man. He shared my every impetus; he knew perfectly, and better perhaps than I, the point where my strength faltered under my will. But I no longer inflict upon Borysthenes' successor the burden of an invalid whose muscles are flabby, and who is too weak to heave himself, unassisted, upon a horse's back. My aide Celer is exercising him at this moment on the road to Praeneste; all my past experiments with swift motion help me now to share the pleasure both of horse and of rider, and to judge the sensations of the màn at full gallop on a day of sun and high wind. When Celer leaps down from his horse I too regain contact with the ground. It is the same for swimming: I have given it up, but I still share the swimmer's delight in water's caress. Running, even for the shortest distance, would today be as impossible for me as for a heavy statue, a Caesar of stone; but I recall my childhood races on the dry hills of Spain, and the game played with myself of pressing on to the last gasp, never doubting that the perfect heart and healthy lungs would reestablish their equilibrium; and with any athlete training for the stadium I have a common understanding which the intelligence alone would not have given me. Thus from each art practiced in its time I derive a knowledge which compensates me in part for pleasures lost. I have supposed, and in my better moments think so still, that it would be possible in this manner to participate in the existence of everyone; such sympathy would be one of the least revocable kinds of immortality. There have been moments when that comprehension tried to go beyond human experience, passing from the swimmer to the wave. But in such a realm, since there is nothing exact left to guide me, I verge upon the world of dream and metamorphosis.

Overeating is a Roman vice, but moderation has always been my delight. Hermogenes has had to change nothing in my diet, except perhaps the impatience which made me devour the first thing served, no matter where or when, in order to satisfy the needs of hunger simply and at once. It is clear that a man of wealth, who has never known anything but voluntary privation, or has experienced hunger only provisionally as one of the more or less exciting incidents of war or of travel, would have but ill grace to boast of undereating. Stuffing themselves on certain feast days has always been the ambition, joy, and natural pride of the poor. At army festivities I liked the aroma of roasted meats and the noisy scraping of kettles, and it pleased me to see that the army banquets (or what passes for a banquet in camp) were just what they always should be, a gay and hearty contrast to the deprivations of working days. I could stand well enough the smell of fried foods in the public squares at the Saturnalia, but the banquets of Rome filled me with such repugnance and boredom that if at times I have expected to die in the course of an exploration or a military expedition I have said to myself, by way of consolation, that at least I should not have to live through another dinner! Do not do me the injustice to take me for a mere ascetic; an operation which is performed two or three times a day, and the purpose of which is to sustain life, surely merits all our care. To eat a fruit is to welcome into oneself a fair living object, which is alien to us but is nourished and protected like us by the earth; it is to consume a sacrifice wherein we sustain ourselves at the expense of things. I have never bitten into a chunk of army bread without marveling that this coarse and heavy concoction can transform itself into blood and warmth, and perhaps into courage. Alas, why does my mind, even in its best days, never possess but a particle of the assimilative powers of the body?

It was in Rome, during the long official repasts, that I began to think of the relatively recent origins of our riches, and of this nation of thrifty farmers and frugal soldiers formerly fed upon garlic and barley now suddenly enabled by our conquests to luxuriate in the culinary arts of Asia, bolting down those complicated viands with the greed of hungry peasants. We Romans cram ourselves with ortolans, drown in sauce, and poison ourselves with spice. An Apicius glories in the succession of courses and the sequence of sweet or sour, heavy or dainty foods which make up the exquisite order of his banquets; these dishes would perhaps be tolerable if each were served separately, and consumed for its own sake, learnedly savored by an expert whose taste and appetite are both unspoiled. But presented pell-mell, in the midst of everyday vulgar profusion, they confound a man's palate and confuse his stomach with a detestable mixture of flavors, odors, and substances in which the true values are lost and the unique qualities disappear. My poor Lucius used to amuse himself by concocting delicacies for me; his pheasant pasties with their skillful blending of ham and spice bore witness to an art which is as exacting as that of a musician or painter, but I could not help regretting the unadulterated flesh of the fine bird. Greece knew better about such things: her resin-steeped wine, her bread sprinkled with sesame seed, fish grilled at the very edge of the sea and unevenly blackened by the fire, or seasoned here and there by the grit of sand. all satisfied the appetite alone without surrounding by too many complications this simplest of our joys. In the merest hole of a place in Aegina or Phaleron I have tasted food so fresh that it remained divinely clean despite the dirty fingers of the tavern waiter; its quantity, though modest, was nevertheless so satisfying that it seemed to contain in the most reduced form possible some essence of immortality. Likewise meat cooked at night after a hunt had that same almost sacramental quality, taking us far back to the primitive origins of the races of men.

Wine initiates us into the volcanic mysteries of the soil, and its hidden mineral riches; a cup of Samos drunk at noon in the heat of the sun or, on the contrary, absorbed of a winter evening when fatigue makes the warm current be felt at once in the hollow of the diaphragm and the sure and burning dispersion spreads along our arteries, such a drink provides a sensation which is almost sacred, and is sometimes too strong for the human head. No feeling so pure comes from the vintage-numbered cellars of Rome; the pedantry of great connoisseurs of wine wearies me. Water drunk more reverently still, from the hands or from the spring itself, diffuses within us the most secret salt of earth and the rain of heaven. But even water is a delight which, sick man that I am, I may now consume only with strict restraint. No matter: in death's agony itself, and mingled with the bitterness of the last potions, I shall try still to taste on my lips its fresh simplicity.

In the schools of philosophy, where it is well to try once for all each mode of life, I have experimented briefly with abstention from meat; later, in Asia, I have seen the Indian Gymnosophists avert their eyes from smoking lamb quarters and gazelle meat served in the tent of Osroës. But this practice, in which your youthful love of austerity finds charm, calls for attentions more complicated than those of culinary refinement itself; and it separates us too much from the common run of men in a function which is nearly always public, and in which either friendship or formality presides. I should prefer to live all my life upon woodcock and fattened goose rather than be accused by my guests, at each meal, of a display of asceticism. As it is, I have had some trouble to conceal from my friends, by the help of dried fruits or the contents of a glass sipped slowly, that the masterpieces of my chefs were made more for them than for me, and that my interest in these courses ended before theirs. A prince lacks the latitude afforded to the philosopher in this respect: he cannot allow himself to be different on too many points at a time; and the gods know that my points of difference were already too numerous, though I flattered myself that many were invisible. As to the religious scruples of the Gymnosophist and his disgust at the sight of bleeding flesh, I should be more affected thereby if I had not sometimes asked myself in what essentials the suffering of grass, when it is cut, differs from the suffering of slaughtered sheep, and if our horror in presence of murdered beasts does not arise from the fact that our sensations belong to the same physical order as theirs. But at certain times of life, for example in periods of ritual fasting or in the course of religious initiations, I have learned the advantage for the mind (and also the dangers) of different forms of abstinence, or even of voluntary starvation, those states approaching giddiness where the body, partly lightened of ballast, enters into a world for which it is not made, and which affords it a foretaste of the cold and emptiness of death. At other moments such experiences have given me the chance to toy with the idea of slow suicide, of decease by inanition which certain philosophers have employed, a kind of debauch in reverse, continued to the point of exhaustion of the human substance. But it never would have pleased me to adhere too closely to a system, and I should not have allowed a scruple to take away my right, say, to stuff myself with sausages, if by chance I so desired, or if that particular food were the only one at hand.

The cynics and the moralists agree in placing the pleasures of love among the enjoyments termed gross, that is, between the desire for drinking and the need for eating, though at the same time they call love less indispensable, since it is something which, they assert, one can go without. I expect about anything from the moralist, but am astonished that the cynic should go thus astray. Probably both fear their own demons, whether resisting or surrendering to them, and they oblige themselves to scorn their pleasure in order to reduce its almost terrifying power, which overwhelms them, and its strange mystery, wherein they feel lost. I shall never believe in the classification of love among the purely physical joys (supposing that any such things exist) until I see a gourmet sobbing with delight over his favorite dish like a lover gasping on a young shoulder. Of all our games, love's play is the only one which threatens to unsettle the soul, and is also the only one in which the player has to abandon himself to the body's ecstasy. To put reason aside is not indispensable for a drinker, but the lover who leaves reason in control does not follow his god to the end. In every act save that of love, abstinence and excess alike involve but one person; any step in the direction of sensuality, however, places us in the presence of the Other, and involves us in the demands and servitudes to which our choice binds us (except in the case of Diogenes, where both the limitations and the merits of reasonable expedient are self-evident). I know no decision which a man makes for simpler or more inevitable reasons, where the object chosen is weighed more exactly for its balance of sheer pleasure, or where the seeker after truth has a better chance to judge the naked human being. Each time, from a stripping down as absolute as that of death, and from a humility which surpasses that of defeat and of prayer, I marvel to see again reforming the complex web of experiences shared and refused, of mutual responsibilities, awkward avowals, transparent lies, and passionate compromises between my pleasures and those of the Other, so many bonds impossible to break but nevertheless so quickly loosened. That mysterious play which extends from love of a body to love of an entire person has seemed to me noble enough to consecrate to it one part of my life. Words for it are deceiving, since the word for pleasure covers contradictory realities comprising notions of warmth, sweetness, and intimacy of bodies, but also feelings of violence and agony, and the sound of a cry. The short and obscene sentence of Poseidonius about the rubbing together of two small pieces of flesh, which I have seen you copy in your exercise books with the application of a good schoolboy, does no more to define the phenomenon of love than the taut cord touched by the finger accounts for the infinite miracle of sounds. Such a dictum is less an insult to pleasure than to the flesh itself, that amazing instrument of muscles, blood, and skin, that red-tinged cloud whose lightning is the soul.

And I admit that the reason stands confounded in presence of the veritable prodigy that love is, and of the strange obsession which makes this same flesh (for which we care so little when it is that of our own body, and which concerns us only to wash and nourish it, and if possible to keep it from suffering) inspire us with such a passion of caresses simply because it is animated by an individuality different from our own, and because it presents certain lineaments of beauty, disputed though they may be by the best judges. Here human logic stops short, as before the revelations of the Mysteries. Popular tradition has not been wrong in regarding love always as a form of initiation, one of the points of encounter of the secret with the sacred. Sensual experience is further comparable to the Mysteries in that the first approach gives to the uninitiated the impression of a ritual which is more or less frightening, and shockingly far removed from the familiar functions of sleeping, eating, and drinking; it appears matter for jest and shame, or even terror. Quite as much as the dance of the Maenads or the frenzy of the Corybantes, love-making carries us into a different world, where at other times we are forbidden to enter, and where we cease to belong as soon as the ardor is spent, or the ecstasy subsides. Nailed to the beloved body like a slave to a cross, I have learned some secrets of life which are now dimmed in my memory by the operation of that same law which ordains that the convalescent, once cured, ceases to understand the mysterious truths laid bare by illness, and that the prisoner, set free, forgets his torture, or the conqueror, his triumph passed, forgets his glory.

I have sometimes thought of constructing a system of human knowledge which would be based on eroticism, a theory of contact wherein the mysterious value of each being is to offer to us just that point of perspective which another world affords. In such a philosophy pleasure would be a more complete but also more specialized form· of approach to the Other, one more technique for getting to know what is not ourselves. In the least sensual encounters it is still in our contacts that emotion begins, or ends: the somewhat repugnant hand of the old woman who presents me her petition, the moist brow of my father in death's agony, the wound which I wash for an injured soldier. Even the most intellectual or the most neutral exchanges are made through this system of body-signals: the sudden enlightenment on the face of a tribune to whom a maneuver is explained on the morning of battle, the impersonal salute of a subordinate who comes to attention as I pass, the friendly glance of a slave at my thanks for the tray which he brings me, or the appreciative grimace of an old friend to whom a rare cameo is given. The slightest and most superficial of contacts are enough for us with most persons, or prove even too much. But when these contacts persist and multiply about one unique being, to the point of embracing him entirely, when each fraction of a body becomes laden for us with meaning as overpowering as that of the face itself, when this one creature haunts us like music and torments us like a problem (instead of inspiring in us, at most, mere irritation, amusement, or boredom), when he passes from the periphery of our universe to its center, and finally becomes for us more indispensable than our own selves, then that astonishing prodigy takes place wherein I see much more an invasion of the flesh by the spirit than a simple play of the body alone.

Such views on love could lead to the career of seducer. If I have not fulfilled that role it is doubtless because I have done something else, if no better. Short of genius, such a career demands attentions and even stratagems for which I was little suited. Those set traps, always the same, and the monotonous routine of perpetual advances, leading no further than conquest itself, have palled on me. The technique of a great seducer requires a facility and an indifference in passing from one object of affection to another which I could never have; however that may be, my loves have left me more often than I have left them, for I have never been able to understand how one could have enough of any beloved. The desire to count up exactly the riches which each new love brings us, and to see it change, and perhaps watch it grow old, accords ill with multiplicity of conquests. I used once to believe that a certain feeling for beauty would serve me in place of virtue, and would render me immune from solicitations of the coarsest kind. But I was mistaken. The lover of beauty ends by finding it everywhere about him, a vein of gold in the basest of ores; by handling fragmentary masterpieces, though stained or broken, he comes to know a collector's pleasure in being the sole seeker after pottery which is commonly passed by. A problem more serious (for a man of taste) is a position of eminence in human affairs, with the risks from adulation and lies which are inherent in the possession of almost absolute power. The idea that anyone should sham in my presence, even in the slightest degree, is enough to make me pity and despise or even hate him. Indeed I have suffered from the inconveniences of my fortune as a poor man does from those of his privations. One step more and I could have accepted the fiction of pretending that one is a seducer when one knows oneself to be merely the master. But that is the road to disgust, or perhaps to fatuity.

One would end by preferring the plain truths of debauchery to the outworn stratagems of seduction if there, too, lies did not prevail. In principle I am ready to admit that prostitution is an art like massage or hairdressing, but for my part I find it hard to get much enjoyment from barbers or masseurs. There is nothing more crude than an accomplice. The sidelong glance of the tavernkeeper who would reserve the best wine for me (and consequently deprive some other customer) sufficed even in my younger days to dull my appetite for the amusements of Rome. It displeases me to have some creature think that he can foresee and profit from my desire, automatically adapting himself to what he supposes to be my taste. At such moments the absurd and deformed reflection of myself which a human brain returns to me would almost make me prefer the ascetic's sorry state. If legend does not exaggerate the excesses of Nero and the erudite researches of Tiberius, those two great consumers of pleasure must have had inert senses indeed to put themselves to the expense of so complicated a machinery, and must have held mankind in singular disdain to let themselves in for such mockery and extortion. And nevertheless, if I have virtually given up these too mechanical forms of pleasure, or have never indulged in them at too great length, I owe it more to chance than to impregnable virtue. I could well fall back into such habits in growing old, just as into any kind of confusion or fatigue, but sickness and approaching death will save me from monotonous repetition of the same procedures, like droning through a lesson too long known by rote.

Of all the joys which are slowly abandoning me, sleep is one of the most precious, though one of the most common, too. A man who sleeps but little and poorly, propped on many a cushion, has ample time to meditate upon this particular delight. I grant that the most perfect repose is almost necessarily a complement to love, that profound rest which is reflected in two bodies. But what interests me here is the specific mystery of sleep partaken of for itself alone, the inevitable plunge risked each night by the naked man, solitary and unarmed, into an ocean where everything changes, the colors, the densities, and even the rhythm of breathing, and where we meet the dead. What reassures us about sleep is that we do come out of it, and come out of it unchanged, since some mysterious ban keeps us from bringing back with us in their true form even the remnants of our dreams. What also reassures us is that sleep heals us of fatigue, but heals us by the most radical of means in arranging that we cease temporarily to exist. There, as elsewhere, the pleasure and the art consist in conscious surrender to that blissful unconsciousness, and in accepting to be slightly less strong, less light, less heavy and less definite than our waking selves. I shall return later to the strange world of our dreams, for I prefer to speak here of certain experiences of pure sleep and pure awakening which border on death and resurrection. I am trying to recapture the exact sensation of such overpowering sleep as that of boyhood where, still fully clad, one toppled over one's books, transported as if by lightning out of mathematics and the law into the midst of a deep and substantial sleep so filled with unused energy that one tasted, as it were, the very essence of being through the closed eyelids. I evoke the short, sudden snatches of slumber on the bare ground, in the forest after tiring days of hunts; the barking of the dogs would awaken me, or their paws planted on my chest. So total was the eclipse that each time I could have found myself to be someone else, and I was perplexed and often saddened by the strict law which brought me back from so far away to re-enter this narrow confine of humanity which is myself. What are those particularities upon which we lay such store, since they count so little for us when we are liberated in sleep, and since for one second before returning, regretfully, into the body of Hadrian I was about to savor almost consciously that new existence without content and without past?

On the other hand, sickness and age have also their prodigies and receive from sleep other forms of benediction. About a year ago, after a singularly exhausting day in Rome, I experienced one of those respites wherein the depletion of one's forces serves to work the same miracle as did the unexploited reserves of former days. I go but rarely to the City now; once there I try to accomplish as much as possible. The day had been disagreeably full: a session at the Senate had been followed by a session in court, and by an interminable discussion with one of the quaestors; then by a religious ceremony which could not be cut short, and upon which it steadily rained. I myself had fitted all these different activities closely together, crowding them in so as to leave between them the least time possible for importunate requests and idle flatteries. The return on horseback was one of my last trips of the kind. I reached the Villa sickened and chilled as we are only when the blood actually refuses, and no longer works in our veins. Celer and Chabrias rushed to my aid, but solicitude can be wearing even when it is sincere. Retiring to my apartment I swallowed a few spoonfuls of a hot broth which I prepare myself, not out of suspicion, as is surmised, but because I thus procure for myself the luxury of being alone. I lay down: sleep seemed as far removed from me as health itself, and as youth or vigor. I dozed off. The sandglass proved to me that I had slept barely an hour, but a brief moment of complete repose, at my age, is equal to sleep which formerly lasted throughout half a revolution of the stars; my time is measured from now on in much smaller units. An hour had sufficed to accomplish the humble and unexpected prodigy: the heat of my blood was rewarming my hands; my heart and my lungs had begun to function with a kind of good will, and life was welling up like a spring which, though not abundant, is faithful. Sleep, in so short a time, had repaired my excesses of virtue with the same impartiality which it would have applied to the repair of my vices. For the divinity of the great restorer consists in bestowing his benefits upon the sleeper without concern for him, exactly as water charged with curative powers cares not at all who may drink from its source.

But if we think so little about a phenomenon which absorbs at least a third of every life it is because a certain modesty is needed to appreciate its gifts. Asleep, Caius Caligula and Aristides the Just are alike; my important but empty privileges are forgotten, and nothing distinguishes me from the black porter who lies guard at my door. What is our insomnia but the mad obstinacy of our mind in manufacturing thoughts and trains of reasoning, syllogisms and definitions of its own, refusing to abdicate in favor of that divine stupidity of closed eyes, or the wise folly of dreams? The man who cannot sleep, and I have had only too many occasions for some months to establish the point for myself, refuses more or less consciously to entrust himself to the flow of things. Brother of Death . . . Isocrates was wrong, and his sentence is a mere exercise in rhetoric. I begin to have some acquaintance with death; it has other secrets, more alien still to our present condition as men. And nevertheless, so intricate and so profound are these mysteries of absence and partial oblivion that we feel half assured that somewhere the white spring of sleep flows into the dark spring of death. I have never cared to gaze, as they slept, upon those I loved; they were resting from me, I know; they were escaping me, too. And every man feels some shame of his visage in the sully of sleep; how often, when I have risen early to read or to study, have I replaced the rumpled pillows myself, and the disordered covers, those almost obscene evidences of our encounters with nothingness, proofs that each night we have already ceased to be.

Little by little this letter, begun in order to tell you of the progress of my illness, has become the diversion of a man who no longer has the energy required for continued application to affairs of state; it has become, in fact, the written meditation of a sick man who holds audience with his memories. I propose now to do more than this: I have formed a project for telling you about my life. To be sure, last year I composed an official summary of my career, to which my secretary Phlegon gave his name. I told as few lies therein as possible; regard for public interest and decency nevertheless forced me to modify certain facts. The truth which I intend to set forth here is not particularly scandalous, or is so only to the degree that any truth creates a scandal. I do not expect your seventeen years to understand anything of it. I desire, all the same, to instruct you and to shock you, as well. Your tutors, whom I have chosen myself, have given you a severe education, well supervised and too much protected, perhaps; from it I hope that eventually great benefit will accrue both to you and to the State. I offer you here, in guise of corrective, a recital stripped of preconceived ideas and of mere abstract principles; it is drawn wholly from the experience of one man, who is myself. I am trusting to this examination of facts to give me some definition of myself, and to judge myself, perhaps, or at the very least to know myself better before I die.

Like everyone else I have at my disposal only three means of evaluating human existence: the study of self, which is the most difficult and most dangerous method, but also the most fruitful; the observation of our fellowmen, who usually arrange to hide their secrets from us, or to make us believe that they have secrets where none exist; and books, with the particular errors of perspective to which they inevitably give rise. I have read nearly everything that our historians and poets have written, and even our story-tellers, although the latter are considered frivolous; and to such reading I owe perhaps more instruction than I have gathered in the somewhat varied situations of my own life. The written word has taught me to listen to the human voice, much as the great unchanging statues have taught me to appreciate bodily motions. On the other hand, but more slowly, life has thrown light for me on the meaning of books.

But books lie, even those that are most sincere. The less adroit, for lack of words and phrases wherein they can enclose life, retain of it but a flat and feeble likeness. Some, like Lucan, make it heavy, and encumber it with a solemnity which it does not possess; others, on the contrary, like Petronius, make life lighter than it is, like a hollow, bouncing ball, easy to toss to and fro in a universe without weight. The poets transport us into a world which is vaster and more beautiful than our own, with more ardor and sweetness, different therefore, and in practice almost uninhabitable. The philosophers, in order to study reality pure, subject it to about the same transformations as fire or pestle make substance undergo: nothing that we have known of a person or of a fact seems to subsist in those ashes or those crystals to which they are reduced. Historians propose to us systems too perfect for explaining the past, with sequence of cause and effect much too exact and clear to have been ever entirely true; they rearrange what is dead, unresisting material, and I know that even Plutarch will never recapture Alexander. The story-tellers and spinners of erotic tales are hardly more than butchers who hang up for sale morsels of meat attractive to flies. I should take little comfort in a world without books, but reality is not to be found in them because it is not there whole.

Direct observation of man is a method still less satisfactory, limited as it frequently is to the cheap reflections which human malice enjoys. Rank, position, all such hazards tend to restrict the field of vision for the student of mankind: my slave has totally different facilities for observing me from what I possess for observing him, but his means to do so are as limited as my own. Every morning for twenty years, old Euphorion has handed me my flask of oil and my sponge, but my knowledge of him ends with his acts of service, and his knowledge of me ends with my bath; any effort on the part of either emperor or slave to learn more straightway produces the effect of an indiscretion. Almost everything that we know about anyone else is at second hand. If by chance a man does confess, he pleads his own cause and his apology is made in advance. If we are observing him, then he is not alone. They have reproached me for liking to read the police reports of Rome, but I learn from them, all the time, matter for amazement; whether friends or suspects, familiars or persons unknown, these people astound me; and their follies serve as excuse for mine. Nor do I tire of comparing the clothed and the unclothed man. But these reports, so artlessly detailed, add to my store of documents without aiding me in the least to render a final verdict. That this magistrate of austere appearance may have committed a crime in no way permits me to know him better. I am henceforth in the presence of two phenomena instead of one, the outer aspect of the magistrate *and* his crime.

As to self-observation, I make it a rule, if only to come to terms with that individual with whom I must live up to my last day, but an intimacy of nearly sixty years' standing leaves still many chances for error. When I seek deep within me for knowledge of myself what I find is obscure, internal, unformulated, and as secret as any complicity. A mcre impersonal approach yields informations as cool and detached as the theories which I could develop on the science of numbers: I employ what intelligence I have to look from above and afar upon my life, which accordingly becomes the life of another. But these two procedures for gaining knowledge are difficult, and require, the one, a descent into oneself, the other, a departure from self. Out of inertia I tend, like everyone else, to substitute for such methods those of mere habit, thus conceiving of my life partly as the public sees it, with judgments ready-made, that is to say poorly made, like a set pattern to which an unskillful tailor laboriously fits the cloth which we bring him. All this is equipment of unequal value; the tools are more or less dulled; but I have no others: it is with them that I must fashion for myself as well as may be some conception of my destiny as man.

When I consider my life, I am appalled to find it a shapeless mass. A hero's existence, such as is described to us, is simple; it goes straight to the mark, like an arrow. Most men like to reduce their lives to a formula, whether in boast or lament, but almost always in recrimination; their memories obligingly construct for them a clear and comprehensible past. My life has contours less firm. As is commonly the case, it is what I have not been which defines me, perhaps, most aptly: a good soldier, but not a great warrior; a lover of art, but not the artist which Nero thought himself to be at his death; capable of crime, but not laden with it. I have come to think that great men are characterized precisely by the extreme position which they take, and that their heroism consists in holding to that extremity throughout their lives. They are our poles, or our antipodes. I have occupied each of the extremes in turn, but have not kept to any one of them; life has always drawn me away. And nevertheless neither can I boast, like some plowman or worthy carter, of a middle-of-the-road existence.

The landscape of my days appears to be composed, like mountainous regions, of varied materials heaped up pell-mell. There I see my nature, itself composite, made up of equal parts of instinct and training. Here and there protrude the granite peaks of the inevitable, but all about is rubble from the landslips of chance. I strive to retrace my life to find in it some plan, following a vein of lead, or of gold, or the course of some subterranean stream, but such devices are only tricks of perspective in the memory. From time to time, in an encounter or an omen, or in a particular series of happenings, I think that I recognize the working of fate, but too many paths lead nowhere at all, and too many sums add up to nothing. To be sure, I perceive in this diversity and disorder the presence of a person; but his form seems nearly always to be shaped by the pressure of circumstances; his features are blurred, like a face reflected in water. I am not of those who say that their actions bear no resemblance to them. Indeed, actions must do so, since they alone give my measure, and are the sole means of engraving me upon the memory of men, or even upon my own memory (and since perhaps the very possibility of continuing to express and modify oneself by action may constitute the real difference between the state of the living and of the dead). But there is between me and these acts which compose me an indefinable hiatus, and the proof of this separation is that I feel constantly the necessity of weighing and explaining what I do, and of giving account of it to myself. In such an evaluation certain works of short duration are surely negligible; yet occupations which have extended over a whole lifetime signify just as little. For example, it seems to me as I write this hardly important to have been emperor.

Besides, a good three-quarters of my life escapes this definition by acts: the mass of my wishes, my desires, and even my projects remains nebulous and fleeting as a phantom; the remainder, the palpable part, more or less authenticated by facts, is barely more distinct, and the sequence of events is as confused as that of dreams. I have a chronology of my own which is wholly unrelated to anything based on the founding of Rome, or on the era of the Olympiads. Fifteen years with the armies have lasted less long than a single morning at Athens; there are people whom I have seen much of throughout my life whom I shall not recognize in Hades. Planes in space overlap likewise: Egypt and the Vale of Tempe are near, indeed, nor am I always in Tibur when I am here. Sometimes my life seems to me so commonplace as to be unworthy even of careful contemplation, let alone writing about it, and is not at all more important, even in my own eyes, than the life of any other person. Sometimes it seems to me unique, and for that very reason of no value, and useless, because it cannot be reduced to the common experience of men. No one thing explains me: neither my vices nor my virtues serve for answer; my good fortune tells more, but only at intervals, without continuity, and above all, without logical reason. Still, the mind of man is reluctant to consider itself as the product of chance, or the passing result of destinies over which no god presides, least of all himself. A part of every life, even a life meriting very little regard, is spent in searching out the reasons for its existence, its starting point, and its source. My own failure to discover these things has sometimes inclined me toward magical explanations, and has led me to seek in the frenzies of the occult for what common sense has not taught me. When all the involved calculations prove false, and the philosophers themselves have nothing more to tell us, it is excusable to turn to the random twitter of birds, or toward the distant mechanism of the stars.

VARIUS MULTIPLEX
MULTIFORMIS

Marullinus, my grandfather, believed in the stars. This tall old man, emaciated and sallow with age, conceded to me much the same degree of affection, without tenderness or visible sign, and almost without words, that he felt for the animals on his farm and for his lands, or for his collection of stones fallen from the sky. He was descended from a line of ancestors long established in Spain, from the period of the Scipios, and was third of our name to bear senatorial rank; before that time our family had belonged to the equestrian order. Under Titus he had taken some modest part in public affairs. Provincial that he was, he had never learned Greek, and he spoke Latin with a harsh Spanish accent which he passed on to me, and for which I was later ridiculed in Rome. His mind, however, was not wholly uncultivated; after his death they found in his house a trunk full of mathematical instruments and books untouched by him for twenty years. He was learned in his way, with a knowledge half scientific, half peasant, that same mixture of narrow prejudice and ancient wisdom which characterized the elder Cato. But Cato was a man of the Roman Senate all his life, and of the war with Carthage, a true representative of the stern Rome of the Republic. The almost impenetrable hardness of Marullinus came from farther back, and from more ancient times. He was a man of the tribe, the incarnation of a sacred and awe-inspiring world of which I have sometimes found vestiges among our Etruscan soothsayers. He always went bareheaded, as I was criticized for doing later on; his horny feet spurned all use of sandals, and his everyday clothing was hardly distinguishable from that of the aged beggars, or of the grave tenant farmers whom I used to see squatting in the sun. They said that he was a wizard, and the village folk tried to avoid his glance. But over animals he had singular powers. I have watched his grizzled head approaching cautiously, though in friendly wise, toward a nest of adders, and before a lizard have seen his gnarled fingers execute a kind of dance.

On summer nights he took me with him to study the sky from the top of a barren hill. I used to fall asleep in a furrow, tired out from counting meteors. He would stay sitting, gazing upward and turning imperceptibly with the stars. He must have known the systems of Philolaus and of Hipparchus, and that of Aristarchus of Samos which was my choice in later years, but these speculations had ceased to interest him. For him the stars were fiery points in the heavens, objects akin to the stones and slow-moving insects from which he also drew portents, constituent parts of a magic universe in which were combined the will of the gods, the influence of demons, and the lot apportioned to men. He had cast my horoscope. One night (I was eleven years old at the time) he came and shook me from my sleep and announced, with the same grumbling laconism that he would have employed to predict a good harvest to his tenants, that I should rule the world. Then, seized with mistrust, he went to fetch a brand from the small fire of root ends kept going to warm us through the colder hours, held it over my hand, and read in my solid, childish palm I know not what confirmation of lines written in the sky. The world for him was all of a piece; a hand served to confirm the stars. His news affected me less than one might think; a child is ready for anything. Later, I imagine, he forgot his own prophecy in that indifference to both present and future which is characteristic of advanced age. They found him one morning in the chestnut woods on the far edge of his domain, dead and already cold, and torn by birds of prey. Before his death he had tried to teach me his art, but with no success; my natural curiosity tended to jump at once to conclusions without burdening itself under the complicated and somewhat repellent details of his science. But the taste for certain dangerous experiments has remained with me, indeed only too much so.

My father, Aelius Hadrianus Afer, was a man weighed down by his very virtues. His life was passed in the thankless duties of civil administration; his voice hardly counted in the Senate. Contrary to usual practice, his governorship of the province of Africa had not made him richer. At home, in our Spanish township of Italica, he exhausted himself in the settlement of local disputes. Without ambitions and without joy, like many a man who from year to year thus effaces himself more and more, he had come to put a fanatic application into minor matters to which he limited himself. I have myself known these honorable temptations to meticulousness and scruple. Experience had produced in my father a skepticism toward all mankind in which he included me, as yet a child. My success, had he lived to see it, would not have impressed him in the least; family pride was so strong that it would not have been admitted that I could add anything to it. I was twelve when this overburdened man left us. My mother settled down, for the rest of her life, to an austere widowhood; I never saw her again from the day that I set out for Rome, summoned hither by my guardian. My memory of her face, elongated like those of most of our Spanish women and touched with melancholy sweetness, is confirmed by her image in wax on the Wall of Ancestors. She had the dainty feet of the women of Gades, in their close-fitting sandals, nor was the gentle swaying of the hips which marks the dancers of that region alien to this virtuous young matron.

I have often reflected upon the error that we commit in supposing that a man or a family necessarily share in the ideas or events of the century in which they happen to exist. The effect of intrigues in Rome barely reached my parents in that distant province of Spain, even though at the time of the revolt against Nero my grandfather had for one night offered hospitality to Galba. We lived on the memory of obscure heroes of archives without renown, of a certain Fabius Hadrianus who was burned alive by the Carthaginians in the siege of Utica, and of a second Fabius, an ill-starred soldier who pursued Mithridates on the roads of Asia Minor. Of the writers of the period my father knew practically nothing: Lucan and Seneca were strangers to him, although like us they were of Spanish origin. My great uncle Aelius, a scholar, confined his reading to the best known authors of the time of Augustus. Such indifference to contemporary fashion kept them from many an error in taste, and especially from falling into turgid rhetoric. Hellenism and the Orient were unknown, or at best regarded frowningly from afar; there was not, I believe, a single good Greek statue in the whole peninsula. Thrift went hand in hand with wealth, and a certain rusticity was always present in our love of pompous ceremony. My sister Paulina was grave, silent, and sullen; she was married young to an old man. The standard of honesty was rigorous, but we were harsh to slaves. There was no curiosity about anything whatsoever; one was careful to think on all subjects what becomes a citizen of Rome. Of these many virtues, if virtues they be, I shall have been the squanderer.

Officially a Roman emperor is said to be born in Rome, but it was in Italica that I was born; it was upon that dry but fertile country that I later superposed so many regions of the world. The official fiction has some merit: it proves that decisions of the mind and of the will do prevail over circumstance. The true birthplace is that wherein for the first time one looks intelligently upon oneself; my first homelands have been books, and to a lesser degree schools. The schools of Spain had suffered from the effects of provincial leisure. Terentius Scaurus' school, in Rome, gave mediocre instruction in the philosophers and the poets but afforded rather good preparation for the vicissitudes of human existence: teachers exercised a tyranny over pupils which it would shame me to impose upon men; enclosed within the narrow limits of his own learning, each one despised his colleagues, who, in turn, had equally narrow knowledge of something else. These pedants made themselves hoarse in mere verbal disputes. The quarrels over precedence, the intrigues and calumnies, gave me acquaintance with what I was to encounter thereafter in every society in which I have lived, and to such experiences was added the brutality of all childhood. And nevertheless I have loved certain of my masters, and those strangely intimate though elusive relations existing between student and teacher, and the Sirens singing somewhere within the cracked voice of him who is first to reveal to you a masterpiece, or to unveil for you a new idea. The greatest seducer was not Alcibiades, after all; it was Socrates.

The methods of grammarians and rhetoricians are perhaps less absurd than I thought them to be during the years when I was subjected to them. Grammar, with its mixture of logical rule and arbitrary usage, proposes to a young mind a foretaste of what will be offered to him later on by law and ethics, those sciences of human conduct, and by all the systems wherein man has codified his instinctive experience. As for the rhetorical exercises in which we were successively Xerxes and Themistocles, Octavius and Mark Antony, they intoxicated me; I felt like Proteus. They taught me to enter into the thought of each man in turn, and to understand that each makes his own decisions, and lives and dies according to his own laws. The reading of the poets had still more overpowering effects; I am not sure that the discovery of love is necessarily more exquisite than the discovery of poetry. Poetry transformed me: initiation into death itself will not carry me farther along into another world than does a dusk of Virgil. In later years I came to prefer the roughness of Ennius, so close to the sacred origins of our race, or Lucretius' bitter wisdom; or to Homer's noble ease the homely parsimony of Hesiod. The most complicated and most obscure poets have pleased me above all; they force my thought to strenuous exercise; I have sought, too, the latest and the oldest, those who open wholly new paths, or help me to find lost trails. But in those days I liked chiefly in the art of verse whatever appealed most directly to the senses, whether the polished metal of Horace, or Ovid's soft texture, like flesh. Scaurus cast me into despair in assuring me that I should never be more than a mediocre poet; that both the gift and the application were wanting. For a long time I thought he was mistaken; somewhere locked away are a volume or two of my love poems, most of them imitated from Catullus. But it is of little concern to me now whether my personal productions are worthless or not.

To my dying day I shall be grateful to Scaurus for having set me early to the study of Greek. I was still a child when for the first time I tried to trace on my tablets those characters of an unknown alphabet: here was a new world and the beginning of my great travels, and also the feeling of a choice as deliberate, but at the same time as involuntary, as that of love. I have loved the language for its flexibility, like that of a supple, perfect body, and for the richness of its vocabulary, in which every word bespeaks direct and varied contact with reality: and because almost everything that men have said best has been said in Greek. There are, I know, other languages, but they are petrified, or have yet to be born. Egyptian priests have shown me their antique symbols; they are signs rather than words, ancient attempts at

classification of the world and of things, the sepulchral speech of
a dead race. During the Jewish War the rabbi Joshua translated
literally for me some texts from Hebrew, that language of sectarians so obsessed by their god that they have neglected the
human. In the armies I grew accustomed to the language of
the Celtic auxiliaries, and remember above all certain of their
songs . . . But barbarian jargons are chiefly important as a reserve
for human expression, and for all the things which they will
doubtless say in time to come. Greek, on the contrary, has its
treasures of experience already behind it, experience both of
man and of the State. From the Ionian tyrants to the Athenian
demagogues, from the austere integrity of an Agesilaus to the
excesses of a Dionysius or a Demetrius, from the treason of
Demaratus to the fidelity of Philopoemen, everything that any
one of us can do to help or to hinder his fellow man has been
done, at least once, by a Greek. It is the same with our personal
decisions: from cynicism to idealism, from the skepticism of
Pyrrho to the mystic dreams of Pythagoras, our refusals or our
acceptances have already taken place; our very vices and virtues
have Greek models. There is nothing to equal the beauty of a
Latin votive or burial inscription: those few words graved on
stone sum up with majestic impersonality all that the world need
ever know of us. It is in Latin that I have administered the empire;
my epitaph will be carved in Latin on the walls of my mausoleum
beside the Tiber; but it is in Greek that I shall have thought and
lived.

At sixteen I returned to Rome after a stretch of preliminary
training in the Seventh Legion, stationed then well into the
Pyrenees, in a wild region of Spain very different from the
southern part of the peninsula where I had passed my childhood.
Acilius Attianus, my guardian, thought it good that some serious
study should counterbalance these months of rough living and
violent hunting. He allowed himself, wisely, to be persuaded by
Scaurus to send me to Athens to the sophist Isaeus, a brilliant
man with a special gift for the art of improvisation. Athens won
me straightway; the somewhat awkward student, a brooding but
ardent youth, had his first taste of that subtle air, those swift
conversations, the strolls in the long golden evenings, and that
incomparable ease in which both discussions and pleasure are

there pursued. Mathematics and the arts, as parallel studies, engaged me in turn; Athens afforded me also the good fortune to follow a course in medicine under Leotychides. The medical profession would have been congenial to me; its principles and methods are essentially the same as those by which I have tried to fulfill my function as emperor. I developed a passion for this science, which is too close to man ever to be absolute, but which, though subject to fad and to error, is constantly corrected by its contact with the immediate and the nude. Leotychides approached things from the most positive and practical point of view; he had developed an admirable system for reduction of fractures. We used to walk together at evening along the shore; this man of universal interests was curious about the structure of shells and the composition of sea mud. But he lacked facilities for experiment and regretted the Museum at Alexandria, where he had studied in his youth, with its laboratories and dissection rooms, its clash of opinions, and its competition between inventive minds. His was a clear, dry intelligence which taught me to value things above words, to mistrust mere formulas, and to observe rather than to judge. It was this bitter Greek who taught me method.

In spite of the legends surrounding me, I have cared little for youth, and for my own youth least of all. This much vaunted portion of existence, considered dispassionately, seems to me often a formless, opaque, and unpolished period, both fragile and unstable. Needless to say I have found a certain number of exquisite exceptions to the rule, and two or three were admirable; of these, Mark, you yourself will have been the most pure. As for me, I was at twenty much what I am today, but not consistently so. Not everything in me was bad, but it could have been: the good or the better parts also lent strength to the worse. I look back with shame on my ignorance of the world, which I thought that I knew, and on my impatience, and on a kind of frivolous ambition and gross avidity which I then had. Must the truth be told? In the midst of the studious life of Athens, where all pleasures, too, received their due, I regretted not Rome itself but the atmosphere of that place where the business of the world is continually done and undone, where are heard the pulleys and gears in the machine of governmental power. The reign of

Domitian was drawing to a close; my cousin Trajan, who had covered himself with glory on the Rhine frontier, ranked now as a popular hero; the Spanish tribe was gaining hold in Rome. Compared with that world of immediate action, the beloved Greek province seemed to me to be slumbering in a haze of ideas seldom stirred by change, and the political passivity of the Hellenes appeared a somewhat servile form of renunciation. My appetite for power, and for money (which is often with us a first form of power), was undeniable, as was the craving for glory (to give that beautiful and impassioned name to what is merely our itch to hear ourselves spoken of). There was mingled confusedly with these desires the feeling that Rome, though inferior in many things, was after all superior in its demand that its citizens should take part in public affairs, those citizens at least who were of senatorial or equestrian rank. I had reached the point where I felt that the most ordinary debate on such a subject as importation of Egyptian wheat would have taught me more about government than would the entire *Republic* of Plato. Even a few years earlier, as a young Roman trained in military discipline, I could see that I had a better understanding than my professors of what it meant to be a Spartan soldier, or an athlete of Pindar's time. I left the mellow light of Athens for the city where men wrapped and hooded in heavy togas battle against February winds, where luxury and debauch are barren of charm, but where the slightest decision taken affects the fate of some quarter of the world. There a young and eager provincial, not wholly obtuse but pursuing at first only vulgar ambitions, was little by little to lose such aspirations in the act of fulfilling them; he was to learn to contend both with men and with things, to command, and what is perhaps in the end slightly less futile, to serve.

Much was unsavory in that accession to power of a virtuous middle class which was hurrying to establish itself in anticipation of a change of regime: political honesty was gaining the upper hand by means of dubious stratagems. The Senate, by gradual transfer of all administrative posts to the hands of its favored dependents, was completing its encirclement of the hard-pressed Domitian; the newcomers, with whom all my family ties allied me, were not perhaps so different from those whom they were about to replace; they were chiefly less soiled by actual possession of power. Provincial cousins and nephews hoped at least for subaltern positions; still they were expected to fill such offices with integrity. I had my share: I was named judge in the court dealing with litigation over inheritances. It was from this modest post that I witnessed the last thrusts in a duel to the death between Domitian and Rome. The emperor had lost hold on the City, where he could no longer maintain himself except by resort to executions, which in turn hastened his own end; the whole army joined in plotting his death. I grasped but little of this fencing match, so much more deadly than those of the arena, and felt only a somewhat arrogant disdain for the tyrant at bay, philosopher's pupil that I then was. Wisely counseled by Attianus, I kept to my work without meddling too much in politics.

That first year in office differed little from the years of study. I knew nothing of law but was fortunate in having Neratius Priscus for colleague in the tribunal. He consented to instruct me, and remained throughout his life my legal counselor and my friend. His was that rare type of mind which, though master of a subject, and seeing it, as it were, from within (from a point of view inaccessible to the uninitiated), nevertheless retains a sense of its merely relative value in the general order of things, and measures it in human terms. Better versed than any of his contemporaries in established procedures, he never hesitated when useful innovations were proposed. It is with his help that I have succeeded in my later years in putting certain reforms into effect. There were other things to think of. My Spanish accent had stayed with me; my first speech in the tribunal brought a burst of laughter. Here I made good use of my intimacy with actors, which had scandalized my family: lessons in elocution throughout long months proved the most arduous but most delightful of my tasks, and were the best guarded of my life's secrets. In those difficult years even dissipation was a kind of study: I was trying to keep up with the young fashionables of Rome, but in that I never completely succeeded. With the cowardice typical of that age, when our courage is wholly physical, and is expended elsewhere, I seldom dared to be myself; in the hope of resembling the others I sometimes subdued and sometimes exaggerated my natural disposition.

I was not much liked. There was, in fact, no reason why I

should have been. Certain traits, for example my taste for the arts, which went unnoticed in the student at Athens, and which was to be more or less generally accepted in the emperor, were disturbing in the officer and magistrate at his first stage of authority. My Hellenism was cause for amusement, the more so in that ineptly I alternated between dissimulating and displaying it. The senators referred to me as 'the Greekling.' I was beginning to have my legend, that strange flashing reflection made up partly of what we do, and partly of what the public thinks about us. Plaintiffs, on learning of my intrigue with a senator's wife, brazenly sent me their wives in their stead, or their sons when I had flaunted my passion for some young mime. There was a certain pleasure in confounding such folk by my indifference. The sorriest lot of all were those who tried to win me with talk about literature.

The technique which I was obliged to develop in those unimportant early posts has served me in later years for my imperial audiences: to give oneself totally to each person throughout the brief duration of a hearing; to reduce the world for a moment to this banker, that veteran, or that widow; to accord to these individuals, each so different though each confined naturally within the narrow limits of a type, all the polite attention which at the best moments one gives to oneself, and to see them, almost every time, make use of this opportunity to swell themselves out like the frog in the fable; furthermore, to devote seriously a few moments to thinking about their business or their problem. It was again the method of the physician: I uncovered old and festering hatreds, and a leprosy of lies. Husbands against wives, fathers against children, collateral heirs against everyone: the small respect in which I personally hold the institution of the family has hardly held up under it all.

It is not that I despise men. If I did I should have no right, and no reason, to try to govern. I know them to be vain, ignorant, greedy, and timorous, capable of almost anything for the sake of success, or for raising themselves in esteem (even in their own eyes), or simply for avoidance of suffering. I know, for I am like them, at least from time to time, or could have been. Between another and myself the differences which I can recognize are too slight to count for much in the final total; I try therefore to maintain a position as far removed from the cold superiority of the philosopher as from the arrogance of a ruling Caesar. The most benighted of men are not without some glimmerings of the divine: that murderer plays passing well upon the flute; this overseer flaying the backs of his slaves is perhaps a dutiful son; this simpleton would share with me his last crust of bread. And there are few who cannot be made to learn at least something reasonably well. Our great mistake is to try to exact from each person virtues which he does not possess, and to neglect the cultivation of those which he has. I might apply here to the search for these partial virtues what I was saying earlier, in sensuous terms, about the search for beauty. I have known men infinitely nobler and more perfect than myself, like your father Antoninus, and have come across many a hero, and even a few sages. In most men I have found little consistency in adhering to the good, but no steadier adherence to evil; their mistrust and indifference, usually more or less hostile, gave way almost too soon, almost in shame, changing too readily into gratitude and respect, which in turn were equally short-lived; even their selfishness could be bent to useful ends. I am always surprised that so few have hated me; I have had only one or two bitter enemies, for whom I was, as is always the case, in part responsible. Some few have loved me: they have given me far more than I had the right to demand, or to hope for: their deaths, and sometimes their lives. And the god whom they bear within them is often revealed when they die.

There is but one thing in which I feel superior to most men: I am freer, and at the same time more compliant, than they dare to be. Nearly all of them fail to recognize their due liberty, and likewise their true servitude. They curse their fetters, but seem sometimes to find them matter for pride. Yet they pass their days in vain license, and do not know how to fashion for themselves the lightest yoke. For my part I have sought liberty more than power, and power only because it can lead to freedom. What interested me was not a philosophy of the free man (all who try that have proved tiresome), but a technique: I hoped to discover the hinge where our will meets and moves with destiny, and where discipline strengthens, instead of restraining, our nature. Understand clearly that here is no question of harsh Stoic

will, which you value too high, nor of some mere abstract choice
or refusal, which grossly affronts the conditions of our universe,
this solid whole, compounded as it is of objects and bodies. No,
I have dreamed of a more secret acquiescence, or of a more supple
response. Life was to me a horse to whose motion one yields,
but only after having trained the animal to the utmost. Since
everything is finally a decision of the mind, however slowly and
imperceptibly made, and involves also the body's assent, I strove
to attain by degrees to that state of liberty, or of submission,
which is almost pure. In this effort gymnastics helped, and
dialectics aided me, too. I sought at first the simple liberty of
leisure moments; each life well regulated has some such intervals,
and he who cannot make way for them does not know how to
live. A step further, and I conceived of a liberty of simultaneity,
whereby two actions or two states would be possible at the same
time; I learned, for example, by modeling myself upon Caesar
to dictate more than one text at a time, and to speak while
continuing to read. I invented a mode of life in which the heaviest
task could be accomplished perfectly without engaging myself
wholly therein; in fact, I have sometimes gone so far as to propose
to myself elimination of the very concept of physical fatigue.

At other moments I practiced a liberty acquired by methods
of alternation: feelings, thoughts, or work had all to be subject
to interruption at any moment, and then resumed; the certainty
of being able to summon or dismiss such preoccupations, like
slaves, robbed them of all chance for tyranny, and freed me of
all sense of servitude. I did a better thing: I organized the day's
activities round some chosen train of thought and did not let it
go; whatever would have distracted or discouraged me from it,
such as projects or work of another kind, words of no import,
or the thousand incidents of the day, were made to take their
place around it as a vine is trained round the shaft of a column.
Sometimes, on the contrary, I made infinite divisions of each
thought and each fact under view, breaking and sectioning them
into a vast number of smaller thoughts and facts, easier thus to
keep in hand. By this method resolutions difficult to take were
broken down into a veritable powder of minute decisions, to be
adopted one by one, each leading to the next, and thereby
becoming, as it were, easy and inevitable.

But it was still to the liberty of submission, the most difficult of all, that I applied myself most strenuously. I determined to make the best of whatever situation I was in; during my years of dependence my subjection lost its portion of bitterness, and even ignominy, if I learned to accept it as a useful exercise. Whatever I had I chose to have, obliging myself only to possess it totally, and to taste the experience to the full. Thus the most dreary tasks were accomplished with ease as long as I was willing to give myself to them. Whenever an object repelled me, I made it a subject of study, ingeniously compelling myself to extract from it a motive for enjoyment. If faced with something unforeseen or near cause for despair, like an ambush or a storm at sea, after all measures for the safety of others had been taken, I strove to welcome this hazard, to rejoice in whatever it brought me of the new and unexpected, and thus without shock the ambush or the tempest was incorporated into my plans, or my thoughts. Even in the throes of my worst disaster, I have seen a moment when sheer exhaustion reduced some part of the horror of the experience, and when I made the defeat a thing of my own in being willing to accept it. If ever I am to undergo torture (and illness will doubtless see to that) I cannot be sure of maintaining the impassiveness of a Thrasea, but I shall at least have the resource of resigning myself to my cries. And it is in such a way, with a mixture of reserve and of daring, of submission and revolt carefully concerted, of extreme demand and prudent concession, that I have finally learned to accept myself.

Had it been too greatly prolonged, this life in Rome would undoubtedly have embittered or corrupted me, or else would have worn me out. My return to the army saved me. Army life has its compromises too, but they are simpler. Departure this time meant travel, and I set out with exultation. I had been advanced to the rank of tribune in the Second Legion Adjutrix, and passed some months of a rainy autumn on the banks of the Upper Danube with no other companion than a newly published volume of Plutarch. In November I was transferred to the Fifth Legion Macedonica, stationed at that time (as it still is) at the mouth of the same river, on the frontiers of Lower Moesia. Snow blocked the roads and kept me from traveling by land. I embarked at Pola, but had barely time on the way to revisit Athens, where later I was so long to reside. News of the assassination of Domitian, announced a few days after my arrival in camp, surprised no one, and was cause for general rejoicing. Trajan was promptly adopted by Nerva; the advanced age of the new ruler made actual succession a matter of months at the most. The policy of conquest on which it was known that my cousin proposed to launch Rome, the regrouping of troops which began, and the progressive tightening of discipline all served to keep the army in a state of excited expectancy. Those Danubian legions functioned with the precision of newly greased military machines; they bore no resemblance to the sleepy garrisons which I had known in Spain. Still more important, the army's attention had ceased to center upon palace quarrels and was turned instead to the empire's external affairs; our troops no longer behaved like a band of lictors ready to acclaim or to murder no matter whom.

The most intelligent among the officers attempted to trace some general plan in these reorganizations in which they took part, hoping to foresee the future, and not their own prospects alone. There were, however, a goodly number of absurdities exchanged by way of comment upon these initial events, and strategic planning as idle as it was ill-founded smeared the surface of the tables at each evening meal. For these professionals, with their firm belief in the beneficence of our authority and in the mission of Rome to govern the world, Roman patriotism assumed brutal forms to which I was not yet accustomed. On the frontiers, just where, for the moment at least, address was needed to conciliate certain of the nomad chieftains, the soldier completely eclipsed the statesman; exaction of labor and requisitions in kind gave rise to abuses too generally condoned. Thanks to incessant divisions among the barbarians the situation to the northeast was about as favorable as it ever could be; I doubt if even the wars which followed have improved matters there to any extent. Frontier incidents cost us few losses, and these were disquieting only because they were continuous. Let us admit that this perpetual vigilance was useful in any case for whetting the military spirit. All the same, I was convinced that a lesser expenditure, coupled with somewhat greater mental effort on our part, would have sufficed to subdue some chieftains and to win others to us. I decided to devote myself especially to this latter task, which everyone else was neglecting.

I was drawn the more to this aim by my love of things foreign; I liked to deal with the barbarians. This great country lying between the mouths of the Danube and the Borysthenes, a triangular area of which I have covered at least two sides, is one of the most remarkable regions of the world, at least for us who are born on the shores of the Interior Sea and are used to the clear, dry line of southern landscape, with its hills and promontories. At times there I worshipped the goddess Earth in the way that we here worship the goddess Rome; I am speaking not so much of Ceres as of a more ancient divinity, anterior even to the invention of the harvest. Our Greek and Latin lands, everywhere supported by bone-structure of rock, have the trim beauty of a male body; the heavy abundance of the Scythian earth was that of a reclining woman. The plain ended only where the sky began. My wonder never ceased in presence of the rivers: that vast empty land was but a slope and a bed for their waters. Our rivers are short; we never feel far from their sources; but the enormous flow which ended there in confused estuaries swept with it the mud of an unknown continent and the ice of uninhabitable regions. The cold of Spain's high plateaus is second to none, but this was the first time that I found myself face to face with true winter, which visits our countries but briefly. There it sets in for a long period of months; farther north it must be unchanging, without beginning and without end. The evening of my arrival in camp the Danube was one immense roadway of ice, red at first and then blue, furrowed by the inner working of currents with tracks as deep as those of chariots. We made use of furs to protect ourselves from the cold. The presence of that enemy, so impersonal as to be almost abstract, produced an indescribable exaltation, and a feeling of energy accrued. One fought to conserve body heat as elsewhere one fights to keep one's courage. There were days when the snow effaced the few differences in level on the steppes; we galloped in a world of pure space and pure atoms. The frozen coating gave transparency to the most ordinary things, and the softest objects took on a celestial rigidity. Each broken reed was a flute of crystal. Assar, my Caucasian guide, chopped through the ice to water our horses at dusk. These animals were, by the way, one of our most useful points of contact with the barbarians: a kind of friendship grew up over the trading and endless bargaining, and out of the respect felt on each side for some act of prowess in horsemanship. At night the campfires lit up the extraordinary leaping of the slender-waisted dancers, and their extravagant bracelets of gold.

Many a time in spring, when the melting snows let me venture farther into the interior, I would turn my back on the southern horizon, which enclosed the seas and islands that we know, and on the western horizon likewise, where at some point the sun was setting on Rome, and would dream of pushing still farther into the steppes or beyond the ramparts of the Caucasus, toward the north or to uttermost Asia. What climates, what fauna, what races of men should I have discovered, what empires ignorant of us as we are of them, or knowing us at most through some few wares transmitted by a long succession of merchants, and as rare for them as the pepper of India or the amber of Baltic regions is for us? At Odessos a trader returning from a voyage of several years' time made me a present of a green stone, of translucent substance held sacred, it seems, in an immense kingdom of which he had at least skirted the edges, but where he had noted neither customs nor gods, grossly centered upon his profit as he was. This exotic gem was to me like a stone fallen from the heavens, a meteor from another world. We know but little as yet of the configuration of the earth, though I fail to understand resignation to such ignorance. I envy those who will succeed in circling the two hundred and fifty thousand Greek stadia so ably calculated by Eratosthenes, the round of which would bring us back to our point of departure. In fancy I took the simple decision of going on, this time on the mere trail to which our roads had now given way. I played with the idea . . . To be alone, without possessions, without renown, with none of the advantages of our own culture, to expose oneself among new men and amid fresh hazards . . . Needless to say it was only a dream, and the briefest dream of all. This liberty that I was inventing ceased to exist upon closer view; I should quickly have rebuilt for myself everything that I had renounced. Furthermore, wherever I went I should only have been a Roman away from Rome. A kind of umbilical cord attached me to the City. Perhaps at that time, in my rank of tribune, I felt still more closely bound to the empire than later as emperor, for the same reason that the thumb joint is less free than the brain. Nevertheless I did have that outlandish dream, at which our ancestors, soberly confined within their Latian fields, would have shuddered; to have harbored the thought, even for a moment, makes me forever different from them.

Trajan was in command of the troops in Lower Germany; the army of the Danube sent me there to convey its felicitations to him as the new heir to the empire. I was three days' march from Cologne, in mid-Gaul, when at the evening halt the death of Nerva was announced. I was tempted to push on ahead of the imperial post, and to be the first to bring to my cousin the news of his accession. I set off at a gallop and continued without stop, except at Treves where my brother-in-law Servianus resided in his capacity as governor. We supped together. The feeble head of Servianus was full of imperial vapors. This tortuous man, who sought to harm me or at least to prevent me from pleasing, thought to forestall me by sending his own courier to Trajan. Two hours later I was attacked at the ford of a river; the assailants wounded my orderly and killed our horses. We managed, however, to lay hold on one of the attacking party, a former slave of my brother-in-law, who told the whole story. Servianus ought to have realized that a resolute man is not so easily turned from his course, at least not by any means short of murder; but before such an act as that his cowardice recoiled. I had to cover some three miles on foot before coming upon a peasant who sold me his horse. I reached Cologne that very night, beating my brother-in-law's courier by only a few lengths. This kind of adventure met with success; I was the better received for it by the army. The emperor retained me there with him as tribune in the Second Legion Fidelis.

Trajan had taken the news of his accession with admirable composure. He had long expected it, and it left his plans unchanged. He remained what he always had been, and what he was to be up to his death, a commander-in-chief; but his virtue was to have acquired, by means of his wholly military conception of discipline, an idea of order in government. Around that idea everything else was organized, in the beginning at least, even his plans for war and his designs for conquest. A soldierly emperor, but not at all a military adventurer. He altered nothing in his way of living; his modesty left room neither for affectation nor for arrogance. While the army was rejoicing he accepted his new responsibilities as a part of the day's ordinary work, and very simply made evident his contentment to his intimates.

He had but little confidence in me. We were cousins, but he was twenty-four years my senior, and had been my co-guardian since my father's death. He fulfilled his family obligations with provincial seriousness, and was ready to do the impossible to advance me, if I proved worthy; if incompetent, to treat me with more severity than anyone else. He had taken my youthful follies with an indignation which was not wholly unjustified, but which is seldom encountered outside the bosom of the family; my debts, in any case, shocked him more than my misdoings. Other things in me disturbed him. Though his learning was limited, he had a touching respect for philosophers and scholars; but it is one thing to admire the great philosophers from afar, and quite another to have at one's side a young lieutenant who dabbles in letters. Not knowing where my principles lay, or my safeguards or restraints, he supposed me to have none, and to be without resource against my own nature. I had, at least, never committed the error of neglecting my duties. My reputation as an officer reassured him, but in his eyes I was no more than a young and promising tribune, who would bear close watching.

An incident of our personal lives soon threatened to be my undoing. A handsome face was my conqueror. I became passionately attached to a youth whom the emperor also fancied. The adventure was dangerous, and was relished as such. A certain secretary Gallus, who had long taken it upon himself to report each of my debts to Trajan, denounced us to the emperor. His irritation knew no bounds; things were bad enough for a while. Some friends, Acilius Attianus among others, did their best to keep him from settling into a permanent and rather ridiculous resentment. He ended by yielding to their entreaties, and the reconciliation, though at first barely sincere on either side, was more humiliating for me than the scenes of anger had been. I admit to having harbored for this Gallus a hatred beyond compare. Many years later he was found guilty of embezzlement of the public funds, and it was with utter satisfaction that I saw myself avenged.

The first expedition against the Dacians got under way the following year. By preference and by political conviction I have always been opposed to a policy based on war, but I should have been either more or less than a man if these great enterprises of Trajan had not intoxicated me. Viewed as a whole, and from afar, those years of war count among my happy years. They were hard at the start, or seemed to me so. At first I held only secondary posts, since Trajan's good will was not yet fully won. But I knew the country, and knew that I was useful. Although barely aware of what was growing within me, winter by winter, encampment after encampment, battle after battle, I began to feel objections to the emperor's policy, objections which at this period it was not my duty, or even my right, to voice; furthermore, nobody would have listened to me. Placed more or less to one side, in fifth or tenth rank, I knew my troops the better for my position; I shared more of their life. I still retained a certain liberty of action, or rather a certain detachment toward action itself, which cannot readily be indulged in once one has attained power, and has passed the age of thirty. There were also advantages special to me: my liking for this harsh land, and my passion for all voluntary (though of course intermittent) forms of privation and discipline. I was perhaps the only one of the young officers who did not regret Rome. The longer the campaign years extended into the mud and the snow the more they brought forth my resources.

There I lived through an entire epoch of extraordinary exaltation, due in part to the influence of a small group of lieutenants around me who had brought back strange gods from the garrisons deep in Asia. The cult of Mithra, less widespread then than it has become since our expedition in Parthia, won me over temporarily by the rigors of its stark asceticism, which drew taut the bowstring of the will, and by its obsession with death, blood, and iron, which elevated the routine harshness of our military lives to the level of a symbol of universal struggle. Nothing could have been more in contradiction to the views which I was beginning to hold about war, but those barbarous rites creating bonds of life and death between the affiliates all served to flatter the most secret aspirations of a young man impatient of the present, uncertain as to the future, and thereby open to the gods. My initiation took place in a turret constructed of wood and reeds on the banks of the Danube, with Marcius Turbo, my fellow officer, for sponsor. I remember that the weight of the bull in its death throes nearly brought down the latticed floor beneath which I lay to receive the bloody aspersion. In recent years I have reflected upon the dangers which this sort of near-secret society might entail for the State under a weak ruler, and I have finally restricted them, but I admit that in presence of an enemy they give their followers a strength which is almost godlike. Each of us believed that he was escaping from the narrow limits of his human state, feeling himself to be at the same time himself and his own adversary, at one with the god who seems to be both the animal victim and the human slayer. Such fantastic dreams, which sometimes terrify me now, were not so very different from the theories of Heraclitus upon the identity of the mark and the bow. They helped me in those days to endure life. Victory and defeat were inextricably mixed like rays of the same sun. These Dacian footsoldiers whom I crushed under my horse's hoofs, those Sarmatian cavalrymen overthrown in the close combat of later years when our rearing horses tore at each other's chests, were all struck down the more easily if I identified myself with them. Had my body been abandoned on the battlefield, stripped of its attire, it would not have differed greatly from theirs. The shock of the final sword thrust would have been the same. I am confessing to you here some extra-ordinary thoughts, among the most secret of my life, and a strange intoxication which I have never again experienced under that same form.

A certain number of deeds of daring, which would have passed unnoticed, perhaps, if performed by a simple soldier, won me a reputation in Rome and a sort of renown in the army. But most of my so-called acts of prowess were little more than idle bravado; I see now with some shame that, mingled with that almost sacred exaltation of which I was just speaking, there was still my ignoble desire to please at any price, and to draw attention upon myself. It was thus that one autumn day when the Danube was swollen by floods I crossed the river on horseback, wearing the full heavy equipment of our Batavian auxiliaries. For this feat of arms, if it was a feat, my horse deserved credit more than I. But that period of heroic foolhardiness taught me to distinguish between the different aspects of courage. The kind of courage which I should like always to possess would be cool and detached, free from all physical excitement and impassive as the calm of a god. I do not flatter myself that I have ever attained it. The semblance of such courage which I later employed was, in my worst days, only a cynical recklessness toward life; in my best days it was only a sense of duty to which I clung. When confronted with the danger itself, however, that cynicism or that sense of duty quickly gave place to a mad intrepidity, a kind of strange orgasm of a man mated with his destiny. At the age which I then was this drunken courage persisted without cessation. A being afire with life cannot foresee death; in fact, by each of his deeds he denies that death exists. If death does take him, he is probably unaware of the fact; it amounts to no more for him than a shock or a spasm. I smile with some bitterness at the realization that now out of any two thoughts I devote one to my own death, as if so much ceremony were needed to decide this worn body for the inevitable. At that time, on the contrary, a young man who would have lost much in not living a few years more was daily risking his future with complete unconcern.

It would be easy to construe what I have just told as the story of a too scholarly soldier who wishes to be forgiven his love for books. But such simplified perspectives are false. Different persons ruled in me in turn, though no one of them for long; each fallen tyrant was quick to regain power. Thus have I played host successively to the meticulous officer, fanatic in discipline, but gaily sharing with his men the privations of war; to the melancholy dreamer intent on the gods; the lover ready to risk all for a moment's rapture; the haughty young lieutenant retiring to his tent to study his maps by lamplight, making clear to his friends his disdain for the way the world goes; and finally the future statesman. But let us not forget, either, the base opportunist who in fear of displeasing succumbed to drunkenness at the emperor's table; the young fellow pronouncing upon all questions with ridiculous assurance; the frivolous wit, ready to lose a friend for the sake of a bright remark; the soldier exercising with mechanical precision his vile gladiatorial trade. And we should include also that vacant figure, nameless and unplaced in history, though as much myself as all the others, the simple toy of circumstance, no more and no less than a body, lying on a camp bed, distracted by an aroma, aroused by a breath of wind, vaguely attentive to some eternal hum of a bee. But little by little a newcomer was taking hold, a stage director and manager. I was beginning to know the names of my actors, and could arrange plausible entrances for them, or exits; I cut short superfluous lines, and came gradually to avoid the most obvious effects. Last, I learned not to indulge too much in monologue. And gradually, in turn, my actions were forming me.

My military successes might have earned me enmity from a lesser man than Trajan. But courage was the only language which he grasped at once; its words went straight to his heart. He came to see in me a kind of second-in-command, almost a son, and nothing of what happened later could wholly separate us. On my side, certain of my newly conceived objections to his views were, at least momentarily, put aside or forgotten in presence of the admirable genius which he displayed with the armies. I have always liked to see a great specialist at work; the emperor, in his own field, had a skill and sureness of hand second to none. Placed at the head of the First Legion Minervia, most glorious of them all, I was assigned to wipe out the last enemy entrenchments in the region of the Iron Gates. After we had surrounded and taken the citadel of Sarmizegethusa I followed the emperor into that subterranean hall where the counselors of King Decebalus had just ended their last banquet by swallowing poison; Trajan gave me the order to set fire to that weird heap of dead men. The same evening, on the steep heights of the battlefield, he transferred to my finger the diamond ring which Nerva had given him, and which had come to be almost a token of imperial succession. That night I fell asleep content.

My newly won popularity diffused over my second stay in Rome something of the feeling of euphoria which I was to know again, but to a much stronger degree, during my years of felicity. Trajan had given me two million sesterces to distribute in public bounty; naturally it was not enough, but by that time I was administering my own estate, which was considerable, and money difficulties no longer troubled me. I had lost most of my ignoble fear of displeasing. A scar on my chin provided a pretext for wearing the short beard of the Greek philosophers. In my attire I adopted a simplicity which I carried to greater extremes after becoming emperor; my time of bracelets and perfumes had passed. That this simplicity was itself still an attitude is of little importance. Slowly I accustomed myself to plainness for its own sake, and to that contrast, which I was later to value, between a collection of gems and the unadorned hands of the collector. To speak further of attire, an incident from which portents were drawn occurred during the year of my tribuneship in Rome. One day of appallingly bad weather, when I was to deliver a public address, I had mislaid my mantle of heavy Gallic wool. Protected only by my toga, which caught the water in its gutterlike folds, I had continually to wipe the rain from my eyes as I pronounced my discourse. Catching cold is an emperor's privilege in Rome, since he is forbidden, regardless of weather, to put anything over the toga: from that day on, every huckster and melon vendor believed in my approaching good fortune.

We talk much of the dreams of youth. Too often we forget its scheming. That, too, is a form of dream, and is no less extravagant than the others. I was not the only one to indulge in such calculations throughout that period of Roman festivities; the whole army rushed into the race for honors. I broke gaily enough into the role of ambitious politician, but I have never been able to play it for long with conviction, or without need of constant help from a prompter. I was willing to carry out with utmost conscientiousness the tiresome duty of recorder of senatorial proceedings; I knew what services would count most. The laconic style of the emperor, though admirable for the armies, did not suffice for Rome; the empress, whose literary tastes were akin to mine, persuaded him to let me compose his speeches. This was the first of the good offices of Plotina. I succeeded all the better for having had practice in that kind of accommodation: in the difficult period of my apprenticeship I had often written harangues for senators who were short of ideas or turns of phrase; they ended by thinking themselves the authors of these pieces.

In working thus for Trajan, I took exactly the same delight as that afforded by the rhetorical exercises of my youth; alone in my room, trying out my effects before a mirror, I felt myself an emperor. In truth I was learning to be one; audacities of which I should not have dreamed myself capable became easy when someone else would have to shoulder them. The emperor's thinking was simple but inarticulate, and therefore obscure; it became quite familiar to me, and I flattered myself that I knew it somewhat better than he did. I enjoyed aping the military style of the commander-in-chief, and hearing him thereafter in the Senate pronounce phrases which seemed typical, but for which I was responsible. On other days, when Trajan kept to his room, I was entrusted with the actual delivery of these discourses, which he no longer even read, and my enunciation, by this time above reproach, did honor to the lessons of the tragic actor Olympus.

Such personal services brought me into intimacy with the emperor, and even into his confidence, but the ancient antipathy went on. It had momentarily given way to the pleasure which an ageing ruler feels on seeing a young man of his blood begin a career which the elder imagines, rather naïvely, is to continue his own. But perhaps that enthusiasm had mounted so high on the battlefield at Sarmizegethusa only because it had come to the surface through so many superposed layers of mistrust. I think still that there was something more there than ineradicable animosity arising from quarrels painfully patched up, from differences of temperament, or merely from habits of mind in a man already growing old. By instinct the emperor detested all indispensable subordinates. He would have understood better on my part a mixture of irregularity and devotion to duty; I seemed to him almost suspect by reason of being technically irreproachable. That fact was apparent when the empress thought to advance my career in arranging for me a marriage with his grandniece. Trajan opposed himself obstinately to the project, adducing my lack of domestic virtues, the extreme youth of the girl, and even the old story of my debts. The empress persisted with like stubbornness; I warmed to the game myself; Sabina, at that age, was not wholly without charm. This marriage, though tempered by almost continuous absence, became for me subsequently a source of such irritation and annoyance that it is hard now to recall it as a triumph at the time for an ambitious young man of twenty-eight.

I was more than ever a member of the family, and was more or less forced to live within it. But everything in that circle displeased me, except for the handsome face of Plotina. Innumerable Spanish cousins were always present at the imperial table, just as later on I was to find them at my wife's dinners during my rare visits to Rome; nor would I even say that later I found them grown older, for from the beginning all those people seemed like centenarians. From them emanated a kind of stale propriety and ponderous wisdom. The emperor had passed almost his whole life with the armies; he knew Rome infinitely less well than did I. With great good will he endeavored to surround himself with the best that the City had to offer, or with what had been presented to him as such. The official set was made up of men wholly admirable for their decency and respectability, but learning did not rest easily upon them, and their philosophy lacked the vigor to go below the surface of things. I have never greatly relished the pompous affability of Pliny; and the sublime rigidity of Tacitus seemed to me to enclose a Republican reactionary's view of the world, unchanged since the death of Caesar. The unofficial circle was obnoxiously vulgar, a deterrent which kept me for the moment from running new risks in that quarter. I nevertheless constrained myself to the utmost politeness toward all these folk, diverse as they were. I was deferent toward some, compliant to others, dissipated when necessary, clever but not too clever. I had need of my versatility; I was many-sided by intention, and made it a game to be incalculable. I walked a tightrope, and could have used lessons not only from an actor, but from an acrobat.

I was reproached at this period for adultery with several of our patrician women. Two or three of these much criticized liaisons endured more or less up to the beginning of my principate. Although Rome is rather indulgent toward debauchery, it has never favored the loves of its rulers. Mark Antony and Titus had a taste of this. My adventures were more modest than theirs, but I fail to see how, according to our customs, a man who could never stomach courtesans and who was already bored to death with marriage might otherwise have come to know the varied world of women. My elderly brother-in-law, the impossible Servianus, whose thirty years' seniority allowed him to stand over me both as schoolmaster and spy, led my enemies in giving out that curiosity and ambition played a greater part in these affairs than love itself; that intimacy with the wives introduced me gradually into the political secrets of the husbands, and that the confidences of my mistresses were as valuable to me as the police reports with which I regaled myself in later years. It is true that each attachment of any duration did procure for me, almost inevitably, the friendship of the fat or feeble husband, a pompous or timid fellow, and usually blind, but I seldom gained pleasure from such a connection, and profited even less. I must admit that certain indiscreet stories whispered in my ear by my mistresses served to awaken in me some sympathy for these much mocked and little understood spouses. Such liaisons, agreeable enough when the women were expert in love, became truly moving when these women were beautiful. It was a study of the arts for me; I came to know statues, and to appreciate at close range a Cnidian Venus or a Leda trembling under the weight of the swan. It was the world of Tibullus and Propertius: a melancholy, an ardor somewhat feigned but intoxicating as a melody in the Phrygian mode, kisses on back stairways, scarves floating across a breast, departures at dawn, and wreaths of flowers left on doorsteps.

I knew almost nothing of these women; the part of their lives which they conceded to me was narrowly confined between two half-opened doors; their love, of which they never ceased talking, seemed to me sometimes as light as one of their garlands; it was like a fashionable jewel, or a fragile and costly fillet, and I suspected them of putting on their passion with their necklaces and their rouge. My own life was not less mysterious to them; they hardly desired to know it, preferring to dream vaguely, and mistakenly, about it; I came to understand that the spirit of the game demanded these perpetual disguises, these exaggerated avowals and complaints, this pleasure sometimes simulated and sometimes concealed, these meetings contrived like the figures of a dance. Even in our quarrels they expected a conventional response from me, and the weeping beauty would wring her hands as if on the stage.

I have often thought that men who care passionately for women attach themselves at least as much to the temple and to the accessories of the cult as to their goddess herself: they delight in fingers reddened with henna, in perfumes rubbed on the skin, and in the thousand devices which enhance that beauty and sometimes fabricate it entirely. These tender idols differed in every respect from the tall females of the barbarians, or from our grave and heavy peasant women; they were born from the golden volutes of great cities, from the vats of the dyers or the baths' damp vapor, like Venus from the foam of Greek seas. They seemed hardly separable from the feverish sweetness of certain evenings in Antioch, from the excited stir of mornings in Rome, from the famous names which they bore, or from that luxury amid which their last secret was to show themselves nude, but never without ornament. I should have desired more: to see the human creature unadorned, alone with herself as she indeed must have been at least sometimes, in illness or after the death of a first-born child, or when a wrinkle began to show in her mirror. A man who reads, reflects, or plans belongs to his species rather than to his sex; in his best moments he rises even above the human. But my fair loves seemed to glory in thinking only as women: the mind, or perhaps the soul, that I searched for was never more than a perfume.

There must have been more to it than that: hidden behind a curtain like a character of comedy awaiting the auspicious moment, I would listen intently to the sounds of an unknown interior, the particular tone of women's chatter, a burst of anger or of laughter, intimate murmurings; all this would cease the moment they knew I was there. The children, and the perpetual preoccupation with clothing or money matters, must again have taken first place once I was gone, though their importance was never mentioned in my presence; even the scorned husband would become essential, and perhaps an object for love. I compared my mistresses with the unsmiling faces of the women of my family, those whose concerns were chiefly domestic, interminably at work on the household accounts, and those who, steeped in family pride, were forever directing the care and repainting of the ancestral busts; I wondered if these frigid matrons would also be embracing a lover in some garden recess, and if my pliant beauties were not waiting merely for my departure to plunge again into some interrupted quarrel with a housekeeper. I tried as best I could to fit together these two aspects of the world of women.

Last year, shortly after the conspiracy in which Servianus came to his end, one of my mistresses of yore chose to travel all the way to the Villa in order to inform against one of her sons-in-law. I took no action upon the denunciation, which could have been inspired as much by a mother-in-law's hatred as by a desire of being useful to me. But the conversation interested me: just as in the inheritance court of old, it was wholly about wills, darkest machinations between relatives, unforeseen or unfortunate marriages. Here again was the narrow domain of women, their hard practical sense and their horizon turned grey the moment that love has ceased to illumine it. A certain acerbity and a kind of harsh loyalty brought to mind my vexatious Sabina. My visitor's features seemed flattened out, melted, as it were, as if the hand of time had passed brutally back and forth over a mask of softened wax; what I had consented, for a moment, to take for beauty had never been more than the first bloom of youth. But artifice reigned there still: the wrinkled face played awkwardly at smiles. Voluptuous memories, if ever there had been any, were completely effaced for me; this was no more than a pleasant exchange with a creature marked like me by sickness or age; I felt the same slightly irritated sympathy that I would have had for an elderly cousin from Spain, or a distant relative coming from Narbonne.

I am trying for a moment to recapture mere curls of smoke, the iridescent bubbles of some childish game. But it is easy to forget . . . So many things have happened since the days of those ephemeral loves that doubtless I no longer recognize their flavor; above all I am pleased to deny that they ever made me suffer. And yet among those mistresses there was one, at least, who was a delight to love. She was both more delicate and more firm than the others, gentler but harder, too; her slender body was rounded like a reed. I have always warmed to the beauty of human hair, that silken and undulating part of a body, but the headdresses of most of our women are towers, labyrinths, ships, or nests of adders. Hers was simply what I liked them to be: the cluster of harvest grapes, or the bird's spread wing. Lying beside me and resting her small proud head against mine, she used to speak with admirable candor of her loves. I liked her intensity and her detachment in loving, her exacting taste in pleasure, and her consuming passion for harrowing her very soul. I have known her to take dozens of lovers, more than she could keep count of; I was only a passer-by who made no demands of fidelity.

She fell in love with a dancer named Bathyllus, so handsome that all follies for his sake were justified in advance. She sobbed out his name in my arms, and my approbation gave her courage. At other times we laughed a great deal together. She died young, on a fever-ridden island to which her family had exiled her after a scandalous divorce. She had feared old age, so I could only rejoice for her, but that is a feeling we never have for those whom we have truly loved. Her need for money was fantastic. One day she asked me to lend her a hundred thousand sesterces. I brought them to her the next morning. She sat down on the floor like some small, trim figure playing at knuckle-bones, emptied the sack on the marble paving, and began to divide the gleaming pile into heaps. I knew that for her, as for all us prodigals, those pieces of gold were not true-ringing specie marked with the head of a Caesar, but a magic substance, a personal currency stamped with the effigy of a chimera and the likeness of the dancer Bathyllus. I had ceased to exist for her; she was alone. Almost plain for the moment, and puckering her brow with delightful indifference to her own beauty, like a pouting schoolboy she counted and recounted upon her fingers those difficult additions. To my eyes she was never more charming.

The news of the Sarmatian incursions reached Rome during the celebration of Trajan's Dacian triumph. These long-delayed festivities lasted eight days. It had taken nearly a year to bring from Africa and from Asia wild animals destined for slaughter in the arena; the massacre of twelve thousand such beasts and the systematic destruction of ten thousand gladiators turned Rome into an evil resort of death. On that particular evening I was on the roof of Attianus' house, with Marcius Turbo and our host. The illuminated city was hideous with riotous rejoicing: that bitter war, to which Marcius and I had devoted four years of our youth, served the populace only as pretext for drunken festival, a brutal, vicarious triumph. It was not the time to announce publicly that these much vaunted victories were not final, and that a new enemy was at our frontiers. The emperor, already absorbed in his projects for Asia, took less and less interest in the situation to the northeast, which he preferred to consider as settled once and for all. That first Sarmatian war was represented as a simple punitive expedition. I was sent out to it with the title of governor of Pannonia, and with full military powers.

The war lasted eleven months, and was atrocious. I still believe the annihilation of the Dacians to have been almost justified; no chief of state can willingly assent to the presence of an organized enemy established at his very gates. But the collapse of the kingdom of Decebalus had created a void in those regions upon which the Sarmatians swooped down; bands starting up from no one knew where infested a country already devastated by years of war and burned time and again by us, thus affording no base for our troops, whose numbers were in any case inadequate; new enemies teemed like worms in the corpse of our Dacian victories. Our recent successes had sapped our discipline: at the advance posts I found something of the gross heedlessness evinced in the feasting at Rome. Certain tribunes gave proof of foolish overconfidence in the face of danger: perilously isolated in a region where the only part we knew well was our former frontier, they were depending for continued victories upon our armament, which I beheld daily diminishing from loss and from wear, and upon reinforcements which I had no hope to see, knowing that all our resources would thereafter be concentrated upon Asia.

Another danger began to threaten: four years of official requisitioning had ruined the villages to our rear; from the time of the first Dacian campaigns, for each herd of oxen or flock of sheep so ostentatiously captured from the enemy I had seen innumerable droves of cattle seized from the inhabitants. If that state of things continued, the moment was approaching when our peasant populations, tired of supporting our burdensome military machine, would end by preferring the barbarians. Pillage by our soldiery presented a less important problem, perhaps, but one which was far more conspicuous. My popularity was such that I could risk imposition of the most rigorous restrictions upon the troops; I made current an austerity which I practiced myself, inventing the cult of the Imperial Discipline, which later I succeeded in extending throughout the army. The rash and the ambitious, who were complicating my task, were sent back to Rome; in their stead I summoned technicians, of whom we had too few. It was essential to repair the defensive works which inflated pride over our recent victories had left singularly neglected; I abandoned entirely whatever would have been too costly to maintain. Civil administrators, solidly installed in the disorder which follows every war, were rising by degrees to the level of semi-independent chieftains, capable of all kinds of extortion from our subjects and of every possible treachery toward us. On that score, as well, I could see in the more or less immediate future the beginning of revolts and divisions to come. I do not believe that we can avoid these disasters, any more than we can escape death, but it depends upon us to postpone them for a few centuries. I got rid of incompetent officials; I had the worst executed. I was discovering myself to be inexorable.

A humid summer gave way to a misty autumn, and then to a cold winter. I had need of my knowledge of medicine, and needed it first of all to treat myself. That life on the frontiers brought me little by little down to the level of the Sarmatian tribesmen: the philosopher's beard changed to that of the barbarian chieftain. I again went through what we had already seen, to the point of revulsion, during the Dacian campaigns. Our enemies burned their prisoners alive; we began to slaughter ours, for lack of means to transport them to slave markets in Rome or Asia. The stakes of our palisades bristled with severed heads. The enemy tortured their hostages; several of my friends perished in this way. One of them dragged himself on his bleeding limbs as far as the camp; he had been so disfigured that I was never able, thereafter, to recall his former aspect. The winter took its toll of victims; groups of horsemen caught in the ice or carried off by the river floods, the sick racked by cough, groaning feebly in their tents, wounded men with frozen extremities. Some admirable spirits gathered round me; this small, closely bound company whose devotion I held had the highest form of virtue, and the only one in which I still believe, namely, the firm determination to be of service. A Sarmatian fugitive whom I had made my interpreter risked his life to return to his people, there to foment revolts or treason; I succeeded in coming to an understanding with this tribe, and from that time on its men fought to protect our advance posts. A few bold strokes, imprudent in themselves but skillfully contrived, demonstrated to the enemy the absurdity of attacking the Roman State. One of the Sarmatian chieftains followed the example of Decebalus: he was found dead in his tent of felt; beside him lay his wives, who had been strangled, and a horrible bundle which contained the bodies of their children. That day my disgust for waste and futility extended to the barbarian losses themselves; I regretted these dead whom Rome might have absorbed and employed one day as allies against hordes more savage still. Our scattered attackers disappeared as they had come, into that obscure region from which no doubt many another storm will break forth. The war had not ended. I was obliged to take it up again and finish it some months after my accession. Order reigned for the moment, at least, on that frontier. I returned to Rome covered with honors. But I had aged.

My first consulate proved also to be a year of campaign, but this time the struggle was secret, though incessant, and was waged on behalf of peace. It was not, however, a struggle carried on alone. Before my return a change of attitude parallel to my own had taken place in Licinius Sura, Attianus, and Turbo alike, as if in spite of the severe censorship which I exercised over my letters these friends had already understood, and were either following me or had gone on ahead. Formerly the ups and downs of my fortunes worried me chiefly because of my friends' solicitude; fears or impatience which I should have borne lightly, if alone, grew oppressive when they had to be concealed from others, or on the contrary revealed, to their distress. I resented the fact that in their affection they felt more concern for me than I did for myself, and that they failed to see beneath the surface agitation that more tranquil being to whom no one thing is wholly important, and who can therefore endure anything. But there was no time thereafter to think about myself, or not to think either. My person began to count less precisely because my point of view was beginning to matter. What was important was that someone should be in opposition to the policy of conquest, envisaging its consequences and the final aim, and should prepare himself, if possible, to repair its errors.

My post on the frontiers had shown me an aspect of victory which does not appear on Trajan's Column. My return to civil administration gave me the chance to accumulate against the military party evidence still more decisive than all the proofs which I had amassed in the army. The ranking personnel of the legions and the entire Praetorian Guard are formed exclusively of native Italian stock; these distant wars were draining off the reserves of a country already underpopulated. Those who survived were as much a loss for this country as the others, since they were forced to settle in the newly conquered lands. Even in the provinces the system of recruiting caused some serious uprisings at about that time. A journey in Spain undertaken somewhat later on in order to inspect the operation of copper mines on my family estates, convinced me of the disorder introduced by war into all branches of the economy; I confirmed my belief in the justice of the protestations of business men whom I knew in Rome. I was not so sanguine as to think that it would always lie within our power to avoid all wars, but I wished them to be no more than defensive; I dreamed of an army trained to maintain order on frontiers less extended, if necessary, but secure. Every new increase in the vast imperial organism seemed to me an unsound growth, like a cancer or dropsical edema which would eventually cause our death.

Not one of these ideas could be presented to the emperor. He had reached that moment in life, different for each one of us, when a man abandons himself to his demon or to his genius, following a mysterious law which bids him either to destroy or outdo himself. On the whole, the achievements of his principate had been admirable, but the labors of peace to which the best of his advisors had ingeniously directed him, those great projects of the architects and legists of his reign, had always counted less for him than a single victory. This man, so nobly parsimonious for his personal needs, was now seized by a passion for expenditure. Barbarian gold raised from the bed of the Danube, the five hundred thousand ingots of King Decebalus, had sufficed to defray the cost of a public bounty and donations to the army (of which I had had my part), as well as the wild luxury of the games and initial outlays for the tremendous venture in Asia. These baneful riches falsified the true state of the finances. The fruits of war were food for new wars.

Licinius Sura died at about that time. He was the most liberal of the emperor's private counselors, so his death was a battle lost for our side. He had always been like a father in his solicitude for me; for some years illness had left him too little strength to fulfill any of his personal ambitions, but he had always enough energy to aid a man whose views appeared to him sane. The conquest of Arabia had been undertaken against his advice; he alone, had he lived, would have been able to save the State the gigantic strain and expense of the Parthian campaign. Ridden by fever, he employed his hours of insomnia in discussing with me plans for reform; they exhausted him, but their success was more important to him than a few more hours of life. At his bedside I lived in advance, and to the last administrative detail, certain of the future phases of my reign. This dying man spared the emperor in his criticisms, but he knew that he was carrying with him to the tomb what reason was left in the regime. Had he lived two or three years longer, I could perhaps have avoided some tortuous devices which marked my accession to power; he would have succeeded in persuading the emperor to adopt me sooner, and openly. But even so the last words of that statesman in bequeathing his task to me were one part of my imperial investiture.

If the group of my followers was increasing, so was that of my enemies. The most dangerous of my adversaries was Lusius Quietus, a Roman with some Arab blood, whose Numidian squadrons had played an important part in the second Dacian campaign, and who was pressing fiercely for the Asiatic war. I detested everything about him, his barbarous luxury, the pretentious swirl of his white headgear bound with cord of gold, his false, arrogant eyes, and his unbelievable cruelty toward the conquered and to those who had offered their submission. The leaders of the military party were destroying themselves in internal strife, but those who remained were thereby only the more entrenched in power, and I was only the more exposed to the mistrust of Palma or to the hatred of Celsus. My own position, happily, was almost impregnable. The civil administration was coming increasingly into my hands, since the emperor now occupied himself exclusively with his plans for war. My friends, who would have been the only persons capable of supplanting me because of their ability or their knowledge of affairs, with noble self-effacement yielded me first place. Neratius Priscus, whom the emperor trusted, daily confined his activities more deliberately within his legal specialty. Attianus organized his life with a view to serving me, and I had the prudent approbation of Plotina. A year before the war I was promoted to the governorship of Syria; later was added the post of military legate. Ordered to organize and supervise our bases, I became one of the levers of command in an undertaking which I knew to be out of all reason. I hesitated for some time, and then accepted. To refuse would have been tantamount to closing the roads to power at a moment when power was more vital to me than ever. It would also have deprived me of the one chance to act as moderator.

During these few years which preceded the great crisis for the State, I had taken a decision which left me forever exposed to the accusation of frivolity by my enemies, and which was in part calculated for that effect, to parry thus all chance of attack. I had gone to spend some months in Greece. Political considerations were no part of this voyage, in appearance at least. It was an excursion for pleasure and for study: I brought back some graven cups, and some books which I shared with Plotina. Of all my official honors, it was there that I received the one accepted with true joy: I was named archon of Athens. I allowed myself some months of effortless work and delights, walks in spring on hillsides strewn with anemones, friendly contact with bare marble. At Chaeronea, where I went to muse upon the heroic friendships of the Sacred Battalion, I spent two days as the guest of Plutarch. I had had my own Sacred Battalion, but, as is often the case with me, my life was less moving to me than history itself. I had some hunting in Arcadia, and went to Delphi to pray. At Sparta, on the edge of the Eurotas, some shepherds taught me an ancient air on the flute, a strange birdsong. Near Megara there was a peasant wedding which lasted the night long; my companions and I joined in the dances, as we should not have dared do in custom-bound Rome.

The traces of Roman crimes were visible on all sides: the walls of Corinth, left in ruins by Mummius, and the spaces within the sanctuaries left empty by Nero's organized theft of statues during his scandalous voyage. Impoverished Greece lived on in an atmosphere of pensive grace, with a kind of lucid subtlety and sober delight. Nothing had changed since the period when the pupil of the rhetorician Isaeus had breathed in for the first time that odor of warm honey, salt, and resin; nothing, in short, had changed for centuries. The sands of the palaestrae were as golden as before; Phidias and Socrates no longer frequented them, but the young men who exercised there still resembled the exquisite Charmides. It seemed to me sometimes that the Greek spirit had not carried the premises of its own genius through to their ultimate conclusions: the harvests were still to be reaped; the grain ripened in the sun and already cut was but little in comparison with the Eleusinian promise of riches hidden in that fair soil. Even among my savage enemies, the Sarmatians, I had found vases of perfect form and a mirror decorated with Apollo's image, gleams from Greece like a pale sun on snow. I could see possibilities of Hellenizing the barbarians and Atticizing Rome, thus imposing upon the world by degrees the only culture which has once for all separated itself from the monstrous, the shapeless, and the inert, the only one to have invented a definition of method, a system of politics, and a theory of beauty. The light disdain of the Greeks, which I have never ceased to feel under their most ardent homage, did not offend me; I found it natural. Whatever virtues may have distinguished me from them, I knew that I should always be less subtle than an Aegean sailor, less wise than an herb vendor of the Agora. I accepted without irritation the slightly haughty condescension of that proud race, according to an entire nation the privileges which I have always so readily conceded to those I loved. But to give the Greeks time to continue and perfect their work some centuries of peace were needed, with those calm leisures and discreet liberties which peace allows. Greece was depending upon us to be her protector, since after all we say that we are her master. I promised myself to stand watch over the defenseless god.

I had held my post as governor of Syria for a year when Trajan joined me in Antioch. He came to inspect the final preparations for the Armenian expedition, which was preliminary in his thoughts to the attack upon the Parthians. Plotina accompanied him as always, and his niece Matidia, my accommodating mother-in-law, who for some years had gone with him in camp as the head of his household. Celsus, Palma, and Nigrinus, my old enemies, still sat in the Council and dominated the general staff. All these people packed themselves into the palace while awaiting the opening of the campaign. Court intrigues flourished as never before. Everyone was laying his bets in expectation of the first throws of the dice of war.

The army moved off almost immediately in a northerly direction. With it departed the vast swarm of high officials, office-seekers, and hangers-on. The emperor and his suite paused for a few days in Commagene for festivals which were already triumphal; the lesser kings of the Orient, gathered at Satala, outdid each other in protestations of loyalty upon which, had I been in Trajan's place, I should have counted little for the future. Lusius Quietus, my dangerous rival, placed in charge of the advance posts, took possession of the shores of Lake Van in the course of a sweeping but absurdly easy conquest; the northern part of Mesopotamia, vacated by the Parthians, was annexed without difficulty; Abgar, king of Osroëne, surrendered in Edessa. The emperor came back to Antioch to take up his winter quarters, postponing till spring the invasion of the Parthian Empire itself, but already determined to accept no overture for peace. Everything had gone according to his plans. The joy of plunging into this adventure, so long delayed, restored a kind of youth to this man of sixty-four.

My views of the outcome remained somber. The Jewish and the Arabian elements were more and more hostile to the war; the great provincial landowners were angered at having to defray costs of troops passing through; the cities objected strenuously to the imposition of new taxes. Just after the emperor's return, a first catastrophe occurred which served as forerunner to all the rest: in the middle of a December night an earthquake laid a fourth of the city of Antioch in ruins within a few seconds. Trajan was bruised by a falling beam, but heroically went on tending the wounded; his immediate following numbered several dead. The Syrian mobs straightway sought to place the blame for the disaster on someone, and the emperor, for once putting aside his principles of tolerance, committed the error of allowing a group of Christians to be massacred. I have little enough sympathy for that sect myself, but the spectacle of old men flogged and children tortured all contributed to the general agitation of spirit and rendered that sinister winter more odious still. There was no money for prompt repair of the effects of the quake; thousands of shelterless people camped at night in the squares. My rounds of inspection revealed to me the existence of a hidden discontent and a secret hatred which the dignitaries who thronged the palace did not even suspect. In the midst of the ruins the emperor was pursuing his preparations for the next campaign: an entire forest was used up in the construction of movable bridges and rafts for the crossing of the Tigris. He had received with joy a whole series of new titles conferred upon him by the Senate, and was impatient to finish with the Orient in order to return to his triumph in Rome. The slightest delay would loose furies which shook him like an access of fever.

The man who restlessly paced the vast halls of that palace built long ago by the Seleucids, and which I had myself embellished (what a spiritless task that was!) with eulogistic inscriptions in his honor and with panoplies of the Dacian war, was no longer the man who had welcomed me to the camp in Cologne nearly twenty years earlier. Even his virtues had aged. His somewhat heavy joviality, which formerly disguised genuine kindness, was now no more than vulgar habit; his firmness had changed to obstinacy; his aptitude for the immediate and the practical had led to a total refusal to think. The tender respect which he felt for the empress and the grumbling affection manifested for his niece Matidia had changed into a senile dependence upon these women, whose counsels, nevertheless, he resisted more and more. His attacks of liver disorder disturbed his physician Crito, though he himself took no thought for it. His pleasures had always lacked art, and they fell still lower as he grew older. It was of little importance that the emperor, when his day's work was over, chose to abandon himself to barrack room debaucheries in company with youths whom he found agreeable, or handsome. It was, on the contrary, rather serious that he could hardly stand wine, and took too much of it; and that his small court of increasingly mediocre subalterns, selected and manipulated by freedmen of dubious character, was so placed as to be present at all my conversations with him and could report them to my adversaries. In daytime I saw him only at staff meetings, which were wholly given over to details of planning, and where the moment never came to express an independent opinion. At all other times he avoided private talks. Wine provided this man of little subtlety with a veritable arsenal of clumsy ruses. His susceptibilities of other years had indeed given way: he insisted that I join him in his pleasures; the noise, the laughter, the feeblest jokes of the young men were always welcomed as so many ways of signifying to me that this was no time for serious business. He waited for the moment when one more glass would deprive me of my reason. Everything reeled about me in this hall where barbaric trophies of wild ox heads seemed to laugh in my face. The wine jars followed in steady succession; a vinous song would spurt forth here and there, or the insolent, beguiling laugh of a page; the emperor, resting an ever more trembling hand upon the table, immured in a drunkenness possibly half feigned, lost far away upon the roads of Asia, sank heavily into his dreams . . .

Unfortunately these dreams had beauty. They were the same as those which had formerly made me think of giving up everything for the sake of following northern routes beyond the Caucasus toward Asia. This fascination, to which the elderly emperor was yielding as if entranced, had lured Alexander before him. That prince had almost made a reality of these same dreams, and had died because of them at thirty. But the gravest danger in these mighty projects lay still more in their apparent soundness; as always, practical reasons abounded for justification of the absurd and for being carried away by the impossible. The problem of the Orient had preoccupied us for centuries; it seemed natural to rid ourselves of it once and for all. Our exchanges of wares with India and the mysterious Land of Silks depended entirely upon Jewish merchants and Arabian exporters who held the franchise for Parthian roads and ports. Once the vast and loosely joined empire of the Arsacid horsemen had been reduced to nothingness we should touch directly upon those rich extremities of the world; Asia once unified would become but a province more for Rome. The port of Alexandria-in-Egypt was the only one of our outlets toward India which did not depend upon Parthian good will; there, too, we were continually confronted with the troublesome demands and revolts of the Jewish communities. Success on the part of Trajan's expedition would have allowed us to disregard that untrustworthy city. But such array of reasoning had never persuaded me. Sound commercial treaties would have pleased me more, and I could already foresee the possibility of reducing the role of Alexandria by creating a second Greek metropolis near the Red Sea, as I did later on in founding Antinoöpolis. I was beginning to know this complicated world of Asia. The simple plan of total extermination which had worked for Dacia was not the right thing in this country of much more abundant and settled population, upon which, besides, the wealth of the world depended. Beyond the Euphrates began for us the land of mirage and danger, the sands where one helplessly sank, and the roads which ended in nothing. The slightest reversal would have resulted in a jolt to our prestige giving rise to all kinds of catastrophe; the problem was not only to conquer but to conquer again and again, perpetually; our forces would be drained off in the attempt. We had tried it already: I thought with horror of the head of Crassus, tossed from hand to hand like a ball in the course of a performance of Euripides' *Bacchantes* which a barbarian king with a smattering of Greek learning had presented on the afternoon of a victory over Rome. Trajan thought to avenge this ancient defeat; I hoped chiefly to keep it from happening again. I could foretell the future with some accuracy, a thing quite possible, after all, when one is informed on a fair number of the elements which make up the present: a few meaningless victories would draw our armies too far on, leaving other frontiers perilously exposed; the dying emperor would cover himself with glory, and we who must go on living would have to resolve all the problems and remedy all the evils.

Caesar was right to prefer the first place in a village to the second in Rome. Not by ambition, nor by vain glory, but

because a man in second place has only the choice between the
dangers of obedience and those of revolt, or those still more
serious dangers of compromise. I was not even second in Rome.
The emperor, though about to set forth upon a hazardous expedition, had not yet designated his successor; each step taken to
advance his projects offered some opportunity to the chiefs of
the general staff. This man, though almost naïve, seemed to me
now more complicated than myself. Only his rough manner
reassured me; in his gruffness he treated me like a son. At other
moments I expected to be supplanted by Palma or cut off by
Quietus as soon as my services could be dispensed with. I had
no real power: I did not even manage to obtain an audience for
the influential members of the Sanhedrin of Antioch, who were
as fearful as we of the surprise moves of the Jewish agitators,
and who would have enlightened Trajan as to the contrivings
of their fellow Jews. My friend Latinius Alexander, who was
descended from one of the ancient royal families of Asia Minor,
and whose name and wealth had great weight, was heeded no
more than I. Pliny, sent out four years before to Bithynia, died
there without having had time to inform the emperor of the
exact state of public opinion and finances, even supposing that
his incurable optimism would have allowed him to do so. The
secret reports of the Lycian merchant Opramoas, who knew
Asian affairs thoroughly, were derided by Palma. The freedmen
took advantage of the morning headaches which followed the
drunken evenings to keep me out of the imperial chamber; the
emperor's orderly, a man named Phoedimus, an honest but
stupid fellow, and set against me, twice refused me entry. On
the contrary, my enemy Celsus, of consular rank, locked himself
in one evening with Trajan for a conference which lasted for
hours, and at the end of which I thought myself lost. I sought
allies where I could; for a price, in gold, I corrupted former slaves
whom otherwise I would willingly have sent to the galleys; I
caressed more than one curly-headed darling. Nerva's diamond
had lost its fire.

And it was then that the wisest of my good geniuses came to
my aid: Plotina. I had known the empress for nearly twenty
years. We were of the same circle and of about the same age. I
had seen her living calmly through almost as constrained an

existence as my own, and one more deprived of future. She had taken my part, without appearing to notice that she did so, in my difficult moments. But it was during the evil days at Antioch that her presence became indispensable to me, as was always her esteem in after times, an esteem which I kept till her death. I grew accustomed to that white-clad figure, in garments as simple as a woman's can be, and to her silences, or to words so measured as to be never more than replies, and these as succinct as possible. Nothing in her appearance or bearing was out of keeping with that palace more ancient than the splendors of Rome: this daughter of a race newly come to power was in no way inferior to the Seleucids. We two were in accord on almost everything. Both of us had a passion for adorning, then laying bare, our souls, and for testing our minds on every touchstone. She leaned toward Epicurean philosophy, that narrow but clean bed whereon I have sometimes rested my thought. The mystery of gods, which haunted me, did not trouble her, nor had she my ardent love for the human body. She was chaste by reason of her disgust with the merely facile, generous by determination rather than by nature, wisely mistrustful but ready to accept anything from a friend, even his inevitable errors. Friendship was a choice to which she devoted her whole being; she gave herself to it utterly, and as I have done only to my loves. She has known me better than anyone has; I have let her see what I carefully concealed from everyone else; for example, my secret lapses into cowardice. I like to think that on her side she has kept almost nothing from me. No bodily intimacy ever existed between us; in its place was this contact of two minds closely intermingled.

Our accord dispensed with explanations and avowals, or reticences: facts themselves sufficed. She observed these more closely than I; under the heavy braids which the fashion demanded her smooth brow was that of a judge. Her memory retained the exact impression of minutest objects; therefore, unlike me, she never had occasion to hesitate too long or to decide too quickly. She could detect at a glance my most secret adversaries, and evaluated my followers with cool detachment. In truth, we were accomplices, but the most trained ear would hardly have been able to catch the tones of a secret accord between us. She never committed the gross error of complaining to me about the emperor, nor the more subtle one of excusing or praising him. On my side, my loyalty was not questioned. Attianus, who had just come from Rome, joined in these discussions, which sometimes lasted all night; but nothing seemed to tire this imperturbable, yet frail, woman. She had managed to have my former guardian named privy councillor, thus eliminating my enemy Celsus. Trajan's mistrust of me, or else the impossibility of finding someone to fill my post in the rear, would keep me in Antioch: I was counting upon these friends to inform me about everything not revealed in the official dispatches. In case of disaster they would know how to rally round me the fidelity of a part of the army. My adversaries would have to reckon with the presence of this aged sufferer from gout, who was setting forth only in order to serve me, and with this woman who could exact of herself the long endurance of a soldier.

I watched them depart, the emperor on horseback, firm and admirably placid, the patient group of women borne in litters, Praetorian guards mingled with the Numidian scouts of the redoubtable Lusius Quietus. The army, which had passed the winter on the banks of the Euphrates, moved forward as soon as its chief arrived; the Parthian campaign was beginning in earnest. First reports were magnificent: Babylon conquered, the Tigris crossed, Ctesiphon fallen. Everything, as always, gave way before the astonishing mastery of this man. The prince of Characene Arabia declared his allegiance, opening thus the entire course of the Tigris to the Roman barges. The emperor embarked for the port of Charax at the head of the Persian Gulf. He was nearing the fabled shores. My fears persisted, but I hid them like something criminal; to be right too soon is to be in the wrong. Worse still, I was beginning to doubt my judgment; had I been guilty of that base incredulity which keeps us from recognizing the grandeur of a man whom we know too well? I had forgotten that certain beings shift the boundaries of destiny and alter history thereby. I had uttered blasphemy against the Genius of the emperor. I was consumed with anxiety at my post: if by chance the impossible were to take place, was I to play no part? Since everything is always easier than to exercise common sense, the desire seized me to don once more the coat of mail of the Sarmatian wars, using Plotina's influence to have myself recalled to the army. I envied the least of our soldiers their lot on the dusty roadways of Asia and the shock of their encounter with Persia's mailed battalions. This time the Senate voted the emperor the right to celebrate not one triumph but a succession of triumphs which would last as long as he lived. I myself did what the occasion demanded: I ordered festivities and went to offer sacrifice on the summit of Mount Casius.

Suddenly the fire which was smoldering in that land of the Orient burst forth everywhere at one time. The Jewish merchants refused to pay tax at Seleucia; Cyrene straightway revolted, and the Oriental element of the city massacred the Greek element; the roads by which Egyptian grain was brought to our troops were cut by a band of Zealots from Jerusalem; at Cyprus the Greek and Roman residents were seized by the Jewish populace, who forced them to slay each other in gladiatorial combats. I succeeded in maintaining order in Syria, but could see flame in the eyes of beggars sitting at the doors of the synagogues, and mute sneers on the heavy lips of the camel drivers, a hatred which after all we did not merit. The Jews and Arabs had made common cause from the beginning against a war which threatened to ruin their commerce; but Israel took advantage of the times to throw itself against a world from which it was excluded by its religious frenzies, its strange rites, and the intransigence of its god. The emperor, returned with all speed to Babylon, delegated Quietus to chastise the rebel cities: Cyrene, Edessa, Seleucia, great Greek centers of the Orient, were set on fire as punishment for treasons planned at mere caravan stops or contrived and directed from jewries. Some time later, in visiting these cities for reconstruction, I passed beneath colonnades in ruins and between rows of broken statues. The emperor Osroës, who had subsidized these revolts, immediately took the offensive; Abgar rose up in resistance to re-enter demolished Edessa; our Armenian allies, on whom Trajan had thought he could depend, lent a helping hand to the Persian war lords. Without warning, the emperor found himself at the center of an immense field of battle where he had to face the enemy on all sides.

He wasted the winter in the siege of Hatra, a virtually impregnable fortress situated in the heart of a desert; it cost our army some thousands of deaths. His stubbornness became more and more a form of personal courage: this ailing man would not let go. I knew from Plotina that Trajan still refused to name his heir, in spite of the admonition of a brief paralytic attack. If this imitator of Alexander were to die, in his turn, of fever or intemperance in some unhealthy corner of Asia this foreign war would be complicated by civil war; a struggle to the death would break out between my supporters and those of Celsus or of Palma. Suddenly reports ceased almost completely; the thin line of communication between the emperor and me was maintained only by the Numidian bands of my worst enemy. It was at this period that I ordered my physician for the first time to mark with red ink on my chest the position of my heart; if it came to the worst, I did not intend to fall, alive, into Lusius Quietus' hands. The difficult task of pacifying the adjacent islands and provinces was now added to the other duties of my office, but the exhausting work of daytime was nothing in comparison with the length of the restless nights. All the problems of the empire fell upon me at once, but my own plight weighed upon me even more. I desired the supreme power. I desired it that I might put my own plans into effect, try my remedies, and restore peace. I wanted it above all in order to become my full self before I died.

I was in my fortieth year. If I were to die at that time, nothing more of me would survive than a name in a series of high functionaries, and an inscription in Greek in honor of an archon of Athens. Ever since that anxious period, each time that I have witnessed the disappearance of a man just at middle age, whose successes and reverses the public thinks it can judge exactly, I have recalled that at the same age I still figured only in my own eyes, and in those of a few friends, who must sometimes have doubted my abilities as I doubted them myself. I have come to the realization that few men fulfill themselves before death, and I have judged their interrupted work with the more pity. This obsession with the possibility of a life frustrated immobilized my thought at one point, drawing everything to it like an abscess. My hunger for power was like the craving for love, which keeps the lover from eating or sleeping, from thinking, or even from loving so long as certain rites remain unperformed. The most urgent tasks seemed vain when I was not the free master over decisions affecting the future; I needed to be assured of reigning in order to recapture the desire to serve. That palace of Antioch, where I was to live some years later on in a virtual frenzy of delight, was for me then but a prison, and perhaps my death cell. I sent messages to the oracles, to Jupiter Ammon, to Castalia, and to Zeus Dolichenus. I summoned Persian Magi; I went so far as to send to the dungeons of Antioch for a criminal intended for crucifixion, whose throat was slit in my presence by a sorcerer in the hope that the soul, floating for an instant between life and death, would reveal the future. The wretch gained thereby escape from slower death, but the questions put remained unanswered. At night I trailed from one window recess to another, from balcony to balcony through the rooms of that palace where the walls were still cracked from the earthquake, here and there tracing my astrological calculations upon the stones, and questioning the trembling stars. But it is on earth that the signs of the future have to be sought.

At last the emperor raised the siege of Hatra and decided to come back over the Euphrates, which never should have been crossed at all. The heat, which was already torrid, and harassing from the Parthian archers rendered that bitter return more disastrous still. On a burning evening in May I rode out beyond the city gates along the banks of the Orontes to meet the small group so worn by anxiety, fever, and fatigue: the ailing emperor, Attianus, and the women. Trajan determinedly kept to his horse as far as the palace door. He could hardly stand; this man once so full of vitality seemed more changed than others are by the approach of death. Crito and Matidia helped him to climb the steps, induced him to lie down, and thereafter established themselves at his bedside. Attianus and Plotina recounted to me those incidents of the campaign which they had not been able to include in their brief dispatches. One of these episodes so moved me as to become forever a personal remembrance, a symbol of my own. As soon as the weary emperor had reached Charax he had gone to sit upon the shore, looking out over the brackish waters of the Persian Gulf. This was still the period when he felt no doubt of victory, but for the first time the immensity of the world overwhelmed him, and the feeling of age, and those limits which circumscribe us all. Great tears rolled down the cheeks of the man ever deemed incapable of weeping. The supreme commander who had borne the Roman eagles to hitherto unexplored shores knew now that he would never embark upon that sea so long in his thoughts: India, Bactria, the whole of that vague East which had intoxicated him from afar, would continue to be for him only names and dreams. On the very next day bad news forced him to turn back. Each time, in my turn, that destiny has denied me my wish I have remembered those tears shed that evening on a distant shore by an old man who, perhaps for the first time, was confronting his own life face to face.

I went the following morning to the emperor's room. I felt filial toward him, or rather, fraternal. The man who had prided himself on living and thinking in every respect like any ordinary soldier of his army was ending his life in complete solitude; lying abed he continued to build up grandiose plans in which no one was any longer interested. As always, his brusque habits of speech served to disfigure his thought; forming his words now with utmost difficulty he talked to me of the triumph which they were preparing for him in Rome. He was denying defeat just as he was denying death. Two days later he had a second attack. My anxious consultations were renewed with Attianus, and with Plotina. The foresight of the empress had just effected the elevation of my old friend to the all-powerful position of commander of the Praetorian cohorts, bringing the imperial guard thus under our control. Happily Matidia, who never left the invalid's chamber, was wholly on our side; in any case, this simple, affectionate woman was like wax in Plotina's hands. But not one of us dared to remind the emperor that the question of the succession was still pendent. Perhaps like Alexander he had decided not to name his heir himself; perhaps, known to himself alone, he had commitments toward the party of Quietus. More likely, he was refusing to face his end. One sees thus in families many an obstinate old man dying intestate. For them it is less a matter of keeping their treasure to the last (or their empire), from which their numbed fingers are already half detached, than of avoiding too early entry into that posthumous state where one no longer has decisions to take, surprises to give, or threats or promises to make to the living. I pitied him; we were too different for him to find in me what most people who have wielded total authority seek desperately on their deathbeds, a docile successor pledged in advance to the same methods, and even to the same errors. But the world about him was void of statesmen: I was the only one whom he could choose without failing in his obligations as a good executive and great prince; this chief so accustomed to evaluate records of service was almost forced to accept me. That was, moreover, an excellent reason to hate me. Little by little his health was restored just enough to allow him to leave his room. He spoke of undertaking a new campaign; he did not believe in it himself. His physician Crito, who feared for him the effects of midsummer heat, succeeded at last in persuading him to re-embark for Rome. The evening before his departure he had me summoned aboard the ship which was to take him back to Italy and named me commander-in-chief in his place. He committed himself that far. But the essential was not done.

Contrary to the orders given me I began negotiations immediately, but in secret, for peace with Osroës. I was banking on the fact that I should probably no longer have to render an accounting to the emperor. Less than ten days later I was awakened in the middle of the night by arrival of a messenger; at once I recognized a confidential envoy of Plotina. He brought two missives. One, official, informed me that Trajan, unable to stand the sea voyage, had been put down at Selinus-in-Cilicia, where he lay gravely ill in the house of a merchant. A second letter, this one secret, told me of his death, which Plotina promised to keep hidden as long as possible, thus giving me the advantage of being the first one warned. I set off immediately for Selinus, after having taken all necessary precautions to assure myself of the loyalty of the Syrian garrisons. I was barely on the way when a new courier brought me official announcement that the emperor was dead. His will, which designated me as his heir, had just been sent to Rome in safe hands. Everything that for ten years' time had been feverishly dreamed of, schemed, discussed or kept silent, was here reduced to a message of two lines, traced in Greek in a small, firm, feminine hand. Attianus, who awaited me on the pier of Selinus, was the first to salute me with the title of emperor.

And it is here, in that interval between the disembarkation of the invalid and the moment of his death, that occurs one of those series of events which will forever be impossible for me to reconstruct, and upon which nevertheless my destiny has been built. Those few days passed by Attianus and the women in that merchant's house determined my life forever after, but concerning them, as later on concerning a certain afternoon on the Nile, I shall never know anything, precisely because it would be of utmost importance to me to know all. Any idler in Rome has his views about these episodes of my life, but I am the least informed of men on that score. My enemies have accused Plotina of taking advantage of the emperor's last moments to make the dying man pen the few words which bequeathed me the power. Calumniators still more lurid-minded have described a curtained bed, the uncertain gleam of a lamp, the physician Crito dictating the last wishes of Trajan in a voice which counterfeited that of the dead man. They have pointed out that the orderly Phoedimus, who hated me, and whose silence could not have been bought by my friends, very opportunely died of a malignant fever the day after the death of his master. There is something in those pictures of violence and intrigue to strike the popular imagination, and even my own. It would not displease me that a handful of reasonable people should have proved capable of verging upon crime in my behalf, nor that the devotion of the empress should have carried her so far. She was well aware of the dangers which a decision *not* taken portended for the State; I respect her enough to believe that she would have agreed to commit a necessary fraud if discretion, common sense, public interest, and friendship had all impelled her to it. Subsequently to these events I have seen this document, so violently contested by my adversaries; I am unable to pronounce either for or against the authenticity of this last dictation of a sick man. Certainly I prefer to think that Trajan himself, relinquishing his personal prejudices before he died, did of his own free will leave the empire to him whom he judged on the whole most worthy. But it must be admitted that the end, in this case, was of more concern to me than the means; the essential is that the man invested with power should have proved thereafter that he deserved to wield it.

The body was burned on the shore, not long after my arrival, as preliminary to the triumphal rites which would be solemnized in Rome. Almost no one was present at the very simple ceremony, which took place at dawn and was only a last episode in the prolonged domestic service rendered by the women to the person of Trajan. Matidia wept unrestrainedly; Plotina's features seemed blurred in the wavering air round the heat of the funeral pyre. Calm, detached, slightly hollow from fever, she remained, as always, cooly impenetrable. Attianus and Crito watched until everything had been duly consumed; the faint smoke faded away in the pale air of unshadowed morning. None of my friends referred to the incidents of those few days which had preceded the emperor's death. Their rôle was evidently to keep silent; mine was to ask no dangerous questions.

That same day the widowed empress and her companions re-embarked for Rome. I returned to Antioch, accompanied along the way by the acclamations of the legions. An extra-ordinary calm had come over me: ambition and fear alike seemed a nightmare of the past. Whatever happened, I had always been determined to defend my chance of empire to the end, but the act of adoption simplified everything. My own life no longer preoccupied me; I could once more think of the rest of mankind.

TELLUS STABILITA

Order was restored in my life, but not in the empire. The world which I had inherited resembled a man in full vigor of maturity who was still robust (though already revealing, to a physician's eyes, some barely perceptible signs of wear), but who had just passed through the convulsions of a serious illness. Negotiations were resumed, this time openly; I let it be generally understood that Trajan himself had told me to do so before he died. With one stroke of the pen I erased all conquests which might have proved dangerous: not only Mesopotamia, where we could not have maintained ourselves, but Armenia, which was too far away and too removed from our sphere, and which I retained only as a vassal state. Two or three difficulties, which would have made a peace conference drag on for years if the principals concerned had had any advantage in lengthening it out, were smoothed over by the skillful mediation of the merchant Opramoas, who was in the confidence of the Satraps. I tried to put into these diplomatic conversations the same ardor that others reserve for the field of battle; I forced a peace. Osroës, moreover, desired peace at least as much as I: the Parthians were concerned only to reopen their trade routes between us and India. A few months after the great crisis I had the joy of seeing the line of caravans re-form on the banks of the Orontes; the oases were again the resort of merchants exchanging news in the glow of their evening fires, each morning repacking along with their goods for transportation to lands unknown a certain number of thoughts, words, and customs genuinely our own, which little by little would take possession of the globe more securely than can advancing legions. The circulation of gold and the passage of ideas (as subtle as that of vital air in the arteries) were beginning again within the world's great body; earth's pulse began to beat once more.

The fever of rebellion subsided in its turn. In Egypt it had been so violent that they had been obliged to levy peasant militia at utmost speed while awaiting reinforcements. Immediately I sent my comrade Marcius Turbo to re-establish order there, a task which he accomplished with judicious firmness. But order in the streets was hardly enough for me; I desired to restore order in the public consciousness, if it were possible, or rather to make order rule there for the first time. A stay of a week in Pelusium was given over entirely to adjusting differences between those eternal incompatibles, Greeks and Jews. I saw nothing of what I should have wished to see: neither the banks of the Nile nor the Museum of Alexandria, nor the temple statues; I barely found time to devote a night to the agreeable debauches of Canopus. Six interminable days were passed in the steaming vat of a courtroom, protected from the heat without by long slatted blinds which slapped to and fro in the wind. At night enormous mosquitoes swarmed round the lamps. I tried to point out to the Greeks that they were not always the wisest of peoples, and to the Jews that they were by no means the most pure. The satiric songs with which these low-class Hellenes were wont to antagonize their adversaries were scarcely less stupid than the grotesque imprecations from the jewries. These races who had lived side by side for centuries had never had the curiosity to get to know each other, nor the decency to accept each other. The exhausted litigants who did not give way till late into the night would find me on my bench at dawn, still engaged in sorting over the rubbish of false testimony; the stabbed corpses which they offered me as evidence for conviction were frequently those of invalids who had died in their beds and had been stolen from the embalmers. But each hour of calm was a victory gained, though precarious like all victories; each dispute arbitrated served as precedent and pledge for the future. It mattered little to me that the accord obtained was external, imposed from without and perhaps temporary; I knew that good like bad becomes a routine, that the temporary tends to endure, that what is external permeates to the inside, and that the mask, given time, comes to be the face itself. Since hatred, stupidity, and delirium have lasting effects, I saw no reason why good will, clarity of mind and just practice would not have their effects, too. Order on the frontiers was nothing if I could not persuade a Jewish peddler and a Greek grocer to live peaceably side by side.

Peace was my aim, but not at all my idol; even to call it my ideal would displease me as too remote from reality. I had considered going so far in my refusal of conquests as to abandon Dacia, and would have done so had it been prudent to break openly with the policy of my predecessor; but it was better to utilize as wisely as possible those gains acquired before my accession and already recorded by history. The admirable Julius Bassus, first governor of that newly organized province, had died in his labors there, as I myself had almost succumbed in my year on the Sarmatian frontiers, exhausted by the thankless task of endless pacification in a country which had supposedly been subdued. I ordered a funeral triumph for him in Rome, an honor reserved ordinarily only for emperors; this homage to a good servitor sacrificed in obscurity was my last, and indirect, protest against the policy of conquest; nor had I need to denounce it publicly from the time that I was empowered to cut it short. On the other hand, military measures had to be taken in Mauretania, where agents of Lusius Quietus were fomenting revolt; nothing, however, required my immediate presence there. It was the same in Britain, where the Caledonians had taken advantage of withdrawal of troops for the war in Asia to decimate the reduced garrisons left on the frontiers. Julius Severus saw to what was most urgent there while awaiting the time when restoration of order in Roman affairs would permit me to undertake that long voyage. But I greatly desired to take charge myself in the Sarmatian war, which had been left inconclusive, and this time to throw in the number of troops requisite to make an end of barbarian depredations. For I refused, here as everywhere, to subject myself to a system. I accepted war as a means toward peace where negotiations proved useless, in the manner of a physician who decides to cauterize only after having tried simples. Everything is so complicated in human affairs that my rule, even if pacific, would have also its periods of war, just as the life of a great captain has, whether he likes it or not, its interludes of peace.

Before heading north for the final settlement of the Sarmatian conflict, I saw Quietus once more. The butcher of Cyrene remained formidable. My first move had been to disband his columns of Numidian scouts, but he still had his place in the Senate, his post in the regular army, and that immense domain of western sands which he could convert at will either into a springboard or a hiding-place. He invited me to a hunt in Mysia, deep in the forests, and skilfully engineered an accident in which with a little less luck or less bodily agility I should certainly have lost my life. It seemed best to appear unsuspecting, to be patient and to wait. Shortly thereafter, in Lower Moesia, at a time when the capitulation of the Sarmatian princes allowed me to think of an early return to Italy, an exchange of dispatches in code with my former guardian warned me that Quietus had come back abruptly to Rome and had just conferred there with Palma. Our enemies were strengthening their positions and realigning their troops. No security was possible so long as we should have these two men against us. I wrote to Attianus to act quickly. The old man struck like lightning. He overstepped his orders and with a single stroke freed me of the last of my avowed foes: on the same day, a few hours apart, Celsus was killed at Baiae, Palma in his villa at Terracina, and Nigrinus at Faventia on the threshold of his summer house. Quietus met his end on the road, on departing from a conference with his fellow conspirators, struck down on the step of the carriage which was bringing him back to the City. A wave of terror broke over Rome. Servianus, my aged brother-in-law, who had seemed resigned to my success but who was avidly anticipating my errors to come, must have felt an impulse of joy more nearly akin to ecstasy than any experience of his whole life. All the sinister rumors which circulated about me found credence anew.

I received this news aboard the ship which was bringing me back to Italy. I was appalled. One is always content to be relieved of one's adversaries, but my guardian had proceeded with the indifference of age for the far-reaching consequences of his act: he had forgotten that I should have to live with the after effects of these murders for more than twenty years. I thought of the proscriptions of Octavius, which had forever stained the memory of Augustus; of the first crimes of Nero, which had been followed by other crimes. I recalled the last years of Domitian, of that merely average man, no worse than another, whom fear had gradually destroyed (his own fear and the fears he caused), dying in his palace like a beast tracked down in the woods. My public life was already getting out of hand: the first line of the inscription bore in letters deeply incised a few words which I could no longer erase. The Senate, that great, weak body, powerful only when persecuted, would never forget that four of its members had been summarily executed by my order; three intriguing scoundrels and a brute would thus live on as martyrs. I notified Attianus at once that he was to meet me at Brundisium to answer for his action.

He was awaiting me near the harbor in one of the rooms of that inn facing toward the East where Virgil died long ago. He came limping to receive me on the threshold, for he was suffering from an attack of gout. The moment that I was alone with him, I burst into upbraiding: a reign which I intended to be moderate, and even exemplary, was beginning with four executions, only one of which was indispensable and for all of which too little precaution had been taken in the way of legal formalities. Such abuse of power would be cause for the more reproach to me whenever I strove thereafter to be clement, scrupulous, and just; it would serve as pretext for proving that my so-called virtues were only a series of masks, and for building about me a trite legend of tyranny which would cling to me perhaps to the end of history. I admitted my fear; I felt no more exempt from cruelty than from any other human fault; I accepted the commonplace that crime breeds crime, and the example of the animal which has once tasted blood. An old friend whose loyalty had seemed wholly assured was already taking liberties, profiting by the weaknesses which he thought that he saw in me; under the guise of serving me he had arranged to settle a personal score against Nigrinus and Palma. He was compromising my work of pacification, and was preparing for me a grim return to Rome, indeed.

The old man asked leave to sit down, and rested his leg, swathed in flannel, upon a stool. While speaking I arranged the coverlet over his ailing foot. He let me run on, smiling meanwhile like a grammarian who listens to his pupil making his way through a difficult recitation. When I had finished, he asked me calmly what I had planned to do with the enemies of the regime. It could be proved, if need were, that these four men had plotted my death; it was to their interest, in any case, to do so. Every transition from one reign to another involved its operations of mopping up; he had taken this task upon himself in order to leave my hands clean. If public opinion demanded a victim, nothing was simpler than to deprive him of his post of Praetorian prefect. He had envisaged such a measure; he was advising me to take it. And if more were needed to conciliate the Senate, he would approve my going as far as relegation to the provinces, or exile.

Attianus had been the guardian from whom money could be wheedled, the counselor of my difficult days, the faithful agent; but this was the first time that I had ever looked attentively at that face with its carefully shaven jowls, at those crippled hands tranquilly clasped over the handle of his ebony cane. I knew well enough the different elements of his life as a prosperous citizen: his wife, whom he loved, and whose health was frail; his married daughters and their children, for whom he was modest but tenacious in his ambitions, as he had been for himself; his love of choice dishes; his decided taste for Greek cameos and for young dancing girls. He had given me precedence over all these things: for thirty years his first care had been to protect me, and next to serve me. To me, who had not yet given first place to anything except to ideas or projects, or at the most to a future image of myself, this simple devotion of man to man seemed prodigious and unfathomable. No one is worthy of it, and I am still unable to account for it. I followed his counsel: he lost his post. His faint smile showed me that he expected to be taken at his word. He knew well that no untimely solicitude toward an old friend would ever keep me from adopting the more prudent course; this subtle politician would not have wished me otherwise. Let us not exaggerate the extent of his disgrace: after some months of eclipse, I succeeded in having him admitted to the Senate. It was the greatest honor that I could offer to this man of equestrian rank. He lived to enjoy the easy old age of a wealthy Roman knight, much sought after for his perfect knowledge of families and public affairs; I have often been his guest at his villa in the Alban Hills. Nevertheless, like Alexander on the eve of a battle, I had made a sacrifice to Fear before entering into Rome: I sometimes count Attianus among my human victims.

*

Attianus had been right in his conjectures: the virgin gold of respect would be too soft without some alloy of fear. The murder of four men of consular rank was received as was the story of the forged will: the honest and pure of heart refused to believe that I was implicated; the cynics supposed the worst, but admired me only the more. As soon as it was known that my resentment had suddenly come to an end Rome grew calm; each person's joy in his own security caused the dead to be promptly forgotten. My clemency was matter for astonishment because it was deemed deliberate and voluntary, chosen each morning in preference to a violence which would have been equally natural to me; my simplicity was praised because it was thought that calculation figured therein. Trajan had had most of the virtues of the average man, but my qualities were more unexpected; one step further and they would have been regarded as a refinement of vice itself. I was the same man as before, but what had previously been despised now passed for sublime: my extreme courtesy, considered by the unsubtle a form of weakness, or even of cowardice, seemed now the smooth and polished sheath of force. They extolled my patience with petitioners, my frequent visits to the sick in the military hospitals, and my friendly familiarity with the discharged veterans. Nothing in all that differed from the manner in which I had treated my servants and tenant farmers my whole life long. Each of us has more virtues than he is credited with, but success alone brings them to view, perhaps because then we may be expected to cease practicing them. Human beings betray their worst failings when they marvel to find that a world ruler is neither foolishly indolent, presumptuous, nor cruel.

I had refused all titles. In the first month of my reign the Senate had adorned me, before I could know of it, with that long series of honorary appellations which is draped like a fringed shawl round the necks of certain emperors. Dacicus, Parthicus, Germanicus: Trajan had loved these brave blasts of martial music, like the cymbals and drums of the Parthian regiments; what had roused echoes and responses in him only irritated or bewildered me. I got rid of all that, and also postponed, for the time, the admirable title of Father of the Country; Augustus accepted that honor only late in life, and I esteemed myself not yet worthy. It was the same for a triumph; it would have been ridiculous to consent to one for a war in which my sole merit had been to force a conclusion. Those who saw modesty in these refusals were as much mistaken as they who reproached me for pride. My motives related less to the effect produced on others than to advantages for myself. I desired that my prestige should be my own, inseparable from my person, and directly measurable in terms of mental agility, strength and achievements. Titles, if they were to come, would come later on; but they would be other titles, evidences of more secret victories to which I dared not yet lay claim. For the moment I had enough to do to become, or merely to be, Hadrian to the utmost.

They accuse me of caring little for Rome. It had beauty, though, during those two years when the State and I were feeling our way with each other, the city of narrow streets, crowded Forums, and ancient, flesh-colored brick. Rome revisited, after the Orient and Greece, was clothed with a strangeness which a Roman born and bred wholly in the City would not find there. I accustomed myself once more to its damp and soot-grimed winters; to the African heat of its summers, tempered by the refreshing cascades of Tibur and by the Alban lakes; to its almost rustic population, bound with provincial attachment to the Seven Hills, but gradually exposed to the influx of all races of the world, driven thither by ambition, enticements to gain, and the hazards of conquest and servitude, the tattooed black, the hairy German, the slender Greek, and the heavy Oriental. I freed myself of certain fastidious restraints: I no longer avoided the public baths at popular hours; I learned to endure the Games, where hitherto I had seen only brutal and stupid waste. My opinion had not changed; I detested these massacres where the beast had not one chance, but little by little I came to feel their ritual value, their effect of tragic purification upon the ignorant multitude. I wanted my festivities to equal those of Trajan in splendor, though with more art and decorum. I forced myself to derive pleasure from the perfect fencing of the gladiators, but only on the condition that no one should be compelled to practice this profession against his will. In the Circus I learned to parley with the crowd from the height of the tribune, speaking through heralds, and not to impose silence upon the throngs save with deference (which they repaid me hundred-fold); likewise never to accord them anything but what they had reasonably the right to expect, nor to refuse anything without explaining my refusal. I did not take my books with me, as you do, into the imperial loge; it is insulting to others to seem to disdain their joys. If the spectacle revolted me, the effort to bear it out was for me a more valuable exercise than the study of Epictetus.

Morals are matter of private agreement; decency is of public concern. Any conspicuous license has always struck me as a tawdry display. I forbade use of the baths by both sexes at the same time, a custom which had given rise to almost continual brawling; I returned to the State treasury the colossal service of silver dishes, melted down by my order, which had been wrought for the hoggish appetite of Vitellius. Our early Caesars have acquired an odious reputation for courting inheritances; I made it a rule to refuse both for myself and for the State any legacy to which direct heirs might think themselves entitled. I tried to reduce the exorbitant number of slaves in the imperial household, and especially to curb their arrogance, which leads them to rival the upper classes and sometimes to terrorize them. One day one of my servants had the impertinence to address a senator; I had the man slapped. My hatred of disorder went so far as to decree flogging in the Circus for spendthrifts sunk in debt. To preserve distinction of rank I insisted that the toga and senatorial robe be worn at all times in public, even though these garments are inconvenient, like everything honorific, and I feel no obligation to wear them myself except when in Rome. I made a practice of rising to receive my friends and of standing throughout my audiences, in reaction against the negligence of a sitting or reclining posture. I reduced the insolent crowd of carriages which cumber our streets, for this luxury of speed destroys its own aim; a pedestrian makes more headway than a hundred conveyances jammed end to end along the twists and turns of the Sacred Way. For visits to private homes I took the habit of being carried inside by litter, thus sparing my host the irksome duty of awaiting me without, or of accompanying me back to the street in the heat of the sun, or in the churlish wind of Rome.

I was again among my own people: I have always had some

affection for my sister Paulina, and Servianus himself seemed less obnoxious than before. My mother-in-law Matidia had come back from the Orient already revealing the first symptoms of a mortal disease; to distract her from her suffering I devised simple dinners, and contrived to inebriate this modest and naïve matron with a harmless drop of wine. The absence of my wife, who had retreated to the country in a fit of ill humor, in no way detracted from these family pleasures. Of all persons she is probably the one whom I have least succeeded in pleasing; to be sure, I have made little effort to do so. I went often to the small house where the widowed empress now gave herself over to the serious delights of meditation and books; there I found unchanged the perfect silence of Plotina. She was withdrawing gently from life; that garden and those light rooms were daily becoming more the enclosure of a Muse, the temple of an empress already among the gods. Her friendships, however, remained exacting; but all things considered, her demands were only reasonable and wise.

I saw my friends again, and felt the subtle pleasure of renewed contact after long absence, of reappraising and of being reappraised. My companion in former pleasures and literary pursuits, Victor Voconius, had died; I made up some sort of funeral oration, provoking smiles in mentioning among the virtues of the deceased a chastity which his poems belied, as did the presence at the funeral of that very Thestylis, him of the honey-colored curls, whom Victor used to call his 'fair torment.' My hypocrisy was less blatant than might appear: every pleasure enjoyed with art seemed to me chaste. I rearranged Rome like a house which the master intends to leave safe in his absence; new collaborators proved their worth, and adversaries now reconciled supped together at the Palatine with my supporters in former trials. At my table Neratius Priscus sketched his legislative plans; there the architect Apollodorus explained his designs; Ceionius Commodus, a wealthy patrician of Etruscan origin, descended from an ancient family of almost royal blood, was the friend who helped me work out my next moves in the Senate; he knew men, as well as wines.

His son Lucius Ceionius, barely eighteen at the time, brought the gay grace of a young prince to these banquets, which I had kept austere. He was already addicted to certain delightful follies:

a passion for concocting rare dishes for his friends, an exquisite mania for arranging flowers, a wild love of travesty, and also of gambling. Martial was his Virgil; he recited those wanton poems with charming effrontery. I made promises which have cost me some trouble since; this dancing young faun filled six months of my life.

I have so often lost sight of Lucius, then found him anew in the course of the years which followed, that perhaps I retain an image of him which is made up of memories superposed, a composite which corresponds to no one phase of his brief existence. The somewhat arrogant arbiter of Roman fashion, the budding orator timidly dependent upon models of style and seeking my advice on a difficult passage, the anxious young officer twisting his thin beard, the invalid exhausted by coughing whom I watched over to his death, none of these existed till much later on. The picture of Lucius the boy is confined to more secret recesses of my memory: a face, a body, a complexion with the pale flush of alabaster, the exact equivalent of an amorous epigram of Callimachus or of certain perfectly turned, unadorned lines of Strato.

But I was eager to leave Rome. My predecessors, up to this time, had absented themselves chiefly for war; for me the great undertakings, the activities of peace, and my life itself began outside Rome's bounds.

There was one last service to perform, the duty of giving to Trajan that triumph which had obsessed his dying dreams. Actually a triumph becomes only the dead. When we are living there is always someone to reproach us for our failings; thus once they mocked Caesar for his baldness and his loves. But the dead are entitled to such inauguration into the tomb, to those few hours of noisy pomp before the centuries of glory and the millenniums of oblivion. Their fortune is safe from all reverses, and even their defeats acquire the splendor of victories. The last triumph of Trajan commemorated not his more or less dubious success over Parthia, but the honorable effort which his whole life had been. We had come together to celebrate the best emperor that Rome had known since the later years of Augustus, the hardest working, the most honest, and the least unjust. His very defects were no more than those distinguishing traits which prove the perfect resemblance between the marble portrait and the face. The emperor's soul ascended to the heavens, borne up along the still spiral of the Trajan Column. My adoptive father became a god: he had taken his place in that series of soldierly incarnations of the eternal Mars who come from century to century to shake and to change the world. As I stood upon the balcony of the Palatine I weighed the differences between us; I was directing myself toward calmer ends. I began to dream of truly Olympian rule.

Rome is no longer confined to Rome: henceforth she must identify herself with half the globe, or must perish. Our homes and terraced roofs of tile, turned by the setting sun to rose and gold, are no longer enclosed, as in the time of our kings, within city walls. Our true ramparts now are thousands of leagues from Rome. I have constructed a good part of these defenses myself along the edges of Germanic forest and British moor. Each time that I have looked from afar, at the bend of some sunny road, toward a Greek acropolis with its perfect city fixed to the hill like a flower to its stem, I could not but feel that the incomparable plant was limited by its very perfection, achieved on one point of space and in one segment of time. Its sole chance of expansion, as for that of a plant, was in its seed; with the pollen of its ideas Greece has fertilized the world. But Rome, less light and less shapely, sprawling to the plain at her river's edge, was moving toward vaster growth: the city has become the State. I should have wished the State to expand still more, likening itself to the order of the universe, to the divine nature of things. Virtues which had sufficed for the small city of the Seven Hills would have to grow less rigid and more varied if they were to meet the needs of all the earth. Rome, which I was first to venture to call 'eternal', would come to be more and more like the mother deities of the cults of Asia, bearer of youths and of harvests, sheltering at her breast both the lions and the hives of bees.

But anything made by man which aspires to eternity must adapt itself to the changing rhythm of nature's great bodies, to accord with celestial time. Our Rome is no longer the village of the days of Evander, big with a future which has already partly passed by; the plundering Rome of the time of the Republic has performed its role; the mad capital of the first Caesars inclines now to greater sobriety; other Romes will come, whose forms I see but dimly, but whom I shall have helped to mold. When I was visiting ancient cities, sacred but wholly dead, and without present value for the human race, I promised myself to save this Rome of mine from the petrification of a Thebes, a Babylon, or a Tyre. She would no longer be bound by her body of stone, but would compose for herself from the words *State, citizenry*, and *republic* a surer immortality. In the countries as yet untouched by our culture, on the banks of the Rhine and the Danube, or the shores of the Batavian Sea, each village enclosed within its wooden palisade brought to mind the reed hut and dunghill where our Roman twins had slept content, fed by the milk of the wolf; these cities-to-be would follow the pattern of Rome. Over separate nations and races, with their accidents of geography and history and the disparate demands of their ancestors or their gods, we should have superposed for ever a unity of human conduct and the empiricism of sober experience, but should have done so without destruction of what had preceded us. Rome would be perpetuating herself in the least of the towns where magistrates strive to demand just weight from the merchants, to clean and light the streets, to combat disorder, slackness, superstition and injustice, and to give broader and fairer interpretation to the laws. She would endure to the end of the last city built by man.

Humanitas, Libertas, Felicitas: those noble words which grace the coins of my reign were not of my invention. Any Greek philosopher, almost every cultured Roman, conceives of the world as I do. I have heard Trajan exclaim, when confronted by a law which was unjust because too rigorous, that to continue its enforcement was to run counter to the spirit of the times. I shall have been the first, perhaps, to subordinate all my actions to this 'spirit of the times', to make of it something other than the inflated dream of a philosopher, or the slightly vague aspirings of some good prince. And I was thankful to the gods, for they had allowed me to live in a period when my allotted task consisted of prudent reorganization of a world, and not of extracting matter, still unformed, from chaos, or of lying upon a corpse in the effort to revive it. I enjoyed the thought that our past was long enough to provide us with great examples, but not so heavy as to crush us under their weight; that our technical developments had advanced to the point of facilitating hygiene in the cities and prosperity for the population, though not to the degree of encumbering man with useless acquisition; that our arts, like trees grown weary with the abundance of their bearing, were still able to produce a few choice fruits. I was glad that our venerable, almost formless religions, drained of all intransigence and purged of savage rites, linked us mysteriously to the most ancient secrets of man and of earth, not forbidding us, however, a secular explanation of facts and a rational view of human conduct. It was, in sum, pleasing to me that even these words *Humanity, Liberty, Happiness*, had not yet lost their value by too much misuse.

I see an objection to every effort toward ameliorating man's condition on earth, namely that mankind is perhaps not worthy of such exertion. But I meet the objection easily enough: so long as Caligula's dream remains impossible of fulfillment, and the entire human race is not reduced to a single head destined for the axe, we shall have to bear with humanity, keeping it within bounds but utilizing it to the utmost; our interest, in the best sense of the term, will be to serve it. My procedure was based on a series of observations made upon myself over a long period; any lucid explanation has always convinced me, all courtesy has won me over, every moment of felicity has almost always left me wise. I lent only half an ear to those well-meaning folk who say that happiness is enervating, liberty too relaxing, and that kindness is corrupting for those upon whom it is practiced. That may be; but, in the world as it is, such reasoning amounts to refusal to nourish a starving man decently for fear that in a few years he may suffer from overfeeding. When useless servitude has been alleviated as far as possible, and unnecessary misfortune avoided, there will still remain as a test of man's fortitude that long series of veritable ills, death, old age and incurable sickness, love unrequited and friendship rejected or betrayed, the mediocrity of a life less vast than our projects and duller than our dreams; in short, all the woes caused by the divine nature of things.

I should say outright that I have little faith in laws. If too severe, they are broken, and with good reason. If too complicated, human ingenuity finds means to slip easily between the meshes of this trailing but fragile net. Respect for ancient laws answers to what is deepest rooted in human piety, but it serves also to pillow the inertia of judges. The oldest codes are a part of that very savagery which they were striving to correct; even the most venerable among them are the product of force. Most of our punitive laws fail, perhaps happily, to reach the greater part of the culprits; our civil laws will never be supple enough to fit the immense and changing diversity of facts. Laws change more slowly than custom, and though dangerous when they fall behind the times are more dangerous still when they presume to anticipate custom. And nevertheless from that mass of outworn routines and perilous innovations a few useful formulas have emerged here and there, just as they have in medicine. The Greek philosophers have taught us to know something more of the nature of man; our best jurists have worked for generations along lines of common sense. I have myself effected a few of those partial reforms which are the only reforms that endure. Any law too often subject to infraction is bad; it is the duty of the legislator to repeal or to change it, lest the contempt into which that rash ruling has fallen should extend to other, more just legislation. I proposed as my aim a prudent avoidance of superfluous decrees, and the firm promulgation, instead, of a small group of well-weighed decisions. The time seemed to have come to evaluate anew all the ancient prescriptions in the interest of mankind.

One day in Spain, in the vicinity of Tarragona, when I was visiting alone a half-abandoned mine, a slave attacked me with a knife. He had passed most of his forty-three years in those subterranean corridors, and not without logic was taking revenge upon the emperor for his long servitude. I managed to disarm him easily enough; under the care of my physicians his violence subsided, and he changed into what he really was, a being not less sensible than others, and more loyal than many. Had the law been applied with savage rigor, he would have been promptly executed; as it was, he became my useful servant. Most men are like this slave: they are only too submissive; their long periods of torpor are interspersed with a few revolts as brutal as they are ineffectual. I wanted to see if well-regulated liberty would not have produced better results, and I am astonished that a similar

experiment has not tempted more princes. This barbarian condemned to the mines became a symbol to me of all our slaves
and all our barbarians. It seemed to me not impossible to treat
them as I had treated this man, rendering them harmless simply
by kindness, provided that first of all they understand that the
hand which disarms them is sure. All nations who have perished
up to this time have done so for lack of generosity: Sparta would
have survived longer had she given her Helots some interest in
that survival; there is always a day when Atlas ceases to support
the weight of the heavens, and his revolt shakes the earth. I
wished to postpone as long as possible, and to avoid, if it can be
done, the moment when the barbarians from without and the
slaves within will fall upon a world which they have been forced
to respect from afar, or to serve from below, but the profits of
which are not for them. I was determined that even the most
wretched, from the slaves who clean the city sewers to the
famished barbarians who hover along the frontiers, should have
an interest in seeing Rome endure.

I doubt if all the philosophy in the world can succeed in
suppressing slavery; it will, at most, change the name. I can well
imagine forms of servitude worse than our own, because more
insidious, whether they transform men into stupid, complacent
machines, who believe themselves free just when they are most
subjugated, or whether to the exclusion of leisure and pleasures
essential to man they develop a passion for work as violent as
the passion for war among barbarous races. To such bondage
for the human mind and imagination I prefer even our avowed
slavery. However that may be, the horrible condition which puts
one man at the mercy of another ought to be carefully regulated
by law. I saw to it that a slave should no longer be anonymous
merchandise sold without regard for the family ties which he has
formed, or a contemptible object whom a judge submits to
torture before taking his testimony, instead of accepting it upon
oath. I prohibited forced entry of slaves into disreputable or
dangerous occupations, forbidding their sale to brothel keepers,
or to schools of gladiators. Let only those who like such professions practice them; the professions will but gain thereby. On
farms, where overseers exploit the strength of slaves, I have
replaced the latter, wherever possible, by free shareholders. Our

collections of anecdotes abound in stories of gourmets who feed their household servants to their fish, but scandalous crimes are readily punishable, and are insignificant in comparison with the thousands of routine atrocities perpetrated daily by correct but heartless people whom no one would think of questioning. There was a great outcry when I banished from Rome a rich and highly esteemed patrician woman who maltreated her aged slaves; any bad son who neglects his old parents shocks the public conscience more, but I see little difference between these two forms of inhumanity.

The condition of women is fixed by strange customs: they are at one and the same time subjected and protected, weak and powerful, too much despised and too much respected. In this chaos of contradictory usage, the practices of society are superposed upon the facts of nature, but it is not easy to distinguish between the two. This confused state of things is in every respect more stable than might appear: on the whole, women want to be just as they are; they resist change, or they utilize it for their one and only aim. The freedom of the women of today, which is greater, or at least more visible, than that of earlier times, is but an aspect of the easier life of a prosperous period; the principles and even the prejudices of old have not been seriously disturbed. Whether sincere or not, the official eulogies and epitaphs continue to attribute to our matrons those same virtues of industry, chastity, and sobriety which were demanded of them under the Republic. These real or supposed changes have in no respect modified the eternal freedom of morals in the humbler classes, nor the perpetual prudery of the bourgeoisie; time alone will prove which of these changes will last. The weakness of women, like that of slaves, lies in their legal status; they take their revenge by their strength in little things, where the power which they wield is almost unlimited. I have rarely seen a household where women do not rule; I have often seen also ruling with them the steward, the cook, or the enfranchised slave. In financial matters they remain legally subject to some form of guardianship, but in practice it is otherwise. In each small shop of the Suburra it is ordinarily the poulterer's or fruiterer's wife who sits firmly ensconced in command of the counter. The wife of Attianus directed the family estate with the acumen of a true businessman. The law should differ as little as possible from accustomed practice, so I have granted women greater liberty to administer or to bequeath their fortunes, and to inherit. I have insisted that no woman should be married without her consent; this form of legalized rape is as offensive as any other. Marriage is their great venture; it is only fair that they should not engage upon it against their will.

One part of our ills comes from the fact that too many men are shamefully rich and too many desperately poor. Happily in our days we tend toward a balance between these two extremes; the colossal fortunes of emperors and freedmen are things of the past: Trimalchio and Nero are dead. But everything is still to be done for the intelligent reorganization of world economy. On coming to power I renounced the voluntary contributions made by the cities to the emperor; they are only a form of theft. I advise you to refuse them in your turn. My wholesale cancellation of private debts to the State was a more hazardous measure, but there was need to start afresh after ten years of wartime financing. Our currency has been dangerously depressed for a century; it is nevertheless by the exchange rate of our gold pieces that Rome's eternity is appraised; it behooves us to give them solid weight and true value in terms of commodities. Our lands are cultivated without plan: only the more fortunate regions, like Egypt, Africa, Tuscany, and a few others, have known how to create peasant communities carefully trained in the culture of vineyards or grain. One of my chief cares has been to promote that class, and to draw instructors from it for more primitive or conservative rural populations with less skill. I have put an end to the scandal of untilled fields neglected by great landowners too little concerned for the public good; any field not cultivated for five years' time belongs hereafter to the farmer who proposes to put it to use. It is much the same for the mines. Most of our rich men make enormous gifts to the State, and to public institutions and the emperor; many do this for their own interest, a few act unselfishly, but nearly all gain thereby in the end. I should have preferred to see their generosity take other forms than that of ostentation in alms, and to teach them to augment their possessions wisely in the interest of the community as they had done hitherto only for the enrichment of their children. With this intention I myself took over the direction of the imperial domains; no one has the right to treat the earth so unproductively as the miser does his pot of gold.

Our merchants are sometimes our best geographers, our best astronomers, and our most learned naturalists. Our bankers number among our ablest judges of men. I made use of these special capacities, but fought with all my strength against their possibilities for encroachment. Subsidies given to shipbuilders had multiplied tenfold our trade with foreign nations; thus I succeeded in reinforcing our costly imperial fleet with but slight expense. So far as importations from the Orient and Africa are concerned, Italy might as well be an island, dependent upon grain dealers for its subsistence, since it no longer supplies itself; the only means of coping with the dangers of this situation is to treat these indispensable men of business as functionaries to be watched over closely. In recent years our older provinces have attained to a state of prosperity which can still perhaps be increased, but it is important that that prosperity should serve for all, and not alone for the bank of Herod Atticus, or for the small speculator who buys up all the oil of a Greek village. No law is too strict which makes for reduction of the countless intermediaries who swarm in our cities, an obscene, fat and paunchy race, whispering in every tavern, leaning on every counter, ready to undermine any policy which is not to their immediate advantage. In time of shortage a judicious distribution from the State granaries helps to check the scandalous inflation of prices, but I was counting most of all on the organization of the producers themselves, the vineyard owners in Gaul and the fishermen in the Black Sea (whose miserable pittance is devoured by importers of caviar and salt fish, middlemen battening on the produce of those dangerous labors). One of my best days was the one on which I persuaded a group of seamen from the Archipelago to join in a single corporation in order to deal directly with retailers in the towns. I have never felt myself more usefully employed as ruler.

For the army, peace is too often only a period of turbulent idleness between two periods of combat: the alternative to inaction or to disorder is first, preparation for a war already determined upon, and then the war itself. I broke with these routines;

my perpetual visits to the advance posts were only one means among many of maintaining that peacetime army in a state of useful activity. Everywhere, on level ground as in the mountains, on the edge of the forest and in the desert, the legions spread or concentrate their buildings, always the same, their drill fields, their barracks, constructed at Cologne to resist the snow, at Lambaesis for shelter from sand storms; likewise their store-houses, from which I ordered all useless materials sold, and their officers' clubs, over which a statue of the emperor presides.

But that uniformity is no more than apparent: those inter-changeable quarters house throngs of auxiliary troops who are never the same; each race contributes to the army its particular strength and its characteristic weapons, the genius of its foot soldiers, horsemen, or archers. There I found, in the rough, that diversity in unity which I sought for the empire as a whole. I authorized the use of native speech for commands, and encour-aged the soldiers in their national war cries; I sanctioned unions between veterans and barbarian women, and gave legal status to their children, trying thus to mitigate the harshness of camp life, and to treat these simple and ignorant men as men. At the risk of rendering them less effectively mobile I intended to attach them to whatever territory they were expected to defend; I did not hesitate to regionalize the army. On an imperial scale I was hoping to re-establish the equivalent of the militias of the early Republic, where each man was wont to defend his field or his farm.

I worked above all to develop the technical efficiency of the legions; my aim was to make use of these military centers as levers of civilization, as wedges strong enough to enter in little by little just where the more delicate instruments of civil life would have been blunted. The army was becoming a connecting link between the forest dwellers, the inhabitants of steppes and marshes, and the more refined urban populations; it offered primary schooling to the barbarians, and a school of endurance and responsibility for the cultured Greeks or our own equestrian youths accustomed to the comforts of Rome. The arduous ele-ments of that life were known to me at first hand, as well as its easier side, with its subterfuges. I abolished special privileges, forbidding too frequent leaves for the officers and ordering the camps cleared of costly gardens, pleasure pavilions, and banquet halls. These superfluous buildings were turned into infirmaries and veterans' homes. We were recruiting our soldiers at too tender an age and keeping them too old, a practice which was both uneconomic and cruel. I changed all that. The August Discipline ought to reflect the humane tendencies of our times.

We emperors are not Caesars; we are functionaries of the State. That plaintiff whom I refused one day to hear to the end was right when she exclaimed that if I had no time to listen to her, I had no time to rule. The apologies which I offered her were not merely a matter of form. But nevertheless time *is* lacking: the more the empire expands the more the different aspects of authority tend to be concentrated in the hands of the chief of state; this man so pressed for time has necessarily to delegate some part of his tasks to others; his genius will consist more and more in surrounding himself with trustworthy personnel. The great crime of Claudius or of Nero was that they indolently allowed their slaves and freedmen to take on these roles of agent and representative of the master, or to serve him as counselor. One portion of my life and my travels has been passed in choosing the administrative heads of a new bureaucracy, in training them, in matching as judiciously as I could the talents to the posts, and in opening possibilities of useful employment to that middle class upon whom the State depends.

I recognize the danger of these armies of civil servants; it can be stated in a word, the fatal increase of routine. This mechanism, wound up for centuries to come, will run awry if we do not watch out; the master must constantly regulate its movements, foreseeing and repairing the effects of wear. But experience shows that in spite of our infinite care in choosing our successors the mediocre emperors will always outnumber the wise, and that at least one fool will reign per century. In time of crisis these bureaus, if well organized, will go on with what must be done, filling the interim (sometimes very long) between two good rulers. Some emperors like to parade behind them whole lines of barbarians, bound at the neck, those interminable processions of the conquered. My cortège will be different; the best of those officials whom I have attempted to train will compose it. Thanks to the members of the Imperial Council I have been able to leave

Rome for years at a time, coming back for only brief stays. I communicated with them by the swiftest of couriers, and in time of danger by semaphore. They have in their turn trained other useful auxiliaries. Their authority is of my making; their efficient activity has left me free to employ myself elsewhere. It is going to let me depart, without too much concern, into death itself.

In my twenty years of rule I have passed twelve without fixed abode. In succession I occupied palatial homes of Asiatic merchants, sober Greek houses, handsome villas in Roman Gaul provided with baths and hot air heat, or mere huts and farms. My preference was still for the light tent, that architecture of canvas and cords. Life at sea was no less diversified than in lodgings on land: I had my own ship, equipped with gymnasium and library, but I was too distrustful of all fixity to attach myself to any one dwelling, even to one in motion. The pleasure bark of a Syrian millionaire, the high galleys of the fleet, the light skiff of a Greek fisherman, each served equally well. The one luxury was speed, and all that favored it, the finest horses, the best swung carriages, luggage as light as possible, clothing and accessories most fitted to the climate. But my greatest asset of all was perfect health: a forced march of twenty leagues was nothing; a night without sleep was no more than a chance to think in peace. Few men enjoy prolonged travel; it disrupts all habit and endlessly jolts each prejudice. But I was striving to have no prejudices and few habits. I welcomed the delight of a soft bed, but liked also the touch and smell of bare earth, some contact with the rough or smooth segments of the world's circumference. I was well inured to all kinds of foods, whether British gruel or African watermelon. Once I tasted that delicacy of certain Germanic tribes, tainted game; it made me vomit, but the experiment had been tried. Though decided in my tastes in love, even there I feared routines. My attendants, reduced in number to the indispensable, or to the exquisite, separated me but little from other people; I took special care to be free in my movements, and to remain accessible to all. The provinces, those great administrative units for which I myself had chosen the emblems (Britannia on her throne of rocks, or Dacia with her scimitar) were entities for me composed of distinct parts, forests where I had sought shade, wells where I had slaked my thirst, chance

encounters at halts, faces known and sometimes loved. I began
to know each mile of our roads, Rome's finest gift, perhaps, to
the world. But best of all, and unforgettable, was the moment
when a road came to an end on a mountainside, and we
hoisted ourselves from crevice to crevice, from boulder to
boulder, to catch the dawn from an Alpine peak, or a height of
the Pyrenees.

A few men before me had traveled over the earth: Pythagoras,
Plato, some dozen philosophers in all, and a fair number of
adventurers. Now for the first time the traveller was also the
master, free both to see and to reform, or to create anew. That
chance fell to me; I reflected that possibly centuries would pass
before there might be another such happy accord between an
office, a temperament, and a world. And it was then that I felt
the advantage of being a newcomer, a man alone, scarcely bound
even by marriage, childless and practically without ancestors, a
Ulysses with no external Ithaca. I must here admit what I have
told no one else: I have never had a feeling of belonging wholly
to any one place, not even to my beloved Athens, nor even to
Rome. Though a foreigner in every land, in no place did I feel
myself a stranger. The different professions which make up the
trade of emperor were practiced along the way: I resumed military life like a garment grown comfortable with use, and fell
back readily into the jargon of the camps, that Latin deformed
by the pressure of barbaric languages and sprinkled with the
usual profanity and obvious jokes; I again grew used to the heavy
equipment of the days of maneuvers, and to that change in
equilibrium in the whole body which the weight of a shield on
the left arm can produce. More arduous were the interminable
duties of accountant, wherever I went, whether for auditing the
records of the province of Asia or those of a small British town
in debt for construction of public baths. I have already spoken
of my function as judge. Comparisons drawn from other employ-
ments came to mind: I thought of the itinerant doctor going
from door to door for care of the sick, of the street department
employee called to repair a pavement or to solder a water main;
of the overseer running back and forth on the ship, encouraging
the oarsmen but sparing his whip as he could. And today, on
the Villa's terrace, watching the slaves treat the orchard trees or

weed the flower beds, I think most of all of the coming and going of a watchful gardener.

The craftsmen whom I took with me on my rounds caused me little concern: their love of travel was as strong as my own. But I had trouble with the writers and scholars. The indispensable Phlegon fusses like an old woman, but he is the only secretary who has held up under the years: he is still with me. The poet Florus, to whom I proposed a Latin secretaryship, proclaimed right and left that he would not have wished to be Caesar, forced to battle the cold of Scythia, or British rain. The long excursions on foot did not appeal to him either. On my side, I gladly left to him the delights of Rome's literary life, the taverns where the same witticisms are exchanged each night and the same mosquitoes are endured in common. To Suetonius I had given the post of curator of archives, thus granting him access to secret documents which he needed for his biographies of the Caesars. This clever man so well named Tranquillus was hardly to be imagined outside a library; he, too, stayed behind in Rome, where he became one of my wife's intimates, a member of that small circle of discontented conservatives who gathered around her to find fault with the ways of the world. This group was little to my liking; I had Tranquillus pensioned off, and he retired to his cottage in the Sabine Hills there to mull undisturbed over the vices of Tiberius. A Greek secretariat was held for some time by Favorinus of Arles. That dwarf with the high treble voice was not devoid of subtlety but his mind was the most given to false deductions of any that I have encountered. We were always disputing, but his erudition charmed me. I was amused at his hypochondria; he dwelt upon his health like a lover attending a cherished mistress. His Hindu servant prepared his rice, imported from the Orient at great expense; unfortunately, this exotic cook spoke Greek badly, and said but little in any language, so he taught me nothing about the marvels of his native land. Favorinus flattered himself on having accomplished three rather rare things in his life: though a Gaul, he had Hellenized himself better than anyone else; though of humble origin, he was constantly quarrelling with the emperor and coming off none the worse for it, a remarkable fact which was, however, entirely to my credit; though impotent, he was continually paying fines for seduction of married women. And it is true that his lady admirers in provincial literary circles caused him difficulties from which I had more than once to extricate him. I wearied of that, and Eudemo took his place. But on the whole I have been unaccountably well served. The respect of that little group of friends and employees has survived, the gods only know how, through the rough intimacies of travel; their discretion has been still more astonishing, if possible, than their fidelity. The Suetoniuses of the future will have few anecdotes to harvest concerning me. What the public knows of my life I have revealed. My friends have kept my secrets, political and otherwise; it is fair to say that I often did the same for them.

To build is to collaborate with earth, to put a human mark upon a landscape, modifying it forever thereby; the process also contributes to that slow change which makes up the history of cities. What thought and care to determine the exact site for a bridge, or for a fountain, and to give a mountain road that perfect curve which is at the same time the shortest . . . The widening of the road to Megara transformed the shore along the Scironian Cliffs; the two thousand odd stadia of paved way, provided with cisterns and military posts, which connected Antinoöpolis with the Red Sea brought an era of security to the desert following an era of danger. For construction of a system of aqueducts in Troas all the revenue from five hundred cities of the province of Asia was not too high a price; an aqueduct for Carthage atoned in some part for the rigors of the Punic Wars. The erecting of fortifications was much like constructing dykes: the object was to find the line on which a shore, or an empire, can be defended, the point where the assault of waves (or barbarians) will be held back, stopped, or utterly broken. The beauty of the gulfs bore fruit with the opening of harbors. The founding of libraries was like constructing more public granaries, amassing reserves against a spiritual winter which by certain signs, in spite of myself, I see ahead.

I have done much rebuilding. To reconstruct is to collaborate with time gone by, penetrating or modifying its spirit, and carrying it toward a longer future. Thus beneath the stones we find the secret of the springs.

Our life is brief: we are always referring to centuries which precede or follow our own as if they were totally alien to us, but I have come close to them in my play with stone. These walls which I reinforce are still warm from contact with vanished bodies; hands yet unborn will caress the shafts of these columns. The more I have meditated upon my death, and especially upon that of another, the more I have tried to add to our lives these virtually indestructible extensions. At Rome I preferred to use our enduring brick; it returns but slowly to the earth, from which it comes, and its imperceptible settling and crumbling leave a mountainous mass even when the edifice has ceased to be visibly what it was built for, a fortress, a circus, or a tomb. In Greece and in Asia I chose the native marble, that fair substance which, once cut, stays so faithful to human measurements and proportions that the plan of an entire temple survives in each fragment of a broken column.

Architecture is rich in possibilities more varied than Vitruvius' four orders would seem to allow; our great stone blocks, like our tones in music, are amenable to endless regrouping. For the Pantheon I turned to the ancient Etruria of augurs and soothsayers; the sunny temple of Venus, on the contrary, is a round of Ionic forms, a profusion of white and pale rose columns clustered about the voluptuous goddess whence sprang the race of Caesar. The Olympieion of Athens, built on the plain, had to be in exact counterpoise to the Parthenon on its hill, vastness opposed to perfection, ardor kneeling before calm, splendor at the feet of beauty. The chapels of Antinous and his temples were magic chambers, commemorating a mysterious passage between life and death; these shrines to an overpowering joy and grief were places of prayer and evocation of the dead; there I gave myself over to my sorrow. My tomb on the bank of the Tiber reproduces, on a gigantic scale, the ancient vaults of the Appian Way, but its very proportions transform it, recalling Ctesiphon and Babylon with their terraces and towers by which man seeks to climb nearer the stars. Sepulchral Egypt provided the plan for the obelisks and rows of sphinxes of that cenotaph which forces upon a vaguely hostile Rome the memory of the friend forever mourned.

The Villa was the tomb of my travels, the last encampment of the nomad, the equivalent, though in marble, of the tents and pavilions of the princes of Asia. Almost everything that appeals to our taste has already been tried in the world of forms; I turned toward the realm of color: jasper as green as the depths of the sea, porphyry dense as flesh, basalt and somber obsidian. The crimson of the hangings was adorned with more and more intricate embroideries; the mosaics of the walls or pavements were never too golden, too white, or too dark. Each building-stone was the strange concretion of a will, a memory, and sometimes a challenge. Each structure was the chart of a dream.

Plotinopolis, Hadrianopolis, Antinoöpolis, Hadriano-therae . . . I have multiplied these human beehives as much as possible. Plumber and mason, engineer and architect preside at the births of cities; the operation also requires certain magical gifts. In a world still largely made up of woods, desert, and uncultivated plain, a city is indeed a fine sight, with its paved streets, its temple to some god or other, its public baths and toilets, a shop where the barber discusses with his clients the news from Rome, its pastry shop, shoestore, and perhaps a bookshop, its doctor's sign, and a theatre, where from time to time a comedy of Terence is played. Our men of fashion complain of the uniformity of our cities; they suffer in seeing everywhere the same statue of the emperor, and the same water pipes. They are wrong: the beauty of Nîmes is wholly different from that of Arles. But that very uniformity, to be found now on three continents, reassures the traveler as does the sight of a milestone; even the dullest of our towns have their comforting significance as shelters and posting stops. A city: that framework constructed by men for men, monotonous if you will, but only as are wax cells laden with honey, a place of meeting and exchange, where peasants come to sell their produce, and linger to gape and stare at the paintings of a portico . . .

My cities were born of encounters, both my own encounters with given corners of the earth and the conjunction of my plans as emperor with the incidents of my personal life. Plotinopolis grew from the need to establish new market towns in Thrace, but also from the tender desire to honor Plotina. Hadrianotherae is designed to serve as a trading town for the forest dwellers of Asia Minor: at first it had been for me a summer retreat, with its forest full of wild game, its hunting lodge of rough hewn logs below the hill of the god Attys, and its headlong stream where we bathed each morning. Hadrianopolis in Epirus reopened an urban center in the heart of an impoverished province: it owes its start to a visit which I made to the oracle of Dodona. Hadrianopolis in Thrace, an agricultural and military outpost strategically placed on the edge of barbarian lands, is populated by veterans of the Sarmatian wars: I know at first hand the strength and the weakness of each one of those men, their names, the number of their years of service, and of their wounds. Antinoöpolis, dearest of all, born on the site of sorrow, is confined to a narrow band of arid soil between the river and the cliffs. I was only the more desirous, therefore, to enrich it with other resources, trade with India, river traffic, and the learned graces of a Greek metropolis. There is not a place on earth that I care less to revisit, but there are few to which I have devoted more pains. It is a veritable city of columns, a perpetual peristyle. I exchange dispatches with its governor, Fidus Aquila, about the propylaea of its temple and the statues of its triumphal arch; I have chosen the names of its district divisions and religious and administrative units, symbolic names both obvious and secret which catalogue all my memories. I myself drew the plan of its Corinthian colonnades and the corresponding alignment of palm trees spaced regularly along the river banks. Countless times have I walked in thought that almost perfect quadrilateral, cut by parallel streets and divided in two by the broad avenue which leads from a Greek theatre to a tomb.

We are crowded with statues and cloyed with the exquisite in painting and sculpture, but this abundance is an illusion, for we reproduce over and over some dozen masterpieces which are now beyond our power to invent. Like other collectors I have had copied for the Villa the Hermaphrodite and the Centaur, the Niobid and the Venus. I have wanted to live as much as possible in the midst of this music of forms. I have encouraged experimentation with the thought and methods of the past, a learned archaism which might recapture lost intentions and lost techniques. I tried those variations which consist of transcribing in red marble a flayed Marsyas, portrayed heretofore only in white, going back thus into the world of painted figures; or of transposing to the pallor of Parian marble the black grain of Egypt's statues, changing the idol to a ghost. Our art is perfect, that is to say, completed, but its perfection can be modulated as finely as can a pure voice: we have still the chance to play with skill the game of perpetual approach to, or withdrawal from, that solution found once for all; we may go to the limit of control, or excess, and enclose within that beauteous sphere innumerable new constructions.

There is advantage in having behind us multiple points of comparison, in being free to follow Scopas intelligently, or to diverge, voluptuously, from Praxiteles. My contacts with the arts of barbarians have led me to believe that each race limits itself to certain subjects and to certain modes among those conceivable; each period, too, makes a selection among the possibilities offered to each race. In Egypt I have seen colossal gods, and kings; on the wrists of Sarmatian prisoners I have found bracelets which endlessly repeat the same galloping horse, or the same serpents devouring each other. But our art (I mean that of the Greeks) has chosen man as its center. We alone have known how to show latent strength and agility in bodies in repose; we alone have made a smooth brow the symbol of wise reflection. I am like our sculptors: the human contents me; I find everything there, even what is eternal. The image of the Centaur sums up for me all forests, so greatly loved, and storm winds never breathe better than in a sea goddess' billowing scarf. Natural objects and sacred emblems have value for me only as they are weighted with human associations: the phallic and funeral pine cone, the vase with doves which suggests siesta beside a fountain, the griffon which carries the beloved to the sky.

The art of portraiture was of slight interest to me. Our Roman busts have value only as records, faces copied to the last wrinkle, with every single wart; stencils of figures with whom we brush elbows in life, and whom we forget as soon as they die. The Greeks, on the contrary, have loved human perfection to the point of caring but little for the varied visages of men. I tend merely to glance at my own likeness, that dark face so changed by the whiteness of marble, those wide-opened eyes, that thin though sensuous mouth, controlled to the point of quivering. But I have been more preoccupied by the face of another. As

soon as he began to count in my life art ceased to be a luxury
and became a resource, a form of succor. I have forced this image
upon the world: there are today more portraits of that youth
than of any illustrious man whatsoever, or of any queen. At first
my desire was to have recorded in sculpture the successive
beauties of a changing form; but later, art became a kind of
magical operation, capable of evoking a countenance lost. Colossal effigies seemed to offer one means of expressing the true
proportions which love gives to those we cherish; I wanted those
images to be enormous, like a face seen at close range, tall and
solemn figures, like visions and apparitions in a terrifying dream,
and as overwhelming as the memory itself has remained. I
demanded perfect execution, nay, perfection pure; in short, that
god who every boy dying at twenty is for those who have loved
him; but I sought also an exact resemblance, the familiar presence
and each irregularity of a face dearer than beauty itself. How
many discussions it cost to keep intact the heavy line of an
eyebrow, that slightly swollen curve of the lip . . . I was counting
desperately on the eternity of stone and the fidelity of bronze to
perpetuate a body which was perishable, or already destroyed,
but I also insisted that the marble, rubbed daily with a mixture
of acid and oil, should take on the shimmer, and almost the
softness, of youthful flesh.

The face was unique, still I found it everywhere; I amalgamated
divinities, sexes, and eternal attributes, the hardy Diana of the
forests with the melancholy Bacchus, the vigorous Hermes of
the palaestrae with the twofold god who sleeps, head on arm,
like a fallen flower. I remarked how much a thoughtful young
man resembles a virile Athena.

My sculptors went slightly astray; the less able fell into the
error of too soft a line, or too obvious; all, however, were more
or less caught up in the dream. There are statues and paintings of
the youth alive, reflecting that immense and changing landscape
which extends from the fifteenth to the twentieth year: the serious
profile of the obedient child; that statue where a sculptor of
Corinth has ventured to retain the careless ease of a young boy
with lounging posture and sloping shoulders, one hand on his
hip, as if he were watching a game of dice at some street corner.
There is that marble where Papias of Aphrodisias has outlined a

body tenderly nude, with the delicate resilience of narcissus. And Aristeas has carved under my direction, in rather rough stonework, that young head so imperious and proud. There are the posthumous portraits, where death has left his mark, those great faces with the knowing lips, laden with secrets which I no longer share, because they are no longer those of the living. There is the bas-relief where the Carian Antonianos has transposed to a divine and melancholy shade the vintager clothed in a tunic of raw silk, his friendly dog nuzzling against his bare leg. And that almost intolerable mask, the work of a sculptor of Cyrene, where pleasure and pain meet on the same face, and seem to break against each other like two waves on the same rock. And those small clay figures sold for a penny which have served as a part of the imperial propaganda: *Tellus Stabilita*, the Genius of the Pacified Earth in the guise of a reclining youth who holds fruits and flowers.

Trahit sua quemque voluptas. Each to his own bent; likewise each to his aim or his ambition, if you will, or his most secret desire and his highest ideal. My ideal was contained within the word *beauty*, so difficult to define despite all the evidence of our senses. I felt responsible for sustaining and increasing the beauty of the world. I wanted the cities to be splendid, spacious and airy, their streets sprayed with clean water, their inhabitants all human beings whose bodies were neither degraded by marks of misery and servitude nor bloated by vulgar riches; I desired that the schoolboys should recite correctly some useful lessons; that the women presiding in their households should move with maternal dignity, expressing both vigor and calm; that the gymnasiums should be used by youths not unversed in arts and in sports; that the orchards should bear the finest fruits and the fields the richest harvests. I desired that the might and majesty of the Roman Peace should extend to all, insensibly present like the music of the revolving skies; that the most humble traveller might wander from one country, or one continent, to another without vexatious formalities, and without danger, assured everywhere of a minimum of legal protection and culture; that our soldiers should continue their eternal pyrrhic dance on the frontiers; that everything should go smoothly, whether workshops or temples; that the sea should be furrowed by brave ships, and the roads resounding to frequent carriages; that, in a world well ordered, the philosophers should have their place, and the dancers also. This ideal, modest on the whole, would be often enough approached if men would devote to it one part of the energy which they expend on stupid or cruel activities; great good fortune has allowed me a partial realization of my aims during the last quarter of a century. Arrian of Nicomedia, one of the best minds of our time, likes to recall to me the beautiful lines of ancient Terpander, defining in three words the Spartan ideal (that perfect mode of life to which Lacedaemon aspired without ever attaining it): *Strength, Justice, the Muses*. Strength was the basis, discipline without which there is no beauty, and firmness without which there is no justice. Justice was the balance of the parts, that whole so harmoniously composed which no excess should be permitted to endanger. Strength and justice together were but one instrument, well tuned, in the hands of the Muses. All forms of dire poverty and brutality were things to forbid as insults to the fair body of mankind, every injustice a false note to avoid in the harmony of the spheres.

In Germany construction or renovation of camps, fortifications, and roads detained me for nearly a year; new bastions, erected over a distance of seventy leagues, reinforced our frontiers along the Rhine. This country of vineyards and rushing streams was wholly familiar to me: there I recrossed the path of the young tribune who had borne news to Trajan of his accession to power. There, too, beyond our farthest fort, built of logs from the spruce forests, lay the same dark, monotonous horizon, the same world which has been closed to us from the time of the imprudent offensive launched by Augustus' legions, the ocean of trees and that vast reserve of fair-haired men. When the task of reorganization was finished, I descended to the mouth of the Rhine along the Belgian and Batavian plains. Desolate dunes cut by stiff grasses made up this northern landscape; at the port of Noviomagus the houses raised on piles stood abreast ships moored at their doors; seabirds perched on their roofs. I liked those forlorn places, though they seemed hideous to my aides, the overcast sky and the muddy rivers channeling their way through a land without form or visible spark, where no god has yet shaped the clay.

I crossed to the Isle of Britain in a ship which was flat as a barge. More than once the wind threw us back toward the coast from which we had sailed: that difficult passage afforded some wonderfully vacant hours. Gigantic clouds rose out of a heavy sea roiled by sand and incessantly stirred in its bed. As formerly in the land of the Dacians and the Sarmatians I had venerated the goddess Earth, I had here a feeling for the first time of a Neptune more chaotic than our own, of an infinite world of waters. In Plutarch I had read a mariner's legend concerning an island in those regions which border the Arctic Sea, where centuries ago the victorious Olympians are said to have exiled the vanquished Titans. There those great captives of rock and wave, eternally lashed by a tireless ocean, never at rest, forever consumed by dreams, continue to defy the Olympian rule with their violence, their anguish, and their burning but perpetually crucified desire. In this myth which is set on the remote edges of the world I came again upon philosophical theories which I had already adopted as my own: each of us has to choose, in the course of his brief life, between endless striving and wise resignation, between the delights of disorder and those of stability, between the Titan and the Olympian . . . To choose between them, or to succeed, at last, in bringing them into accord.

The civil reforms effected in Britain are part of my administrative work of which I have spoken elsewhere. What imports here is that I was the first emperor to settle pacifically in that island situated on the boundaries of the known world, where before me only Claudius had ventured for several days' time in his capacity as commander-in-chief. For an entire winter Londinium became, by my choice, what Antioch had been by necessity at the time of the Parthian war, the virtual center of the world. Thus each of my voyages changed the center of gravity for imperial power, placing it for some time along the Rhine, or on the banks of the Thames, and permitting me to estimate what would have been the strength and the weakness of such a capital. That stay in Britain made me envisage a hypothetical empire governed from the West, an Atlantic world. Such imaginary perspectives have no practical value; they cease, however, to be absurd as soon as the calculator extends his computations sufficiently far into the future.

Barely three months before my arrival the Sixth Legion Victrix had been transferred to British territory. It replaced the unhappy Ninth Legion, cut to pieces by the Caledonians during the uprisings which made the grim aftermath, in Britain, of our Parthian expedition. Two measures were necessary to prevent the return of a like disaster. Our troops were reinforced by creation of a native auxiliary corps at Eboracum. From the top of a green knoll, I watched the first maneuvers of this newly formed British army. At the same time the erection of a wall cutting the island in two in its narrowest part served to protect the fertile, guarded areas of the south from the attacks of northern tribes. I myself inspected a substantial part of those constructions begun everywhere at the same time along an earthwork eighty miles in length; it was my chance to try out, on that carefully defined space running from coast to coast, a system of defense which could afterward be applied anywhere else. But already that purely military project was proving an aid to peace and to development of prosperity in that part of Britain; villages sprang up, and there was a general movement of settlers toward our frontiers. The trench-diggers of the legion were aided in their task by native crews; the building of the wall was for many of these mountain dwellers, so newly subdued, the first irrefutable proof of the protective power of Rome; their pay was the first Roman money to pass through their hands. This rampart became the emblem of my renunciation of the policy of conquest: below the northernmost bastion I ordered the erection of a temple to the god Terminus.

Everything enchanted me in that rainy land: the shreds of mist on the hillsides, the lakes consecrated to nymphs wilder than ours, the melancholy, grey-eyed inhabitants. I took as a guide a young tribune of the British auxiliary corps, a fair-haired god who had learned Latin and who spoke some halting Greek; he even attempted timidly to compose love verses in that tongue. One cold autumn night he served as interpreter between me and a Sibyl. We were sitting in the smoky hut of a Celtic woodcutter, warming our legs clad in clumsy, heavy trousers of rough wool, when we saw creeping toward us an ancient creature drenched

and disheveled by rain and wind, wild and furtive as any animal
of the wood. She fell upon the small oaten loaves which lay
baking upon the hearth. My guide coaxed this prophetess, and
she consented to examine for me the smoke rings, the sudden
sparks, and those fragile structures of embers and ashes. She saw
cities a-building, and joyous throngs, but also cities in flames,
with bitter lines of captives, who belied my dreams for peace;
there was a young and gentle visage which she took for the
face of a woman and in which I refused to believe; then a
white spectre, which was perhaps only a statue, since that would
be an object far stranger than any phantom for this denizen
of forest and heath. And vaguely, at a distance of some years,
she saw my death, which I could well have predicted without
her.

There was less need for my presence in prosperous Gaul and
wealthy Spain than in Britain. Narbonensian Gaul reminded me
of Greece, whose graces had spread that far, the same fine schools
of eloquence, the same porticoes under a cloudless sky. I stopped
in Nîmes to plan a basilica to be dedicated to Plotina and destined
one day to become her temple. Some family ties endeared this
city to the empress and so made its clear, sun-warmed landscape
the dearer to me.

But the revolt in Mauretania was flaming still. I cut short
my journey through Spain, with no stop between Corduba
and the sea even for a moment in Italica, the city of my
childhood and my ancestors. At Gades I embarked for
Africa.

The handsome tattooed warriors of the Atlas mountains were
still molesting the African coastal cities. For a very few days
there I went through the Numidian equivalent of the Sarmatian
battles; I again saw tribes subdued one by one and the surrender
of haughty chiefs, prostrating themselves in the open desert in a
chaos of women and packs and kneeling beasts. But this time
the sand took the place of snow.

It would have been good, for once, to pass the spring in Rome,
to find there the Villa begun, to have capricious Lucius and his
caresses again, and the friendship of Plotina. But that stay in
town was broken almost at once by alarming rumors of war.
Peace with the Parthians had been concluded scarcely three years

before, but already some grave incidents were occurring on the Euphrates. I set forth at once for the East.

I had made up my mind to settle these frontier disturbances by a less routine method than that of sending in the legions. A meeting was arranged with Osroës. I took with me his daughter, who had been captured in infancy, at the time of Trajan's occupation of Babylon, and held thereafter in Rome as a hostage. She was a thin child with enormous eyes. Her presence, and that of her women attendants, was something of an encumbrance on a journey which had above all to be made with speed. This cluster of creatures in veils was jolted along on camelback across the Syrian desert. The curtains of their canopies were kept severely closed, but each evening at the halt I sent to inquire if the princess had need of anything.

In Lycia I stopped for an hour to persuade Opramoas, the merchant, who had already demonstrated his capacities for negotiation, to go with me into Parthia. The urgency of the moment restricted his customary display. Wealth and luxury had left him soft, but he was none the less admirable as a traveling companion, for he knew the desert and all its dangers.

The meeting was to take place on the left bank of the Euphrates, not far from Doura. We crossed the river on a raft. Along the bank the soldiers of the Parthian guard formed a dazzling line; their armor was of gold, and was matched in splendor by their horses' trappings. My ever-attendant Phlegon was decidedly pale, and even the officers who accompanied me were in some fear; this meeting could prove a trap. But Opramoas, alert to every air stirring in Asia, was wholly at ease in this mingling of silence and tumult, immobility and sudden gallop, and in all this magnificence thrown on the desert like a carpet on the sand. As for me, I was wondrous free from concern; like Caesar on his bark, I was entrusting myself to those planks which carried my Fortune. I gave proof of this confidence by restoring the Parthian princess immediately to her father, instead of holding her in our lines until my departure. I promised also to give back the golden throne of the Arsacid dynasty, which Trajan had taken as spoil. We had no use for the thing, but Oriental superstition held it in great esteem.

The high ceremony of these sessions with Osroës was purely external. In substance they differed little from talks between two neighbors who are trying to arrive at some peaceable settlement over a boundary dispute. I had to do with a sophisticated, Greek-speaking barbarian, not at all obtuse, not necessarily more perfidious than I, but vacillating to the point of seeming untrustworthy. My peculiar mental disciplines helped me to grasp this elusive intelligence: seated facing the Parthian emperor, I learned to anticipate, and soon to direct, his replies; I entered into his game; last, I imagined myself as Osroës bargaining with Hadrian. I detest futile discussions where each party knows in advance that he will, or will not, give way; truth in business appeals to me most of all as a means of simplifying and advancing matters. The Parthians feared us; we, in turn, held them in dread, and from the mating of our two fears would come war. The Satraps were pressing toward this war for ends of their own; I could see at once that Osroës, like me, had his Quietus and his Palma. Pharasmanes, the most turbulent of those semi-independent border princes, was even more a danger for the Parthian Empire than for us. It has been charged against me that I kept those base and corruptible lords in hand by resort to subsidies; the money was well spent. For I was too confident of the superiority of our forces to be governed by false pride, so was ready for any concession of mere prestige, but for nothing else. The greatest difficulty was to persuade Osroës that if my promises were few it was because I meant to keep them. But he did believe me, in the end, or acted as if he did. The accord concluded between us in the course of that visit has endured; for fifteen years nothing has troubled the peace on the frontiers for either side. I count on you, Marcus, to continue this state of things after my death.

One evening in Osroës' tent, during a feast given in my honor, I observed among the women and long-eyelashed pages a naked, emaciated man who sat utterly motionless. His eyes were wide open, but he seemed to see nothing of that confusion of acrobats and dancers, or those dishes laden with viands. I addressed him through my interpreter but he deigned no reply, for this was indeed a sage. His disciples, however, were more loquacious; these pious beggars came from India, and their master belonged to the powerful caste of Brahmans. I gathered that his meditations led him to believe that the whole universe is only a tissue of

illusion and error; for him self-denial, renunciation, death were
the sole means of escape from this changing flood of forms
whereon, on the contrary, our Heraclitus had willingly been
borne along. Beyond the world of the senses he hoped to rejoin
the sphere of the purely divine, that unmoving firmament of
which Plato, too, had dreamed.

I got some inkling, therefore, in spite of the bungling of my
interpreters, of conceptions not unlike those of certain of our
philosophers, but expressed by this Indian with more absolute
finality. He had reached the state where nothing was left, except
his body, to separate him from intangible deity, without substance or form, and with which he would unite; he had resolved
to burn himself alive that next morning. Osroës invited me to
the solemnity. A pyre of fragrant woods was prepared; the man
leaped into it and disappeared without one cry. His disciples gave
no sign of sorrow; for them it was not a funeral ceremony.

I pondered these things far into the night which followed.
There I lay on a carpet of finest wool on the floor of a tent
hung with gleaming brocades. A page massaged my feet. From
without came the few sounds of that Asiatic night: the whispering
of slaves at my door; the soft rustle of a palm, and Opramoas'
snores behind a curtain; the stamp of a horse's hoof; from farther
away, in the women's quarters, the melancholy murmur of a
song. All of that had left the Brahman unmoved. In his veritable
passion of refusal he had given himself to the flames as a lover
to a bed. He had cast off everything and everyone, and finally
himself, like so many garments which served to conceal from
him that unique presence, the invisible void which was his
all.

I felt myself to be different, and ready for wider choice.
Austerity, renunciation, negation were not wholly new to me; I
had been drawn to them young (as is almost always the case), at
the age of twenty. I was even younger when a friend in Rome
took me to see the aged Epictetus in his hovel in the Suburra,
shortly before Domitian ordered his exile. As in his slave days,
when a brutal master failed to extract from him even one cry,
though the beating broke his leg, so now grown old and frail he
was patiently bearing the slow torments of gravel; yet he seemed
to me to enjoy a liberty which was almost divine. His crutches,

his pallet, the earthenware lamp and wooden spoon in its vessel of clay were objects of admiration to me, the simple tools of a pure life.

But Epictetus gave up too many things, and I had been quick to observe that nothing was more dangerously easy for me than mere renunciation. This Indian, more logically, was rejecting life itself. There was much to learn from such pure-hearted fanatics, but on the condition of turning the lesson from the meaning originally intended. These sages were trying to rediscover their god above and beyond the ocean of forms, and to reduce him to that quality of the unique, intangible, and incorporeal which he had foregone in the very act of becoming universe. I perceived differently my relations with the divine. I could see myself as seconding the deity in his effort to give form and order to a world, to develop and multiply its convolutions, extensions, and complexities. I was one of the segments of the wheel, an aspect of that unique force caught up in the multiplicity of things; I was eagle and bull, man and swan, phallus and brain all together, a Proteus who is also a Jupiter.

And it was at about this time that I began to feel myself divine. Don't misunderstand me: I was still, and more than ever, the same man, fed by the fruits and flesh of earth, and giving back to the soil their unconsumed residue, surrendering to sleep with each revolution of the stars, and nearly beside myself when too long deprived of the warming presence of love. My strength and agility, both of mind and of body, had been carefully maintained by purely human disciplines. What more can I say except that all that was lived as god-like experience? The dangerous experiments of youth were over, and its haste to seize the passing hour. At forty-eight I felt free of impatience, assured of myself, and as near perfection as my nature would permit, in fact, eternal. Please realize that all this was wholly on the plane of the intellect; the delirium, if I must use the term, came later on. I was god, to put it simply, because I was man. The titles of divinity which Greece conferred upon me thereafter served only to proclaim what I had long since ascertained for myself. I even believe that I could have felt myself god had I been thrown into one of Domitian's prisons, or confined to the pits of a mine. If I make bold to such pretensions, it is because the feeling seems to me hardly extraordinary, and in no way unique. Others besides me have felt it, or will do so in time to come.

I have already mentioned that my titles added virtually nothing to this astonishing certitude; on the contrary, the feeling was confirmed in performing the simplest routines of my function as emperor. If Jupiter is brain to the world, then the man who organizes and presides over human affairs can logically consider himself as a part of that all-governing mind. Humanity, rightly or not, has almost always conceived of its god in terms of Providence; my duties forced me to serve as the incarnation of this Providence for one part of mankind. The more the State increases in size and power, extending its strict, cold links from man to man, the more does human faith aspire to exalt the image of a human protector at the end of this mighty chain. Whether I wished it or not, the Eastern populations of the empire already considered me a god. Even in the West, and even in Rome, where we are not officially declared divine till after death, the instinctive piety of the common people tends more and more to deify us while we are still alive. The Parthians, in gratitude to the Roman who had established and maintained peace, were soon to erect temples in my honor; even at Vologasia, in the very heart of that vast world beyond our frontiers, I had my sanctuary. Far from reading in this adoration a risk of arrogant presumption, or madness, for the man who accepts it, I found therein a restraint, and indeed an obligation to model myself upon something eternal, trying to add to my human capacity some part of supreme wisdom. To be god demands more virtues, all things considered, than to be emperor.

I was initiated at Eleusis eighteen months later. In one sense this visit to Osroës had been a turning point in my life. Instead of going back to Rome I had decided to devote some years to the Greek and Oriental provinces of the empire; Athens was coming more and more to be the center of my thought, and my home. I wished to please the Greeks, and also to Hellenize myself as much as possible, but though my motives for this initiation were in part political, it proved nevertheless to be a religious experience without equal. These ancient rites serve only to symbolize what happens in human life, but the symbol has a deeper purport than the act, explaining each of our motions in terms of celestial mechanism. What is taught at Eleusis must remain secret; it has, besides, the less danger of being divulged in that its nature is ineffable. If formulated, it would result only in commonplaces; therein lies its real profundity. The higher degrees which were later conferred upon me in the course of private talks with the Hierophant added almost nothing to that first emotion which I shared in common with the least of the pilgrims who made the same ritual ablutions and drank at the spring. I had heard the discords resolving into harmonies; for one moment I had stood on another sphere and contemplated from afar, but also from close by, that procession which is both human and divine, wherein I, too, had my place, this our world where suffering existed still, but error was no more. From such a perspective our human destiny, that vague design in which the least practiced eye can trace so many flaws, gleamed bright like the patterns of the heavens.

And it is here that I can best speak of a habit which led me throughout my life along paths less secret than those of Eleusis, but after all parallel to them, namely, the study of the stars. I have always been friend to astronomers and client to astrologers. The science of the latter is questionable, but if false in its details it is perhaps true in the total implication; for if man is part and parcel of the universe, and is ruled by the same laws as govern the sky, it is not unreasonable to search the heavens for the patterns of our lives, and for those impersonal attractions which induce our successes and our errors. On autumn evenings I seldom failed to greet Aquarius to the south, that heavenly Cup Bearer and Giver of Gifts under whose sign I was born. Nor did I forget to note in each of their passages Jupiter and Venus, who govern my life, nor to measure the dangerous influence of Saturn.

But if this strange refraction of human affairs upon the stellar vault preoccupied many of my waking hours, I was still more deeply absorbed in celestial mathematics, the abstract speculations to which those flaming spheres give rise. I was inclined to believe, along with certain of our more daring philosophers, that earth, too, takes part in that daily and nightly round which the sacred processions of Eleusis are intended to reproduce in human terms. In a world which is only a vortex of forces and whirl of atoms, where there is neither high nor low, periphery nor center, I could ill conceive of a globe without motion, or a fixed point which would not move.

At other times I was haunted in my nightly vigils by the problem of precession of the equinoxes, as calculated long ago by Hipparchus of Alexandria. I could see in this passage and return the mathematical demonstration of those same mysteries which Eleusis represents in mere fable and symbol. In our times the Spike of Virgo is no longer at the point of the map where Hipparchus marked it, but such variation itself completes a cycle, and serves to confirm the astronomer's hypotheses. Slowly, ineluctably, this firmament will become again what it was in Hipparchus' time; it will be again what it is in the time of Hadrian. Disorder is absorbed in order, and change becomes part of a plan which the astronomer can know in advance; thus the human mind reveals its participation in the universe by formulating such exact theorems about it, just as it does at Eleusis, by ritual outcry and dance. Both the man and the stars which are the objects of his gaze roll inevitably toward their ends, marked somewhere in the sky; but each moment of that descent is a pause, a guide mark, and a segment of a curve itself as solid as a chain of gold. Each movement in space brings us back to a point which, because we happen to be on it, seems to us a center.

From the nights of my childhood, when Marullinus first pointed out to me the constellations above, my curiosity for the world of the spheres has not abated. In the watches of camp life I looked with wonder at the moon as it raced through the clouds of barbarian skies; in later years, in the clear nights of Attica, I listened while Theron of Rhodes, the astronomer, explained his system of the world. In mid-Aegean, lying flat on the deck of a ship, I have followed the slow oscillation of the mast as it moved among the stars, swaying first from the red eye of Taurus to the tears of the Pleiades, then from Pegasus to the Swan. I answered as well as I could the naïve questions so gravely put by the youth gazing with me at that same sky. Here at the Villa I have built an observatory, but I can no longer climb its steps. Once in my life I did a rarer thing. I made sacrifice to the constellations of an entire night. It was after my visit to Osroës, coming back through the Syrian desert: lying on my back, wide awake but abandoning for some hours every human concern, I gave myself up from nightfall to dawn to this world of crystal and flame. That was the most glorious of all my voyages. Overhead shone the great star of the constellation of Lyra, destined to be the polar star for men who will live tens of thousands of years after we have ceased to be. In the last light of the horizon Castor and Pollux gleamed faintly; the Serpent gave way to the Archer; next the Eagle mounted toward the zenith, wings widespread, and beneath him appeared the constellation at that time unnamed by astronomers, but to which I have since given that most cherished of names.

The night, which is never so black as people think who live and sleep indoors, was at first more dark, and then grew lighter. The fires, left burning to frighten the jackals, went out; their dying coals made me think of my grandfather warming himself as he stood in his vineyard, and of his prophecies, which by then had become the present, and were soon to be the past. I have tried under many a form to join the divine, and have known more than one ecstasy; some of these have been atrocious, others overpoweringly sweet, but the one of the Syrian night was strangely lucid. It inscribed within me the heavenly motions with greater precision than any partial observation would ever have allowed me to attain. I know exactly, at the hour of this writing, what stars are passing here at Tibur above this stuccoed and painted ceiling; and elsewhere, far away, over a tomb. Some years later it was death which was to become the object of my constant contemplation, the thought to which I was to give every faculty of my mind not absorbed by the State. And who speaks of death speaks also of that mysterious world to which, perhaps, we gain access by death. After such long reflection, and so many experiments, some of them reprehensible, I still know nothing of what goes on behind death's dark curtain. But the Syrian night remains as my conscious experience of immortality.

SAECULUM AUREUM

The summer following my meeting with Osroës was passed in Asia Minor: I made a stop in Bithynia in order to supervise in person the annual felling in the State forests there. At Nicomedia, that lustrous, well-ordered, and learned city, I stayed with the procurator of the province, Cneius Pompeius Proculus, who lived in the ancient palace of King Nicomedus, where voluptuous memories of the young Julius Caesar abound. Breezes from the Propontis fanned those cool, shaded rooms. Proculus was a man of taste; he arranged some readings for my pleasure. Some visiting sophists and several small groups of students and poetry-lovers met together in the gardens, beside a spring consecrated to Pan. From time to time a servant would dip a great jar of porous clay into the cooling waters; even the most limpid verses lacked the sparkle of that clear stream.

One late afternoon we were reading an abstruse work of Lycophron, whom I enjoy for his daring juxtaposition of sounds, figures and allusions, a complex system of echoes and mirrors. A little apart from the others a young boy was listening to those difficult strophes, half attentive, half in dream; I thought at once of some shepherd, deep in the woods, vaguely aware of a strange bird's cry. He had brought neither tablet nor style. Seated on the edge of the water's basin he trailed a hand idly over the fair, placid surface: His father, I learned, had held a small post in administration of the vast imperial domains; left young to a grandfather's care the boy had been sent to study in Nicomedia, and to reside there with a former guest of his parents, a shipowner and builder of the town who seemed rich to that modest family.

I kept him on after the others had gone. He had read little, and knew almost nothing of the world; though childishly trusting, he was also disposed to reflection. I had seen Claudiopolis, his native city, so I led him to speak of his home on the edge of the great pine forests which furnish masts for our ships; of the hilltop temple of Attys, whose strident music he loved; of the superb horses of his country and its strange gods. His voice was low, and his Greek had the accent of Asia. Suddenly aware of my attention, or of my gaze, perhaps, he grew confused, flushed, and fell back into one of those stubborn silences to which I was soon to become accustomed. An intimacy gradually developed. He accompanied me thereafter in all my voyages, and the fabulous years began.

Antinous was Greek; I traced the story of this ancient but little known family back to the time of the first Arcadian settlers along the shores of the Propontis. But Asia had produced its effect upon that rude blood, like the drop of honey which clouds and perfumes a pure wine. I could detect in him mystic superstitions like those of a disciple of Apollonius, and the religious adoration, as well, of an Oriental subject for his monarch. His presence was extraordinarily silent: he followed me like some animal, or a familiar spirit. He had the infinite capacity of a young dog for play and for swift repose, and the same fierceness and trust. This graceful hound, avid both for caresses and commands, took his post at my feet.

I admired his almost haughty indifference for all that was not his delight or his cult; it served him in place of disinterestedness and scruple, and of all virtues painfully acquired. I marveled at his gentleness, which had aspects of hardness, too, and the somber devotion to which he gave his whole being. And yet this submission was not blind; those lids so often lowered in acquiescence or in dream were not always so; the most attentive eyes in the world would sometimes look me straight in the face, and I felt myself judged. But I was judged as is a god by his adorer: my harshness and sudden suspicions (for I had them later on) were patiently and gravely accepted. I have been absolute master but once in my life, and over but one being.

If I have said nothing yet of a beauty so apparent it is not merely because of the reticence of a man too completely conquered. But the faces which we try so desperately to recall escape us: it is only for a moment . . . I see a head bending under its dark mass of hair, eyes which seemed slanting, so long were the lids, a young face broadly formed, as if for repose. This tender body

varied all the time, like a plant, and some of its alterations were
those of growth. The boy changed; he grew tall. A week of
indolence sufficed to soften him completely; a single afternoon
at the hunt made the young athlete firm again, and fleet; an
hour's sun would turn him from jasmine to the color of honey.
The boyish limbs lengthened out; the face lost its delicate childish
round and hollowed slightly under the high cheekbones; the full
chest of the young runner took on the smooth, gleaming curves
of a Bacchante's breast; the brooding lips bespoke a bitter ardor,
a sad satiety. In truth this visage changed as if I had molded it
night and day.

When I think back on these years I seem to return to the Age
of Gold. Trouble was no more: past efforts were repaid by an
ease which was almost divine. Travel was play, a pleasure well
known, controlled, and skilfully planned. Work, though incessant, was only a form of delight. My life, where everything came
late, power and happiness, too, now acquired the splendor of
high noon, the luminous glow of siesta time when everything,
the objects of the room and the figure lying beside one, bathes
in golden shade. Passion satisfied has its innocence, almost as
fragile as any other: the remainder of human beauty was relegated
to the rank of mere spectacle, and ceased to be game for my
pursuit. This adventure, begun casually enough, served to enrich
but also to simplify my life: the future was matter for slight
concern; I ceased to question the oracles; the stars were no longer
anything more than admirable patterns upon the vault of heaven.
Never before had I noted with such elation the glimmer of dawn
on the distant islands, the coolness of caves sacred to nymphs
and haunted by birds of passage, the low flight of quail at dusk.
I reread the poets; some seemed better to me than before, but
most of them worse. I wrote verses myself which appeared less
inadequate than usual.

There was Bithynia and its sea of trees, the forests of cork-oak
and pine; and the hunting lodge with latticed galleries where the
boy, once again in familiar haunts, would cast off his dagger and
belt of gold, scattering his arrows at random to roll with the
dogs on the leather divans. The plains had stored up the long
summer's heat; haze rose from the meadows along the Sangarius
where herds of wild horses ran. At break of day we used to go

down to the river to bathe, brushing tall grass in our path still wet with dew, while above us hung the thin crescent moon which Bithynia takes for her emblem. This country received every privilege and even added my name to its own.

Winter overtook us at Sinope; there, in almost Scythian cold, I officially inaugurated the work of enlarging the port, already begun at my order by the navy's men. On our way to Byzantium, outside each village the local officials had enormous fires built up for my guards to warm themselves. We crossed the Bosphorus in full beauty of storm and snow. Then came long rides in the Thracian Forest, with stinging wind swelling the folds of our cloaks. I remember the steady beat of rain on the leaves and the tent top; the halt at the workers' camp where Hadrianopolis was to be built, and ovations there from the veterans of the Dacian wars; the soft, wet earth out of which walls and towers soon would rise. In spring an inspection of the Danube garrisons took me back to Sarmizegethusa, which today is no more than a prosperous village; a bracelet of King Decebalus now graced the wrist of the young Bithynian.

The return to Greece was made from the north: I lingered in the valley of Tempe, all splashed as it is with streams; then on to blond Euboea, and Attica's wine-rose hills. Athens we barely touched, but at Eleusis, for my initiation into the Mysteries, I passed three days and three nights mingled with the pilgrims attending the autumn feast; the only precaution taken for me was to forbid the men to wear their daggers.

I took Antinous to the Arcadia of his ancestors: its forests were still as impenetrable as in the days of those wolf hunters of old. Sometimes, with a crack of the whip, a horseman would startle a viper. On the stony heights the sun burned hot as in summer and the lad, resting against the boulders, head bowed low and his hair lightly stirred by the breeze, would sleep like some daylight Endymion. A hare which my young hunter had tamed with great effort was caught and torn by the hounds, sole woe of shadowless days. The people of Mantinea uncovered some traces of kinship with that family of Bithynian colonists, hitherto unknown; the city, where the boy was later to have his temples, was enriched by me and adorned. Its immemorial sanctuary of Neptune had fallen in ruins, yet was so venerable that all entrance to it had been forbidden: mysteries more ancient than mankind itself were perpetuated behind those never-opening doors. I built a new temple, far more vast than the old and wholly enclosing the ancient edifice, which will lie hereafter within like the stone at the heart of a fruit. On the road not far from Mantinea I restored the tomb where Epaminondas, slain in the heat of battle, is laid to rest with the young companion struck down at his side; a column whereon a poem is inscribed was erected by my order to commemorate this example of a time when everything, viewed at a distance, seems to have been noble, and simple, too, whether tenderness, glory, or death.

On the Isthmus the Games were celebrated with a splendor unparalleled since ancient times; my hope, in reviving these Hellenic festivals, was to make Greece a living unity once more. We were drawn by the hunt to the valley of the Helicon, then in its last bronzed red of autumn; at the spring of Narcissus we paused, near the Sanctuary of Love; there we offered a trophy, the pelt of a young she-bear fixed by nails of gold to the temple wall, to Eros, that god who is wisest of all.

The ship lent me by Erastos, the merchant of Ephesus, to sail the Archipelago, idled at anchor in Phaleron Bay; I had come back to Athens like a man coming home. I ventured to add to the beauty of this city, trying to perfect what was already admirable. For the first time Athens was to grow again, taking on new life after long decline. I doubled the city in extent: along the Ilissus I planned a new Athens, the city of Hadrian joined to the city of Theseus. Everything had to be rearranged, or constructed anew. Six centuries earlier the great temple consecrated to the Olympian Zeus had been left abandoned almost as soon as the structure was started. My workmen took up the task and Athens again felt the joy of activity such as she had not known since the days of Pericles: I was completing what one of the Seleucids had aspired in vain to finish, and was making amends in kind for the depredations of our Sulla. To inspect the work I went daily in and out of a labyrinth of machines and intricate pulleys, of half-dressed columns and marble blocks haphazardly piled, gleaming white against the blue sky. There was something of the excitement of the naval shipyards; a mighty vessel had been salvaged and was being fitted out for the future.

In the evenings the art of building gave way to that of music, which is architecture, too, though invisible. I am somewhat practiced in all the arts, but music is the only one to which I have steadily kept and in which I profess to some skill. At Rome I had to dissemble this taste, but could indulge it with discretion in Athens. The musicians used to gather in a court where a cypress grew, near a statue of Hermes. There were only six or seven of them, an orchestra of reeds and lyres; to these we sometimes added a professional with a cithara. My instrument was chiefly the long flute. We played ancient tunes, some almost forgotten, and newer works as well, composed for me. I liked the hard vigor of the Dorian airs, but certainly had no aversion to voluptuous or passionate melodies, or to the poignant, subtly broken rhythms which sober, fearful folk reject as intoxicating for the senses and the soul. Through the strings of his lyre I could see the profile of my young companion, gravely absorbed in his part in the group, his fingers moving with care along the taut cords.

That perfect winter was rich in friendly intercourse: the opulent Atticus, whose bank was financing my constructions (though not without profit therefrom), invited me to his gardens in Kephissia where he lived surrounded by a court of lecturers and writers then in fashion; his son, young Herod, a subtle wit, proved indispensable at my Athenian suppers. He had certainly lost the timidity which once left him speechless before me, on the occasion of his embassy to the Sarmatian frontier on behalf of the youth of Athens to congratulate me on my accession; but his growing vanity now seemed to me no more than mildly ridiculous. Herod's rival in eloquence, and in wealth, was the rhetorician Polemo, glory of Laodicea, who beguiled me by his Oriental style, shimmering and full as the goldbearing waves of Pactolus; this clever craftsman in words lived as he discoursed, with splendor.

But the most precious of all these encounters was that with Arrian of Nicomedia, the best of my friends. Younger than I by some twelve years, he had already begun that outstanding political and military career in which he continues to distinguish himself and to serve the State. His experience in government, his knowledge of hunting, horses, and dogs, and of all bodily exercise, raised him infinitely above the mere word-mongers of the time. In his youth he had been prey to one of those strange passions of the soul without which, perhaps, there can be no true wisdom, nor true greatness: two years of his life had been passed at Nicopolis in Epirus in the cold, bare room where Epictetus lay dying; he had set himself the task of gathering and transcribing, word for word, the last sayings of that aged and ailing philosopher. That period of enthusiasm had left its mark upon him; from it he retained certain admirable moral disciplines, and a kind of grave simplicity. In secret he practiced austerities which no one even suspected. But his long apprenticeship to Stoic duty had not hardened him into self-righteousness; he was too intelligent not to realize that the heights of virtue, like those of love, owe their special value to their very rarity, to their quality of unique achievement and sublime excess. Now he was striving to model himself upon the calm good sense and perfect honesty of Xenophon. He was writing the history of his country, Bithynia; I had placed this province, so long ill governed by proconsuls, under my personal jurisdiction; Arrian advised me in my plans for reform. This assiduous reader of Socratic dialogue treated my young favorite with tender deference, for he knew full well the rich stores of heroism, devotion, and even wisdom, on which Greece has drawn to ennoble love between friends. These two Bithynians spoke the soft speech of Ionia, where word endings are almost Homeric in form. I later persuaded Arrian to employ this dialect in his writings.

At that period Athens had its philosopher of the frugal life: in a cabin of the village of Colonus, Demonax was leading an exemplary but merry existence. He was no Socrates, for he lacked both the subtlety and the ardor, but I relished his waggish good humor. Another of these good-hearted friends was the actor Aristomenes, a spirited performer of ancient Attic comedy. I used to call him my Greek partridge; short, fat, happy as a child (or a bird), he was better informed than anyone else on religious rituals, poetry, and cookery of former days. He was long a source of amusement and instruction to me. At about that time Antinous chose as his tutor the philosopher Chabrias, a Platonist with leanings toward Orphic teachings, and the most innocent of men; he developed a kind of watchdog fidelity to the boy which was later transferred to me. Eleven years of court life have not changed him; he is still the same honest, pious creature, chastely absorbed in his dreams, blind to all intrigue and deaf to rumor. He annoys me at times, but I shall part with him only at my death.

My relations with the Stoic philosopher Euphrates were of shorter duration. He had retired to Athens after brilliant successes in Rome. I engaged him as my reader, but the suffering which he had long endured from a liver abscess, and the resulting weakness, convinced him that his life no longer offered him anything worth the living. He asked my permission to quit my service by suicide. I have never been opposed to voluntary departure from life, and had considered it as a possible end in my hour of crisis before Trajan's death. The problem of suicide which has obsessed me since seemed then of easy solution. Euphrates received the authorization which he sought; I had it carried to him by my young Bithynian, perhaps because it would have pleased me myself to receive from the hands of such a messenger this final response. The philosopher came to the palace that same evening for a conversation which differed in no respect from all preceding visits; he killed himself the next day. We talked over the incident several times; the boy remained somber for some days thereafter. This ardent young creature held death in horror; I had not observed that he already gave it much thought. For my part I could ill conceive that anyone would willingly leave a world which seemed to me so fair, or fail to exhaust to the end, despite all its evils, its utmost possibility of thought and of contact, and even of seeing. I have indeed changed since that time.

The years merge: my memory forms but a single fresco whereon are crowded the events and travels of several seasons. The luxuriously fitted bark of the merchant Erastos turned its prow first toward the Orient, then to the south, and only at last toward Italy, which was fast becoming for me the Occident. We twice touched Rhodes; Delos, blinding white, was visited on an April morning, and later on under full moon of the summer solstice; storms on the coast of Epirus allowed me to prolong a stay in Dodona. In Sicily we delayed a few days to explore the mystery of the Syracusan springs, Arethusa and Cyane, fair nymphs of blue waters. There I thought again of Licinius Sura, the statesman devoting his scant leisure to study of the marvels of hydraulics. They had told me much of the curious colors of dawn on the Ionian Sea, when beheld from the heights of Aetna. I decided to make the ascent of the mountain. We passed from the region of vines to the beds of lava, and on to the snow; the agile youth fairly ran on those steep slopes, but the scientists who went with me climbed by muleback. At the summit a shelter had been built for us to await the dawn. It came: an immense rainbow arched from horizon to horizon; on the icy crest strange fires blazed; earth and sea spread out to view as far as Africa, within sight, and as Greece, which we merely guessed at. That was truly an Olympian height in my life. All was there, the golden fringe of cloud, the eagles, and the cupbearer of immortality.

Halcyon seasons, solstice of my days . . . Far from exaggerating my former happiness, I must struggle against too weak a portrayal; even now the recollection overpowers me. More sincere than most men, I can freely admit the secret causes of this felicity: that calm so propitious for work and for discipline of the mind seems to me one of the richest results of love. And it puzzles me that these joys, so precarious at best, and so rarely perfect in the course of human life, however we may have sought or received them, should be regarded with such mistrust by the so-called wise, who denounce the danger of habit and excess in sensuous delight, instead of fearing its absence or its loss; in tyrannizing over their senses they pass time which would be better occupied in putting their souls to rights, or embellishing them. At that period I paid as constant attention to the greater securing of my happiness, to enjoying and judging it, too, as I had always done for the smallest details of my acts; and what is the act of love, itself, if not a moment of passionate attention on the part of the body? Every bliss achieved is a masterpiece; the slightest error turns it awry, and it alters with one touch of doubt; any heaviness detracts from its charm, the least stupidity renders it dull. My own felicity is in no way responsible for those of my imprudences which shattered it later on; in so far as I have acted in harmony with it I have been wise. I think still that someone wiser than I might well have remained happy till his death.

It was some time later, in Phrygia, on the borderlands where Greece melts into Asia, that I formed the clearest and most complete idea of the nature of this happiness. We were camping in a wild and desert place, on the site of the tomb of Alcibiades, who died there a victim of machinations of the Satraps. His grave had been neglected for several centuries; I ordered a statue of Parian marble for the effigy of that man so beloved by Greece. I also arranged for commemorative rites to be celebrated annually there. The neighboring villagers joined with the members of my escort for the first of these ceremonies; a young bull was sacrificed, and part of its flesh put aside for the night's feast. A horse race was improvised upon the plain, and dances likewise. The Bithynian took part with a kind of fiery grace, and later that evening beside the last fire he sang. The upraised head showed the curve of the fine, strong throat.

I like to measure myself alongside the dead; that night I compared my life with the life of that great artist in pleasure, no longer young, who fell pierced by arrows on this spot, defended to the end by a beloved companion and wept over by an Athenian courtesan. My young years made no pretension to the prestige of Alcibiades' youth, but my versatility equalled or surpassed his own. I had tasted as many delights, had reflected more, and had done far more work; I knew, like him, the strange felicity of being loved. Alcibiades had seduced everyone and everything, even History herself; and nevertheless he left behind him mounds of Athenian dead, abandoned in the quarries of Syracuse, his own country on verge of collapse, and the gods of the crossroads drunkenly mutilated by his hands. I had governed a world infinitely larger than that of his time, and had kept peace therein; I had rigged it like a fair ship made ready for a voyage which might last for centuries; I had striven my utmost to encourage in man the sense of the divine, but without at the same time sacrificing to it what is essentially human. My bliss was my reward.

There was Rome still. But I was no longer obliged to feel my way there, to reassure and to please. The achievements of my administration were not to be denied; the gates of the temple of Janus, open in time of war, remained closed; my plans were bearing fruit: the prosperity of the provinces flowed back upon the capital. I no longer refused the title which they had proposed to me at the time of my accession, Father of the Country.

Plotina was no more. On a previous sojourn in the City I had seen her for the last time, this woman with the tired smile whom official nomenclature named my mother, and who was so much more, my sole friend among women. This time there was only her funeral urn, placed in the chamber below Trajan's Column. I attended in person the ceremonies for her apotheosis, and contrary to imperial custom wore mourning for the full nine days. But death made little change in an intimacy which for years had dispensed with mere presence; the empress remained for me what she always had been, a mind and a spirit with which mine had united.

Some of the great works of construction were nearing completion: the Colosseum, restored and cleansed of reminders of Nero which still haunted its site, was no longer adorned with the image of that emperor, but with a colossal statue of the Sun, Helios the King, in allusion to my family name of Aelius. They were putting the last touches to the Temple of Venus and Rome, erected likewise on the site of the scandalous House of Gold, where Nero had grossly displayed a luxury ill acquired. *Roma, Amor*: the divinity of the Eternal City was now for the first time identified with the Mother of Love, inspirer of every joy. It was a basic concept in my life. The Roman power was thus taking on that cosmic and sacred character, that pacific, protective form which I aspired to give it. At times it occurred to me to identify the late empress with that wise Venus, my heavenly counselor.

More and more the different gods seemed to me merged mysteriously in one Whole, emanations infinitely varied, but all equally manifesting the same force; their contradictions were only expressions of an underlying accord. The construction of a temple of All Gods, a Pantheon, seemed increasingly desirable to me. I had chosen a site on the ruins of the old public baths given by Agrippa, Augustus' son-in-law, to the people of Rome. Nothing remained of the former structure except a porch and a marble plaque bearing his dedication to the Roman citizens; this inscription was carefully replaced, just as before, on the front of the new temple. It mattered little to me to have my name recorded on this monument, which was the product of my very thought. On the contrary, it pleased me that a text of more than a century ago should link this new edifice to the beginning of our empire, to that reign which Augustus had brought to peaceful conclusion. Even in my innovations I liked to feel that I was, above all, a continuator. Farther back, beyond Trajan and Nerva, now become officially my father and my grandfather, I looked for example even to those twelve Caesars so mistreated by Suetonius: the clear-sightedness of Tiberius, without his harshness; the learning of Claudius, without his weakness; Nero's taste for the arts, but stripped of all foolish vanity; the kindness of Titus, stopping short of his sentimentality; Vespasian's thrift, but not his absurd miserliness. These princes had played their part in human affairs; it devolved upon me, to choose hereafter from among their acts what should be continued, consolidating the best things, correcting the worst, until the day when other men, either more or less qualified than I, but charged with equal responsibility, would undertake to review my acts likewise.

The dedication of the Temple of Venus and Rome was a kind of triumph, celebrated by chariot races, public spectacles, and distribution of spices and perfumes. The twenty-four elephants which had transported the enormous blocks of building stone, reducing thereby the forced labor of slaves, figured in the procession, great living monoliths themselves. The date chosen for this festival was the anniversary of Rome's birth, the eighth day following the Ides of April in the eight hundred and eighty-second year after the founding of the City. Never had a Roman spring been so intense, so sweet and so blue.

On the same day, with graver solemnity, as if muted, a dedicatory ceremony took place inside the Pantheon. I myself had revised the architectural plans, drawn with too little daring by Apollodorus: utilizing the arts of Greece only as ornamentation, like an added luxury, I had gone back for the basic form of the structure to primitive, fabled times of Rome, to the round temples of ancient Etruria. My intention had been that this sanctuary of All Gods should reproduce the likeness of the terrestrial globe and of the stellar sphere, that globe wherein are enclosed the seeds of eternal fire, and that hollow sphere containing all. Such was also the form of our ancestors' huts where the smoke of man's earliest hearths escaped through an orifice at the top. The cupola, constructed of a hard but light-weight volcanic stone which seemed still to share in the upward movement of flames, revealed the sky through a great hole at the center, showing alternately dark and blue. This temple, both open and mysteriously enclosed, was conceived as a solar quadrant. The hours would make their round on that caissoned ceiling, so carefully polished by Greek artisans; the disk of daylight would rest suspended there like a shield of gold; rain would form its clear pool on the pavement below; prayers would rise like smoke toward that void where we place the gods.

This solemnity was for me one of those moments when all things converge. Standing beside me in that well of daylight was my entire administrative staff; these men were the materials which composed the destiny of my mature years, by then already more than half completed. I could discern the austere vigor of Marcius Turbo, faithful servitor of the State; the frowning dignity of Servianus, whose grumblings, whispered ever lower, no longer reached my ears; the regal elegance of Lucius Ceionius; and slightly to one side, in that luminous shade which is best for divine apparitions, the dreamy visage of the young Greek in whom I had embodied my Fortune. My wife, present there also, had just received the title of empress.

For a long time, already, I had been more inclined toward the fables of loves and quarrels of the gods than to the clumsy commentaries of philosophers upon the nature of divinity; I was willing to be the terrestrial image of that Jupiter who is the more god in that he is also man, who supports the world, incarnating justice and giving order to the universe, but who is at the same time the lover of Ganymedes and Europas, the negligent husband of a bitter Juno. Disposed that day to see everything without shadow, in fancy I likened the empress to that goddess in whose honor, during a recent visit to Argos, I had consecrated a golden peacock adorned with precious stones. I could have freed myself by divorce from this unloved woman; had I been a private citizen I should not have hesitated to do so. But she troubled me very little, and nothing in her conduct justified so public an insult. As a young wife, she had taken offense at my ways, but only in much the same manner as her uncle had been irked by my debts. She was now confronted with manifestations of a passion which promised to endure, but she seemed not to notice them. Like many a woman little sensitive to love she poorly divined its power; such ignorance precluded the possibilities of tolerance and jealousy alike. She took umbrage only if her titles or her security were threatened, and such was not the case.

Nothing was left of that youthful charm which had briefly attracted me to her in former days; this Spanish woman grown prematurely old was grave and hard. I owed it to her natural coldness that she never took a lover, and was pleased that she wore her matronly veils with dignity; they were almost the veils of a widow. I rather liked to have the profile of an empress on the Roman coins, with an inscription on the reverse, sometimes to Matronly Virtue, sometimes to Tranquillity. Often now I thought of that symbolical marriage which takes place on the night of the Eleusinian festivities between the high priestess and the hierophant, and which is not a union or even a contact, but is a rite, and is sacred as such.

From the top of a terrace on the night following these celebrations I watched Rome ablaze. Those festive bonfires were surely as brilliant as the disastrous conflagrations lighted by Nero; they were almost as terrifying, too. Rome the crucible, but also the furnace, the boiling metal, the hammer, and the anvil as well, visible proof of the changes and repetitions of history, one place in the world where man will have most passionately lived. The great fire of Troy from which a fugitive had escaped, taking with him his aged father, his young son, and his household goods, had passed down to us that night in this flaming festival. I thought also, with something like awe, of conflagrations to come. These millions of lives past, present, and future, these structures newly arisen from ancient edifices and followed themselves by structures yet to be born, seemed to me to succeed each other in time like waves; by chance it was at my feet that night that this great surf swept to shore. I say nothing of those moments of rapture when the sacred cloth, the imperial purple, which I so seldom consented to wear, was thrown over the shoulders of the youth who was fast becoming for me my Genius; it pleased me, certainly, to place that rich red against the pale gold of a body, but I wanted above all to compel my Fortune and my Bliss, those uncertain, intangible entities, to assume this visible, earthly form, to acquire the warmth and reassuring weight of flesh. The solid walls of the Palatine Palace, which I occupied so little, but which I had just rebuilt, seemed to sway like a ship at sea; the curtains drawn back to admit the night air were like those of a high cabin aft, and the cries of the crowd were the sound of wind in the sails. The massive reef in the distance, perceptible in the dark, that gigantic base of my tomb so newly begun on the banks of the Tiber, suggested to me no regret at the moment, no terror nor vain meditation upon the brevity of life.

Little by little the light changed. For two years and more the very passage of time had been marked in the progress of a young life perfecting itself, growing radiant, and mounting to its zenith: the grave voice accustoming itself to cry orders to pilots and to masters of the hunt; the lengthened stride of the runner; the limbs of the horseman more expertly mastering his mount. The schoolboy of Claudiopolis who had learned by heart long fragments of Homer was now enamored of voluptuous, abstruse poems, or infatuated with certain passages of Plato. My young shepherd was turning into a young prince. He was no longer a mere boy, eager to jump down from his horse at the halts to offer spring water cupped in his hands: the donor now knew the immense worth of his gifts. At the hunts organized in Tuscany, in Lucius' domains, it had pleased me to place this perfect visage in among the heavy and care-laden faces of high officials, or alongside the sharp Oriental profiles and the broad, hairy faces of barbarian huntsmen, thus obliging the beloved to maintain also the difficult role of friend. In Rome intrigues had been woven around that young head, and low devices used to secure his influence, or to supplant it. He had known enough to despise all that, or ignore it; absorption in his one thought endowed this youth of eighteen with a capacity for indifference which the wisest of men might envy. But the beautiful lips had taken on a bitter line already observed by the sculptors.

Here I give the moralists occasion for easy triumph. My critics are ready to point out the consequences of aberration and excess in what befell me; it is the harder for me to refute them in that I fail to see what the error is, or where the excess lies. I try to review my crime, if it is one, in its true proportions. I tell myself that suicide is not rare, and that it is common to die at twenty; that the death of Antinous is a problem and a catastrophe for me alone. It is possible that such a disaster was inseparable from too exuberant joy, and from a plentitude of experience which I would have refused to forego either for myself or for my companion in danger. Even my remorse has gradually become a form of possession, though bitter, and a way of assuring myself that, to the end, I have been the sorry master of his destiny. But I am well aware that other factors exist, namely, the will and decision of that fair stranger who each loved one is, and remains for us, in spite of everything. In taking upon myself the entire fault I reduce the young figure to proportions of a wax statuette which I might have shaped, and crushed, in my hands. I have no right to detract from the extraordinary masterpiece which he made of his departure; I must leave to the boy the credit for his own death.

It goes without saying that I lay no blame upon the physical desire, ordinary enough, which determined my choice in love. Similar passions had often occurred in my life; these frequent adventures so far had cost no more than a minimum of pledges, troubles, or lies. My brief fancy for Lucius had involved me in only a few follies easy to mend. There was nothing to keep this supreme affection from following the same course, nothing except precisely that unique quality which distinguished it from the others. Mere habit would have led us to that inglorious but safe ending which life brings to all who accept its slow dulling from wear. I should have seen passion change into friendship, as the moralists would have it do, or into indifference, as is more often the case. A young person would have grown away from me at about the time that our bonds would have begun to weigh me down; other sensual routines, or the same under other forms, would have been established in his life; the future would have held a marriage neither worse nor better than many another, a post in provincial administration, or the direction of some rural domain in Bithynia. Or otherwise, there would have been simple inertia, and court life continued in some subaltern position; to put it at the worst, one of those careers of fallen favorites who turn into confidants or panders. Wisdom, if I understand it at all, consists of admitting each of such possibilities and dangers, which make up life itself, while trying to ward off the worst. But we were not wise, neither the boy nor I.

I had not awaited the coming of Antinous to feel myself a god, but success was multiplying around me the sense of vertiginous heights. The seasons seemed to collaborate with the poets and musicians of my escort to make our existence one continuous Olympian festival. The day of my arrival in Carthage a five-year drought came to an end; the crowds, wild with joy at the downpour, acclaimed me as dispenser of blessings from above; great works of public construction for Africa thereafter were only a means of channeling such celestial prodigality. A short time before, in the course of a stop in Sardinia, we took refuge in a peasant's hut during a storm; Antinous helped our host broil a few slices of tuna over the coals, and I felt like Zeus visiting Philemon in company with Hermes. The youth half reclining on a couch, knees upraised, was that same Hermes untying his sandals; it was Bacchus who gathered grapes or tasted for me the cup of red wine; the fingers hardened by the bowstring were those of Eros. Amid so many fantasies, and surrounded by such wonders, I sometimes forgot the purely human, the boy who vainly strove to learn Latin, who begged the engineer Decrianus for lessons in mathematics, then quickly gave up, and who at the slightest reproach used to take himself off to the prow of the ship to gaze broodingly at the sea.

The African journey had its culmination in the newly completed camp at Lambaesis, under blazing July sun; my companion donned cuirass and military tunic with boyish delight; for these few days I was the nude but helmeted Mars taking part in the camp sports, the athletic Hercules who revelled in the feeling of still youthful vigor. In spite of the heat and the long labors of digging and grading completed before my arrival, the army functioned, like everything else, with divine facility: it would have been impossible to force a runner to one more hurdle, to demand of a horseman a single new jump without spoiling the value of the maneuvers themselves, and breaking into that exact equilibrium which constitutes their beauty. I had to point out to the officers only one slight error, a group of horses left without cover during a feigned attack on open ground; my prefect Cornelianus satisfied me in every respect. Intelligent order governed these masses of men and beasts of burden, these barbarian women with their sturdy children who crowded round the headquarters to kiss my hands. This was not servile obedience; that wild energy was applied to the support of my program for security; nothing had cost too much, and nothing had been neglected. I thought of having Arrian compose a treatise on tactics and discipline as perfect as is a body well-formed.

In Athens, three months later, the dedication of the Olympieion was occasion for festivals which recalled the Roman solemnities, but what in Rome had been celebrated on earth seemed there to occur in the heavens. Late on a luminous day of autumn I took my station in that porch which had been conceived on the superhuman scale of Zeus himself; the marble temple, built on the spot where Deucalion had watched the Deluge recede, seemed to lose its weight and float like a great white cloud; even my ritual robe was in tone with the evening colors on nearby Hymettus. I had entrusted Polemo with the inaugural discourse. It was at this time that Greece granted me those divine appellations wherein I could recognize both a source of prestige and the most secret aim of my life's work: Evergetes, Olympian, Epiphanios, Master of All. And the most beautiful of all these titles, and most difficult to merit, Ionian and Friend of Greece. There was much of the actor in Polemo, but the play of features in a great performer sometimes translates the emotion shared by a whole people, and a whole century. He raised his eyes to the heavens and gathered himself together before his exordium, seeming to assemble within him all gifts held in that moment of time: I had collaborated with the ages, and with Greek life itself; the authority which I wielded was less a power than a mysterious force, superior to man but operating effectively only through the intermediary of a human person; the marriage of Rome with Athens had been accomplished; the future once more held the hope of the past; Greece was stirring again like a vessel, long becalmed, caught anew in the current of the wind. Just then a moment's melancholy came over me; I could not but reflect that these words of completion and perfection contained within them the very word *end*;

perhaps I had offered only one more object as prey to Time the Devourer.

We were taken next inside the temple where the sculptors were still at work; the immense, half-assembled statue of Zeus in ivory and gold seemed to lighten somewhat that dim shade; at the foot of the scaffolding lay the great python brought from India at my order to be consecrated in this Greek sanctuary. Already reposing in its filigree basket, the divine snake, emblem of Earth on which it crawls, has long been associated with the nude youth who symbolizes the emperor's Genius. Antinous, entering more and more into that role, himself fed the monster its ration of wing-clipped wrens. Then, raising his arms, he prayed. I knew that this prayer, made for me, was addressed to no one but myself, though I was not god enough to grasp its sense, nor to know if it would some day be answered. There was comfort in leaving that silence and pale twilight to regain the city streets, where lamps were alight, to feel the friendliness of the crowd and hear the vendors' cries in the dusty evening air. The young face which was soon to adorn so many coins of the Greek world was becoming a familiar presence for the people, and a sign.

I did not love less; indeed I loved more. But the weight of love, like that of an arm thrown tenderly across a chest, becomes little by little too heavy to bear. Passing interests reappeared: I remember the hard, elegant youth who was with me during a stay in Miletus, but whom I gave up. I recall that evening in Sardis when the poet Strato escorted us from brothel to brothel, and we surrounded ourselves with conquests of doubtful value. This same Strato, who had preferred obscurity in the freedom of Asia's taverns to life in my court, was a man of exquisite sensibility, a mocking wit quick to assert the vanity of all that is not pleasure itself, in order perhaps to excuse himself for having sacrificed to it everything else. And there was that night in Smyrna when I forced the beloved one to endure the presence of a courtesan. His conception of love had remained austere because it was centered on but one being; his disgust now verged on nausea. Later on he got used to that sort of thing. Such idle experiments on my part are explained well enough by a taste for dissipation; there was also mingled therein the thought of inventing a new kind of intimacy in which the companion in pleasure would not cease to be the beloved and the friend; there was the desire to instruct him, too, giving him some of the experiences which had been those of my own youth. And possibly, though less clearly avowed, there was some intention of lowering him slowly to the level of routine pleasures which involve no commitments.

A certain dread of bondage impelled me to wound this umbrageous affection, which threatened to encumber my life. On a journey to Troas we visited the plain of the Scamander in time of catastrophe: I had come to see the flood and appraise its damage at first hand; the waters, under a strangely green sky, were making mere islets of the mounds of the ancient tombs. I took a moment to pay homage at the tomb of Hector; Antinous stood dreaming over Patroclus' grave but I failed to recognize in the devoted young fawn who accompanied me an emulator of Achilles' friend: when I derided those passionate loyalties which abound chiefly in books the handsome boy was insulted, and flushed crimson. Frankness was rapidly becoming the one virtue to which I constrained myself; I was beginning to realize that our observance of that heroic code which Greece had built around the attachment of a mature man for a younger companion is often no more for us than hypocrisy and pretence. More sensitive to Rome's prejudices than I was aware, I recalled that although they grant sensuality a rôle they see only shameful folly in love; I was again seized by my mania for avoiding exclusive dependence on any one being. Shortcomings which were merely those of youth, and as such were inseparable from my choice, began to exasperate me. In this passion of wholly different order I was finally reinstating all that had irritated me in my Roman mistresses: perfumes, elaborate attire, and the cool luxury of jewels took their place again in my life. Fears almost without justification had entered that brooding heart; I have seen the boy anxious at the thought of soon becoming nineteen. Dangerous whims and sudden anger shaking the Medusa-like curls above that stubborn brow alternated with a melancholy which was close to stupor, and with a gentleness more and more broken. Once I struck him; I shall remember forever those horrified eyes. But the offended idol remained an idol, and my expiatory sacrifices began.

All the sacred Mysteries of Asia, with their strident music, served now to add to this voluptuous unrest. The period of Eleusis had indeed gone by. Initiations into strange or secret cults (practices tolerated rather than approved, and which the legislator in me regarded with distrust) appealed at that moment of life when dance leaves us reeling and song ends in outcry. In Samothrace I had been initiated into the Mysteries of the Cabiri, ancient and obscene rites as sacred as flesh and blood; at the Cave of Trophonius milk-fed serpents glided about my ankles; the Thracian feasts of Orpheus taught me savage brotherhood rites. The statesman who had imposed severe penalties upon all forms of mutilation now consented to attend the orgies of Cybele: I witnessed the hideous whirling of bleeding dancers; fascinated as a kid in presence of a snake, my young companion watched with terror these men who were electing to answer the demands of age and of sex with a response as final as that of death itself, and perhaps more dreadful.

But the height of horror was reached during a stay in Palmyra, where the Arab merchant, Meles Agrippa, entertained us for three weeks in the lap of splendid and barbaric luxury. One day in the midst of the drinking, this Meles, who was a high official in the Mithraic cult but who took somewhat lightly his priestly duties, proposed to Antinous that he share in the blood baptism. The youth knew that I had formerly been inducted in a ceremony of the same kind; he offered himself with fervor as a candidate. I saw no reason to object to this fantasy; only a minimum of purificatory rites and abstinence was required. I agreed to serve myself as sponsor, together with Marcus Ulpius Castoras, my secretary for the Arabian language. We descended into the sacred cave at the appointed hour; the Bithynian lay down to receive the bloody aspersion. But when I saw his body, streaked with red, emerging from the ditch, his hair matted with sticky mud and his face spattered with stains which could not be washed away but had to be left to wear off themselves, I felt only disgust and abhorrence for all such subterranean and sinister cults. Some days later I forbade access to the black Mithraeum for all troops stationed at Emesa.

Warnings there were: like Mark Antony before his last battle I heard receding into the night the music of the change of guard as the protecting gods withdrew . . . I heard, but paid no heed. My assurance was like that of a horseman whom some talisman protects from every fall. At Samosata an assembly of lesser kings of the Orient was held under my auspices; during the mountain hunts, Abgar himself, king of Osroëne, taught me the art of falconry; great beats engineered like scenes on a stage drove whole herds of antelope into nets of purple. Antinous was given two panthers for this chase; he had to pull back with all his strength to hold them in as they strained at their heavy yoke of gold. Under cover of all these splendors negotiations were concluded; the bargaining invariably ended in my favor; I continued to be the player who wins at every throw.

The winter was passed in that palace of Antioch where in other days I had besought soothsayers to enlighten me as to the future. But from now on the future had nothing to bring me, nothing at least which could count as a gift. My harvests were in; life's heady wine filled the vats to overflowing. I had ceased to control my own destiny, it is true, but the disciplines so carefully worked out in earlier years seemed now to me no more than the first stage of a man's vocation; they were like those chains which a dancer makes himself wear in order to leap the higher after casting them off. On certain points austerity was still the rule: I continued to forbid the serving of wine before the second watch at night; I remembered the sight of Trajan's trembling hand on those same tables of polished wood. But there are other forms of inebriation. Though no shadow was cast on my days, whether death, defeat, or that subtle undoing which is self-inflicted, or age (which nevertheless would surely come), yet I was hurrying, as if each one of those hours was the most beautiful, but also the last of all.

My frequent sojourns in Asia Minor had put me in touch with a small group of scholars seriously concerned with the study of magic arts. Each century has its particular daring: the boldest minds of our time, weary of a philosophy which grows more and more academic, are venturing to explore those frontiers forbidden to mankind. In Tyre, Philo of Byblus had revealed to me certain secrets of ancient Phoenician magic; he continued in my suite to Antioch. There Numenius was giving a new interpretation to Plato's myths on the nature of the soul; his theories remained somewhat timid, but they would have led far a hardier intelligence than his own. His disciples could summon spirits; for us that was a game like many another. Strange faces which seemed made of the very marrow of my dreams appeared to me in the smoke of the incense, then wavered and dissolved, leaving me only the feeling that they resembled some known, living visage. All that was no more, perhaps, than a mere juggler's trick, but in this case the juggler knew his trade.

I went back to the study of anatomy, barely approached in my youth, but now it was no longer a question of sober consideration of the body's structure. I was seized with curiosity to investigate those intermediate regions where the soul and the flesh inter-mingle, where dream echoes reality, or sometimes even precedes it, where life and death exchange attributes and masks. My physician Hermogenes disapproved of such experiments, but nevertheless he acquainted me with a few practitioners who worked along these lines. I tried with them to find the exact seat of the soul and the bonds which attach it to the body, and to measure the time which it takes to detach itself. Some animals were sacrificed to this research. The surgeon Satyrus took me into his hospital to witness death agonies. We speculated together: is the soul only the supreme development of the body, the fragile evidence of the pain and pleasure of existing? Is it, on the contrary, more ancient than the body, which is modeled on its image and which serves it momentarily, more or less well, as instrument? Can it be called back inside the flesh, re-establishing with the body that close union and mutual combustion which we name life? If souls possess an identity of their own, can they be interchanged, going from one being to another like a segment of fruit or the sip of wine which two lovers exchange in a kiss? Every philosopher changes his opinion about these things some twenty times a year; in my case skepticism contended with desire to know, and enthusiasm with irony. But I felt convinced that our brain allows only the merest residue of facts to filter through to us: I began to be more and more interested in the obscure world of sensation, dark as night, but where blinding suns mysteriously flash and revolve.

Near this same period Phlegon, who was a collector of ghost stories, told us one evening the tale of *The Bride of Corinth*, vouching for its authenticity. That adventure, wherein love brings a soul back to earth and temporarily grants it a body, moved each one of us, though at different depths. Several tried to set up a similar experiment: Satyrus attempted to evoke his master Aspasius, with whom he had made one of those pacts (never kept) according to which those who die promise to give information to the living. Antinous made me a promise of the same nature, which I took lightly, having no reason to believe that the boy would not survive me. Philo sought to bring back his dead wife. I permitted the names of my father and my mother to be pronounced, but a certain delicacy kept me from evoking Plotina. Not one of these attempts succeeded. But some strange doors had been opened.

A few days before the departure from Antioch I went to offer sacrifice, as in other years, on the summit of Mount Casius. The ascent was made by night; just as for Aetna, I took with me only a small number of friends used to climbing. My purpose was not simply to accomplish a propitiatory rite in that very sacred sanctuary; I wished to see from its height the phenomenon of dawn, that daily miracle which I never have contemplated without some secret cry of joy. At the topmost point the sun brightens the copper ornaments of the temple and the faces smile in full light while Asia's plains and the sea are still plunged in darkness; for the briefest moment the man who prays on that peak is sole beneficiary of the morning.

Everything was prepared for a sacrifice; we climbed with horses at first, then on foot, along perilous paths bordered with broom and shrubs which we knew at night by their pungent perfumes. The air was heavy; that spring was as burning as summer elsewhere. For the first time while ascending a mountain I had trouble breathing; I was obliged to lean for a moment on the shoulder of my young favorite. We were a hundred steps from the summit when a storm broke which Hermogenes had expected for some time, for he was expert in meteorology. The priests came out to receive us under flashes of lightning; the small band, drenched to the skin, crowded around the altar laid for the sacrifice. Just as it was to take place a thunderbolt burst above us and killed both the victim and the attendant with knife in hand. When the first moment of horror had passed, Hermogenes

bent with a physician's curiosity over the stricken pair; Chabrias
and the high priest cried out in admiration that the man and fawn
thus sacrificed by this divine sword were uniting with the eternity
of my Genius; that these lives, by substitution, were prolonging
mine. Antinous gripping fast to my arm was trembling, not
from terror, as I then supposed, but under the impact of a
thought which I was to understand only later on. In his dread of
degradation, that is to say, of growing old, he must have promised himself long ago to die at the first sign of decline, or even
before. I have come to think now that that promise, which so
many of us have made to ourselves but without holding to it,
went far back for him, to the period of Nicomedia and the
encounter at the edge of the spring. It explained his indolence,
his ardor in pleasure, his sadness, and his total indifference to all
future. But it was still essential that this departure should have
no air of revolt, and should contain no complaint. The lightning
of Mount Casius had revealed to him a way out: death could
become a last form of service, a final gift, and the only one which
seemed left for him to give. The illumination of dawn was as
nothing compared with the smile which arose on that overwhelmed countenance.

Some days later I saw that same smile again, but more hidden,
and ambiguously veiled: at supper, Polemo, who dabbled in
chiromancy, wished to examine the hand of the youth, that palm
which alarmed even me by its astonishing fall of stars. But the boy
withdrew it and closed it gently, almost chastely. He intended to
keep the secret of his game, and that of his end.

We made a stop at Jerusalem. There I took occasion to study
the plan for a new capital which I proposed to construct on the
site of the Jewish city laid low by Titus. Good administration in
Judaea and increasing commerce with the Orient showed the
need for developing a great metropolis at this intersection of
routes. I had in mind the usual Roman capital: Aelia Capitolina
would have its temples, its markets, its public baths, and its
sanctuary of the Roman Venus. My recent absorption in passionate and tender cults led me to choose a grotto on Mount Moriah
as best suited for celebrating the rites of Adonis. These projects
roused indignation in the Jewish masses: the wretched creatures

actually preferred their ruins to a city which would afford them the chance of gain, of knowledge, and of pleasure. When our workmen approached those crumbling walls with pickaxes they were attacked by the mob. I went ahead notwithstanding: Fidus Aquila, who was soon to employ his genius for planning in the construction of Antinoöpolis, took up the work at Jerusalem. I refused to see in those heaps of rubble the rapid growth of hatred.

A month later we arrived at Pelusium. I arranged to restore the tomb of Pompey there: the deeper I delved into affairs of the Orient the more I admired the political genius of that vanquished opponent of the great Julius. Pompey, in endeavoring to bring order to this uncertain world of Asia, sometimes seemed to me to have worked more effectively for Rome than Caesar himself. That reconstruction was one of my last offerings to History's dead; I was soon to be forced to busy myself with other tombs.

Our arrival in Alexandria was kept discreetly quiet. The triumphal entry was postponed until the empress should come. Though she traveled little she had been persuaded to pass the winter in the milder climate of Egypt; Lucius, but poorly recovered from a persistent cough, was to try the same remedy. A small fleet of vessels was assembled for a voyage on the Nile with a program comprising official inspections, festivals, and banquets which promised to be as tiring as those of a season at the Palatine. I myself had organized all that: the luxury and display of a court were not without political value in this ancient country accustomed to royal pomp.

But I had therefore the more desire to devote these few days which would precede the arrival of my guests to hunting. In Palmyra, Meles Agrippa had arranged some parties for us in the desert, but we had not gone far enough to see lions. Two years earlier Africa had provided the chance for some marvelous wild animal hunts; Antinous, then too young and inexperienced, had had no permission to take a significant part. In that respect I lacked courage for him in a way that I should not have dreamed for myself. Yielding, as always, I promised him now the chief rôle in this lion hunt. The time had passed for treating him as a child, and I was proud of his young strength.

We set off for the oasis of Ammon, some days' journey from Alexandria, that same place where long ago Alexander had learned from the priests of his divine birth. The natives were reporting a particularly dangerous animal in the area which often attacked men as well as beasts. At night around the camp fire we gaily compared our exploits-to-be with those of Hercules. But the first days brought us only a few gazelles. Then we decided to take up a position, the two of us, near a sandy pool all overgrown with rushes. The lion was supposed to come there at dusk to drink. The negroes were instructed to drive him toward us with the noise of conch horns, cymbals, and cries; the rest of our escort had been left some distance away. The air was heavy and still; there was no need even to consider the direction of the wind. We could hardly have passed the tenth hour of the day, for Antinous called my attention to the red water lilies still wide open on the pond. Suddenly the royal beast appeared in a turmoil of trampled reeds and turned his handsome head toward us, one of the most godlike faces that danger can assume. Placed somewhat behind I had no time to restrain the boy; he imprudently spurred his horse and hurled first his spear and then his two javelins, with skill, but from too close range. Pierced in the neck, the animal fell to earth, lashing the ground with his tail; the whirl of sand kept us from distinguishing more than a reddening, confused mass. At last the lion regained his feet and mustered his strength to spring upon horse and rider, now disarmed. I had foreseen this danger; happily Antinous' mount did not stir: our horses had been admirably trained for this sort of game. I interposed my horse, exposing the right flank; I was used to such action and it was not very difficult for me to dispatch the beast, already mortally stricken. He collapsed for the second time; the muzzle rolled in the mire and a stream of dark blood ran into the water. The mighty cat, color of the desert, of honey, of the sun itself, expired with a majesty greater than man's. Antinous leaped down from his horse, which was covered with foam and trembling still; our companions rejoined us and the negroes dragged the immense prey back to the camp.

A feast was improvised; lying flat on his stomach before a platter of copper, the youth handed us our portions of lamb roasted beneath the coals. In his honor we drank palm wine. His exultation mounted like song. Perhaps he exaggerated the significance of the aid which I had given him, forgetting that I would have done as much for any hunter in danger; we felt, nevertheless, that we had gone back into that heroic world where lovers die for each other. Pride and gratitude alternated in his joy like the strophes of an ode. The blacks did wonders: soon under the starry sky the skin was swinging suspended on two stakes at the entrance of my tent. Despite the aromatics applied to it, its wild odor haunted us all night long. The next morning, after a meal of fruits, we left the camp; at the moment of departure we caught sight of what was left of the royal beast of the day before: by that time it was only a red carcass in a ditch, surmounted by a cloud of flies.

Some days later we returned to Alexandria. The poet Pancrates arranged a special entertainment for me at the Museum; in a music room was assembled a collection of fine and rare instruments. Old Dorian lyres, heavier and more complicated than ours today, stood side by side with curved citharas of Persia and Egypt; there were Phrygian pipes shrill as eunuchs' voices, and delicate Indian flutes, the name of which I do not know. For a long time an Ethiopian beat upon some African drums. Then a woman played a triangular harp of melancholy tone; her cool beauty would have won me had I not already decided to simplify my life by reducing it to what was for me the essential. My favorite musician, Mesomedes of Crete, used the water organ to accompany the recitation of his poem *The Sphinx*, a disturbing, undulating work, as elusive as the sand before the wind. The concert hall gave on an inner court where some water lilies were growing in the fountain's basin; they lay wide open in the almost furious heat of a late August afternoon. During an interlude, Pancrates urged us to inspect more closely these flowers of rare type, red as blood, which bloomed only at the end of summer. At once we recognized our scarlet lilies of the oasis of Ammon; Pancrates was suddenly fired by the thought of the wounded beast expiring among the flowers. He proposed to me that he versify this episode of our hunt; the lion's blood would be represented as tinting the lilies. The formula is not new: I nevertheless gave him the commission. This Pancrates, who was completely the court poet, improvised on the spot a few pleasant verses in Antinous' honor: the rose, the hyacinth, and the celandine were valued less in his hexameters than those scarlet cups which would hereafter bear the name of the chosen one. A slave was ordered to wade into the water to gather an armful of the blossoms. The youth accustomed to homage gravely accepted the wax-like flowers with the limp, snaky stems; the petals closed like eyelids when night fell.

In the midst of these pleasures the empress arrived. The long crossing had told on her: she was growing frail without ceasing to be hard. Her political associations no longer caused me annoyance, as in the period when she had foolishly encouraged Suetonius; she now had only inoffensive women writers about her. The confidante of the moment was a certain Julia Balbilla, whose Greek verse was fairly good. The empress and her suite established themselves in the Lyceum, from which they rarely went out. Lucius, on the contrary, was as always avid for all delights, including alike those of the mind and of the eye.

At twenty-six he had lost almost nothing of that arresting beauty which aroused acclamations from the youth in the streets of Rome. He was still absurd, ironic, and gay. His caprices of other days had now turned to manias: he made no move without his head cook; his gardeners composed astonishing flower plantings for him even aboard ship; he took his bed with him wherever he went, modeled on his own design of four mattresses stuffed with four special kinds of aromatics, on top of which he lay surrounded by his young mistresses like so many cushions. His pages, painted, powdered, and attired like Zephyrs and Eros, complied as well as they could with mad whims which were sometimes cruel: I had to intervene to keep the young Boreas, whose slenderness Lucius admired, from letting himself die of hunger. All that was more exasperating than charming. We visited together everything to be visited in Alexandria: the Lighthouse, the Mausoleum of Alexander and that of Mark Antony, where Cleopatra triumphs eternally over Octavia, the temples, the workshops and factories, and even the quarter of the embalmers. From a reputable sculptor I purchased an entire lot of Venuses, Dianas, and Hermes for Italica, my native city, which I had in mind to modernize and adorn. The priest of the temple of Serapis offered me a service of opaline glass, but I sent it to Servianus, with whom, out of regard for my sister Paulina, I tried to keep passable relations, at least at a distance. Great building projects took shape in the course of all these somewhat tedious rounds.

The religions in Alexandria are as varied as the trades; the quality of the product, however, is more doubtful. The Christians especially distinguish themselves there by a multiplication of sects which is, to say the least, useless; two charlatans among them, Valentinus and Basilides, were intriguing against each other, closely watched over by the Roman police. As for the Egyptian populace, the lowest level took advantage of each of their own ritual festivities to throw themselves, cudgel in hand, upon foreigners; the death of the bull Apis provokes more uprisings in that city than an imperial succession in Rome. Fashionable people change gods there as elsewhere they change doctors, and with about as much success. But gold·is their only idol: nowhere have I seen more shameless importuning. Grandiose inscriptions were displayed all about to commemorate my benefactions, but my refusal to exempt the inhabitants from a tax which they were quite able to pay soon alienated that rabble from me. The two young men who accompanied me were insulted more than once: Lucius was reproached for his lavish expenditures, which, it must be admitted, were excessive, and Antinous for his obscure origin, on the subject of which ran absurd rumors; both were blamed for the ascendancy which they were supposed to have over me. This last assumption was ridiculous: Lucius, whose judgment in public affairs was surprisingly acute, nevertheless had no political influence whatsoever; Antinous did not aspire to it. The young patrician, knowing the ways of the world, merely laughed at the jibes, but they were cause for suffering to Antinous.

The Alexandrian Jews, egged on by their coreligionists in Judaea, did their best to aggravate a situation already bad. The synagogue of Jerusalem delegated Akiba to me, its most venerable member; almost a nonagenarian, and knowing no Greek, he came with the mission of prevailing upon me to abandon projects already under way at Jerusalem. Aided by my interpreters I held several colloquies with him which, on his part, were mere pretext for monologue. In less than an hour I felt able to define his thought exactly, though not subscribing to it; he made no corresponding effort concerning my own. This fanatic did not even suspect any reasoning possible on premises other than those he set forth. I offered his despised people a place among the others in the Roman community; Jerusalem, however, speaking through Akiba, signified its intention of remaining, to the end, the fortress of a race and of a god isolated from human kind. That savage determination was expressed with tiresome deviousness: I had to listen to a long line of argument, subtly deduced step by step, proving Israel's superiority. At the end of eight days even this obstinate negotiator became aware that he was pursuing the wrong course, so he announced his departure. I abhor defeat, even for others, and it moves me the more when the vanquished is an old man. The ignorance of Akiba, and his refusal to accept anything outside his sacred books or his own people, endued him with a kind of narrow innocence. But it was difficult to feel sympathy for this bigot. Longevity seemed to have bereft him of all human suppleness: that gaunt body and dried mind had the locust's hard vigor. It seems that he died a hero later on for the cause of his people, or rather, for his law. Each of us dedicates himself to his own gods.

The distractions which Alexandria affords began to wane. Phlegon, who knew the local curiosities everywhere, whether procuress or famous hermaphrodite, proposed to take us to a local magician. This go-between for two worlds, the invisible and our own, lived in Canopus. We went there at night by boat along the torpid waters of the canal, a dismal ride. A silent hostility reigned, as always, between the two young men: the intimacy into which I was forcing them augmented their aversion for each other. Lucius hid this feeling under a mocking condescension; my young Greek enclosed himself in one of his dark moods. I happened to be rather tired; a few days before, on coming back from a race in full sun, I had had a brief fainting fit which only Antinous and the black Euphorion had witnessed. They had been unduly alarmed, and I had forbidden them to disclose the matter.

Canopus is no more than a tawdry stage-setting: the magician's house was situated in the most sordid part of that pleasure resort. We disembarked at a tumble-down terrace. The sorceress awaited us inside her house, surrounded by the dubious tools of her trade.

She seemed competent; there was nothing of the stage witch about her; she was not even old.

Her predictions were sinister. For some time the oracles everywhere had been foretelling annoyances for me of every sort, political troubles, palace intrigues, and serious illness. I now believe that some decidedly human influences were at work upon those voices from below, sometimes to warn me, more often to frighten me. The true condition of one part of the Orient was more clearly explained therein than in the reports of our proconsuls. I took these so-called revelations with calm, since my respect for the invisible world did not go so far as to give credence to such divine claptrap: ten years before, soon after my accession to power, I had ordered the closing of the oracle of Daphne, near Antioch, which had foretold my rule, for fear that it might do the same for the first pretender who should appear. But it is always annoying to hear talk of trouble.

After having disturbed us to the best of her ability the prophetess offered her aid: one of those magical sacrifices in which Egyptian sorcerers specialize would suffice to put everything right with destiny. My explorations in Phoenician magic had already shown me that the horror of these forbidden practices lies less in what is revealed to us than in what they hide from our sight; if my abomination of human sacrifice had not been well known this practitioner would probably have advised the immolation of a slave. As it was she contented herself with speaking of some pet animal.

Had it been at all possible the sacrificial victim should have belonged to me; it could not be a dog, which is an animal considered unclean in Egyptian superstition; a bird would have done, but I do not travel with an aviary. My young master proposed his falcon. The conditions would be fulfilled thereby; I had given him this beautiful bird after I had myself received it from the king of Osroëne. The boy fed it himself; it was one of the rare possessions to which he was attached. At first I refused; he insisted, gravely; I gathered that he attributed some extraordinary significance to the offer, so I accepted, out of affection. Provided with the most detailed instructions, my courier Menecrates went to fetch the bird from our apartments in the Serapeion. Even at a gallop the errand would take, in all, more than two hours.

There was no question of passing the interval in the dirty hole of the magician, and Lucius complained of the dampness aboard the boat. Phlegon found an expedient: we installed ourselves as well as we could in the house of a procuress after the inmates of the place had been disposed of. Lucius decided to sleep; I made use of the time to dictate some dispatches, and Antinous stretched out at my feet. Phlegon's reed pen scratched away under the lamp. The last watch of the night was beginning when Menecrates brought back the bird, the glove, the hood, and the chain.

We returned to the house of the magician. Antinous removed the falcon's hood and for some moments caressed its little head, so sleepy and so wild, then handed it to the enchantress, who began a series of magic passes. The bird, fascinated, fell asleep again. It was important that the victim should not struggle, and that the death should appear voluntary. Rubbed over with ritual honey and attar of roses, the animal, now inert, was placed in the bottom of a tub filled with Nile water; in drowning thus it was to be assimilated to Osiris borne along on the river's current; the bird's earthly years were added to mine, and the little soul, issue of the sun, was united with the Genius of him for whom the sacrifice was made; the invisible Genius could hereafter appear to me and serve me under this form. The long manipulations which followed were no more interesting than some preparation for cooking. Lucius began to yawn. The ceremonies imitated human funerals in every detail: the fumigations and the psalm singing dragged on until dawn. The bird was finally enclosed in a casket lined with aromatic substances and the magician buried it in our presence at the edge of the canal, in an abandoned cemetery. When she had finished she crouched under a tree to count one by one the gold pieces which Phlegon paid her.

We re-embarked. An unusually cold wind was blowing. Lucius, seated near me, drew closer the embroidered cotton coverlets with the tips of his slender fingers; for politeness' sake we continued to exchange remarks at broken intervals about business and scandal in Rome. Antinous, lying in the bottom of the boat, had leaned his head on my knees, pretending to sleep in order to keep apart from a conversation which did not include him. My hand passed over his neck, under his heavy hair; thus even in the dullest or most futile moments I kept some feeling of contact with the great objects of nature, the thick growth of the forests, the muscular back of the panther, the regular pulsation of springs; but no caress goes so deep as the soul. The sun was shining when we reached the Serapeion, and the melon merchants were crying their wares in the streets. I slept until time for the session of the local Council, which I attended. I learned later that Antinous took advantage of my absence to persuade Chabrias to go with him to Canopus. He went back to the house of the magician.

The first of the month of Athyr, the second year of the two hundred and twenty-sixth Olympiad . . . That is the anniversary of the death of Osiris, the god of the dying; along the river piercing cries of lamentation had resounded from all the villages for three days' time. My Roman guests, less accustomed than I to the mysteries of the East, showed a certain curiosity for those ceremonies of another race. For me, on the contrary, they were tiring and irritating to the extreme. I had ordered my boat anchored at some distance from the others, far from any habitation; but a half-abandoned temple of the time of the Pharaohs stood near the river bank and had still its school of priests, so I did not entirely escape the sound of wailing.

On the preceding evening Lucius invited me to supper on his boat. I went there at sunset. Antinous refused to go with me, so I left him alone in my stern deck cabin lying on his lion skin, playing at knucklebones with Chabrias. Half an hour later, just as night fell, he changed his mind and called for a boat. Aided by a single oarsman, and pulling against the current, he rowed the considerable distance which separated us from the other boats. His entry into the deck tent where the supper was given interrupted the applause for the contortions of a dancing girl. He had arrayed himself in a long Syrian robe, sheer as the skin of a fruit and strewn over with flowers and chimeras. In order to row more easily he had freed his right arm from its sleeve; sweat was trembling on the smooth chest. Lucius tossed him a garland which he caught in mid-air; his gaiety, almost strident, did not abate for one moment, though hardly sustained by a single cup of Greek wine. We returned together in my boat with six oarsmen, followed by the cutting 'good night' of Lucius from above. The wild gay mood persisted. But in the morning I happened by chance to touch a face wet with tears. I asked him impatiently the cause for such crying; he replied humbly, excusing himself on the ground of fatigue. I accepted the lie and fell back to sleep. His true agony took place in that bed, there beside me.

The mail from Rome had just come, and the day went by in reading and answering it. As usual Antinous went silently about the room; I know not at what moment that fair creature passed out of my life. Toward the twelfth hour Chabrias entered, in great agitation. Contrary to all regulations the youth had left the boat without stating his purpose or the length of his intended absence; two hours at least had gone by since his departure. Chabrias recalled some strange things said the evening before, and a recommendation made that very morning, concerning me. He voiced his fears. We descended in haste to the river bank. As if by instinct the old tutor made for a chapel on the water's edge, a small structure apart which was one of the outbuildings of the temple, and which he and Antinous had visited together. On an offering table lay ashes still warm from a sacrifice; turning them with his fingers, Chabrias drew forth a lock of hair, almost intact.

There was no longer anything for us to do but to search the shore. A series of reservoirs which must once have served for sacred ceremonies extended to a bend of the river; on the edge of the last basin Chabrias perceived in the rapidly lowering dusk a folded garment and sandals. I descended the slippery steps; he was lying at the bottom, already sunk in the river's mud. With Chabrias' aid I managed to lift the body, which had suddenly taken on the weight of stone. Chabrias hailed some boatmen who improvised a stretcher from sail cloth. Hermogenes, called in haste, could only pronounce him dead. That body, once so responsive, refused to be warmed again or revived. We took him aboard. Everything gave way; everything seemed extinguished. The Olympian Zeus, Master of All, Saviour of the World – all toppled together, and there was only a man with greying hair sobbing on the deck of a boat.

Two days went by before Hermogenes could get me to think of the funeral. The sacrificial rites with which Antinous had chosen to surround his death showed us a course to follow: it would not be for nothing that the day and hour of that end had coincided with the moment when Osiris descends into the tomb. I crossed the river to Hermopolis, to its quarter of embalmers. I had seen their work in Alexandria and knew to what outrages I was submitting this body; but fire is horrible too, searing and charring the beloved flesh; and in the earth it rots. The crossing was brief; squatting in a corner of the stern cabin Euphorion chanted in a low voice I know not what African dirge; this hoarse, half-muffled song seemed to me almost my own cry. We transferred the beloved dead into a room cleanly flushed with water which reminded me of the clinic of Satyrus; I aided the castmaker to oil the face before the wax was applied. All the metaphors took on meaning: I held that heart in my hands. When I left the empty body it was no more than an embalmer's preparation, the first stage of a frightful masterpiece, a precious substance treated with salt and gum of myrrh, and never again to be touched by sun or air.

On the return I visited the temple near which the sacrifice had been consummated; I spoke with the priests. Their sanctuary would be renovated to become a place of pilgrimage for all Egypt; their college, enriched and augmented, would be consecrated hereafter to the service of my god. Even in my most obtuse moments I had never doubted that that young presence was divine. Greece and Asia would worship him in our manner, with games and dances, and with ritual offerings placed at the feet of a nude, white statue. Egypt, who had witnessed the death agony, would have also her part in the apotheosis: it would be the most secret and somber part, and the harshest, for this country would play the eternal role of embalmer to his body. For centuries to come priests with shaven heads would recite litanies repeating that name which for them had no value, but for me held all. Each year the sacred barge would bear that effigy along the river; the first of the month of Athyr mourners would walk on that shore where I had walked.

Every hour has its immediate duty, its special injunction which dominates all others: the problem of the moment was to defend from death the little that was left to me. Phlegon had assembled on the shore the architects and engineers of my suite, as I had ordered; sustained by a kind of clearsighted frenzy I made them follow me along the stony hills; I explained my plan, the development of forty-five stadia of encircling wall, and I marked in the sand the position of the triumphal arch and that of the tomb. Antinoöpolis was to be born; it would already be some check to death to impose upon that sinister land a city wholly Greek, a bastion which would hold off the nomads of Erythrea, a new market on the route to India. Alexander had celebrated the funeral of Hephaestion with devastation and mass slaughter of prisoners. I preferred to offer to the chosen one a city where his cult would be forever mingled with the coming and going on the public square, where his name would be repeated in the casual talk of evening, where youths would toss crowns to each other at the banqueting hour. But on one point my thought fluctuated: it seemed impossible to abandon this body to foreign soil. Like a man uncertain of his next stop who reserves lodgings in several hostelries at a time, I ordered a monument for him at Rome, on the banks of the Tiber near my own tomb, but thought also of the Egyptian chapels which I had had built at the Villa by caprice, and which were suddenly proving tragically useful. A date was set for the funeral at the end of the two months demanded by the embalmers. I entrusted Mesomedes with the composition of funeral choruses. Late into the night I went back aboard; Hermogenes prepared me a sleeping potion.

The journey up the river continued, but my course lay on the Styx. In prisoners' camps on the banks of the Danube I had once seen wretches continually beating their heads against a wall with a wild motion, both mad and tender, endlessly repeating the same name. In the underground chambers of the Colosseum I had been shown lions pining away because the dog with which their keepers had accustomed them to live had been taken away. I tried to collect my thoughts: Antinous was dead. As a child I had wept and wailed over the corpse of Marullinus torn to shreds by crows, but had cried as does a mere animal, in the night. My father had died, but a boy orphaned at the age of twelve noticed no more than disorder in the house, his mother's tears, and his own terror; he knew nothing of the anguish which the dying man had experienced. My mother had died much later, about the time of my mission in Pannonia; I do not recall the exact date. Trajan had been only a sick man who must be made to make a will. I had not seen Plotina die. Attianus had died; he was old. During the Dacian wars I had lost comrades whom I had believed that I loved ardently; but we were young, and life and death were equally intoxicating and easy. Antinous was dead. I remembered platitudes frequently heard: 'One can die at any age,' or 'They who die young are beloved by the gods.' I myself had shared in that execrable abuse of words; I had talked of dying of sleep, and dying of boredom. I had used the word *agony*, the word *mourning*, the word *loss*. Antinous was dead.

Love, wisest of gods . . . But love had not been to blame for that negligence, for the harshness and indifference mingled with passion like sand with the gold borne along by a stream, for that blind self-content of a man too completely happy, and who is growing old. Could I have been so grossly satisfied? Antinous was dead. Far from loving too much, as doubtless Servianus was proclaiming at that moment in Rome, I had not been loving enough to force the boy to live on. Chabrias as a member of an Orphic cult held suicide a crime, so he tended to insist upon the sacrificial aspect of that ending; I myself felt a kind of terrible joy at the thought that that death was a gift. But I was the only one to measure how much bitter fermentation there is at the bottom of all sweetness, or what degree of despair is hidden under abnegation, what hatred is mingled with love. A being deeply wounded had thrown this proof of devotion at my very face; a boy fearful of losing all had found this means of binding me to him forever. Had he hoped to protect me by such a sacrifice he must have deemed himself unloved indeed not to have realized that the worst of ills would be to lose him.

The tears ceased; the dignitaries who approached me were no longer obliged to avoid glancing at me (as if weeping were a thing obscene). Visits to model farms and irrigation canals were renewed; it mattered little how the hours were spent. Countless wild rumors were already afoot with regard to my disaster; even on the boats accompanying mine some atrocious stories were circulating against me; I let them talk, the truth being not of the kind to cry in the streets. Then, too, the most malicious lies were accurate in their way; they accused me of having sacrificed him and, in a sense, I had done so. Hermogenes, who faithfully relayed these echoes to me from without, transmitted some messages from the empress; she behaved decently (people usually do in the presence of death). But such compassion was based on a misapprehension: I was to be pitied provided that I console myself rather promptly. I myself thought that I was somewhat calmed, and was almost embarrassed by the fact. Little did I know what strange labyrinths grief contains, or that I had yet to walk therein.

They tried to divert me. Some days after we reached Thebes I learned that the empress and her suite had gone twice to the base of the colossal statue of Memnon, hoping to hear the mysterious sound emitted from the stone at dawn, a well-known phenomenon which all travelers wish to witness. The prodigy had not occurred, but with superstitious awe they imagined that it would take place if I were present, so I agreed to accompany the women the next day; any means would do to shorten those interminable nights of autumn. Early that morning, at about the eleventh hour, Euphorion came to my cabin to relight the lamp and help me put on my clothes. I stepped on deck; the sky, still wholly dark, was truly the iron sky of Homer's poems, indifferent to man's woes and joys alike. More than twenty days had passed since this thing had happened. I descended to the small boat for the short trip, which was not without tremorous cries from the women.

They landed us near the Colossus. A strip of dull rose extended along the East; still another day was beginning. The mysterious sound occurred three times, resembling the snap of a breaking bowstring. The inexhaustible Julia Balbilla produced on the spot a whole series of poems. The women undertook to visit the temples, but I accompanied them only part way, along walls monotonously covered with hieroglyphs. I had had enough of those colossal figures of kings all alike, sitting side by side, their long flattened feet planted straight before them; in such inert blocks of stone there is nothing which signifies life for us, neither grief nor sensuous delight, nor movement which gives limbs their freedom, nor that capacity which composes a world round a pensive head. The priests who guided me seemed almost as ill-informed as myself about those extinguished lives, though from time to time some discussion arose over a name. They knew vaguely that each of these monarchs had inherited a kingdom, governed over his peoples, and begotten a successor; nothing besides remained. Those obscure dynasties extended farther back than Rome, farther than Athens, back beyond the day when Achilles died before the walls of Troy, earlier than the astronomic cycle of five thousand years calculated by Meno for Julius Caesar.

Feeling tired, I dismissed the priests and rested for a while in the shade of the Colossus before returning to the boat. The massive legs were covered to the knees with inscriptions traced in Greek by sightseers: names, dates, a prayer, a certain Servius Suavis, a certain Eumenius who had been in that same place six centuries before me, a certain Panion who had visited Thebes just six months ago . . . Six months ago . . . A fancy seized me which I had not known since childhood days, when I used to carve my name in the bark of chestnut trees on the Spanish estate; the emperor who steadily refused to have his appelations and titles inscribed upon the buildings and monuments of his own construction now took his dagger to scratch a few Greek letters on that hard stone, an abridged and familiar form of his name, AΔPIANO . . . It was one more thrust against time: a name, a life sum (of which the innumerable elements would never be known), a mere mark left by a man wholly lost in that succession of centuries. Suddenly I remembered that it was the twenty-seventh day of the month of Athyr, the fifth day before our kalends of December. It was the birthday of Antinous; the boy would have been twenty that day had he been still alive.

I went back aboard; the wound closed too quickly had opened again; I stifled my cries in the cushion which Euphorion slipped under my head. That corpse and I were drifting apart, carried in different directions by two currents of time. The fifth day before the kalends of December, the first day of the month of Athyr: with each passing moment that body was sinking deeper, that death was more imbedded. Once more I climbed the treacherous ascent; with my very nails I strove to exhume that day dead and gone. Phlegon had sat facing the door, but remembered the successive entries and departures in the cabin only for the ray of light which had disturbed him each time that a hand pushed the blind. Like a man accused of a crime I strove to account for each hour: some dictation, a reply to the Senate of Ephesus; at which of those phrases did that agony take place? I tried to gauge the

play of the footbridge under his tread, to reconstitute the dry
bank and the flat paving stones; then the knife cutting the curl at
the edge of his temple, the inclined body and knee bent to allow
the hand to untie the sandal; the unique manner of opening the
lips as he closed his eyes. It must have cost a desperate resolution
indeed for so fine a swimmer to smother in that black silt. In my
thoughts I tried to go as far as that revolution through which we
all shall pass, when the heart gives out and the brain stops short
as the lungs cease to draw in life. I shall undergo a similar
convulsion; I, too, shall die. But each passing is different; my
attempts to picture his last agony came to no more than mere
fabrication, for he had died alone.

I fought against my grief, battling as if it were gangrene: I
recalled his occasional stubbornness and lies; I told myself that
he would have changed, growing older and heavy. Such efforts
proved futile; instead, like some painstaking workman who toils
to copy a masterpiece, I exhausted myself in tasking my memory
for fanatic exactitude, evoking that smooth chest, high and
rounded as a shield. Sometimes the image leaped to mind of
itself, and a flood of tenderness swept over me: once again I
caught sight of an orchard in Tibur, and the youth gathering up
autumn fruits in his tunic, for lack of a basket. I had lost
everything at once, the companion of the night's delights and
the young friend squatting low to his heels to help Euphorion
with the folds of my toga. If one were to believe the priests, the
shade was also in torment, regretting the warm shelter of its
body and haunting its familiar habitations with many a moan,
so far and yet so near, but for the time too weak to signify his
presence to me. If that were true my deafness was worse than
death itself. But after all had I so well understood, on that
morning, the living boy who sobbed at my side?

One evening Chabrias called me to show me a star, till then
hardly visible, in the constellation of the Eagle; it flashed like a
gem and pulsated like a heart. I chose it for his star and his sign.
Each night I would follow its course until utterly wearied; in
that part of the sky I have seen strange radiance. Folk thought
me mad, but that was of little consequence.

Death is hideous, but life is too. Everything seemed awry.
The founding of Antinoöpolis was a ludicrous endeavor, after

all, just one more city to shelter fraudulent trading, official extortion, prostitution, disorder, and those cowards who weep for a while over their dead before forgetting them. Apotheosis was but empty ceremony: such public honors would serve only to make of the boy a pretext for adulation or irony, a posthumous object of cheap desire, or of scandal, one of those legends already tainted which clutter history's recesses. Perhaps my grief itself was only a form of license, a vulgar debauch: I was still the one who profited from the experience and tasted it to the full, for the beloved one was giving me even his death for my indulgence. A man frustrated was weeping over himself.

Ideas jarred upon each other; words ground on without meaning; voices rasped and buzzed like locusts in the desert or flies on a dung pile; our ships with sails swelling out like doves' breasts were carriers for intrigue and lies; on the human countenance stupidity reigned. Death, in its aspect of weakness or decay, came to the surface everywhere: the bad spot on a fruit, some imperceptible rent at the edge of a hanging, a carrion body on the shore, the pustules of a face, the mark of scourges on a bargeman's back. My hands seemed always somewhat soiled. At the hour of the bath, as I extended my legs for the slaves to shave, I looked with disgust upon this solid body, this almost indestructible machine which absorbed food, walked, and managed to sleep, and would, I knew, reaccustom itself one day or another to the routines of love. I could no longer bear the presence of any but those few servants who remembered the departed one; in their way they had loved him. My sorrow found an echo in the rather foolish mourning of a masseur, or of the old negro who tended the lamps. But their grief did not keep them from laughing softly amongst themselves as they took the evening air along the river bank. One morning as I leaned on the taffrail I noticed a slave at work in the quarters reserved for the kitchens; he was cleaning one of those chickens which Egypt hatches by the thousands in its dirty incubators; he gathered the slimy entrails into his hands and threw them into the water. I had barely time to turn away to vomit. At our stop in Philae, during a reception offered us by the governor, a child of three met with an accident: son of a Nubian porter and dark as bronze, he had crept into the balconies to watch the dancing, and fell from that height. They did the best they could to hide the whole thing; the porter held back his sobs for fear of disturbing his master's guests, and was led out with the body through the kitchen doors; in spite of such precautions I caught a glimpse of his shoulders rising and falling convulsively, as under the blows of a whip. I had the feeling of taking that father's grief to myself much as I had taken on the sorrow of Hercules, of Alexander, of Plato, each of whom wept for a dead friend. I sent a few gold pieces to this poor fellow; one could do nothing more. Two or three days later I saw him again; he was contentedly picking at lice as he lay in the sun at the doorway.

Messages flooded in; Pancrates sent me his poem, finished at last; it was only a mediocre assemblage of Homeric hexameters, but the name which figured in almost every line made it more moving for me than many a masterpiece. Numenius sent me a *Consolation* written according to the usual formulas for such works; I passed a night reading it, although it contained every possible platitude. These feeble defenses raised by man against death were developed along two lines: the first consisted in presenting death to us as an inevitable evil, and in reminding us that neither beauty, youth, nor love escapes decay; life and its train of ills are thus proved even more horrible than death itself, and it is better, accordingly, to die than to grow old. Such truths are cited to incline us toward resignation, but they justify chiefly despair. The second line of argument contradicts the first, but our philosophers care little for such niceties: the theme was no longer resignation to death but negation of it. Only the soul was important, they said, arrogantly positing as a fact the immortality of that vague entity which we have never seen function in the absence of the body, and the existence of which they had not yet taken the trouble to prove. I was not so certain: since the smile, the expression of the eyes, the voice, these imponderable realities, had ceased to be, then why not the soul, too? Was it necessarily more immaterial than the body's heat? They attached no importance to those remains wherein the soul no longer dwelt; that body, however, was the only thing left to me, my sole proof that the living boy had existed. The immortality of the race was supposed to make up in some way for each individual death, but it was hardly consoling to me that whole generations of

Bithynians would succeed each other to the end of time along the banks of the Sangarius. We speak of glory, that fine word which swells the heart, but there is willful confusion between it and immortality, as if the mere trace of a person were the same thing as his presence. They would have had me see the resplendent god in place of the corpse, but I had created that god; I believed in him, in my way, but a brilliant posthumous destiny in the midst of the stellar spheres failed to compensate for so brief a life; the god did not take the place of the living being I had lost.

I was incensed by man's mania for clinging to hypotheses while ignoring facts, for mistaking his dreams for more than dreams. I felt otherwise about my obligations as the survivor. That death would be in vain if I lacked the courage to look straight at it, keeping in mind those realities of cold and silence, of coagulated blood and inert members which men cover up so quickly with earth, and with hypocrisy; I chose to grope my way in the dark without recourse to such weak lamps. I could feel that those around me began to take offence at a grief of such duration; furthermore, the violence of my sorrow scandalized them more than its cause. If I had given way to the same tears for the death of a brother or a son I should have been equally reproached for crying like a woman. The memory of most men is an abandoned cemetery where lie, unsung and unhonored, the dead whom they have ceased to cherish. Any lasting grief is reproof to their neglect.

We came back down the river to the point where Antinoöpolis was beginning to rise. There were fewer boats in our party than before; Lucius, whom I had seen but little again, had returned to Rome, where his young wife was newly delivered of a son. His departure freed me of a goodly number of curious and troublesome onlookers. The work already started was altering the line of the shore; the plan of buildings-to-be became visible in the clearings between mounds of earth dug up everywhere for foundations; but I no longer recognized the exact place of the sacrifice. The embalmers delivered their handiwork; the slender coffin of cedar was placed inside a porphyry sarcophagus standing upright within the innermost room of the temple. I approached the dead boy timidly. He seemed as if costumed: the stiff Egyptian headdress covered his hair. His legs tightly bound in strips of linen were now only a long white bundle, but the profile of the young falcon had not changed; the lashes cast a shadow which I knew on the painted cheeks. Before they finished the wrapping of the hands I was urged to admire the gold fingernails.

The litanies began; the departed one, speaking through the priests, declared himself to have been perpetually truthful, perpetually chaste, perpetually compassionate and just, and boasted of virtues which, had he practiced them as described, would have set him forever apart from the living. The stale odor of incense filled the room, and through the smoky cloud I tried to give myself the illusion of a smile on those lips; the beautiful, immobile features seemed to tremble. I watched the magic passes whereby the priests force the soul of the dead to incarnate some portion of itself inside the statues which are to conserve his memory; there were other injunctions, stranger still. When all was over, the gold mask cast from the wax funeral mold was laid in place, perfectly fitting the features. That fair, incorruptible surface was soon to absorb within itself its own possibilities for radiance and warmth; it was to lie forever in that case hermetically closed, like some inert symbol of immortality. A sprig of acacia was placed on his chest, and some dozen men lifted the heavy cover into position.

But I hesitated still about where to place the tomb. I recalled that in ordering rites of apotheosis everywhere, with funeral games, issues of coins, and statues in the public squares, I had made an exception for Rome, fearing to augment that animosity which more or less surrounds any foreign favorite. I told myself that I should not always be there to protect that sepulchre. The monument envisaged at the gates of Antinoöpolis seemed too public also, and far from safe. I followed the priests' advice. On a mountainside in the Arabic range, some three leagues from the new city, they indicated to me one of those caverns formerly intended by Egypt's kings to serve as their funeral vaults. A team of oxen drew the sarcophagus up that grade; it was lowered with ropes to those subterranean corridors, and was then slid into position to lean against a wall of rock. The youth from Claudiopolis was descending into the tomb like a Pharaoh, or a Ptolemy. There we left him, alone. He was entering upon that endless tenure, without air, without light, without change of season, compared with which every life seems short; such was the stability to which he had attained, such perhaps was the peace. Centuries as yet unborn within the dark womb of time would pass by thousands over that tomb without restoring life to him, but likewise without adding to his death, and without changing the fact that he had been.

Hermogenes took my arm to help me go up again to the open air; it was almost a joy to be above ground once more, to catch sight of the cold blue sky between two slabs of tawny rock. The remainder of the voyage was brief. At Alexandria the empress re-embarked for Rome.

DISCIPLINA AUGUSTA

I returned to Greece by the land route. The journey was long. I had reason to think that this would be my last official tour in the Orient, and I was the more anxious, therefore, to see everything for myself. Antioch, where I stopped for some weeks, appeared to me under a new light; I was less impressed than before by the spell of its theaters and festivals, by the delights of the pleasure gardens of Daphne, and by the brilliant color in its passing crowds. I was increasingly aware of the eternal frivolity of the populace, mocking and malicious like the people of Alexandria, and of the stupidity of their so-called intellectual activities; likewise of the vulgar display of luxury on the part of the rich. Hardly one of these leading citizens grasped in its entirety my program for public works and reforms in Asia; they were satisfied to profit by them for their city, and above all for themselves. For a short time I considered advancing Smyrna or Pergamum to the detriment of the arrogant Syrian capital, but the faults of Antioch are those inherent in any metropolis; no great city can escape them. My disgust with urban life made me apply myself even more, if possible, to agrarian reform; I put the finishing touches to the long and complex reorganization of the imperial domains in Asia Minor; the peasants were the better off for it, and the State, too. Crossing Thrace, I went to revisit Hadrianopolis, where veterans of the Dacian and Sarmatian campaigns had settled in great numbers, attracted by land grants and reductions in taxes. The same plan was to be put into operation in Antinoöpolis. I had long since made comparable exemptions everywhere for doctors and professors in the hope of favoring the survival and development of a serious, well-educated middle class. I know the deficiences of this class, but only through it does a State endure.

Athens remained the stop of my choice; I marveled that its

beauty depended so little upon memories, whether my own or those of history; that city seemed new with each new day. I stayed this time with Arrian. He had been initiated like me at Eleusis, so was accordingly adopted by one of the great priestly families of Attica, the Kerykes, as I had been by the family of the Eumolpides. He had married into the Kerykes family; his wife was a proud and elegant young Athenian. The two of them gave me every care. Their house was only a few steps from the new library with which I had just endowed Athens, and which offered every aid to meditation, or to the repose which must precede it: comfortable chairs and adequate heating for winters which are often so sharp; stairways giving ready access to the galleries where books are kept; a luxury of alabaster and gold, quiet and subdued. Particular attention had been paid to the choice of lamps, and to their placing. I felt more and more the need to gather together and conserve our ancient books, and to entrust the making of new copies to conscientious scribes. This noble task seemed to me no less urgent than aid to veterans or subsidies to prolific families of the poor; I warned myself that it would take only a few wars, and the misery that follows them, or a single period of brutality or savagery under a few bad rulers to destroy forever the ideas passed down with the help of these frail objects in fiber and ink. Each man fortunate enough to benefit to some degree from this legacy of culture seemed to me responsible for protecting it and holding it in trust for the human race.

During that period I read a great deal. I had encouraged Phlegon to compose a series of chronicles, under the name of *Olympiads*, which would continue Xenophon's *Hellenica* and which would come down to my reign, a bold plan in that it reduced Rome's vast history to a mere sequel of that of Greece. Phlegon's style is annoyingly dry, but it would already be something done to have untangled and assembled the facts. The project inspired me to reread the historians of other days; their works, judged in the light of my own experience, filled me with somber thoughts; the energy and good intentions of each statesman seemed of slight avail before this flood so fortuitous and so fatal, this torrent of happenings too confused to be foreseen or directed, or even appraised. The poets, too, engaged me; I liked to conjure those few clear, mellow voices out of a distant past. Theognis became a friend, the aristocrat, the exile, observing human activities without illusion and without indulgence, ever ready to denounce the faults and errors which we call our woes. This clear-sighted man had known love's poignant delights; his liaison with Cyrnus, in spite of suspicions, jealousies, and mutual grievances, had endured into the old age of the one and the mature years of the other: the immortality which he was wont to promise to that youth of Megara was more than an empty assurance, since their two memories have come down to me through a space of more than six centuries. But among the ancient poets Antimachus especially won me: I liked his rich but abstruse style, his ample though highly concentrated phrases, like great bronze cups filled with a heavy wine. I preferred his account of Jason's expedition to the more romantic *Argonautica* by Apollonius: Antimachus understood better the mystery of voyages and horizons, and how ephemeral a shadow man throws on this abiding earth. He had wept passionately over the death of his wife, Lydia, and had given her name to a long poem made up of all manner of legends of grief and mourning. That Lydia, whom perhaps I should have taken no notice of as a living being, became a familiar figure for me, dearer than many a feminine face in my own existence. Such poems, though almost forgotten, were little by little restoring to me my faith in immortality.

I revised my own works, the love poems, the occasional pieces, and the ode to the memory of Plotina. One day, perhaps, someone would wish to read all that. A group of obscene verses were matter for hesitation, but I ended, after all, by including them. Our best and most cultivated men write such things. They make a game of it; I should have preferred mine to be more than that, to reflect exactly the naked truth. But there as elsewhere the commonplace entraps us; I was beginning to understand that it takes more than audacity of mind to free us from banality, and that the poet triumphs over routines or imposes his thought upon words by efforts quite as long and persevering as those of my work of emperor. For my part I could aspire only to the rare good luck of the amateur: it would already be considerable if from all this rubble two or three verses were to survive. At about this time, however, I outlined a rather ambitious work, half in

prose, half in verse, wherein I intended to include the curious
facts observed in the course of my life, together with my meditations and certain dreams, mingling the serious and the ironic;
all this would have been bound together by the merest thread, a
sort of *Satyricon*, but harsher. In it I should have set forth a
philosophy which had become my own, the Heraclitean idea of
change and return. But I have put aside that project as far too
vast.

In that same year I held several conversations with the priestess
who had formerly initiated me at Eleusis (and whose name must
remain secret) in order to discuss and establish details of the cult
of Antinous, one by one. The great Eleusiac symbols continued
to exert upon me their calming effect; the world has no meaning,
perhaps, but if it does have one, that meaning is expressed at
Eleusis more wisely and nobly than anywhere else. It was under
this woman's influence that I undertook to plan the administrative
divisions of Antinoöpolis, its demes, its streets, its city blocks,
on the model of the world of the gods, and at the same time to
include therein a reflection of my own life. All the deities were
to be represented, Hestia and Bacchus, divinities of the hearth
and of the orgy, the gods of the heavens and those of the
underworld. I placed my imperial ancestors there, too, Trajan
and Nerva, now an integral part of that system of symbols.
Plotina figured; the good Matidia was there, in the likeness of
Demeter; my wife herself, with whom at the time my relations
were cordial enough, made one of that procession of divinities.
Some months later I bestowed the name of my sister Paulina
upon a district of Antinoöpolis; I had finally broken off with her
as the wife of Servianus, but she had now died and thus had
regained her unique position of sister in that city of memories.
The site of sorrow was becoming the ideal center for reunions
and recollections, the Elysian Fields of a life, the place where
contradictions are resolved and where everything, within its
rank, is equally sacred.

Standing at a window in Arrian's house under night skies alive
with stars, I thought of those words which the Egyptian priests
had had carved on Antinous' tomb: *He has obeyed the command of
heaven.* Can it be that the sky intimates its orders to us, and that
only the best among us hear them while the remainder of man-

kind is aware of no more than oppressive silence? The priestess of Eleusis and Chabrias both thought so. I should have liked them to be right. In my mind I could see the palm of that hand again, smoothed by death, as I had looked on it for the last time that morning at the embalmers'; the lines which had previously disquieted me were no longer visible; the surface was like a wax tablet from which an instruction, once carried out, had been erased. But such lofty affirmations enlighten without rewarming us, like the light of stars, and the night all around us is darker still. If the sacrifice of Antinous had been thrown into the balance in my favor in some divine scale, the results of that terrible gift of self were not yet manifest; the benefits were neither those of life nor even those of immortality. I hardly dared seek a name for them. Sometimes, at rare intervals, a feeble gleam pulsed without warmth on my sky's horizon; but it served to improve neither the world nor myself; I continued to feel more deteriorated than saved.

It was near this period that Quadratus, a bishop of the Christians, sent me a defense of his faith. I had made it a principle to maintain towards that sect the strictly equitable line of conduct which had been Trajan's in his better days: I had just reminded the provincial governors that the protection of the law extends to all citizens, and that defamers of Christians would be punished if they levelled accusations against that group without proof. But any tolerance shown to fanatics is immediately mistaken by them for sympathy with their cause; though I can hardly imagine that Quadratus was hoping to make a Christian of me, he assuredly strove to convince me of the excellence of his doctrine, and to prove, above all, that it offered no harm to the State. I read his work, and was even enough interested to have Phlegon assemble some information about the life of the young prophet named Jesus who had founded the sect, but who died a victim of Jewish intolerance about a hundred years ago. This young sage seems to have left behind him some teachings not unlike those of Orpheus, to whom at times his disciples compare him. In spite of Quadratus' singularly flat prose I could discern through it the appealing charm of virtues of simple folk, their kindness, their ingenuousness, and their devotion to each other. All of that strongly resembled the fraternities which slaves or poor citizens found almost everywhere in honor of our gods in the crowded quarters of our cities. Within a world which remains, despite all our efforts, hard and indifferent to men's hopes and trials, these small societies for mutual aid offer the unfortunate a source of comfort and support.

But I was aware, too, of certain dangers. Such glorification of virtues befitting children and slaves was made at the expense of more virile and more intellectual qualities; under that narrow, vapid innocence I could detect the fierce intransigence of the sectarian in presence of forms of life and of thought which are not his own, the insolent pride which makes him value himself above other men, and his voluntarily circumscribed vision. I speedily tired of Quadratus' captious arguments, and of those scraps of wisdom ineptly borrowed from the writings of our philosophers. Chabrias, ever preoccupied to offer the gods the worship due them, was disturbed by the progress of sects of this kind among the populace of large cities; he feared for the welfare of our ancient religions, which yoke men to no dogma whatsoever, but lend themselves, on the contrary, to interpretations as varied as nature itself; they allow austere spirits who desire to do so to invent for themselves a higher morality, but they do not bind the masses by precepts so strict as to engender immediate constraint and hypocrisy. Arrian shared these views. I passed a whole evening discussing with him the injunction which consists in loving another as oneself; it is too foreign to the nature of man to be followed with sincerity by the average person, who will never love anyone but himself, and it is not at all suited to the philosopher, who is little given to self-love.

On many points, however, the thinking of our philosophers also seemed to be limited and confused, if not sterile. Three quarters of our intellectual performances are no more than decorations upon a void; I wondered if that increasing vacuity was due to the lowering of intelligence or to moral decline; whatever the cause, mediocrity of mind was matched almost everywhere by shocking selfishness and dishonesty. I had directed Herod Atticus to supervise the construction of a chain of aqueducts in the Troad; he made use of that trust to squander public funds in shameful fashion, and when called to render an accounting sent back the insolent reply that he was rich enough to cover all deficits; such wealth was itself a scandal. His father, who had but recently died, had made a discreet arrangement to disinherit him by multiplying bounties to the Athenian citizenry; young Herod refused outright to pay the paternal legacy, and a law suit ensued which is still going on. In Smyrna my erstwhile intimate, Polemo, had the effrontery to oust a deputation of senators from Rome who had thought it reasonable to count on his hospitality. Your father Antoninus, the gentlest of men, was enraged; statesman and sophist finally came to blows over the matter; such pugilism, if unworthy of an emperor-to-be, was still more disgraceful for a Greek philosopher. Favorinus, that greedy dwarf whom I had showered with money and honors, was peddling witticisms on all sides at my expense: the thirty legions which I commanded were, according to him, my only strong arguments in the philosophical bouts wherein I had the vanity to indulge, and wherein, he explained, he took care to leave the last word to the emperor. That was to tax me with both presumption and stupidity, but it amounted, above all, to admission of singular cowardice on his part. Pedants are always annoyed when others know their narrow specialty as well as they do themselves, and everything now served as pretext for their ugly remarks: because I had added the much neglected works of Hesiod and Ennius to the school curriculum, those routine minds promptly attributed to me the desire to dethrone Homer, and the gentle Virgil as well (whom nevertheless I was always quoting). There was nothing to be done with people of that sort.

Arrian was better than that. I liked to talk with him on all subjects. He had retained a fervent and profoundly serious memory of the Bithynian youth; I was grateful to him for ranking that love, which he had witnessed, with the famous mutual attachments of antiquity; from time to time we spoke of it, but although no lie was uttered I frequently had the impression of a certain falsity in our words; the truth was being covered beneath the sublime. I was almost as much disappointed by Chabrias: his blind devotion to Antinous had been like that of an aged slave for a young master, but, absorbed as he was in the worship of the new god, he seemed to have lost all remembrance of the living boy. My black Euphorion had at least observed our life at closer range. Arrian and Chabrias were dear to me, and I felt

myself in no way superior to those two decent men, but sometimes it seemed to me that I was the only person struggling to
keep his eyes wholly open.

Yes, Athens remained exquisite, and I did not regret the choice
of Greek disciplines for my life. Everything in us which is human,
or well-ordered and clearly thought out comes to us from them.
But I was beginning to feel that Rome's seriousness, even if
somewhat heavy, and its sense of continuity and love of the
concrete, had all been needed for the full realization of what was
for Greece still only an admirable idea, a splendid impulse of the
soul. Plato had written the *Republic* and glorified the Just, but
we were the ones who were striving, warned by our own errors,
to make the State a machine fit to serve man, with the least
possible risk of crushing him. The word *philanthropy* is Greek,
but the legist Salvius Julianus and I are the ones who are working
to change the wretched condition of the slaves. Rome had taught
me prudence and assiduous application to detail, those virtues
which temper the boldness of broad general views.

There were times, too, when deep within myself I would
come upon those vast, melancholy landscapes of Virgil, and his
twilights veiled by tears; if I searched deeper still I would encounter the burning sadness of Spain and its stark violence; I reflected
upon the varied blood, Celtic, Iberian, Punic perhaps, which
must have infiltrated into the veins of those Roman colonists in
Italica; I recalled that my father had been surnamed 'the African.'
Greece had helped me evaluate those elements in my nature
which were not Greek. Likewise for Antinous: I had made him
the very image and symbol of that country so passionate for
beauty, and he would be, perhaps, the last of its gods; yet the
refinements of Persia and the savagery of Thrace had met in
Bithynia with the shepherds of ancient Arcadia; that slightly
arched nose recalled profiles of Osroës' pages; the broad visage
and high cheekbones were those of the Thracian horsemen who
gallop along the shores of the Bosphorus, and who burst forth
at night into wild, sad song. No formula is so complete as to
contain all.

That year I completed the revision of the Athenian consti-
tution, a reform begun by me long before. For the new instrument I went back, in so far as possible, to Cleisthenes' ancient

democratic laws. Governmental costs were lightened by reducing the number of officials; I tried, too, to put a stop to the farming of taxes, a disastrous system unfortunately still employed here and there by local administrations. University endowments, established at about the same period, helped Athens to become once more an important center of learning. Beauty lovers who flocked to that city before my time had been content to admire its monuments without concern for the growing poverty of the inhabitants. On the contrary, I had done my utmost to increase the resources of that poor land. One of the great projects of my reign was realized shortly before my departure, the establishment of annual assemblies in Athens wherein delegates from all the Greek world would hereafter transact all affairs for Greece, thus restoring this small, perfect city to its due rank of metropolis. The plan had taken shape only after delicate negotiations with cities jealous of Athens' supremacy and still nursing ancient resentments against her; little by little, however, common sense and even some enthusiasm carried the day. The first of those assemblies coincided with the opening of the Olympieion for public worship; that temple was becoming more than ever the symbol of a reawakened Greece.

On that occasion a series of spectacles was given, with marked success, in the theater of Dionysos; my seat there was beside that of the Hierophant, and only slightly higher; thereafter the priest of Antinous had his place, too, among the notables and the clergy. I had had the stage of the theater enlarged and ornamented with new bas-reliefs; on one of these friezes my young Bithynian was receiving a kind of eternal right of citizenship from the Eleusinian goddesses. In the Panathenaic stadium, transformed for a few hours into a forest of mythological times, I staged a hunt in which some thousand wild animals figured; thus was revived for the brief space of the festival that primitive and rustic town of Hippolytus, servitor of Diana, and of Theseus, companion of Hercules. A few days later I left Athens. Nor have I returned there since.

The administration of Italy, left for centuries wholly in the hands of the praetors, had never been definitely codified. The Perpetual Edict, which settles the issue once and for all, dates from this period of my life. For years I had been corresponding with Salvius Julianus about these reforms, and my return to Rome served to hasten their completion. The Italian cities were not to be deprived of their civil liberties; on the contrary, we had everything to gain, in that respect as in others, if we did not forcibly impose upon them an artificial uniformity. I am even surprised that such townships, many of which are older than Rome, should be so ready to renounce their customs (some of them wise, indeed) in order to follow the capital in every respect. My purpose was simply to diminish that mass of contradictions and abuses which eventually turn legal procedure into a wilderness where decent people hardly dare venture, and where bandits abound. Such endeavors obliged me to travel frequently from one place to another about the country. I made several stays in Baiae, in the former villa of Cicero which I had purchased early in my reign; this province of Campania interested me, for it reminded me of Greece. On the edge of the Adriatic, in the small city of Hadria whence my ancestors had emigrated to Spain nearly four centuries earlier, I was honored with the highest municipal offices. Near that stormy sea whose name I bear, I came upon some of my family urns in a ruined cemetery. There I meditated on those men, of whom I knew nothing but from whom I sprang, and whose race would end with me.

In Rome they were enlarging my mausoleum, since Decrianus had cleverly redrawn the plans; they are still at work upon it, even now. The idea for those circular galleries came from Egypt, and likewise the ramps descending to underground chambers; I had conceived of a colossal tomb to be reserved not for myself alone, or for my immediate successors, but as the eventual resting-place of future emperors for centuries to come; princes yet to be born have thus their places already marked in this palace of death. I saw also to the ornamentation of the cenotaph erected on the Field of Mars in memory of Antinous; a barge from Alexandria had discharged its loads of sphinxes and obelisks for this work. A new project long occupied me, and has not ceased to do so, namely, the construction of the Odeon, a model library provided with halls for courses and lectures to serve as a center of Greek culture in Rome. I made it less splendid than the new library at Ephesus, built three or four years before, and gave it

less grace and elegance than the library of Athens, but I intend
to make this foundation a close second to, if not the equal of,
the Museum of Alexandria; its further development will rest with
you. In working upon it I often think of the library established by
Plotina in Trajan's Forum, with that noble inscription placed by
her order over its door: *Dispensary to the Soul.*

The Villa was near enough completion to have my collections
transported to it, my musical instruments and the several thousand books purchased here and there in the course of my travels.
I gave a series of banquets where everything was assembled with
care, both the menu for the repasts and the somewhat restricted
list of my guests. My goal was to have all in harmony with the
calm beauty of these gardens and these halls, to have fruits as
exquisite as the music, and the sequence of courses as perfect as
the chasing on the silver plates. For the first time I took an
interest in the choice of foods, giving orders that the oysters
must come from Lucrinus and the crayfish be taken from the
rivers of Gaul. My dislike of the combined pomposity and
negligence which too often characterize an emperor's table led
me to rule that all viands be shown to me before they were
presented to any of my guests, even to the least of them. I insisted
upon verifying the accounts of cooks and caterers myself; there
were times when I recalled that my grandfather had been miserly.

Neither the small Greek theater of the Villa, nor the Latin
theater, hardly larger, had been completed, but I had a few plays
produced in them nevertheless, tragedies, pantomimes, musical
dramas, and old local farces. I delighted above all in the subtle
gymnastics of the dance, and discovered a weakness for women
with castanets, who reminded me of the region of Gades and the
first spectacles which I had attended as a child. I liked that brittle
sound, those uplifted arms, the furling and unfurling of veils,
the dancer who changed now from woman to cloud, and then
to bird, who became sometimes the ship and sometimes the
wave. For one of these creatures I even took a fancy, though
briefly enough. Nor had the kennels and studs been neglected in
my absence; I came back to the rough coats of the hounds, the
silken horses, the fair pack of the pages. I arranged a few hunting
parties in Umbria, on the shore of Lake Trasimene, or nearer
Rome, in the Alban woods.

Pleasure had regained its place in my life; my secretary Onesimus served me as purveyor. He knew when to avoid certain resemblances, or when, just the reverse, it was better to seek them out. But such a hurried and half attentive lover was hardly loved in return. Now and then I met with a being finer and gentler than the rest, someone worth hearing talk, and perhaps worth seeing again. Those happy chances were rare, though I may have been to blame. Ordinarily I did no more than appease (or deceive) my hunger. At other times my indifference to such games was like that of an old man.

In my wakeful hours I took to pacing the corridors of the Villa, proceeding from room to room, sometimes disturbing a mason at work as he laid a mosaic. I would examine, in passing, a Satyr of Praxiteles and then would pause before the effigies of the beloved dead. Each room had its own, and each portico. Sheltering the flame of my lamp with my hand, I would lightly touch that breast of stone. Such encounters served to complicate the memory's task; I had to put aside like a curtain the pallor of the marble to go back, in so far as possible, from those motionless contours to the living form, from the hard texture of Paros or Pentelikon to the flesh itself. Again I would resume my round; the statue, once interrogated, would relapse into darkness; a few steps away my lamp would reveal another image; these great white figures differed little from ghosts. I reflected bitterly upon those magic passes whereby the Egyptian priests had drawn the soul of the dead youth into the wooden effigies which they use in their rites; I had done like them; I had cast a spell over stones which, in their turn, had spellbound me; nevermore should I escape from their cold and silence, henceforth closer to me than the warmth and voices of the living; it was with resentment that I gazed upon that dangerous countenance and its elusive smile. Still, a few hours later, once more abed, I would decide to order another statue from Papias of Aphrodisias; I would insist upon a more exact modeling of the cheeks, just where they hollow almost insensibly under the temples, and a gentler inclination of the head toward the shoulder; I would have the garlands of vine leaves or the clusters of precious stones give way to the glory of the unadorned hair. I took care to have the weight of these bas-reliefs and these busts reduced by drilling out the inside, thus leaving them easier to transport. The best likenesses among them have accompanied me everywhere; it no longer matters to me whether they are good works of art or not.

In appearance my life was reasonable; I applied myself more steadily than ever to my task as emperor, exerting more discrimination, perhaps, if less ardor than before. I had somewhat lost my zest for new ideas and new contacts, and that flexibility of mind which used once to help me enter into another's thought, and to learn from it while I judged it. My curiosity, wherein I could formerly trace the mainspring of my thinking and one of the bases of my method, was now aroused only over futile details: I opened letters addressed to my friends, to their indignation; such a glimpse into their loves and domestic quarrels amused me for the moment. But an element of suspicion was mingled therein: for a few days I was even prey to the dread of being poisoned, that horrible fear which I had previously beheld in the eyes of the ailing Trajan, and which a ruler dare not avow, since it would seem grotesque so long as unjustified by the event. Such an obsession may seem surprising in one who was already deep in meditation upon death, but I do not pretend to be more consistent than others. When confronted by the least stupidity or the commonest petty contriving I was seized with inward fury and wild impatience (nor did I exempt myself from my own disgust). For example, Juvenal, in one of his *Satires*, was bold enough to attack the actor Paris, whom I liked. I was tired of that pompous, tirading poet; I had little relish for his coarse disdain of the Orient and Greece, or for his affected delight in the so-called simplicity of our forefathers; his mixture of detailed descriptions of vice with virtuous declamation titillates the reader's senses without shaking him from his hypocrisy. As a man of letters, however, he was entitled to certain consideration; I had him summoned to Tibur to tell him myself of his sentence to exile. This scorner of the luxuries and pleasures of Rome would be able hereafter to study provincial life and manners at first hand; his insults to the handsome Paris had drawn the curtain on his own act.

Favorinus, towards that same time, settled into his comfortable exile in Chios (where I should have rather liked to dwell myself), whence his biting voice came no longer to my ears. At about this period, too, I ordered a wisdom vendor chased ignomini-

ously from a banquet hall, an ill-washed Cynic who complained
of dying of hunger, as if that breed merited anything else. I took
great pleasure in seeing the prater packed off, bent double by
fear, midst the barking of dogs and the mocking laughter of the
pages. Literary and philosophical riff-raff no longer impressed
me.

The least setback in political affairs exasperated me just as did
the slightest inequality in a pavement at the Villa, or the smallest
dripping of wax on the marble surface of a table, the merest
defect of an object which one would wish to keep free of imperfec-
tions and stains. A report from Arrian, recently appointed governor of Cappadocia, cautioned me against Pharasmanes, who
was continuing in his small kingdom along the Caspian Sea to
play that double game which had cost us dear under Trajan. This
petty prince was slyly pushing hordes of barbarian Alani toward
our frontiers; his quarrels with Armenia endangered peace in the
Orient. When summoned to Rome he refused to come, just as
he had already refused to attend the conference at Samosata four
years before. By way of excuse he sent me a present of three
hundred robes of gold, royal garments which I ordered worn in
the arena by criminals loosed to wild beasts. That rash gesture
solaced me like the action of one who scratches himself nearly
raw.

I had a secretary, a very mediocre fellow, whom I retained
because he knew all the routines of the chancellery, but who
provoked me by his stubborn, snarling self-sufficiency: he refused to try new methods, and had a mania for arguing endlessly
over trivial details. This fool irritated me one day more than
usual; I raised my hand to slap him; unhappily, I was holding a
style, which blinded his right eye. I shall never forget that howl
of pain, that arm awkwardly bent to ward off the blow, that
convulsed visage from which the blood spurted. I had Hermogenes sent for at once, to give the first care, and the oculist Capito
was then consulted. But in vain; the eye was gone. Some days
later the man resumed his work, a bandage across his face. I sent
for him and asked him humbly to fix the amount of compensation
which was his due. He replied with a wry smile that he asked of
me only one thing, another right eye. He ended, however, by
accepting a pension. I have kept him in my service; his presence

serves me as a warning, and a punishment, perhaps. I had not wished to injure the wretch. But I had not desired, either, that a boy who loved me should die in his twentieth year.

Jewish affairs were going from bad to worse. The work of construction was continuing in Jerusalem, in spite of the violent opposition of Zealot groups. A certain number of errors had been committed, not irreparable in themselves but immediately seized upon by fomenters of trouble for their own advantage. The Tenth Legion Fretensis has a wild boar for its emblem; when its standard was placed at the city gates, as is the custom, the populace, unused to painted or sculptured images (deprived as they have been for centuries by a superstition highly unfavorable to the progress of the arts), mistook that symbol for a swine, the meat of which is forbidden them, and read into that insignificant affair an affront to the customs of Israel. The festivals of the Jewish New Year, celebrated with a din of trumpets and rams' horns, give rise every year to brawling and bloodshed; our authorities accordingly forbade the public reading of a certain legendary account devoted to the exploits of a Jewish heroine who was said to have become, under an assumed name, the concubine of a king of Persia, and to have instigated a savage massacre of the enemies of her despised and persecuted race. The rabbis managed to read at night what the governor Tineus Rufus forbade them to read by day; that barbarous story, wherein Persians and Jews rivaled each other in atrocities, roused the nationalistic fervor of the Zealots to frenzy. Finally, this same Tineus Rufus, a man of good judgment in other respects and not uninterested in Israel's traditions and fables, decided to extend to the Jewish practice of circumcision the same severe penalties of the law which I had recently promulgated against castration (and which was aimed especially at cruelties perpetrated upon young slaves for the sake of exorbitant gain or debauch). He hoped thus to obliterate one of the marks whereby Israel claims to distinguish itself from the rest of human kind. I took the less notice of the danger of that measure, when I received word of it, in that many wealthy and enlightened Jews whom one meets in Alexandria and in Rome have ceased to submit their children to a practice which makes them ridiculous in the public baths

and gymnasiums; and they even arrange to conceal the evidence
on themselves. I was unaware of the extent to which these banker
collectors of myrrhine vases differed from the true Israel.

As I said, nothing in all that was beyond repair, but the hatred,
the mutual contempt, and the rancor were so. In principle,
Judaism has its place among the religions of the empire; in
practice, Israel has refused for centuries to be one people among
many others, with one god among the gods. The most primitive
Dacians know that their Zalmoxis is called Jupiter in Rome; the
Phoenician Baal of Mount Casius has been readily identified with
the Father who holds Victory in his hand, and of whom Wisdom
is born; the Egyptians, though so proud of their myths some
thousands of years old, are willing to see in Osiris a Bacchus
with funeral attributes; harsh Mithra admits himself brother to
Apollo. No people but Israel has the arrogance to confine truth
wholly within the narrow limits of a single conception of the
divine, thereby insulting the manifold nature of the Deity, who
contains all; no other god has inspired his worshipers with disdain
and hatred for those who pray at different altars. I was only the
more anxious to make Jerusalem a city like the others, where
several races and several beliefs could live in peace; but I was
wrong to forget that in any combat between fanaticism and
common sense the latter has rarely the upper hand. The clergy
of the ancient city were scandalized by the opening of schools
where Greek literature was taught; the rabbi Joshua, a pleasant,
learned man with whom I had frequently conversed in Athens,
but who was trying to excuse himself to his people for his foreign
culture and his relations with us, now ordered his disciples not
to take up such profane studies unless they could find an hour
which was neither day nor night, since Jewish law must be
studied night and day. Ismael, an important member of the
Sanhedrin, who supposedly adhered to the side of Rome, let his
nephew Ben-Dama die rather than accept the services of the
Greek surgeon sent to him by Tineus Rufus. While here in Tibur
means were still being sought to conciliate differences without
appearing to yield to demands of fanatics, affairs in the East took
a turn for the worse; a Zealot revolt triumphed in Jerusalem.

An adventurer born of the very dregs of the people, a fellow
named Simon who entitled himself Bar-Kochba, Son of the Star,

played the part of firebrand or incendiary mirror in that revolt. I could judge this Simon only by hearsay; I have seen him but once face-to-face, the day a centurion brought me his severed head. Yet I am disposed to grant him that degree of genius which must always be present in one who rises so fast and so high in human affairs; such ascendancy is not gained without at least some crude skill. The Jews of the moderate party were the first to accuse this supposed Son of the Star of deceit and imposture; I believe rather that his untrained mind was of the type which is taken in by its own lies, and that guile in his case went hand in hand with fanaticism. He paraded as the hero whom the Jewish people had awaited for centuries in order to gratify their ambitions and their hate; this demagogue proclaimed himself Messiah and King of Israel. The aged Akiba, in a foolish state of exaltation, led the adventurer through the streets of Jerusalem, holding his horse by the bridle; the high priest Eleazar rededicated the temple, said to be defiled from the time that uncircumcised visitors had crossed its threshold. Stacks of arms hidden underground for nearly twenty years were distributed to the rebels by agents of the Son of the Star; they also had recourse to weapons formerly rejected for our ordnance as defective (and purposely constructed thus by Jewish workers in our arsenals over a period of years). Zealot groups attacked isolated Roman garrisons and massacred our soldiers with refinements of cruelty which recalled the worst memories of the Jewish revolt under Trajan; Jerusalem finally fell wholly into the hands of the insurgents, and the new quarters of Aelia Capitolina were set burning like a torch. The first detachments of the Twenty-Second Legion Deiotariana, sent from Egypt with utmost speed under the command of the legate of Syria, Publius Marcellus, were routed by bands ten times their number. The revolt had become war, and war to the bitter end.

Two legions, the Twelfth Fulminata and the Sixth Ferrata, came immediately to reinforce the troops already stationed in Judaea; some months later, Julius Severus took charge of the military operations. He had formerly pacified the mountainous regions of Northern Britain, and brought with him some small contingents of British auxiliaries accustomed to fighting on difficult terrain. Our heavily equipped troops and our officers trained to the square or the phalanx formation of pitched battles were hard put to it to adapt themselves to that war of skirmishes and surprise attacks which, even in open country, retained the techniques of street fighting. Simon, a great man in his way, had divided his followers into hundreds of squadrons posted on mountain ridges or placed in ambush in caverns and abandoned quarries, or even hidden in houses of the teeming suburbs of the cities. Severus was quick to grasp that such an elusive enemy could be exterminated, but not conquered; he resigned himself to a war of attrition. The peasants, fired by Simon's enthusiasm, or terrorized by him, made common cause with the Zealots from the start; each rock became a bastion, each vineyard a trench; each tiny farm had to be starved out, or taken by assault. Jerusalem was not recaptured until the third year, when last efforts to negotiate proved futile; what little of the Jewish city had been spared by the destruction under Titus was now wiped out. Severus closed his eyes for a long time, voluntarily, to the flagrant complicity of the other large cities now become the last fortresses of the enemy; they were later attacked and reconquered in their turn, street by street and ruin by ruin.

In those times of trial my place was with the army, and in Judaea. I had utter confidence in my two lieutenants, but it was all the more fitting, therefore, that I should be present to share responsibility for decisions which, however carried out, promised atrocities to come. At the end of a second summer of campaign I made my preparations for travel, but with bitterness; once more Euphorion packed up my toilet kit, wrought long ago by an artisan of Smyrna and somewhat dented by wear, my case of books and maps, and the ivory statuette of the Imperial Genius with his lamp of silver; I landed at Sidon early in autumn.

The army is the first of my callings; I have never gone back into it without feeling repaid for my constraints there by certain inner compensations; I do not regret having passed the last two active years of my existence in sharing with the legions the harshness and desolation of that Palestine campaign. I had become again the man clad in leather and iron, putting aside all that is not immediate, sustained by the routines of a hard life, though somewhat slower than of old to mount my horse, or to dismount, somewhat more taciturn, perhaps more somber, surrounded as ever (the gods alone know why) by a devotion from the troops which was both religious and fraternal. During this last stay in the army I made an encounter of inestimable value: I took a young tribune named Celer, to whom I was attached, as my aide-de-camp. You know him; he has not left me. I admired that handsome face of a casqued Minerva, but on the whole the senses played as small a part in this affection as they can so long as one is alive. I recommend Celer to you: he has all the qualities to be sought in an officer placed in second rank; his very virtues will always keep him from pushing into first place. Once again, but in circumstances somewhat different from those of other days, I had come upon one of those beings whose destiny is to devote himself, to love, and to serve. Since I have known him Celer has had no thought which was not for my comfort or my security; I lean still upon that firm shoulder.

In the spring of the third year of campaign the army laid siege to the citadel of Bethar, an eagle's nest where Simon and his partisans held out for nearly a year against the slow tortures of hunger, thirst, and despair, and where the Son of the Star saw his followers perish one by one but still would not surrender. Our army suffered almost as much as the rebels, for the latter, on retiring, had burned the forests, laid waste the fields, slaughtered the cattle, and polluted the wells by throwing our dead therein; these methods from savage times were hideous in a land naturally arid and already consumed to the bone by centuries of folly and fury. The summer was hot and unhealthy; fever and dysentery decimated our troops, but an admirable discipline continued to rule in those legions, forced to inaction and yet obliged to be constantly on the alert; though sick and harassed, they were sustained by a kind of silent rage in which I, too, began to share. My body no longer withstood as well as it once did the fatigues of campaign, the torrid days, the alternately suffocating or chilly nights, the harsh wind, and the gritty dust; I sometimes left the bacon and boiled lentils of the camp mess in my bowl, and went hungry. A bad cough stayed with me well into the summer, nor was I the only one in such case. In my dispatches to the Senate I suppressed the formula which is regulation for the opening of official communications: *The emperor and the army are well*. The emperor and the army were,

on the contrary, dangerously weary. At night, after the last
conversation with Severus, the last audience with fugitives from
the enemy side, the last courier from Rome, the last message
from Publius Marcellus or from Rufus, whose respective tasks
were to wipe up outside Jerusalem and, to reorganize Gaza,
Euphorion would measure my bath water sparingly into a tub
of tarred canvas; I would lie down on my bed and try to think.

There is no denying it; that war in Judaea was one of my
defeats. The crimes of Simon and the madness of Akiba were
not of my making, but I reproached myself for having been blind
in Jerusalem, heedless in Alexandria, impatient in Rome. I had
not known how to find words which would have prevented, or
at least retarded, this outburst of fury in a nation; I had not
known in time how to be either supple enough or sufficiently
firm. Surely we had no reason to be unduly disturbed, and still
less need to despair; the blunder and the reversal had occurred
only in our relations with Israel; everywhere else at this critical
hour we were reaping the reward of sixteen years of generosity
in the Orient. Simon had supposed that he could count on a
revolt in the Arab world similar to the uprising which had
darkened the last years of Trajan's reign; even more, he had
ventured to bank on Parthian aid. He was mistaken, and that
error in calculation was causing his slow death in the besieged
citadel of Bethar: the Arab tribes were drawing apart from
the Jewish communities; the Parthians remained faithful to the
treaties. The synagogues of the great Syrian cities proved undecided or lukewarm, the most ardent among them contenting
themselves with sending money in secret to the Zealots; the
Jewish population of Alexandria, though naturally so turbulent,
remained calm; the abscess in Jewish affairs remained local,
confined within the arid region which extends from Jordan to
the sea; this ailing finger could safely be cauterized, or amputated.
And nevertheless, in a sense, the evil days which had immediately
preceded my reign seemed to begin over again. In the past
Quietus had burned down Cyrene, executed the dignitaries of
Laodicea, and recaptured a ruined Edessa . . . The evening courier had just informed me that we had re-established ourselves on
the heap of tumbled stones which I called Aelia Capitolina and
which the Jews still called Jerusalem; we had burned Ascalon,

and had been forced to mass executions of rebels in Gaza . . . If sixteen years of rule by a prince so pacifically inclined were to culminate in the Palestine campaign, then the chances for peace in the world looked dim ahead.

I raised myself on my elbow, uneasy on the narrow camp bed. To be sure, there were some Jews who had escaped the Zealot contagion: even in Jerusalem the Pharisees spat on the ground before Akiba, treating that fanatic like an old fool who threw to the wind the solid advantages of the Roman peace, and shouting to him that grass would grow from his mouth before Israel's victory would be seen on this earth. But I preferred even false prophets to those lovers of order at all costs who, though despising us, counted on us to protect them from Simon's demands upon their gold (placed for safety with Syrian bankers), and upon their farms in Galilee. I thought of the deserters from his camp who, a few hours back, had been sitting in my tent, humble, conciliatory, servile, but always managing to turn their backs to the image of my Genius. Our best agent, Elias Ben-Abayad, who played the role of informer and spy for Rome, was justly despised by both camps; he was nevertheless the most intelligent man in the group, a liberal mind but a man sick at heart, torn between love for his people and his liking for us and for our culture; he too, however, thought essentially only of Israel. Joshua Ben-Kisma, who preached appeasement, was but a more timid, or more hypocritical Akiba. Even in the rabbi Joshua, who had long been my counselor in Jewish affairs, I had felt irreconcilable differences under that compliance and desire to please, a point where two opposite kinds of thinking meet only to engage in combat. Our territories extended over hundreds of leagues and thousands of stadia beyond that dry, hilly horizon, but the rock of Bethar was our frontier; we could level to dust the massive walls of that citadel where Simon in his frenzy was consummating his suicide, but we could not prevent that race from answering us 'No.'

A mosquito hummed over me; Euphorion, who was getting along in years, had failed to close exactly the thin curtains of gauze; books and maps left on the ground rattled in the low wind which crept under the tent wall. Sitting up on my bed, I drew on my boots and groped for my tunic and belt with its dagger, then went out to breathe the night air. I walked through the wide, straight streets of the camp, empty at that late hour, but lighted like city streets; sentries saluted formally as I passed; alongside the barracks which served for hospital I caught the stale stench of the dysenterics. I proceeded towards the earthwork which separated us from the precipice, and from the enemy. A sentinel, perilously outlined by the moon, was making his round with long, even tread; his passage and return was one part of the movement of that immense machine in which I was the pivot; for a moment I was stirred by the spectacle of that solitary form, that brief flame burning in the breast of a man midst a world of dangers. An arrow whistled by, hardly more irksome than the mosquito which had troubled me in my tent; I stood looking out, leaning against the rampart of sandbags.

For some years now people have credited me with strange insight, and with knowledge of divine secrets. But they are mistaken; I have no such power. It is true, however, that during those nights of Bethar some disturbing phantoms passed before my eyes. The perspectives afforded the mind from the height of those barren hills were less majestic than these of the Janiculum, and less golden than those of Cape Sunion; they offered the reverse and the nadir. I admitted that it was indeed vain to hope for an eternity for Athens and for Rome which is accorded neither to objects nor men, and which the wisest among us deny even to the gods. These subtle and complex forms of life, these civilizations comfortably installed in their refinements of ease and of art, the very freedom of mind to seek and to judge, all this depended upon countless rare chances, upon conditions almost impossible to bring about, and none of which could be expected to endure. We should manage to destroy Simon; Arrian would be able to protect Armenia from Alani invasions. But other hordes would come, and other false prophets. Our feeble efforts to ameliorate man's lot would be but vaguely continued by our successors; the seeds of error and of ruin contained even in what is good would, on the contrary, increase to monstrous proportions in the course of centuries. A world wearied of us would seek other masters; what had seemed to us wise would be pointless for them, what we had found beautiful they would abominate. Like the initiate to Mithraism the human race has need, perhaps, of a periodical bloodbath and descent into the grave. I could see the return of barbaric codes, of implacable gods, of unquestioned despotism of savage chieftains, a world broken up into enemy states and eternally prey to insecurity. Other sentinels menaced by arrows would patrol the walls of future cities; the stupid, cruel, and obscene game would go on, and the human species in growing older would doubtless add new refinements of horror. Our epoch, the faults and limitations of which I knew better than anyone else, would perhaps be considered one day, by contrast, as one of the golden ages of man.

Natura deficit, fortuna mutatur, deus omnia cernit. Nature fails us, fortune changes, a god beholds all things from on high: I fingered the stone of a ring on which on a day of bitter depression I had had those few sad words engraved. I went deeper in disillusion, and perhaps into blasphemy: I was beginning to find it natural, if not just, that we should perish. Our literature is nearing exhaustion, our arts are falling asleep; Pancrates is not Homer, nor is Arrian a Xenophon; when I have tried to immortalize Antinous in stone no Praxiteles has come to hand. Our sciences have been at a standstill from the times of Aristotle and Archimedes; our technical development is inadequate to the strain of a long war; even our pleasure-lovers grow weary of delight. More civilized ways of living and more liberal thinking in the course of the last century are the work of a very small minority of good minds; the masses remain wholly ignorant, fierce and cruel when they can be so, and in any case limited and selfish; it is safe to wager that they will never change. Our effort has been compromised in advance by too many greedy procurators and publicans, too many suspicious senators, too many brutal centurions. Nor is time granted oftener to empires than to men to learn from past errors. Although a weaver would wish to mend his web or a clever calculator would correct his mistakes, and the artist would try to retouch his masterpiece if still imperfect or slightly damaged, Nature prefers to start again from the very clay, from chaos itself, and this horrible waste is what we term natural order.

I raised my head and moved slightly in order to limber myself. From the top of Simon's citadel vague gleams reddened the sky, unexplained manifestations of the nocturnal life of the enemy. The wind was blowing from Egypt; a whirl of dust passed by like a specter; the flattened rims of the hills reminded me of the Arabic range in moonlight. I went slowly back, drawing a fold of my cloak over my mouth, provoked with myself for having devoted to hollow meditations upon the future a night which I could have employed to prepare the work of the next day, or to sleep. The collapse of Rome, if it were to come about, would concern my successors; in that eight hundred and forty-seventh year of the Roman era my task consisted of stifling the revolt in Judaea and bringing back from the Orient, without too great loss, an ailing army. In crossing the esplanade I slipped at times on the blood of some rebel executed the evening before. I lay down on my bed without undressing, to be awakened two hours later by the trumpets at dawn.

All my life long I had been on the best of terms with my body; I had implicitly counted upon its docility, and its strength. That close alliance was beginning to dissolve; my body was no longer at one with my will and my mind, and with what after all, however ineptly, I must call my soul; the ready comrade of other days was only a slave sulking at his task. In fact, my body was afraid of me; continually now I was aware of the obscure presence of fear, of a feeling of constriction in my chest which was not yet pain, but the first step toward it. I had long been used to insomnia, but from this time on sleep was worse than vigil; hardly would I doze off before there were frightful awakenings. I was subject to headaches which Hermogenes attributed to the heat of the climate and the helmet's weight; by evening, after prolonged fatigue, I sank into a chair like one falling; rising to receive Rufus or Severus was an effort for which I had to prepare well in advance; when seated I leaned heavily on the arms of my chair, and my thigh muscles trembled like those of an exhausted runner. The slightest motion became actual labor, and of such labors life was now composed.

An accident almost ridiculous, a mere childish indisposition, brought to light the true malady beneath that appalling fatigue. During a meeting of the general staff I had a nosebleed, but took little notice of it at first; it persisted, however, until time for the evening meal; I awoke at night to find myself drenched in blood. I called Celer, who slept in the next tent, and he in his turn roused Hermogenes, but the horrid warm flood went on. With careful hands the young officer wiped away the liquid which smirched my face. At dawn I was seized with retching as are the condemned in Rome who open their veins in their bath. They warmed my chilled body the best they could with the aid of blankets and hot packs; to staunch the blood Hermogenes prescribed snow; it was not to be had in camp; coping with innumerable difficulties Celer had it brought from the summit of Mount Hermon. I learned later that they had despaired of my life, and I myself felt attached to it by no more than the merest thread, as imperceptible as the too rapid pulse which now dismayed my physician. But the sudden, inexplicable hemorrhage came to an end; I got up again and strove to live as before, but did not succeed. When, but poorly restored to health, I had imprudently attempted an evening ride, I received a second warning, more serious than the first. For the space of a second I felt my heartbeats quicken, then slow down, falter, and cease; I seemed to fall like a stone into some black well which is doubtless death. If death it was, it is a mistake to call it silent: I was swept down by cataracts, and deafened like a diver by the roaring of waters. I did not reach bottom, but came to the surface again, choking for breath. All my strength in that moment, which I thought my last, had been concentrated into my hand as I clutched at Celer, who was standing beside me; he later showed me the marks of my fingers upon his shoulder. But that brief agony was, like all bodily experiences, indescribable, and remains the secret of him who has lived through it, whether he would tell it or no. Since that time I have passed similar crises, though never identical, and no doubt one does not go twice (and still live) through that terror and that night. Hermogenes finally diagnosed an initial stage of hydropic heart; there was no choice but to accept the orders given me by this illness, which had suddenly become my master, and to consent to a long period of inaction, if not of rest, limiting the perspectives of my life for a time to the frame of a bed. I was almost ashamed of such an ailment, wholly internal and barely visible, without fever, abscess, or intestinal pain, with its only

symptom a somewhat hoarser breathing and a livid mark left by
the sandal strap across the swollen foot.

An extraordinary silence reigned round my tent; the entire
camp of Bethar seemed to have become a sick room. The
aromatic oil which burned below my Genius rendered the close
air of this canvas cage heavier still; the pounding of my arteries
made me think vaguely of the island of the Titans on the edge
of night. At other moments the insufferable noise changed to
that of galloping horses thudding down on wet earth; the mind
so carefully reined in for nearly fifty years was wandering; the
tall body was floating adrift; I resigned myself to be that tired
man who absently counted the star-and-diamond pattern of his
blanket. I gazed at the white blur of a marble bust in the shadow;
a chant in honor of Epona, goddess of horses, which used to be
sung by my Spanish nurse, a tall, somber woman who looked
like a Fate, came back to me from the depths of more than half
a century's time. The long days, and after them the nights,
seemed measured out not by the clepsydra but by the brown
drops which Hermogenes counted one by one into a cup of glass.

At evening I mustered my strength to listen to Rufus' report:
the war was nearing its end; Akiba, who had ostensibly retired
from public affairs since the outbreak of hostilities, was devoting
himself to the teaching of rabbinic law in the small city of Usfa
in Galilee; his lecture room had become the center of Zealot
resistance; secret messages were transcribed from one cipher to
another by the hands of this nonagenarian and transmitted to the
partisans of Simon; the fanatic students who surrounded the old
man had to be sent off by force to their homes. After long
hesitation Rufus decided to ban the study of Jewish law as
seditious; a few days later Akiba, who had disregarded that
decree, was arrested and put to death. Nine other Doctors of the
Law, the heart and soul of the Zealot faction, perished with him.
I had approved all these measures by nods of assent. Akiba and
his followers died persuaded to the end that they alone were
innocent, they alone were just; not one of them dreamed of
admitting his share in responsibility for the evils which weighed
down his people. They would be enviable if one could envy the
blind. I do not deny these ten madmen the title of heroes, but in
no case were they sages.

Three months later, from the top of a hill on a cold morning in February, I sat leaning against the trunk of a leafless fig-tree to watch the assault which preceded by only a few hours the capitulation of Bethar. I saw the last defenders of the fortress come out one by one, haggard, emaciated, hideous to view but nevertheless superb, like all that is indomitable. At the end of the same month I had myself borne to the place called Abraham's Well, where the rebels in the urban centers, taken with weapons in hand, had been assembled to be sold at auction: children sneering defiance, already turned fierce and deformed by implacable convictions, boasting loudly of having brought death to dozens of legionaries; old men immured in somnambulistic dreams; women with fat, heavy bodies and others stern and stately, like the Great Mother of the Oriental cults; all these filed by under the cool scrutiny of the slave merchants; that multitude passed before me like a haze of dust. Joshua Ben-Kisma, leader of the so-called moderates, who had lamentably failed in his role of peacemaker, succumbed at about that time to the last stages of a long illness; he died calling down upon us foreign wars and victory for Parthia. On the other hand, the Christianized Jews, whom we had not disturbed and who harbored resentment against the rest of the Hebrews for having persecuted their prophet, saw in us the instrument of divine wrath. The long series of frenzies and misconceptions was thus continuing.

An inscription placed on the site of Jerusalem forbade the Jews, under pain of death, to re-establish themselves anew upon that heap of rubble; it reproduced word for word the interdict formerly inscribed on the temple door, forbidding entrance to the uncircumcised. One day a year, on the ninth of the month of Ab, the Jews have the right to come to weep in front of a ruined wall. The most devout refused to leave their native land; they settled as well as they could in the regions least devastated by the war. The most fanatical emigrated to Parthian territory; others went to Antioch, to Alexandria, and to Pergamum; the clever ones made for Rome, where they prospered. Judaea was struck from the map and took the name of Palestine by my order. In those four years of war fifty fortresses and more than nine hundred villages and towns had been sacked and destroyed; the enemy had lost nearly six hundred thousand men; battles, endemic fevers, and epidemics had taken nearly ninety thousand of ours. The labors of war were followed immediately by reconstruction in that area; Aelia Capitolina was rebuilt, though on a more modest scale; one has always to begin over again.

I rested for some time in Sidon, where a Greek merchant lent me his house and his gardens. In March those inner courts were already carpeted with roses. I had regained my strength, and was even discovering surprising resources in this body which at first had been prostrated by the violence of the initial attack. But we have understood nothing about illness so long as we have not recognized its odd resemblance to war and to love, its compromises, its feints, its exactions, that strange and unique amalgam produced by the mixture of a temperament and a malady. I was better, but in order to contrive with my body, to impose my wishes upon it or to cede prudently to its will, I devoted as much art as I had formerly employed in regulating and enlarging my world, in building the being who I am, and in embellishing my life. I resumed the exercises of the gymnasium, but with moderation; although my physician no longer forbade me the use of a horse, riding was now no more than a means of transport; I had to forego the dangerous jumps of other days. In the course of any work or any pleasure, neither work nor pleasure was now the essential; my first concern was to get through it without fatigue. A recovery which seemed so complete astonished my friends; they tried to believe that the illness had been due merely to excessive efforts in those years of war, and would not recur. I judged otherwise; I recalled the great pines of Bithynia's forests which the woodsman notches in passing, and which he will return next season to fell. Towards the end of spring I embarked for Italy on a large galley of the fleet, taking with me Celer, now become indispensable, and Diotimus of Gadara, a young Greek of slave origin encountered in Sidon, who had beauty.

The route of return crossed the Archipelago; for the last time in my life, doubtless, I was watching the dolphins leap in that blue sea; with no thought henceforth of seeking for omens I followed the long straight flight of the migrating birds, which sometimes alighted in friendly fashion to rest on the deck of the ship; I drank in the odor of salt and sun on the human skin, the perfume of lentisk and terebinth from the isles where each voyager longs to dwell, but knows in advance that he will not pause. Diotimus read me the poets of his country; he has had that perfect instruction in letters which is often given to young slaves endowed with bodily graces in order to increase further their value; as night fell I would lie in the stern, protected by the purple canopy, listening till darkness came to efface both those lines which describe the tragic incertitude of our life, and those which speak of doves and kisses and garlands of roses. The sea was exhaling its moist, warm breath; the stars mounted one by one to their stations; the ship inclining before the wind made straight for the Occident, where showed the last shreds of red; phosphorescence glittered in the wake which stretched out behind us, soon covered over by the black masses of the waves. I said to myself that only two things of importance awaited me in Rome: one was the choice of my successor, of interest to the whole empire; the other was my death, of concern to me alone.

Rome had prepared me a triumph, which this time I accepted. I no longer protested against these vain but venerable customs; anything which honors man's effort, even if only for a day, seemed to me salutary in presence of a world so prone to forget. I was celebrating more than the suppression of the Jewish revolt; in a sense more profound, and known to me alone, I had triumphed. I included the name of Arrian in these honors. He had just inflicted a series of defeats on the hordes of the Alani which would throw them back for a long time to come into that obscure center of Asia which they had thought to leave for good; Armenia had been saved; the reader of Xenophon was revealing himself as the emulator of that general, showing that the race of scholars who could also command and fight, if need be, was not extinct. That evening, on returning to my house in Tibur, it was with a weary but tranquil heart that I received from Diotimus' hands the incense and wine of the daily sacrifice to my Genius.

While still a private citizen I had begun to buy up and unite these lands, spread below the Sabine Halls along clear streams, with the patient tenacity of a peasant who parcel by parcel rounds out his vineyard; later on, between two imperial tours, I had camped in these groves then in prey of architects and masons; a youth imbued with all the superstitions of Asia used often to urge devoutly that the trees be spared. On the return from my longest travel in the Orient I had worked in a kind of frenzy to perfect this immense stage-setting for a play then already three-quarters completed. I was coming back to it this time to end my days as reasonably as possible. Everything here was arranged to facilitate work as well as pleasure: the chancellery, the audience halls, and the court where I judged difficult cases in last appeal all saved me the tiring journeys between Tibur and Rome. I had given each of these edifices names reminiscent of Greece: the Pœcile, the Academy, the Prytaneum. I knew very well that this small valley planted with olive trees was not Tempe, but I was reaching the age when each beauteous place recalls another, fairer still, when each delight is weighted with the memory of past joys. I was willing to yield to nostalgia, that melancholy residue of desire. I had even given the name of Styx to a particularly somber corner of the park, and the name of Elysian Fields to a meadow strewn with anemones, thus preparing myself for that other world where the torments resemble those of this world, but where joys are nebulous, and inferior to our joys. But most important of all, in the heart of this retreat I had built for myself a refuge more private still, an islet of marble at the center of a pool surrounded by colonnades; this gave me a room wholly apart, connected with, or rather, separated from the shore by a turning bridge so light that with one hand I could make it slide in its grooves. Into this summer pavilion I had two or three beloved statues moved, and the small bust of Augustus as a child, which Suetonius had given me in the period when we still were friends; I used to go there at the hour of siesta to sleep or to think, or to read. My dog would stretch out across the doorway, extending his paws somewhat stiffly now; reflections played on the marble; Diotimus would rest his cheek, to cool himself, against the smooth surface of an urn; my thoughts were on my successor.

I have no children, nor is that a regret. To be sure, in time of weakness and fatigue, when one lacks the courage of one's convictions, I have sometimes reproached myself for not having taken the precaution to engender a son, to follow me. But such a vain regret rests upon two hypotheses, equally doubtful: first, that a son necessarily continues us, and second, that the strange mixture of good and evil, that mass of minute and odd particularities which make up a person, deserves continuation. I have put my virtues to use as well as I could, and have profited from my vices likewise, but I have no special concern to bequeath myself to anyone. It is not by blood, anyhow, that man's true continuity is established: Alexander's direct heir is Caesar, and not the frail infant born of a Persian princess in an Asiatic citadel; Epaminondas, dying without issue, was right to boast that he had Victories for daughters. Most men who figure in history have but mediocre offspring, or worse; they seem to exhaust within themselves the resources of a race. A father's affection is almost always in conflict with the interests of a ruler. Were it otherwise, then an emperor's son would still have to suffer the drawbacks of a princely education, the worst possible school for a future prince. Happily, in so far as our State has been able to formulate a rule for imperial succession, that rule has been adoption: I see there the wisdom of Rome. I know the dangers of choice, and its possible errors; I am well aware, too, that blindness is not reserved to paternal affections alone; but any decision in which intelligence presides, or where it at least plays a part, will always seem to me infinitely superior to the vague wishes of chance and unthinking nature. The power to the worthiest! It is good and fitting that a man who has proved his competence in handling the affairs of the world should choose his replacement, and that a decision of such grave consequence should be both his last privilege and his last service rendered to the State. But this important choice seemed to me more difficult than ever to make.

I had bitterly reproached Trajan for having evaded the problem for twenty years before he resolved to adopt me, and for having decided the matter only upon his deathbed. But nearly eighteen years had passed since my accession to power and I in my turn, despite the dangers of an adventurous life, had put off till the last my choice of a successor. Hundreds of rumors were circulating, almost all of them false; countless hypotheses had been built up; but what was supposed my secret decision was only my hesitation and my doubt. All around me good functionaries abounded, but not one of them had the necessary breadth of view. Forty years of integrity made Marcius Turbo a likely candidate, my friend and companion of yore and my incomparable prefect of the

Praetorian Guard; but he was my age, too old. Julius Severus, an excellent general and a good administrator for Britain, knew little of the complex affairs of the Orient; Arrian had given proof of all the qualities expected of a statesman, but he was Greek, and the time has not yet come to place a Greek emperor over Rome and its prejudices.

Servianus was living still: such longevity looked like deliberate calculation on his part, an obstinate form of waiting. He had waited for sixty years. In Nerva's time he had been both disappointed and encouraged by the adoption of Trajan; he was hoping for more, but the rise to power of this cousin incessantly occupied with the army seemed at least to assure him a considerable place in the State, perhaps second place. There, too, he was mistaken, for he had obtained only a rather empty share of honors. He waited for that time when he had stationed his slaves to attack me from an ambush in a poplar grove, along the Moselle; the duel-to-the-death begun on that morning between the young man and the man of fifty had gone on for twenty years; he had turned the mind of the sovereign against me, exaggerating my escapades and making the most of my slightest error. Such an enemy is an excellent schoolmaster: Servianus has taught me much, all in all, about prudence. After my accession to power he had had sufficient subtlety to appear to accept the inevitable; he disclaimed all connection with the plot of the four consular conspirators, and I had preferred not to remark the stains on those fingers still visibly soiled. On his side he had limited himself to mere whispered protest, and only in private pronounced my actions outrageous. With support in the Senate from that small but powerful faction of life-long conservatives who were hindering my reforms he had comfortably installed himself in the rôle of silent critic of my reign. Little by little he had alienated my sister Paulina from me. Their only child was a daughter, married to a certain Salinator, a man of high birth whom I had raised to the consulship, but who had died young of consumption. My niece did not long survive him; their one child, Fuscus, was set against me by this pernicious grandfather.

But the hatred between us kept within certain bounds: I did not begrudge him his part in public functions, though I took care, nevertheless, not to stand beside him in ceremonies where his advanced age would have given him precedence over the emperor. On each return to Rome I agreed, for appearances' sake, to attend one of those family meals where one keeps on one's guard; we exchanged letters; his were not without wit. In the long run, however, I had become disgusted with such dreary pretense; the possibility of discarding the mask in every respect is one of the rare advantages which I find in growing old: I had refused to be present at the funeral of Paulina. In the camp of Bethar, in the worst hours of physical distress and discouragement, the supreme bitterness had been to tell myself that Servianus was nearing his goal, and nearing it by my fault; that octogenarian so niggard of his strength would manage to survive an invalid of fifty-seven years; if I should die intestate he would contrive to obtain both the votes of the malcontents and the approval of those who thought that they were remaining faithful to me in electing my brother-in-law; he would profit from our slender kinship to undermine my work. In order to calm my fears I used to say to myself that the empire could find worse masters; Servianus after all was not without qualities; even the dull Fuscus would one day perhaps be worthy to reign. But all the energy which I had left was summoned to refuse this lie, and I wished to live if only to crush that viper.

On coming back to Rome I saw much of Lucius again. In former days I had made commitments to him which ordinarily one hardly troubles to fulfill, but which I had kept. It is not true, however, that I had promised him the imperial purple; such things are not done. But for nearly fifteen years I had paid his debts, hushed up his scandals, and answered his letters without delay; delightful letters they were, but they always ended with requests for money for himself, or for advancement for his friends. He was too much mingled with my life for me to exclude him from it had I wished to do so, but I wished nothing of the sort. His conversation was brilliant: this young man whom people judged superficial had read more, and more intelligently, than the writers who make such works their profession. In everything his taste was exquisite, whether for people, objects, manners, or the most exact fashion of scanning a line of Greek verse. In the Senate, where he was considered able, he had made a reputation as an orator: his speeches were at the same time terse and ornate, and served immediately upon utterance as models for the professors of eloquence. I had had him named praetor, and then consul: he had fulfilled these functions well. Some years earlier I had arranged a marriage for him with the daughter of Nigrinus, one of the consular conspirators executed at the beginning of my reign; that union became the emblem of my policy of conciliation. It was but moderately successful: the young woman complained of being neglected, but she had three children by him, one of whom was a son. To her almost continual repining he would reply with frigid politeness that one marries for one's family's sake and not for oneself, and that so weighty a contract ill accords with the carefree play of love. His complicated system demanded mistresses for display and willing slaves for sensuous delights. He was killing himself in pursuit of pleasure, but was doing so like an artist who destroys himself in completing a masterpiece: it is not for me to reproach him in that.

I watched him live: my opinion of him was constantly changing, a thing which rarely happens except for those persons to whom we are closely attached; we are satisfied to judge others more in general, and once for all. Sometimes a studied insolence and hardness, or a coldly frivolous remark would disturb me; more often, however, I let myself be carried along by his swift and nimble intelligence; an astute comment seemed suddenly to reveal the future statesman. I spoke of all this to Marcius Turbo, who after his tiring day as Praetorian prefect came every evening to talk over current business and play his game of dice with me; together we re-examined in utmost detail Lucius' possibilities for suitably fulfilling the career of emperor. My friends were amazed at my scruples; some of them counseled me, with a shrug of the shoulders, to take whatever decision I liked; such people imagine that one bequeaths half the world to someone as one would leave a country house to a friend. I reflected further about it by night: Lucius had hardly reached thirty; what was Caesar at thirty years but a young patrician submerged in debts and sullied by scandal? As in the bad days of Antioch, before my adoption by Trajan, I thought with a pang that nothing is slower than the true birth of a man: I had myself passed my thirtieth year before the Pannonian campaign had opened my eyes to the responsibilities of power; Lucius seemed to me at times more accomplished than

I was at that age. I made up my mind abruptly, after a crisis of suffocation graver than the others, which warned me that I had no more time to lose.

I adopted Lucius, who took the name of Aelius Caesar. He was carefree even in his ambition, and though demanding was not grasping, having always been accustomed to obtain everything; he took my decision with casual ease. I had the imprudence to mention that this fair-haired prince would be admirably handsome clad in the purple; the maliciously inclined hastened to assert that I was giving an empire in return for a voluptuous intimacy of earlier days. Such a charge shows no understanding of the way that the mind of a ruler functions (provided that in some degree he merits his post and his title). If like considerations had figured, then Lucius would not have been the only one on whom I could have fixed my choice.

My wife had just died in her residence at the Palatine, which she had preferred to the end to Tibur, and where she lived surrounded by a small court of friends and Spanish relations, who were all that she cared about. The polite evasions, the proprieties, the feeble efforts towards understanding had gradually terminated between us, and had left exposed only antipathy, irritation, and rancor, and, on her part, hatred. I paid her a visit in the last days; sickness had further soured her morose and acid disposition; that interview was occasion for her for violent recrimination; she gained relief thereby, but was indiscreet in speaking thus before witnesses. She congratulated herself on dying childless: my sons would doubtless have resembled me, she said, and she would have had the same aversion for them as for their father. That avowal, in which such bitterness rankled, is the only proof of love which she has ever given me. My Sabina: I searched for the few passably good memories which are left of someone when we take the trouble to look back for them; I recalled a basket of fruit which she had sent me for my birthday, after a quarrel; while passing by litter through the narrow streets of the town of Tibur and before the small summer house which had once belonged to my mother-in-law Matidia, I thought bitterly of some nights of a summer long ago, when I had tried in vain to arouse some amorous feeling for this young bride so harsh and so cold. The death of my wife was less moving for me than the loss of the good Arete, the housekeeper at the Villa, stricken that same winter by fever. Because the illness to which the empress succumbed had been but poorly diagnosed by the physicians, and towards the last caused her cruel intestinal pain, I was accused of having had her poisoned, and that wild rumor was readily believed. It goes without saying that so superfluous a crime had never tempted me.

The death of Sabina perhaps pushed Servianus to risk his all: her influence in Rome had been wholly at his disposal; with her fell one of his most respected supports. And further, he had just entered upon his ninetieth year; like me, he had no more time to lose. For some months now he had tried to draw around him small groups of officers of the Praetorian Guard; sometimes he ventured to exploit the superstitious respect which great age inspires in order to assume imperial authority within his four walls. I had recently reinforced the secret military police, a distasteful institution, I admit, but one which the event proved useful. I knew all about those supposedly secret assemblies, wherein the aged Ursus was teaching the art of conspiracy to his grandson. The nomination of Lucius did not surprise the old man; he had long taken my incertitude on this subject for a well dissimulated decision; but he chose to act at the moment when the legal adoption was still a matter of controversy in Rome. His secretary, Crescens, weary of forty years of faithful service badly repaid, divulged the project, the date and place of attack, and the names of the accomplices. My enemies had not taxed their imagination; they simply copied outright the assault premeditated long before by Quietus and Nigrinus: I was to be struck down during a religious ceremony at the Capitol; my adopted son was to fall with me.

I took my precautions that very night: our enemy had lived only too long; I would leave Lucius a heritage cleansed of dangers. Towards the twelfth hour, on a gray dawn of February, a tribune bearing a sentence of death for Servianus and his grandson presented himself to my brother-in-law; his instructions were to wait in the vestibule until the order which he brought had been executed. Servianus sent for his physician, and all was decently performed. Before dying he expressed the wish that I should expire in the slow torments of incurable illness, without having like him the privilege of brief agony. His prayer has already been granted.

I had not ordered this double execution light-heartedly, but I felt no regret for it thereafter, and still less remorse. An old score had been paid at last; that was all. Age has never seemed to me an excuse for human malevolence; I should even be inclined to consider advanced years as the less excuse for such dangerous ill-will. The sentencing of Akiba and his acolytes had cost me longer hesitation; of the two old men I should still prefer the fanatic to the conspirator. As to Fuscus, however mediocre he might be and however completely his odious grandfather might have alienated him from me, he was the grandson of Paulina. But bonds of blood are truly slight (despite assertions to the contrary) when they are not reinforced by affection; this fact is evident in any family where the least matter of inheritance arises. The youth of Fuscus moved me somewhat more to pity, for he had barely reached eighteen. But interests of State required this conclusion, which the aged Ursus had seemed voluntarily to render inevitable. And from then on I was too near my own death to take time for meditation upon those two endings.

For a few days Marcius Turbo doubled his vigilance; the friends of Servianus could have sought revenge. But nothing came of it, neither attack nor sedition, nor even complaints. I was no longer the newcomer trying to win public opinion after the execution of four men of consular rank; nineteen years of just rule arbitrated in my favor; my enemies were execrated as a group, and the crowd approved me for having rid myself of a traitor. Fuscus was commiserated, but without being judged innocent. The Senate, I well knew, would not pardon me for having once more struck down one of its members, but it kept quiet, and would remain quiet until my death. As formerly, also, an admixture of clemency soon mitigated the dose of severity: not one of the partisans of Servianus was disturbed. The only exception to this rule was the eminent Apollodorus, the malevolent depositary of my brother-in-law's secrets, who perished with him. That talented man had been the favorite architect of my predecessor; he had piled up the great stone blocks of Trajan's Column with art. We did not care much for each other: he had of old derided my unskilled amateur paintings, my conscientious still-lifes of pumpkins and gourds; I had on my side, with a young man's presumption, criticized his works. Later on he had disparaged mine: he knew nothing of the finest period of Greek art; that literal mind reproached me for having filled our temples with colossal statues which, if they were to rise, would batter their brows against the vaults of their sanctuaries. An inane criticism that, and one to hurt Phidias even more than me. But the gods do not rise; they rise neither to warn us nor to protect us, nor to recompense nor to punish. Nor did they rise on that night to save Apollodorus.

By spring the health of Lucius began to cause me rather grave concern. One morning in Tibur we went down from the bath to the palaestra where Celer was exercising with other youths; someone proposed one of those contests where each participant runs bearing his shield and his spear. Lucius managed to excuse himself from the sport, as he usually did, but finally yielded to our friendly raillery; in equipping himself he complained of the weight of the bronze shield; compared with the firm beauty of Celer that slender body seemed frail. After a few strides he fell breathless, and spit blood. The incident had no sequel, and he recovered without difficulty; but I had been alarmed. I should not have been so soon reassured. I resisted these first symptoms of his illness with the stupid confidence of a man who had long been robust, and who had implicit faith in the undepleted reserves of youth and in the capacities of bodies to function as they should. It is true that he was mistaken, too; some light flame sustained him, and his vivacity created the same illusion for him as for us. My best years had been passed in travel and in camp, or on the frontiers; I had known at first hand the values of a rude life, and the salubrious effect of frozen or desert regions. I decided to name Lucius governor of that same Pannonia where I had had my first experience in rule. The situation on that frontier was less critical than formerly; his task would be limited to the peaceful work of civil administration or to routine military inspections. Such difficult country would rouse him from Rome's easy ways; he would get better acquainted with that immense world which the City governs, and on which she depends. He dreaded those distant climes, and would not understand that life could be enjoyed elsewhere than in Rome. He accepted, however, with the compliance which he always showed when he wished to please me.

Throughout the summer I read with care both his official reports and those more secret communications from Domitius Rogatus, my confidential informant whom I had sent with him as a secretary instructed to watch over him. These accounts satisfied me: Lucius demonstrated in Pannonia that he was capable of the seriousness which I expected of him, but from which he might have relaxed, perhaps, after my death. He even conducted himself rather brilliantly in a series of cavalry skirmishes at the advance posts. In the provinces, as everywhere else, he succeeded in charming everyone around him; his dry and somewhat imperious manner did him no disservice; at least this would not be a case of one of those easy-going princes who is governed by a coterie. But with the very beginning of autumn he caught cold. He was thought to be well again soon, but the cough recurred and the fever persisted, setting in for good. A temporary gain was followed by a sudden relapse the next spring. The bulletins from the physicians appalled me; the public postal service, which I had just established with its relays of horses and carriages over vast territories, seemed to function only in order to bring me news of the invalid more promptly each morning. I could not pardon myself for having been inhumane towards him in the fear of being, or seeming, too indulgent. As soon as he was recovered enough to travel I had him brought back to Italy.

In company with the aged Rufus of Ephesus, a specialist in phthisis, I went to the port of Baiae to await my fragile Aelius Caesar. The climate of Tibur, though better than that of Rome, is nevertheless not mild enough for affected lungs; I had decided to have him spend the late autumn in that safer region. The ship anchored in the middle of the bay; a light tender brought the sick man and his physician ashore. His haggard face seemed thinner still under the fringe of beard with which he had let his cheeks be covered, in the hope of resembling me. But his eyes had kept their hard fire, the gleam of precious stones. His first words to me were to remind me that he had come back only at my command; that his administration had incurred no reproach; that he had obeyed me in everything. He spoke like a schoolboy who justifies the way that he has spent his day. I established him in that villa of Cicero where he had formerly passed a season with me when he was eighteen. He had the elegance never to speak of those times.

The first few days seemed like a victory over the disease; this return to Italy was already a remedy in itself; at that time of year the countryside there was wine-red in hue. But the rains began; a damp wind blew from the strong sea; the old house built in the time of the Republic lacked the more modern comforts of the villa in Tibur; I watched Lucius dispiritedly warming his slender fingers, laden with rings, over the brazier. Hermogenes had returned but a short time before from the Orient, where I had sent him to refurnish and augment his provision of medicaments; he tried on Lucius the effects of a mud impregnated with powerful mineral salts; these applications were reputed to cure everything. But they were of no more help to his lungs than to my arteries.

Illness exposed the worst aspects of that hard and frivolous nature: his wife paid him a visit; as always, their interview ended in bitter words; she did not come back again. His son was brought to see him, a beautiful child of seven, laughing and gay, and just at the toothless age; Lucius beheld him without interest. He asked eagerly for political news from Rome, but more as a gambler would than a statesman. Such levity, however, was a form of courage on his part; he would awaken from long afternoons of pain or torpor to throw his whole being into one of those sparkling conversations of his former days; that face wet with sweat still knew how to smile; the emaciated body rose with grace to receive the physician. He would be to the end the prince formed of ivory and gold.

At night, unable to sleep, I would take up my station in the invalid's room; Celer, who disliked Lucius, but who is too loyal not to serve with care those dear to me, consented to share my vigil; from the covers came the sound of rattled breathing. A feeling of bitterness swept over me, deep as the sea: he had never loved me; our relations had quickly become those of the spendthrift son and the indulgent father; that life had run out without ever having known great hopes or serious thoughts and ardent passions; he had squandered his years as a prodigal scatters gold coin. I had leaned for support upon a ruined wall: I thought with anger of the enormous sums expended for his adoption, three hundred million sesterces distributed to the soldiers. In a sense, my good fortune had followed me, though sadly: I had satisfied my old desire to give Lucius all that can be given, but the State would not suffer for it now; I should not risk being dishonored by that choice. In the very depths of my being I was even fearing that he might get better; if by chance he should drag on some years still, I could not leave the empire to such a shade.

Without ever asking questions he seemed to penetrate my thoughts on this point; his eyes followed anxiously my slightest motion. I had named him consul for the second time; he worried because he could not fulfill the functions of that office; the dread of displeasing me aggravated his condition. *Tu Marcellus eris* . . . I repeated to myself Virgil's lines devoted to the nephew of Augustus, likewise designated to rule, and whom death stopped short on the way. *Manibus date lilia plenis* . . . *Purpureos spargam flores* . . . The lover of flowers would receive only futile funeral wreaths from me.

He believed that he was better, and wished to return to Rome. The physicians, who no longer disputed among themselves except as to the length of time left him to live, counseled me to do whatever he liked; I took him back by short stages to the Villa. His formal presentation to the Senate as heir to the empire was to take place during the session which would follow almost immediately upon the New Year. According to custom, he was supposed on that occasion to address to me a speech of thanks; this piece of eloquence had preoccupied him for months, and together we had smoothed over its difficult passages. He was working at it on the morning of the first of January, when he was suddenly taken with hemorrhage; he grew faint, and leaned against the back of his chair, closing his eyes. Death was no more than dizziness for this light creature. It was New Year's Day: in order not to interrupt the public and private festivities, I restricted immediate proclamation of the news of his passing; it was not announced officially until the following day. He was buried quietly on his family estate. The evening before that ceremony the Senate sent a delegation to me bearing its condolences, and offering the honors of divinization to Lucius, to which he was entitled as the emperor's adopted son. But I refused: this whole affair had already cost only too much to the State. I confined myself to having some funeral chapels constructed for him, and statues erected here and there in different places where he had lived: this poor Lucius was not a god.

This time each moment counted. But I had had ample leisure for reflection at the invalid's bedside; my plans were made. In the Senate I had remarked a certain Antoninus, a man of about fifty, of a provincial family distantly related to that of Plotina. He had impressed me by the deferent but tender care with which he surrounded his father-in-law, an old man partially paralyzed, who sat beside him. I read through his records; this honest man had proved himself in every post that he had held an irreproachable official. My choice fell on him. The more I frequent Antoninus the more my esteem for him tends to change into profound respect. This simple man possesses a virtue which I had thought little about up to this time, even when I happened to practice it, namely, kindness. He is not devoid of the modest faults of a sage: in applying his intelligence to the meticulous accomplishment of daily tasks he concerns himself more with the present than the future; his experience of life is limited by his very virtues; his travel has been confined to certain official missions, though these have been well fulfilled. He is little versed in the arts. He yields only unwillingly to innovation; the provinces, for example, will never represent for him the immense possibilities for development that they have always signified for me; he will continue rather than expand my work, but he will continue it well; in him the State will have an honest servitor and a good master.

But the space of one generation seemed to me but a small thing when the problem was to safeguard the security of the world; I wanted if possible to prolong further this line created by prudent adoption, and to prepare for the empire one more relay on the road of time. Upon each return to Rome I had never failed to visit my old friends, the Verus family, Spanish like me, and among the most liberal members of the upper magistracy. I have known you from your cradle, young Annius Verus, who by my provision now call yourself Marcus Aurelius. During one of the

most glorious years of my life, in the period which is marked
for me by the erection of the Pantheon, I had you elected, out
of friendship for your family, to the sacred college of the Arval
Brethren, over which the emperor presides, and which devoutly
perpetuates our ancient Roman religious customs. I held you by
the hand during the sacrifice which took place that year on the
bank of the Tiber, and with tender amusement watched your
childish face (you were only five years old at the time), frightened
by the cries of the immolated swine, but trying bravely to imitate
the dignified demeanor of your elders. I concerned myself with
the education of this almost too sober little boy, helping your
father to choose the best masters for you, Verus, the Most
Veracious: I used so to play on your name; you are perhaps the
only being who has never lied to me.

I have seen you read with passion the writings of the philosophers, and clothe yourself in harsh wool, sleeping on the bare
floor and forcing your somewhat frail body to all the mortifica-
tions of the Stoics. There is some excess in all that, but excess is
a virtue at the age of seventeen. I sometimes wonder on what
reef that wisdom will founder, for one always founders: will it
be a wife, or a son too greatly beloved, one of those legitimate
snares (to sum it up in a word) where overscrupulous, pure hearts
are caught? Or will it be more simply age, illness, fatigue, or the
disillusion which says to us that if all is vain, then virtue is, too?
I can imagine in place of your candid, boyish countenance your
weary visage as an older man. I am aware that your severity, so
carefully acquired, has beneath it some sweetness, and some
weakness, perhaps; I divine in you the presence of a genius which
is not necessarily that of the statesman; the world will doubtless
be forever the better off, however, for having once seen such
qualities operating in conjunction with supreme authority. I have
arranged the essentials for your adoption by Antoninus; under
the new name by which you will one day be designated in the
list of emperors you are now and henceforth my grandson. I
believe that I may be giving mankind the only chance it will ever
have to realize Plato's dream, to see a philosopher pure of heart
ruling over his fellow men.

You have accepted these honors only with reluctance; your
rank obliges you to live in court; Tibur, this place where to the

very end I am assembling whatever pleasures life has, disturbs you for your young virtue. I watch you wandering gravely under these rose-covered alleys, and smile to see you drawn towards the fair human objects who cross your path; you hesitate tenderly between Veronica and Theodoros, but quickly renounce them both in favor of that chaste phantom, austerity. You have not concealed from me your melancholy disdain for these short-lived splendors, nor for this court, which will disperse after my death. You scarcely care for me; your filial affection goes more toward Antoninus; in me you discern a kind of wisdom which is contrary to what your masters teach you, and in my abandonment to the life of the senses you see a mode of life opposed to the severity of your own, but which nevertheless is parallel to it. Never mind: it is not necessary that you understand me. There is more than one kind of wisdom, and all are essential in the world; it is not bad that they should alternate.

Eight days after the death of Lucius, I had myself taken by litter to the Senate; I asked permission to enter thus into the council chamber, and to remain lying against my pile of cushions as I gave my address. Speaking tires me: I requested the senators to form a close circle around me, in order not to be obliged to force my voice. I pronounced Lucius' eulogy; these few lines took the place on that session's program of the discourse which he was to have given on that same day. Thereafter I announced my decision: I nominated Antoninus, and named you also. I had counted upon completely unanimous adherence, and obtained it. I expressed a last wish, which was acceded to like the others: I asked that Antoninus should also adopt Lucius' son, who will in this way become your brother; you two will govern together, and I rely upon you as the elder to look after his welfare. I want the State to conserve something of Lucius.

On returning home, for the first time in many a day I was tempted to smile. I had played my game singularly well. The followers of Servianus, conservatives hostile to my administration, had not capitulated; all the courtesies which I had paid to this great and ancient, but outworn, senatorial body were no compensation to them for the two or three blows which I had dealt them. They would undoubtedly take advantage of the moment of my death to try to annul my acts. But my worst enemies would not dare to reject their most upright representative, nor the son of one of their most respected members as well. My public duty was done: I could now return to Tibur, going back into that retreat which is called illness, to experiment with my suffering, to taste fully what delights are left to me, and to resume in peace my interrupted dialogue with a shade. My imperial heritage was safe in the hands of the devoted Antoninus and the grave Marcus Aurelius; Lucius himself would survive in his son. All that was not too badly arranged.

PATIENTIA

Arrian wrote me thus:

*I have completed the circumnavigation of the Black Sea, in conformity
with the orders received. We ended the circuit at Sinope, whose inhabitants are still grateful to you for the vast work of enlarging and repairing
the port, brought successfully to conclusion under your supervision some
years back . . . By the way, they have erected a statue in your honor
which is not fine enough, nor a good enough likeness; pray send them
another, in white marble . . . At Sinope it was not without emotion
that I looked down on that same sea from the hilltops whence our
Xenophon first beheld it of old, and whence you yourself contemplated
it not so long ago . . .*

*I have inspected the coastal garrisons: their commandants merit the
highest praise for excellent discipline, for use of latest methods in training,
and for the quality of their engineering . . . Wherever the coasts are
wild and still rather little known I have had new soundings taken, and
have rectified, where necessary, the indications of earlier navigators . . .*

*We have skirted Colchis. Knowing how interested you are in what
the ancient poets recount, I questioned the inhabitants about Medea's
enchantments and the exploits of Jason. But they seemed not to know
of these stories . . .*

*On the northern shore of that inhospitable sea we touched upon a
small island of great import in legend, the isle of Achilles. As you know,
Thetis is supposed to have brought her son to be reared on this islet
shrouded in mist; each evening she would rise from the depths of the sea
and would come to talk with her child on the strand. Nowadays the
place is uninhabited; only a few goats graze there. It has a temple to
Achilles. Terns, gulls, and petrels, all kinds of sea birds frequent this
sanctuary, and its porch is cooled by the continual fanning of their wings
still moist from the sea. But this isle of Achilles is also, as it should be,
the isle of Patroclus, and the innumerable votive offerings which decorate*

the temple walls are dedicated sometimes to Achilles and sometimes to his friend, for of course whoever loves Achilles cherishes and venerates Patroclus' memory. Achilles himself appears in dream to the navigators who visit these parts: he protects them and warns them of the sea's dangers, as Castor and Pollux do elsewhere. And the shade of Patroclus appears at Achilles' side.

I report these things to you because I think them worthy to be known, and because those who told them to me have experienced them themselves, or have learned them from credible witnesses . . . Achilles sometimes seems to me the greatest of men in his courage, his fortitude, his learning and intelligence coupled with bodily skill, and his ardent love for his young companion. And nothing in him seems to me nobler than the despair which made him despise life and long for death when he had lost his beloved.

I laid down the voluminous report of the governor of Armenia Minor, admiral of the expeditionary fleet. As always Arrian has worked well. But this time he is doing more than that: he offers me a gift which I need if I am to die in peace; he sends me a picture of my life as I should have wished it to be. Arrian knows that what counts is something which will not figure in official biographies and which is not written on tombs; he knows also that the passing of time only adds one more bewilderment to grief. As seen by him the adventure of my existence takes on meaning and achieves a form, as in a poem; that unique affection frees itself from remorse, impatience, and vain obsessions as from so much smoke, or so much dust; sorrow is decanted and despair runs pure. Arrian opens to me the vast empyrean of heroes and friends, judging me not too unworthy of it. My hidden study built at the center of a pool in the Villa is not internal enough as a refuge; I drag this body there, grown old, and suffer there. My past life, to be sure, affords me certain retreats where I escape from at least some part of my present afflictions: the snowy plain along the Danube, the gardens of Nicomedia, Claudiopolis turned gold in the harvest of flowering saffron, Athens (no matter what street), an oasis where water lilies ripple above the ooze, the Syrian desert by starlight on the return from Osroës' camp. But these beloved places are too often associated with premises which have led to some error, some disappointment, some repulse known to me alone: in my bad moments all my roads to success seem only to lead to Egypt, to a sick room in Baiae, or to Palestine. And worse still, the fatigue of my body transmits itself to my memories: recollection of the stairways of the Acropolis is almost insupportable to a man who pants as he mounts the garden steps; the thought of July sun on the drill-field of Lambaesis overwhelms me as if I were now exposing my head there bare. Arrian offers me something better. Here in Tibur, in the full heat of May, I listen for the waves' slow complaint on the beach of the isle of Achilles; I breathe there in cool, pure air; I wander effortlessly over the temple terrace bathed in the fresh sea spray; I catch sight of Patroclus . . . That place which I shall never see is becoming my secret abode, my innermost haven. I shall doubtless be there at the moment of my death.

In former years I had given the philosopher Euphrates permission for suicide. Nothing seemed simpler: a man has the right to decide how long he may usefully live. I did not then know that death can become an object of blind ardor, of a hunger like that of love. I had not foreseen those nights when I should be wrapping my baldric around my dagger in order to force myself to think twice before drawing it. Arrian alone has penetrated the secret of this unsung battle against emptiness, barrenness, fatigue, and the disgust for existing which brings on a craving for death. There is no getting over it: the old fever has prostrated me more than once; I would shudder to feel it coming on, like a sick man aware of an approaching attack. Everything served me as means to postpone the hour of the nightly struggle: work, conversations wildly prolonged until dawn, caresses, my books. An emperor is not supposed to take his own life unless he is forced to do so for reasons of State; even Mark Antony had the excuse of a lost battle. And my strict Arrian would think less highly of this despair brought with me from Egypt had I not triumphed over it. My own legislation forbade soldiers that voluntary death which I accorded to sages; I felt no freer to desert than any other legionary. But I know what it is to fondle the harsh fibres of a rope or the edge of a knife.

Gradually I turned my dread desire into a rampart against itself: the fact that the possibility of suicide was ever present helped me to bear life with less impatience, just as a sedative potion within hand's reach serves to calm a man afflicted with insomnia. By some inner contradiction this obsession with death ceased only after the first symptoms of illness came to distract me from that one thought; I began to interest myself anew in this life which was leaving me; in Sidon's gardens I wanted intensely to enjoy my body for some years more.

One desires to die, but not to suffocate; sickness disgusts us with death, and we wish to get well, which is a way of wishing to live. But weakness and suffering, with manifold bodily woes, soon discourage the invalid from trying to regain ground: he tires of those respites which are but snares, of that faltering strength, those ardors cut short, and that perpetual lying in wait for the next attack. I kept sly watch upon myself: that dull chest pain, was it only a passing discomfort, the result of a meal absorbed too fast, or was I to expect from the enemy an assault which this time would not be repulsed? I no longer entered the Senate without saying to myself that the door had perhaps closed behind me as finally as if I had been awaited, like Caesar, by fifty conspirators armed with knives. During the suppers at Tibur I feared to distress my guests by the discourtesy of a sudden and final departure; I was afraid to die in my bath, or in the embrace of young arms. Functions which formerly were easy to perform or even agreeable, become humiliating now that they have become more laborious; one wearies of the silver vase handed each morning to be examined by the physician. The principal ailment brings with it a whole train of secondary afflictions: my hearing is less acute than before; even yesterday I was forced to ask Phlegon to repeat a whole sentence; no crime would have cost me more shame.

The months which followed the adoption of Antoninus were bad indeed: the stay in Baiae and the return to Rome, with the negotiations accompanying it, overtaxed what strength I had left. The obsession with death again took hold of me, but this time the reasons were plain to see, and could be told; my worst enemy would have had no cause to smile over my despair. There was nothing now to restrain me: people would have understood that the emperor, withdrawn to his country house after having arranged all matters of State, had taken the necessary measures to facilitate his ending. But the solicitude of my friends amounts to constant surveillance: every invalid is a prisoner. I no longer have the force which it would take to drive the dagger in at the exact place, marked at one time with red ink under my left breast; I should only have added to the present ills a repulsive mixture of bandages and bloody sponges, and surgeons discussing at the foot of my bed. To prepare a suicide I needed to take the same precautions as would an assassin to plan his crime.

I thought first of my huntsman, Mastor, the handsome, half-savage Sarmatian who had followed me for years like a devoted wolf-dog. He was sometimes entrusted to keep watch by night at my door. I took advantage of a moment's solitude to call him in and explain what I wanted of him: at first he did not understand. Then my meaning dawned; the barbarian face under the fair shaggy hair contracted with terror. He believes me immortal: morning and evening he sees physicians enter my room and hears me groan at each punction without his faith being shaken thereby; for him it was as if the master of the gods, thinking to tempt him, had descended from Olympus to entreat of him a death-blow. He tore away the sword which I had seized from him, and fled howling. That night he was found in the depths of the park, uttering strange gibberish in his native jargon. They calmed this terrified creature as well as they could; no one spoke to me again of the incident. But the next morning I noticed that Celer had exchanged the metal style on the writing table within reach of my bed for a reed pen.

I sought a better ally. I had complete confidence in Iollas, a young physician from Alexandria whom Hermogenes had chosen last summer as his substitute during his absence. We often talked together, for I liked to build up hypotheses with him on the nature and origin of things, and took pleasure in his intelligence, both daring and dreamy, and in the dark fire of those deep-set eyes. I knew that in Alexandria he had found in the palace archives the formulae for extraordinarily subtle poisons compounded long ago by Cleopatra's chemists. An excuse came for me to get rid of Hermogenes for several hours: he had to examine candidates for the chair of medicine which I had just founded at the Odeon; there was thus the chance for a secret talk with Iollas. He understood me at once; he pitied me; he could but admit that I was right. But his Hippocratic oath forbade him to dispense a nocent drug to a patient, under any pretext whatsoever; he refused, standing fast in his professional honor. I insisted; I made absolute demand; I employed every means to try to draw his pity, or to corrupt him; he will be the last man whom I shall have implored. Finally won over, he promised me to go and seek the dose of poison. I awaited him in vain until evening. Late in the night I learned with horror that he had just been found dead in his laboratory, with a glass phial in his hands. That heart clean of all compromise had found this means of abiding by his oath while denying me nothing.

The next day Antoninus was announced; this true friend could barely hold back his tears. The idea that a man whom he had come to love and to venerate as a father suffered enough to seek out death was to him insupportable; it seemed to him that he must have failed in his obligations as a good son. He promised me to add his efforts to those of my entourage in order to nurse me and relieve my pain, to make my life smooth and easy to the last, even to cure me perhaps. He depended upon me to continue the longest time possible in guiding and instructing him; he felt himself responsible towards the whole empire for the remainder of my days.

I know what these pathetic protestations and naïve promises are worth; nevertheless I derive some relief and comfort from them. Antoninus' simple words have convinced me; I am regaining possession of myself before I die. The death of Iollas, faithful to his duty as physician, exhorts me to conform, to the end, to the proprieties of my profession as emperor. *Patientia*: yesterday I saw Domitius Rogatus, now become procurator of the mint and entrusted with a new issue of coins; I have chosen for it this legend, which will be my last watchword. My death had seemed to me the most personal of my decisions, my supreme redoubt as a free man; I was mistaken. The faith of millions of Mastors must not be shaken, nor other Iollases put to so sore a trial. I have realized that suicide would appear to signify indifference, or ingratitude perhaps, to the little group of devoted friends who surround me; I do not wish to bequeath to them the hideous picture of a man racked by pain who cannot endure one torture more.

Other considerations came slowly to mind during the night which followed Iollas' death; life has given me much, or at least I have known how to obtain a great deal from it; in this moment as in the time of my felicity, but for wholly opposite reasons, it seems to me that existence has nothing more to offer: I am not sure, however, that I have not something more to learn from it. I shall listen for its secret instructions to the end. All my life long I have trusted in the wisdom of my body; I have tried to distinguish between and enjoy the varied sensations which this friend has provided me: I no longer refuse the death agony prepared for me, this ending slowly elaborated within my arteries and inherited perhaps from some ancestor, or born of my temperament, formed little by little from each of my actions throughout my life. The time of impatience has passed; at the point where I now am, despair would be in as bad taste as hope itself. I have ceased to hurry my death.

There is still much to be done. My estates in Africa, inherited from my mother-in-law, Matidia, must be turned into models of agricultural development; the peasants of Borysthenes, the village established in Thrace in memory of a good horse, are entitled to aid after a severe winter; on the contrary, subsidies should not be granted to the rich cultivators of the Nile Valley, who are ever ready to take advantage of the emperor's solicitude. Julius Vestinus, prefect of Education, sends me his report on the opening of public grammar schools. I have just completed the revision of Palmyra's commercial code: it takes everything into account, from the entrance fees for caravans to the tax set for prostitutes. At the moment, we are assembling a congress of physicians and magistrates to determine the utmost duration of a pregnancy, thus putting an end to interminable legal squabbles. Cases of bigamy are increasing in number in the veterans' settlements; I am doing my best to persuade these men not to make wrong use of the new laws which permit them to marry, and I counsel them to abstain prudently from taking more than one wife at a time! In Athens a Pantheon is in process of construction on the model of the Pantheon in Rome; I am composing the inscription to be placed on its walls, and shall enumerate therein (as examples and commitments for the future) my services to the Greek cities and to barbarian peoples; the services rendered to Rome are matters of course.

The struggle goes on against brutal misuse of judiciary power: I have had to reprimand the governor of Cilicia who took it into his head to execute under torture the cattle thieves in his province, as if simple death were not enough to punish a man and dispose of him. Both the State and the municipalities were abusing their power to condemn men to forced labor in order to procure workers at no cost; I have prohibited that practice not only with regard to free men but for forced labor of slaves as well; it is important, however, to watch sharply lest this detestable system re-establish itself under other names. In certain parts of the territory of ancient Carthage child sacrifice still prevails, so means must be devised to forbid the priests of Baal the pleasure of feeding their fires. In Asia Minor the rights of heirs of the Seleucids have been shamefully disregarded by our civil tribunals, ever prejudiced against the former kings; I have repaired that long-standing injustice. In Greece the trial of Herod Atticus still goes on. Phlegon's dispatch box, with his erasers of pumice stone and his sticks of red wax, will be with me to the end.

As in the days of my felicity, people believe me to be a god; they continue to give me that appellation even though they are offering sacrifices to the heavens for the restoration of the Imperial Health. I have already told you the reasons for which such a belief, salutary for them, seems to me not absurd. A blind old woman has come on foot from Pannonia, having undertaken that exhausting journey in order to ask me to touch her eyes; she has recovered her sight under my hands, as her fervor had led her to expect; her faith in the emperor-god explains this miracle. Other prodigies have occurred, and invalids say that they have seen me in their dreams, as the pilgrims to Epidaurus have visions of Æsculapius; they claim that they have awakened cured, or at least improved. I do not smile at the contrast between my powers as a thaumaturge and my own illness; I accept these new privileges with gravity. The old blind woman who made her way to the emperor from the depths of a barbarian province has become for me what the slave of Tarragona had formerly been, namely, a symbol of the populations of the empire whom I have both ruled and served. Their immense confidence repays me for twenty years of work which was itself congenial to me.

Phlegon has recently read me verses of a Jew of Alexandria who also attributes to me superhuman powers; without irony I welcomed that description of an elderly prince who is seen going back and forth over all the roads of the earth, descending to the treasures of the mines, reawakening the generative forces of the soil, and everywhere establishing peace and prosperity; the initiate who has restored the shrines of all races, the connoisseur in magic arts, the seer who raised a youth to the heavens. I shall have been better understood by this enthusiastic Jew than by many a senator and proconsul; this adversary now won over looks upon me almost as does Arrian; I am amazed to have become for people just what I sought to be, after all, and I marvel that this success is made up of so little.

Old age and death, as they approach, begin to add their majesty to this prestige; men step reverently from my path; they no longer compare me, as they once did, to serene and radiant Zeus, but to Mars Gradivus, god of long campaigns and austere discipline, or to grave Numa, inspired by the gods. Of late this pale, drawn visage, these fixed eyes and this tall body held straight by force of will, suggest to them Pluto, god of shades. Only a few intimates, a few tried and cherished friends, escape such dread contagion of respect. The young lawyer Fronto, this future magistrate who will doubtless be one of the good servants of your reign, came to discuss with me an address of mine to be made in the Senate; his voice was trembling, and I read in his face that same reverence mingled with fear. The tranquil joys of human friendship are no longer for me; men adore and venerate me far too much to love me.

A happy fate not unlike that of certain gardeners has been allotted me: everything that I have tried to implant in the human imagination has taken root there. The cult of Antinous seemed like the wildest of my enterprises, the overflow of a grief which concerned me alone. But our epoch is avid for gods; it prefers the most ardent deities, and the most sorrowful, those who mingle with the wine of life a bitter honey from beyond the grave. At Delphi the youth has become the Hermes who guards the threshold, master of the dark passages leading to the shades. Eleusis, where his age and status as a stranger formerly prevented him from being initiated with me, now makes of him the young Bacchus of the Mysteries, prince of those border regions which lie between the senses and the soul. His ancestral Arcadia associates him with Pan and Diana, woodland divinities; the peasants of Tibur identify him with the gentle Aristaeus, king of the bees. In Asia his worshippers liken him to their tender gods devoured by summer heat or broken by autumn storms. Far away, on the edge of barbarian lands, the companion of my hunts and travels has assumed the aspect of the Thracian Horseman, that mysterious figure seen riding through the copses by moonlight and carrying away souls of the dead in the folds of his cloak.

All of that could be merely an excrescence of the official cult, a form of public flattery or the adulation of priests greedy for subsidies. But the young face is escaping from me to respond to the aspirations of simpler hearts: by one of those shifts of balance inherent in the nature of things that somber but exquisite youth has taken his place in popular devotion as the support of the weak and the poor, and the comforter of dead children. His image on the coins of Bithynia, that profile of the youth of fifteen with floating locks and delighted, truthful smile (which he kept for so short a time), is hung at the neck of new-born infants to serve as an amulet; it is nailed up likewise in village cemeteries on the small tombs. In recent years, when I used to think of my own death, like a pilot unmindful of himself but trembling for the ship's passengers and cargo, I would tell myself bitterly that this remembrance would founder with me; that young being so carefully embalmed in the depths of my memory seemed obliged thus to perish for a second time. That fear, though justifiable, has been in part allayed; I have compensated for this premature death as well as I could; an image, a reflection, some feeble echo will survive for at least a few centuries. Little more can be done in matters of immortality.

I have again seen Fidus Aquila, governor of Antinoöpolis, as he passed on his way to his new post at Sarmizegethusa. He has described to me the annual rites celebrated now on the banks of the Nile in honor of the dead god, to which pilgrims come by thousands from the regions of the North and the South, with offerings of beer and of grain, and with prayers; every third year anniversary games are held in Antinoöpolis as well as in Alexandria, and in Mantinea and my beloved Athens. These triennial festivities will recur this autumn, but I do not hope to last out until this ninth return of the month of Athyr. It is the more important, therefore, that each detail of such solemnities be determined in advance. The oracle of the dead youth functions inside the secret chamber of the ancient Egyptian temple restored by my care; its priests distribute daily some hundreds of responses already prepared for all those questions which human hope or anguish may pose. I have incurred reproach for having composed several of these answers myself. I did not intend, in so doing, to be lacking in respect towards my god, or in compassion for the soldier's wife who asks if her husband will come back alive from a garrison in Palestine, for the invalid hungering for comfort, for some merchant whose ships ride the waves of the Red Sea, for a couple who desire a son; at the most I was continuing in this way the games of logographs and versified charades at which we used sometimes to play together. Likewise there was comment because here in the Villa, around that chapel of Canopus where his cult is celebrated in Egyptian fashion, I have encouraged the establishment of various pleasure pavilions like those of the suburb of Alexandria which bears that name, and have offered their facilities and distractions to my guests, sometimes participating in them myself. He had grown used to that kind of thing. And then, one does not enclose oneself for years in a unique thought without reintroducing into it, little by little, all the mere routines of a life.

I have done all they say to do. I have waited, and sometimes I have prayed. *Audivi voces divinas* . . . The light-headed Julia Balbilla believed that she heard the mysterious voice of Memnon at dawn; I have listened for the night's faintest sounds. I have used the unctions of oil and essence of roses which attract the shades; I have set out the bowl of milk, the handful of salt, the drop of blood, supports of their former existence. I have lain down on the marble pavement of the small sanctuary; the light of the stars made its way through the openings of the wall, producing reflections here and there, strange, pale gleams. I have recalled to myself the orders whispered by the priests in the ear of the dead, and the itinerary written on the tomb: *And he will recognize the way . . . And the guardians of the threshold will let him pass . . . And he will come and go around those who love him for millions of days . . .* Sometimes, after long intervals, I have thought to feel the slight stir of an approach, a touch as light as the contact of eyelashes and warm as the hollow of a hand. *And the shade of Patroclus appears at Achilles' side . . .* I shall never know if that warmth, that sweetness, did not emanate simply from deep within me, the last efforts of a man struggling against solitude and the cold of night. But the question, which arises also in the presence of our living loves, has ceased to interest me now; it matters little to me whether the phantoms whom I evoke come from the limbo of my memory or from that of another world. My soul, if I possess one, is made of the same substance as are the specters; this body with swollen hands and livid nails, this sorry mass almost half-dissolved, this sack of ills, of desires and dreams, is hardly more solid or consistent than a shade. I differ from the dead only in my faculty to suffocate some moments longer; in one sense their existence seems to me more assured than my own. Antinous and Plotina are at least as real as myself.

Meditation upon death does not teach one how to die; it does not make the departure more easy, but ease is no longer what I seek. Beloved boy, so willful and brooding, your sacrifice will have enriched not my life but my death. Death's approach re-establishes between us a kind of close complicity: the living beings who surround me, my devoted if sometimes importunate servitors, will never know how little the world interests the two of us now. I think with disgust of those doleful symbols of the Egyptian tombs: the hard scarab, the rigid mummy, the frog which signifies eternal parturition. To believe the priests, I have left you at the place where the separate elements of a person tear apart like a worn garment under strain, at that sinister crossroads between what was and what will be, and what exists eternally. It is conceivable, after all, that such notions are right, and that death is made up of the same confused, shifting matter as life. But none of these theories of immortality inspire me with confidence; the system of retributions and punishments makes little impression upon a judge well aware of the difficulties of judging.

On the other hand, the opposite solution seems to me also too simple, the neat reduction to nothingness, the hollow void where Epicurus' disdainful laughter resounds.

I try now to observe my own ending: this series of experiments conducted upon myself continues the long study begun in Satyrus' clinic. So far the modifications are as external as those to which time and inclement weather subject any edifice, leaving its architecture and basic material unaltered; I sometimes think that through the crevices I see and touch upon the indestructible foundation, the rock eternal. I am what I always was; I am dying without essential change. At first view the robust child of the gardens in Spain and the ambitious officer regaining his tent and shaking the snowflakes from his shoulders seem both as thoroughly obliterated as I shall be when I shall have gone through the funeral fire; but they are still there; I am inseparable from those parts of myself. The man who howled his grief upon a dead body has not ceased to wail in some corner of my being, in spite of the superhuman, or perhaps subhuman calm into which I am entering already; the voyager immured within the ever sedentary invalid is curious about death because it spells departure. That force which once was I seems still capable of actuating several more lives, or of raising up whole worlds. If by miracle some centuries were suddenly to be added to the few days now left to me I would do the same things over again, even to committing the same errors; I would frequent the same Olympian heights and even the same Infernos. Such a conclusion is an excellent argument in favor of the utility of death, but at the same time it inspires certain doubts as to death's total efficacity.

In certain periods of my life I have noted down my dreams; I have discussed their significance with priests and philosophers, and with astrologers. That faculty for dreaming, though deadened for many years, has been restored to me in the course of these months of agony; the incidents of my waking hours seem less real, and sometimes less irksome, than those of dream. If this larval and spectral world, where the platitudinous and the absurd swarm in even greater abundance than on earth, affords us some notion of the state of the soul when separated from the body, then I shall doubtless pass my eternity in regretting the exquisite control which our senses now provide, and the adjusted perspectives offered by human reason.

And nevertheless I sink back with a certain relief into those insubstantial regions of dream; there I possess for a moment some secrets which soon escape me again; there I drink at the sacred springs. The other day I was in the oasis of Ammon, on the afternoon of the lion hunt. I was in high spirits; everything went as in the time of my former vigor: the wounded lion collapsed to the ground, then rose again; I pressed forward to strike the final blow. But this time my rearing horse threw me; the horrible, bleeding mass of the beast rolled over me, and claws tore at my chest; I came to myself in my room in Tibur, crying out for aid. More recently still I have seen my father, though I think of him rather seldom. He was lying on his sick bed in a room of our house in Italica, where I ceased to dwell soon after his death. On his table he had a phial full of a sedative potion which I begged him to give me. I awoke before he had time to reply. It surprises me that most men are so fearful of ghosts when they are so ready to speak to the dead in their dreams.

Presages are also increasing: from now on everything seems like an intimation and a sign. I have just dropped and broken a precious stone set in a ring; my profile had been carved thereon by a Greek artist. The augurs shake their heads gravely, but my regret is for that pure masterpiece. I have come to speak of myself, at times, in the past tense: in the Senate, while discussing certain events which had taken place after the death of Lucius, I have caught myself more than once mentioning those circumstances, by a slip of the tongue, as if they had occurred after my own death. A few months ago, on my birthday, as I was mounting the steps of the Capitol by litter, I found myself face to face with a man in mourning; furthermore, he was weeping, and I saw my good Chabrias turn pale. At that period I still went about and was able to continue performing in person my duties as high pontiff and as Arval Brother, and to celebrate myself the ancient rites of this Roman religion which, in the end, I prefer to most of the foreign cults. I was standing one day before the altar, ready to light the flame; I was offering the gods a sacrifice for Antoninus. Suddenly the fold of my toga covering my brow slipped and fell to my shoulder, leaving me bare-headed; thus I passed from the rank of sacrificer to that of victim. Verily, it is my turn.

My patience is bearing fruit; I suffer less, and life has become almost sweet again. I have ceased to quarrel with physicians; their foolish remedies have killed me, but their presumption and hypocritical pedantry are work of our making: if we were not so afraid of pain they would tell fewer lies. Strength fails me now for the angers of old; I know from a reliable source that Platorius Nepos, for whom I have had great affection, has taken advantage of my confidence; I have not tried to confound him with the evidence, nor have I ordered a punishment. The future of the world no longer disturbs me; I do not try still to calculate, with anguish, how long or how short a time the Roman peace will endure; I leave that to the gods. Not that I have acquired more confidence in their justice, which is not our justice, or more faith in human wisdom; the contrary is true. Life is atrocious, we know. But precisely because I expect little of the human condition, man's periods of felicity, his partial progress, his efforts to begin over again and to continue, all seem to me like so many prodigies which nearly compensate for the monstrous mass of ills and defeats, of indifference and error. Catastrophe and ruin will come; disorder will triumph, but order will too, from time to time. Peace will again establish itself between two periods of war; the words *humanity*, *liberty*, and *justice* will here and there regain the meaning which we have tried to give them. Not all our books will perish, nor our statues, if broken, lie unrepaired; other domes and other pediments will arise from our domes and pediments; some few men will think and work and feel as we have done, and I venture to count upon such continuators, placed irregularly throughout the centuries, and upon this kind of intermittent immortality.

If ever the barbarians gain possession of the world they will be forced to adopt some of our methods; they will end by resembling us. Chabrias fears that the pastophor of Mithra or the bishop of Christ may implant himself one day in Rome, replacing the high pontiff. If by ill fate that day should come, my successor officiating in the vatical fields along the Tiber will already have ceased to be merely the chief of a gang, or of a band of sectarians, and will have become in his turn one of the universal figures of authority. He will inherit our palaces and our archives, and will differ from rulers like us less than one might suppose. I accept with calm these vicissitudes of Rome eternal.

The medicaments have no effect on me now; my limbs are more swollen than ever, and I sleep sitting up instead of reclining. One advantage of death will be to lie down again on a bed. It is now my turn to console Antoninus. I remind him that death has long seemed to me the most fitting solution of my own problem; as always, my wishes are finally being fulfilled, but in a slower and more indirect way than I had expected. I can be glad that illness has left me lucid to the end, and I rejoice to have escaped the trials of old age, with its hardening and stiffening, its aridity and cruel absence of desire. If my calculations are exact, my mother died at about the age which I am today; my life has already been half again as long as that of my father, who died at forty. Everything is prepared: the eagle entrusted with bearing the emperor's soul to the gods is held in reserve for the funeral ceremony. My mausoleum, on top of which they are just now planting the cypresses, designed to form a black pyramid high in the sky, will be completed about in time to receive the ashes while yet still warm. I have requested Antoninus to see that Sabina is transported there later on; at her death I did not have divine honors conferred upon her, as was after all her due; it would not be bad to have that neglect repaired. And I would like the remains of Aelius Caesar to be placed at my side.

They have brought me to Baiae; in this July heat the journey has been an ordeal, but I breathe better near the sea. On the shore the waves make their murmur of rustling silk and whispered caress. I can still enjoy the pale rose light of the long evenings. But I hold these tablets now only to occupy my hands, which in spite of me agitate. I have sent for Antoninus; a courier dispatched at full speed has left for Rome. Sound of the hoofs of Borysthenes, gallop of the Thracian Rider . . .

The little group of intimates presses round my bed. Chabrias moves me to pity: tears ill become the wrinkles of age. Celer's handsome face is, as always, strangely calm; he applies himself steadily to nursing me without letting anything be seen of what might add to a patient's anxiety or fatigue. But Diotimus is sobbing, his head buried in the cushions. I have assured his future; he does not like Italy; he will be able to realize his dream, which is to return to Gadara and open a school of eloquence there with a friend; he has nothing to lose by my death. And nevertheless the slight shoulder moves convulsively under the folds of his tunic; on my fingers I feel those tender tears. To the last, Hadrian will have been loved in human wise.

Little soul, gentle and drifting, guest and companion of my body, now you will dwell below in pallid places, stark and bare; there you will abandon your play of yore. But one moment still, let us gaze together on these familiar shores, on these objects which doubtless we shall not see again . . . Let us try, if we can, to enter into death with open eyes . . .

TO THE DEIFIED AUGUST HADRIAN

SON OF TRAJAN CONQUEROR OF THE PARTHIANS
GRANDSON OF NERVA
HIGH PONTIFF
HONORED FOR THE XXIIND TIME
WITH THE TRIBUNICIAN POWER
THREE TIMES CONSUL TWO TIMES HAILED IN TRIUMPH
FATHER OF HIS COUNTRY
AND TO HIS DEIFIED SPOUSE
SABINA
ANTONINUS THEIR SON DEDICATES THIS MEMORIAL

TO LUCIUS AELIUS CAESAR
SON OF THE DEIFIED HADRIAN
TWO TIMES CONSUL

BIBLIOGRAPHICAL NOTE

A reconstruction of an historical figure and of the world of his time written in the first person borders on the domain of fiction, and sometimes of poetry; it can therefore dispense with formal statement of evidence for the historical facts concerned. Its human significance, however, is greatly enriched by close adherence to those facts. Since the main object of the author here has been to approach inner reality, if possible, through careful examination of what the documents themselves afford, it seems advisable to offer the reader some discussion of the principal materials employed, though not to present a complete bibliography, which would extend beyond the scope of the present volume. Some brief indication will also be given of the comparatively few changes, all of secondary importance, which add to, or cautiously modify, what history has told us.

The reader who likes to consider sources at first hand will not necessarily know where to find the principal ancient texts relating to Hadrian, or even what they are, since most of them come down to us from writers of the late classical period who are relatively little read, and who are ordinarily familiar only to specialists. Our two chief authorities are the Greek historian Dio Cassius and the Latin chronicler known by the name of Spartianus. Dio's *Roman History*, written about forty years after Hadrian's death but surviving, unfortunately, only in abridged form, devotes a chapter to this emperor. Somewhat more than a century after Dio, and apparently writing independently of his Greek predecessor, Spartianus composed a *Life of Hadrian*, one of the most substantial texts of the *Historia Augusta*, and a *Life of Aelius Caesar*, a slighter work of that same collection. The latter biography presents a very plausible likeness of Hadrian's adopted son, and is superficial only because, after all, the subject was so

himself. These two writers had access to documents no longer
extant, among others an autobiography published by Hadrian
under the name of his freedman Phlegon, as well as a collection
of the emperor's letters assembléd by this same secretary. Neither
Dio nor Spartianus is great as historian or biographer, but their
very lack of art, and, to a certain degree, their lack of system,
leave them singularly close to actuality. On the whole, modern
research has confirmed their assertions in striking manner, and
it is in great part upon their piecemeal accumulation of facts that
the present interpretation is based.

Mention may also be made, without attempting a comprehensive listing, of some details gleaned in other *Lives* of the *Historia
Augusta*, in particular in the biographies of Antoninus and of
Marcus Aurelius by Julius Capitolinus. Some phrases have been
taken from Aurelius Victor's *Book of the Caesars* and from the
unknown author of the *Epitome*, professedly the work of Aurelius
Victor, too. Both these writers, though only some half century
later than Spartianus, already conceive of Hadrian's life as almost
legendary, but the splendor of their rhetoric puts them in a class
apart. The historians Eutropius and Ammianus Marcellinus, also
of the latter half of the fourth century, add little to the information
given by earlier writers on Hadrian. Likewise the notice on this
emperor in the *Lexicon* of the tenth-century Byzantine scholar
Suidas, and the few pages devoted to him by the historian
Zonaras, of the twelfth century, hardly do more than repeat Dio;
but two other notices in Suidas provide each a fact little known
about one episode in Hadrian's life, namely that a *Consolation*
was addressed to him by the philosopher Numenios, and that
Mesomedes, the court musician, composed music for the funeral
of Antinous.

From Hadrian himself we have a certain number of works of
unquestioned authenticity: from his official life there is administrative correspondence and there are fragments of discourses
or reports, like the noted address to the troops at Lambaesis,
conserved for the most part in inscriptions; also his legal decisions, handed down by the jurists. From his personal life we
have poems mentioned by authors of his time, such as his
celebrated *Animula Vagula Blandula*, or occurring as votive inscriptions, like the poem to Eros and the Uranian Aphrodite on

the temple wall at Thespiae (G. Kaibel, *Epigr. Gr.* 811). Three letters supposedly written by Hadrian, and concerning his personal life, are of doubtful authenticity (*Letter to Matidia, Letter to Servianus, Letter addressed by the Dying Emperor to Antoninus*, to be found respectively in the collection of Dositheus, in the *Vita Saturnini* of Vopiscus, and in a fragment of Fayum papyrus, edited by Grenfell and Hunt, *Fayum Towns and Their Papyri*, 1900). All three of these letters, nevertheless, are decidedly characteristic of the man to whom they are attributed, and therefore certain indications which they afford have been used in this book.

References or allusions to Hadrian or to his entourage are to be found scattered through most of the writers of the second and third centuries, and serve to complete suggestions in the chronicles, or fill in lacunae there. Thus, to cite only a few examples, the episode of the hunt in Libya is taken from a fragment of a poem of Pancrates, *The Hunt of Hadrian and Antinous*, found in Egypt and published in 1911 in the collection, *Oxyrhynchus Papyri*, VIII, No. 1085; Athenaeus, Aulus Gellius, and Philostratus have furnished numerous details on the sophists and poets of the imperial court; both the Younger Pliny and Martial add a few touches to the somewhat sketchy information left to us by Apuleius and by Trajan's historians for two of Hadrian's friends, Voconius and Licinius Sura. The description of Hadrian's grief at the death of Antinous is drawn from the historians of the reign, but also from certain passages in the Church Fathers, who though indeed disapproving are sometimes more understanding on this subject, and above all more varied in their approach to it, than the usual blanket references to their opinions would reveal. We have allusions to that grief also in the writings of the emperor's friend Arrian, from whom actual passages have been incorporated in these *Memoirs* (*Letter from Arrian to the Emperor Hadrian on the Occasion of the Circumnavigation of the Black Sea*, a text questioned by some scholars, but accepted by others as genuine except for minor interpolations). For the war in Palestine, certain details known to be authentic have been extracted from the *Talmud*, where they lie imbedded in an immense amount of legendary material; they serve to supplement the principal account of that war as given in Eusebius' *Ecclesiastical*

History. Details of the exile of Favorinus come from a fragment of that writer in a manuscript of the Vatican Library published in 1931 (M. Norsa and G. Vitelli, *Il Papiro Vaticano Greco* II, in *Studi e Testi*, LIII); the horrible episode of the secretary blinded in one eye occurs in a treatise of Galen, who was physician to Marcus Aurelius; the picture of the dying Hadrian is built upon the somber portrait which Fronto, an intimate of Marcus Aurelius, gives of the emperor in his last years.

Statues, reliefs, inscriptions, and coins have provided factual details not recorded by ancient writers. Certain glimpses into the savagery of the Dacian and Sarmatian wars, such as prisoners burned alive and counselors of King Decebalus poisoning themselves on the day of their capitulation, are afforded by the scenes on Trajan's Column (W. Froehner, *La Colonne Trajane*, 1865; I. A. Richmond, *Trajan's Army on Trajan's Column, Papers of the British School at Rome*, XIII, 1935). Certain inscriptions serve as points of departure for episodes constructed in this work: thus the three poems of Julia Balbilla carved on the legs of the Colossus of Memnon, and Hadrian's own name carved on that statue as well, help to build the visit to Thebes (J. A. Letronne, *Recueil des Inscriptions grecques et latines de l'Egypte*, II, 1848, and R. Cagnat, *Inscr. Graec. ad res Rom. pert.*, I, 1186–7). The day of the year on which Antinous was born is given as it occurs on an inscription left by a fraternity of workmen and slaves in Lanuvium, who chose that new deity for their patron and protector in the year 133 (*Corp. Inscr. Lat.* XIV, 2112). This precision as to the day has been questioned by Mommsen but has been accepted since his time by less hypercritical scholars. The several phrases presented in these *Memoirs* as if inscribed on the tomb of the favorite are taken from the long text in hieroglyphs on the obelisk of the Pincio in Rome, telling of Antinous' funeral and detailing the ritual of his cult. (A. Erman, *Obelisken Römischer Zeit*, in *Mitt. d. deutsch. arch. Inst., Röm. Abt.*, XI, 1896; O. Marucchi, *Gli Obelischi Egiziani di Roma*, 1898). The coins of the reign suggest many details for the voyages described; the legends on some of these coins have furnished titles for the parts of this book (with two exceptions, one drawn from Aurelius Victor), and have often provided the keynotes for Hadrian's meditations themselves.

To discuss briefly the study of Hadrian and his period by

modern and contemporary writers it may first be noted that already in the seventeenth and eighteenth centuries all historians of Rome from Tillemont to Gibbon have touched upon this emperor, but their works, substantial as they are (the critical spirit which animates the article on Hadrian in Bayle's *Dictionnaire*, for example, remains unrivaled in its kind), belong henceforth to History's history. Nearer our time even the brilliant sketch by Renan in the first chapter of *L'Eglise Chrétienne* shows equally the marks of age. Nor is there a complete modern biography, properly speaking, to which the reader can be referred without reservation. The earliest work of the kind, that of Gregorovius, published in 1851 (revised edition 1884), is not without life and color, but is weak in everything that concerns Hadrian as administrator and prince, and is in great part outdated by researches of the past half century. The more methodical study of O. Th. Schulz, *Leben des Kaisers Hadrian*, Leipzig, 1904, is less rich in humanistic erudition than Gregorovius and is also outdated in part. The more recent biography by B. W. Henderson, *The Life and Principate of the Emperor Hadrian, A.D.* 76–138, published in 1923, though lengthy, gives only a superficial idea of Hadrian's thought and of the intellectual currents of his time, making too little use of available sources.

But important specialized studies abound; in many respects modern scholarship has thrown new light upon the history of Hadrian's reign and administration. To cite only a few such studies, recent or at least relatively recent, and easily accessible, there are in English the chapter devoted to Hadrian's social and financial reforms in the masterly work of M. Rostovtzeff, *Social and Economic History of the Roman Empire*, 1926; the valuable studies, respectively, of R. H. Lacey, *The Equestrian Officials of Trajan and Hadrian: Their Careers, with some Notes on Hadrian's Reforms*, Princeton, 1917; of Paul Alexander, *Letters and Speeches of the Emperor Hadrian*, Harv. Stud. in Class. Phil., XLIX, 1938; of W. D. Gray, *A Study of the Life of Hadrian Prior to his Accession*, Smith Coll. Stud. in Hist., 1919; of F. Pringsheim, *The Legal Policy and Reforms of Hadrian*, Journ. of Rom. Stud., XXIV, 1934; of R. G. Collingwood and J. N. L. Myres, *Roman Britain and the English Settlements*, 2nd ed., 1937, which includes an excellent chapter on Hadrian's visit to the British Isles. Jocelyn Toynbee offers a valuable interpretation of Hadrian's liberal and pacific policies in her *Roman Empire and Modern Europe, Dublin Review*, Jan., 1945. Among French scholarly studies may be mentioned the chapters devoted to Hadrian in *Le Haut-Empire Romain* of Léon Homo, 1933, and in *L'Empire Romain* of E. Albertini, 1936; the analysis of Trajan's Parthian campaigns and Hadrian's peace policy in *Histoire de l'Asie* by René Grousset, Vol. 1, 1921 (followed closely for the description of the Parthian campaigns in these *Memoirs*); the study of the literary productions of Hadrian in *Les Empereurs et les Lettres latines* by Henri Bardon, 1944; the respective works of Paul Graindor, *Athènes sous Hadrien*, 1934, Cairo, of Louis Perret, *La Titulature impériale d'Hadrien*, 1929, and of Bernard d-Or' geval, *L'Empereur Hadrien, son oeuvre législative et administrative*, 1950. But the most comprehensive studies of the sources for Hadrian and his chronology are still those of the German School, J. Dürr, *Die Reisen des Kaisers Hadrian*, Vienna, 1881; J. Plew, *Quellenuntersuchungen zur Geschichte des Kaisers Hadrian*, Strassburg, 1890; E. Kornemann, *Kaiser Hadrian und der letzte grosse Historiker von Rom*, Leipzig, 1905; and especially the admirable short work of Wilhelm Weber, *Untersuchungen zur Geschichte des Kaisers Hadrianus*, Leipzig, 1907. By the same Weber is the striking essay *Hadrian*, published in English in the *Cambridge Ancient History*, XI (*The Imperial Peace*), 1936, pp. 294–324. For the study of Hadrian's coins (apart from those of Antinous, to be discussed below) in relation to the events of the reign, consult H. Mattingly and E. A. Sydenham, *The Roman Imperial Coinage*, II, 1926; P. L. Strack, *Untersuchungen zur römischen Reichsprägung des zweiten Jahrhunderts*, II, Stuttgart, 1933.

Much material about Hadrian is to be found in studies made on his associates, and on problems which led to, or followed, the war in Palestine. For Trajan's reign, and in particular for his wars, see (apart from the text of Grousset mentioned above) R. Paribeni, *Optimus Princeps*, Messina (1927); M. Durry, *Le règne de Trajan d'après les monnaies, Revue Hist.*, LVII, 1932; R. P. Longden, *Nerva and Trajan*, and *The Wars of Trajan*, chapters in *Cambridge Ancient History*, XI, 1936; and Wilhelm Weber, *Traian und Hadrian*, in *Meister der Politik* I², Stuttgart, 1923. On Aelius Caesar, A. S. L. Farquharson, *On the Names of Aelius Caesar*,

Class. Quar. II, 1908, and J. Carcopino, *L'Hérédité dynastique chez les Antonins*, 1950 (whose hypotheses have been set aside as unconvincing in favor of a more literal interpretation of the texts). On the affair of the four 'consulars,' see especially A. von Premerstein, *Das Attentat der Konsulare auf Hadrian in Jahre 118*, in *Klio*, 1908; J. Carcopino, *Lusius Quiétus, l'homme de Qwrnyn*, in *Istros*, 1934. On the Greek entourage of Hadrian, see more particularly A. von Premerstein, *C. Julius Quadratus Bassus*, in *Sitz. Bayr. Akad. d. Wiss.*, 1934; P. Graindor, *Un Milliardaire antique: Hérode Atticus et sa famille*, Cairo, 1930; A. Boulanger, *Aelius Aristide et la sophistique dans la province d'Asie au IIe siècle de notre ère*, in *Bib. des Ec. Fr. d'Athènes et de Rome*, 1923; K. Horna, *Die Hymnen des Mesomedes*, Leipzig, 1928; G. Martellotti, *Mesomede*, in *Scuola di Filol. Class.*, Rome, 1929; H. C. Puech, *Numénius d'Apamée*, in *Mélanges Bidez*, Brussels, 1934. On the Jewish war, for studies in English see especially A. L. Sachar, *A History of the Jews*, 1950; S. Lieberman, *Greek in Jewish Palestine*, 1942; and the articles of W. D. Gray, *The Founding of Aelia Capitolina and the Chronology of the Jewish War under Hadrian*, and *New Light from Egypt on the Early Reign of Hadrian*, Amer. Journ. of Semit. Lang. and Lit., 1923; R. Harris, *Hadrian's Decree of Expulsion of the Jews from Jerusalem*, Harv. Theol. Rev. XIX, 1926; W. Stinespring, *Hadrian in Palestine*, Amer. Orient. Soc. LIX, 1939. See also, apart from the German works already cited, A. von Premerstein, *Alexandrinische und jüdische Gesandte vor Kaiser Hadrian*, in *Hermes*, LVII, 1922. In French, Renan's account of Hadrian's war in Palestine, in *L'Eglise Chrétienne*, 1879, is essential still. The archaeologists of Israel, too, are now steadily bringing new contributions to our still limited knowledge of the history and topography of this war.

What we know of Antinous, and of the posthumous cult which was built up around him, is derived from a limited number of ancient texts, both historical and literary and most of them brief, and some of which have been cited already in this *Note*; from a few inscriptions, like that of the very important text on the obelisk of the Pincio mentioned above; and from the innumerable statues, bas-reliefs, and coins of the Bithynian favorite which have come down to us. That is to say, history, iconography, and esthetic evaluation are here inseparable. Up to the time of the

Renaissance, the very reprobation with which Christian tradition had surrounded the deified youth helped to keep his memory alive; from the sixteenth century on, the statues discovered in Roman vineyards, as well as the counterfeits of forgers, have served to enrich the princely and papal collections with his image. In 1764 Winckelmann, in his *Geschichte der Kunst des Alterthums*, presented with a kind of fervor the first comprehensive study of Antinous portraiture, based on the statues to be seen in the Rome of his time. Such example was soon to be followed in the course of the nineteenth century by numerous essays in the fields of historical scholarship or esthetics; unequal in value, these studies are chiefly significant for what they reveal of the tastes or the moral conventions of their period. Among them should be noted especially the *Antinous* of L. Dietrichson (Christiania, 1884), a work which though based on somewhat confused idealism, and decidedly outdated from the point of view of iconographic research, nevertheless lists with almost passionate care all the ancient texts and inscriptions known about Antinous at that time. The study of F. Laban, *Der Gemütsausdruck des Antinous*, Berlin, 1891, enumerates different reactions in those German studies of esthetics from Winckelmann to the end of the nineteenth century which discuss Antinous portraiture, but it hardly touches upon the actual iconography and history of Hadrian's favorite. The essay on Antinous by J. Addington Symonds in his *Sketches in Italy and Greece*, 1900, is singularly penetrating, although the tone is now outmoded and the information on some points is outdated by recent research; unlike Laban, he tries with the help of literary and artistic documentation to approach the young Bithynian as a living reality. Symonds is one of the first critics to note the conscious revival by Hadrian of Greek erotic tradition (Note 4, p. 21, *A Problem in Greek Ethics*, privately printed, 1883, reimpressions, 1901, 1908). The important study published in 1923 by Pirro Marconi, *Antinoo. Saggio sull'Arte dell' Età Adrianea*, (*Mon. Ant. R. Accad. Lincei*, XXIX), provides a very nearly complete catalogue of statues and bas-reliefs of the favorite known at that date, with good photographic illustration; although poor in discussion of esthetic values, this work marks a great advance in the iconography of the subject (still incomplete today). Marconi's careful scrutiny and comparison of the individual statues adds a few points to our knowledge of the history of Antinous himself and spells an end to the hazy dreaming in which even the best romantic critics had indulged with regard to that youth. The brief study of E. Holm, *Das Bildnis des Antinous*, Leipzig, 1933, is typical of the narrowly specialized dissertation in which iconography is wholly dissociated from psychology and from history. The second volume of Robert West's *Römische Porträt-Plastik*, Munich, 1941, contains notices (sometimes too absolute on points still open to question) on the life and portraits of Antinous, accompanied by good photographic reproduction of some of the best known statues and relief figures of Hadrian's favorite. The long essay of G. Blum, *Numismatique d'Antinoos, Journ. Int. d'Arch. Numismatique*, XVI, Athens, 1914, is still indispensable for the study of the coins of Antinous, for which it offers the only attempt, to date, in complete cataloguing and analysis. For the coins of Antinous struck in Asia Minor, consult W. H. Waddington, E. Babelon and Th. Reinach, *Recueil général des Monnaies Grecques d'Asie-Mineure*, I–IV, 1904–12, and I, 2nd ed., 1925; for his Alexandrine coins, J. Vogt, *Die Alexandrinischen Münzen*, I–II, Stuttgart, 1924; and for some of his coins in Greece, C. Seltman, *Greek Sculpture and Some Festival Coins*, in *Hesperia*, the *Journ. Amer. School of Class. Stud. at Athens*, XVII, 1948.

Without mentioning the discussions of portraiture of Antinous in general appraisals of Hadrianic art, which will be referred to below, we should indicate here the great number of books, articles, and archaeological notices containing descriptions of portraits of the young Bithynian newly discovered or identified, or new appreciations of those portrayals; for example, R. Lanciani and C. L. Visconti, *Delle Scoperte . . .* in *Bulletino Communale di Roma*, XIV, 1886, pp. 189–90, 208–14; G. Rizzo, *Antinoo-Silvano*, in *Ausonia*, III, 1908; P. Gauckler, *Le Sanctuaire syrien du Janicule*, 1912; R. Bartoccini, *Le Terme di Lepcis (Leptis Magna)*, in *Africa Italiana*, 1929; S. Reinach, *Les têtes des médaillons de l'Arc de Constantin*, in *Rev Arch.*, Série 4, XV, 1910; H. Bulle, *Ein Jagddenkmal des Kaisers Hadrian*, in *Jahr. d. arch. Inst.*, XXXIV, 1919; E. Buschor, *Die Hadrianischen Jagdbilder*, in *Mitt. d. deutsch. arch. Inst., Röm. Abt.* XXXVIII-IX, 1923–24; H. Kähler, *Hadrian und seine Villa bei Tivoli*, Berlin, 1950, note 151, pp. 177–9; C.

Seltman, *Approach to Greek Art,* 1948. Such new research on points of iconography or numismatics has made it possible to ascertain certain aspects of the cult of Antinous and even certain dates in that short life.

As to the religious atmosphere which seems to have surrounded Antinous' death, see especially W. Weber, *Drei Untersuchungen zur aegyptisch-griechischen Religion,* Heidelberg, 1911; likewise P. Graindor, *Athènes sous Hadrien* (cited above among specialized studies on Hadrian), p. 13. The problem of the exact location of the tomb of Antinous is still unsolved, despite the arguments of C. Hülsen, *Das Grab des Antinous,* in *Mitt. d. deutsch. arch. Inst., Röm. Abt.,* XI, 1896, and in *Berl. Philol. Wochenschr.,* March 15, 1919, and the opposite view of Kähler on this point (note 158, p. 179, of his work already cited). And finally should be noted the valuable chapter of Father A. J. Festugière, *La Valeur religieuse des papyrus magiques* in his book *L'Idéal religieux des Grecs et l'Evangile,* 1932, especially for its analysis of the sacrifice of the *Esies* (death by immersion with consequent attainment of divine status for the victim); though without reference to the story of Hadrian's favorite, this study nevertheless throws light upon practices known to us hitherto only through an outworn literary tradition, and thus allows this legend of voluntary sacrifice to be taken out of the storehouse of operatic episode and fitted again into the very exact framework of a specific occult tradition.

Most books on the general subjects of Greco-Roman and late Greek art give much space to the art which is termed Hadrianic. Mention is made here only of a few of the more substantial accessible works, all of which could have been also included among the good modern appreciations of Antinous portraiture above: H. B. Walters, *The Art of the Romans,* 1911, 2nd ed., 1928; Eugenie Strong, Chapter XV on *The Golden Age of Hadrian* in *Art in Ancient Rome,* II, 1929; G. Rodenwaldt, *Die Kunst der Antike (Hellas und Rom),* in *Propyläen-Kunstgeschichte,* III, 2, Berlin, 1930, and *Art from Nero to the Antonines,* in *Cambridge Ancient History,* XI, 1936. The work of Jocelyn Toynbee, *The Hadrianic School: A Chapter in the History of Greek Art,* 1934, is essential for Hadrianic motifs in coins and reliefs, and for their cultural and political implications. For Hadrianic portraiture in general, in addition to the book of West mentioned above, may be noted, among others, the work of P. Graindor, *Bustes et Statues-Portraits de l'Egypte Romaine* (no date), and of F. Poulsen, *Greek and Roman Portraits* in *English Country Houses*, 1923. This much abridged list may be terminated with reference to only a few studies on Hadrian's architectural constructions: that of P. Graindor, *Athènes sous Hadrian* (mentioned above) for his buildings in Greece; for his military architecture that of J. C. Bruce, *Handbook to the Roman Wall*, ed. by Ian A. Richmond, 10th ed., 1947, and of R. G. Collingwood, *Roman Britain*, cited above among specialized studies on Hadrian. For the Villa Adriana, the works of Gaston Boissier, *Promenades archéologiques, Rome et Pompei*, 1886, and Pierre Gusman, *La Villa impériale de Tibur*, 1904, are still essential; more recent works are those of R. Paribeni, *La Villa dell' Imperatore Adriano a Tivoli*, Milan (1927), and H. Kähler, *Hadrian und seine Villa bei Tivoli*, cited above on the subject of Antinous.

As to Antinoöpolis, we know something of its appearance from travelers' accounts in the seventeenth and eighteenth centuries (a sentence from a Sieur Paul Lucas, who described the ruins in 1714, in the second edition of his *Voyage au Levant*, has been incorporated in the present work), but our detailed information comes from the admirable drawings of Edmé Jomard, made for the monumental *Description de l'Egypte* (Vol. IV, Paris, 1817), begun at Napoleon's order during the Egyptian campaign. They offer a very moving record of the ruined city, completely destroyed since that time. For, about the year 1860, the ancient materials of the triumphal arch, the colonnades, and the theater were converted into cement or used otherwise to build factories in a neighboring Arab town. The French archaeologist Albert Gayet was the first to excavate on the site of Antinoöpolis, at the end of the last century; among his many findings were mummies of officiating attendants in the Antinous cult, together with their funeral equipment, but hardly a vestige was recovered of anything dating from the actual time of the city's founding by Hadrian. Gayet's *Exploration des Ruines d'Antinoé*, in *Annales* of the Guimet Museum, XXVI, 3, 1897, and other notes published in those *Annales* on that subject, through rather unmethodical, remain essential for study of the site. The papyri of Antinoöpolis and those of Oxyrhynchus, in the same district, in successive publication since 1898, have afforded no new details about the architecture of the Hadrianic city or the cult of the favorite there, but they provide a very complete list of its religious and administrative divisions, which evidently come down from Hadrian himself and bear witness to the strong influence of Eleusinian ritual on his thought. Weber, *Untersuchungen zur Geschichte des Kaisers Hadrianus*, and Graindor, *Athènes sous Hadrien*, both cited before, give some discussion of this list, as do two other studies: E. Kühn, *Antinoöpolis, Ein Beitrag zur Geschichte des Hellenismus in römischen Aegypten*, Göttingen, 1913, and B. Kübler, *Antinoupolis*, Leipzig, 1914. The brief article of M. J. de Johnson, *Antinoe and its Papyri*, in *Journ. of Egypt. Arch.*, I, 1914, gives an excellent summary of the topography of the ancient city. The Italian archaeologist Evaristo Breccia has also studied the site of Antinoöpolis, and has contributed an article on the subject to the *Enciclopedia Italiana* (1928) which includes a useful bibliography.

History has its rules, though they are not always followed even by professional historians; poetry, too, has its laws. The two are not necessarily irreconcilable. The perspectives chosen for this narrative made necessary some rearrangements of detail, together with certain simplifications or modifications intended to eliminate repetitions, lagging, or confusion which only didactic explanation would have dispelled. It was important that these adjustments, all relating only to very small points, should in no way change the spirit or the significance of the incident or the fact in question. In other cases, the lack of authentic details for some given episode of Hadrian's life has obliged the writer to prudent filling in of such lacunae from information furnished by contemporary texts treating of analogous experiences or events; these joinings had, of course, to be kept to the indispensable minimum. And last, this work, which tries to evoke Hadrian not only as he was but also as his contemporaries saw him, and sometimes imagined him, could even make some sparing use of legendary material, provided that the material thus chosen corresponded to the conception that the men of his time (and he himself, perhaps) had of his personality. The method of making such changes and additions is best explained by specific examples, with which this *Note* is hereby concluded.

The character Marullinus is built upon a name, that of an ancestor of Hadrian, and upon a tradition which says that an uncle (and not the grandfather) of the future emperor foretold the boy's fortune; the portrait of the old man and the circumstances of his death are imaginary. The character Gallus is based on an historical Gallus who played the part described here, but the detail of his final discomfiture is created only in order to emphasize one of Hadrian's traits most often mentioned, his capacity for bitter resentment. The episode of Mithraic initiation is invented; that cult was already in vogue in the army at the time, and it is possible, but not proved, that Hadrian desired to be initiated into it while he was still a young officer. Likewise, it is only a possibility that Antinous submitted himself to the ritual blood bath in Palmyra; Turbo, Meles Agrippa, and Castoras are all historical figures, but their participation in the respective initiations is invented. Hadrian's meeting with the Gymnosophist is not given by history; it has been built from first- and second-century texts which describe episodes of the same kind. All details concerning Attianus are authentic except for one or two allusions to his private life, of which we know nothing. The chapter on the mistresses has been constructed out of two lines of Spartianus (XI, 7–8) on this subject; the effort has been to stay within the most plausible general outlines, supplementing by invention where it was essential to do so.

Pompeius Proculus was indeed governor of Bithynia, but was not surely so in 123-124 during the emperor's visit in those years. Strato of Sardis, an erotic poet and compiler of the twelfth book of the *Greek Anthology*, probably lived in Hadrian's time; there is nothing to prove that he saw the emperor in person, but it was tempting to make these two men meet. The visit of Lucius to Alexandria in 130 is deduced (as Gregorovius has already done) from a text often contested, the *Letter to Servianus*, discussed above, nor does the passage of this letter which refers to Lucius require such interpretation. We do not know, therefore, if he was in Egypt at that time, but almost all the details given for him at this period are drawn from his biography by Spartianus. The story of Antinous' sacrifice is traditional (Dio, LXIX, 11; Spartianus XIV, 7); the detail of the magic operations is suggested by recipes from Egyptian papyri on magic, but the incidents of the evening in Canopus are invented. The episode of the fall of a child from a balcony, during a banquet, placed in these *Memoirs* in the course of Hadrian's stop at Philae, is drawn from a report in the *Oxyrhynchus Papyri* and took place in reality nearly forty years after Hadrian's journey in Egypt. The two examples of miracles reported by Spartianus as supposedly performed by the emperor in his last years have been blended into one. The association of Apollodorus with the Servianus conspiracy is only a hypothesis, but one which can perhaps be defended.

Chabrias, Celer, and Diotimus are mentioned several times by Marcus Aurelius, who, however, indicates only their names and their passionate loyalty to Hadrian's memory. They have been introduced into this reconstruction in order to evoke something of the court of Tibur during the last years of the reign: Chabrias represents the circle of Platonist or Stoic philosophers who surrounded the emperor; the military element is represented by Celer (not to be confused with that Celer mentioned by Philostratus and Aristides as secretary for Greek correspondence); Diotimus stands for the group of imperial *éroménoi* (the term long established by tradition for young favorites). Three names of actual associates of the emperor have thus served as points of departure for three characters who are, for the most part, invented. The physician Iollas, on the contrary, is an actual person for whom we lack the true name; nor do we know if he came originally from Alexandria. The freedman Onesimus was in Hadrian's service, but we do not know if his role was that of procurer for Hadrian; the name of Crescens as a secretary of Servianus is authenticated by an inscription, but history does not tell us that he betrayed his master. Opramoas was a great merchant of Hadrian's time who aided Hadrian and his army, but there is nothing to prove that he accompanied Hadrian to the Euphrates. Arrian's wife is known to us by an inscription, but we do not know if she was 'proud and elegant' as Hadrian says here. Only a few minor characters are wholly invented, the slave Euphorion, the actors Olympus and Bathyllus, the physician Leotychides, the young British tribune, and the guide Assar. The two sorceresses, of the Island of Britain and of Canopus respectively, are created to suggest the world of fortune tellers and dealers in occult sciences with whom Hadrian liked to surround himself. The feminine name of *Arete* comes from an authentic poem of Hadrian (*Inscr. Graec.*, XIV, 1089), but is given only arbitrarily here to the housekeeper of the Villa; the name of the courier Menecrates is taken from the *Letter of the King Fermès to the Emperor Hadrian* (H. Osmont, *Bibliothèque de l'Ecole des Chartres*, Vol. 74, 1913), a text of wholly legendary content which comes to us from a medieval manuscript and of which history, properly speaking, can make no use; the *Letter* could, however, have borrowed this particular name from other documents now lost. In the passages concerning young Marcus Aurelius the names *Veronica* and *Theodoros* are modifications, in part for the sake of euphony, of the two names *Benedicta* and *Theodotus* given in the *Meditations of Marcus Aurelius* 1, xvii, 7).

The brief sketch of the family background of Antinous is not historical, but attempts to take into consideration the social conditions which prevailed at that time in Bithynia. On certain controversial points, such as the cause for enforced retirement of Suetonius, the origin of Antinous, whether slave or free, the active participation of Hadrian in the Palestinian war, the dates of apotheosis of Sabina and of interment of Aelius Caesar in the Castel Sant Angelo, it has been necessary to choose between hypotheses of historians, but the effort has been to make that choice only with good reason. In other cases, like that of the adoption of Hadrian by Trajan, or of the death of Antinous, the author has tried to leave that very incertitude which before it existed in history doubtless existed in life itself.

❋❋ ❋❋

REFLECTIONS ON THE COMPOSITION OF MEMOIRS OF HADRIAN

The idea for this book and the first writing of it, in whole or in part, and in various forms, date from the period between 1924 and 1929, between my twentieth and twenty-fifth year. All those manuscripts were destroyed, deservedly.

★

In turning the pages of a volume of Flaubert's correspondence much read and heavily underscored by me about the year 1927 I came again upon this admirable sentence: 'Just when the gods had ceased to be, and the Christ had not yet come, there was a unique moment in history, between Cicero and Marcus Aurelius, when man stood alone.' A great part of my life was going to be spent in trying to define, and then to portray, that man existing alone and yet closely bound with all being.

★

I resumed work on the book in 1934; after prolonged research some fifteen pages were written which seemed to me final in form. Then the project was abandoned, only to be taken up again several times between 1934 and 1937.

★

There was a long period in which I thought of the work in the form of a series of dialogues, where all the voices of those times would be heard. But whatever I did, the details seemed to take undue precedence; the parts threatened the balance of the whole; Hadrian's voice was drowned out by all the others. I was not succeeding in my attempt to reconstruct that world as seen and heard by one man.

★

From the version of 1934 only one sentence has been retained: 'I begin to discern the profile of my death.' Like a painter who has chosen a landscape, but who constantly shifts his easel now

right, now left, I had at last found a point from which to view
the book.

★

Take a life that is known and completed, recorded and fixed
by History (as much as lives ever can be fixed), so that its entire
course may be seen at a single glance; more important still,
choose the moment when the man who lived that existence
weighs and examines it, and is, for the briefest span, capable of
judging it. Try to manage so that he stands before his own life
in much the same position as we stand when we look at it.

★

Mornings spent at the Villa Adriana; innumerable evenings
passed in small cafés around the Olympieion; the constant back
and forth over Greek seas; roads of Asia Minor. In order to make
full use of these memories of mine they had first to recede as far
from me as is the Second Century.

★

Experiments with time: eighteen days, eighteen months, eighteen years, or eighteen centuries. The motionless survival of
statues which, like the head of the *Mondragone Antinous* in the
Louvre, are still living in a past time, a *time that has died*. The
problem of time foreshortened in terms of human generations:
some five and twenty aged men, their withered hands interlinked
to form a chain, would be enough to establish an unbroken
contact between Hadrian and ourselves.

★

In 1937, during a first stay in the United States, I did some
reading for this book in the libraries at Yale; I wrote the visit
to the physician, and the passage on renunciation of bodily exercise. These fragments, re-worked, are still part of the present
version.

★

In any case, I was too young. There are books which one
should not attempt before having passed the age of forty. Earlier
than that one may well fail to recognize those great natural
boundaries which from person to person, and from century to
century, separate the infinite variety of mankind; or, on the
contrary, one may attach too much importance to mere administrative barriers, to the customs houses or the sentry boxes erected

between man and man. It took me years to learn how to calculate exactly the distances between the emperor and myself.

*

I ceased to work on the book (except for a few days, in Paris) between 1937 and 1939.

*

Some mention of T. E. Lawrence reminded me that his tracks in Asia Minor cross and recross those of Hadrian. But the background for Hadrian is not the desert; it is Athens and her hills. The more I thought of these two men, the more the adventure of one who rejects life (and first of all rejects himself) made me desirous of presenting, through Hadrian, the point of view of the man who accepts all experience, or at least who refuses on one score only to accept elsewhere. It goes without saying, of course, that the asceticism of the one and the hedonism of the other are at many points interchangeable.

*

In October of 1939 the manuscript was left behind in Europe, together with the greater part of the notes; I nevertheless took with me to the United States the several résumés of my former readings at Yale and a map of the Roman Empire at the time of Trajan's death which I had carried about with me for years; also the profile photograph of the *Antinous* of the Archaeological Museum in Florence, purchased there in 1926, the young face gravely sweet.

*

From 1939 to 1948 the project was wholly abandoned. I thought of it at times, but with discouragement, and almost with indifference, as one thinks of the impossible. And with something like shame for ever having ventured upon such an undertaking.

*

The lapse into despair of a writer who does not write.

*

In the worst hours of apathy and dejection I would go for solace to Hartford's fine museum, seeking out a Canaletto painting of Rome, the Pantheon standing brown and gold against the blue sky of a late afternoon in summer; and each time I would come away from it comforted, and once again at peace.

*

About the year 1941 I had discovered by chance, in an artists' supply shop in New York, four Piranesi engravings which G . . . and I bought. One of them, a *View of Hadrian's Villa* which I had not known before, is an interior of the chapel of Canopus, from which were taken in the Seventeenth Century the *Antinous* in Egyptian style and the accompanying basalt statues of priestesses, all to be seen today in the Vatican. The foreground shows a round structure, burst open like a skull, from which fallen trees and brush hang vaguely down, like strands of hair. The genius of Piranesi, almost mediumistic, has truly caught the element of hallucination here: he has sensed the long-continued rituals of mourning, the tragic architecture of an inner world. For several years I looked at this drawing almost daily, without a thought for my former enterprise, which I supposed that I had given up. Such are the curious detours of what is called oblivion.

*

In the spring of 1947, while sorting over some papers I burned the notes taken at Yale; they seemed to have become by that time completely useless.

*

Still, Hadrian's name appears in an essay on Greek myth which I wrote in 1943 and which Roger Caillois published during those war years in *Les Lettres Françaises*, in Buenos Aires. Then in 1945 the figure of the drowned Antinous, borne along somehow on that Lethean current, came again to the surface in an unfinished essay, *Canticle of the Soul and its True Freedom*, written just before the advent of a serious illness.

*

Keep in mind that everything recounted here is thrown out of perspective by what is left unsaid: these notes serve only to mark the lacunae. There is nothing, for example, of what I was doing during those difficult years, nor of the thinking, the work, the worries and anxieties, *or* the joys; nor of the tremendous repercussion of external events and the perpetual testing of oneself upon the touchstone of fact. And I pass also in silence over the experiences of illness, and over other, more profound experiences which they bring in their train; and over the perpetual search for, or presence of, love.

*

Never mind. That disjunction, that break in continuity, that 'night of the soul' which so many of us experienced at the time, each in his own way (and so often in far more tragic and final form than did I), was essential, perhaps, in order to force me into trying to bridge not only the distance which separated me from Hadrian, but, above all, the distance which separated me from my true self.

*

Everything turns out to be valuable that one does for one's self without thought of profit. During those years in an unfamiliar land I had kept on with the reading of authors from classical antiquity: the red or green cloth-bound volumes of Loeb-Heinemann editions had become a country of my own. Thus, since one of the best ways to reconstruct a man's thinking is to rebuild his library, I had actually been working for years, without knowing it, to refurnish the bookshelves at Tibur in advance. Now I had only to imagine the swollen hands of a sick man holding the half-rolled manuscripts.

*

Do, from within, the same work of reconstruction which the nineteenth-century archaeologists have done from without.

*

In December of 1948 I received from Switzerland a trunk which I had stored there during the war, with its contents of family papers and letters some ten years old. I sat down by the fire to work my way through the débris, as if to take some gloomy inventory after a death. I passed several evenings alone at the task, undoing the separate packets and running through them before destroying that accumulation of correspondence with people whom I had forgotten, and who had forgotten me, some of them still alive, others dead. A few of the pages bore dates of a generation ago, and even the names had quite gone from my mind. As I unfolded and threw mechanically into the fire that exchange of dead thoughts between a Marie and a François or a Paul, long since disappeared, I came upon four or five typewritten sheets, the paper of which had turned yellow. The salutation told me nothing: 'My dear Mark . . .' *Mark* . . . What friend or love, what distant relative was this? I could not recall the name at all. It was several minutes before I remembered that *Mark* stood here for *Marcus Aurelius*, and that I had in hand a fragment of the lost manuscript. From that moment there was no question but that this book must be taken up again, whatever the cost.

*

That same night I re-opened two of the volumes which had also just been returned to me, remnants of a library in large part lost. One was Dio Cassius in Henri Estienne's beautiful printing, and the other a volume of an ordinary edition of *Historia Augusta*, the two principal sources for Hadrian's life, purchased at the time that I was intending to write this book. Everything that the world, and I, had gone through in the interval now served to enrich these chronicles of an earlier age, and threw upon that imperial existence certain other lights and other shades. Once I had thought chiefly of the man of letters, the traveller, the poet, the lover; none of that had faded, to be sure, but now for the first time I could see among all those figures, standing out with great clarity of line, the most official and yet the most hidden form of all, that of the emperor. The fact of having lived in a world which is toppling around us had taught me the importance of the Prince.

*

I fell to making, and then re-making, this portrait of a man who was *almost* wise.

*

Only one other figure in history has tempted me with nearly the same insistence: Omar Khayyám, the poet-astronomer. But the life of Khayyám is that of the pure contemplator, and of the somber skeptic, too; the world of action meant little to him. Furthermore, I do not know Persia, nor do I know its language.

*

Another thing virtually impossible, to take a feminine character as a central figure, to make Plotina, for example, rather than Hadrian, the axis of my narrative. Women's lives are much too limited, or else too secret. If a woman does recount her own life she is promptly reproached for being no longer truly feminine. It is already hard enough to give some element of truth to the utterances of a man.

*

I left for Taos, in New Mexico, taking with me the blank sheets for a fresh start on the book (the swimmer who plunges into the water with no assurance that he will reach the other shore). Closed inside my compartment as if in a cubicle of some Egyptian tomb, I worked late into the night between New York and Chicago; then all the next day, in the restaurant of a Chicago station where I awaited a train blocked by storms and snow; then again until dawn, alone in the observation car of a Santa Fé limited, surrounded by black spurs of the Colorado mountains, and by the eternal pattern of the stars. Thus were written at a single impulsion the passages on food, love, sleep, and the knowledge of men. I can hardly recall a day spent with more ardor, or more lucid nights.

★

I pass as rapidly as possible over three years of research, of interest to specialists alone, and over the development of a method akin to controlled delirium, of interest, probably, to none but madmen. And yet this term *delirium* smacks too much of romanticism; let us say, rather, a constant participation, as intensely aware as possible, in *that which has been.*

★

One foot in scholarship, the other in magic arts, or, more accurately and without metaphor, absorption in that *sympathetic magic* which operates when one transports oneself, in thought, into another's body and soul.

★

Portrait of a voice. If I have chosen to write these *Memoirs of Hadrian* in the first person it is in order to dispense with any intermediary, in so far as possible, even were that intermediary myself. Surely Hadrian could speak more forcibly and more subtly of his life than could I.

★

Those who put the historical novel in a category apart are forgetting that what every novelist does is only to interpret, by means of the techniques which his period affords, a certain number of past events; his memories, whether consciously or unconsciously recalled, whether personal or impersonal, are all woven of the same stuff as History itself. The work of Proust is a reconstruction of a lost past quite as much as is *War and*

Peace. The historical novel of the 1830s, it is true, tends toward melodrama, and to cloak-and-dagger romance; but not more than does Balzac's magnificent *Duchess of Langeais*, or his startling *Girl with the Golden Eyes*, both of wholly contemporary setting. Flaubert painstakingly rebuilds a Carthaginian palace by charging his description with hundreds of minute details, thus employing essentially the same method as for his picture of Yonville, a village of his own time and of his own Normandy. In our day, when introspection tends to dominate literary forms, the historical novel, or what may for convenience's sake be called by that name, must take the plunge into time recaptured, and must fully establish itself within some inner world.

*

Time itself has nothing to do with the matter. It is always surprising to me that my contemporaries, masters as they consider themselves to be over space, apparently remain unaware that one can contract the distance between centuries at will.

*

We lose track of everything, and of everyone, even ourselves. The facts of my father's life are less known to me than those of the life of Hadrian. My own existence, if I had to write of it, would be reconstructed by me from externals, laboriously, as if it were the life of someone else: I should have to turn to letters, and to the recollections of others, in order to clarify such uncertain memories. What is ever left but crumbled walls, or masses of shade? Here, where Hadrian's life is concerned, try to manage so that the lacunae of our texts coincide with what he himself might have forgotten.

*

Which is not to suggest, as is too often done, that historical truth is never to be attained, in any of its aspects. With this kind of truth, as with all others, the problem is the same: one errs *more* or *less*.

*

The rules of the game: learn everything, read everything, inquire into everything, while at the same time adapting to one's ends the *Spiritual Exercises* of Ignatius of Loyola, or the method of Hindu ascetics, who for years, and to the point of exhaustion, try to visualize ever more exactly the images which they create beneath their closed eyelids. Through hundreds of card notes pursue each incident to the very moment that it occurred; endeavor to restore the mobility and suppleness of life to those visages known to us only in stone. When two texts, or two assertions, or perhaps two ideas, are in contradiction, be·ready to reconcile them rather than cancel one by the other; regard them as two different facets, or two successive stages, of the same reality, a reality convincingly human just because it is complex. Strive to read a text of the Second Century with the eyes, soul, and feelings of the Second Century; let it steep in that mother solution which the facts of its own time provide; set aside, if possible, all beliefs and sentiments which have accumulated in successive strata between those persons and us. And nevertheless take advantage (though prudently, and solely by way of preparatory study) of all possibilities for comparison and cross-checking, and of new perspectives slowly developed by the many centuries and events separating us from a given text, a fact, a man; make use of such aids more or less as guide-marks along the road of return toward one particular point in time. Keep one's own shadow out of the picture; leave the mirror clean of the mist of one's own breath; take only what is most essential and durable in us, in the emotions aroused by the senses or in the operations of the mind, as our point of contact with those men who, like us, nibbled olives and drank wine, or gummed their fingers with honey, who fought bitter winds and blinding rain, or in summer sought the plane tree's shade; who took their pleasures, thought their own thoughts, grew old, and died.

*

Several times I have had physicians 'diagnose' the brief passages in the chronicles which deal with Hadrian's illness. Indications not so different, after all, from the clinical descriptions of Balzac's last days.

*

Make good use, the better to understand Hadrian's malady, of the first symptoms of a heart ailment.

*

'What's Hecuba to him?' Hamlet asks when a strolling player weeps over that tragic queen. Thus the Prince of Denmark is forced to admit that this actor who sheds genuine tears has managed to establish with a woman dead for three thousand years a more profound relationship than he himself has with his own father, so recently buried, and whose wrongs he does not feel fully enough to seek swift revenge.

★

The human substance and structure hardly change: nothing is more stable than the curve of a heel, the position of a tendon, or the form of a toe. But there are periods when the shoe is less deforming than in others. In the century of which I speak we are still very close to the undisguised freedom of the bare foot.

★

In crediting Hadrian with prophetic insight I was keeping within the realm of plausibility as long as such prognostics remained vague and general. The impartial analyst of human affairs ordinarily makes few mistakes as to the ultimate course of events, but he begins to err seriously when he tries to foresee the exact way that events will work out, their turning points and details. Napoleon on Saint Helena predicted that a century after his death Europe would have turned either revolutionary or Cossack; he stated the two terms of the problem extremely well, but could not imagine one superposed upon the other. On the whole, however, it is only out of pride or gross ignorance, or cowardice, that we refuse to see in the present the lineaments of times to come. Those sages of the ancient world, unbound by dogma of any kind, thought as we do in terms of physics, or rather, of physiology, as applied to the whole universe: they envisaged the end of man and the dying out of this sphere. Both Plutarch and Marcus Aurelius knew full well that gods, and civilizations, pass and die. We are not the first to look upon an inexorable future.

★

My attribution of clairvoyance to the emperor was, in any case, only a means of bringing into play the almost Faustian element of his character, as it appears, for example, in the *Sibylline Verses* and in the writings of Aelius Aristides, or in the portrait of Hadrian grown old, as sketched by Fronto. Rightly or not, the contemporaries of this dying man ascribed to him something more than human powers.

★

If this man had not maintained peace in the world, and revived the economy of the empire, his personal fortunes and misfortunes would have moved me less.

*

One can never give enough time to the absorbing study of relationships between texts. The poem on the hunting trophy consecrated by Hadrian at Thespiae to the God of Love and to the Uranian Venus, 'on the hills of Helicon, beside Narcissus' spring', can be dated as of the autumn of the year 124; at about that same time the emperor passed through Mantinea, where, according to Pausanius, he had the tomb of Epaminondas rebuilt, and wrote a poem to be inscribed upon it. The Mantinean inscription is now lost, but Hadrian's act of homage is to be fully understood, perhaps, only if we view it in relation to a passage of Plutarch's *Morals* which tells us that Epaminondas was buried in that place between two young friends struck down at his side. If for date of the meeting of the emperor and Antinous we accept the stay in Asia Minor of 123–124, which is in any case the most plausible date and the best supported by iconographical evidence, these two poems then would form a part of what might be called the Antinous cycle; both are inspired by that same Greece of heroic lovers which Arrian evoked later on, after the death of the favorite, when he compared the youth to Patroclus.

*

A certain number of persons whose portraits one would wish to develop: Plotina, Sabina, Arrian, Suetonius. But Hadrian could see them only in part, from the point of view at which he was standing. Antinous himself has to be presented by refraction, through the emperor's memories, that is to say, in passionately meticulous detail, not devoid of a few errors.

*

All that can be said of the temperament of Antinous is inscribed in any one of his likenesses. 'Eager and impassionated tenderness, sullen effeminacy': Shelley, with a poet's admirable candor, says the essential in six words, while most of the nineteenth-century art critics and historians could only expatiate upon the subject with righteous declamation, or else idealize about it, vaguely and hypocritically.

*

We are rich in portraits of Antinous; they range in quality from the mediocre to the incomparable. Despite variations due to the skill of the respective sculptors or to the age of the model, or to differences between portraits made from life and those executed to commemorate the youth after death, all are striking and deeply moving because of the incredible realism of the face, always immediately recognizable and nevertheless so diversely interpreted, and because they are examples, unique in classical antiquity, of survival and repetition in stone of a countenance which was neither that of a statesman nor of a philosopher, but simply of one who was loved. Among these portraits the two most beautiful are the least known: they are also the only ones which transmit to us the name of the sculptor. One is the bas-relief signed by Antonianos of Aphrodisias and found some fifty years ago on the property of an agronomic institute, the Fundi Rustici, in the Committee Room of which it is now placed. Since no guidebook of Rome indicates its existence in that city already so crowded with statues, tourists do not know about it. This work of Antonianos has been carved in Italian marble, so it was certainly executed in Italy, and doubtless in Rome, either because that artist was already established in the capital, or because he had been brought back by Hadrian on one of the emperor's travels. It has exquisite delicacy. The young head, pensively inclined, is framed by the tendrils of a vine twined in supple arabesque; the brevity of life comes inevitably to mind, the sacrificial grape and the fruit-scented air of an evening in autumn. Unhappily, the marble has suffered from storage in a cellar during the recent war-years: its whiteness is temporarily obscured and earth-stained, and three fingers of the figure's left hand have been broken. Thus do gods pay for the follies of men.

[The preceding paragraph appeared for the first time six years ago; meanwhile this bas-relief was acquired by a Roman banker, Arturo Osio, a whimsical man who probably would have stirred the imagination of Stendhal or of Balzac. Signor Osio has lavished upon this fair object the same solicitous attention that he gives to the animals on his property at the edge of Rome, where they run free in their natural state, and to the trees which he has planted by the thousand on his shore estate at Orbetello. A rare virtue, this last, for Stendhal was writing as early as 1828, 'The Italians loathe trees;' and what would he say today when real estate speculators, trying to pack more and more colossal apartment houses into Rome, are circumventing the city's laws to protect its handsome umbrella pines? Their method is simply to kill the trees by injections of hot water. A rare luxury, too, though one which many a man of wealth could enjoy, is this landowner's animation of woods and fields with creatures at full liberty, and that not for the pleasure of hunting them down, but for reconstituting a veritable Eden. The love for statues of classical antiquity, those great peaceful objects which seem so solid and yet are so easily destroyed, is an uncommon taste among private collectors in these agitated times, cut off from both past and future. The new possessor of the bas-relief of Antonianos, acting on the advice of experts, has just had it cleaned by a specialist whose light, slow rubbing by hand has removed the rust and moisture stains from the marble and restored its soft gleam, like that of alabaster or of ivory.]*

*

The second of these masterpieces is the famous sardonyx known as the Marlborough Gem, because it once belonged to that family collection, now dispersed. For more than thirty years this fine intaglio seemed to have been lost, or hidden away, but in January of 1952 it came to light in a public sale in London; the informed taste of the great collector Giorgio Sangiorgi has brought it back to Rome. I am indebted to him for the chance to see and to handle this unique gem. A signature, though no longer complete, can be read around the edge; it is thought, and doubtless correctly, to be that of the sculptor of the bas-relief, Antonianos of Aphrodisias. So skilfully has the master-carver enclosed that perfect profile within the narrow compass of a sardonyx that this bit of stone stands as testimony to a great lost art quite as much as does any statue or any relief. The proportions of the work make us forget the dimensions of the object. At some time during the Byzantine period the gem was set in a nugget of solid gold, and in this form passed from collector to collector, none of whose names we know, until it reached Venice; it is mentioned as part of a great seventeenth-century collection there. In the next century it was purchased by the celebrated

* Addition of 1958.

dealer in antiques, Gavin Hamilton, and brought to England, whence it now returns to Rome, its starting-point. Of all objects still above ground today it is the one of which we can assume with some assurance that it has often been held in Hadrian's hands.

*

One has to go into the most remote corners of a subject in order to discover the simplest things, and things of most general literary interest. It is only in studying Phlegon, secretary to Hadrian, that I learned that we owe to this forgotten personage the first, and one of the finest, of the great ghost stories, that somber, sensuous *Bride of Corinth* which inspired Goethe's ballad, and likewise the *Corinthian Wedding* of Anatole France. It must be said, however, that Phlegon also took down, with the same avid and uncritical curiosity for everything beyond ordinary experience, some absurd stories of two-headed monsters, and of hermaphrodites got with child. Such was the stuff of the conversations, on some days, at least, at the imperial table.

*

Those who would have preferred a *Journal* of Hadrian to his *Memoirs* forget that a man of action rarely keeps a journal; it is almost always later on, and in a period of prolonged inactivity, that he does his recollecting, makes his notations, and, very often, has cause for wonder at the course his life has taken.

*

If all other documents were lacking, the *Letter of Arrian to the Emperor Hadrian on the Circumnavigation of the Black Sea* would suffice to recreate in broad outline that great imperial figure: the scrupulous exactitude of the chief-of-state who would know all details; his interest in the work both of war and of peace; his concern for good likenesses in statues, and that these should be finely wrought; his passion for the poetry and legend of an earlier day. And that society, rare in any period, but destined to vanish completely after the time of Marcus Aurelius, wherein the scholarly administrator can still address his prince as a friend, however subtly shaded his deference and his respect. Everything is there: the nostalgia for ancient Greece and its ideals, discreet allusion to a lost love and to mystical consolation sought by the bereaved survivor, the haunting appeal of unknown lands and barbarous climes. The evocation of desert wastes peopled only by sea-birds, so profoundly romantic in spirit, calls to mind the exquisite vase found in Villa Hadriana, to be seen today in the Museum of the Terme in Rome; there on a field of marble snow a flock of wild heron are spreading their wings to fly away, in utter solitude.

★

Note of 1949: the more I strive for an exact portrait the farther I diverge from the kind of book, and of man, who would please the public. Only a few students of human destiny will understand.

★

In our time the novel devours all other forms; one is almost forced to use it as the medium of expression. This study of the destiny of a man called Hadrian would have been cast in the form of a tragedy in the Seventeenth Century, or of an essay, perhaps, in the period of the Renaissance.

★

This book is the condensation of a vast work composed for myself alone. I had taken the habit of writing each night, in almost automatic fashion, the result of those long, self-induced visions whereby I could place myself intimately within another period of time. The merest word, the slightest gesture, the least perceptible implications were noted down; scenes now summed up in a line or two, in the book as it is, passed before me in fullest detail, and as if in slow motion. Added all together, these accounts would have afforded material for a volume of several thousand pages, but each morning I would burn the work of the night before. In such fashion I wrote a great number of decidedly abstruse meditations, and several descriptions bordering on the obscene.

★

He who seeks passionately for truth, or at least for accuracy, is frequently the one best able to perceive, like Pilate, that truth is not absolute or pure. Hence, mingled with his most direct assertions we find hesitations, deviousness, and reservations which a more conventional mind would not evince. At certain moments, though very seldom, it has even occurred to me that the emperor was lying. In such cases I had to let him lie, like the rest of us.

★

The utter fatuity of those who say to you, 'By "Hadrian" you mean yourself!' Almost as unsubtle as those who wonder why one should choose a subject so remote in time and in space. The sorcerer who pricks his thumb before he evokes the shades knows well that they will heed his call only because they can lap his blood. He knows, too, or ought to know, that the voices who speak to him are wiser and more worthy of attention than are his own clamorous outcries.

★

It did not take me long to realize that I had embarked upon the life of a very great man. From that time on, still more respect for truth, closer attention, and, on my part, ever more silence.

★

In a sense, every life that is recounted is offered as an example; we write in order to attack or to defend a view of the universe, and to set forth a system of conduct which is our own. It is none the less true, however, that nearly every biographer disqualifies himself by over-idealizing his subject or by deliberate disparagement, by exaggerated stress on certain details or by cautious omission of others. Thus a character is arbitrarily constructed, taking the place of the man to be understood and explained. A human life cannot be graphed, whatever people may say, by two virtual perpendiculars, representing what a man believed himself to be and what he wished to be, plus a flat horizontal for what he actually was; rather, the diagram has to be composed of three curving lines, extended to infinity, ever meeting and ever diverging.

★

Whatever one does, one always rebuilds the monument in his own way. But it is already something gained to have used only the original stones.

★

Every being who has gone through the adventure of living *is* myself.

★

This Second Century appeals to me because it was the last century, for a very long period of time, in which men could think and express themselves with full freedom. As for us, we are perhaps already very far from such times as that.

★

On the 26th of December, 1950, on an evening of freezing cold and in the almost polar silence of Mount Desert Island, off the Atlantic shore, I was striving to live again through the smothering heat of a day in July, in the year 138 in Baiae, to feel the weight of a sheet on weary, heavy limbs, and to catch the barely perceptible sound of that tideless sea as from time to time it reached a man whose whole attention was concentrated upon other murmurs, those of his approaching death. I tried to go as far as the last sip of water, the last spasm of pain, the last image in his mind. Now the emperor had but to die.

★

This book bears no dedication. It ought to have been dedicated to G.F . . . and would have been, were there not a kind of impropriety in putting a personal inscription at the opening of a work where, precisely, I was trying to efface the personal. But even the longest dedication is too short and too commonplace to honor a friendship so uncommon. When I try to define this asset which has been mine now for years, I tell myself that such a privilege, however rare it may be, is surely not unique; that in the whole adventure of bringing a book successfully to its conclusion, or even in the entire life of some fortunate writers, there must have been sometimes, in the background, perhaps, someone who will not let pass the weak or inaccurate sentence which we ourselves would retain, out of fatigue; someone who would re-read with us for the twentieth time, if need be, a questionable page; someone who takes down for us from the library shelves the heavy tomes in which we may find a helpful suggestion, and who persists in continuing to peruse them long after weariness has made us give up; someone who bolsters our courage and approves, or sometimes disputes, our ideas; who shares with us, and with equal fervor, the joys of art and of living, the endless work which both require, never easy but never dull; someone who is neither our shadow nor our reflection, nor even our complement, but simply himself; someone who leaves us ideally free, but who nevertheless obliges us to be fully what we are. *Hospes Comesque.*

★

In December, 1951, learned of the fairly recent death of the German historian Wilhelm Weber, and in April, 1952, of the

death of the scholar Paul Graindor, both of whose works I have
so much used. A few days ago talked with G.B . . . and J.F . . .
who had known the engraver Pierre Gusman in Rome at the
time that he was drawing, with passion, all the different parts of
the Villa. The feeling of belonging to a kind of *Gens Aelia*, of
being, as it were, one of the throng of secretaries who had served
the great man, of participating in the change of that imperial
guard which poets and humanists mount in relay around any
great memory. Thus (and it is doubtless the same for specialists
in the study of Napoleon, or for lovers of Dante), over the ages
is formed a circle of kindred spirits, moved by the same interests
and sympathies, or concerned with the same problems.

★

The pedants of comedy, Vadius and Blazius still exist, and
their fat cousin Basil is ever about. Once and once only have I
happened to be confronted with that mixture of insults and coarse
jokes; with extracts truncated or skillfully deformed, so as to
make our sentences say some absurdity which they do not say;
with captious arguments built up by assertions both vague and
peremptory enough to win ready credence from the reader respectful of academic trappings and lacking the time, or the desire,
to look up the sources for himself. Characteristic, all of it, of a
certain species which, fortunately, is rare. On the contrary, what
genuine good will have so many scholars shown who could
just as readily, in these times of excessive specialization, have
disdained outright any literary effort at reconstruction of the past
which might seem to them to trespass on their domain . . . Too
many of them have graciously, and of their own accord, taken
trouble to rectify some error already in print, or to confirm a
detail, support a hypothesis, expedite new research, for me not
to express here a word of gratitude to such well-disposed readers.
Each book which sees a new edition owes something to the
discriminating people who have read it.

★

Do the best one can. Do it over again. Then still improve,
even if ever so slightly, those retouches. 'It is myself that I
re-make,' said the poet Yeats in speaking of his revisions.

★

Yesterday, at the Villa, I thought of the thousands of lives, silent and furtive as those of wild beasts, unthinking as those of plants, who have followed in succession here between Hadrian's time and ours: gypsies of Piranesi's day, pillagers of the ruins, beggars, goatherds, and peasants lodged as best they could in some corner of the rubble. At the end of an olive grove, in an ancient corridor partly cleared, G . . . and I came upon a shepherd's bed of rushes, with his improvised clothes-peg stuck between two blocks of Roman cement, and the ashes of his fire not yet cold. A sense of intimacy with humble, ordinary things, a little like what one feels at the Louvre when, after closing hour, the cots of the guardians appear in among the statues.

[Nothing need be changed in 1958 in the preceding paragraph; the clothes-peg of the shepherd is still there, though not his bed. G . . . and I have again sat resting on the grass of the Vale of Tempe, among the violets, at that sacred moment of the year when everything begins anew, in spite of the threats which man today is everywhere raising overhead. But nevertheless the Villa has suffered pernicious change. Not all of it, to be sure: a whole which the centuries have slowly destroyed, but have also formed, is not so quickly altered. By an error seldom committed in Italy certain dubious 'embellishments' have followed in the wake of excavations and necessary repairs. Olive groves have been cut down to make way for a highly conspicuous parking lot, complete with shop and counter service of the type prevalent at exposition grounds, thus transforming the Poecilium's noble solitude into a city square; visitors may drink from a cement fountain which offers water through an absurd plaster mask, a would-be imitation of the antique; another mask, even more pointless, decorates the wall of the great pool, where a flotilla of ducks now holds forth. Still more plaster graces the Canal: casts of the garden statues found here in recent diggings have been placed on pedestals and lined up somewhat arbitrarily along its banks; the originals, fairly average Greco-Roman work, do not deserve the honor of so conspicuous a position, but neither do they merit the indignity of being copied in such hideous material, both swollen and unsubstantial. This new décor gives to the once melancholy Canopus something of the air of a studio set, ready for a film version of 'life in Imperial Rome'.

There is nothing more easily destroyed than the equilibrium of the fairest places. A text remains intact regardless of our whims of interpretation, and survives our commentaries; but the slightest imprudence inflicted upon stone, the shortest macadamized road cut through a field where grass has peacefully grown for centuries, does something irreparable, and for ever. The beauty goes, and the authenticity likewise.]*

★

There are places where one has chosen to live, invisible abodes which one makes for oneself quite outside the current of time. I have lived in Tibur, and shall die there, perhaps, as Hadrian did on Achilles' Isle.

★

No. Once more I have gone back to the Villa, to its garden pavilions built for privacy and for repose, to the vestiges of a luxury free of pomp, and as little imperial as possible, conceived of rather for the wealthy connoisseur who tries to combine the pleasures of art with the charms of rural life. In the Pantheon I have watched for the exact spot where sunlight would fall on a morning of April 21, and along the Mausoleum's halls have retraced that funeral path so often walked by the friends of the emperor's last days, Chabrias, Diotimus, and Celer. But I have ceased to feel the immediate presence of those beings, the living reality of those events; they are near me still, but of the past, neither more nor less now than the memories of my own life. Our commerce with others does not long endure; it ceases once satisfaction is obtained, the lesson learned, the service rendered, the book complete. What I could say has been said; what I could learn has been learned. Let us turn, for the time that is left to us, to other work.

* Addition of 1958.

Critical acclaim for Ian Rankin

'Rankin weaves his plots with a menacing ease . . . His prose is understated, yet his canvas of Scotland's criminal underclass has a panoramic breadth. His ear for dialogue is as sharp as a switchblade. This is, quite simply, crime writing of the highest order'
Daily Express

'A series that shows no signs of flagging . . . Assured, sympathetic to contemporary foibles, humanistic, this is more than just a police procedural as the character of Rebus grows in moral stature . . . Rankin is the head capo of the MacMafia' *Time Out*

'Rankin has followed one success with another. Sardonic and assured, the novel has a powerful and well-paced narrative. What is striking is the way Rankin uses his laconic prose as a literary paint stripper, scouring away pretensions to reveal the unwholesome reality beneath' *Independent*

'Rankin strips Edinburgh's polite façade to its gritty skeleton' *The Times*

'A teeming Ellroy-esque evocation of life at the sharp end in modern Scotland . . . Rankin is the finest Scottish crime writer to emerge since William McIlvanney' *GQ*

'Rebus resurgent . . . A brilliantly meshed plot which delivers on every count on its way to a conclusion as unexpected as it is inevitable. Eleventh in the series. Still making waves' *Literary Review*

'His fiction buzzes with energy . . . Essentially, he is a romantic storyteller in the tradition of Robert Louis Stevenson . . . His prose is as vivid and terse as the next man's yet its flexibility and rhythm give it potential for lyrical expression which is distinctly Rankin's own' *Scotland on Sunday*

'Top notch . . . the bleakness is unrelenting, but it quite suits Mr Rankin who does his best work in the dark' *New York Times*

'The internal police politics and corruption in high places are both portrayed with bone-freezing accuracy. This novel should come with a wind-chill factor warning' *Daily Telegraph*

'Detective Inspector Rebus makes the old-style detectives with their gentle or bookish backgrounds, Alleyn, Morse, Dalgliesh, look like wimps . . . Rankin is brilliant at conveying the genuine stench of seedy places on the dark side of Scotland' *Sunday Telegraph*

'It's the banter and the energy, the immense carnival of scenes and characters, voices and moods that set Rankin apart. His stories are like a transmission forever in the red zone, at the edge of burnout. This is crime ficiton at its best' *Washington Post*

Born in the Kingdom of Fife in 1960, Ian Rankin graduated from the University of Edinburgh and has since been employed as grape-picker, swineherd, taxman, alcohol researcher, hi-fi journalist and punk musician. His first Rebus novel, *Knots & Crosses*, was published in 1987 and the Rebus books have now been translated into 26 languages. Ian Rankin has been elected a Hawthornden Fellow, and is a past winner of the prestigious Chandler-Fulbright Award, as well as two CWA short-story 'Daggers' and the 1997 CWA Macallan Gold Dagger for Fiction for *Black & Blue*, which was also shortlisted for the Mystery Writers of America 'Edgar' award for Best Novel. *Black & Blue*, *The Hanging Garden*, *Dead Souls* and *Mortal Causes* have been televised on ITV, starring John Hannah as Inspector Rebus. *Dead Souls*, the tenth novel in the series, was shortlisted for the CWA Gold Dagger Award in 1999. An Alumnus of the Year at Edinburgh University, he has also been awarded four honorary doctorates, from the University of Abertay Dundee in 1999, from the University of St Andrews in 2001, in 2003 from the University of Edinburgh and in 2005 from the Open University. In 2002 Ian Rankin was awarded an OBE for services to literature. In 2004 *Resurrection Men* won the Edgar Award for Best Novel. In 2005 *Fleshmarket Close* won the Crime Thriller of the Year award at the British Book Awards. Ian is the winner of the Crime Writers' Association Diamond Dagger 2005. In 2005 he was also awarded the Grand Prix du Littérature Policier (France), the Deutsche Krimi Prize (Germany) and the Icons of Scotland award. He lives in Edinburgh with his wife and two sons. Visit his website at www.ianrankin.net.

By Ian Rankin

The Inspector Rebus series
Knots & Crosses
Hide & Seek
Tooth & Nail
Strip Jack
The Black Book
Mortal Causes
Let It Bleed
Black & Blue
The Hanging Garden
Death Is Not The End (*novella*)
Dead Souls
Set in Darkness
The Falls
Resurrection Men
A Question of Blood
Fleshmarket Close

Other novels
The Flood
Watchman
Westwind

Writing as Jack Harvey
Witch Hunt
Bleeding Hearts
Blood Hunt

Short stories
A Good Hanging and Other Stories
Beggars Banquet

Omnibus editions
Rebus: The Early Years
(Knots & Crosses, Hide & Seek, Tooth & Nail)
Rebus: The St Leonard's Years
(Strip Jack, The Black Book, Mortal Causes)
Rebus: The Lost Years
(Let It Bleed, Black & Blue, The Hanging Garden)
Rebus: Capital Crimes (Dead Souls, Set in Darkness, The Falls)

All Ian Rankin's titles are available on audio. Also available:
Jackie Leven Said by Ian Rankin and Jackie Leven.

Ian Rankin

A Good Hanging

and other stories

An Orion paperback

First published in Great Britain in 1992
by Century
This paperback edition published in 1998
by Orion Books Ltd,
Orion House, 5 Upper St Martin's Lane,
London WC2H 9EA

Reissued 2005

2

Both the author and publisher acknowledge first
publication of 'Playback' in *Writer's Crimes 22* (Macmillan).

Printed and bound in Great Britain by
Clays Ltd, St Ives plc

The Orion Publishing Group's policy is to use papers that
are natural, renewable and recyclable products and
made from wood grown in sustainable forests. The logging
and manufacturing processes are expected to conform to
the environmental regulations of the country of origin.

www.orionbooks.co.uk

To my editor, Euan Cameron,
who had faith from the first

Contents

Playback   1

The Dean Curse   23

Being Frank   49

Concrete Evidence   63

Seeing Things   87

A Good Hanging   109

Tit for Tat   137

Not Provan   157

Sunday   175

Auld Lang Syne   189

The Gentlemen's Club   205

Monstrous Trumpet   225

Playback

It was the perfect murder.

Perfect, that is, so far as the Lothian and Borders Police were concerned. The murderer had telephoned in to confess, had then panicked and attempted to flee, only to be caught leaving the scene of the crime. End of story.

Except that now he was pleading innocence. Pleading, yelling and screaming it. And this worried Detective Inspector John Rebus, worried him all the way from his office to the four-storey tenement in Leith's trendy dockside area. The tenements here were much as they were in any working-class area of Edinburgh, except that they boasted colour-splashed roller blinds or Chinese-style bamboo affairs at their windows, and their grimy stone facades had been power-cleaned, their doors now boasting intruder-proof intercoms. A far cry from the greasy Venetian blinds and kicked-in passageways of the tenements in Easter Road or Gorgie, or even in nearby parts of Leith itself, the parts the developers were ignoring as yet.

The victim had worked as a legal secretary, this much Rebus knew. She had been twenty-four years old. Her name was Moira Bitter. Rebus smiled at that. It was a guilty smile, but at this hour of the morning any smile he could raise was something of a miracle.

He parked in front of the tenement, guided by a uniformed officer who had recognised the badly dented front bumper of Rebus's car. It was rumoured that the dent had come from knocking down too many old ladies, and who was Rebus to deny it? It was the stuff of legend and it

1

gave him prominence in the fearful eyes of the younger recruits.

A curtain twitched in one of the ground-floor windows and Rebus caught a glimpse of an elderly lady. Every tenement, it seemed, tarted up or not, boasted its elderly lady. Living alone, with one dog or four cats for company, she was her building's eyes and ears. As Rebus entered the hallway, a door opened and the old lady stuck out her head.

'He was going to run for it,' she whispered. 'But the bobby caught him. I saw it. Is the young lass dead? Is that it?' Her lips were pursed in keen horror. Rebus smiled at her but said nothing. She would know soon enough. Already she seemed to know as much as he did himself. That was the trouble with living in a city the size of a town, a town with a village mentality.

He climbed the four flights of stairs slowly, listening all the while to the report of the constable who was leading him inexorably towards the corpse of Moira Bitter. They spoke in an undertone: stairwell walls had ears.

'The call came at about 5 a.m., sir,' explained PC MacManus. 'The caller gave his name as John MacFarlane and said he'd just murdered his girlfriend. He sounded distressed by all accounts, and I was radioed to investigate. As I arrived, a man was running down the stairs. He seemed in a state of shock.'

'Shock?'

'Sort of disorientated, sir.'

'Did he say anything?' asked Rebus.

'Yes, sir, he told me, "Thank God you're here. Moira's dead." I then asked him to accompany me upstairs to the flat in question, called in for assistance, and the gentleman was arrested.'

Rebus nodded. MacManus was a model of efficiency, not a word out of place, the tone just right. Everything by rote and without the interference of too much thought. He would go far as a uniformed officer, but Rebus doubted the

2

young man would ever make CID. When they reached the fourth floor, Rebus paused for breath then walked into the flat.

The hall's pastel colour scheme extended to the living-room and bedroom. Mute colours, subtle and warming. There was nothing subtle about the blood though. The blood was copious. Moira Bitter lay sprawled across her bed, her chest a riot of colour. She was wearing apple-green pyjamas, and her hair was silky blonde. The police pathologist was examining her head.

'She's been dead about three hours,' he informed Rebus. 'Stabbed three or four times with a small sharp instrument, which, for the sake of convenience, I'm going to term a knife. I'll examine her properly later on.'

Rebus nodded and turned to MacManus, whose face had a sickly grey tinge to it.

'Your first time?' Rebus asked. The constable nodded slowly. 'Never mind,' Rebus continued. 'You never get used to it anyway. Come on.'

He led the constable out of the room and back into the small hallway. 'This man we've arrested, what did you say his name was?'

'John MacFarlane, sir,' said the constable, taking deep breaths. 'He's the deceased's boyfriend apparently.'

'You said he seemed in a state of shock. Was there anything else you noticed?'

The constable frowned, thinking. 'Such as, sir?' he said at last.

'Blood,' said Rebus coolly. 'You can't stab someone in the heat of the moment without getting blood on you.'

MacManus said nothing. Definitely not CID material and perhaps realising it for the very first time. Rebus turned from him and entered the living-room. It was almost neurotically tidy. Magazines and newspapers in their rack beside the sofa. A chrome and glass coffee table bearing nothing more than a clean ashtray and a paperback

3

romance. It could have come straight from an Ideal Home exhibition. No family photographs, no clutter. This was the lair of an individualist. No ties with the past, a present ransacked wholesale from Habitat and Next. There was no evidence of a struggle. No evidence of an encounter of any kind: no glasses or coffee cups. The killer had not loitered, or else had been very tidy about his business.

Rebus went into the kitchen. It, too, was tidy. Cups and plates stacked for drying beside the empty sink. On the draining-board were knives, forks, teaspoons. No murder weapon. There were spots of water in the sink and on the draining-board itself, yet the cutlery and crockery were dry. Rebus found a dishtowel hanging up behind the door and felt it. It was damp. He examined it more closely. There was a small smudge on it. Perhaps gravy or chocolate. Or blood. Someone had dried something recently, but what?

He went to the cutlery drawer and opened it. Inside, amidst the various implements was a short-bladed chopping knife with a heavy black handle. A quality knife, sharp and gleaming. The other items in the drawer were bone dry, but this chopping knife's wooden handle was damp to the touch. Rebus was in no doubt: he had found his murder weapon.

Clever of MacFarlane though to have cleaned and put away the knife. A cool and calm action. Moira Bitter had been dead three hours. The call to the police station had come an hour ago. What had MacFarlane done during the intervening two hours? Cleaned the flat? Washed and dried the dishes? Rebus looked in the kitchen's swing-bin, but found no other clues, no broken ornaments, nothing that might hint at a struggle. And if there had been no struggle, if the murderer had gained access to the tenement and to Moira Bitter's flat without forcing an entry ... if all this were true, Moira had known her killer.

Rebus toured the rest of the flat, but found no other clues. Beside the telephone in the hall stood an answering machine. He played the tape, and heard Moira Bitter's voice.

'Hello, this is Moira. I'm out, I'm in the bath, or I'm otherwise engaged.' (A giggle.) 'Leave a message and I'll get back to you, unless you sound boring.'

There was only one message. Rebus listened to it, then wound back the tape and listened again.

'Hello, Moira, it's John. I got your message. I'm coming over. Hope you're not "otherwise engaged". Love you.'

John MacFarlane: Rebus didn't doubt the identity of the caller. Moira sounded fresh and fancy-free in her message. But did MacFarlane's response hint at jealousy? Perhaps she *had* been otherwise engaged when he'd arrived. He lost his temper, blind rage, a knife lying handy. Rebus had seen it before. Most victims knew their attackers. If that were not the case, the police wouldn't solve so many crimes. It was a blunt fact. You double bolted your door against the psychopath with the chainsaw, only to be stabbed in the back by your lover, husband, son or neighbour.

John MacFarlane was as guilty as hell. They would find blood on his clothes, even if he'd tried cleaning it off. He had stabbed his girlfriend, then calmed down and called in to report the crime, but had grown frightened at the end and had attempted to flee.

The only question left in Rebus's mind was the why? The why and those missing two hours.

Edinburgh through the night. The occasional taxi rippling across setts and lone shadowy figures slouching home with hands in pockets, shoulders hunched. During the night hours, the sick and the old died peacefully, either at home or in some hospital ward. Two in the morning until four: the dead hours. And then some died horribly, with terror in their eyes. The taxis still rumbled past, the night people kept moving. Rebus let his car idle at traffic lights, missing the change to green, only coming to his senses as amber turned red again. Glasgow Rangers were coming to town on Saturday. There would be casual violence. Rebus felt comfortable with the thought. The worst football hooligan could probably not have stabbed with the same ferocity as Moira Bitter's killer. Rebus lowered his eyebrows. He was rousing himself to fury, keen for confrontation. Confrontation with the murderer himself.

John MacFarlane was crying as he was led into the interrogation room, where Rebus had made himself look comfortable, cigarette in one hand, coffee in the other. Rebus had expected a lot of things, but not tears.

'Would you like something to drink?' he asked. MacFarlane shook his head. He had slumped into the chair on the other side of the desk, his shoulders sagging, head bowed, and the sobs still coming from his throat. He mumbled something.

'I didn't catch that,' said Rebus.

'I said I didn't do it,' MacFarlane answered quietly. 'How could I do it? I love Moira.'

Rebus noted the present tense. He gestured towards the tape machine on the desk. 'Do you have any objections to my making a recording of this interview?' MacFarlane shook his head again. Rebus switched on the machine. He flicked ash from his cigarette onto the floor, sipped his coffee, and waited. Eventually, MacFarlane looked up. His eyes were stinging red. Rebus stared hard into those eyes, but still said nothing. MacFarlane seemed to be calming. Seemed, too, to know what was expected of him. He asked for a cigarette, was given one, and started to speak.

'I'd been out in my car. Just driving, thinking.'

Rebus interrupted him. 'What time was this?'

'Well,' said MacFarlane, 'ever since I left work, I suppose. I'm an architect. There's a competition on just now to design a new art gallery and museum complex in Stirling. Our partnership's going in for it. We were

discussing ideas most of the day, you know, brainstorming.'
He looked up at Rebus again, and Rebus nodded.
Brainstorm: now there was an interesting word.

'And after work,' MacFarlane continued, 'I was so fired
up I just felt like driving. Going over the different options
and plans in my head. Working out which was strongest –'

He broke off, realising perhaps that he was talking in a
rush, without thought or caution. He swallowed and
inhaled some smoke. Rebus was studying MacFarlane's
clothes. Expensive leather brogues, brown corduroy trousers, a thick white cotton shirt, the kind cricketers wore,
open at the neck, a tailor-made tweed jacket. MacFarlane's
3-Series BMW was parked in the police garage, being
searched. His pockets had been emptied, a Liberty print tie
confiscated in case he had ideas about hanging himself. His
brogues, too, were without their laces, these having been
confiscated along with the tie. Rebus had gone through the
belongings. A wallet, not exactly bulging with money but
containing a fair spread of credit cards. There were more
cards, too, in MacFarlane's personal organiser. Rebus
flipped through the diary pages, then turned to the sections
for notes and for addresses. MacFarlane seemed to lead a
busy but quite normal social life.

Rebus studied him now, across the expanse of the old
table. MacFarlane was well-built, handsome if you liked
that sort of thing. He looked strong, but not brutish.
Probably he would make the local news headlines as
'Secretary's Yuppie Killer'. Rebus stubbed out his cigarette.

'We know you did it, John. That's not in dispute. We
just want to know why.'

MacFarlane's voice was brittle with emotion. 'I swear I
didn't, I swear.'

'You're going to have to do better than that.' Rebus
paused again. Tears were dripping onto MacFarlane's
corduroys. 'Go on with your story,' he said.

MacFarlane shrugged. 'That's about it,' he said, wiping his nose with the sleeve of his shirt.

Rebus prompted him. 'You didn't stop off anywhere for petrol or a meal or anything like that?' He sounded sceptical. MacFarlane shook his head.

'No, I just drove until my head was clear. I went all the way to the Forth Road Bridge. Turned off and went into Queensferry. Got out of the car to have a look at the water. Threw a few stones in for luck.' He smiled at the irony. 'Then drove round the coast road and back into Edinburgh.'

'Nobody saw you? You didn't speak to anyone?'

'Not that I can remember.'

'And you didn't get hungry?' Rebus sounded entirely unconvinced.

'We'd had a business lunch with a client. We took him to The Eyrie. After lunch there, I seldom need to eat until the next morning.'

The Eyrie was Edinburgh's most expensive restaurant. You didn't go there to eat, you went there to spend money. Rebus was feeling peckish himself. The canteen did a fine bacon buttie.

'When did you last see Miss Bitter alive?'

At the word 'alive', MacFarlane shivered. It took him a long time to answer. Rebus watched the tape revolving. 'Yesterday morning,' MacFarlane said at last. 'She stayed the night at my flat.'

'How long have you known her?'

'About a year. But I only started going out with her a couple of months ago.'

'Oh? And how did you know her before that?'

MacFarlane paused. 'She was Kenneth's girlfriend,' he said at last.

'Kenneth being –'

MacFarlane's cheeks reddened before he spoke. 'My best

friend,' he said. 'Kenneth was my best friend. You could say I stole her from him. These things happen, don't they?'

Rebus raised an eyebrow. 'Do they?' he said. MacFarlane bowed his head again.

'Can I have a coffee?' he asked quietly. Rebus nodded, then lit another cigarette.

MacFarlane sipped the coffee, holding it in both hands like a shipwreck survivor. Rebus rubbed his nose and stretched, feeling tired. He checked his watch. Eight in the morning. What a life. He had eaten two bacon rolls and a string of rind curled across the plate in front of him. MacFarlane had refused food, but finished the first cup of coffee in two gulps and gratefully accepted a second.

'So,' Rebus said, 'you drove back into town.'

'That's right.' MacFarlane took another sip of coffee. 'I don't know why, but I decided to check my answering machine for calls.'

'You mean when you got home?'

MacFarlane shook his head. 'No, from the car. I called home from my car-phone and got the answering machine to play back any messages.'

Rebus was impressed. 'That's clever,' he said.

MacFarlane smiled again, but the smile soon vanished. 'One of the messages was from Moira,' he said. 'She wanted to see me.'

'At that hour?' MacFarlane shrugged. 'Did she say why she wanted to see you?'

'No. She sounded ... strange.'

'Strange?'

'A bit ... I don't know, distant maybe.'

'Did you get the feeling she was on her own when she called?'

'I've no idea.'

'Did you call her back?'

9

'Yes. Her answering machine was on. I left a message.'

'Would you say you're the jealous type, Mr Mac-Farlane?'

'What?' MacFarlane sounded surprised by the question. He seemed to give it serious thought. 'No more so than the next man,' he said at last.

'Why would anyone want to kill her?'

MacFarlane stared at the table, shaking his head slowly.

'Go on,' said Rebus, sighing, growing impatient. 'You were saying how you got her message.'

'Well, I went straight to her flat. It was late, but I knew if she was asleep I could always let myself in.'

'Oh?' Rebus was interested. 'How?'

'I had a spare key,' MacFarlane explained.

Rebus got up from his chair and walked to the far wall and back, deep in thought.

'I don't suppose,' he said, 'you've got any idea *when* Moira made that call?'

MacFarlane shook his head. 'But the machine will have logged it,' he said. Rebus was more impressed than ever. Technology was a wonderful thing. What's more, he was impressed by MacFarlane. If the man was a murderer, then he was a very good one, for he had fooled Rebus into thinking him innocent. It was crazy. There was nothing to point to him not being guilty. But all the same, a feeling was a feeling, and Rebus most definitely had a feeling.

'I want to see that machine,' he said. 'And I want to hear the message on it. I want to hear Moira's last words.'

It was interesting how the simplest cases could become so complex. There was still no doubt in the minds of those around Rebus – his superiors and those below him – that John MacFarlane was guilty of murder. They had all the proof they needed, every last bit of it circumstantial.

MacFarlane's car was clean: no bloodstained clothes

stashed in the boot. There were no prints on the chopping-knife, though MacFarlane's prints were found elsewhere in the flat, not surprising given that he'd visited that night, as well as on many a previous one. No prints either on the kitchen sink and taps, though the murderer had washed a bloody knife. Rebus thought that curious. And as for motive: jealousy, a falling-out, a past indiscretion discovered. The CID had seen them all.

Murder by stabbing was confirmed and the time of death narrowed down to a quarter of an hour either side of three in the morning. MacFarlane claimed that at that time he was driving towards Edinburgh, but had no witnesses to corroborate the claim. There was no blood to be found on MacFarlane's clothing, but, as Rebus himself knew, that didn't mean the man wasn't a killer.

More interesting, however, was that MacFarlane denied making the call to the police. Yet someone – in fact, whoever murdered Moira Bitter – *had* made it. And more interesting even than this was the telephone answering machine.

Rebus went to MacFarlane's flat in Liberton to investigate. The traffic was busy coming into town, but quiet heading out. Liberton was one of Edinburgh's many anonymous middle-class districts, substantial houses, small shops, a busy thoroughfare. It looked innocuous at midnight, and was even safer by day.

What MacFarlane had termed a 'flat' comprised, in fact, the top two storeys of a vast, detached house. Rebus roamed the building, not sure if he was looking for anything in particular. He found little. MacFarlane led a rigorous and regimented life and had the home to accommodate such a lifestyle. One room had been turned into a makeshift gymnasium, with weightlifting equipment and the like. There was an office for business use, a study for private use. The main bedroom was decidedly masculine in taste, though a framed painting of a naked woman had been removed from one wall and tucked behind a chair. Rebus thought he detected Moira Bitter's influence at work.

In the wardrobe were a few pieces of her clothing and a pair of her shoes. A snapshot of her had been framed and placed on MacFarlane's bedside table. Rebus studied the photograph for a long time, then sighed and left the bedroom, closing the door after him. Who knew when John MacFarlane would see his home again?

The answering machine was in the living-room. Rebus played the tape of the previous night's calls. Moira Bitter's voice was clipped and confident, her message to the point: 'Hello.' Then a pause. 'I need to see you. Come round as soon as you get this message. Love you.'

MacFarlane had told Rebus that the display unit on the machine showed time of call. Moira's call registered at 3.50 a.m., about forty-five minutes after her death. There was room for some discrepancy, but not three-quarters of an hour's worth. Rebus scratched his chin and pondered. He played the tape again. 'Hello.' Then the pause. 'I need to see you.' He stopped the tape and played it again, this time with the volume up and his ear close to the machine. That pause was curious and the sound quality on the tape was poor. He rewound and listened to another call from the same evening. The quality was better, the voice much clearer. Then he listened to Moira again. Were these recording machines infallible? Of course not. The time displayed could have been tampered with. The recording itself could be a fake. After all, whose word did he have that this *was* the voice of Moira Bitter? Only John MacFarlane's. But John MacFarlane had been caught leaving the scene of a murder. And now Rebus was being presented with a sort of an alibi for the man. Yes, the tape could well be a fake, used by MacFarlane to substantiate his story, but stupidly not put into use until after the time of death. Still,

12

from what Rebus had heard from Moira's own answering machine, the voice was certainly similar to her own. The lab boys could sort it out with their clever machines. One technician in particular owed him a rather large favour.

Rebus shook his head. This still wasn't making much sense. He played the tape again and again.

'Hello.' Pause. 'I need to see you.'

'Hello.' Pause. 'I need to see you.'

'Hello.' Pause. 'I need –'

And suddenly it became a little clearer in his mind. He ejected the tape and slipped it into his jacket pocket, then picked up the telephone and called the station. He asked to speak to Detective Constable Brian Holmes. The voice, when it came on the line, was tired but amused.

'Don't tell me,' Holmes said, 'let me guess. You want me to drop everything and run an errand for you.'

'You must be psychic, Brian. Two errands really. Firstly, last night's calls. Get the recording of them and search for one from John MacFarlane, claiming he'd just killed his girlfriend. Make a copy of it and wait there for me. I've got another tape for you, and I want them both taken to the lab. Warn them you're coming –'

'And tell them it's priority, I know. It's *always* priority. They'll say what they always say: give us four days.'

'Not this time,' Rebus said. 'Ask for Bill Costain and tell him Rebus is collecting on his favour. He's to shelve what he's doing. I want a result today, not next week.'

'What's the favour you're collecting on?'

'I caught him smoking dope in the lab toilets last month.'

Holmes laughed. 'The world's going to pot,' he said. Rebus groaned at the joke and put down the receiver. He needed to speak with John MacFarlane again. Not about lovers this time, but about friends.

Rebus rang the doorbell a third time and at last heard a voice from within.

'Jesus, hold on! I'm coming.'

The man who answered the door was tall, thin, with wire-framed glasses perched on his nose. He peered at Rebus and ran his fingers through his hair.

'Mr Thomson?' Rebus asked. 'Kenneth Thomson?'

'Yes,' said the man, 'that's right.'

Rebus flipped open his ID. 'Detective Inspector John Rebus,' he said by way of introduction. 'May I come in?'

Kenneth Thomson held open the door. 'Please do,' he said. 'Will a cheque be all right?'

'A cheque?'

'I take it you're here about the parking tickets,' said Thomson. 'I'd have got round to them eventually, believe me. It's just that I've been hellish busy, and what with one thing and another ...'

'No, sir,' said Rebus, his smile as cold as a church pew, 'nothing to do with parking fines.'

'Oh?' Thomson pushed his glasses back up his nose and looked at Rebus. 'Then what's the problem?'

'It's about Miss Moira Bitter,' said Rebus.

'Moira? What about her?'

'She's dead, sir.'

Rebus had followed Thomson into a cluttered room overflowing with bundles of magazines and newspapers. A hi-fi sat in one corner, and covering the wall next to it were shelves filled with cassette tapes. These had an orderly look to them, as though they had been indexed, each tape's spine carrying an identifying number.

Thomson, who had been clearing a chair for Rebus to sit on, froze at the detective's words.

'Dead?' he gasped. 'How?'

'She was murdered, sir. We think John MacFarlane did it.'

'John?' Thomson's face was quizzical, then sceptical, then resigned. 'But why?'

14

'We don't know that yet, sir. I thought you might be able to help.'

'Of course I'll help if I can. Sit down, please.'

Rebus perched on the chair, while Thomson pushed aside some newspapers and settled himself on the sofa.

'You're a writer, I believe,' said Rebus.

Thomson nodded distractedly. 'Yes,' he said. 'Freelance journalism, food and drink, travel, that sort of thing. Plus the occasional commission to write a book. That's what I'm doing now, actually. Writing a book.'

'Oh? I like books myself. What's it about?'

'Don't laugh,' said Thomson, 'but it's a history of the haggis.'

'The haggis?' Rebus couldn't disguise a smile in his voice, warmer this time: the church pew had been given a cushion. He cleared his throat noisily, glancing around the room, noting the piles of books leaning precariously against walls, the files and folders and newsprint cuttings. 'You must do a lot of research,' he said appreciatively.

'Sometimes,' said Thomson. Then he shook his head. 'I still can't believe it. About Moira, I mean. About John.'

Rebus took out his notebook, more for effect than anything else. 'You were Miss Bitter's lover for a while,' he stated.

'That's right, Inspector.'

'But then she went off with Mr MacFarlane.'

'Right again.' A hint of bitterness had crept into Thomson's voice. 'I was very angry at the time, but I got over it.'

'Did you still see Miss Bitter?'

'No.'

'What about Mr MacFarlane?'

'No again. We spoke on the telephone a couple of times. It always seemed to end in a shouting match. We used to be like, well, it's a cliché, I suppose, but we used to be like brothers.'

'Yes,' said Rebus, 'so Mr MacFarlane told me.'

'Oh?' Thomson sounded interested. 'What else did he say?'

'Not much really.' Rebus rose from his perch and went to the window, holding aside the net curtain to stare out onto the street below. 'He said you'd known each other for years.'

'Since school,' Thomson added.

Rebus nodded. 'And he said you drove a black Ford Escort. That'll be it down there, parked across the street?'

Thomson came to the window. 'Yes,' he agreed, uncertainly, 'that's it. But I don't see what –'

'I noticed it as I was parking my own car,' Rebus continued, brushing past Thomson's interruption. He let the curtain fall and turned back into the room. 'I noticed you've got a car alarm. I suppose you must get a lot of burglaries around here.'

'It's not the most salubrious part of town,' Thomson said. 'Not all writers are like Jeffrey Archer.'

'Did money have anything to do with it?' Rebus asked. Thomson paused.

'With what, Inspector?'

'With Miss Bitter leaving you for Mr MacFarlane. He's not short of a bob or two, is he?'

Thomson's voice rose perceptibly. 'Look, I really can't see what this has to do with –'

'Your car was broken into a few months ago, wasn't it?' Rebus was examining a pile of magazines on the floor now. 'I saw the report. They stole your radio and your car phone.'

'Yes.'

'I notice you've replaced the car phone.' He glanced up at Thomson, smiled, and continued browsing.

'Of course,' said Thomson. He seemed confused now, unable to fathom where the conversation was leading.

'A journalist would need a car phone, wouldn't he?'

Rebus observed. 'So people could keep in touch, contact him at any time. Is that right?'

'Absolutely right, Inspector.'

Rebus threw the magazine back onto the pile and nodded slowly. 'Great things, car phones.' He walked over towards Thomson's desk. It was a small flat. This room obviously served a double purpose as study and living-room. Not that Thomson entertained many visitors. He was too aggressive for many people, too secretive for others. So John MacFarlane had said.

On the desk there was more clutter, though in some appearance of organisation. There was also a neat word processor, and beside it a telephone. And next to the telephone sat an answering machine.

'Yes,' Rebus repeated. 'You need to be in contact.' Rebus smiled towards Thomson. 'Communication, that's the secret. And I'll tell you something else about journalists.'

'What?' Unable to comprehend Rebus's direction, Thomson's tone had become that of someone bored with a conversation. He shoved his hands deep into his pockets.

'Journalists are hoarders.' Rebus made this sound like some great wisdom. His eyes took in the room again. 'I mean, near-pathological hoarders. They can't bear to throw things away, because they never know when something might become useful. Am I right?'

Thomson shrugged.

'Yes,' said Rebus, 'I bet I am. Look at these cassettes, for example.' He went to where the rows of tapes were neatly displayed. 'What are they? Interviews, that sort of thing?'

'Mostly, yes,' Thomson agreed.

'And you still keep them, even though they're years old?'

Thomson shrugged again. 'So I'm a hoarder.'

But Rebus had noticed something on the top shelf, some brown cardboard boxes. He reached up and lifted one down. Inside were more tapes, marked with months and

17

years. But these tapes were smaller. Rebus gestured with the box towards Thomson, his eyes seeking an explanation.

Thomson smiled uneasily. 'Answering machine messages,' he said.

'You keep these, too?' Rebus sounded amazed.

'Well,' Thomson said, 'someone may agree to something over the phone, an interview or something, then deny it later. I need them as records of promises made.'

Rebus nodded, understanding now. He replaced the brown box on its shelf. He still had his back to Thomson when the telephone rang, a sharp electronic sound.

'Sorry,' Thomson apologised, going to answer it.

'Not at all.'

Thomson picked up the receiver. 'Hello?' He listened, then frowned. 'Of course,' he said finally, holding the receiver out towards Rebus. 'It's for you, Inspector.'

Rebus raised a surprised eyebrow and accepted the receiver. It was, as he had known it would be, Detective Constable Holmes.

'Okay,' Holmes said. 'Costain no longer owes you that favour. He's listened to both tapes. He hasn't run all the necessary tests yet, but he's pretty convinced.'

'Go on.' Rebus was looking at Thomson, who was sitting, hands clasping knees, on the arm of the chair.

'The call we received last night,' said Holmes, 'the one from John MacFarlane admitting to the murder of Moira Bitter, originated from a portable telephone.'

'Interesting,' said Rebus, his eyes on Thomson. 'And what about the other one?'

'Well, the tape you gave me seems to be twice-removed.'

'What does that mean?'

'It means,' said Holmes, 'that according to Costain it's not just a recording, it's the recording of a recording.'

Rebus nodded, satisfied.

'Okay, thanks, Brian.' He put down the receiver.

'Good news or bad?' Thomson asked.

'A bit of both,' answered Rebus thoughtfully. Thomson had risen to his feet.

'I feel like a drink, Inspector. Can I get you one?'

'It's a bit early for me, I'm afraid,' Rebus said, looking at his watch. It was eleven o'clock: opening time. 'All right,' he said, 'just a small one.'

'The whisky's in the kitchen,' Thomson explained. 'I'll just be a moment.'

'Fine, sir, fine.'

Rebus listened as Thomson left the room and headed off towards the kitchen. He stood beside the desk, thinking through what he now knew. Then, hearing Thomson returning from the kitchen, floor-boards bending beneath his weight, he picked up the wastepaper basket from below the desk, and, as Thomson entered the room, proceeded to empty the contents in a heap on the sofa.

Thomson stood in the doorway, a glass of whisky in each hand, dumbstruck. 'What on earth are you doing?' he spluttered at last. But Rebus ignored him and started to pick through the now strewn contents of the bin, talking as he searched.

'It was pretty close to being fool-proof, Mr Thomson. Let me explain. The killer went to Moira Bitter's flat and talked her into letting him in despite the late hour. He murdered her quite callously, let's make no mistake about that. I've never seen so much premeditation in a case before. He cleaned the knife and returned it to its drawer. He was wearing gloves, of course, knowing John MacFarlane's fingerprints would be all over the flat, and he cleaned the knife precisely to disguise the fact that he *had* worn gloves. MacFarlane, you see, had not.'

Thomson took a gulp from one glass, but otherwise seemed rooted to the spot. His eyes had become vacant, as though picturing Rebus's story in his mind.

'MacFarlane,' Rebus continued, still rummaging, 'was summoned to Moira's flat. The message did come from her. He knew her voice well enough not to be fooled by someone else's voice. The killer sat outside Moira's flat, sat waiting for MacFarlane to arrive. Then the killer made one last call, this one to the police, in the guise of an hysterical MacFarlane. We know this last call was made on a car phone. The lab boys are very clever that way. The police are hoarders, too, you see, Mr Thomson. We make recordings of emergency calls made to us. It won't be hard to voice-print that call and try to match it to John MacFarlane. But it won't be John MacFarlane, will it?' Rebus paused for effect. 'It'll be you.'

Thomson gave a thin smile, but his grip on the two glasses had grown less steady, and whisky was dribbling from the angled lip of one of them.

'Ah-ha.' Rebus had found what he was looking for in the contents of the bin. With a pleased-as-punch grin on his unshaven, sleepless face, he pinched forefinger and thumb together and lifted them for his own and Thomson's inspection. He was holding a tiny sliver of brown recording tape.

'You see,' he continued, 'the killer had to lure MacFarlane to the murder scene. Having killed Moira, he went to his car, as I've said. There he had his portable telephone and a cassette recorder. He was a hoarder. He had kept all his answering machine tapes, including messages left by Moira at the height of their affair. He found the message he needed and he spliced it. He played this message to John MacFarlane's answering machine. All he had to do after that was wait. The message MacFarlane received was "Hello. I need to see you." There was a pause after the "hello". And that pause was where the splice was made in the tape, excising this.' Rebus looked at the sliver of tape. 'The one word "Kenneth". "Hello, Kenneth, I need to see you." It was Moira Bitter talking to you, Mr Thomson, talking to you a long time ago.'

Thomson hurled both glasses at once, so that they

arrowed in towards Rebus, who ducked. The glasses collided above his head, shards raining down on him. Thomson had reached the front door, had hauled it open even, before Rebus was on him, lunging, pushing the younger man forwards through the doorway and onto the tenement landing. Thomson's head hit the metal rails with a muted chime and he let out a single moan before collapsing. Rebus shook himself free of glass, feeling one or two tiny pieces nick him as he brushed a hand across his face. He brought a hand to his nose and inhaled deeply. His father had always said whisky would put hairs on his chest. Rebus wondered if the same miracle might be effected on his temples and the crown of his head ...

It had been the perfect murder.

Well, almost. But Kenneth Thomson had reckoned without Rebus's ability actually to believe someone inno-cent despite the evidence against him. The case against John MacFarlane had been overwhelming. Yet Rebus, feeling it to be wrong, had been forced to invent other scenarios, other motives and other means to the fairly chilling end. It wasn't enough that Moira had died – died at the hands of someone she knew. MacFarlane had to be implicated in her murder. The killer had been out to tag them both. But it was Moira the killer hated, hated because she had broken a friendship as well as a heart.

Rebus stood on the steps of the police station. Thomson was in a cell somewhere below his feet, somewhere below ground level. Confessing to everything. He would go to jail, while John MacFarlane, perhaps not realising his luck, had already been freed.

The streets were busy now. Lunchtime traffic, the reliable noises of the everyday. The sun was even managing to burst from its slumber. All of which reminded Rebus that his day was over. Time, all in all he felt, for a short

visit home, a shower and a change of clothes, and, God and
the Devil willing, some sleep.

The Dean Curse

The locals in Barnton knew him either as 'the Brigadier' or as 'that Army type who bought the West Lodge'. West Lodge was a huge but until recently neglected detached house set in a walled acre and a half of grounds and copses. Most locals were relieved that its high walls hid it from general view, the house itself being too angular, too gothic for modern tastes. Certainly, it was very large for the needs of a widower and his unsmiling daughter. Mrs MacLennan, who cleaned for the Brigadier, was pumped for information by curious neighbours, but could say only that Brigadier-General Dean had had some renovations done, that most of the house was habitable, that one room had become a library, another a billiard-room, another a study, another a makeshift gymnasium and so on. The listeners would drink this in deeply, yet it was never enough. What about the daughter? What about the Brigadier's background? What happened to his wife?

Shopkeepers too were asked for their thoughts. The Brigadier drove a sporty open-topped car which would pull in noisily to the side of the road to allow him to pop into this or that shop for a few things, including, each day at the same time, a bottle of something or other from the smarter of the two off-licences.

The grocer, Bob Sladden, reckoned that Brigadier-General Dean had been born nearby, even that he had lived for a few childhood years in West Lodge and so had retired there because of its carefree connections. But Miss Dalrymple, who at ninety-three was as old as anyone in that part of Barnton, could not recall any family named Dean living at West Lodge. Could not, indeed, recall any Deans ever living in this 'neck' of Barnton, with the exception of Sam Dean. But when pressed about Sam Dean, she merely shook her head and said, 'He was no good, that one, and got what he deserved. The Great War saw to him.' Then she would nod slowly, thoughtfully, and nobody would be any further forward.

Speculation grew wilder as no new facts came to light, and in The Claymore public bar one afternoon, a bar never patronised by the Brigadier (and who'd ever heard of an Army man not liking his drink?), a young out-of-work plasterer named Willie Barr came up with a fresh proposition.

'Maybe Dean isn't his real name.'

But everyone around the pool table laughed at that and Willie just shrugged, readying to play his next shot. 'Well,' he said, 'real name or not, I wouldn't climb over that daughter of his to get to any of you lot.'

Then he played a double off the cushion, but missed. Missed not because the shot was difficult or he'd had too many pints of Snakebite, but because his cue arm jerked at the noise of the explosion.

It was a fancy car all right, a Jaguar XJS convertible, its bodywork a startling red. Nobody in Barnton could mistake it for anyone else's car. Besides, everyone was used to it revving to its loud roadside halt, was used to its contented ticking-over while the Brigadier did his shopping. Some complained – though never to his face – about the noise, about the fumes from the exhaust. They couldn't say why he never switched off the ignition. He always seemed to want to be ready for a quick getaway. On this particular afternoon, the getaway was quicker even than usual, a squeal of tyres as the car jerked out into the road and sped past the shops. Its driver seemed ready actually to disregard the red stop light at the busy junction. He never got the chance. There was a ball of flames where the car had been and the heart-stopping sound of the explosion. Twisted metal flew into the air, then down again, wounding passers-by, burning skin. Shop windows blew in, shards of fine glass finding soft targets. The traffic lights turned to green, but nothing moved in the street.

For a moment, there was a silence punctuated only by the arrival on terra firma of bits of speedometer, headlamp, even steering-wheel. Then the screaming started, as people realised they'd been wounded. More curdling still though were the silences, the dumb horrified faces of people who would never forget this moment, whose shock would disturb each wakeful night.

And then there was a man, standing in a doorway, the doorway of what had been the wine merchant's. He carried a bottle with him, carefully wrapped in green paper, and his mouth was open in surprise. He dropped the bottle with a crash when he realised his car was not where he had left it, realising that the roaring he had heard and thought he recognised was that of his own car being driven away. At his feet, he saw one of his driving gloves lying on the pavement in front of him. It was still smouldering. Only five minutes before, it had been lying on the leather of his passenger seat. The wine merchant was standing beside him now, pale and shaking, looking in dire need of a drink. The Brigadier nodded towards the carcass of his sleek red Jaguar.

'That should have been me,' he said. Then: 'Do you mind if I use your telephone?'

John Rebus threw *The Dain Curse* up in the air, sending it spinning towards his living-room ceiling. Gravity caught up with it just short of the ceiling and pulled it down hard, so that it landed open against the uncarpeted floor. It was a cheap copy, bought secondhand and previously much read.

But not by Rebus; he'd got as far as the beginning of the third section, 'Quesada', before giving up, before tossing what many regard as Hammett's finest novel into the air. Its pages fell away from the spine as it landed, scattering chapters. Rebus growled. The telephone had, as though prompted by the book's demise, started ringing. Softly, insistently. Rebus picked up the apparatus and studied it. It was six o'clock on the evening of his first rest-day in what seemed like months. Who would be phoning him? Pleasure or business? And which would he prefer it to be? He put the receiver to his ear.

'Yes?' His voice was non-committal.

'DI Rebus?' It was work then. Rebus grunted a response. 'DC Coupar here, sir. The Chief thought you'd be interested.' There was a pause for effect. 'A bomb's just gone off in Barnton.'

Rebus stared at the sheets of print lying all around him. He asked the Detective Constable to repeat the message.

'A bomb, sir. In Barnton.'

'What? A World War Two leftover you mean?'

'No, sir. Nothing like that. Nothing like that at all.'

There was a line of poetry in Rebus's head as he drove out towards one of Edinburgh's many quiet middle-class districts, the sort of place where nothing happened, the sort of place where crime was measured in a yearly attempted break-in or the theft of a bicycle. That was Barnton. The line of poetry hadn't been written about Barnton. It had been written about Slough.

It's my own fault, Rebus was thinking, for being disgusted at how far-fetched that Hammett book was. Entertaining, yes, but you could strain credulity only so far, and Dashiell Hammett had taken that strain like the anchor-man on a tug-o'-war team, pulling with all his might. Coincidence after coincidence, plot after plot, corpse following corpse like something off an assembly line.

Far-fetched, definitely. But then what was Rebus to make of his telephone call? He'd checked: it wasn't 1st April. But then he wouldn't put it past Brian Holmes or one of his other colleagues to pull a stunt on him just because he was having a day off, just because he'd carped on about it for the previous few days. Yes, this had Holmes' fingerprints all over it. Except for one thing.

The radio reports. The police frequency was full of it; and when Rebus switched on his car radio to the local commercial channel, the news was there, too. Reports of an explosion in Barnton, not far from the roundabout. It is thought a car has exploded. No further details, though there are thought to be many casualties. Rebus shook his head and drove, thinking of the poem again, thinking of anything that would stop him focussing on the truth of the news. A car bomb? *A car bomb?* In Belfast, yes, maybe even on occasion in London. But here in Edinburgh? Rebus blamed himself. If only he hadn't cursed Dashiell Hammett, if only he hadn't sneered at his book, at its exaggerations and its melodramas, if only … Then none of this would have happened.

But of course it would. It had.

The road had been blocked off. The ambulances had left with their cargo. Onlookers stood four deep behind the orange and white tape of the hastily erected cordon. There was just the one question: how many dead? The answer seemed to be: just the one. The driver of the car. An Army bomb disposal unit had materialised from somewhere and, for want of anything else to do, was checking the shops either side of the street. A line of policemen, aided so far as Rebus could judge by more Army personnel, was moving slowly up the road, mostly on hands and knees, in what an outsider might regard as some bizarre slow-motion race. They carried with them polythene bags, into which they dropped anything they found. The whole scene was one of brilliantly organised confusion and it didn't take Rebus longer than a couple of minutes to detect the mastermind behind it all – Superintendent 'Farmer' Watson. 'Farmer' only behind his back, of course, and a nickname which matched both his north-of-Scotland background and his at times agricultural methods. Rebus decided to skirt around his superior officer and glean what he could from the various less senior officers present.

He had come to Barnton with a set of preconceptions and it took time for these to be corrected. For example, he'd premised that the person in the car, the as-yet-unidentified deceased, would be the car's owner and that this person would have been the target of the bomb attack (the evidence all around most certainly pointed to a bomb, rather than spontaneous combustion, say, or any other more likely explanation). Either that or the car might be stolen or borrowed, and the driver some sort of terrorist, blown apart by his own device before he could leave it at its intended destination. There were certainly Army installations around Edinburgh: barracks, armouries, listening posts. Across the Forth lay what was left of Rosyth naval dockyard, as well as the underground installation at Pitreavie. There were targets. Bomb meant terrorist meant target. That was how it always was.

But not this time. This time there was an important difference. The apparent target escaped, by dint of leaving his car for a couple of minutes to nip into a shop. But while he was in the shop someone had tried to steal his car, and that person was now drying into the tarmac beneath the knees of the crawling policemen. This much Rebus learned before Superintendent Watson caught sight of him, caught sight of him smiling wryly at the car thief's luck. It wasn't every day you got the chance to steal a Jaguar XJS ... but what a day to pick.

'Inspector!' Farmer Watson beckoned for Rebus to join him, which Rebus, ironing out his smile, did.

Before Watson could start filling him in on what he already knew, Rebus himself spoke.

'Who was the target, sir?'

'A man called Dean.' Meaningful pause. 'Brigadier-General Dean, retired.'

Rebus nodded. 'I thought there were a lot of Tommies about.'

'We'll be working with the Army on this one, John. That's how it's done, apparently. And then there's Scotland Yard, too. Their anti-terrorist people.'

'Too many cooks if you ask me, sir.'

Watson nodded. 'Still, these buggers are supposed to be specialised.'

'And we're only good for solving the odd drunk driving or domestic, eh, sir?'

The two men shared a smile at this. Rebus nodded towards the wreck of the car. 'Any idea who was behind the wheel?'

Watson shook his head. 'Not yet. And not much to go on either. We may have to wait till a mum or girlfriend reports him missing.'

'Not even a description?'

'None of the passers-by is fit to be questioned. Not yet anyway.'

'So what about Brigadier-General Whassisname?'

'Dean.'

'Yes. Where is he?'

'He's at home. A doctor's been to take a look at him, but he seems all right. A bit shocked.'

'A bit? Someone rips the arse out of his car and he's a *bit* shocked?' Rebus sounded doubtful. Watson's eyes were fixed on the advancing line of debris collectors.

'I get the feeling he's seen worse.' He turned to Rebus. 'Why don't you have a word with him, John? See what you think.'

Rebus nodded slowly. 'Aye, why not,' he said. 'Anything for a laugh, eh, sir?'

Watson seemed stuck for a reply, and by the time he'd formed one Rebus had wandered back through the cordon, hands in trouser pockets, looking for all the world like a man out for a stroll on a balmy summer's evening. Only then did the Superintendent remember that this was Rebus's day off. He wondered if it had been such a bright idea to send him off to talk to Brigadier-General Dean. Then he smiled, recalling that he had brought John Rebus out here precisely because something didn't quite feel right. If he could feel it, Rebus would feel it too, and would burrow deep to find its source – as deep as necessary and, perhaps, deeper than was seemly for a Superintendent to go.

Yes, there were times when even Detective Inspector John Rebus came in useful.

It was a big house. Rebus would go further. It was bigger than the last hotel he'd stayed in, though of a similar style: closer to Hammer Films than *House and Garden*. A hotel in Scarborough it had been; three days of lust with a divorced school-dinner lady. School-dinner ladies hadn't been like that in Rebus's day ... or maybe he just hadn't been paying attention.

He paid attention now. Paid attention as an Army uniform opened the door of West Lodge to him. He'd already had to talk his way past a mixed guard on the gate – an apologetic PC and two uncompromising squaddies. That was why he'd started thinking back to Scarborough – to stop himself punching those squaddies in their square-chinned faces. The closer he came to Brigadier-General Dean, the more aggressive and unlovely the soldiers seemed. The two on the gate were like lambs compared to the one on the main door of the house, yet he in his turn was meekness itself compared to the one who led Rebus into a well-appointed living-room and told him to wait.

Rebus hated the Army – with good reason. He had seen the soldier's lot from the inside and it had left him with a resentment so huge that to call it a 'chip on the shoulder' was to do it an injustice. Chip? Right now it felt like a whole transport cafe! There was only one thing for it. Rebus made for the sideboard, sniffed the contents of the decanter sitting there and poured himself an inch of whisky. He was draining the contents of the glass into his mouth when the door opened.

Rebus had brought too many preconceptions with him today. Brigadier-Generals were squat, ruddy-faced men, with stiff moustaches and VSOP noses, a few silvered wisps of Brylcreemed hair and maybe even a walking stick. They retired in their seventies and babbled of campaigns over dinner.

Not so Brigadier-General Dean. He looked to be in his mid- to late-fifties. He stood over six feet tall, had a youthful face and vigorous dark hair. He was slim too, with no sign of a retirement gut or a port drinker's red-veined cheeks. He looked twice as fit as Rebus felt and for a moment the policeman actually caught himself straightening his back and squaring his shoulders.

'Good idea,' said Dean, joining Rebus at the sideboard. 'Mind if I join you?' His voice was soft, blurred at the edges, the voice of an educated man, a civilised man. Rebus tried hard to imagine Dean giving orders to a troop of hairy-fisted Tommies. Tried, but failed.

'Detective Inspector Rebus,' he said by way of introduction. 'Sorry to bother you like this, sir, but there are a few questions –'

Dean nodded, finishing his own drink and offering to replenish Rebus's.

'Why not?' agreed Rebus. Funny thing though: he could

swear this whisky wasn't whisky at all but whiskey – Irish whiskey. Softer than the Scottish stuff, lacking an edge.

Rebus sat on the sofa, Dean on a well-used armchair. The Brigadier-General offered a toast of *slainte* before starting on his second drink, then exhaled noisily.

'Had to happen sooner or later, I suppose,' he said.

'Oh?'

Dean nodded slowly. 'I worked in Ulster for a time. Quite a long time. I suppose I was fairly high up in the tree there. I always knew I was a target. The Army knew, too, of course, but what can you do? You can't put bodyguards on every soldier who's been involved in the conflict, can you?'

'I suppose not, sir. But I assume you took precautions?'

Dean shrugged. 'I'm not in *Who's Who* and I've got an unlisted telephone number. I don't even use my rank much, to be honest.'

'But some of your mail might be addressed to Brigadier-General Dean?'

A wry smile. 'Who gave you that impression?'

'What impression, sir?'

'The impression of rank. I'm not a Brigadier-General. I retired with the rank of Major.'

'But the –'

'The what? The locals? Yes, I can see how gossip might lead to exaggeration. You know how it is in a place like this, Inspector. An incomer who keeps himself to himself. A military air. They put two and two together then multiply it by ten.'

Rebus nodded thoughtfully. 'I see.' Trust Watson to be wrong even in the fundamentals. 'But the point I was trying to make about your mail still stands, sir. What I'm wondering, you see, is how they found you.'

Dean smiled quietly. 'The IRA are quite sophisticated these days, Inspector. For all I know, they could have hacked into a computer, bribed someone in the know, or maybe it was just a fluke, sheer chance.' He shrugged. 'I suppose we'll have to think of moving somewhere else now, starting all over again. Poor Jacqueline.'

'Jacqueline being?'

'My daughter. She's upstairs, terribly upset. She's due to start university in October. It's her I feel sorry for.'

Rebus looked sympathetic. He felt sympathetic. One thing about Army life and police life – both could have a devastating effect on your personal life.

'And your wife, sir?'

'Dead, Inspector. Several years ago.' Dean examined his now empty glass. He looked his years now, looked like someone who needed a rest. But there was something other about him, something cool and hard. Rebus had met all types in the Army – and since. Veneers could no longer fool him, and behind Major Dean's sophisticated veneer he could glimpse something other, something from the man's past. Dean hadn't just been a good soldier. At one time he'd been lethal.

'Do you have any thoughts on how they might have found you, sir?'

'Not really.' Dean closed his eyes for a second. There was resignation in his voice. 'What matters is that they *did* find me.' His eyes met Rebus's. 'And they can find me again.'

Rebus shifted in his seat. Christ, what a thought. What a, well, time-bomb. To always be watching, always expecting, always fearing. And not just for yourself.

'I'd like to talk to Jacqueline, sir. It may be that she'll have some inkling as to how they were able to –'

But Dean was shaking his head. 'Not just now, Inspector. Not yet. I don't want her – well, you understand. Besides, I'd imagine that this will all be out of your hands by tomorrow. I believe some people from the Anti-Terrorist Branch are on their way up here. Between them and the Army … well, as I say, it'll be out of your hands.'

Rebus felt himself prickling anew. But Dean was right,

33

wasn't he? Why strain yourself when tomorrow it would be someone else's weight? Rebus pursed his lips, nodded, and stood up.

'I'll see you to the door,' said the Major, taking the empty glass from Rebus's hand.

As they passed into the hallway, Rebus caught a glimpse of a young woman – Jacqueline Dean presumably. She had been hovering by the telephone-table at the foot of the staircase, but was now starting up the stairs themselves, her hand thin and white on the bannister. Dean, too, watched her go. He half-smiled, half-shrugged at Rebus.

'She's upset,' he explained unnecessarily. But she hadn't looked upset to Rebus. She had looked like she was moping.

The next morning, Rebus went back to Barnton. Wooden boards had been placed over some of the shop windows, but otherwise there were few signs of yesterday's drama. The guards on the gate to West Lodge had been replaced by beefy plainclothes men with London accents. They carried portable radios, but otherwise might have been bouncers, debt collectors or bailiffs. They radioed the house. Rebus couldn't help thinking that a shout might have done the job for them, but they were in love with technology; you could see that by the way they held their radio-sets. He'd seen soldiers holding a new gun the same way.

'The guvnor's coming down to see you,' one of the men said at last. Rebus kicked his heels for a full minute before the man arrived.

'What do you want?'

'Detective Inspector Rebus. I talked with Major Dean yesterday and –'

The man snapped. 'Who told you his rank?'

'Major Dean himself. I just wondered if I might –'

'Yes, well there's no need for that, Inspector. We're in charge now. Of course you'll be kept informed.'

The man turned and walked back through the gates with a steady, determined stride. The guards were smirking as they closed the gates behind their 'guvnor'. Rebus felt like a snubbed schoolboy, left out of the football game. Sides had been chosen and there he stood, unwanted. He could smell London on these men, that cocky superiority of a self-chosen elite. What did they call themselves? C13 or somesuch, the Anti-Terrorist Branch. Closely linked to Special Branch, and everyone knew the trade name for Special Branch – Smug Bastards.

The man had been a little younger than Rebus, well-groomed and accountant-like. More intelligent, for sure, than the gorillas on the gate, but probably well able to handle himself. A neat pistol might well have been hidden under the arm of his close-fitting suit. None of that mattered. What mattered was that the captain was leaving Rebus out of his team. It rankled; and when something rankled, it rankled hard.

Rebus had walked half a dozen paces away from the gates when he half-turned and stuck his tongue out at the guards. Then, satisfied with this conclusion to his morning's labours, he decided to make his own inquiries. It was eleven-thirty. If you want to find out about someone, reasoned a thirsty Rebus, visit his local.

The reasoning, in this case, proved false: Dean had never been near The Claymore.

'The daughter came in though,' commented one young man. There weren't many people in the pub at this early stage of the day, save a few retired gentlemen who were in conversation with three or four reporters. The barman, too, was busy telling his life story to a young female hack, or rather, into her tape recorder. This made getting served difficult, despite the absence of a lunchtime scrum. The young man had solved this problem, however, reaching behind the bar to refill his glass with a mixture of cider and lager, leaving money on the bartop.

'Oh?' Rebus nodded towards the three-quarters full glass. 'Have another?'

'When this one's finished I will.' He drank greedily, by which time the barman had finished with his confessions – much (judging by her face) to the relief of the reporter. 'Pint of Snakebite, Paul,' called the young man. When the drink was before him, he told Rebus that his name was Willie Barr and that he was unemployed.

'You said you saw the daughter in here?' Rebus was anxious to have his questions answered before the alcohol took effect on Barr.

'That's right. She came in pretty regularly.'

'By herself?'

'No, always with some guy.'

'One in particular, you mean?'

But Willie Barr laughed, shaking his head. 'A different one every time. She's getting a bit of a name for herself. And,' he raised his voice for the barman's benefit, 'she's not even eighteen, I'd say.'

'Were they local lads?'

'None I recognised. Never really spoke to them.' Rebus swirled his glass, creating a foamy head out of nothing.

'Any Irish accents among them?'

'In here?' Barr laughed. 'Not in here. Christ, no. Actually, she hasn't been in for a few weeks, now that I think of it. Maybe her father put a stop to it, eh? I mean, how would it look in the Sunday papers? Brigadier's daughter slumming it in Barnton.'

Rebus smiled. 'It's not exactly a slum though, is it?'

'True enough, but her boyfriends ... I mean, there was more of the car mechanic than the estate agent about them. Know what I mean?' He winked. 'Not that a bit of rough ever hurt *her* kind, eh?' Then he laughed again and suggested a game or two of pool, a pound a game or a fiver if the detective were a betting man.

But Rebus shook his head. He thought he knew now why

Willie Barr was drinking so much: he was flush. And the reason he was flush was that he'd been telling his story to the papers – for a price. *Brigadier's Daughter Slumming It*. Yes, he'd been telling tales all right, but there was little chance of them reaching their intended audience. The Powers That Be would see to that.

Barr was helping himself to another pint as Rebus made to leave the premises.

It was late in the afternoon when Rebus received his visitor, the Anti-Terrorist accountant.

'A Mr Matthews to see you,' the Desk Sergeant had informed Rebus, and 'Matthews' he remained, giving no hint of rank or proof of identity. He had come, he said, to 'have it out' with Rebus.

'What were you doing in The Claymore?'

'Having a drink.'

'You were asking questions. I've already told you, Inspector Rebus, we can't have –'

'I know, I know.' Rebus raised his hands in a show of surrender. 'But the more furtive you lot are, the more interested I become.'

Matthews stared silently at Rebus. Rebus knew that the man was weighing up his options. One, of course, was to go to Farmer Watson and have Rebus warned off. But if Matthews were as canny as he looked, he would know this might have the opposite effect from that intended. Another option was to talk to Rebus, to ask him what he wanted to know.

'What do you want to know?' Matthews said at last.

'I want to know about Dean.'

Matthews sat back in his chair. 'In strictest confidence?'

Rebus nodded. 'I've never been known as a clipe.'

'A clipe?'

'Someone who tells tales,' Rebus explained. Matthews was thoughtful.

'Very well then,' he said. 'For a start, Dean is an alias, a very necessary one. During his time in the Army Major Dean worked in Intelligence, mostly in West Germany but also for a time in Ulster. His work in both spheres was very important, crucially important. I don't need to go into details. His last posting was West Germany. His wife was killed in a terrorist attack, almost certainly IRA. We don't think they had targeted her specifically. She was just in the wrong place with the wrong number plates.'

'A car bomb?'

'No, a bullet. Through the windscreen, point-blank. Major Dean asked to be ... he was invalided out. It seemed best. We provided him with a change of identity, of course.'

'I thought he looked a bit young to be retired. And the daughter, how did she take it?'

'She was never told the full details, not that I'm aware of. She was in boarding school in England.' Matthews paused. 'It was for the best.'

Rebus nodded. 'Of course, nobody'd argue with that. But why did – Dean – choose to live in Barnton?'

Matthews rubbed his left eyebrow, then pushed his spectacles back up his sharply sloping nose. 'Something to do with an aunt of his,' he said. 'He spent holidays there as a boy. His father was Army, too, posted here, there and everywhere. Never the most stable upbringing. I think Dean had happy memories of Barnton.'

Rebus shifted in his seat. He couldn't know how long Matthews would stay, how long he would continue to answer Rebus's questions. And there were so many questions.

'What about the bomb?'

'Looks like the IRA, all right. Standard fare for them, all the hallmarks. It's still being examined, of course, but we're pretty sure.'

'And the deceased?'

'No clues yet. I suppose he'll be reported missing sooner or later. We'll leave that side of things to you.'

'Gosh, thanks.' Rebus waited for his sarcasm to penetrate, then, quickly: 'How does Dean get on with his daughter?'

Matthews was caught off-guard by the question. He blinked twice, three times, then glanced at his wristwatch.

'All right, I suppose,' he said at last, making show of scratching a mark from his cuff. 'I can't see what ... Look, Inspector, as I say, we'll keep you fully informed. But meantime –'

'Keep out of your hair?'

'If you want to put it like that.' Matthews stood up. 'Now I really must be getting back –'

'To London?'

Matthews smiled at the eagerness in Rebus's voice. 'To Barnton. Don't worry, Inspector, the more *you* keep out of *my* hair, the quicker I can get out of yours. Fair enough?' He shot a hand out towards Rebus, who returned the almost painful grip.

'Fair enough,' said Rebus. He ushered Matthews from the room and closed the door again, then returned to his seat. He slouched as best he could in the hard, uncomfortable chair and put his feet up on the desk, examining his scuffed shoes. He tried to feel like Sam Spade, but failed. His legs soon began to ache and he slid them from the surface of the desk. The coincidences in Dashiell Hammett had nothing on the coincidence of someone nicking a car seconds before it exploded. Someone must have been watching, ready to detonate the device. But if they were watching, how come they didn't spot that Dean, the intended victim, wasn't the one to drive off?

Either there was more to this than met the eye, or else there was less. Rebus was wary – very wary. He'd already made far too many prejudgments, had already been proved wrong too many times. Keep an open mind, that was the secret. An open mind and an inquiring one. He nodded his head slowly, his eyes on the door.

'Fair enough,' he said quietly. 'I'll keep out of your hair, Mr Matthews, but that doesn't necessarily mean I'm leaving the barber's.'

The Claymore might not have been Barnton's most salubrious establishment, but it was as Princes Street's Caledonian Hotel in comparison with the places Rebus visited that evening. He began with the merely seedy bars, the ones where each quiet voice seemed to contain a lifetime's resentment, and then moved downwards, one rung of the ladder at a time. It was slow work; the bars tended to be in a ring around Edinburgh, sometimes on the outskirts or in the distant housing schemes, sometimes nearer the centre than most of the population would dare to think.

Rebus hadn't made many friends in his adult life, but he had his network of contacts and he was as proud of it as any grandparent would be of their extended family. They were like cousins, these contacts; mostly they knew each other, at least by reputation, but Rebus never spoke to one about another, so that the extent of the chain could only be guessed at. There were those of his colleagues who, in Major Dean's words, added two and two, then multiplied by ten. John Rebus, it was reckoned, had as big a net of 'snitches' as any copper on the force bar none.

It took four hours and an outlay of over forty pounds before Rebus started to catch a glimpse of a result. His basic question, though couched in vague and imprecise terms, was simple: have any car thieves vanished off the face of the earth since yesterday?

One name was uttered by three very different people in three distinct parts of the city: Brian Cant. The name meant little to Rebus.

'It wouldn't,' he was told. 'Brian only shifted across here

from the west a year or so ago. He's got form from when he was a nipper, but he's grown smart since then. When the Glasgow cops started sniffing, he moved operations.' The detective listened, nodded, drank a watered-down whisky, and said little. Brian Cant grew from a name into a description, from a description into a personality. But there was something more.

'You're not the only one interested in him,' Rebus was told in a bar in Gorgie. 'Somebody else was asking questions a wee while back. Remember Jackie Hanson?'

'He used to be CID, didn't he?'

'That's right, but not any more ...'

Not just any old banger for Brian Cant: he specialised in 'quality motors'. Rebus eventually got an address: a third-floor tenement flat near Powderhall race-track. A young man answered the door. His name was Jim Cant, Brian's younger brother. Rebus saw that Jim was scared, nervous. He chipped away at the brother quickly, explaining that he was there because he thought Brian might be dead. That he knew all about Cant's business, but that he wasn't interested in pursuing this side of things, except insofar as it might shed light on the death. It took a little more of this, then the brother opened up.

'He said he had a customer interested in a car,' Jim Cant explained. 'An Irishman, he said.'

'How did he know the man was Irish?'

'Must have been the voice. I don't think they met. Maybe they did. The man was interested in a specific car.'

'A red Jaguar?'

'Yeah, convertible. Nice cars. The Irishman even knew where there was one. It seemed a cinch, that's what Brian kept saying. A cinch.'

'He didn't think it would be hard to steal?'

'Five seconds' work, that's what he kept saying. I thought it sounded too easy. I told him so.' He bent over in his chair, grabbing at his knees and sinking his head between them. 'Ach, Brian, what the hell have you done?'

Rebus tried to comfort the young man as best he could with brandy and tea. He drank a mug of tea himself, wandering through the flat, his mind thrumming. Was he blowing things up out of all proportion? Maybe. He'd made mistakes before, not so much errors of judgment as errors of jumping the gun. But there was something about all of this ... Something.

'Do you have a photo of Brian?' he asked as he was leaving. 'A recent one would be best.' Jim Cant handed him a holiday snap.

'We went to Crete last summer,' he explained. 'It was magic.' Then, holding the door open for Rebus: 'Don't I have to identify him or something?'

Rebus thought of the scrapings which were all that remained of what may or may not have been Brian Cant. He shook his head. 'I'll let you know,' he said. 'If we need you, we'll let you know.'

The next day was Sunday, day of rest. Rebus rested in his car, parked fifty yards or so along the road from the gates to West Lodge. He put his radio on, folded his arms and sank down into the driver's seat. This was more like it. The Hollywood private eye on a stakeout. Only in the movies, a stakeout could be whittled away to a few minutes' footage. Here, it was measured in a slow ticking of seconds ... minutes ... quarter hours.

Eventually, the gates opened and a figure hurried out, fairly trotting along the pavement as though released from bondage. Jacqueline Dean was wearing a denim jacket, short black skirt and thick black tights. A beret sat awkwardly on her cropped dark hair and she pressed the palm of her hand to it from time to time to stop it sliding off altogether. Rebus locked his car before following her. He kept to the other side of the road, wary not so much from fear that she might spot him but because C13 might have put a tail on her, too.

She stopped at the local newsagent's first and came out heavy-laden with Sunday papers. Rebus, making to cross the road, a Sunday-morning stroller, studied her face. What was the expression he'd thought of the first time he'd seen her? Yes, *moping*. There was still something of that in her liquid eyes, the dark shadows beneath. She was making for the corner shop now. Doubtless she would appear with rolls or bacon or butter or milk. All the things Rebus seemed to find himself short of on a Sunday, no matter how hard he planned.

He felt in his jacket pockets, but found nothing of comfort there, just the photograph of Brian Cant. The window of the corner shop, untouched by the blast, contained a dozen or so personal ads, felt-tipped onto plain white postcards. He glanced at these, and past them, through the window itself to where Jacqueline was making her purchases. Milk and rolls: elementary, my dear Conan Doyle. Waiting for her change, she half-turned her head towards the window. Rebus concentrated on the postcards. 'Candy, Masseuse' vied for attention with 'Pram and carry-cot for sale', 'Babysitting considered', and 'Lada, seldom used'. Rebus was smiling, almost despite himself, when the door of the shop tinkled open.

'Jacqueline?' he said. She turned towards him. He was holding open his ID. 'Mind if I have a word, Miss Dean?'

Major Dean was pouring himself a glass of Irish whiskey when the drawing-room door opened.

'Mind if I come in?' Rebus's words were directed not at Dean but at Matthews, who was seated in a chair by the window, one leg crossed over the other, hands gripping the arm-rests. He looked like a nervous businessman on an airplane, trying not to let his neighbour see his fear.

'Inspector Rebus,' he said tonelessly. 'I thought I could feel my scalp tingle.'

Rebus was already in the room. He closed the door behind him. Dean gestured with the decanter, but Rebus shook his head.

'How did you get in?' Matthews asked.

'Miss Dean was good enough to escort me through the gate. You've changed the guard detail again. She told them I was a friend of the family.'

Matthews nodded. 'And are you, Inspector? Are you a friend of the family?'

'That depends on what you mean by friendship.'

Dean had seated himself on the edge of his chair, steadying the glass with both hands. He didn't seem quite the figure he had been on the day of the explosion. A reaction, Rebus didn't doubt. There had been a quiet euphoria on the day; now came the aftershock.

'Where's Jacqui?' Dean asked, having paused with the glass to his lips.

'Upstairs,' Rebus explained. 'I thought it would be better if she didn't hear this.'

Matthews' fingers plucked at the arm-rests. 'How much does she know?'

'Not much. Not yet. Maybe she'll work it out for herself.'

'So, Inspector, we come to the reason why you're here.'

'I'm here,' Rebus began, 'as part of a murder inquiry. I thought that's why you were here, too, Mr Matthews. Maybe I'm wrong. Maybe you're here to cover up rather than bring to light.'

Matthews' smile was momentary. But he said nothing.

'I didn't go looking for the culprits,' Rebus went on. 'As you said, Mr Matthews, that was *your* department. But I did wonder who the victim was. The accidental victim, as I thought. A young car thief called Brian Cant, that would be my guess. He stole cars to order. A client asked him for a red open-top Jag, even told him where he might find one. The client told him about Major Dean. Very specifically about Major Dean, right down to the fact that every day he'd nip into the wine-shop on the main street.' Rebus turned to Dean. 'A bottle of Irish a day, is it, sir?'

Dean merely shrugged and drained his glass.

'Anyway, that's what your daughter told me. So all Brian Cant had to do was wait near the wine-shop. You'd get out of your car, leave it running, and while you were in the shop he could drive the car away. Only it bothered me that the client – Cant's brother tells me he spoke with an Irish accent – knew so much, making it easy for Cant. What was stopping this person from stealing the car himself?'

'And the answer came to you?' Matthews suggested, his voice thick with irony.

Rebus chose to avoid his tone. He was still watching Dean. 'Not straight away, not even then. But when I came to the house, I couldn't help noticing that Miss Dean seemed a bit strange. Like she was waiting for a phone call from someone and that someone had let her down. It's easy to be specific now, but at the time it just struck me as odd. I asked her about it this morning and she admitted it's because she's been jilted. A man she'd been seeing, and seeing regularly, had suddenly stopped calling. I asked her about him, but she couldn't be very helpful. They never went to his flat, for example. He drove a flashy car and had plenty of money, but she was vague about what he did for a living.'

Rebus took a photograph from his pocket and tossed it into Dean's lap. Dean froze, as though it were some hair-trigger grenade.

'I showed her a photograph of Brian Cant. Yes, that was the name of her boyfriend – Brian Cant. So you see, it was small wonder she hadn't heard from him.'

Matthews rose from the chair and stood before the window itself, but nothing he saw there seemed to please him, so he turned back into the room. Dean had found the courage to lift the photograph from his leg and place it on the floor. He got up too, and made for the decanter.

'For Christ's sake,' Matthews hissed, but Dean poured regardless.

Rebus's voice was level. 'I always thought it was a bit of a coincidence, the car being stolen only seconds before exploding. But then the IRA use remote control devices, don't they? So that someone in the vicinity could have triggered the bomb any time they liked. No need for all these long-term timers and what have you. I was in the SAS once myself.'

Matthews raised an eyebrow. 'Nobody told me that,' he said, sounding impressed for the first time.

'So much for Intelligence, eh?' Rebus answered. 'Speaking of which, you told me that Major Dean here was in Intelligence. I think I'd go further. Covert operations, that sort of thing? Counter-intelligence, subversion?'

'Now you're speculating, Inspector.'

Rebus shrugged. 'It doesn't really matter. What matters is that someone had been spying on Brian Cant, an ex-policeman called Jackie Hanson. He's a private detective these days. He won't say anything about his clients, of course, but I think I can put two and two together without multiplying the result. He was working for you, Major Dean, because you were interested in Brian Cant. Jacqueline was serious about him, wasn't she? So much so that she might have forsaken university. She tells me they were even talking of moving in together. You didn't want her to leave. When you found out what Cant did for a … a living, I suppose you'd call it, you came up with a plan.' Rebus was enjoying himself now, but tried to keep the pleasure out of his voice.

'You contacted Cant,' he went on, 'putting on an Irish accent. Your Irish accent is probably pretty good, isn't it,

Major? It would need to be, working in counter-intelligence. You told him all about a car – your car. You offered him a lot of money if he'd steal it for you and you told him precisely when and where he might find it. Cant was greedy. He didn't think twice.' Rebus noticed that he was sitting very comfortably in his own chair, whereas Dean looked ... the word that sprang to mind was 'rogue'. Matthews, too, was sparking internally, though his surface was all metal sheen, cold bodywork.

'You'd know how to make a bomb, that goes without saying. Wouldn't you, Major? Know thine enemy and all that. Like I say, I was in the SAS myself. What's more, you'd know how to make an IRA device, or one that looked like the work of the IRA. The remote was in your pocket. You went into the shop, bought your whiskey, and when you heard the car being driven off, you simply pressed the button.'

'Jacqueline.' Dean's voice was little more than a whisper. 'Jacqueline.' He rose to his feet, walked softly to the door and left the room. He appeared to have heard little or nothing of Rebus's speech. Rebus felt a pang of disappointment and looked towards Matthews, who merely shrugged.

'You cannot, of course, prove any of this, Inspector.'

'If I put my mind to it I can.'

'Oh, I've no doubt, no doubt.' Matthews paused. 'But will you?'

'He's mad, you've got to see that.'

'Mad? Well, he's unstable. Ever since his wife ...'

'No reason for him to murder Brian Cant.' Rebus helped himself to a whisky now, his legs curiously shaky. 'How long have you known?'

Matthews shrugged again. 'He tried a similar trick in Germany, apparently. It didn't work that time. So what do we do now? Arrest him? He'd be unfit to plead.'

'However it happens,' Rebus said, 'he's got to be made safe.'

'Absolutely.' Matthews was nodding agreement. He came to the sideboard. 'A hospital, somewhere he can be treated. He was a good soldier in his day. I've read his record. A good soldier. Don't worry, Inspector Rebus, he'll be "made safe" as you put it. He'll be taken care of.' A hand landed on Rebus's forearm. 'Trust me.'

Rebus trusted Matthews – about as far as he could spit into a Lothian Road headwind. He had a word with a reporter friend, but the man wouldn't touch the story. He passed Rebus on to an investigative journalist who did some ferreting, but there was little or nothing to be found. Rebus didn't know Dean's real name. He didn't know Matthews' first name or rank or even, to be honest, that he had been C13 at all. He might have been Army, or have inhabited that indefinite smear of operations somewhere between Army, Secret Service and Special Branch.

By the next day, Dean and his daughter had left West Lodge and a fortnight later it appeared in the window of an estate agent on George Street. The asking price seemed surprisingly low, if your tastes veered towards *The Munsters*. But the house would stay in the window for a long time to come.

Dean haunted Rebus's dreams for a few nights, no more. But how did you make safe a man like that? The Army had designed a weapon and that weapon had become misadjusted, its sights all wrong. You could dismantle a weapon. You could dismantle a man, too, come to that. But each and every piece was still as lethal as the whole. Rebus put aside fiction, put aside Hammett and the rest and of an evening read psychology books instead. But then they too, in their way, were fiction, weren't they? And so, too, in time became the case that was not a case of the man who had never been.

Being Frank

It wasn't easy, being Frank.

That's what everybody called him, when they weren't calling him a dirty old tramp or a scrounger or a layabout. Frank, they called him. Only the people at the hostel and at the Social Security bothered with his full name: Francis Rossetti Hyslop. Rossetti, he seemed to remember, not after the painter but after his sister the poet, Christina. Most often, a person – a person in authority – would read that name from the piece of paper they were holding and then look up at Frank, not quite in disbelief, but certainly wondering how he'd come so low.

He couldn't tell them that he was climbing higher all the time. That he preferred to live out of doors. That his face was weatherbeaten, not dirty. That a plastic bag was a convenient place to keep his possessions. He just nodded and shuffled his feet instead, the shuffle which had become his trademark.

'Here he comes,' his companions would cry. 'Here comes The Shuffler!' Alias Frank, alias Francis Rossetti Hyslop.

He spent much of the spring and autumn in Edinburgh. Some said he was mad, leaving in the summer months. That, after all, was when the pickings were richest. But he didn't like to bother the tourists, and besides, summer was for travelling. He usually walked north, through Fife and into Kinross or Perthshire, setting up camp by the side of a loch or up in the hills. And when he got bored, he'd move on. He was seldom moved on by gamekeepers or the police. Some of them he knew of old, of course. But others he encountered seemed to regard him more and more as some rare species, or, as one had actually said, a 'national monument'.

It was true, of course. Tramp meant to walk and that's what tramps used to do. The term 'gentleman of the road' used to be accurate. But the tramp was being replaced by the beggar: young, fit men who didn't move from the city and who were unrelenting in their search for spare change. That had never been Frank's way. He had his regulars of course, and often he only had to sit on a bench in The Meadows, a huge grassy plain bordered by tree-lined paths, and wait for the money to appear in his lap.

That's where he was when he heard the two men talking. It was a bright day, a lunchtime and there were few spaces to be had on the meagre supply of Meadows benches. Frank was sitting on one, arms folded, eyes closed, his legs stretched out in front of him with one foot crossed over the other. His three carrier bags were on the ground beside him, and his hat lay across his legs – not because he was hot especially, but because you never knew who might drop a coin in while you were dozing, or pretending to doze.

Maybe his was the only bench free. Maybe that's why the men sat down beside him. Well, 'beside him' was an exaggeration. They squeezed themselves onto the furthest edge of the bench, as far from him as possible. They couldn't be comfortable, squashed up like that and the thought brought a moment's smile to Frank's face.

But then they started to talk, not in a whisper but with voices lowered. The wind, though, swept every word into Frank's right ear. He tried not to tense as he listened, but it was difficult. Tried not to move, but his nerves were jangling.

'It's war,' one said. 'A council of war.'

War? He remembered reading in a newspaper recently about terrorists. Threats. A politician had said something about vigilance. Or was it vigilantes? A council of war: it sounded ominous. Maybe they were teasing him, trying to scare him from the bench so that they could have it for themselves. But he didn't think so. They were speaking in undertones; they didn't think he could hear. Or maybe they simply knew that it didn't matter whether an old tramp heard them or not. Who would believe him?

This was especially true in Frank's case. Frank believed that there was a worldwide conspiracy. He didn't know who was behind it, but he could see its tentacles stretching out across the globe. Everything was connected, that was the secret. Wars were connected by arms manufacturers, the same arms manufacturers who made the guns used in robberies, who made the guns used by crazy people in America when they went on the rampage in a shopping-centre or hamburger restaurant. So already you had a connection between hamburgers and dictators. Start from there and the thing just grew and grew.

And because Frank had worked this out, he wondered from time to time if *they* were after him. The dictators, the arms industry, or maybe even the people who made the buns for the hamburger chains. Because he *knew*. He wasn't crazy; he was sure of that.

'If I was,' he told one of his regulars, 'I wouldn't wonder if I was or not, would I?'

And she'd nodded, agreeing with him. She was a student at the university. A lot of students became regulars. They lived in Tollcross, Marchmont, Morningside, and had to pass through The Meadows on their way to the university buildings in George Square. She was studying psychology, and she told Frank something.

'You've got what they call an active fantasy life.'

Yes, he knew that. He made up lots of things, told himself stories. They whiled away the time. He pretended he'd been an RAF pilot, a spy, minor royalty, a slave-trader in Africa, a poet in Paris. But he *knew* he was making all these stories up, just as he knew that there really was a conspiracy.

And these two men were part of it.

'Rhodes,' one of them was saying now.

A council of war in Rhodes. So there was a Greek connection, too. Well, that made sense. He remembered stories about the generals and their junta. The terrorists were using Greece as their base. And Edinburgh was called the 'Athens of the north'. Yes! Of course! That's why they were basing themselves in Edinburgh too. A symbolic gesture. Had to be.

But who would believe him? That was the problem, being Frank. He'd told so many stories in the past, given the police so much information about the conspiracy, that now they just laughed at him and sent him on his way. Some of them thought he was looking for a night in the cells and once or twice they'd even obliged, despite his protests.

No, he didn't want to spend another night locked up. There was only one thing for it. He'd follow the men and see what he could find. Then he'd wait until tomorrow. They were talking about tomorrow, too, as if it was the start of their campaign. Well, tomorrow was Sunday and with a bit of luck if Frank hung around The Meadows, he'd bump into another of his regulars, one who might know exactly what to do.

Sunday morning was damp, blustery. Not the sort of day for a constitutional. This was fine by John Rebus: it meant there'd be fewer people about on Bruntsfield Links. Fewer men chipping golf-balls towards his head with a wavering cry of 'Fore!' Talk about crazy golf! He knew the Links had been used for this purpose for years and years, but all the same there were so many paths cutting through that it was a miracle no one had been killed.

He walked one circuit of the Links, then headed as usual

across Melville Drive and into The Meadows. Sometimes he'd stop to watch a kickabout. Other times, he kept his head down and just walked, hoping for inspiration. Sunday was too close to Monday for his liking and Monday always meant a backlog of work. Thinking about it never did any good, of course, but he found himself thinking of little else.

'Mr Rebus!'

But then The Meadows offered other distractions, too.

'Mr Rebus!'

'Hello, Frank.'

'Sit yourself down.'

Rebus lowered himself onto the bench. 'You look excited about something.'

Frank nodded briskly. Though he was seated, he shuffled his feet on the earth, making little dance movements. Then he looked around him, as though seeking interlopers.

Oh no, thought Rebus, here we go again.

'War,' Frank whispered. 'I heard two men talking about it.'

Rebus sighed. Talking to Frank was like reading one of the Sunday rags – except sometimes the stories *he* told were more believable. Today didn't sound like one of those days.

'Talking about war? Which war?'

'Terrorism, Mr Rebus. Has to be. They've had a council of war at Rhodes. That's in Greece.'

'They were Greek, were they?'

Frank wrinkled his face. 'I don't think so. I can give you a description of them though. They were both wearing suits. One was short and bald, the other one was young, taller, with black hair.'

'You don't often see international terrorists wearing suits these days, do you?' Rebus commented. Actually, he thought to himself, that's a lie: they're becoming more smartly dressed all the time.

In any case, Frank had an answer ready. 'Need a disguise though, don't they? I followed them.'

'Did you?' A kickabout was starting nearby. Rebus concentrated on the kick-off. He liked Frank, but there were times ...

'They went to a bed and breakfast near the Links.'

'Did they now?' Rebus nodded slowly.

'And they said it was starting *today*. Today, Mr Rebus.'

'They don't hang about, do they? Anything else?'

Frank frowned, thinking. 'Something about lavatories, or laboratories. Must have been laboratories, mustn't it? And money, they talked about that. Money they needed to set it up. That's about it.'

'Well, thanks for letting me know, Frank. I'll keep my ears open, see if I can hear any whispers. But listen, don't go following people in future. It could be dangerous, understand?'

Frank appeared to consider this. 'I see what you mean,' he said at last, 'but I'm tougher than I look, Mr Rebus.'

Rebus was standing now. 'Well, I'd better be getting along.' He slipped his hands into his pockets. The right hand emerged again holding a pound note. 'Here you go, Frank.' He began to hand the money over, then withdrew it again. Frank knew what was coming and grinned.

'Just one question,' Rebus said, as he always did. 'Where do you go in the winter?'

It was a question a lot of his cronies asked him. 'Thought you were dead,' they'd say each spring as he came walking back into their lives. His reply to Rebus was the same as ever: 'Ah, that would be telling, Mr Rebus. That's *my* secret.'

The money passed from one hand to the other and Rebus sauntered off towards Jawbone Walk, kicking a stone in front of him. Jawbone because of the whale's jawbone which made an arch at one end of the path. Frank knew that. Frank knew lots of things. But he knew, too, that

Rebus hadn't believed him. Well, more fool him. For over a year now they'd played this little game: where did Frank go in the winter? Frank wasn't sure himself why he didn't just say, I go to my sister's place in Dunbar. Maybe because it was the truth. Maybe because it *was* a secret.

Rebus looked to him like a man with secrets, too. Maybe one day Rebus would set out for a walk and never return home, would just keep on walking the way Frank himself had done. What was it the girl student had said?

'Sometimes I think we're *all* gentlemen of the road. It's just that most of us haven't got the courage to take that first step.'

Nonsense: that first step was the easiest. It was the hundredth, the thousandth, the millionth that was hard. But not as hard as going back, never as hard as that.

Rebus had counted the steps up to his second-floor flat many, many times. It always added up to the same number. So how come with the passing years there seemed to be more? Maybe it was the height of each step that was changing. Own up, John. For once, own up: it's *you* that's changing. You're growing older and stiffer. You never used to pause on the first-floor landing, never used to linger outside Mrs Cochrane's door, breathing in that smell unique to blackcurrant bushes and cat-pee.

How could one cat produce that amount of odour? Rebus had seen it many a time: a fat, smug-looking creature with hard eyes. He'd caught it on his own landing, turning guiltily to look at him before sprinting for the next floor up. But it was inside Mrs Cochrane's door just now. He could hear it mewling, clawing at the carpet, desperate to be outside. He wondered. Maybe Mrs Cochrane was ill? He'd noticed that recently her brass nameplate had become tarnished. She wasn't bothering to polish it any more. How old was she anyway? She seemed to have come with the tenement, almost as if they'd constructed the thing around her. Mr and Mrs Costello on the top floor had been here nigh-on twenty-five years, but they said she'd been here when they arrived. Same brass nameplate on her door. Different cat, of course, and a husband, too. Well, he'd been dead by the time Rebus and his wife – now ex-wife – had moved here, what, was it ten years ago now?

Getting old, John. Getting old. He clamped his left hand onto the bannister and somehow managed the last flight of steps to his door.

He started a crossword in one of the newspapers, put some jazz on the hi-fi, drank a pot of tea. Just another Sunday. Day of rest. But he kept catching glimpses of the week ahead. No good. He made another pot of tea and this time added a dollop of J&B to the mixture in his mug. Better. And then, naturally, the doorbell rang.

Jehovah's Witnesses. Well, Rebus had an answer ready for them. A friend in the know had said that Roman Catholics are taught how to counter the persuasive arguments of the JWs. Just tell them you're a Catholic and they'll go away.

'I'm Catholic,' he said. They didn't go away. There were two of them, dressed in dark suits. The younger one stood a little behind the older one. This didn't matter, since he was a good foot taller than his elder. He was holding a briefcase. The chief, however, held only a piece of paper. He was frowning, glancing towards this. He looked at Rebus, sizing him up, then back to the paper. He didn't appear to have heard what Rebus said.

'I'm Catholic,' Rebus repeated, but hollowly.

The man shook his head. Maybe they were foreign missionaries, come to convert the heathen. He consulted his scrap of paper again.

'I think this is the wrong address,' he said. 'There isn't a Mr Bakewell here?'

'Bakewell?' Rebus started to relax. A simple mistake; they weren't JWs. They weren't salesmen or cowboy builders or tinkers. Simply, they'd got the wrong flat. 'No,' he said. 'No Mr Bakewell here. And his tart's not here either.'

Oh, they laughed at that. Laughed louder than Rebus had expected. They were still laughing as they made their apologies and started back downstairs. Rebus watched them until they were out of sight. He'd stopped laughing almost before they'd begun. He checked that his keys were in his pocket, then slammed shut his door – but with himself still out on the landing.

Their footsteps sent sibilant echoes up towards the skylight. What was it about them? If pressed, he couldn't have said. There was just *something*. The way the smaller, older man had seemed to weigh him up in a moment, then mentioned Bakewell. The way the younger man had laughed so heartily, as if it were such a release. A release of what? Tension, obviously.

The footsteps had stopped. Outside Mrs Cochrane's door. Yes, that was the ting-ting-ting of her antiquated doorbell, the kind you pulled, tightening and releasing the spring on a bell inside the door. The door which was now being pulled open. The older man spoke.

'Mrs Cochrane?' Well, they'd got that name right. But then it was on her nameplate, wasn't it? *Anyone* could have guessed at it.

'Aye.' Mrs Cochrane, Rebus knew, was not unique in making this sound not only questioning but like a whole sentence. Yes, I'm Mrs Cochrane, and who might you be and what do you want?

'Councillor Waugh.'

Councillor! No, no, there was no problem: Rebus had paid his Poll Tax, always put his bin-bags out the night before, never earlier. They might be after Bakewell, but Rebus was in the clear.

'It's about the roadworks.'

'Roadworks?' echoed Mrs Cochrane.

Roadworks? thought Rebus.

'Yes, roadworks. Digging up the roads. You made a complaint about the roads. I've come to talk to you about it.'

'Roadworks? Here, you mean?'

He was patient, Rebus had to grant him that. 'That's right, Mrs Cochrane. The road outside.'

There was a bit more of this, then they all went indoors to talk over Mrs Cochrane's grievances. Rebus opened his own door and went in, too. Then, realising, he slapped his hand against his head. These were the two men Shuffling Frank had been talking about! Of course they were, only Frank had misheard: council of war was Councillor Waugh; Rhodes was roads. What else had Frank said? Something about money: well, that might be the money for the repairs. That it was all planned to start on Sunday: and here they were, on Sunday, ready to talk to the residents about roadworks.

What roadworks? The road outside was clear, and Rebus hadn't heard any gossip concerning work about to start. Something else Frank had heard them say. Lavatories or laboratories. Of course, his own cherished conspiracy theory had made him plump for 'laboratories', but what if he'd misheard again? Where did lavatories fit into the scheme? And if, as seemed certain, these were the two men, what was a local councillor doing staying at a bed and breakfast? Maybe he owned it, of course. Maybe it was run by his wife.

Rebus was a couple of paces further down his hall when it hit him. He stopped dead. Slow, John, slow. Blame the whisky, maybe. And Jesus, wasn't it so obvious when you thought of it? He went back to his door opened it quietly, and slipped out onto the landing.

There was no such thing as silent movement on an Edinburgh stairwell. The sound of shoe on stone, a sound like sandpaper at work, was magnified and distorted, bouncing off the walls upwards and downwards. Rebus slipped off his shoes and left them on his landing, then started downstairs. He listened outside Mrs Cochrane's door. Muffled voices from the living-room. The layout of her flat was the same as Rebus's own: a long hallway off which were half a dozen doors, the last of which – actually around a corner – led to the living-room. He crouched down and pushed open the letterbox. The cat was just inside the door and it swiped at him with its paw. He let the hinge fall back.

Then he tried the doorhandle, which turned. The door opened. The cat swept past him and down the stairs. Rebus began to feel that the odds were going his way. The door was open just wide enough to allow him to squeeze inside. Open it an inch or two further, he knew, and it creaked with the almightiest groan. He tiptoed into the hallway. Councillor Waugh's voice boomed from the living-room.

'Bowel trouble. Terrible in a man so young.'

Yes, he'd no doubt be explaining why his assistant was taking so long in the lavatory: that was the excuse they always made. Well, either that or a drink of water. Rebus passed the toilet. The door wasn't locked and the tiny closet was empty. He pushed open the next door along – Mrs Cochrane's bedroom. The young man was closing the wardrobe doors.

'Well,' said Rebus, 'I hope you didn't think *that* was the toilet.'

The man jerked around. Rebus filled the doorway. There was no way past him; the only way to get out was to go through him, and that's what the man tried, charging at the doorway, head low. Rebus stood back a little, giving himself room and time, and brought his knee up hard, aiming for the bridge of the nose but finding mouth instead. Well, it was an imprecise science, wasn't it? The man flew backwards like a discarded ragdoll and fell onto the bed. Flat out, to Rebus's satisfaction.

They'd heard the noise of course, and the 'councillor' was already on his way. But he, too, would need to get past Rebus to reach the front door. He stopped short. Rebus nodded slowly.

'Very wise,' he said. 'Your colleague's going to need some new teeth when he wakes up. I'm a police officer by the way. And you, "councillor", are under arrest.'

'Arresting the councillor?' This from Mrs Cochrane, who had appeared in the hall.

'He's no more a councillor than I am, Mrs Cochrane. He's a conman. His partner's been raking through your bedroom.'

'What?' She went to look.

'Bakewell,' Rebus said, smiling. They would try the same ruse at every door where they didn't fancy their chances. Sorry, wrong address, and on to the next potential sucker until they found someone old enough or gullible enough. Rebus was trying to remember if Mrs Cochrane had a telephone. Yes, there was one in her living-room, wasn't there? He gestured to his prisoner.

'Let's go back into the living-room,' he said. Rebus could call the station from there …

Mrs Cochrane was back beside him. 'Blood on my good quilt,' she muttered. Then she saw that Rebus was in his stocking-soles. 'You'll get chilblains, son,' she said. 'Mark my words. You should take better care of yourself. Living on your own like that. You need somebody to look after you. Mark my words. He told me he was a councillor. Would you credit it? And me been wanting to talk to them for ages about the dogs' mess on the Links.'

'Hello, Shuffler.'

'Mr Rebus! Day off is it? Don't usually see you around here during the week.'

Frank was back on his bench, a newspaper spread out on his lap. One of yesterday's papers. It contained a story about some black magic conspiracy in the United States. Wealthy people, it was reckoned, influential people, taking part in orgies and rituals. Yes, and the arms manufacturers would be there, too. That's how they got to know the politicians and the bankers. It all connected.

'No, I'm off to work in a minute. Just thought I'd stop by. Here.' He was holding out a ten-pound note. Frank looked at it suspiciously, moved his hand towards it, and took it. What? Didn't Rebus even want to ask him the question?

'You were right,' Rebus was saying. 'What you told me about those two men, dead right. Well, nearly dead right. Keep your ears open, Frank. And in future, I'll try to keep *my* ears open when you talk to me.'

And then he turned and was walking away, back across the grass towards Marchmont. Frank stared at the money. Ten pounds. Enough to finance another long walk. He needed a long walk to clear his head. Now that they'd had the council of war at Rhodes, the laboratories would be making potions for satanic rituals. They'd put the politicians in a trance, and ... No, no, it didn't bear thinking about.

'Mr Rebus!' he called. 'Mr Rebus! I go to my sister's! She lives in Dunbar! That's where I go in the winter!'

But if the distant figure heard him, it made no sign. Just kept on walking. Frank shuffled his feet. Ten pounds would buy a transistor radio, or a pair of shoes, a jacket, or a new hat, maybe a little camping stove. That was the problem with having money: you ended up with decisions to make. And if you bought anything, where would you put it? He'd need either to ditch something, or to start on another carrier-bag.

That was the problem, being Frank.

Concrete Evidence

'It's amazing what you find in these old buildings,' said the contractor, a middle-aged man in safety helmet and overalls. Beneath the overalls lurked a shirt and tie, the marks of his station. He was the chief, the gaffer. Nothing surprised him any more, not even unearthing a skeleton.

'Do you know,' he went on, 'in my time, I've found everything from ancient coins to a pocket-watch. How old do you reckon he is then?'

'We're not even sure it *is* a he, not yet. Give us a chance, Mr Beesford.'

'Well, when can we start work again?'

'Later on today.'

'Must be gey old though, eh?'

'How do you make that out?'

'Well, it's got no clothes on, has it? They've perished. Takes time for that to happen, plenty of time ...'

Rebus had to concede, the man had a point. Yet the concrete floor beneath which the bones had been found ... *it* didn't look so old, did it? Rebus cast an eye over the cellar again. It was situated a storey or so beneath road-level, in the basement of an old building off the Cowgate. Rebus was often in the Cowgate; the mortuary was just up the road. He knew that the older buildings here were a veritable warren, long narrow tunnels ran here, there and, it seemed, everywhere, semi-cylindrical in shape and just about high enough to stand up in. This present building was being given the full works – gutted, new drainage system, rewiring. They were taking out the floor in the cellar to lay new drains and also because there seemed to be damp – certainly there was a fousty smell to the place – and its cause needed to be found.

They were expecting to find old drains, open drains perhaps. Maybe even a trickle of a stream, something which would lead to damp. Instead, their pneumatic drills found what remained of a corpse, perhaps hundreds of years old. Except, of course, for that concrete floor. It couldn't be more than fifty or sixty years old, could it? Would clothing deteriorate to a visible nothing in so short a time? Perhaps the damp could do that. Rebus found the cellar oppressive. The smell, the shadowy lighting provided by portable lamps, the dust.

But the photographers were finished, and so was the pathologist, Dr Curt. He didn't have too much to report at this stage, except to comment that he preferred it when skeletons were kept in cupboards, not confined to the cellar. They'd take the bones away, along with samples of the earth and rubble around the find, and they'd see what they would see.

'Archaeology's not really my line,' the doctor added. 'It may take me some time to bone up on it.' And he smiled his usual smile.

It took several days for the telephone call to come. Rebus picked up the receiver.

'Hello?'

'Inspector Rebus? Dr Curt here. About our emaciated friend.'

'Yes?'

'Male, five feet ten inches tall, probably been down there between thirty and thirty-five years. His left leg was broken at some time, long before he died. It healed nicely. But the little finger on his left hand had been dislocated and it did *not* heal so well. I'd say it was crooked all his adult life. Perfect for afternoon tea in Morningside.'

'Yes?' Rebus knew damned well Curt was leading up to something. He knew, too, that Curt was not a man to be hurried.

'Tests on the soil and gravel around the skeleton show traces of human tissue, but no fibres or anything which might have been clothing. No shoes, socks, underpants, nothing. Altogether, I'd say he was buried there in the altogether.'

'But did he die there?'

'Can't say.'

'All right, what did he die *of*?'

There was an almost palpable smile in Curt's voice. 'Inspector, I thought you'd never ask. Blow to the skull, a blow of considerable force to the back of the head. Murder, I'd say. Yes, definitely murder.'

There were, of course, ways of tracing the dead, of coming to a near-infallible identification. But the older the crime, the less likely this outcome became. Dental records, for example. They just weren't *kept* in the 50s and 60s the way they are today. A dentist practising then would most probably be playing near-full-time golf by now. And the record of a patient who hadn't been in for his check-up since 1960? Discarded, most probably. Besides, as Dr Curt pointed out, the man's teeth had seen little serious work, a few fillings, a single extraction.

The same went for medical records, which didn't stop Rebus from checking. A broken left leg, a dislocated left pinkie. Maybe some aged doctor would recall? But then again, maybe not. Almost certainly not. The local papers and radio were interested, which was a bonus. They were given what information the police had, but no memories seemed to be jogged as a result.

Curt had said he was no archaeologist; well, Rebus was no historian either. He knew other cases – contemporary cases – were yammering for his attention. The files stacked up on his desk were evidence enough of that. He'd give this one a few days, a few hours of his time. When the dead ends started to cluster around him, he'd drop it and head back for the here and now.

Who owned the building back in the 1950s? That was easy enough to discover: a wine importer and merchant. Pretty much a one-man operation, Hillbeith Vintners had held the premises from 1948 until 1967. And yes, there was a Mr Hillbeith, retired from the trade and living over in Burntisland, with a house gazing out across silver sands to the grey North Sea.

He still had a cellar, and insisted that Rebus have a 'wee taste' from it. Rebus got the idea that Mr Hillbeith liked visitors – a socially acceptable excuse for a drink. He took his time in the cellar (there must have been over 500 bottles in there) and emerged with cobwebs hanging from his cardigan, holding a dusty bottle of something nice. This he opened and sat on the mantelpiece. It would be half an hour or so yet at the very least before they could usefully have a glass.

Mr Hillbeith was, he told Rebus, seventy-four. He'd been in the wine trade for nearly half a century and had 'never regretted a day, not a day, nor even an hour'. Lucky you, Rebus thought to himself.

'Do you remember having that new floor laid in the cellar, Mr Hillbeith?'

'Oh, yes. That particular cellar was going to be for best claret. It was just the right temperature, you see, and there was no vibration from passing buses and the like. But it was damp, had been ever since I'd moved in. So I got a building firm to take a look. They suggested a new floor and some other alterations. It all seemed fairly straightforward and their charges seemed reasonable, so I told them to go ahead.'

'And when was this, sir?'

'1960. The spring of that year. There you are, I've got a

great memory where business matters are concerned.' His small eyes beamed at Rebus through the thick lenses of their glasses. 'I can even tell you how much the work cost me … and it was a pretty penny at the time. All for nothing, as it turned out. The cellar was still damp, and there was always that *smell* in it, a very unwholesome smell. I couldn't take a chance with the claret, so it became the general stock-room, empty bottles and glasses, packing-cases, that sort of thing.'

'Do you happen to recall, Mr Hillbeith, was the smell there *before* the new floor was put in?'

'Well, certainly there was *a* smell there before the floor was laid, but the smell afterwards was different somehow.' He rose and fetched two crystal glasses from the china cabinet, inspecting them for dust. 'There's a lot of nonsense talked about wine, Inspector. About decanting, the type of glasses you must use and so on. Decanting can help, of course, but I prefer the feel of the bottle. The bottle, after all, is part of the wine, isn't it?' He handed an empty glass to Rebus. 'We'll wait a few minutes yet.'

Rebus swallowed drily. It had been a long drive. 'Do you recall the name of the firm, sir, the one that did the work?'

Hillbeith laughed. 'How could I forget? Abbot & Ford, they were called. I mean, you just don't forget a name like that, do you? Abbot & Ford. You see, it sounds like Abbotsford, doesn't it? A small firm they were, mind. But you may know one of them, Alexander Abbot.'

'Of Abbot Building?'

'The same. He went on to make quite a name for himself, didn't he? Quite a fortune. Built up quite a company, too, but he started out small like most of us do.'

'How small, would you say?'

'Oh, small, small. Just a few men.' He rose and stretched an arm towards the mantelpiece. 'I think this should be ready to taste, Inspector. If you'll hold out your glass –'

Hillbeith poured slowly, deliberately, checking that no

lees escaped into the glass. He poured another slow, generous measure for himself. The wine was reddish-brown. 'Robe and disc not too promising,' he muttered to himself. He gave his glass a shake and studied it. 'Legs not promising either.' He sighed. 'Oh dear.' Finally, Hillbeith sniffed the glass anxiously, then took a swig.

'Cheers,' said Rebus, indulging in a mouthful. A mouthful of vinegar. He managed to swallow, then saw Hillbeith spit back into the glass.

'Oxidisation,' the old man said, sounding cruelly tricked. 'It happens. I'd best check a few more bottles to assess the damage. Will you stay, Inspector?' Hillbeith sounded keen.

'Sorry, sir,' said Rebus, ready with his get-out clause. 'I'm still on duty.'

Alexander Abbot, aged fifty-five, still saw himself as the force behind the Abbot Building Company. There might be a dozen executives working furiously beneath him, but the company had grown from *his* energy and from *his* fury. He was Chairman, and a busy man too. He made this plain to Rebus at their meeting in the executive offices of ABC. The office spoke of business confidence, but then in Rebus's experience this meant little in itself. Often, the more dire straits a company was in, the healthier it tried to look. Still, Alexander Abbot seemed happy enough with life.

'In a recession,' he explained, lighting an overlong cigar, 'you trim your workforce pronto. You stick with regular clients, good payers, and don't take on too much work from clients you don't know. They're the ones who're likely to welch on you or go bust, leaving nothing but bills. Young businesses ... they're always hit hardest in a recession, no back-up you see. Then, when the recession's over for another few years, you dust yourself off and go touting for business again, re-hiring the men you laid off. That's where we've always had the edge over Jack Kirkwall.'

Kirkwall Construction was ABC's main competitor in

the Lowlands, when it came to medium-sized contracts. Doubtless Kirkwall was the larger company. It, too, was run by a 'self-made' man, Jack Kirkwall. A larger-than-life figure. There was, Rebus quickly realised, little love lost between the two rivals.

The very mention of Kirkwall's name seemed to have dampened Alexander Abbot's spirits. He chewed on his cigar like it was a debtor's finger.

'You started small though, didn't you, sir?'

'Oh aye, they don't come much smaller. We were a pimple on the bum of the construction industry at one time.' He gestured to the walls of his office. 'Not that you'd guess it, eh?'

Rebus nodded. 'You were still a small firm back in 1960, weren't you?'

'1960. Let's think. We were just starting out. It wasn't ABC then, of course. Let's see. I think I got a loan from my dad in 1957, went into partnership with a chap called Hugh Ford, another self-employed builder. Yes, that's right. 1960, it was Abbot & Ford. Of course it was.'

'Do you happen to remember working at a wine merchant's in the Cowgate?'

'When?'

'The spring of 1960.'

'A wine merchant's?' Abbot furrowed his brow. 'Should be able to remember that. Long time ago, mind. A wine merchant's?'

'You were laying a new floor in one of his cellars, amongst other work. Hillbeith Vintners.'

'Oh, aye, Hillbeith, it's coming back now. I remember him. Little funny chap with glasses. Gave us a case of wine when the job was finished. Nice of him, but the wine was a bit off as I remember.'

'How many men were working on the job?'

Abbot exhaled noisily. 'Now you're asking. It was over thirty years ago, Inspector.'

'I appreciate that, sir. Would there be any records?'

Abbot shook his head. 'There might have been up to about ten years ago, but when we moved into this place a lot of the older stuff got chucked out. I regret it now. It'd be nice to have a display of stuff from the old days, something we could set up in the reception. But no, all the Abbot & Ford stuff got dumped.'

'So you don't remember how many men were on that particular job? Is there anyone else I could talk to, someone who might –'

'We were small back then, I can tell you that. Mostly using casual labour and part-timers. A job that size, I wouldn't think we'd be using more than three or four men, if that.'

'You don't recall anyone going missing? Not turning up for work, that sort of thing?'

Abbot bristled. 'I'm a stickler for time-keeping, Inspector. If anyone had done a bunk, I'd remember, I'm pretty sure of that. Besides, we were careful about who we took on. No lazy buggers, nobody who'd do a runner halfway through a job.'

Rebus sighed. Here was one of the dead ends. He rose to his feet. 'Well, thanks anyway, Mr Abbot. It was good of you to find time to see me.' The two men shook hands, Abbot rising to his feet.

'Not at all, Inspector. Wish I could help you with your little mystery. I like a good detective story myself.' They were almost at the door now.

'Oh,' said Rebus, 'just one last thing. Where could I find your old partner Mr Ford?'

Abbot's face lost its animation. His voice was suddenly that of an old man. 'Hugh died, Inspector. A boating accident. He was drowned. Hell of a thing to happen. Hell of a thing.'

Two dead ends.

* * *

Mr Hillbeith's telephone call came later that day, while Rebus was ploughing through the transcript of an interview with a rapist. His head felt full of foul-smelling glue, his stomach acid with caffeine.

'Is that Inspector Rebus?'

'Yes, hello, Mr Hillbeith. What can I do for you?' Rebus pinched the bridge of his nose and screwed shut his eyes.

'I was thinking all last night about that skeleton.'

'Yes?' In between bottles of wine, Rebus didn't doubt.

'Well, I was trying to think back to when the work was being done. It might not be much, but I definitely recall that there were four people involved. Mr Abbot and Mr Ford worked on it pretty much full-time, and there were two other men, one of them a teenager, the other in his forties. They worked on a more casual basis.'

'You don't recall their names?'

'No, only that the teenager had a nickname. Everyone called him by that. I don't think I ever knew his real name.'

'Well, thanks anyway, Mr Hillbeith. I'll get back to Mr Abbot and see if what you've told me jogs his memory.'

'Oh, you've spoken to him then?'

'This morning. No progress to report. I didn't realise Mr Ford had died.'

'Ah, well, that's the other thing.'

'What is?'

'Poor Mr Ford. Sailing accident, wasn't it?'

'That's right.'

'Only I remember that, too. You see, that accident happened just after they'd finished the job. They kept talking about how they were going to take a few days off and go fishing. Mr Abbot said it would be their first holiday in years.'

Rebus's eyes were open now. 'How soon was this after they'd finished your floor?'

'Well, directly after, I suppose.'

'Do you remember Mr Ford?'

'Well, he was very quiet. Mr Abbot did all the talking, really. A very quiet man. A hard worker though, I got that impression.'

'Did you notice anything about his hands? A misshapen pinkie?'

'Sorry, Inspector, it *was* a long time ago.'

Rebus appreciated that. 'Of course it was, Mr Hillbeith. You've been a great help. Thank you.'

He put down the receiver. A long time ago, yes, but still murder, still calculated and cold-blooded murder. Well, a path had opened in front of him. Not much of a path perhaps, a bit overgrown and treacherous. Nevertheless ... Best foot forward, John. Best foot forward.

Of course, he kept telling himself, he was still ruling possibilities out rather than ruling them in, which was why he wanted to know a little more about the boating accident. He didn't want to get the information from Alexander Abbot.

Instead, the morning after Hillbeith's phone-call, Rebus went to the National Library of Scotland on George IV Bridge. The doorman let him through the turnstile and he climbed an imposing staircase to the reading room. The woman on the desk filled in a one-day reader's card for him, and showed him how to use the computer. There were two banks of computers, being used by people to find the books they needed. Rebus had to go into the reading room and find an empty chair, note its number and put this on his slip when he'd decided which volume he required. Then he went to his chair and sat, waiting.

There were two floors to the reading room, both enveloped by shelves of reference books. The people working at the long desks downstairs seemed bleary. Just another morning's graft for them; but Rebus found it all fascinating. One person worked with a card index in front of him, to which he referred frequently. Another seemed asleep, head resting on arms. Pens scratched across countless sheets of paper. A few souls, lost for inspiration, merely chewed on their pens and stared at the others around them, as Rebus was doing.

Eventually, his volume was brought to him. It was a bound edition of the *Scotsman*, containing every issue for the months from January to June, 1960. Two thick leather buckles kept the volume closed. Rebus unbuckled these and began to turn the pages.

He knew what he was looking for, and pretty well where to find it, but that didn't stop him browsing through football reports and front page headlines. 1960. He'd been busy trying to lose his virginity and supporting Hearts. Yes, a long time ago.

The story hadn't quite made the front page. Instead, there were two paragraphs on page three. 'Drowning Off Lower Largo.' The victim, Mr Hugh Ford, was described as being twenty-six years of age (a year old than the survivor, Mr Alex Abbot) and a resident of Duddingston, Edinburgh. The men, on a short fishing-holiday, had taken a boat out early in the morning, a boat hired from a local man, Mr John Thomson. There was a squall, and the boat capsized. Mr Abbot, a fair swimmer, had made it back to the shore. Mr Ford, a poor swimmer, had not. Mr Ford was further described as a 'bachelor, a quiet man, shy according to Mr Abbot, who was still under observation at the Victoria Hospital, Kirkcaldy'. There was a little more, but not much. Apparently, Ford's parents were dead, but he had a sister, Mrs Isabel Hammond, somewhere out in Australia.

Why hadn't Abbot mentioned any of this? Maybe he wanted to forget. Maybe it still gave him the occasional bad dream. And of course he would have forgotten all about the Hillbeith contract precisely because this tragedy happened so soon afterwards. So soon. Just the one line of print really bothered Rebus; just that one sentence niggled.

'Mr Ford's body has still not been recovered.'

* * *

Records might get lost in time, but not by Fife Police. They sent on what they had, much of it written in fading ink on fragile paper, some of it typed – badly. The two friends and colleagues, Abbot and Ford, had set out on Friday evening to the Fishing-Net Hotel in Largo, arriving late. As arranged, they'd set out early next morning on a boat they'd hired from a local man, John Thomson. The accident had taken place only an hour or so after setting out. The boat was recovered. It had been overturned, but of Ford there was no sign. Inquiries were made. Mr Ford's belongings were taken back to Edinburgh by Mr Abbot, after the latter was released from hospital, having sustained a bump to the head when the boat went over. He was also suffering from shock and exhaustion. Mr Ford's sister, Mrs Isabel Hammond, was never traced.

They had investigated a little further. The business run jointly by Messrs Abbot and Ford now became Mr Abbot's. The case-notes contained a good amount of information and suspicion – between the lines, as it were. Oh yes, they'd investigated Alexander Abbot, but there had been no evidence. They'd searched for the body, had found none. Without a body, they were left with only their suspicions and their nagging doubts.

'Yes,' Rebus said quietly to himself, 'but what if you were looking for the body in the wrong place?' The wrong place at the wrong time. The work on the cellar had ended on Friday afternoon and by Saturday morning Hugh Ford had ceased to exist.

The path Rebus was on had become less overgrown, but it was still rock-strewn and dangerous, still a potential dead-end.

The Fishing-Net Hotel was still in existence, though apparently much changed from its 1960 incarnation. The present owners told Rebus to arrive in time for lunch if he could and it would be on the house. Largo was north of Burntisland but on the same coastline. Alexander Selkirk, the original of Defoe's Robinson Crusoe, had a connection with the fishing village. There was a small statue of him somewhere which Rebus had been shown as a boy (but only after much hunting, he recalled). Largo was picturesque, but then so were most, if not all, of the coastal villages in Fife's 'East Neuk'. But it was not yet quite the height of the tourist season and the customers taking lunch at the Fishing-Net Hotel were businessmen and locals.

It was a good lunch, as picturesque as its surroundings but with a bit more flavour. And afterwards, the owner, an Englishman for whom life in Largo was a long-held dream come true, offered to show Rebus round, including 'the very room your Mr Ford stayed in the night before he died'.

'How can you be sure?'

'I looked in the register.'

Rebus managed not to look too surprised. The hotel had changed hands so often since 1960, he despaired of finding anyone who would remember the events of that weekend.

'The register?'

'Yes, we were left a lot of old stuff when we bought this place. The store-rooms were choc-a-bloc. Old ledgers and what have you going back to the 1920s and 30s. It was easy enough to find 1960.'

Rebus stopped in his tracks. 'Never mind showing me Mr Ford's room, would you mind letting me see that register?'

He sat at a desk in the manager's office with the register open in front of him, while Mr Summerson's finger stabbed the line. 'There you are, Inspector, H. Ford. Signed in at 11.50 p.m., address given as Duddingston. Room number seven.'

It wasn't so much a signature as a blurred scrawl and

above it, on a separate line, was Alexander Abbot's own more flowing signature.

'Bit late to arrive, wasn't it?' commented Rebus.

'Agreed.'

'I don't suppose there's anyone working here nowadays who worked in the hotel back then?'

Summerson laughed quietly. 'People do retire in this country, Inspector.'

'Of course, I just wondered.' He remembered the newspaper story. 'What about John Thomson? Does the name mean anything to you?'

'Old Jock? Jock Thomson? The fisherman?'

'Probably.'

'Oh, yes, he's still about. You'll almost certainly find him down by the dockside or else in the Harbour Tavern.'

'Thanks. I'd like to take this register with me if I may?'

Jock Thomson sucked on his pipe and nodded. He looked the archetype of the 'old salt', from his baggy cord trousers to his chiselled face and silvery beard. The only departure from the norm was, perhaps, the Perrier water in front of him on a table in the Harbour Tavern.

'I like the fizz,' he explained after ordering it, 'and besides, my doctor's told me to keep off the alcohol. Total abstinence, he said, total abstinence. Either the booze goes, Jock, or the pipe does. No contest.'

And he sucked greedily on the pipe. Then complained when his drink arrived without 'the wee slice of lemon'. Rebus returned to the bar to fulfil his mission.

'Oh aye,' said Thomson, 'remember it like it was yesterday. Only there's not much to remember, is there?'

'Why do you say that?'

'Two inexperienced laddies go out in a boat. Boat tips. End of story.'

'Was the weather going to be bad that morning?'

'Not particularly. But there *was* a squall blew up. Blew

up and blew out in a matter of minutes. Long enough though.'

'How did the two men seem?'

'How do you mean?'

'Well, were they looking forward to the trip?'

'Don't know, I never saw them. The younger one, Abbot was it? He phoned to book a boat from me, said they'd be going out early, six or thereabouts. I told him he was daft, but he said there was no need for me to be on the dockside, if I'd just have the boat ready and tell him which one it was. And that's what I did. By the time I woke up that morning, he was swimming for the shore and his pal was food for the fish.'

'So you never actually saw Mr Ford?'

'No, and I only saw the lad Abbot afterwards, when the ambulance was taking him away.'

It was fitting into place almost too easily now. And Rebus thought, sometimes these things are only visible with hindsight, from a space of years. 'I don't suppose,' he ventured, 'you know anyone who worked at the hotel back then?'

'Owner's moved on,' said Thomson, 'who knows where to. It might be that Janice Dryman worked there then. Can't recall if she did.'

'Where could I find her?'

Thomson peered at the clock behind the bar. 'Hang around here ten minutes or so, you'll bump into her. She usually comes in of an afternoon. Meantime, I'll have another of these if you're buying.'

Thomson pushed his empty glass over to Rebus. Rebus, most definitely, was buying.

Miss Dryman – 'never married, never really saw the point' – was in her early fifties. She worked in a gift-shop in town and after her stint finished usually nipped into the Tavern for a soft drink and 'a bit of gossip'. Rebus asked what she would like to drink.

'Lemonade, please,' she said, 'with a drop of whisky in it.' And she laughed with Jock Thomson, as though this were an old and cherished joke between them. Rebus, not used to playing the part of straight-man, headed yet again for the bar.

'Oh yes,' she said, her lips poised above the glass. 'I was working there at the time all right. Chambermaid and general dogsbody, that was me.'

'You wouldn't see them arrive though?'

Miss Dryman looked as though she had some secret to impart. '*Nobody* saw them arrive, I know that for a fact. Mrs Dennis who ran the place back then, she said she'd be buggered if she'd wait up half the night for a couple of fishermen. They knew what rooms they were in and their keys were left at reception.'

'What about the front door?'

'Left unlocked, I suppose. The world was a safer place back then.'

'Aye, you're right there,' added Jock Thomson, sucking on his sliver of lemon.

'And Mr Abbot and Mr Ford knew this was the arrangement?'

'I suppose so. Otherwise it wouldn't have worked, would it?'

So Abbot knew there'd be nobody around at the hotel, not if he left it late enough before arriving.

'And what about in the morning?'

'Mrs Dennis said they were up and out before she knew anything about it. She was annoyed because she'd already cooked the kippers for their breakfast before she realised.'

So nobody saw them in the morning either. In fact ...

'In fact,' said Rebus, 'nobody saw Mr Ford at all. Nobody at the hotel, not you, Mr Thomson, nobody.' Both drinkers conceded this.

'I saw his stuff though,' said Miss Dryman.

'What stuff?'

'In his room, his clothes and stuff. That morning. I didn't know anything about the accident and I went in to clean.'

'The bed had been slept in?'

'Looked like it. Sheets all rumpled. And his suitcase was on the floor, only half unpacked. Not that there was much *to* unpack.'

'Oh?'

'A single change of clothes, I'd say. I remember them because they seemed mucky, you know, not fresh. Not the sort of stuff *I'd* take on holiday with me.'

'What? Like he'd been working in them?'

She considered this. 'Maybe.'

'No point wearing clean clothes for fishing,' Thomson added. But Rebus wasn't listening.

Ford's clothes, the clothes he had been working in while laying the floor. It made sense. Abbot bludgeoned him, stripped him and covered his body in fresh cement. He'd taken the clothes away with him and put them in a case, opening it in the hotel room, ruffling the sheets. Simple, but effective. Effective these past thirty years. The motive? A falling out perhaps, or simple greed. It was a small company, but growing, and perhaps Abbot hadn't wanted to share. Rebus placed a five-pound note on the table.

'To cover the next couple of rounds,' he said, getting to his feet. 'I'd better be off. Some of us are still on duty.'

There were things to be done. He had to speak to his superior, Chief Inspector Lauderdale. And that was for starters. Maybe Ford's Australian sister could be traced this time round. There had to be someone out there who could acknowledge that Ford had suffered from a broken leg in youth, and that he had a crooked finger. So far, Rebus could think of only one person – Alexander Abbot.

Somehow, he didn't think Abbot could be relied on to tell the truth, the whole truth.

Then there was the hotel register. The forensics lab could ply their cunning trade on it. Perhaps they'd be able to say for certain that Ford's signature was merely a bad rendition of Abbot's. But again, he needed a sample of Ford's handwriting in order to substantiate that the signature was not genuine. Who did he know who might possess such a document? Only Alexander Abbot. Or Mr Hillbeith, but Mr Hillbeith had not been able to help.

'No, Inspector, as I told you, it was Mr Abbot who handled all the paperwork, all that side of things. If there is an invoice or a receipt, it will be in his hand, not Mr Ford's. I don't recall ever seeing Mr Ford writing anything.'

No through road.

Chief Inspector Lauderdale was not wholly sympathetic. So far all Rebus had to offer were more suppositions to add to those of the Fife Police at the time. There was no proof that Alexander Abbot had killed his partner. No proof that the skeleton was Hugh Ford. Moreover, there wasn't even much in the way of circumstantial evidence. They could bring in Abbot for questioning, but all he had to do was plead innocence. He could afford a good lawyer; and even bad lawyers weren't stupid enough to let the police probe too deeply.

'We need proof, John,' said Lauderdale, 'concrete evidence. The simplest proof would be that hotel signature. If we prove it's not Ford's, then we have Abbot at that hotel, Abbot in the boat and Abbot shouting that his friend has drowned, *all* without Ford having been there. That's what we need. The rest of it, as it stands, is rubbish. You know that.'

Yes, Rebus knew. He didn't doubt that, given an hour alone with Abbot in a darkened alley, he'd have his confession. But it didn't work like that. It worked through the law. Besides, Abbot's heart might not be too healthy. BUSINESSMAN, 55, DIES UNDER QUESTIONING. No, it had to be done some other way.

The problem was, there *was* no other way. Alexander Abbot was getting away with murder. Or was he? Why did his story have to be false? Why did the body have to be Hugh Ford's? The answer was: because the whole thing seemed to fit. Only, the last piece of the jigsaw had been lost under some sofa or chair a long time ago, so long ago now that it might remain missing forever.

He didn't know why he did it. If in doubt, retrace your steps ... something like that. Maybe he just liked the atmosphere. Whatever, Rebus found himself back in the National Library, waiting at his desk for the servitor to bring him his bound volume of old news. He mouthed the words of 'Yesterday's Papers' to himself as he waited. Then, when the volume appeared, he unbuckled it with ease and pulled open the pages. He read past the April editions, read through into May and June. Football results, headlines – and what was this? A snippet of business news, barely a filler at the bottom right-hand corner of a page. About how the Kirkwall Construction Company was swallowing up a couple of smaller competitors in Fife and Midlothian.

'The 1960s will be a decade of revolution in the building industry,' said Managing Director Mr Jack Kirkwall, 'and Kirkwall Construction aims to meet that challenge through growth and quality. The bigger we are, the better we are. These acquisitions strengthen the company, and they're good news for the workforce, too.'

It was the kind of sentiment which had lasted into the 1980s. Jack Kirkwall, Alexander Abbot's bitter rival. Now there was a man Rebus ought to meet ...

The meeting, however, had to be postponed until the

following week. Kirkwall was in hospital for a minor operation.

'I'm at that age, Inspector,' he told Rebus when they finally met, 'when things go wrong and need treatment or replacing. Just like any bit of well-used machinery.'

And he laughed, though the laughter, to Rebus's ears, had a hollow centre. Kirkwall looked older than his sixty-two years, his skin saggy, complexion wan. They were in his living-room, from where, these days, he did most of his work.

'Since I turned sixty, I've only really wandered into the company headquarters for the occasional meeting. I leave the daily chores to my son, Peter. He seems to be managing.' The laughter this time was self-mocking.

Rebus had suggested a further postponement of the meeting, but when Jack Kirkwall knew that the subject was to be Alexander Abbot, he was adamant that they should go ahead.

'Is he in trouble then?'

'He might be,' Rebus admitted. Some of the colour seemed to reappear in Kirkwall's cheeks and he relaxed a little further into his reclining leather chair. Rebus didn't want to give Kirkwall the story. Kirkwall and Abbot were still business rivals, after all. Still, it seemed, enemies. Given the story, Kirkwall might try some underhand tactic, some rumour in the media, and if it got out that the story originally came from a police inspector, well. Hello, being sued and goodbye, pension.

No, Rebus didn't want that. Yet he did want to know whether Kirkwall knew anything, knew of any reason why Abbot might wish, might *need* to kill Ford.

'Go on, Inspector.'

'It goes back quite a way, sir. 1960, to be precise. Your firm was at that time in the process of expansion.'

'Correct.'

'What did you know about Abbot & Ford?'

Kirkwall brushed the palm of one hand over the knuckles of the other. 'Just that they were growing, too. Of course, they were younger than us, much smaller than us. ABC still is much smaller than us. But they were cocky, they were winning some contracts ahead of us. I had my eye on them.'

'Did you know Mr Ford at all?'

'Oh yes. Really, he was the cleverer of the two men. I've never had much respect for Abbot. But Hugh Ford was quiet, hardworking. Abbot was the one who did the shouting and got the firm noticed.'

'Did Mr Ford have a crooked finger?'

Kirkwall seemed bemused by the question. 'I've no idea,' he said at last. 'I never actually met the man, I merely knew *about* him. Why? Is it important?'

Rebus felt at last that his meandering, narrowing path had come to the lip of a chasm. Nothing for it but to turn back.

'Well,' he said, 'it would have clarified something.'

'You know, Inspector, my company *was* interested in taking Abbot & Ford under our wing.'

'Oh?'

'But then with the accident, that tragic accident. Well, Abbot took control and he wasn't at all interested in any offer we had to make. Downright rude, in fact. Yes, I've always thought that it was such a *lucky* accident so far as Abbot was concerned.'

'How do you mean, sir?'

'I mean, Inspector, that Hugh Ford was on our side. He wanted to sell up. But Abbot was against it.'

So, Rebus had his motive. Well, what did it matter? He was still lacking that concrete evidence Lauderdale demanded.

'... Would it show up from his handwriting?'

Rebus had missed what Kirkwall had been saying. 'I'm sorry, sir, I didn't catch that.'

'I said, Inspector, if Hugh Ford had a crooked finger, would it show from his handwriting?'

'Handwriting?'

'Because I had his agreement to the takeover. He'd written to me personally to tell me. Had gone behind Abbot's back, I suppose. I bet Alex Abbot was mad as hell when he found out about that.' Kirkwall's smile was vibrant now. 'I always thought that accident was a bit too lucky where Abbot was concerned. A bit too neat. No proof though. There was never any proof.'

'Do you still have the letter?'

'What?'

'The letter from Mr Ford, do you still have it?'

Rebus was tingling now, and Kirkwall caught his excitement. 'I never throw anything away, Inspector. Oh yes, I've got it. It'll be upstairs.'

'Can I see it? I mean, can I see it now?'

'If you like,' Kirkwall made to stand up, but paused. '*Is* Alex Abbot in trouble, Inspector?'

'If you've still got that letter from Hugh Ford, then, yes, sir, I'd say Mr Abbot could be in very grave trouble indeed.'

'Inspector, you've made an old man very happy.'

It was the letter against Alex Abbot's word, of course, and he denied everything. But there was enough now for a trial. The entry in the hotel, while it was *possibly* the work of Alexander Abbot was *certainly* not the work of the man who had written the letter to Jack Kirkwall. A search warrant gave the police the powers to look through Abbot's home and the ABC headquarters. A contract, drawn up between Abbot and Ford when the two men had gone into partnership, was discovered to be held in a solicitor's safe. The signature matched that on the letter to Jack Kirkwall. Kirkwall himself appeared in court to give evidence. He seemed to Rebus a different man altogether from the person he'd met previously: sprightly, keening, enjoying life to the full.

From the dock, Alexander Abbot looked on almost reproachfully, as if this were just one more business trick in a life full of them. Life, too, was the sentence of the judge.

Seeing Things

To be honest, if you were going to see Christ anywhere in Edinburgh, the Hermitage was perfect.

Or, to give it its full title, the Hermitage of Braid, named after the Braid Burn which trickled through the narrow, bushy wilderness between Blackford Hill and Braid Hills Road. Across this road, the Hermitage became a golf course, its undulations cultivated and well-trodden, but on sunny weekend afternoons, the Hermitage itself was as wild a place as your imagination wished it to be. Children ran in and out of the trees or threw sticks into the burn. Lovers could be seen hand-in-hand as they tackled the tricky descent from Blackford Hill. Dogs ran sniffing to stump and post, watched, perhaps, by punks seated atop an outcrop. Can would be tipped to mouth, the foam savoured. Picnic parties would debate the spot most sheltered from the breeze.

It was sometimes hard to believe that the place was in Edinburgh, that the main entrance to the Hermitage was just off the busy Comiston Road at the southern reach of Morningside. The protesters – such as they were – had held vigil at these gates for a couple of days, singing songs and handing out their 'No Popery' pamphlets. Occasionally a megaphone would appear, so that they could deliver their rant. A seller of religious nick-nacks and candles had set up his pitch across the road from the protesters, and at a canny distance along the road from them. The megaphone was most often directed towards him, there being no other visible target.

A rant was occurring as Inspector John Rebus arrived. Would the day of judgment be like this, he wondered, accepting a leaflet. Would the loudest voices belong to the saved? *Megaphones will be provided*, he thought to himself as he passed through the gates. He studied the leaflet. No Popery, indeed.

'Why ever not?' And so asking, he crumpled the paper and tossed it into the nearest wastepaper-bin. The voice followed him as though it had a mission and he was it.

'There must be NO idolatry! There is but ONE God and it is HE ye should worship! Do not turn YOUR face to graven IMAGES! The Good Book is the ONLY truth ye NEED!'

Rave on …

They were a minority of course, far outweighed by the curious who came to see. But they in their turn looked as though they might be outnumbered very soon by the shrine-builders. Rebus liked to think of himself as a Christian, albeit with too many questions and doubts to ally himself with either side, Catholic or Protestant. He could not escape the fact that he had been born a Protestant; but his mother, a religious woman, had died young, and his father had been indifferent.

Rebus hadn't even been aware of any difference between Catholic and Protestant until he'd started school. His pre-schooldays best friend was a Catholic, a boy called Miles Skelly. Come their first day at school, the boys had been split up, sent to schools on different sides of town. Parted like this daily, they soon grew to have new friends and stopped playing together.

That had been Rebus's first lesson in 'the divide'. But he had nothing against Catholics. The Protestant community might call them 'left-footers', but Rebus himself kicked a ball with his left foot. He did, however, mistrust the shrine mentality. It made him uneasy: statues which wept or bled or moved. Sudden visions of the Virgin Mary. A face imprinted on a shroud.

A faith should be just that, Rebus reasoned. And if you held belief, what need had you of miracles, especially ones that seemed more the province of the Magic Circle than of the divine? So the closer he came to the spot itself, the shakier became his legs. There was a tangle of undergrowth, and in front of it a stunted tree. Around this tree had been arranged candles, small statues, photographs, written prayers, flowers, all in the last two or three days. It was quite a transformation. A knot of people knelt nearby, but at a respectful distance. Their heads were bowed in prayer. Others sat, arms out behind them, supporting themselves on the grass. They wore beatific smiles, as though they could hear or see something Rebus couldn't. He listened hard, but heard only whispers of prayer, the distant barking of dogs. He looked, but saw only a tree, though it had to be admitted that the sunlight seemed to catch it in a particularly striking way, picking it out from the undergrowth behind it.

There was a rustling from beyond the tree itself. Rebus moved around the congregation – there was no other word for the gathering – towards the undergrowth, where several police cadets were on their hands and knees, not in worship this time but searching the ground.

'Anything?'

One of the figures straightened up, pressing his fingers into his spine as he exhaled. Rebus could hear the vertebrae crackling.

'Nothing, sir, not a blasted thing.'

'Language, Holmes, language. Remember, this is a holy site.'

Detective Constable Brian Holmes managed a wry smile. He'd been smiling a lot this morning. For once he'd been put in charge and it didn't matter to him that he was in a damp copse, or that he was in charge of a shower of disgruntled cadets, or that he had twigs in his hair. He was in charge. Not even John Rebus could take that away from him.

Except that he could. And did.

'All right,' Rebus said, 'that's enough. We'll have to make do with what we've got. Or rather, what the lab boys have got.'

The cadets rose mercifully to their feet. One or two brushed white chalky powder from their knees, others scraped at dirt and grass stains. 'Well done, lads,' Rebus admitted. 'Not very exciting, I know, but that's what police work is all about. So if you're joining for thrills and spills, think again.'

That should have been *my* speech, Holmes thought to himself as the cadets grinned at Rebus's words. They would agree with anything he said, anything he did. He was an Inspector. He was *the* Inspector Rebus. Holmes felt himself losing height and density, becoming like a patch of low mist or a particularly innocuous shadow. Rebus was in charge now. The cadets had all but forgotten their former leader. They had eyes for only one man, and that man was ordering them to go and drink some tea.

'What's up, Brian?'

Holmes, watching the cadets shuffle away, realised Rebus was speaking to him. 'Sorry?'

'You look like you've found a tanner and lost a shilling.'

Holmes shrugged. 'I suppose I'm thinking about how I could have had one-and-six. No news yet on the blood?'

'Just that it's every bit as messianic as yours and mine.'

'What a surprise.'

Rebus nodded towards the clearing. 'Try telling them that. They'll have an answer for you.'

'I know. I've already been ticked off for desecration. You know they've started posting an all-night guard?'

'What for?'

'In case the Wee Frees chop down the tree and run away with it.'

They stared at one another, then burst out laughing. Hands quickly went to mouths to stifle the sound. Desecration upon desecration.

'Come on,' said Rebus, 'you look like you could do with a cuppa yourself. My treat.'

'Now that *is* a miracle,' said Holmes, following his superior out of the trees. A tall, muscled man was approaching. He wore denims and a white T-shirt. A large wooden cross swung from his neck, around which was also tied a red kerchief. His beard was as thick and black as his hair.

'Are you police officers?'

'Yes,' Rebus said.

'Then I think you should know, they're trying to steal the tree.'

'Steal it, sir?'

'Yes, steal it. We've got to keep watch twenty-four hours. Last night, one of them had a knife, but there were too many of us, thank God.'

'And you are?'

'Steven Byrne.' He paused. 'Father Steven Byrne.'

Rebus paused too, digesting this new information. 'Well, Father, would you recognise this man again? The one with the knife?'

'Yes, probably.'

'Well, we could go down to the station and have a look at some photographs.'

Father Byrne seemed to be appraising Rebus. Acknowledging that he was being taken seriously, he nodded slowly. 'Thank you, I don't think that'll be necessary. But I thought you ought to know. Things might turn nasty.'

Rebus bit back a comment about turning the other cheek. 'Not if we can help it,' he said instead. 'If you see the man again, Father, let us know straight away. Don't try anything on your own.'

Father Byrne looked around him. 'There aren't so many telephones around here.' His eyes were twinkling with humour. An attractive man, thought Rebus. Even a touch charismatic.

'Well,' he said, 'we'll try to make sure a patrol car comes by and checks on things. How would that be?'

Father Byrne nodded. Rebus made to move away. 'Bless you,' he heard the man saying. Rebus kept walking, but for some reason his cheeks had turned deep red. But it was right and proper, after all, wasn't it? Right that he should be blessed.

'Blessed are the peacemakers,' he quoted, as the megaphone came back into range.

The story was a simple one. Three girls had been in the Hermitage one late afternoon. School over, they'd decided to cut through the park, climb Blackford Hill and come down the other side towards their homes. A long way round for a short-cut, as Rebus had put it at the time.

They were sensible girls, from good Catholic homes. They were fifteen and all had future plans that included university and a career as well as marriage. They didn't seem inclined to fantasy or exaggeration. They stuck to the same story throughout. They'd been about thirty yards or so from the tree when they'd seen a man. One second he wasn't there, the next he was. Dressed in white and with a glow all around him. Long wavy dark hair and a beard. A very pale face, they were definite about that. He leaned with one hand against the tree, the other to his side. His right side – again, all three concurred on this. Then he took the hand away, and they saw that there was blood on his side. A dark red patch. They gasped. They looked to each other for confirmation that they'd seen what they had seen. When they looked again, the figure had vanished.

They ran to their separate homes, but over dinner the story came out in each of the three households. Disbelieved, perhaps, for a moment. But then why would the girls lie? The parents got together and went to the Hermitage. They were shown the place, the tree. There was no sign of anyone. But then one of the mothers shrieked before crossing herself.

'Look at that!' she cried. 'Just look at it!'

It was a smeared red mark, still wet on the bark of the tree. Blood.

The parents went to the police and the police made an initial search of the area, but in the meantime, the neighbour of one of the families telephoned a friend who was a stringer on a Sunday newspaper. The paper ran the story of the 'Hermitage Vision' and the thing began to grow. The blood, it was said, hadn't dried. And this was true, though as Rebus knew it could well have something to do with the reaction of blood and bark. Footprints were found, but so many and so varied that it was impossible to say when they'd been made or by whom. The parents, for example, had searched the area thoroughly, destroying a lot of potential evidence. There were no bloodstains on the ground. No patients with side wounds had been treated in any of the city's hospitals or by any doctor.

The description of the figure was vague: tallish, thinnish, the long hair and beard of course – but was the hair brown or black? The girls couldn't be sure. Dressed in white – 'like a gown', one of them remembered later. But by then the story had become public property; how far would that distort her memories of the evening? And as for the glow. Well, Rebus had seen how the sun hit that particular spot. Imagine a lowish sun, creeping towards evening. That would explain the glow – to a rational man.

But then the zealous – of both sides – appeared. The believers and the doubters, carrying candles or toting megaphones. It was a quiet time for news: the media loved it. The girls photographed well. When they appeared on TV, the trickle of visitors to the site became a flood. Coach-loads headed north from Wales and England. Organised parties were arriving from Ireland. A Parisian magazine had picked up on the mystery; so, it was rumoured, had a Bible-thumping cable channel from the USA.

Rebus wanted to raise his hands and turn back the tide. Instead of which that tide rolled straight over him. Superintendent Watson wanted answers.

'I don't like all this hocus-pocus,' he said, with Presbyterian assuredness and an Aberdonian lilt. 'I want something tangible. I want an explanation, one I can *believe*. Understood?'

Understood. Rebus understood it; so did Chief Inspector Lauderdale. Chief Inspector Lauderdale understood that *he* wanted Rebus to do something about it. Rebus understood that hands were being washed; that his alone were to work on the case. If in doubt, delegate. That was where Brian Holmes and his cadets entered the picture. Having found no new clues – no clues *period* – Rebus decided to back off. Media interest was already dying. Some local historian would now and again come up with a 'fact' or a 'theory' and these would revive the story for a while – the hermit who'd lived in the Hermitage, executed for witchcraft in 1714 and said still to haunt the place, that sort of thing, but it couldn't last. It was like poking at embers without feeding them. A momentary glow, no more. When the media interest died, so would that of the fringe lunatics. There had already been copycat 'visions' in Cornwall, Caerphilly and East Croydon. The Doubting Thomases were appear-ing. What's more, the blood had gone, washed away in an overnight deluge which also extinguished the candles around the tree.

A recurrence of the 'vision' was needed if the thing were not to die. Rebus prayed each night for a quick and merciful release. It didn't come. Instead there was a 4 a.m. phone call.

'This better be worth it.'

'It is.'

'Go on then.'

'How soon can you get to the Hermitage?'

Rebus sat up in bed. 'Talk to me.'

'They've found a body, Well, that's putting it a bit strongly. Let's say they've found a trunk.'

A trunk it was, and not the sort you stuck travel labels on either.

'Dear God in heaven,' Rebus whispered, staring at the thing. 'Who found it?'

Holmes didn't look too good himself. 'One of the tree people,' he said. 'Wandered over here looking for a place to do his number twos. Had a torch with him. Found this. I think you could say he's in a state of shock. Apparently, so are his trousers.'

'I can't say I blame them.' A generator hummed in the background, providing juice for the three tall halogen lamps which lit the clearing. Some uniformed officers were cordoning off the area with strips of orange tape. 'So nobody's touched it?'

'Nobody's been near it.'

Rebus nodded, satisfied. 'Better keep it that way till forensics get here. Where the hell's the pathologist?'

Holmes nodded over Rebus's shoulder. 'Speak of the devil,' he said.

Rebus turned. Two men in sombre Crombie-style coats were walking briskly towards the scene. One carried a black surgeon's bag, the other had his hands firmly in his pockets, protection from the chill air. The halogen had fooled a few of the local birds, who were chirping their hearts out. But morning wasn't far away.

Chief Inspector Lauderdale nodded curtly towards

Rebus, reckoning this greeting enough under the circumstances. The pathologist, Dr Curt, was, however (and despite his name), as voluble as ever.

'Top of the morning to you, Inspector.' Rebus, knowing Dr Curt of old, waited for the inevitable joke. The doctor obliged, gesturing towards the body. 'Not often I get a trunk call these days.'

Rebus, as was expected of him, groaned. The doctor beamed. Rebus knew what came next: the corny newspaper headlines. Again, Dr Curt obliged. 'Corpse in the coppice baffles cops,' he mused brightly, donning overshoes and coveralls before making for the corpse itself.

Chief Inspector Lauderdale looked stunned. He shuffled closer to Rebus. 'Is he always like this?'

'Always.'

The doctor had crouched down to inspect the body. He asked for the position of the lamps to be changed, then started his examination. But there was time for a last twist of the head towards Rebus.

'I'm afraid we're too late,' Dr Curt called out. 'Poor chap's dead.'

Chuckling to himself, he set to work, bringing a tape-recorder out of his case and mumbling into it from time to time.

Lauderdale watched for a minute. It was about fifty-nine seconds too long. He turned to Rebus again. 'What can you tell me?'

'About Dr Curt? Or about the deceased?'

'About the deceased.'

Rebus pushed fingers through his hair, scratching at the scalp. He was mentally listing the bad puns still available to Dr Curt – he got legless, he's out of 'arm's way, lost his head, hadn't paid his bills so got cut off, was for the chop anyway, had no bleeding right, worked as a hack, take a butcher's at him …

'Inspector?'

Rebus started. 'What?'

Lauderdale stared at him hard.

'Oh,' Rebus said, remembering. 'Well, he's naked of course. And they haven't severed *every* limb, so we know for sure that it *is* a he. Nothing else yet, sir. Come first light, we'll search the area for the missing appendages. One thing I'm pretty sure of, he wasn't butchered here.'

'Oh?'

'No blood, sir. Not that I can see.'

'Gentlemen!' It was Curt, calling to them, waving his arm for them to join him. They, too, had to slip on the elastic shoes, like ill-fitting polythene bags, and the coveralls. The forensics people would want to cover every inch of the ground around the victim's body. It didn't do to leave erroneous 'clues' like fibres from your jacket or a dropped coin.

'What is it, Doctor?'

'First, let me tell you that he's male, aged anywhere between thirty-five and fifty. Either dissolute thirty-five or a fairly well-preserved fifty. Stocky, too, unless the legs are in ridiculous proportion to the trunk. I can give a better guesstimate once we've had him on the slab.' His smile seemed directed at Lauderdale especially. 'Been dead a day or more. He was brought here in this condition, of course.'

'Of course,' said Lauderdale. 'No blood.'

The doctor nodded, still smiling. 'But there's something else. Look here.' He pointed to what was left of the right shoulder. 'Do you see this damage?' He circled the shoulder with his finger. They had to bend closer to see what he was talking about. The shoulder had been attacked with a knife, like someone had tried to peel it. It all looked clumsy and amateurish compared to the other neat examples.

'A tattoo,' Rebus said. 'Got to be.'

'Quite right, Inspector. They've tried removing it. *After* they dumped the trunk here. They must have spotted that there was still part of the tattoo left, enough to help us identify the victim. So ...' He moved his finger from the shoulder stump to the ground beneath it. Rebus could just make out the shreds of skin.

'We can piece it back together,' Rebus stated.

'Of course we can!' The doctor stood up. 'They must think we're stupid. They go to all this trouble, then leave something like that.' He shook his head slowly. Rebus held his breath, waiting. The doctor's face brightened. 'It's years since I last did a jigsaw,' he said, opening his bag, placing his things back in it, and closing it with a loud snap. 'An open and shut case,' he said, moving back towards the cordon.

After he'd gone, off to his slab to await delivery of the body, Lauderdale lingered to see that everything was running smoothly. It was, as Rebus assured him. Lauderdale then bid him goodnight. Rebus didn't think anyone had ever 'bid' him goodnight before; wasn't sure anyone had *ever* bid anyone goodnight, outside of books and plays. It was especially strange to be bid goodnight at dawn. He could swear there was a cock crowing in the distance, but who in Morningside would keep chickens?

He looked for Holmes and found him over beside the tree-dwellers. Overnight, a guard-duty worked in shifts, two or three people at a time for two hours at a stretch. Holmes was chatting, seeming casual. He shifted his weight from foot to foot, as though cramp or cold were seeping through his socks.

Hadn't a leg to stand on: that was another one Dr Curt could have used.

'You seem very cheerful this morning, Inspector. But then each morning is a cause for celebration in itself.' Intent on Holmes, Rebus hadn't noticed the other figure who, like him, was making his way towards the tree. Dressed in jeans, tartan shirt and lumber jacket, but with the same wooden cross. It was Father Byrne. Sky-blue eyes, piercing eyes, the pupils like tiny points of ink. The smile spreading from the lips and mouth towards the eyes and cheeks. The man's very beard seemed to take part in the process.

'I don't know about cheerful, Father Byrne —'

'Please, call me Steven.'

'Well, as I was saying, I don't know about cheerful. You know there was a murder last night?'

Now the eyes opened wide. 'A murder? Here?'

'Well, not strictly speaking, no. But the body was dumped here. We'll need to talk to anyone who was here yesterday. They may have seen something.'

Holmes waved a notebook. 'I've already collected some names and addresses.'

'Good lad. Have there been any more threats, Father?'

'Threats?'

'You remember, the man with the knife.'

'No, not that I know of.'

'Well, I really would like you to come down the station and see if you can pick him out from some photographs.'

'Now?'

'Sometime today.' Rebus paused. 'At your convenience.'

Father Byrne caught the meaning of the pause. 'Well, of course. If you think it will help. I'll come this morning. But you don't think …? Surely not.'

Rebus shrugged. 'Probably just a coincidence, Father. But you have to admit, it *is* quite a coincidence. Someone comes down here with a knife. Some days later, a body appears not three hundred yards away. Yes, coincidence.' That pause again. 'Wouldn't you say?'

But Father Byrne didn't seem to have an answer for that.

No, it was no coincidence, Rebus was sure of that. Fine, if you were going to dump a body the Hermitage was as good a spot as any. But not in a clearing, where it would be stumbled upon sooner rather than later. And not so close to the famous tree, where, as everyone knew, people were to be found round-the-clock, making dumping a body nearby a risky procedure. Too risky. There had to be a reason. There had to be some meaning. Some message.

Yes, some *message*.

And wasn't three hundred yards a long way to go for number twos? Well, that one was cleared up quickly. The man admitted that he hadn't gone off alone. He'd gone with his girlfriend. After finding the body, the man had sent her home. Partly because she was in shock; partly to avoid any 'slur on her character'. Father Byrne passed this news on to Rebus when he came to the station to look through the mug-shots – without success.

A new sort of tourist now visited the Hermitage, to view a new kind of 'shrine'. They wanted to see the spot where the trunk had been discovered. Locals still brought their dogs, and lovers still followed the route of the burn; but they wore fixed looks on their faces, as though unwilling to accept that the Hermitage, *their* Hermitage, had become something else, something they never believed it could be.

Rebus, meantime, played with a jigsaw. The tattoo was coming together, though it was a slow business. Errors were made. And one error, once made, led to more pieces being placed incorrectly, until the whole thing had to be broken up and started again. Blue was the predominant colour, along with some patches of red. The dark, inked lines tended to be straight. It looked like a professional job. Tattoo parlours were visited, but the description given was too vague as yet. Rebus showed yet another configuration of the pieces to Brian Holmes: it was the fifth such photograph in a week. The lab had provided their own dotted outline of how they thought the design might continue. Holmes nodded.

'It's a Kandinsky,' he said. 'Or one of his followers. Solid bars of colour. Yes, definitely a Kandinsky.'

Rebus was amazed. 'You mean Kandinsky did this tattoo?'

Holmes looked up from the photograph, grinned sheepishly. 'Sorry, I was making a joke. Or trying to. Kandinsky was a painter.'

'Oh,' Rebus sounded disappointed. 'Yes,' he said, 'yes, of course he was. Right.'

Feeling guilty at having raised his superior's hopes, Holmes concentrated all the harder on the photo. 'Could be a swastika,' he offered. 'Those lines ...'

'Yes.' Rebus turned the photograph towards him, then slapped a hand against it. 'No!' Holmes flinched. 'No, Brian, not a swastika ... a Union Jack! It's a bloody Union Jack!'

Once the lab had the design in front of them, it was a straightforward job of following it in their reconstruction. Not just a Union Jack, though, as they found. A Union Jack with the letters UFF slurred across it, and a machine gun half-hidden behind the letters.

'Ulster Freedom Fighters,' Rebus murmured. 'Right, let's get back to those tattoo parlours.'

A CID officer in Musselburgh came up with the break. A tattooist there thought he recognised the design as the work of Tam Finlayson, but Finlayson had retired from the business some years ago, and tracing him was hard work. Rebus even feared for a moment that the man might be dead and buried. He wasn't. He was living with his daughter and son-in-law in Brighton.

A Brighton detective visited the address and telephoned Edinburgh with details. Shown the photograph, Finlayson had flinched, then had taken, as the daughter put it, 'one of his turns'. Pills were administered and finally Finlayson was in a state to talk. But he was scared, there was no doubt of that. Reassured, though, by the information that the tattoo belonged to a corpse, the tattooist owned up. Yes, it was his work. He'd done it maybe fifteen years before. And the customer? A young man called Philips. Rab Philips. Not a terrorist, just a tearaway looking for a cause.

'Rab Philips?' Rebus stared at his telephone. '*The* Rab Philips?' Who else? A dim, small-time villain who'd spent enough time in prison, that university of life, to become a clever small-time villain. And who had grown, matured, if you like, into a big-game player. Well, not quite Premier League, but not Sunday kickabout either. He'd certainly been keeping himself to himself these past couple of years. No gossip on the street about him; no dirt; no news at all really.

Well, there was news now. Pubs and clubs were visited, drinks bought, occasionally an arm twisted and the information began to trickle in. Philips' home was searched, his wife questioned. Her story was that he'd told her he was going to London for a few days on a business trip. Rebus nodded calmly and handed her a photograph.

'Is that Rab's tattoo?'

She went pale. Then she went into hysterics.

Meanwhile, Philips' cronies and 'associates' had been rounded up and questioned. One or two were released and picked up again, released and picked up. The message was clear: CID thought they knew more than they were telling and unless they told what they knew, this process would go on indefinitely. They were nervous, of course, and who could blame them? They couldn't know who would now take over their ex-boss's terrain. There were people out there with grudges and knives. The longer they hung about in police stations, the more of a liability they would appear.

They told what they knew, or as much as CID needed to know. That was fine by Rebus. Rab Philips, they said, had started shifting drugs. Nothing serious, mostly cannabis, but in hefty quantities. Edinburgh CID had done much to clear up the hard drug problem in the city, mainly by clearing out the dealers. New dealers would always appear, but they were small-fry. Rab Philips, though, had been so quiet for so long that he was not a suspect. And besides, the drugs were merely passing through Edinburgh; they weren't staying there. Boats would land them on the Fife coast or further north. They would be brought to Edinburgh and from there transferred south. To England. Which meant, in effect, to London. Rebus probed for an Ulster connection, but nobody had anything to tell him.

'So who are the drugs going to in London?'

Again, nobody knew. Or nobody was saying. Rebus sat at his desk, another jigsaw to work on now, but this time in his head – a jigsaw of facts and possibilities. Yes, he should have known from the start. Dismemberment equals gangland. A betrayal, a double-cross. And the penalty for same. Rebus reached for his telephone again and this time put in a call to London.

'Inspector George Flight, please.'

Trust Flight to make it all seem so easy. Rebus gave him the description and an hour later Flight came back with a name. Rebus added some details and Flight went visiting. This time, the phone call came to Rebus's flat. It was late evening and he was lying half-asleep in his chair, the telephone waiting on his lap.

Flight was in good humour. 'I'm glad you told me about the wound,' he said. 'I asked him a few questions, noticed he was a bit stiff. As he stood up to show me out, I slapped him on his right side. I made it seem sort of playful. You know, not malicious like.' He chuckled. 'You should have seen him, John. Doubled over like a bloody pen-knife. It started bleeding again, of course. The silly sod hadn't had it seen to. I wouldn't wonder if it's gone septic or something.'

'When did he get back from Edinburgh?'

'Couple of days ago. Think we can nail him?'

'Maybe. We could do with some evidence though. But I think I can do something about that.'

As Rebus explained to Brian Holmes, it had been more than a 'hunch'. A hunch was, as Dr Curt himself might put it, a stab in the dark. Rebus had a little more light to work by. He told the story as they drove through early-morning Edinburgh towards the Hermitage. The three girls had seen a man appearing from the trees. A wounded man. It seemed clear now that he'd been stabbed in some skirmish nearer to, or by the side of, Braid Hills Road. A switch of drugs from one car to another. An attempted double-cross. He'd been wounded and had fled down the hill into the Hermitage itself, coming into the clearing at the same time as the girls, making himself scarce when he saw them.

Because, of course, he had something to hide: his wound. He had patched himself up, but had stuck around Edinburgh, looking for revenge. Rab Philips had been grabbed, dismembered and his body dumped in the Hermitage as a message to Philips' gang. The message was: you don't mess with London.

Then the wounded villain had finally headed back south. But he was the antithesis of Philips; he wore flashy clothes. 'Probably a white coat,' Rebus had told George Flight. 'White trousers. He's got long hair and a beard.'

Flight had bettered the description. 'It's a white trench-coat,' he'd said. 'And yellow trousers, would you believe. A real old ex-hippy this one.' His name was Shaun McLafferty. 'Everyone on the street knows Shaun,' Flight went on. 'I didn't know he'd started pushing dope though. Mind you, he'd try anything, that one.'

McLafferty. 'He wouldn't,' Rebus asked, 'be Irish by any chance?'

'London Irish,' said Flight. 'I wouldn't be surprised if the IRA was creaming ten per cent off his profits. Maybe more. After all, he either pays up or they take over. It happens.'

Maybe it was as simple as that then. An argument over 'the divide'. An IRA supporter finding himself doing business with a UFF tattoo. The kind of mix old Molotov himself would have appreciated.

'So,' Brian Holmes said, having digested all this, 'Inspector Flight paid a visit to McLafferty?'

Rebus nodded. 'And he was wounded in his right side. Stab wound, according to George.'

'So why,' Holmes said, 'are we here?'

They had parked the car just outside the gates and were now walking into the Hermitage.

'Because,' Rebus said, 'we still lack evidence.'

'What evidence?'

But Rebus wasn't saying; perhaps because he didn't know the answer himself. They were approaching the tree. There was no sign of the once ubiquitous guard, but a familiar figure was kneeling before the tree.

'Morning, Father.'

Father Byrne looked up. 'Good morning, Inspector. You too, Constable.'

Rebus looked around him. 'All alone?'

Byrne nodded. 'Enthusiasm seems to have waned, Inspector. No more megaphones, or coach parties, or cameras.'

'You sound relieved.'

'Believe me, I am.' Father Byrne held out his arms. 'I much prefer it like this, don't you?'

Rebus was obliged to nod his agreement. 'Anyway,' he said, 'we think we can explain what the girls saw.'

Father Byrne merely shrugged.

'No more guard-duties?' Rebus asked.

'The men stopped bothering us.'

Rebus nodded thoughtfully. His eyes were on the tree. 'It wasn't you they were after, Father. It was the tree. But not for the reason you think. Brian, give me a hand, will you?'

A literal hand. Rebus wanted Holmes to form a stirrup from his hands, so that Rebus could place a foot on them and be hoisted up into the tree. Holmes steadied himself against the tree and complied, not without a silent groan. It was feasible that Rebus weighed a good three and a half stones more than him. Still, ours is not to reason why ... and *heave!*

Rebus scrabbled with his hands, finding knot-holes, moss, but nothing else, nothing hidden. He peered upwards, seeking any fissure in the bark, any cranny. Nothing.

'All right, Brian.'

Gratefully, Holmes lowered Rebus groundwards. 'Anything?'

Rebus shook his head. He was gnawing his bottom lip.

'Are you going to tell me what we're looking for?'

'McLafferty had something else to hide from the girls, something on top of the fact that he'd been stabbed. Let's think.' McLafferty had come through the copse, the undergrowth, had rested for a second against the tree, fled back through the copse.

'Chalk!' Rebus thumped the tree with his fist.

'Pardon?'

'Chalk! That morning I came to check on you. When the cadets got up, their knees had white, powdery chalk on them.'

'Yes?'

'Well look!' Rebus led Holmes into the copse. 'There's no white rock here. No bits of chalky stone. That wasn't bloody chalk.' He fell to his knees and began to burrow furiously, raking his hands through the earth.

The girls' parents had messed up the ground, making the white powder inconspicuous. Enough to mark a trouser-knee, but hardly noticeable otherwise. Certainly, nothing a cadet would bother with. And besides, they'd been looking for something *on* the ground, not below it.

'Ah!' He paused, probed a spot with his fingers, then began to dig around it. 'Look,' he said, 'just the one packet and it's burst. That's what it was. Must have burst when

McLafferty was burying it. Better call for forensics, Brian. His blood and his prints will be all over it.'

'Right, sir.' Stunned, Brian Holmes sprinted from the clearing, then stopped and turned back. 'Keys,' he explained. Rebus fished his car-keys from his pocket and tossed them to him. Father Byrne, who had been a spectator throughout, came a little closer.

'Heroin, Father. Either that or cocaine. Bigger profits than cannabis, you see. It all comes down to money in the end. They were doing a deal. McLafferty got himself stabbed. He was holding a packet when it happened. Got away somehow, ran down here before he had time to think. He knew he'd better get rid of the stuff, so he buried it. The men who were bothering you, McLafferty's men, it was *this* they were after. Then they got Rab Philips instead and went home satisfied. If it wasn't for your all-night vigil, they'd've had this stuff too.'

Rebus paused, aware that he couldn't be making much sense to the priest. Father Byrne seemed to read his mind and smiled.

'For a minute there, Inspector,' he said, 'I thought you were speaking in tongues.'

Rebus grinned, too, feeling breathless. With McLafferty's prints on the bag, they would have the evidence they needed. 'Sorry you didn't get your miracle,' he said.

Father Byrne's smile broadened. 'Miracles happen every day, Inspector. I don't need to have them invented for me.'

They turned to watch as Holmes came wandering back towards them. But his eyes were concentrating on an area to the left of them. 'They're on their way,' he said, handing Rebus's keys back to him.

'Fine.'

'Who was that by the way?

'Who?'

'The other man.' Holmes looked from Rebus to Byrne back to Rebus again. 'The other man,' he repeated. 'The one who was standing here with you. When I was coming back, he was …' He was pointing now, back towards the gate, then over towards the left of the tree. But his voice died away.

'No, never mind,' he said. 'I thought … I just, no never mind. I must be –'

'Seeing things?' Father Byrne suggested, his fingers just touching the wooden cross around his neck.

'That's right, yes. Yes, seeing things.'

Ghosts, thought Rebus. Spirits of the wood. Rab Philips maybe, or the Hermitage Witch. My God, those two would have a lot to talk about, wouldn't they?

A Good Hanging

I

It was quite some time since a scaffold had been seen in Parliament Square. Quite some time since Edinburgh had witnessed a hanging, too, though digging deeper into history the sight might have been common enough. Detective Inspector John Rebus recalled hearing some saloon-bar story of how criminals, sentenced to hang, would be given the chance to run the distance of the Royal Mile from Parliament Square to Holyrood, a baying crowd hot on their heels. If the criminal reached the Royal Park before he was caught, he would be allowed to remain there, wandering in safety so long as he did not step outside the boundary of the park itself. True or not, the tale conjured up the wonderful image of rogues and vagabonds trapped within the confines of Arthur's Seat, Salisbury Crags and Whinny Hill. Frankly, Rebus would have preferred the noose.

'It's got to be a prank gone wrong, hasn't it?'

A prank. Edinburgh was full of pranks at this time of year. It was Festival time, when young people, theatrical people, flooded into the city with their enthusiasm and their energy. You couldn't walk ten paces without someone pressing a handbill upon you or begging you to visit their production. These were the 'Fringe lunatics' as Rebus had not very originally, but to his own satisfaction, termed them. They came for two or three or four weeks, mostly from London and they squeezed into damp sleeping-bags on bedsit floors throughout the city, going home much paler, much more tired and almost always the poorer. It was not unusual for the unlucky Fringe shows, those given a venue on the outskirts, those with no review to boast of, starved of publicity and inspiration, for those unfortunate shows to play to single-figure audiences, if not to an audience of a single figure.

Rebus didn't like Festival time. The streets became clogged, there seemed a despair about all the artistic fervour and, of course, the crime rate rose. Pickpockets loved the festival. Burglars found easy pickings in the overpopulated, underprotected bedsits. And, finding their local pub taken over by the 'Sassenachs', the natives were inclined to throw the occasional punch or bottle or chair. Which was why Rebus avoided the city centre during the Festival, skirting around it in his car, using alleyways and half-forgotten routes. Which was why he was so annoyed at having been called here today, to Parliament Square, the heart of the Fringe, to witness a hanging.

'Got to be a prank,' he repeated to Detective Constable Brian Holmes. The two men were standing in front of a scaffold, upon which hung the gently swaying body of a young man. The body swayed due to the fresh breeze which was sweeping up the Royal Mile from the direction of Holyrood Park. Rebus thought of the ghosts of the royal park's inmates. Was the wind of their making? 'A publicity stunt gone wrong,' he mused.

'Apparently not, sir,' Holmes said. He'd been having a few words with the workmen who were trying to erect a curtain of sorts around the spectacle so as to hide it from the view of the hundreds of inquisitive tourists who had gathered noisily outside the police cordon. Holmes now consulted his notebook, while Rebus, hands in pockets, strolled around the scaffold. It was of fairly ramshackle construction, which hadn't stopped it doing its job.

'The body was discovered at four-fifty this morning. We don't think it had been here long. A patrol car passed this way at around four and they didn't see anything.'

'That doesn't mean much,' Rebus interrupted in a mutter.

Holmes ignored the remark. 'The deceased belonged to a Fringe group called Ample Reading Time. They come from the University of Reading, thus the name.'

'It also makes the acronym ART,' Rebus commented.

'Yes, sir,' said Holmes. His tone told the senior officer that Holmes had already worked this out for himself. Rebus wriggled a little, as though trying to keep warm. In fact, he had a summer cold.

'How did we discover his identity?' They were in front of the hanging man now, standing only four or so feet below him. Early twenties, Rebus surmised. A shock of black curly hair.

'The scaffold has a venue number pinned to it,' Holmes was saying. 'A student hall of residence just up the road.'

'And that's where the ART show's playing?'

'Yes, sir.' Holmes consulted the bulky Fringe programme which he had been holding behind his notebook. 'It's a play of sorts called "Scenes from a Hanging".' The two men exchanged a look at this. 'The blurb,' Holmes continued, consulting the company's entry near the front of the programme, 'promises "thrills, spills and a live hanging on stage".'

'A live hanging, eh? Well, you can't say they didn't deliver. So, he takes the scaffold from the venue, wheels it out here – I notice it's on wheels, presumably to make it easier to trundle on and off the stage – and in the middle of the night he hangs himself, without anyone hearing anything or seeing anything.' Rebus sounded sceptical.

'Well,' said Holmes, 'be honest, sir.' He was pointing towards and beyond the crowd of onlookers. 'Does anything look suspicious in Edinburgh at this time of year?'

Rebus followed the direction of the finger and saw that a twelve-foot-high man was enjoying a grandstand view of the spectacle, while somewhere to his right someone was juggling three saucepans high into the air. The stilt-man walked towards the pans, grabbed one from mid-air and set it on his head, waving down to the crowd before moving off. Rebus sighed.

'I suppose you're right, Brian. Just this once you may be right.'

A young DC approached, holding a folded piece of paper towards them. 'We found this in his trousers back-pocket.'

'Ah,' said Rebus, 'the suicide note.' He plucked the sheet from the DC's outstretched hand and read it aloud.

' "Pity it wasn't *Twelfth Night*".'

Holmes peered at the line of type. 'Is that it?'

'Short but sweet,' said Rebus. '*Twelfth Night*. A play by Shakespeare and the end of the Christmas season. I wonder which one he means?' Rebus refolded the note and slipped it into his pocket. 'But is it a suicide note or not? It could just be a bog-standard note, a reminder or whatever, couldn't it? I still think this is a stunt gone wrong.' He paused to cough. He was standing beside the cobblestone inset of the Heart of Midlothian, and like many a Scot before him, he spat for luck into the centre of the heart-shaped stones. Holmes looked away and found himself gazing into the dead man's dulled eyes. He turned back as Rebus was fumbling with a handkerchief.

'Maybe,' Rebus was saying between blows, 'we should have a word with the rest of the cast. I don't suppose they'll have much to keep them occupied.' He gestured towards the scaffold. 'Not until they get back their prop. Besides, we've got a job to do, haven't we?'

II

'Well, I say we keep going!' the voice yelled. 'We've got an important piece of work here, a play people should *see*. If anything, David's death will bring audiences *in*. We shouldn't be pushing them away. We shouldn't be packing our bags and crawling back south.'

'You sick bastard.'

Rebus and Holmes entered the makeshift auditorium as the speaker of these last three words threw himself forwards and landed a solid punch against the side of the speech-maker's face. His glasses flew from his nose and slid along the floor, stopping an inch or two short of Rebus's scuffed leather shoes. He stooped, picked up the spectacles and moved forward.

The room was of a size, and had an atmosphere, that would have suited a monastery's dining-hall. It was long and narrow, with a stage constructed along its narrow face and short rows of chairs extending back into the gloom. What windows there were had been blacked-out and the hall's only natural light came from the open door through which Rebus had just stepped, to the front left of the stage itself.

There were five of them in the room, four men and a woman. All looked to be in their mid- to late-twenties. Rebus handed over the glasses.

'Not a bad right-hook that,' he said to the attacker, who was looking with some amazement at his own hand, as though hardly believing it capable of such an action. 'I'm Inspector Rebus, this is Detective Sergeant Holmes. And you are?'

They introduced themselves in turn. Sitting on the stage was Pam, who acted. Beside her was Peter Collins, who also acted. On a chair in front of the stage, legs and arms crossed and having obviously enjoyed tremendously the one-sided bout he had just witnessed, sat Marty Jones.

'I don't act,' he said loudly. 'I just design the set, build the bloody thing, make all the props and work the lights and the music during the play.'

'So it's your scaffold then?' commented Rebus. Marty Jones looked less confident.

'Yes,' he said. 'I made it a bit too bloody well, didn't I?'

'We could just as easily blame the rope manufacturer, Mr Jones,' Rebus said quietly. His eyes moved to the man with the spectacles, who was nursing a bruised jaw.

'Charles Collins,' the man said sulkily. He looked towards where Peter Collins sat on the stage. 'No relation. I'm the director. I also wrote "Scenes from a Hanging".'

Rebus nodded. 'How have the reviews been?'

Marty Jones snorted.

'Not great,' Charles Collins admitted. 'We've only had four,' he went on, knowing if he didn't say it someone else would. 'They weren't exactly complimentary.'

Marty Jones snorted again. Stiffening his chin, as though to take another punch, Collins ignored him.

'And the audiences?' Rebus asked, interested.

'Lousy.' This from Pam, swinging her legs in front of her as though such news was not only quite acceptable, but somehow humorous as well.

'Average, I'd say,' Charles Collins corrected. 'Going by what other companies have been telling me.'

'That's the problem with staging a new play, isn't it?' Rebus said knowledgeably, while Holmes stared at him. Rebus was standing in the midst of the group now, as though giving them a pre-production pep talk. 'Trying to get audiences to watch new work is always a problem. They prefer the classics.'

'That's right,' Charles Collins agreed enthusiastically. 'That's what I've been telling —' with a general nod in everyone's direction, 'them. The classics are "safe". That's why we need to challenge people.'

'To excite them,' Rebus continued, 'to shock them even. Isn't that right, Mr Collins? To give them a spectacle?'

Charles Collins seemed to see where Rebus's line, devious though it was, was leading. He shook his head.

'Well, they got a spectacle all right,' Rebus went on, all enthusiasm gone from his voice. 'Thanks to Mr Jones's scaffold, the people got a shock. Someone was hanged. I think his name's David, isn't it?'

'That's right.' This from the attacker. 'David Caulfield.' He looked towards the writer/director. 'Supposedly a friend of ours. Someone we've known for three years. Someone we never thought could ...'

'And you are?' Rebus was brisk. He didn't want anyone breaking down just yet, not while there were still questions that needed answers.

'Hugh Clay.' The young man smiled bitterly. 'David always said it sounded like "ukulele".'

'And you're an actor?'

Hugh Clay nodded.

'And so was David Caulfield?'

Another nod. 'I mean, we're not really professionals. We're students. That's all. Students with pretensions.'

Something about Hugh Clay's voice, its tone and its slow rhythms, had made the room darken, so that everyone seemed less animated, more reflective, remembering at last that David Caulfield was truly dead.

'And what do you think happened to him, Hugh? I mean, how do you think he died?'

Clay seemed puzzled by the question. 'He killed himself, didn't he?'

'Did he?' Rebus shrugged. 'We don't know for certain. The pathologist's report may give us a better idea.' Rebus turned to Marty Jones, who was looking less confident all the time. 'Mr Jones, could David have operated the scaffold by himself?'

'That's the way I designed it,' Jones replied. 'I mean, David worked it himself every night. During the hanging scene.'

Rebus pondered this. 'And could someone else have worked the mechanism?'

Jones nodded. 'No problem. The neck noose we used was a dummy. The real noose was attached around David's chest, under his arms. He held a cord behind him and at the right moment he pulled the cord, the trapdoor opened and he fell about a yard. It looked pretty bloody realistic. He had to wear padding under his arms to stop bruising.' He glanced at Charles Collins. 'It was the best bit of the show.'

'But,' said Rebus, 'the scaffold could easily be rejigged to work properly?'

Jones nodded. 'All you'd need is a bit of rope. There's plenty lying around backstage.'

'And then you could hang yourself? Really hang yourself?'

Jones nodded again.

'Or someone could hang you,' said Pam, her eyes wide, voice soft with horror.

Rebus smiled towards her, but seemed to be thinking about something else. In fact, he wasn't thinking of anything in particular: he was letting them stew in the silence, letting their minds and imaginations work in whatever way they would.

At last, he turned to Charles Collins. 'Do you think David killed himself?'

Collins shrugged. 'What else?'

'Any particular reason why he would commit suicide?'

'Well,' Collins looked towards the rest of the company. 'The show,' he said. 'The reviews weren't very complimentary about David's performance.'

'Tell me a little about the play.'

Collins tried not to sound keen as he spoke. Tried, Rebus noticed, but failed. 'It took me most of this year to write,' he said. 'What we have is a prisoner in a South American country, tried and found guilty, sentenced to death. The play opens with him standing on the scaffold, the noose around his neck. Scenes from his life are played out around him, while his own scenes are made up of soliloquies dealing with the larger questions. What I'm asking the audience to do is to ask themselves the same questions he's asking himself on the scaffold. Only the answers are perhaps more urgent, more important for him, because they're the last things he'll ever know.'

Rebus broke in. The whole thing sounded dreadful. 'And David would be on stage the entire time?' Collins nodded. 'And how long was that?'

'Anywhere between two hours and two and a half –' with a glance towards the stage, 'depending on the cast.'

'Meaning?'

'Sometimes lines were forgotten, or a scene went missing.' (Peter and Pam smiled in shared complicity.) 'Or the pace just went.'

' "Never have I prayed so ardently for a death to take place", as one of the reviews put it,' Hugh Clay supplied. 'It was a problem of the play. It didn't have anything to do with David.'

Charles Collins looked ready to protest. Rebus stepped in. 'But David's mentions weren't exactly kind?' he hinted.

'No,' Clay admitted. 'They said he lacked the necessary *gravitas* whatever that means.'

' "Too big a part for too small an actor",' interrupted Marty Jones, quoting again.

'Bad notices then,' said Rebus. 'And David Caulfield took them to heart?'

'David took everything to heart,' explained Hugh Clay. 'That was part of the problem.'

'The other part being that the notices were true,' sniped Charles Collins. But Clay seemed prepared for this.

' "Overwritten and messily directed by Charles Collins",' he quoted. Another fight seemed to be on the cards. Rebus blew his nose noisily.

'So,' he said. 'Notices were bad, audiences were poor. And you didn't decide to remedy this situation by staging a little publicity stunt? A stunt that just happened – nobody's fault necessarily – to go wrong?'

There were shakes of the head, eyes looked to other eyes, seemingly innocent of any such plans.

'Besides,' said Marty Jones, 'you couldn't hang yourself accidentally on that scaffold. You either had to mean to do it yourself, or else someone had to do it for you.'

More silence. An impasse seemed to have been reached. Rebus collapsed noisily into a chair. 'All things considered,' he said with a sigh, 'you might have been better off sticking to *Twelfth Night*.'

'That's funny,' Pam said.

'What is?'

'That's the play we did last year,' she explained. 'It went down very well, didn't it?' She had turned to Peter Collins, who nodded agreement.

'We got some good reviews for that,' he said. 'David was a brilliant Malvolio. He kept the cuttings pinned to his bedroom wall, didn't he, Hugh?'

Hugh Clay nodded. Rebus had the distinct feeling that Peter Collins was trying to imply something, perhaps that Hugh Clay had seen more of David Caulfield's bedroom walls than was strictly necessary.

He fumbled in his pocket, extracting the note from below the handkerchief. Brian Holmes, he noticed, was staying very much in the wings, like the minor character in a minor scene. 'We found a note in David's pocket,' Rebus said without preamble. 'Maybe your success last year explains it.' He read it out to them. Charles Collins nodded.

'Yes, that sounds like David all right. Harking back to past glories.'

'You think that's what it means?' Rebus asked conversationally.

Collins nodded. 'You should know, Inspector, that actors are conceited. The greater the actor, the greater the ego. And David was, I admit, on occasion a very gifted actor.'

He was speechifying again, but Rebus let him go on. Perhaps it was the only way a director could communicate with his cast.

'It would be just like David to get depressed, suicidal even, by bad notices, and just like him to decide to stage as showy an exit as he could, something to hit the headlines. I happen to think he succeeded splendidly.'

No one seemed about to contradict him on this, not even David Caulfield's stalwart defender, Hugh Clay. It was Pam who spoke, tears in her eyes at last.

'I only feel sorry for Marie,' she said.

Charles Collins nodded. 'Yes, Marie's come into her own in "Scenes from a Hanging".'

'She means,' Hugh Clay said through gritted teeth, 'she feels sorry for Marie because Marie's lost David, not because Marie can no longer act in your bloody awful play.'

Rebus felt momentary bemusement, but tried not to show it. Marty Jones, however, had seen all.

'The other member of ART,' he explained to Rebus. 'She's back at the flat. She wanted to be left on her own for a bit.'

'She's pretty upset,' Peter Collins agreed.

Rebus nodded slowly. 'She and David were …?'

'Engaged,' Pam said, the tears falling now, Peter Collins' arm snaking around her shoulders. 'They were going to be married after the Fringe was finished.'

Rebus stole a glance towards Holmes, who raised his eyebrows in reply. Just like every good melodrama, the raised eyebrows said. A twist at the end of every bloody act.

III

The flat the group had rented, at what seemed to Rebus considerable expense, was a dowdy but spacious second-floor affair on Morrison Street, just off Lothian Road.

Rebus had been to the block before, during the investigation of a housebreaking. That had been years ago, but the only difference in the tenement seemed to be the installation of a communal intercom at the main door. Rebus ignored the entry-phone and pushed at the heavy outside door. As he had guessed, it was unlocked anyway.

'Bloody students,' had been one of Rebus's few voiced comments during the short, curving drive down the back of the Castle towards the Usher Hall and Lothian Road. But then Holmes, driving, had been a student, too, hadn't he? So Rebus had not expanded on his theme. Now they climbed the steep winding stairwell until they arrived at the second floor. Marty Jones had told them that the name on the door was BLACK. Having robbed the students of an unreasonable rent (though no doubt the going rate), Mr and Mrs Black had departed for a month-long holiday on the proceeds. Rebus had borrowed a key from Jones and used it to let Holmes and himself in. The hall was long, narrow and darker than the stairwell. Off it were three bedrooms, a bathroom, a kitchen and the living-room. A young woman, not quite out of her teens, came out of the kitchen carrying a mug of coffee. She was wearing a long baggy T-shirt and nothing else, and there was a sleepy, tousled look to her, accompanying the red streakiness of her eyes.

'Oh,' she said, startled. Rebus was quick to respond.

'Inspector Rebus, miss. This is Detective Constable Holmes. One of your friends lent us a key. Could we have a word?'

'About David?' Her eyes were huge, doe-like, her face small and round. Her hair was short and fair, the body slender and brittle. Even in grief – perhaps especially in grief – she was mightily attractive, and Holmes raised his eyebrows again as she led them into the living-room.

Two sleeping bags lay on the floor, along with paperback books, an alarm clock, mugs of tea. Off the living-room was a box-room, a large walk-in cupboard. These were often used by students to make an extra room in a temporary flat and light coming from the half-open door told Rebus that this was still its function. Marie went into the room and switched off the light, before joining the two policemen.

'It's Pam's room,' she explained. 'She said I could lie down there. I didn't want to sleep in our ... in my room.'

'Of course,' Rebus said, all understanding and sympathy.

'Of course,' Holmes repeated. She signalled for them to sit, so they did, sinking into a sofa the consistency of marshmallow. Rebus feared he wouldn't be able to rise again without help and struggled to keep himself upright. Marie meantime had settled, legs beneath her, with enviable poise on the room's only chair. She placed her mug on the floor, then had a thought.

'Would you like ...?'

A shake of the head from both men. It struck Rebus that there was something about her voice. Holmes beat him to it.

'Are you French?'

She smiled a pale smile, then nodded towards the Detective Constable. 'From Bordeaux. Do you know it?'

'Only by the reputation of its wine.'

Rebus blew his nose again, though pulling the hankie from his pocket had been a struggle. Holmes took the hint and closed his mouth. 'Now then, Miss ...?' Rebus began.

'Hivert, Marie Hivert.'

Rebus nodded slowly, playing with the hankie rather than trying to replace it in his pocket. 'We're told that you were engaged to Mr Caulfield.'

Her voice was almost a whisper. 'Yes. Not officially, you understand. But there was – a promise.'

'I see. And when was this promise made?'

'Oh, I'm not sure exactly. March, April. Yes, early April I think. Springtime.'

'And how were things between David and yourself?' She seemed not quite to understand. 'I mean,' said Rebus, 'how did David seem to you?'

She shrugged. 'David was David. He could be –' she raised her eyes to the ceiling, seeking words, 'impossible, nervous, exciting, foul-tempered.' She smiled. 'But mostly exciting.'

'Not suicidal?'

She gave this serious thought. 'Oh yes, I suppose,' she admitted. 'Suicidal, just as actors can be. He took criticism to heart. He was a perfectionist.'

'How long had you known him?'

'Two years. I met him through the theatre group.'

'And you fell in love?'

She smiled again. 'Not at first. There was a certain ... competitiveness between us, you might say. It helped our acting. I'm not sure it helped our relationship altogether. But we survived.' Realising what she had said, she grew silent, her eyes dimming. A hand went to her forehead as, head bowed, she tried to collect herself.

'I'm sorry,' she said, collapsing into sobs. Holmes raised his eyebrows: someone should be here with her. Rebus shrugged back: she can handle it on her own. Holmes' eyebrows remained raised: can she? Rebus looked back at the tiny figure, engulfed by the armchair. Could actors always tell the real world from the illusory?

We survived. It was an interesting phrase to have used. But then she was an interesting young woman.

She went to the bathroom to splash water on her face and while she was gone Rebus took the opportunity to rise awkwardly to his feet. He looked back at the sofa.

'Bloody thing,' he said. Holmes just smiled.

When she returned, composed once more, Rebus asked if David Caulfield might have left a note somewhere. She shrugged. He asked if she minded them having a quick look round. She shook her head. So, never men to refuse a gift,

Rebus and Holmes began looking.

The set-up was fairly straightforward. Pam slept in the box-room, while Marty Jones and Hugh Clay had sleeping-bags on the living-room floor. Marie and David Caulfield had shared the largest of the three bedrooms, with Charles and Peter Collins having a single room each. Charles Collins' room was obsessively tidy, its narrow single bed made up for the night and on the quilt an acting-copy of 'Scenes from a Hanging', covered in marginalia and with several long speeches, all Caulfield's, seemingly excised. A pencil lay on the typescript, evidence that Charles Collins was taking the critics' view to heart himself and attempting to shorten the play as best he could.

Peter Collins' room was much more to Rebus's personal taste, though Holmes wrinkled his nose at the used underwear underfoot, the contents of the hastily unpacked rucksack scattered over every surface. Beside the unmade bed, next to an overflowing ashtray, lay another copy of the play. Rebus flipped through it. Closing it, his attention was caught by some doodlings on the inside cover. Crude heart shapes had been constructed around the words 'I love Edinburgh'. His smile was quickly erased when Holmes held the ashtray towards him.

'Not exactly Silk Cut,' Holmes was saying. Rebus looked. The butts in the ashtrays were made up of cigarette papers wrapped around curled strips of cardboard. They were called 'roaches' by those who smoked dope, though he couldn't remember why. He made a tutting sound.

'And what were we doing in here when we found these?' he asked. Holmes nodded, knowing the truth: they probably couldn't charge Peter Collins even if they'd wanted to, since there was no reason for their being in his room. *We were looking for someone else's suicide note* probably wouldn't impress a latter-day jury.

The double room shared by Marie Hivert and David Caulfield was messiest of all. Marie helped them sift through a few of Caulfield's things. His diary proved a dead end, since he had started it faithfully on 1st January but the entries ceased on 8th January. Rebus, having tried keeping a diary himself, knew the feeling.

But in the back of the diary were newspaper clippings, detailing Caulfield's triumph in the previous year's *Twelfth Night*. Marie, too, had come in for some praise as Viola, but the glory had been Malvolio's. She wept again a little as she read through the reviews. Holmes said that he'd make another cup of coffee. Did he want her to fetch Pam from the theatre? She shook her head. She'd be all right. She promised she would.

While Marie sat on the bed and Holmes filled the kettle, Rebus wandered back into the living-room. He peered into the box-room, but saw little there to interest him. Finally, he came back to the sleeping-bags on the floor. Marie was coming back into the room as he bent to pick up the paperback book from beside one sleeping-bag. It was Tom Wolfe's *Bonfire of the Vanities*. Rebus had a hardback copy at home, still unopened. Something fell from the back of the book, a piece of card. Rebus retrieved it from the floor. It was a photograph of Marie, standing on the Castle ramparts with the Scott Monument behind her. The wind blew her hair fiercely against her face and she was attempting to sweep the hair out of her eyes as she grinned towards the camera. Rebus handed the picture to her.

'Your hair was longer then,' he said.

She smiled and nodded, her eyes till moist. 'Yes,' she said. 'That was in June. We came to look at the venue.'

He waved the book at her. 'Who's the Tom Wolfe fan?'

'Oh,' she said, 'it's doing the rounds. I think Marty's reading it just now.' Rebus flipped through the book again, his eyes lingering a moment on the inside cover. 'Tom Wolfe's had quite a career,' he said before placing the book, face down as it had been, beside the sleeping-bag. He pointed towards the photograph. 'Shall I put it back?' But she shook her head.

'It was David's,' she said. 'I think I'd like to keep it.'

Rebus smiled an avuncular smile. 'Of course,' he said. Then he remembered something. 'David's parents. Have you been in touch at all?'

She shook her head, horror growing within her. 'Oh God,' she said, 'they'll be devastated. David was very close to his mother and father.'

'Well,' said Rebus, 'give me the details and I'll phone them when I get back to the station.'

She frowned. 'But I don't … No, sorry,' she said, 'all I know is that they live in Croydon.'

'Well, never mind,' said Rebus, knowing, in fact, that the parents had already been notified, but interested that Caulfield's apparent fiancée should know their address only vaguely. If David Caulfield had been so close to his mother and father, wouldn't they have been told of the engagement? And once told, wouldn't they have wanted to meet Marie? Rebus's knowledge of English geography wasn't exactly Mastermind material, but he was fairly sure that Reading and Croydon weren't at what you would call opposite ends of the country.

Interesting, all very interesting. Holmes came in carrying three mugs of coffee, but Rebus shook his head, suddenly the brisk senior officer.

'No time for that, Holmes,' he said. 'There's plenty of work waiting for us back at the station.' Then, to Marie: 'Take care of yourself, Miss Hivert. If there's anything we can do, don't hesitate.'

Her smile was winning. 'Thank you, Inspector.' She turned to Holmes, taking a mug from him. 'And thank you, too, constable,' she said. The look on Holmes' face kept Rebus grinning all the way back to the station.

IV

There the grin promptly vanished. There was a message

marked URGENT from the police pathologist asking Rebus to call him. Rebus pressed the seven digits on his new-fangled telephone. The thing had a twenty-number memory and somewhere in that memory was the single-digit number that would connect him with the pathologist, but Rebus could never remember which number was which and he kept losing the sheet of paper with all the memory numbers on it.

'It's four,' Holmes reminded him, just as he'd come to the end of dialling. He was throwing Holmes a kind of half-scowl when the pathologist himself answered.

'Oh, yes, Rebus. Hello there. It's about this hanging victim of yours. I've had a look at him. Manual strangulation, I'd say.'

'Yes?' Rebus, his thoughts on Marie Hivert, was waiting for some punch-line.

'I don't think you understand me, Inspector. *Manual* strangulation. From the Latin *manus*, meaning the hand. From the deep body temperature, I'd say he died between midnight and two in the morning. He was strung up on that contraption some time thereafter. Bruising around the throat is definitely consistent with thumb-pressure especially.'

'You mean someone strangled him?' Rebus said, really for Holmes' benefit.

'I *think* that's what I've been telling you, yes. If I find out anything more, I'll let you know.'

'Are the forensics people with you?'

'I've contacted the lab. They're sending someone over with some bags, but to be honest, we started off on this one thinking it was simple suicide. We may have inadvertently destroyed the tinier scraps of evidence.'

'Not to worry,' Rebus said, a father-confessor now, easing guilt. 'Just get what you can.'

He put down the receiver and stared at his Detective

Constable. Or, rather, stared *through* him. Holmes knew that there were times for talking and times for silence, and that this fell into the latter category. It took Rebus a full minute to snap out of his reverie.

'Well I'll be buggered,' he said. 'We've been talking with a murderer this morning, Brian. A cold-blooded one at that. And we didn't even know it. I wonder whatever happened to the famous police "nose" for a villain. Any idea?'

Holmes frowned. 'About what happened to the famous police "nose"?'

'No,' cried Rebus, exasperated. 'I mean, any idea who did it?'

Holmes shrugged, then brought the Fringe programme back out from where it had been rolled up in his jacket pocket. He started turning pages. 'I think,' he said, 'there's an Agatha Christie playing somewhere. Maybe we could get a few ideas?'

Rebus's eyes lit up. He snatched the programme from Holmes' hands. 'Never mind Agatha Christie,' he said, starting through the programme himself. 'What we want is Shakespeare.'

'What, *Macbeth*? *Hamlet*? *King Lear*?'

'No, not a tragedy, a good comedy, something to cheer the soul. Ah, here we go.' He stabbed the open page with his finger. '*Twelfth Night*. That's the play for us, Brian. That's the very play for us.'

The problem, really, in the end was: which *Twelfth Night*? There were three on offer, plus another at the Festival proper. One of the Fringe versions offered an update to gangster Chicago, another played with an all-female cast and the third boasted futuristic stage-design. But Rebus wanted traditional fare, and so opted for the Festival performance. There was just one hitch: it was a complete sell-out.

Not that Rebus considered this a hitch. He waited while Holmes called his girlfriend, Nell Stapleton, and apologised to her about some evening engagement he was breaking, then the two men drove to the Lyceum, tucked in behind the Usher Hall so as to be almost invisible to the naked eye.

'There's a five o'clock performance,' Rebus explained. 'We should just make it.' They did. There was a slight hold-up while Rebus explained to the house manager that this really was police business and not some last-minute culture beano, and a place was found for them in a dusty corner to the rear of the stalls. The lights were dimming as they entered.

'I haven't been to a play in years,' Rebus said to Holmes, excited at the prospect. Holmes, bemused, smiled back, but his superior's eyes were already on the stage, where the curtain was rising, a guitar was playing and a man in pale pink tights lay across an ornate bench, looking as cheesed off with life as Holmes himself felt. Why did Rebus always have to work from instinct, and always alone, never letting anyone in on whatever he knew or thought he knew? Was it because he was afraid of failure? Holmes suspected it was. If you kept your ideas to yourself, you couldn't be proved wrong. Well, Holmes had his own ideas about this case, though he was damned if he'd let Rebus in on them.

'If music be the food of love …' came the voice from the stage. And that was another thing – Holmes was starving. It was odds-on the back few rows would soon find his growling stomach competition for the noises from the stage.

'Will you go hunt, my lord?'

'What, Curio?'

'The hart.'

'Why, so I do, the noblest that I have …'

Holmes sneaked a glance towards Rebus. To say the older man's attention was rapt would have been understating the case. He'd give it until the end of Act One, then sneak out to the nearest chip shop. Leave Rebus to his

Shakespeare; Holmes was a nationalist when it came to literature. A pity Hugh MacDiarmid had never written a play.

In fact, Holmes went for a wander, up and down Lothian Road as far as the Caledonian Hotel to the north and Tollcross to the south. Lothian Road was Edinburgh's fast-food centre and the variety on offer brought with it indecision. Pizza, burgers, kebabs, Chinese, baked potatoes, more burgers, more pizza and the once-ubiquitous fish and chip shop (more often now an offshoot of a kebab or burger restaurant). Undecided, he grew hungrier, and stopped for a pint of lager in a noisy barn of a pub before finally settling for a fish supper, naming himself a nationalist in cuisine as well as in writing.

By the time he returned to the theatre, the players were coming out to take their applause. Rebus was clapping as loudly as anyone, enjoyment evident on his face. But when the curtain came down, he turned and dragged Holmes from the auditorium, back into the foyer and out onto the street.

'Fish and chips, eh?' he said. 'Now there's an idea.'

'How did you know?'

'I can smell the vinegar coming off your hands. Where's the chippie?'

Holmes nodded in the direction of Tollcross. They started walking. 'So did you learn anything?' Holmes asked. 'From the play, I mean?'

Rebus smiled. 'More than I'd hoped for, Brian. If you'd been paying attention, you'd have noticed it, too. The only speech that mattered was way back in Act One. A speech made by the Fool, whose name is Feste. I wonder who played Feste in ART's production last year? Actually, I think I can guess. Come on then, where's this chip shop? A man could starve to death on Lothian Road looking for something even remotely edible.'

'It's just off Tollcross. It's nothing very special.'

'So long as it fills me up, Brian. We've got a long evening ahead of us.'

'Oh?'

Rebus nodded vigorously. 'Hunting the heart, Brian.' He winked towards the younger man. 'Hunting the heart.'

V

The door of the Morrison Street flat was opened by Peter Collins. He looked surprised to see them.

'Don't worry, Peter,' Rebus said, pushing past him into the hall. 'We're not here to put the cuffs on you for possession.' He sniffed the air in the hall, then tutted. 'Already? At this rate you'll be stoned before *News at Ten*.'

Peter blushed.

'All right if we come in?' Rebus asked, already sauntering down the hall towards the living-room. Holmes followed him indoors, smiling an apology. Peter closed the door behind them.

'They're mostly out,' Peter called.

'So I see,' said Rebus, in the living-room now. 'Hello, Marie, how are you feeling?'

'Hello again, Inspector. I'm a little better.' She was dressed, and seated primly on the chair, hands resting on her knees. Rebus looked towards the sofa, but thought better of sitting down. Instead he rested himself on the sofa's fairly rigid arm. 'I see you're all getting ready to go.' He nodded towards the two rucksacks parked against the living-room wall. The sleeping-bags from the floor had been folded away, as had books and alarm clocks.

'Why bother to stay?' Peter said. He flopped onto the sofa and pushed a hand through his hair. 'We thought we'd drive down through the night. Be back in Reading by dawn with any luck.'

Rebus nodded at this. 'So the show does *not* go on?'

'It'd be a bit bloody heartless, don't you think?' This from Peter Collins, with a glance towards Marie.

'Of course,' Rebus agreed. Holmes had stationed himself between the living-room door and the rucksacks. 'So where is everyone?'

Marie answered. 'Pam and Marty have gone for a last walk around.'

'And Charles is almost certainly off getting drunk somewhere,' added Collins. 'Rueing his failed show.'

'And Hugh?' asked Rebus. Collins shrugged.

'I think,' Marie said, 'Hugh went off to get drunk, too.'

'But for different reasons, no doubt,' Rebus speculated.

'He was David's best friend,' she answered quietly.

Rebus nodded thoughtfully. 'Actually, we just bumped into him – literally.'

'Who?' asked Peter.

'Mr Clay. He seems to be in the middle of a pub crawl the length of Lothian Road. We were coming out of a chip shop and came across him weaving his way to the next watering-hole.'

'Oh?' Collins didn't sound particularly interested.

'I told him where the best pubs in this neighbourhood are. He didn't seem to know.'

'That was good of you,' Collins said, voice heavy with irony.

'Nice of them all to leave you alone, isn't it though?'

The question hung in the air. At last, Marie spoke. 'What do you mean?'

But Rebus shifted on his perch and left the comment at that. 'No,' he said instead, 'only I thought Mr Clay might have had a better idea of the pubs, seeing how he was here last year, and then again in June to look at the venue. But of course, as he was good enough to explain, he *wasn't* here in June. There were exams. Some people had to study harder than others. Only three of you came to Edinburgh in June.' Rebus raised a finger shiny with chip-fat. 'Pam, who has what I'd call a definite crush on you, Peter.' Collins smiled at this, but weakly. Rebus raised a second and then third finger. 'And you two. Just the three of you. That, I presume, is where it started.'

'What?' The blood had drained from Marie's face, making her somehow more beautiful than ever. Rebus shifted again, seeming to ignore her question.

'It doesn't really matter who took that photo of you, the one I found in *Bonfire of the Vanities*.' He was staring at her quite evenly now. 'What matters is that it was there. And on the inside cover someone had drawn a couple of hearts, very similar to some I happened to see on Peter's copy of the play. It matters that on his copy of the play, Peter has also written the words "I love Edinburgh".' Peter Collins was ready to protest, but Rebus studiously ignored him, keeping his eyes on Marie's, fixing her, so that there might only have been the two of them in the room.

'You told me,' he continued, 'that you'd come to Edinburgh to check on the venue. I took that "you" to mean all of you, but Hugh Clay has put me right on that. You came without David, who was too busy studying to make the trip. And you told me something else earlier. You said your relationship with him had "survived". Survived what? I asked myself afterwards. The answer seems pretty straightforward. Survived a brief fling, a fling that started in Edinburgh and lasted the summer.'

Now, only now, did he turn to Peter Collins. 'Isn't that right, Peter?'

Collins, his face mottled with anger, made to rise.

'Sit down,' Rebus ordered, standing himself. He walked towards the fireplace, turned and faced Collins, who looked to be disappearing into the sofa, reducing in size with the passing moments. 'You love Edinburgh,' he went on, 'because that's where your little fling with Marie started. Fair enough, these things are never anyone's fault, are they? You managed to keep it fairly secret. The Tom Wolfe book belongs to you, though, and that photo you'd kept in it –

maybe forgetting it was there – that photo might have been a giveaway, but then again it could all be very innocent, couldn't it?

'But it's hard to keep something like that so secret when you're part of a very small group. There were sixteen of you in ART last year; that might have made it manageable. But not when there were only seven of you. I'm not sure who else knows about it. But I am sure that David Caulfield found out.' Rebus didn't need to turn round to know that Marie was sobbing again. He kept staring at Peter Collins. 'He found out, and last night, late and backstage, perhaps drunk, the two of you had a fight. Quite dramatic in its way, isn't it? Fighting over the heroine and all that. But during the fight you just happened to strangle the life out of David Caulfield.' He paused, waiting for a denial which didn't come.

'Perhaps,' he continued, 'Marie wanted to go to the police. I don't know. But if she did, you persuaded her not to. Instead, you came up with something more dramatic. You'd make it look like suicide. And by God, what a suicide, the kind that David himself might just have attempted.' Rebus had been moving forward without seeming to, so that now he stood directly over Peter Collins.

'Yes,' he went on, 'very dramatic. But the note was a mistake. It was a bit too clever, you see. You thought everyone would take it as a reference to David's success in last year's production, but you knew yourself that there was a double meaning in it. I've just been to see *Twelfth Night*. Bloody good it was, too. You played Feste last year, didn't you, Peter? There's one speech of his … how does it go?' Rebus seemed to be trying to remember. 'Ah yes: "Many a good hanging prevents a bad marriage." Yes, that's it. And that's when I knew for sure.'

Peter Collins was smiling thinly. He gazed past Rebus towards Marie, his eyes full and liquid. His voice when he spoke was tender. ' "Many a good hanging prevents a bad marriage; and for turning away, let summer bear it out." '

'That's right,' Rebus said, nodding eagerly. 'Summer bore it out, all right. A summer fling. That's all. Not worth killing someone for, was it, Peter? But that didn't stop you. And the hanging was so apt, so neat. When you recalled the Fool's quote, you couldn't resist putting that note in David's pocket.' Rebus was shaking his head. 'More fool you, Mr Collins. More fool you.'

Brian Holmes went home from the police station that night in sombre mood. The traffic was slow, too, with theatre-goers threading in and out between the near-stationary cars. He rolled down the driver's-side window, trying to make the interior less stuffy, less choked, and instead let in exhaust fumes and balmy late-evening air. Why did Rebus have to be such a clever bugger so much of the time? He seemed always to go into a case at an odd angle, like someone cutting a paper shape which, apparently random, could then be folded to make an origami sculpture, intricate and recognisable.

'Too clever for his own good,' he said to himself. But what he meant was that his superior was too clever for Holmes' own good. How was he expected to shine, to be noticed, to push forwards towards promotion, when it was always Rebus who, two steps ahead, came up with the answers? He remembered a boy at school who had always beaten Holmes in every subject save History. Yet Holmes had gone to university; the boy to work on his father's farm. Things could change, couldn't they? Though all he seemed to be learning from Rebus was how to keep your thoughts to yourself, how to be devious, how to, well, how to *act*. Though all this were true, he would still be the best understudy he possibly could be. One day, Rebus wouldn't be there to come up with the answers, or – occasion even more to be relished – would be unable to find the answers.

And when that time came, Holmes would be ready to take the stage. He felt ready right now, but then he supposed every understudy must feel that way.

A flybill was thrown through his window by a smiling teenage girl. He heard her pass down the line of cars, yelling 'Come and see our show!' as she went. The small yellow sheet of paper fluttered onto the passenger seat and stayed there, face up, to haunt Holmes all the way back to Nell. Growing sombre again, it occurred to him how different things might have been if only Priestley had called the play *A Detective Constable Calls* instead.

Tit for Tat

Before he'd arrived in Edinburgh in 1970, Inspector John Rebus had fixed in his mind an image of tenement life. Tenements were things out of the Gorbals in the early years of the century, places of poverty and despair, safe havens for vermin and disease. They were the enforced homes of the poorest of the working class, a class almost without a class, a sub-class. Though tenements rose high into the air, they might as well have been dug deep into the ground. They were society's replacement for the cave.

Of course, in the 1960s the planners had come up with something even more outrageous – the tower-block. Even cities with plenty of spare land started to construct these space-saving horrors. Perhaps the moral rehabilitation of the tenement had something to do with this new contender. Nowadays, a tenement might contain the whole of society in microcosm – the genteel spinster on the ground floor, the bachelor accountant one floor above, then the bar-keeper, and above the barkeeper, always it seemed right at the top of the house, the students. This mix was feasible only because the top two floors contained flats rented out by absentee landlords. Some of these landlords might own upwards of one hundred separate flats – as was spectacu-larly the case in Glasgow, where the figure was even rumoured, in one or two particulars, to rise into four figures.

But in Edinburgh, things were different. In Edinburgh, the New Town planners of the nineteenth century had come up with streets of fashionable houses, all of them, to

Rebus's latter-day eyes, looking like tenements. Some prosperous areas of the city, such as Marchmont where Rebus himself lived, boasted almost nothing *but* tenements. And with the price of housing what it was, even the meaner streets were seeing a kind of renaissance, stone-blasted clean by new owner-occupiers who kept the cooking-range in the living-room as an 'original feature'.

The streets around Easter Road were as good an example as any. The knock-on effect had reached Easter Road late. People had to decide first that they couldn't afford Stockbridge, then that they couldn't quite afford any of the New Town or its immediate surroundings, and at last they might arrive in Easter Road, not by chance but somehow through fate. Soon, an enterprising soul saw his or her opportunity and opened a delicatessen or a slightly upmarket cafe, much to the bemusement of the 'locals'. These were quiet, accepting people for the most part, people who liked to see the tenement buildings being restored even if they couldn't understand why anyone would pay good money for bottled French water. (After all, you were always told to steer clear of the water on foreign holidays, weren't you?)

Despite this, the occasional Alfa Romeo or Golf GTi might find itself scratched maliciously, as might a too-clean 2CV or a coveted Morris Minor. But arson? Attempted murder? Well, that was a bit more serious. That was a very serious turn of events indeed. The trick was one perfected by racists in mixed areas. You poured petrol through the letter-box of a flat, then you set light to a rag and dropped it through the letter-box, igniting the hall carpet and ensuring that escape from the resulting fire was made difficult if not impossible. Of course, the noise, the smell of petrol meant that usually someone inside the flat was alerted early on, and mostly these fires did not spread. But sometimes ... sometimes.

'His name's John Brodie, sir,' the police constable

informed Rebus as they stood in the hospital corridor. 'Age thirty-four. Works for an insurance company in their accounts department.'

None of which came as news to Rebus. He had been to the second-floor flat, just off Easter Road, reeking of soot and water now; an unpleasant clean-up ahead. The fire had spread quickly along the hall. Some jackets and coats hanging from a coat-stand had caught light and sent the flames licking along the walls and ceiling. Brodie, asleep in bed (it all happened around one in the morning) had been wakened by the fire. He'd dialled 999, then had tried putting the fire out himself, with a fair degree of success. A rug from the living-room had proved useful in snuffing out the progress of the fire along the hall and some pans of water had dampened things down. But there was a price to pay – burns to his arms and hands and face, and smoke inhalation. Neighbours, alerted by the smoke, had broken down the door just as the fire engine was arriving. CID, brought to the scene by a police constable's suspicions, had spoken with some of the neighbours. A quiet man, Mr Brodie, they said. A decent man. He'd only moved in a few months before. Worked for an insurance company. Nobody thought he smoked, but they seemed to assume he'd left a cigarette burning somewhere.

'Careless that. Even supposing we *do* live in Auld Reekie.' And the first-floor occupier had chuckled to himself, until his wife yelped from their flat that there was water coming in through the ceiling. The man looked helpless and furious.

'Insurance should cover it,' Rebus commented, pouring oil on troubled ... no, not the best image that. The husband went off to investigate further and the other tenement dwellers began slouching off to bed, leaving Rebus to head into the burnt-out hallway itself.

But even without the Fire Officer, the cause of the fire

had been plain to Rebus. Chillingly plain. The smell of petrol was everywhere.

He took a look round the rest of the flat. The kitchen was tiny, but boasted a large sash-window looking down onto back gardens and across to the back of the tenement over the way. The bathroom was smaller still, but kept very neat. No ring of grime around the bath, no strewn towels or underpants, nothing steeping in the sink. A very tidy bachelor was Mr Brodie. The living-room, too, was uncluttered. A series of framed prints more or less covered one wall. Detailed paintings of birds. Rebus glanced at one or two: willow warbler, bearded tit. The rooms would need to be redecorated, of course, otherwise the charred smell would always be there. Insurance would probably cover it. Brodie was an insurance man, wasn't he? He'd know. Maybe he'd even squeeze a cheque out of the company without too much haggling.

Finally, Rebus went into the bedroom. Messier here, mostly as a result of the hurriedly flung-back bedclothes. Pyjama bottoms lying crumpled on the bed itself. Slippers and a used mug sitting on the floor beside the bed, and in one corner, next to the small wardrobe, a tripod atop which was fixed a good make of SLR camera. On the floor against the wall was a large-format book, *Better Zoom Pictures*, with a photograph of an osprey on the front. Probably one of the Loch Garten ospreys, thought Rebus. He'd taken his daughter there a couple of times in the past. Tourists, plenty of them, he had seen, but ospreys were there none.

If anyone had asked him what he thought most odd about the flat, he would have answered: there's no television set. What did Mr Brodie do for company then of an evening?

For no real reason, Rebus bent down and peered beneath the bed itself, and was rewarded with a pile of magazines. He pulled one out. Soft porn, a 'readers' wives' special. He pushed it back into place. The tidy bachelor's required bedtime companion. And, partly, an answer to his earlier question.

He left the flat and sought out one or two of the still wakeful neighbours. No one had seen or heard anything. Access to the tenement itself was easy; you just pushed open the communal front door, the lock of which had broken recently and was waiting to be fixed.

'Any reason,' Rebus asked, 'why anyone would bear Mr Brodie a grudge?'

That gave them pause. No smouldering cigarette then, but arson. But there were shakes of rumpled heads. No reason. A very quiet man. Kept himself to himself. Worked in insurance. Always stopped for a chat if you met him on the stairs. Always cleaned the stairs promptly when his turn came, not like some they could mention. Probably paid his rent promptly, too. Tea was being provided in the kitchen of one of the first-floor flats, where the 'Auld Reekie' wag was being consoled.

'I only painted that ceiling three months back. Do you know how much textured paint costs?'

Soon enough everyone found the answer. The man's wife looked bored. She smiled towards the tea-party's hostess.

'Wasn't that first fireman dishy?' she said.

'Which one?'

'The one with the blue eyes. The one who told us not to worry. He could give me a fireman's lift anytime.'

The hostess snorted into her tea. Rebus made his excuses and left.

Rebus had dealt with racist arson attacks before. He'd even come across 'anti-yuppie' attacks, usually in the form of graffiti on cars or the outside walls of property. A warehouse conversion in Leith had been sprayed with the slogan HOUSES FOR THE NEEDY, NOT THE GREEDY. The attack on Brodie seemed more personal, but it was worth considering all the possible motives. He was crossing things off from a list in his mind as he drove to the hospital. Once there, he talked to the police constable in the corridor and, after nodding his head a few times, he entered the ward where John Brodie had been 'made comfortable'. Despite the hour, Brodie was far from asleep. He was propped up against a pillow, his arms lying out in front of him on top of the sheets. Thick creamy white cotton pads and delicate-looking bandages predominated. Part of his hair had been shaved away, so that burns to the scalp could be treated. He had no eyebrows, and only remnants of eyelashes. His face was round and shiny; easy to imagine it breaking into a chuckle, but probably not tonight.

Rebus picked a chair out from a pile against the far wall and sat down, only then introducing himself.

Brodie's voice was shaky. 'I know who did it.'

'Oh?' Rebus kept his voice low, in deference to the sleeping bodies around him. This was not quite how he'd expected the conversation to begin.

Brodie swallowed. 'I know who did it and I know *why* she did it. But I don't want to press charges.'

Rebus wasn't about to say that this decision was not up to Brodie himself. He didn't want the man clamming up. He wanted jaw-jaw. He nodded as if in agreement. 'Is there anything I can get you?' he said, inviting further confessions, as though from one friend to another.

'She must be a bit cracked,' Brodie went on, as though Rebus hadn't spoken at all. 'I told the police that at the time. She's doolally, I said. Must be. Well, this proves it, doesn't it?'

'You think she needs help?'

'Maybe. Probably.' He seemed deep in thought for a moment. 'Yes, almost certainly. I mean, it's going a bit far, isn't it? Even if you think you've got grounds. But she didn't have grounds. The police *told* her that.'

'But they didn't manage to convince her.'

'That's right.'

Rebus thought he was playing this fairly well. Obviously, Brodie was in shock. Maybe he was even babbling a bit, but as long as he was kept talking, Rebus would be able to piece together whatever the story was that he was trying to tell. There was a wheezy, dry laugh from the bed.

Brodie's eyes twinkled. 'You don't know what I'm talking about, do you?' Rebus was obliged to shake his head. 'Of course you don't. Well, I'll have a sip of water and then I'll tell you.'

And he did.

The morning was bright but grey: 'sunshine and showers', the weatherman would term it. It wasn't quite autumn yet. The too-short summer might yet have some surprises. Rebus waited in his room – his desk located not too far from the radiator – until the two police constables could be found. They were uneasy when they came in, until he reassured them. Yes, as requested, they had brought their notebooks with them. And yes, they remembered the incident very well indeed.

'It started with anonymous phone calls,' one of them began. 'They seemed to be genuine enough. Miss Hooper told us about one of them in particular. Her phone rings. Man on the other end identifies himself as a police inspector and tells her there's an anonymous caller who's going through the Edinburgh directory trying number after number. He says her number might come up soon, but the police have put a trace on her line. So can she keep the man talking for as long as possible.'

'Oh yes.' Really, Rebus didn't need to hear the rest. But he listened patiently to the constable's story.

'Later on that day, a man did ring. He asked her some very personal questions and she kept him talking. Afterwards, she rang the police station to see if they'd caught him. Only, of course, the name the so-called inspector had given wasn't known to the station. It was the anonymous caller himself, setting her up.'

Rebus shook his head slowly. It was old, but clever. 'So she complained about anonymous calls?'

'Yes, sir. But then the calls stopped. So that didn't seem too bad. No need for an operator to intercept or a change of number or anything.'

'How did Miss Hooper seem at the time?'

The constable shrugged and turned to his colleague, who now spoke. 'A bit nervy, sir. But that was understandable, wasn't it? A very nice lady, I'd say. Not married. I don't think she even had a boyfriend.' He turned his head towards his colleague. 'Didn't she say something like that, Jim?'

'I think so, yes.'

'So then what happened?' asked Rebus.

'A few weeks later, this would be just over a week ago, we had another call from Miss Hooper. She said a man in the tenement across the back from her was a peeping tom. She'd seen him at a window, aiming his binoculars towards her building. More particularly, she thought, towards her own flat. We investigated and spoke to Mr Brodie. He appeared quite concerned about the allegations. He showed us the binoculars and admitted using them to watch from his kitchen window. But he assured us that he was bird-watching.' The other constable smiled at this. ' "Bird-watching," he said.'

'Ornithology,' said Rebus.

'That's right, sir. He said he was very interested in birds, a bird-fancier sort of thing.' Another smile. They were obviously hoping Rebus would come to enjoy the joke with them. They were wrong, though they didn't seem to sense this just yet.

'Go on,' he said simply.

'Well, sir, there did seem to be a lot of pictures of birds in his flat.'

'You mean the prints in the living-room?'

'That's right, sir, pictures of an ornithological nature.'

Now the other constable interrupted. 'You won't believe it, sir. He said he was watching the tenement and the garden because he'd seen some ...' pause for effect ... 'bearded tits.'

Now both the young constables were grinning.

'I'm glad you find your job so amusing,' Rebus said. 'Because I don't think frightening phone calls, peeping toms and arson attacks are material for jokes!'

The grins disappeared.

'Get on with it,' Rebus demanded. The constables looked at one another.

'Not much more to tell, sir,' said the one called Jim. 'The gentleman, Mr Brodie, seemed genuine enough. But he promised to be a bit more careful in future. Like I say, he seemed genuinely concerned. We informed Miss Hooper of our findings. She didn't seem entirely convinced.'

'Obviously not,' said Rebus, but he did not go on to clarify. Instead, he dismissed the two officers and sat back in his chair. Brodie suspected Hooper of the arson attack, not, it would appear, without reason. What was more, Brodie had said he couldn't think of any other enemies he might have made. Either that or he wasn't about to tell Rebus about them. Rebus leaned back in his chair and rested his arm along the radiator, enjoying its warmth. The next person to speak to, naturally, was Miss Hooper herself. Another day, another tenement.

'Bearded tits,' Rebus said to himself. This time, he allowed himself a smile.

'It's your lucky day,' Miss Hooper told him. 'Normally I don't come home for lunch, but today I just felt like it.'

Lucky indeed. Rebus had knocked on the door of Miss

Hooper's first-floor flat but received no answer. Eventually, another door on the landing had opened, revealing a woman in her late forties, stern of face and form.

'She's not in,' the woman had stated, unnecessarily.

'Any idea when she'll be back?'

'Who are you then?'

'Police.'

The woman pursed her lips. The nameplate above her doorbell, to the left of the door itself, read McKAY. 'She works till four o'clock. She's a schoolteacher. You'll catch her at school if you want her.'

'Thank you. Mrs McKay, is it?'

'It is.'

'Could I have a word?'

'What about?'

By now, Rebus was standing at Mrs McKay's front door. Past her, he caught sight of a dark entrance hall strewn with bits and pieces of machinery, enough to make up most, but not quite all, of a motorbike.

'About Miss Hooper,' he said.

'What about her?'

No, she was not about to let him in. He could hear her television blaring. Lunchtime game-show applause. The resonant voice of the questionmaster. Master of the question.

'Have you known her long?'

'Ever since she moved in. Three, four years. Aye, four years.' She had folded her arms now, and was resting one shoulder against the door-jamb. 'What's the problem?'

'I suppose you must know her quite well, living on the same landing?'

'Well enough. She comes in for a cuppa now and again.' She paused, making it quite clear to Rebus that this was not an honour *he* was about to receive.

'Have you heard about the fire?'

'Fire?'

'Across the back.' Rebus gestured in some vague direction with his head.

'Oh aye. The fire engine woke me right enough. Nobody hurt though, was there?'

'What makes you say that?'

She shuffled now, unfolding her arms so one hand could rub at another. 'Just ... what I heard.'

'A man was injured, quite seriously. He's in hospital.'

'Oh.'

And then the main door opened and closed. Sound of feet on stone echoing upwards.

'Oh, here's Miss Hooper now,' said Mrs McKay. Said with relief, Rebus thought to himself. Said with relief ...

Miss Hooper let him in and immediately switched on the kettle. She hoped he wouldn't mind if she made herself a sandwich? And would he care for one himself? Cheese and pickle or peanut butter and apple? No, on second thoughts, she'd make some of both, and he could choose for himself.

A teacher? Rebus could believe it. There was something in her tone, in the way she seemed to have to utter all of her thoughts aloud, and in the way she asked questions and then answered them herself. He could see her standing in her classroom, asking her questions and surrounded by silence.

Alison Hooper was in her early thirties. Small and slim, almost schoolboyish. Short straight brown hair. Tiny earrings hooked into tiny ears. She taught in a primary school only ten minutes' walk from her flat. The flat itself was scattered with books and magazines, from many of which had been cut illustrations, clearly intended to find their way into her classroom. Mobiles hung from her living-room ceiling: some flying pigs, an alphabet, teddy bears waving from aeroplanes. There were colourful rugs on her walls, but no rugs at all on the stripped floor. She had a breathy, nervous way with her and an endearing

147

twitch to her nose. Rebus followed her into the kitchen and watched her open a loaf of brown sliced bread.

'I usually take a packed lunch with me, but I slept in this morning and didn't have time to make it. I could have eaten in the canteen, of course, but I just felt like coming home. Your lucky day, Inspector.'

'You had trouble sleeping last night then?'

'Well, yes. There was a fire in the tenement across the back.' She pointed through her window with a buttery knife. 'Over there. I heard sirens and the fire-engine's motor kept rumbling away, so I couldn't for the life of me get back to sleep.'

Rebus went across to the window and looked out. John Brodie's tenement stared back at him. It could have been any tenement anywhere in the city. Same configuration of windows and drainpipes, same railing-enclosed drying-green. He angled his head further to look into the back garden of Alison Hooper's tenement. Movement there. What was it? A teenager working on his motorbike. The motorbike standing on the drying-green, and all the tools and bits and pieces lying on a piece of plastic which had been spread out for the purpose. The nearby garden shed stood with its door propped open by a wooden stretcher. Through the doorway Rebus could see yet more motorbike spares and some oil cans.

'The fire last night,' he said, 'it was in a flat occupied by Mr John Brodie.'

'Oh!' she said, her knife-hand pausing above the bread. 'The peeping tom?' Then she swallowed, not slow on the uptake. 'That's why you're here then.'

'Yes. Mr Brodie gave us your name, Miss Hooper. He thought perhaps —'

'Well, he's right.'

'Oh?'

'I mean, I do have a grudge. I do think he's a pervert. Not that I seem able to convince the police of that.' Her

148

voice was growing shriller. She stared at the slices of bread in a fixed, unblinking way. 'No, the police don't seem to think there's a problem. But I know. I've talked to the other residents. We *all* know.' Then she relaxed, smiled at the bread. She slapped some peanut butter onto one slice. Her voice was calm. 'I do have a grudge, Inspector, but I did not set fire to that man's flat. I'm even pleased that he wasn't injured.'

'Who says he wasn't?'

'What?'

'He's in hospital.'

'Is he? I thought someone said there'd been no –'

'Who said?'

She shrugged. 'I don't know. One of the other teachers. Maybe they'd heard something on the radio. I don't know. Tea or coffee?'

'Whatever you're having.'

She made two mugs of decaffeinated instant. 'Let's go through to the living-room,' she said.

There, she gave him the story of the phone calls, and the story of the man with the binoculars.

'Bird-watching my eye,' she said. 'He was looking into people's windows.'

'Hard to tell, surely.'

She twitched her nose. 'Looking into people's windows,' she repeated.

'Did anyone else see him?'

'He stopped after I complained. But who knows? I mean, it's easy enough to see someone during the day. But at night, in that room of his with the lights turned off. He could sit there all night watching us. Who would know?'

'You say you spoke to the other residents?'

'Yes.'

'All of them?'

'One or two. That's enough, word gets round.'

I'll bet, thought Rebus. And he had another thought,

which really was just a word: tenementality. He ate the spicy sandwich and the sickly sandwich quickly, drained his mug and said he'd leave her to finish her lunch in peace. ('Finish your piece in peace,' he'd nearly said, but hadn't, just in case she didn't get the joke.) He walked downstairs, but instead of making along the passage to the front door, turned right and headed towards the tenement's back door.

Outside, the biker was fitting a bulb to his brake-light. He took the new bulb from a plastic box and tossed the empty box onto the sheet of plastic.

'Mind if I take that?' asked Rebus. The youth looked round at him, saw where he was pointing, then shrugged and returned to his work. There was a small cassette recorder playing on the grass beside him. Heavy Metal. The batteries were low and the sound was tortuous.

'Can if you like,' he said.

'Thanks.' Rebus lifted the box by its edges and slipped it into his jacket pocket. 'I use them to keep my flies in.'

The biker turned and grinned.

'Fishing flies,' Rebus explained, smiling himself. 'It's just perfect for keeping my fishing flies in.'

'No flies on you, eh?' said the youth.

Rebus laughed. 'Are you Mrs McKay's son?' he asked.

'That's right.' The bulb was fitted, the casing was being screwed back into place.

'I'd test that before you put the casing on. Just in case it's a dud. You'd only have to take it apart again.'

The boy looked round again. 'No flies on you,' he repeated. He took the casing off again.

'I've just been up seeing your mum.'

'Oh aye?' The tone told Rebus that the boy's parents were either separated, or else the father was dead. You're her latest, are you? the tone implied. Mum's latest fancy-man.

'She was telling me about the fire.'

The boy examined the casing closely. 'Fire?'

'Last night. Have you noticed any of your petrol-cans disappearing? Or maybe one's got less in than you thought?'

Now, the red see-through casing might have been a gem under a microscope. But the boy was saying nothing.

'My name's Rebus, by the way, Inspector Rebus.'

Rebus had a little courtroom conversation with himself on the way back to the station.

And did the suspect drop anything when you revealed your identity to him?

Yes, he dropped his jaw.

Dropped his jaw?

That's right. He looked like a hairless ape with a bad case of acne. And he lost his nut.

Lost his nut?

A nut he'd been holding. It fell into the grass. He was still looking for it when I left.

What about the plastic box, Inspector, the one in which the new brake-light bulb had been residing? Did he ask for it back?

I didn't give him the chance. It's my intention *never* to give a sucker an even chance.

Back at the station, comfortable in his chair, the desk solid and reliable in front of him, the heater solid and reliable behind, Rebus thought about fire, the easy assassin. You didn't need to get your hands on a gun. Didn't even need to buy a knife. Acid, poison, again, difficult to find. But fire ... fire was everywhere. A disposable lighter, a box of matches. Strike a match and you had fire. Warming, nourishing, dangerous fire. Rebus lit a cigarette, the better to help him think. There wouldn't be any news from the lab for some time yet. Some time. Something was niggling. Something he'd heard. What was it? A saying came to mind: prompt payment will be appreciated. You used to get that on the bottom of invoices. Prompt payment.

Probably pays his rent promptly, too.

Well, well. Now there was a thing. Owner-occupier. Not every owner *did* occupy, and not every occupier was an owner. Rebus recalled that Detective Sergeant Hendry of Dunfermline CID was a keen bird-watcher. Once or twice, on courses or at conferences, he'd collared Rebus and bored him with tales of the latest sighting of the Duddingston bittern or the Kilconquhar red-head smew. Like all hobbyists, Hendry was keen to have others share his enthusiasm. Like all anti-hobbyists, Rebus would yawn with more irony than was necessary.

Still, it was worth a phone-call.

'I'll have to call you back, John,' said a busy DS Hendry. 'It's not the sort of thing I could tell you offhand. Give me your number at home and I'll ring you tonight. I didn't know you were interested.'

'I'm not, believe me.'

But his words went unheeded. 'I saw siskins and twite earlier in the year.'

'Really?' said Rebus. 'I've never been one for country and western music. Siskins and Twite, eh? They've been around for years.'

By the following morning, he had everything he needed. He arrived as Mrs McKay and her son were eating a late breakfast. The television was on, providing the noise necessary to their lives. Rebus had come accompanied by two other officers, so that there could be no doubting he meant business. Gerry McKay's jaw dropped again as Rebus began to speak. The tale itself was quickly told. John Brodie's front door had been examined, the metal letterbox checked for fingerprints. Some good, if oily, prints had been found, and these matched those found on the plastic box Rebus had taken from Gerry McKay. There could be no doubting that Gerry McKay had pushed open John Brodie's letterbox. If Gerry would accompany the officers to the station.

'Mum!' McKay was on his feet, yelling, panicky. 'Mum, tell them! Tell them!'

Mrs McKay had a face as dark as ketchup. Rebus was glad he had brought the other officers. Her voice trembled when she spoke. 'It wasn't Gerry's idea,' she said. 'It was mine. If there's anyone you want to talk to about it, it should be me. It was my idea. Only, I knew Gerry'd be faster getting in and out of the stairwell. That's all. He's got nothing to do with it.' She paused, her face turning even nastier. 'Besides, that wee shite deserved all he got. Dirty, evil little runt of a man. You didn't see the state Alison was in. Such a nice wee girl, wouldn't say boo to a goose, and to be got into a state like that. I couldn't let him get away with it, hell. And if it were up to you lot, he'd have gotten off scot-free, wouldn't he? It's nothing to do with Gerry.'

'It'll be taken into account at the trial,' Rebus said quietly.

John Brodie looked not to have moved since Rebus had left him. His arms still lay on the top of the bed-cover, and he was still propped up against a pillow.

'Inspector Rebus,' he said. 'Back again.'

'Back again,' said Rebus, placing a chair by the bed and seating himself. 'The doctor says you're doing fine.'

'Yes,' said Brodie.

'Anything I can get you?' Brodie shook his head. 'No? Juice? A bit of fruit maybe? How about something to read? I notice you like girlie mags. I saw one in your flat. I could get you a few of those if you like.' Rebus winked. 'Readers' wives, eh? Amateurs. That's your style. All those blurry Polaroid shots, heads cut off. That's what you like, eh, John?'

But John Brodie was saying nothing. He was looking at

his arms. Rebus drew the chair closer to the bed. Brodie flinched, but could not move.

'*Panurus biarmicus*,' Rebus hissed. Now Brodie looked blankly at him. Rebus repeated the words. Still Brodie looked blank. 'Go on,' Rebus chided, 'take a guess.'

'I don't know what you're talking about.'

'No?' Rebus was wide-eyed. 'Curious that. Sounds like the name of a disease, doesn't it? Maybe you know it better as the bearded tit.'

'Oh.' Brodie smiled shyly, and nodded. 'Yes, the bearded tit.'

Rebus smiled too, but coldly. 'You didn't know, you didn't have a clue. Shall I tell you something about the bearded tit? No, better yet, Mr Brodie, you tell *me* something about it.' He sat back and folded his arms expectantly.

'What?'

'Go on.'

'Look, what's all this about?'

'It's quite simple, you see.' Rebus sat forward again. 'The bearded tit isn't commonly found in Scotland. I got that from an expert. Not commonly found, that's what he said. More than that, its habitat – and I'm quoting here – is "extensive and secluded reed-beds". Do you see what I'm getting at? You'd hardly call Easter Road a reed-bed, would you?'

Brodie raised his head a little, his thin lips very straight and wide. He was thinking, but he wasn't talking.

'You see what I'm getting at, don't you? You told those two constables that you were watching bearded tits from your window. But that's just not true. It couldn't possibly be true. You said the name of the first bird that came into your head, and it came into your head because there was a drawing on your living-room wall. I saw it myself. But it's not you that's the bird-watcher, John. It's your landlord and landlady. You rented the place furnished and you haven't changed anything. It's their drawings on the wall. They got in touch about the insurance, you see. Wondering whether the fire was accidental. They saw a bit about it in the newspaper. They could appreciate that they hadn't heard from you, what with you being in hospital and all, but they wanted to sort out the insurance. So I was able to ask them about the birds on the wall. *Their* birds, John, not yours. It was quick thinking of you to come up with the story. It even fooled those two PCs. It might have fooled me. That book about zoom photography, even that had a picture of birds on the front.' He paused. 'But you're a peeper, John, that's all. That's what you are, a nasty little voyeur. Miss Hooper was right all the time.'

'Was it her who –?'

'You'll find out soon enough.'

'It's all lies, you know. Hearsay, circumstantial. You've no proof.'

'What about the photos?'

'What photos?'

Rebus sighed. 'Come on, John. All that gear in your bedroom. Tripod, camera, zoom lenses. Photographing birds, were you? I'd be interested to see the results. Because it wasn't just binoculars, was it? You took piccies, too. In your wardrobe, are they?' Rebus checked his watch. 'With luck I'll have the search warrant inside the hour. Then I intend to take a good look round your flat, John. I intend taking a *very* good look.'

'There's nothing there.' He was shaking now, his arms moving painfully in their gauze bandages. 'Nothing. You've no right. Someone tried to kill ... No right. They tried to kill me.'

Rebus was willing to concede a point. 'Certainly they tried to scare you. We'll see what the courts decide.' He rose to his feet. Brodie was still twittering on. Twit, twit, twit. It would be a while before he'd be able to use a camera again.

'Do you want to know something else, John?' Rebus said, unable to resist one of his parting shots. 'Something about the bearded tit? It's classified as a *babbler*.' He smiled a smile of warm sunshine. 'A babbler!' he repeated. 'Looks to me like you're a bit of a babbler yourself. Well,' he picked up the chair and pretended to be considering something, 'at any rate, I'd certainly classify you as a tit.'

He returned that evening to his own tenement and his roaring gas fire. But there was a surprise awaiting him on the doorhandle of his flat. A reminder from Mrs Cochrane downstairs. A reminder that it was his week for washing the stairs and that he hadn't done it yet and it was nearly the end of the week and when was he going to do it? Rebus sent a roar into the stairwell before slamming shut the door behind him. It was only a moment before other doors started to open, faces peering out, and another Edinburgh tenement conversation began, multi-storeyed, undertone and echoing.

Not Provan

How badly did Detective Inspector John Rebus want to nail Willie Provan? Oh, badly, very badly indeed. Rebus visualised it as a full-scale crucifixion, each nail going in slowly, the way Willie liked to put the boot and the fist slowly, methodically, into the victims of his violence.

Rebus had first encountered Willie Provan five years before, as a schoolkid spiralling out of control. Both parents dead, Willie had been left in the charge of a dotty and near-deaf aunt. He had taken charge of her house, had held wild parties there, parties to which the police were eventually, habitually called by neighbours at the end of their tether.

Entering the house had been like stepping into an amateur production of *Caligula*: naked, under-aged couples so drunk or drugged they could not complete the act which so interested them; emptied tins of solvent, polythene bags encrusted with the dregs of the stuff. A whiff of something animal, something less-than-human in the air. And, in a small back room upstairs, the aunt, locked in and sitting up in her bed, a cold cup of tea and a half-eaten sandwich on the table beside her.

By the time he left school, Willie was already a legend. Four years on the dole had benefited him little. But he had learned cunning, and so far the police had been unable to put him away. He remained a thorn in Rebus's side. Today, Rebus felt someone might just come along and pluck that thorn out.

He sat in the public gallery and watched the court proceedings. Near him were a few of Willie Provan's

friends, members of his gang. They called themselves the
Tiny Alice, or T-Alice. No one knew why. Rebus glanced
over towards them. Sleeves rolled up, sporting tattoos and
unshaven grins. They were the city's sons, the product of
an Edinburgh upbringing, but they seemed to belong to
another culture, another civilisation entirely, reared on
Schwarzenegger videos and bummed cigarettes. Rebus
shivered, feeling he understood them better than he liked to
admit.

The case against Provan was solid and satisfying. On a
cup-tie evening several months ago, a football fan had been
heading towards the Heart of Midlothian ground. He was
late, his train from Fife having been behind time. He was
an away supporter and he was on his own in Gorgie.

An arm snaked around his neck, yanked him into a
tenement stairwell, and there Willie Provan had kicked and
punched him into hospitalisation. For what reason? Rebus
could guess. It had nothing to do with football, nothing
with football hooliganism. Provan pretended a love of
Hearts, but had never, to Rebus's knowledge, attended a
game. Nor could he name more than two or three players in
the current team's line-up.

Nevertheless, Gorgie was his patch, his territory. He had
spotted an invader and had summarily executed him, in his
own terms. But his luck had run out. A woman had heard
some sounds from the stairwell and had opened her door to
investigate. Provan saw her and ran off. But she had given
the police a good description and had later identified
Provan as the attacker. Moreover, a little while after the
attack, a constable, off duty and happening to pass
Tynecastle Park, had spotted a young man, apparently
disorientated. He had approached the man and asked him if
he was all right, but at that point some members of T-Alice
had appeared from their local pub, directly opposite the
Hearts ground and had taken the man inside.

The constable thought little of it, until he heard about

the assault and was given a description of the attacker. The description matched that of the disorientated man, and that man turned out to be Willie Provan. With Provan's previous record, this time he would go down, Rebus was sure of that. So he sat and he watched and he listened.

He watched the jurors, too. They winced, perceptibly as they were told of the injuries to the victim, injuries which still, several months on, kept him in hospital, unable to walk and with respiratory difficulties to boot. To boot. Ha! Rebus let a short-lived smile wrinkle his face. Yes, the jury would convict. But Rebus was most interested in one juror in particular, an intense young man who was taking copious notes, sending intelligent written questions to the judge, studying photographs and diagrams with enthusiasm. The model juror, ready to see that justice was done and all was fair and proper. At one point, the young man looked up and caught Rebus watching him. After that, he gave Rebus some of his attention, but still scribbled his notes and checked and rechecked what he had written.

The other jurors were solemn, looked bored even. Passive spectators at a one-horse race. Guilty. Probably by the end of the day. Rebus would sit it out. The prosecution had finished its case, and the defence case had already begun. The usual stuff when an obviously guilty party pleaded not guilty: trying to catch out prosecution witnesses, instilling mistrust, trying to persuade the jury that things were not as cut and dried as they seemed, that there was probable cause for doubt. Rebus sat back and let it wash over him. Provan would go down.

Then came the iceberg, ripping open the bow of Rebus's confidence.

The defence counsel had called the off-duty constable, the one who had spotted Provan outside the Hearts ground. The constable was young, with a bad case of post-juvenile acne. He tried to stand to attention as the questions were put to him, but when flustered would raise a hand towards

159

his scarred cheeks. Rebus remembered his own first time on the witness stand. A Glasgow music-hall stage could not have been more terrifying.

'And what time do you say it was when you first saw the accused?' The defence counsel had a slight Irish brogue, and his eyes were dark from want of sleep. His cheap ballpoint pen had burst, leaving black stains across his hands. Rebus felt a little sorry for him.

'I'm not sure, sir.'

'You're not sure?' The words came slowly. The inference was: this copper is a bit thick, isn't he? How can you the jury trust him? For the counsel was staring at the jury as he spoke and this seemed to unnerve the constable further. A hand rubbed against a cheek.

'Roughly then,' continued the defence counsel. 'Roughly what time was it?'

'Sometime between seven-thirty and eight, sir.'

The counsel nodded, flipping through a sheaf of notes. 'And what did you say to the accused?' As the constable was about to reply, the counsel interrupted, still with his face towards the jury. 'I say "the accused" because there's no disagreement that the person the constable saw outside the football ground was my client.' He paused. 'So constable, what did you say?'

' "Are you all right?" Something like that.'

Rebus glanced towards where Provan sat in the dock. Provan was looking terribly confident. His clear blue eyes were sparkling and he sat forwards in his chair, keen to catch the dialogue going on before him. For the first time, Rebus felt an uneasy stab: the thorn again, niggling him. What was going on?

'You asked him if he was all right.' It was a statement. The counsel paused again. Now the prosecution counsel was frowning: he too was puzzled by this line of questioning. Rebus felt his hands forming into fists.

'You asked him if he was all right, and he replied? What exactly *did* he reply?'

'I couldn't really make it out, sir.'

'Why was that? Were his words slurred perhaps?'

The constable shrugged. 'A little, maybe.'

'A little? Mmm.' The counsel looked at his notes again. 'What about the noise from the stadium?'

'Sir?'

'You were directly outside the ground. There was a cup-tie being played in front of thousands of spectators. It was noisy, wasn't it?'

'Yes, sir,' agreed the constable.

'In fact, it was *very* noisy, wasn't it, Constable Davidson? It was *extraordinarily* noisy. That was why you couldn't hear my client's reply. Isn't that the case?'

The constable shrugged again, not sure where any of this was leading, happy enough to agree with the defence. 'Yes, sir,' he said.

'In fact, as you approached my client, you may remember that there was a sudden upsurge in the noise from the ground.'

The constable nodded, seeming to remember. 'That's right, yes. I think a goal had just been scored.'

'Indeed, a goal had been scored. Just after you had first spotted my client, as you were walking towards him. A goal was scored, the noise was terrific. You shouted your question to my client, and he replied, but his words were drowned out by the noise from the ground. His friends saw him from the Goatfell public house and came to his aid, leading him inside. The noise was still very great, even then. They were shouting to you to let you know they would take care of him. Isn't that right?'

Now, the counsel turned to the constable, fixing him with his dark eyes.

'Yes, sir.'

The counsel nodded, seeming satisfied. Willie Provan,

too, looked satisfied. Rebus's nerves were jangling. He was reminded of a song lyric: *there's something happening here, but you don't know what it is.* Something was most definitely happening here, and Rebus didn't like it. The defence counsel spoke again.

'Do you know what the score was that night?'

'No, sir.'

'It was one-nil. The home team won by a single goal, the single goal you heard from outside the ground. A single goal scored –' picking up the notes for effect, turning again to face the jury, 'in the fifteenth minute of the game, a game that kicked off ... when? Do you happen to recall?'

The constable knew now, knew where this was leading. His voice when he spoke had lost a little of its life. 'It was a seven-thirty kick-off.'

'That's right, it was. So you see, Police Constable Davidson, it was seven forty-five when you saw my client outside the ground. I don't think you would contest that now, would you? And yet we heard Mrs McClintock say that it was twenty to eight when she heard a noise on her stairwell and went to her door. She was quite specific because she looked at her clock before she went to the door. Her call to the police was timed at seven forty-two, just two minutes later.'

Rebus didn't need to hear any more, tried to shut his ears to it. The tenement where the assault had taken place was over a mile from Tynecastle Park and the Goatfell pub. To have been where he was when the constable had approached him, Provan would have had to run, in effect, a four-minute mile. Rebus doubted he was capable of it, doubted everything now. But looking at Provan he could *see* the little prick was guilty. He was as guilty as hell and he was about to get away scot bloody free. Rebus's knuckles were white, his teeth were gritted. Provan looked up at him and smiled. The thorn was in Rebus's side again, working away relentlessly, bleeding the policeman to death.

* * *

It couldn't be true. It just couldn't. The trial wasn't over yet. Things had been strung out over the afternoon, the prosecution clearly flustered and playing for time, wondering what tactic to try next, what question to ask. He had lasted the afternoon and court had been adjourned after the summings up. It was all to do with time, as the defence counsel contended. The prosecution tried to negate the time factor and rely instead on the one and only witness. He asked: can we be certain a goal had been scored at that precise moment when PC Davidson approached the accused? Is it not better to trust the identification of the witness, Mrs McClintock, who had actually disturbed the attacker in the course of the assault? And so on. But Rebus knew the case was doomed. There was too much doubt now, way too much. Not guilty, or maybe that Scots get-out clause of 'not proven', whatever. If only the victim had caught a glimpse of Provan, if only. If, if, if. The jury would assemble again tomorrow at ten-thirty, retire to their room and emerge before lunch with a decision which would make Provan a free man. Rebus shook his head.

He was sitting in his car, not up to driving. Just sitting there, the key in the ignition, trying to think things through. But going around in circles, no clear direction, his mind filled with Provan's smile, a smile he would happily tear from that face. Illegal thoughts coursed through his head, ways of fixing Provan, ways of putting him inside. But no: it had to be clean, it had to be *right*. Justification was only part of the process; justice demanded more.

At last, he gave an audible growl, the sound of a caged animal, and turned the ignition, starting the car, heading nowhere in particular. At home he would only brood. A pub might be an idea. There were a few pubs, their clientele almost silent, where a man might drink in solitude and quiet. A kind of a wake for The Law. Damn it, no, he knew where he was headed. Tried not to know, but knew all the same. He was driving towards Gorgie, driving deep into Willie Provan's territory, into the gangland ruled by Tiny Alice. He was heading into the Wild West End of Edinburgh.

The streets were narrow, tenements rising on either side. A cold October wind was blowing, forcing people to angle their walk into the wind, giving them the jack-knife look of a Lowry painting. They were all coming home from work. It was dark, the headlamps of cars and buses like torches in a cave. Gorgie always seemed dark. Even on a summer's day it seemed dark. It had something to do with the narrowness of the streets and the height of the tenements; they seemed like trees in the Amazon, blocking out the light to the pallid vegetation beneath.

Rebus found Cooper Road and parked on the opposite side of the street from number 42. He switched off his engine and wondered what to do now. He was treading dangerously: not the physical danger of the T-Alice, but the more enveloping danger of involvement in a case. If he spoke with Mrs McClintock and the defence counsel were to learn of it, Rebus might be in serious trouble. He wasn't even sure he should be in the vicinity of the crime. Should he turn back? No. Provan was going to get off anyway, whether because of an unconvinced jury or a procedural technicality. Besides, Rebus wasn't getting involved. He was just in the area, that was all.

He was about to get out of the car when he saw a man dressed in duffel coat and jeans shuffle towards the door of number 42 and stop there, studying it. The man pushed at the door and it opened. He looked around before entering the stairwell, and Rebus recognised with a start the intent face of the keen juror from Provan's trial.

Now *this* might be trouble. This might be very bad indeed. What the hell was the juror doing here anyway? The answer seemed simple enough: he was becoming involved, the same as Rebus. Because he, too, could not believe Provan's luck. But what was he doing at number

42? Was he going to talk to Mrs McClintock? If so, he faced certain disqualification from the jury. Indeed, it was Rebus's duty as a police officer, having seen the juror enter that stairwell, to report this fact to the court officials.

Rebus gnawed at his bottom lip. He could go in and warn the juror, of course, but then he, a policeman, would be guilty of approaching a juror on the very evening prior to a judgment. That could mean more than a slapped wrist and a few choice words from the Chief Super. That could mean the end of his career.

Suddenly, Rebus's mind was made up for him. The door of the tenement was heaved open and out ran the juror, an eye on his watch as he turned left and sprinted towards Gorgie Road. Rebus smiled with relief and shook his head.

'You little bugger,' he murmured in appreciation. The juror was timing the whole thing. It was all a matter of time, so the defence had said, and the juror wanted to time things for himself. Rebus started the car and drove off, following behind the juror until the young man discovered a short cut and headed off down an alleyway. Unable to follow, Rebus fed into the traffic on the main road and found himself in the rush hour jams, heading west out of town. It didn't matter: he knew the juror's destination.

Turning down a sidestreet, Rebus rounded a bend and came immediately upon Tynecastle Park. The Goatfell was ahead of him on the other side of the street. Rebus stopped the car on some double yellow lines by the stadium side of the road. Opposite the Goatfell, the juror was doubled over on the pavement, hands pressing into his sides, exhausted after the run and trying to regain his breath. Rebus examined his watch. Eight minutes since the juror had started off from the tenement. The only witness placed the attack at seven-forty, absolutely certain in her mind that this had been the time. The goal had been scored at seven forty-five. Perhaps Mrs McClintock's clock had been wrong? It could be that simple, couldn't it? But they'd have a hell of a job proving it in court, and no jury would convict on the possibility of a dodgy clock.

Besides, her call to the police had been logged, hadn't it? There was no room for manoeuvre on the time, unless … Rebus tapped his fingers against the steering wheel. The juror had recovered some of his equilibrium, and was now staring at the Goatfell. *Don't do it, son*, Rebus intoned mentally. *Don't*.

The juror looked both ways as he crossed the road and, once across, he looked both ways again before pushing open the door of the Goatfell and letting it rattle shut behind him. Rebus groaned and screwed shut his eyes.

'Stupid little …' He pulled the keys from the ignition, and leaned across the passenger seat to lock the passenger side door. You couldn't be too careful around these parts. He stared at his radio. He could call for back-up, *should* call for back-up, but that would involve explanations. No, he was in this one alone.

He opened his own door and swivelled out of his seat, closing the door after him. Pausing to lock the door, he hesitated. After all, you never knew when a quick getaway might be needed. He left the door unlocked. Then, having taken three steps in the direction of the Goatfell, he stopped again and returned to the car, this time unlocking the passenger-side door, too.

You can't afford to get involved, John, he told himself. But his feet kept moving forwards. The front of the Goatfell was uninviting, its bottom half a composition of large purple and black tiles, some missing, the others cracked and chipped and covered in graffiti. The top half was constructed from glass panels, some frosted, some bottle glass. From the fact that there seemed no rhyme or reason to the pattern of these different panels, Rebus guessed that many a fight or thrown stone had seen most of the original panels replaced over time with whatever was available and cheap. He stopped for a moment at the solid wooden door, considering his madness, his folly. Then he pushed open the door and went inside.

The interior was, if anything, less prepossessing than the exterior. Red stubbled linoleum, plastic chairs and long wooden benches, a pool table, its green baize torn in several places. The lone gaming machine coughed up a few coins for an unshaven man who looked as though he had spent most of his adult life battling with it. At one small table sat three thick-set men and a dozing greyhound. Behind the pool table, three more men, younger, shuffling, were arguing over selections from the jukebox. And at the bar stood a solitary figure – the juror – being served with a half pint of lager by the raw-faced barman.

Rebus went to the far end of the bar, as far from the juror as he could get and, keeping his face towards the optics, waited to be served.

'What'll it be?' The barman's question was not unfriendly.

'Half of special and a Bell's,' replied Rebus. This was his gambit in any potentially rough pub. He could think of no good reason why; somehow it just seemed like the right order. He remembered the roughest drinking den he'd ever encountered, deep in a Niddrie housing scheme. He'd given his order and the barman asked, in all seriousness, whether he wanted the two drinks in the same glass. That had shaken Rebus, and he hadn't lingered.

Served with two glasses this evening, one foaming, the other a generous measure of amber, he thanked the barman with a nod and the exact money. But the barman was already turning away, walking back to the conversation he had been having at the other end of the bar before Rebus had walked in, the conversation he'd been having with the juror.

'Aye, that was some game all right. Pity you missed it.'

'Well,' explained the juror, 'what with being away for so long. I've kind of lost touch with their fortunes.'

'Fortune had nothing to do with that night. Cracker of a goal. I must've seen it on the telly a dozen times. Should have been goal of the season.'

The juror sighed. 'Wish I'd been here to see it.'

'Where did you say you'd been again?'

'Europe mostly. Working. I'm only back for a few weeks, then I'm off again.'

Rebus had to admit that the juror made a convincing actor. Of course, there might be a grain of truth in his story, but Rebus doubted it. All the same, good actor or no, he was digging too deep too soon into the barman's memory of that night.

'When did you say the goal was scored?'

'Eh?' The barman seemed puzzled.

'How far into the game,' explained the juror.

'I don't know. Fifteen, twenty minutes, something like that. What difference does it make?'

'Oh, nothing, no, no difference. I was just wondering.'

But the barman was frowning, suspicious now. Rebus felt his grip on the whisky glass tightening.

There's no need for this, son. I know the answer now. It was you that led me to it, but I know now. Just drink your drink and let's get out of here.

Then, as the question and answer session between the juror and barman began again, Rebus glanced into a mirror and his heart dipped fast. The three young men had turned from the wall-mounted jukebox and were now in the process of starting a game of pool. Rebus recognised one of them from the public gallery. Tattoos. Tattoos had sat in the public gallery most of the morning and a little of the afternoon. He seemed not to have recognised Rebus. More to the point, he had not yet recognised the juror – but he would. Rebus had no doubt in his mind about that. Tattoos had spent a long portion of the day staring at fifteen faces, fifteen individuals who, collectively, could put his good friend Willie Provan away for a stretch. Tattoos would recognise the juror, and God alone could tell what would happen then.

God was in a funny mood. Tattoos, standing back while one of the other two T-Alice members played a thunderous break-shot, glanced towards the bar and saw the juror. Perhaps because Rebus was much further away, and partly hidden from view by the juror, Tattoos gave him no heed. But his eyes narrowed as he spotted the juror and Rebus could feel the young man trying to remember where he'd seen the drinker at the bar before. Where and when. Not too long ago. But not to speak to; just a face, a face in a crowd. On a bus? No. In a shop? No. But just a short time ago.

A grunt from one of the other players told Tattoos it was his turn. He lifted a cue from against the wall and bent low over the table, potting an easy ball. Meantime, Rebus had missed the low-voiced conversation between the juror and the barman. From the look on the juror's face, however, it was clear he had discovered something of import: the same 'something' Rebus had deduced while sitting in his car. Keen to leave now that he had his answer, the juror finished his drink.

Tattoos was walking around the table to his next shot. He looked again towards the bar, then towards the table. Then towards the bar again. Rebus, watching this in the wall mirror, saw Tattoos' jaw visibly drop open. Damn him, he had finally placed the juror. He placed his cue on the table and started slowly towards the bar. Rebus felt the tide rising around him. Here he was, where he shouldn't be, following a jury member on the eve of a retiral for verdict and now said juror was about to be approached by a friend of the accused.

For 'approached' read 'nobbled', or at the very least 'scared off'.

There was nothing for it. Rebus finished off the whisky and pushed the half pint away.

169

Tattoos had reached his quarry, who was just turning to go. Tattoos pointed an unnecessary finger.

'It's you, isn't it? You're on my pal's case. One of the jury. Christ, it *is* you.' Tattoos sounded as though he would have been less surprised to have encountered the entire Celtic team supping in his local. He grabbed hold of the juror's shoulder. 'Come on, I want a wee word.'

The juror's face, once red from running, had drained of all colour. Tattoos was hauling him towards the pub door.

'Easy, Dobbs!' called the barman.

'Not your concern, shite-face!' Tattoos, aka Dobbs, growled, tugging the door open and propelling the juror through it, out onto the street.

The bar fell quiet again. The dog, who had awakened at the noise, rested its head back on its paws. The pool game continued. A record came on the jukebox.

'Turn it up a bit!' yelled one of the pool players. 'I can hardly hear it!'

Rebus nodded to the barman in a gesture of farewell. Then he, too, made for the door.

Outside, he knew he must act quickly. At any sign of trouble, members of T-Alice would crawl out of the woodwork like so many termites. Tattoos had pinned the juror to a shop-front window between the Goatfell and Rebus's car. Rebus's attention was drawn from the conflict to the car itself. Its doors were open! He could see two kids playing inside it, crawling over its interior, pretending they were at the wheel of a racing car. Rebus hissed and moved forwards. He was almost passing Tattoos and the juror when he yelled:

'Get out of my bloody car!'

Even Tattoos turned at this and as he did so Rebus hammered a clenched fist into his nose. It had to be fast: Rebus didn't want Tattoos to be able ever to identify him. The sound of the nose flattening was dull and unmistakable. Tattoos let go of the juror and held his hands to his face. Rebus hit him again, this time in proper boxing fashion, knuckles against the side of the jaw. Tattoos fell against the glass shop-front and sank to the pavement.

It was Rebus's turn to grab the juror's shoulder, marching him towards the car with no words of explanation. The juror went quietly, glancing back just the once towards the prone body.

Seeing Rebus approach, brimstone in his eyes, the two boys ran from the car. Rebus watched them go, committing their faces to memory. Future Willie Provans.

'Get in,' he said to the juror, shoving him towards the passenger side. They both shut the car doors after them. Rebus's police radio was missing, and wires protruded from beneath the dashboard, evidence of an attempted hot-wiring. Rebus was relieved the attempt hadn't worked. Otherwise he would be trapped in Gorgie, surrounded by hostile natives. It didn't bear thinking about.

The car started first time and Rebus revved it hard as he drove off, never looking back.

'I know you,' said the juror. 'You were in the public gallery, too.'

'That's right.'

The juror grew quiet. 'You're not one of …?'

'I want to see Willie Provan behind bars. That's all you need to know, and I don't want to know anything about you. I just want you to go home, go back to court tomorrow, and do your duty.'

'But I know how he –'

'So do I.' Rebus stopped at a red traffic light and checked in the mirror. No one was following. He turned to the juror. 'It was a cup-tie, a big crowd,' he said. 'And ever since Hillsborough, the football bosses and the police have been careful about big crowds.'

'That's right.' The juror was bursting to come out with it first. 'So they held up the game for ten minutes to let everybody in. The barman told me.'

Rebus nodded. The game had been a seven-thirty kick-off all right, but that intended kick-off time had been delayed. The goal, scored fifteen minutes into the game, had been scored at seven fifty-five, *not* seven forty-five, giving Provan plenty of time to make the one-mile trip from Cooper Road to the Goatfell. The truth would have come out eventually, but it might have taken a little time. The situation, however, was still dangerous. The light turned green, and Rebus moved off.

'So you think Provan is guilty?' he asked the juror.

'I know he is. It's obvious.'

Rebus nodded. 'He could still get away with it.'

'How?'

'If,' Rebus explained carefully, 'it comes to light that you and I have been doing a little snooping. You'll be thrown off the jury. It could go to a retrial, or some technicality might arise which would see Provan go free. We can't let that happen, can we?'

Rebus heard his own words. They sounded calm. Yet inside him the adrenalin was racing and his fist was pleasantly sore from use.

'No,' answered the juror, as Rebus had hoped he would.

'So,' continued Rebus, 'what I propose is that I have a quiet word with the prosecution counsel. Let's let him stand up in court and come out with the solution. That way no problems or technicalities arise. You just stay quiet and let the process work through.'

The juror seemed disheartened. This was his feat, after all, his sleuthing had turned things around. And for what?

'There's no glory in it, I'm afraid,' said Rebus. 'But at least you'll have the satisfaction of knowing Provan is inside, not out there, waiting to pick off another victim.' Rebus nodded through the windscreen and the juror stared at the city streets, thinking it over.

'Okay,' he said at last. 'Yes, you're right.'

'So we keep it quiet?'

'We keep it quiet,' the juror agreed. Rebus nodded slowly. This might shape up all right after all. The whisky was warming his veins. A quiet word to the prosecution, maybe by way of a typed and anonymous note, something that would keep Rebus out of the case. It was a pity he couldn't be in court tomorrow for the revelation. But the last thing he wanted was to encounter a broken-nosed Tattoos. A pity though; he wanted to see Provan's face and he wanted to catch Provan's eyes and he wanted to give him a great big pitiless smile.

'You can stop here,' said the juror, waking Rebus from his reverie. They were approaching Princes Street. 'I just live down Queens –'

'Don't tell me,' Rebus said abruptly. The juror looked at him.

'Technicalities?' he ventured. Rebus smiled and nodded. He pulled the car over to the side of the road. The juror opened his door, got out, but then bent down into the car again.

'I don't even know who you are,' he said.

'That's right,' said Rebus, reaching across and pulling shut the door. 'You don't.'

He drove off into the Edinburgh evening. No thorn jabbed him now. By tomorrow there would be another. And then he'd have to report the theft of his radio. There would be smiles at that, smiles and, behind his back if not to his face, laughter.

John Rebus could laugh, too.

Sunday

Where was that light coming from? Bright, hot light. Knives in the night. Last night, was it? No, the night before. Just another Friday in Edinburgh. A drug haul at a dance hall. A few of the dealers trying to run for it. Rebus cornering one. The man, sweating, teeth bared, turning before Rebus's eyes into an animal, something wild, predatory, scared. And cornered. The glint of a knife …

But that was Friday, the night before last. So this was Sunday. Yes! Sunday morning. (Afternoon, maybe.) Rebus opened his eyes and squinted into the sunshine, streaming through his uncurtained window. No, not sunshine. His bedside lamp. Must have been on all night. He had come to bed drunk last night, drunk and tired. Had forgotten to close the curtains. And now warming light, birds resting on the window-ledge. He stared into a small black eye, then checked his watch. Ten past eight. Morning then, not afternoon. Early morning.

His head was the consistency of syrup, his limbs stiff. He'd been fit as a young man; not fitness daft, but fit all the same. But one day he had just stopped caring. He dressed quickly, then checked and found that he was running out of clean shirts, clean pants, clean socks. Today's chore then: doing the laundry. Ever since his wife had left him, he had taken his dirty washing to a public launderette at the top of Marchmont Road, where a service wash cost very little and the manageress always used to fold his clean clothes away very neatly, a smile on her scrupulous lips. But in a fit of madness one Saturday afternoon, he had walked calmly into an electrical shop and purchased a washer/dryer for the flat.

He pressed the dirty bundle into the machine and found he was down to one last half-scoop of washing powder. What the hell, it would have to do. There were various buttons and controls on the machine's fascia, but he only ever used one programme: Number 5 (40 Degrees), full load, with ten minutes' tumble dry at the end. The results were satisfactory, if never perfect. He switched the machine on, donned his shoes and left the flat, double-locking the door behind him.

His car, parked directly outside the main entrance to the tenement, scowled at him. *I need a wash, pal.* It was true, but Rebus shook his head. Not today, today was his day off, the only day this week. Some other time, some other free time. Who was he kidding? He'd drive into a car wash one afternoon between calls. His car could like it or lump it.

The corner shop was open. Rebus had seldom seen it closed. He bought ground coffee, rolls, milk, margarine, a packet of bacon. The bacon, through its plastic wrapping, had an oily, multi-coloured look to it, but its sell-by date seemed reasonable. Pigs: very intelligent creatures. How could one intelligent creature eat another? Guilty conscience, John? It must be Sunday. Presbyterian guilt, Calvinist guilt. Mea culpa, he thought to himself, taking the bacon to the check-out till. Then he turned back and bought some washing powder, too.

Back in the flat, the washing machine was churning away. He put Coleman Hawkins on the hi-fi (not too loud; it was only quarter to nine). Soon the church bells would start ringing, calling the faithful. Rebus would not answer. He had given up church-going. Any day but Sunday he might have gone. But Sunday, Sunday was the only day off he had. He remembered his mother, taking him with her to church every Sunday while his father stayed at home in bed with tea and the paper. Then one Sunday, when he was twelve or thirteen, his mother had said he could choose: go with her or stay with his father. He stayed and saw his little brother's jealous eyes glance at him, desperate to be of an age where he would be given the same choice.

Ah me, John, Sunday morning. Rubbedy-rrub of the washing machine, the coffee's aroma wafting up from the filter. (Getting short on filters, but no panic: he only used them on Sunday.) He went into the bathroom. Suddenly, staring at the bath itself, he felt an overwhelming urge to steep himself in hot water. Wednesdays and Saturdays: those were his usual days for a bath. Go on, break the rules. He turned on the hot tap, but it was a mere trickle. Damn! the washing machine was being fed all the flat's hot water. Oh well. Bath later. Coffee now.

At five past nine, the Sunday papers thudded through the letterbox. *Sunday Post, Mail,* and *Scotland on Sunday.* He seldom read them, but they helped the day pass. Not that he got bored on a Sunday. It was the day of rest, so he rested. A nice lazy day. He refilled his coffee mug, went back into the bathroom and walked over to the toilet to examine a roughly circular patch on the wall beside it, a couple of feet up from floor level. The patch was slightly discoloured and he touched it with the palm of his hand. Yes, it was damp. He had first noticed the patch a week ago. Damp, slightly damp. He couldn't think why. There was no dampness anywhere else, no apparent source of the damp. Curious, he had peeled away the paper from the patch, had scratched at the plaster wall. But no answer had emerged. He shook his head. That would irritate him for the rest of the day. As before, he went to the bedroom and returned with an electric hair-drier and an extension flex. He plugged the hair-drier into the flex, and rested the drier on the toilet seat, aimed towards the patch, then switched on the hair-drier and tested that it was hitting the spot. That would dry things out a bit, but he knew the patch would return.

Washing machine rumbling. Hair-drier whirring. Coleman Hawkins in the living-room. He went into the living-room. Could do with a tidy, couldn't it? Hoover, dust. Car sitting outside waiting to be washed. Everything could wait. There were the papers to be read. There they were on the table, just next to his briefcase. The briefcase full of documents for his attention, half-completed case-notes, reminders of appointments, all the rubbish he hadn't found time for during the week at the station. All the so-important paperwork, without which his life would be milk and honey. Some toast perhaps? Yes, he would eat some toast.

He checked his watch: ten past eleven. He had switched off the hairdrier, but left it sitting on the toilet, the extension lead snaking across the floor to the wall-socket in the hall. The washing machine was silent, spent. One more cup of coffee left in the pot. He had flicked through the papers, looking for the interesting, the unusual. Same old stories: court cases, weekend crime, sport. There was even a paragraph on Friday night's action. He skipped that, but remembered all the same. Bright knife's flat edge, caught in the lamplight. Sour damp smell in the alleyway. Feet standing in something soft. Don't look down, look at him, look straight at him, the cornered animal. Look at him, talk to him with your eyes, try to calm him, or quell him.

There were birds on the window sill, chirping, wanting some crumbled up crusts of bread, but he had no bread worth the name left in the flat; just fresh rolls, too soft to be thrown out. Ach, he'd never eat six rolls though, would he? One or two would go stale and then he'd give them to the birds. So why not give them some in advance, while the rolls are soft and sweet?

In the kitchen he prepared the broken pieces of bread on a plate, then took it to the birds on the window-ledge. Hell: what about lunch? Sunday afternoon lunch. In the freezer compartment, he found a steak. How long would it take to defrost? Damn! he meant to pick up the microwave during the week. The shop had called him to say they'd fixed the fault. He was supposed to have collected it on Friday, but he'd been too busy. So: defrost in a low oven. And wine. Yes, open a bottle. He could always drink just one or two glasses, then keep the rest of the bottle for some other occasion. Last Christmas, a friend had given him a vacuum-tube. It was supposed to keep wine fresh after opening. Where had he put it? In the cupboard beside the wine: that would make sense. But there was no gadget to be found.

He chose a not-bad bottle, bought from a reliable wine merchant in Marchmont and stood it on the table in the living-room. Beside his briefcase. Let the sediment settle. That's what Sunday was all about, wasn't it? Maybe he could try one of the crosswords. It was ages since he'd done a crossword. A glass of wine and a crossword while he waited for the meat to thaw. Sediment wouldn't be settled yet, but what the hell. He opened the bottle and poured an inch into his glass. Glanced at his watch again. It was half past eleven. A bit early to be drinking. Cheers.

You could break the rules on a Sunday, couldn't you?

Christ, what a week it had been at work. Everything from a senile rapist to a runaway blind boy. A shotgun robbery at a bookmaker's shop and an apparently accidental drowning at the docks. Drunk, the victim had been. Dead drunk. Fished about a bottle of whisky and a recently dismembered kebab from his stomach. Annual crime figures for the Lothians were released: murder slightly up on the previous year, sexual assaults well up, burglaries up, street crime down a little, motoring offences significantly reduced. The clear-up rate for housebreakings in some parts of Edinburgh was standing at less than five per cent. Rebus was not exactly a fascist, not quite a totalitarian, but he knew that given wider powers of entry and search, that final figure could be higher. There were high-rise blocks where a flat on the twelfth floor would be broken into time after time. Was someone climbing twelve flights to break in? Of course not: someone in the block was responsible, but without the powers of immediate and indiscriminate search, they'd never find the culprit.

And that was the tip of the whole polluted iceberg. Maniacs were put back on the streets by institutions unable or unwilling to cope. Rebus had never seen so many beggars in Edinburgh as in this past year. Teenagers (and younger) up to grandparents, dossing, cadging the occasional quid or cigarette. Christ, it depressed him to think of it almost as much as it did to pretend he could ignore it. He stalked through to the kitchen and felt the steak. It was still solid at its core. He lifted the nearly dry clothes out of the machine and draped them over the cold radiators throughout the flat. More music on the hi-fi. Art Pepper this time, a little louder, the hour being respectable. Not that the neighbours ever complained. Sometimes he could see in their eyes that they wanted to complain – complain about his noise, his irregular comings and goings, the way he revved his car or coughed his way up the stairwell. They wanted to complain, but they daren't, for fear that he would somehow 'stitch them up' or would prove not to be amenable to some favour they might ask one day. They all watched the TV police dramas and thought they must know their neighbour pretty well. Rebus shook his head and poured more wine: two inches deep in the glass this time. They knew nothing about him. Nothing. He didn't have a TV, hated all the game shows and the cop shows and the news programmes. Not having a TV had set him apart from his colleagues at the station: he found he had little to discuss with them of a morning. His mornings were quieter and saner for it.

He checked the damp patch in the bathroom again, letting his hand rest against it for half a minute. Mmm: it still wasn't completely dry. But then maybe his hands were damp from the washing he had been carrying. What the hell. Back in the bedroom, he picked up some books from the floor and stacked them against a wall, beside other columns of paperbacks and hardbacks, read and unread. One day he would get time to read them. They were like contraband: he couldn't stop himself buying them, but then he never really did anything with them once he'd bought them. The buying was the thing, that sense of ownership. Perhaps somewhere in Britain someone had exactly the same collection of books as him, but he doubted it. The range was too eclectic, everything from secondhand rugby yearbooks to dense philosophical works. Meaningless, really; without pattern. So much of his working life was spent to a pattern, a modus operandi. A series of rules for the possible (not probable) solving of crimes. One of the rules would have it that he get through the briefcase full of work before Monday morning and, preferably, while still sober.

Bell. Bell?

Bell. Someone at his front door. Jesus, on a *Sunday*? Not on a Sunday, please, God. The wrong door: they'd got the wrong door. Give them a minute and they would realise their mistake. Bell again. Bloody hell's bells. Right then, he would answer it.

He pulled the door open slowly, peering around it. Detective Constable Brian Holmes was standing on the tenement landing.

'Brian?'

'Hello, sir. Hope you don't mind. I was in the neighbourhood and thought I'd … you know.'

Rebus held open the door. 'Come in.'

He led Holmes through the hall, stepping over the electric flex. Holmes stared at the flex, an alarmed look on his face.

'Don't worry,' said Rebus, pausing at the threshold of

181

the living-room. 'I'm not going to jump in the bath with an electric fire. Just drying out a damp patch.'

'Oh.' Holmes sounded unconvinced. 'Right.'

'Sit down,' said Rebus. 'I've just opened a bottle of wine. Would you like some?'

'Bit early for me,' Holmes said, glancing towards Rebus's glass.

'Well, coffee then. I think there's still some in the pot.'

'No thanks, I'm fine.'

They were both seated, Rebus in his usual chair, Holmes perched on the edge of the sofa. Rebus knew why the younger officer was here, but he was damned if he would make it easy for him.

'In the neighbourhood you say?'

'That's right. I was at a party last night in Mayfield. Afterwards, I stopped the night.'

'Oh?'

Holmes smiled. 'No such luck, I slept on the sofa.'

'It's still off with Nell then?'

'I don't know. Sometimes she ... let's change the subject.'

He flipped one of the newspapers over so that he could study the back page. 'Did you see the boxing last night?'

'I don't have a television.'

Holmes looked around the room, then smiled again. 'Neither you do. I hadn't noticed.'

'I'll bear that in mind when you come up for promotion, Constable.' Rebus took a large gulp of wine, watching Holmes over the rim of the glass. Holmes was looking less comfortable by the second.

'Any plans for the day?'

'Such as?'

Holmes shrugged. 'I don't know. I thought maybe you had a Sunday routine. You know: clean the car, that sort of thing.'

Rebus nodded towards the briefcase on the table. 'Paperwork. That'll keep me busy most of the day.'

Holmes nodded, flicking through the paper until he came, as Rebus knew he would, to the piece about the nightclub bust.

'It's at the bottom of the page,' Rebus said. 'But then you know that, don't you? You've already seen it.' He rose from his chair sharply and walked to the hi-fi, turning the record over. Alto sax bloomed from the speakers. Holmes still hadn't said anything. He was pretending to read the paper, but his eyes weren't moving. Rebus returned to his seat.

'Was there really a party, Brian?'

'Yes.' Holmes paused. 'No.'

'And you weren't just passing?'

'No. I wanted to see how you were.'

'And how am I?'

'You look fine.'

'That's because I *am* fine.'

'Are you sure?'

'Perfectly.'

Holmes sighed and threw aside the paper. 'I'm glad to hear it. I was worried, John. We were all a bit shaken up.'

'I've killed someone before, Brian. It wasn't the first time.'

'Yes, but Christ, I mean …' Holmes got up and walked to the window, looking down on the street. A nice quiet street in a quiet part of town. Net curtains and trim front gardens, the gardens of professional people, lawful people, people who smiled at you in shops or chatted in a bus queue.

But Rebus's mind flashed again to the dark alleyway, a distant streetlamp, the cornered drug dealer. He had thrown packets from his pockets onto the ground as he had run. Like sowing seed. Small polythene bags of drugs soft and hard. Sowing them in the soft mud, every year a new crop.

Then the blinding light. The flat steel of a knife. Not a huge knife, but how big did a knife need to be? An inch of blade would be enough. Anything more was excess. It was a very excessive knife indeed, curved, serrated edge, a commando special. The kind you could buy from a camping shop. The kind *anybody* could buy from a camping shop. A serious knife for outdoor pursuits. Rebus had the idea they called them 'survival' knives.

The man – not much more than a boy in reality, eighteen or nineteen – had not hesitated. He slid the knife out from the waistband of his trousers. He lunged, one swipe, two swipes. Rebus wasn't fit, but his reactions were fast. On the third swipe, he snapped out a hand and caught the wrist, twisting it all the way. The knife fell to the ground. The dealer cried out in pain and dropped to one knee. No words had passed between the two men. There was no real need for words.

But then Rebus had realised that his opponent was not on his knees as a sign of defeat. He was scrabbling around for the knife and found it with his free hand. Rebus let go of the dead wrist and pinned the man's left arm to his body, but the arm was strong and the blade sheared through Rebus's trousers, cutting a red line up across his thigh. Rebus brought his knee up hard into his adversary's crotch and felt the body go limp. He repeated the action, but the dealer wasn't giving up. The knife was rising again. Rebus grabbed the wrist with one hand, the other going for the man's throat. Then he felt himself being spun and pushed hard up against the wall of the alley. The wall was damp, smelling of mould. He pressed a thumb deep into the dealer's larynx, still wrestling with the knife. His knee thudded into the man's groin again. And then, as the strength in the knife-arm eased momentarily, Rebus yanked the wrist and pushed.

Pushed hard, driving the dealer across the alley and against the other wall. Where the man gasped, gurgled, eyes bulging. Rebus stood back and released his grasp on the wrist, the wrist which held the knife, buried up to the hilt in the young man's stomach.

'Oh shit,' he whispered. 'Oh shit, oh shit, oh shit.'

The dealer was staring in surprise at the handle of the knife. His hand fell away from it, but the knife itself stayed put. He shuffled forward, walking past Rebus, who could only stand and watch, making for the entrance to the alleyway. The tip of the knife was protruding through the back of the dealer's jacket. He made it to the mouth of the alley before falling to his knees.

'Sir?'

'Mmm?' Rebus looked up and saw that Holmes was studying him from the window. 'What is it, Brian?'

'Are you okay?'

'I told you, I'm fine.' Rebus tipped the last of the wine down his throat and placed the glass on the floor, trying to control the trembling in his hand.

'It's just that … well, I've never —'

'You've never killed anyone.'

'That's right,' Holmes came back to the sofa. 'I haven't.' He sat down, hands pressed between his knees, leaning slightly forwards as he spoke. 'What does it feel like?'

'Feel like?' Rebus smiled with half his mouth. 'It doesn't feel like anything. I don't even think about it. That's the best way.'

Holmes nodded slowly. Rebus was thinking: *get to the point*. And then Holmes came to the point.

'Did you mean to do it?' he asked.

Rebus had no hesitation. 'It was an accident. I didn't know it had happened until it did happen. We got into a clinch and somehow the knife ended up where it ended up. That's all. That's what I told them back at the station and that's what I'll tell any inquiry they shove at me. It was an accident.'

'Yes,' said Holmes quietly, nodding. 'That's what I thought.'

Accidents will happen, won't they?

Like burning the steak. Like finishing the bottle when you'd meant to have just a couple of glasses. Like punching a dent in the bathroom wall. Accidents happened and most of them happened in the home.

Holmes refused the offer of lunch and left. Rebus sat in the chair for a while, just listening to jazz, forgetting all about the steak. He only remembered it when he went to open another bottle of wine. The corkscrew had found its way back into the cutlery drawer, and he plucked out a knife by mistake. A small sharp-bladed knife with a wooden handle. He kept this knife for steaks especially.

It was good of Holmes to look in, no matter what the motive. And it was good of him not to stay, too. Rebus needed to be alone, needed time and space enough to think. He had told Holmes he never thought about it, never thought about death. That was a lie; he thought about it all the time. This weekend he was replaying Friday night, going over the scene time and time again in his head. Trying to answer the question Holmes himself had asked: was it an accident? But every time Rebus went through it, the answer became more and more vague. The hand was holding the knife, and then Rebus was angling that hand away from himself, propelling the hand and the body behind it backward into the wall of the alley. Angling the hand ... That was the vital moment. When he grabbed the wrist so that the knife was pointing towards the dealer, what had been going through his mind then? The thought that he was saving himself? Or that he was about to kill the dealer?

Rebus shook his head. It was no clearer now than it had been at the time. The media had chalked it up yesterday as self-defence and the internal inquiry would come to the same conclusion. Could he have disarmed the young man? Probably. Would the man have killed Rebus, given the chance? Certainly. Had he lived, would he have become Prime Minister, or fascist dictator, or Messiah? Would he have seen the error of his ways, or would he have gone on dispensing the only thing he had to sell? What about his parents, his family, his friends who had known him at school, who had known him as a child: what would they be thinking now? Were the photograph albums and the paper hankies out? Pictures of the dealer as a boy, dressed up as a cowboy on his birthday, pictures of him splashing in the bath as a baby. Memories of someone John Rebus had never known.

He shook his head again. Thinking about it would do no good, but it was the only way to deal with it. And yes, he felt guilty. He felt soiled and defeated and bad. But he would stop feeling bad, and then eventually he would stop feeling anything at all. He had killed before; it might be he would kill again. You never knew until the moment itself.

And sometimes even then, you still didn't know, and would continue not to know. Holmes mentioned Mayfield. Rebus knew of a church in Mayfield with an evening service on a Sunday. A church with a restrained congregation and a minister not overly keen on prying into one's affairs. Maybe he would go there later. Meantime, he felt like a walk. He would walk through The Meadows and back across Bruntsfield Links, with a diversion towards the ice-cream shop near Tollcross. Maybe he'd bump into his friend Frank.

For this was Sunday, his day off, and he could do whatever he liked, couldn't he? After all, Sunday was a day for breaking the rules. It was the only day he could afford.

Auld Lang Syne

Places Detective Inspector John Rebus did not want to be at midnight on Hogmanay: number one, the Tron in Edinburgh.

Which was perhaps, Rebus decided, why he found himself at five minutes to midnight pushing his way through the crowds which thronged the area of the Royal Mile outside the Tron Kirk. It was a bitter night, a night filled with the fumes of beer and whisky, of foam licking into the sky as another can was opened, of badly sung songs and arms around necks and stooped, drunken proclamations of undying love, proclamations which would be forgotten by morning.

Rebus had been here before, of course. He had been here the previous Hogmanay, ready to root out the eventual troublemakers, to break up fights and crunch across the shattered glass covering the setts. The best and worst of the Scots came out as another New Year approached: the togetherness, the sharpness, the hugging of life, the inability to know when to stop, so that the hug became a smothering stranglehold. These people were drowning in a sea of sentiment and sham. *Flower of Scotland* was struck up by a lone voice for the thousandth time, and for the thousandth time a few more voices joined in, all falling away at the end of the first chorus.

'Gawn yirsel there, big man.'

Rebus looked around him. The usual contingent of uniformed officers was going through the annual ritual of having hands shaken by a public suddenly keen to make friends. It was the WPCs Rebus felt sorry for, as another slobbering kiss slapped into the cheek of a young female officer. The police of Edinburgh knew their duty: they always offered one sacrificial lamb to appease the multitude. There was actually an orderly queue standing in front of the WPC waiting to kiss her. She smiled and blushed. Rebus shivered and turned away. Four minutes to midnight. His nerves were like struck chords. He hated crowds. Hated drunken crowds more. Hated the fact that another year was coming to an end. He began to push through the crowd with a little more force than was necessary.

People Detective Inspector John Rebus would rather not be with at midnight on Hogmanay: number one, detectives from Glasgow CID.

He smiled and nodded towards one of them. The man was standing just inside a bus shelter, removed from the general scrum of the road itself. On top of the shelter, a Mohican in black leather did a tribal dance, a bottle of strong lager gripped in one hand. A police constable shouted for the youth to climb down from the shelter. The punk took no notice. The man in the bus shelter smiled back at John Rebus. He's not waiting for a bus, Rebus thought to himself, he's waiting for a bust.

Things Detective Inspector John Rebus would rather not be doing at midnight on Hogmanay: number one, working.

So he found himself working, and as the crowd swept him up again, he thought of Dante's *Inferno*. Three minutes to midnight. Three minutes away from hell. The Scots, pagan at their core, had always celebrated New Year rather than Christmas. Back when Rebus was a boy, Christmases were muted. New Year was the time for celebration, for first-footing, black bun, madeira cake, coal wrapped in silver foil, stovies during the night and steak pie the following afternoon. Ritual after ritual. Now he found himself observing another ritual, another set of procedures. A meeting was about to take place. An exchange would be made: a bag filled with money for a parcel full of dope. A consignment of heroin had entered Scotland via a west coast fishing village. The CID in Glasgow had been tipped off, but failed to intercept the package. The trail had gone cold for several days, until an informant came up with the vital information. The dope was in Edinburgh. It was about to be handed on to an east coast dealer. The dealer was known to Edinburgh CID, but they'd never been able to pin a major possession charge on him. They wanted him badly. So did the west coast CID.

'It's to be a joint operation,' Rebus's boss had informed him, with no trace of irony on his humourless face. So now here he was, mingling with the crowds, just as another dozen or so undercover officers were doing. The men about to make the exchange did not trust one another. One of them had decided upon the Tron as a public enough place to make the deal. With so many people around, a double-cross was less likely to occur. The Tron at midnight on Hogmanay: a place of delirium and riot. No one would notice a discreet switch of cases, money for dope, dope for money. It was perfect.

Rebus, pushing against the crowd again, saw the money-man for the very first time. He recognised him from photographs. Alan Lyons, 'Nal' to his friends. He was twenty-seven years old, drove a Porsche 911 and lived in a detached house on the riverside just outside Haddington. He had been one of Rab Philips' men until Philips' demise. Now he was out on his own. He listed his occupation as 'entrepreneur'. He was sewerage.

Lyons was resting his back against a shop window. He smoked a cigarette and gave the passers-by a look that said he was not in the mood for handshakes and conversation. A glance told Rebus that two of the Glasgow crew were keeping a close watch on Lyons, so he did not linger. His interest now was in the missing link, the man with the package. Where was he? A countdown was being chanted all around him. A few people reckoned the New Year was less than ten seconds away; others, checking their watches, said there was a minute left. By Rebus's own watch, they were already into the New Year by a good thirty seconds. Then, without warning, the clock chimes rang and a great cheer went up. People were shaking hands, hugging, kissing. Rebus could do nothing but join in.

'Happy New Year.'

'Happy New Year, pal.'

'Best of luck, eh?'

'Happy New Year.'

'All the best.'

'Happy New Year.'

Rebus shook a Masonic hand, and looked up into a face he recognised. He returned the compliment – 'Happy New Year' – and the man smiled and moved on, hand already outstretched to another well-wisher, another stranger. But this man had been no stranger to Rebus. Where the hell did he know him from? The crowd had rearranged itself, shielding the man from view. Rebus concentrated on the memory of the face. He had known it younger, less jowly, but with darker eyes. He could hear the voice: a thick Fife accent. The hands were like shovels, miner's hands. But this man was no miner.

He had his radio with him, but trapped as he was in the midst of noise there was no point trying to contact the others on the surveillance. He wanted to tell them something. He wanted to tell them he was going to follow the mystery man. Always supposing, that was, he could find him again in the crowd.

And then he remembered: Jackie Crawford. Dear God, it was Jackie Crawford!

People Rebus did not want to shake hands with as the old year became the new: number one, Jackie 'Trigger' Crawford.

Rebus had put Crawford behind bars four years ago for

armed robbery and wounding. The sentence imposed by the judge had been a generous stretch of ten years. Crawford had headed north from court in a well-guarded van. He had not gained the nickname 'Trigger' for his quiet and homely outlook on life. The man was a headcase of the first order, gun happy and trigger happy. He'd taken part in a series of bank and building society robberies; short, violent visits to High Streets across the Lowlands. That nobody had been killed owed more to strengthened glass and luck than to Crawford's philanthropy. He'd been sent away for ten, he was out after four. What was going on? Surely, the man could not be out and walking the streets *legally*? He had to have broken out, or at the very least cut loose from some day-release scheme. And wasn't it a coincidence that he should bump into Rebus, that he should be here in the Tron at a time when the police were waiting for some mysterious drug pedaller?

Rebus believed in coincidence, but this was stretching things a bit too far. Jackie Crawford was somewhere in this crowd, somewhere shaking hands with people whom, a scant four years before, he might have been terrorising with a sawn-off shotgun. Rebus had to do something, whether Crawford was the 'other man' or not. He began squeezing through the crowd again, this time ignoring proffered hands and greetings. He moved on his toes, craning his head over the heads of the revellers, seeking the square-jawed, wiry-haired head of his prey. He was trying to recall whether there was some tradition in Scotland that ghosts from your past came to haunt you at midnight on Hogmanay. He thought not. Besides, Crawford was no ghost. His hands had been meaty and warm, his thumb pressing speculatively against Rebus's knuckles. The eyes which had glanced momentarily into Rebus's eyes had been clear and blue, but uninterested.

Had Crawford recognised his old adversary? Rebus couldn't be sure. There had been no sign of recognition, no raising of eyebrows or opening of the mouth. Just three mumbled words before moving on to the next hand. Was Crawford drunk? Most probably: few sane and sober individuals visited the Tron on this night of all nights. Good: a drunken Crawford would have been unlikely to recognise him. Yet the voice had been quiet and unslurred, the eyes focussed. Crawford had not seemed drunk, had not acted drunk. Sober as a judge, in fact. This, too, worried Rebus.

But then, *everything* worried him this evening. He couldn't afford any slip-ups from the operation's Edinburgh contingent. It would give too much ammo to the Glasgow faction: there was a certain competitive spirit between the two forces. For 'competitive spirit' read 'loathing'. Each would want to claim any arrest as *its* victory; and each would blame any foul-up on the other.

This had been explained to him very clearly by Chief Inspector Lauderdale.

'But surely, sir,' Rebus had replied, 'catching these men is what's most important.'

'Rubbish, John,' Lauderdale had replied. 'What's important is that we don't look like arseholes in front of McLeish and his men.'

Which, of course, Rebus had already known: he just liked winding his superior up a little the better to watch him perform. Superintendent Michael McLeish was an outspoken and devout Catholic, and Rebus's chief did not like Catholics. But Rebus hated bigots, and so he wound up Lauderdale whenever he could and had a name for him behind his back: the Clockwork Orangeman.

The crowd was thinning out as Rebus headed away from the Tron and uphill towards the castle. He was, he knew, moving away from the surveillance and should inform his fellow officers of the fact, but if his hunch was right, he was also following the man behind the whole deal. Suddenly he caught sight of Crawford, who seemed to be moving purposefully out of the crowd, heading onto the pavement and giving a half-turn of his head, knowing he was being followed.

So he had recognised Rebus, and now had seen him hurrying after him. The policeman exhaled noisily and pushed his way through the outer ring of the celebrations. His arms ached, as though he had been swimming against a strong current, but now that he was safely out of the water, he saw that Crawford had vanished. He looked along the row of shops, separated each from the other by narrow, darkened closes. Up those closes were the entrances to flats, courtyards surrounded by university halls of residence, and many steep and worn steps leading from the High Street down to Cockburn Street. Rebus had to choose one of them. If he hesitated, or chose wrongly, Crawford would make good his escape. He ran to the first alley and, glancing down it, listening for footsteps, decided to move on. At the second close, he chose not to waste any more time and ran in, passing dimly-lit doorways festooned with graffiti, dank walls and frozen cobbles. Until, launching himself down a flight of steps into almost absolute darkness, he stumbled. He flailed for a hand-rail to stop him from falling, and found his arm grabbed by a powerful hand, saving him.

Crawford was standing against the side of the alley, on a platform between flights of steps. Rebus sucked in air, trying to calm himself. There was a sound in his ears like the aftermath of an explosion.

'Thanks,' he spluttered.

'You were following me.' The voice was effortlessly calm.

'Was I?' It was a lame retort and Crawford knew it. He chuckled.

'Yes, Mr Rebus, you were. You must have gotten a bit of a shock.'

Rebus nodded. 'A bit, yes, after all these years, Jackie.'

'I'm surprised you recognised me. People tell me I've changed.'

'Not that much.' Rebus glanced down at his arm, which was still in Crawford's vice-like grip. The grip relaxed and fell away.

'Sorry.'

Rebus was surprised at the apology, but tried not to let it show. He was busy covertly studying Crawford's body, looking for any bulge big enough to be a package or a gun.

'So what were you doing back there?' he asked, not particularly interested in the answer, but certainly interested in the time it might buy him.

Crawford seemed amused. 'Bringing in the New Year, of course. What else would I be doing?'

It was a fair question, but Rebus chose not to answer it. 'When did you get out?'

'A month back.' Crawford could sense Rebus's suspicion. 'It's legit. Honest to God, Sergeant, as He is my witness. I haven't done a runner or anything.'

'You ran from *me*. And it's Inspector now, by the way.'

Crawford smiled again. 'Congratulations.'

'Why did you run?'

'Was I running?'

'You know you were.'

'The reason I was running was because the last person I wanted to see tonight of all nights was you, Inspector Rebus. You spoilt it for me.'

Rebus frowned. He was *looking* at Trigger Crawford, but felt he was talking to somebody else, someone calmer and less dangerous, someone, well, *ordinary*. He was confused, but still suspicious. 'Spoilt what exactly?'

'My New Year resolution. I came here to make peace with the world.'

It was Rebus's turn to smile, though not kindly. 'Make peace, eh?'

'That's right.'

'No more guns? No more armed robberies?'

Crawford was shaking his head slowly. Then he held open his coat. 'No more shooters, Inspector. That's a promise. You see, I've made my own peace.'

Peace or piece? Rebus couldn't be sure. He was reaching into his own jacket pocket, from which he produced a police radio. Crawford looked on the level. He even sounded on the level, but facts had to be verified. So he called in and asked for a check to be made on John Crawford, nickname 'Trigger'. Crawford smiled shyly at the mention of that name. Rebus held onto the radio, waiting for the computer to do its stuff, waiting for the station to respond.

'It's been a long time since anyone called me Trigger,' Crawford said. 'Quite some time.'

'How come they released you after four?'

'A bit less than four, actually,' corrected Crawford. 'They released me because I was no longer a threat to society. You'll find that hard to believe. In fact, you'll find it *impossible* to believe. That's not my fault, it's yours. You think men like me can never go straight. But we can. You see, something happened to me in prison. I found Jesus Christ.'

Rebus knew the look on his face was a picture, and it caused Crawford to smile again, still shyly. He looked down at the tips of his shoes.

'That's right, Inspector. I became a Christian. It wasn't any kind of blinding light. It took a while. I got bored inside and I started reading books. One day I picked up the Bible and just opened it at random. What I read there seemed to make sense. It was the Good News Bible, written in plain English. I read bits and pieces, just flicked through it. Then I went to one of the Sunday services, mainly because there were a few things I couldn't understand and I wanted to ask the minister about them. And he helped me a bit. That's how it started. It changed my life.'

Rebus could think of nothing to say. He thought of himself as a Christian, too, a sceptical Christian, a little like Crawford himself perhaps. Full of questions that needed answering. No, this couldn't be right. He was *nothing* like Crawford. Nothing at all like him. Crawford was an animal; his kind never changed. Did they? Just because he had never met a 'changed man', did that mean such a thing did not exist? After all, he'd never met the Queen or the Prime Minister either. The radio crackled to life in his hand.

'Rebus here,' he said, and then listened.

It was all true. The details from Crawford's file were being read to him. Model prisoner. Bible class. Recommended for early release. Personal tragedy.

'Personal tragedy?' Rebus looked at Crawford.

'Ach, my son died. He was only in his twenties.'

Rebus, having heard enough, had already switched off the radio. 'I'm sorry,' he said. Crawford just shrugged, shrugged shoulders beneath which were tucked no hidden shotguns, and slipped his hands into his pockets, pockets where no pistols lurked. But Rebus held out a hand towards him.

'Happy New Year,' he said.

Crawford stared at the hand, then brought out his own right hand. The two men shook warmly, their grips firm.

'Happy New Year,' said Crawford. Then he glanced back up the close. 'Look, Inspector, if it's all right with you I think I'll go back up the Tron. It was daft of me to run away in the first place. There are plenty of hands up there I've not shaken yet.'

Rebus nodded slowly. He understood now. For Crawford, the New Year was something special, a new start in more ways than one. Not everyone was given that chance.

'Aye,' he said. 'On you go.'

Crawford had climbed three steps before he paused. 'Incidentally,' he called, 'what were *you* doing at the Tron?'

'What else would I be doing there on New Year?' replied Rebus. 'I was working.'

'No rest for the wicked, eh?' said Crawford, climbing the slope back up to the High Street.

Rebus watched until Crawford disappeared into the gloom. He knew he should follow him. After all, he *was* still working. He was sure now that Crawford had been speaking the truth, that he had nothing to do with the drug deal. Their meeting had been coincidence, nothing more. But who would have believed it? Trigger Crawford a 'model prisoner'. And they said mankind no longer lived in an age of miracles.

Rebus climbed slowly. There seemed more people than ever on the High Street. He guessed things would be at their busiest around half past midnight, with the streets emptying quickly after that. If the deal was going to go through, it would take place before that time. He recognised one of the Glasgow detectives heading towards him. As he spotted Rebus, the detective half-raised his arms.

'Where have you been? We thought you'd buggered off home.'

'Nothing happening then?'

The detective sighed. 'No, nothing at all. Lyons looks a bit impatient. I don't think he's going to give it much longer himself.'

'I thought your informant was air-tight?'

'As a rule. Maybe this will be the exception.' The detective smiled, seemingly used to such disappointments in his life. Rebus had noticed earlier that the young man possessed badly chewed fingernails and even the skin around the nails was torn and raw-looking. A stressed young man. In a few years he would be overweight and then would become heart attack material. Rebus knew that he himself was heart attack material: h.a.m., they called it back at the station. You were lean (meaning fit) or you were ham. Rebus was decidedly the latter.

'So anyway, where were you?'

'I bumped into an old friend. Well, to be precise an old adversary. Jackie Crawford.'

'Jackie Crawford? You mean Trigger Crawford?' The young detective was rifling through his memory files. 'Oh yes, I heard he was out.'

'Did you? Nobody bothered to tell me.'

'Yes, something about his son dying. Drug overdose. All the fire went out of Crawford after that. Turned into a Bible basher.'

They were walking back towards the crowd. Back towards where Alan Lyons waited for a suitcase full of heroin. Rebus stopped dead in his tracks.

'Drugs? Did you say his son died from drugs?'

The detective nodded. 'The big H. It wasn't too far from my patch. Somewhere in Partick.'

'Did Crawford's son live in Glasgow then?'

'No, he was just visiting. He stayed here in Edinburgh.' The detective was not as slow as some. He knew what Rebus was thinking. 'Christ, you don't mean ...?'

And then they were both running, pushing their way through the crowd, and the detective from Glasgow was shouting into his radio, but there was noise all around him, yelling and cheering and singing, smothering his words. Their progress was becoming slower. It was like moving through water chest-high. Rebus's legs felt useless and sore and there was a line of sweat trickling down his spine. Crawford's son had died from heroin, heroin purchased most probably in Edinburgh, and the man behind most of the heroin deals in Edinburgh was waiting somewhere up ahead. Coincidence? He had never really believed in coincidences, not really. They were convenient excuses for shrugging off the unthinkable.

What had Crawford said? Something about coming here tonight to make peace. Well, there were ways and ways of making peace, weren't there? 'If any mischief should follow, then thou shalt give life for life.' That was from Exodus. A dangerous book, the Bible. It could be made to say anything, its meaning in the mind of the beholder.

What was going through Jackie Crawford's mind? Rebus dreaded to think. There was a commotion up ahead, the crowd forming itself into a tight semi-circle around a shop-front. Rebus squeezed his way to the front.

'Police,' he shouted. 'Let me through, please.'

Grudgingly, the mass of bodies parted just enough for him to make progress. Finally he found himself at the front, staring at the slumped body of Alan Lyons. A long smear ran down the shop window to where he lay and his chest was stained dark red. One of the Glasgow officers was trying unsuccessfully to stem the flow of blood, using his own rolled-up coat, now sopping wet. Other officers were keeping back the crowd. Rebus caught snatches of what they were saying.

'Looked like he was going to shake hands.'

'Looked like he was hugging him.'

'Then the knife ...'

'Pulled out a knife.'

'Stabbed him twice before we could do anything.'

'Couldn't do anything.'

A siren had started nearby, inching closer. There were always ambulances on standby near the Tron on Hogmanay. Beside Lyons, still gripped in his left hand, was the bag containing the money for the deal.

'Will he be all right?' Rebus said to nobody in particular, which was just as well since nobody answered. He was remembering back a month to another dealer, another knife ... Then he saw Crawford. He was being restrained on the edge of the crowd by two more plainclothes men. One held his arms behind him while the other frisked him for weapons. On the pavement between where Crawford stood and Alan Lyons lay dying or dead there was a fairly ordinary looking knife, small enough to conceal in a sock or a waistband, but enough for the job required. More than an inch of blade was excess. The other detective was beside Rebus.

'Aw, Christ,' he said. But Rebus was staring at Crawford and Crawford was staring back, and in that moment they understood one another well enough. 'I don't suppose,' the detective was saying, 'we'll be seeing the party with the merchandise. Always supposing he was going to turn up in any event.'

'I'm not so sure about that,' answered Rebus, turning his gaze from Crawford. 'Ask yourself this: how did Crawford know Lyons would be in the High Street tonight?' The detective did not answer. Behind them, the crowd was pressing closer for a look at the body and then making noises of revulsion before opening another can of lager or half-bottle of vodka. The ambulance was still a good fifty yards away. Rebus nodded towards Crawford.

'He knows where the stuff is, but he's probably dumped it somewhere. Somewhere nobody can ever touch it. It was just bait, that's all. Just bait.'

And as bait it had worked. Hook, line and bloody sinker. Lyons had swallowed it, while Rebus, equally fooled, had swallowed something else. He felt it sticking in his throat like something cancerous, something no amount of coughing would dislodge. He glanced towards the prone body again and smiled involuntarily. A headline had come to mind, one that would never be used.

LYONS FED TO THE CHRISTIAN.

Someone was being noisily sick somewhere behind him. A bottle shattered against a wall. The loudest voices in the crowd were growing irritable and hard-edged. In fifteen minutes or so, they would cease to be revellers and would be transformed into trouble-makers. A woman shrieked from one of the many darkened closes. The look on Jackie Crawford's face was one of calm and righteous triumph. He offered no resistance to the officers. He had known they were watching Lyons, had known he might kill Lyons but he would never get away. And still he had driven home the knife. What else was he to do with his freedom?'

The night was young and so was the year. Rebus held out his hand towards the detective.

'Happy New Year,' he said. 'And many more of them.'

The young man stared at him blankly. 'Don't think you're blaming us for this,' he said. 'This was your fault. You let Crawford go. It's Edinburgh's balls-up, not ours.'

Rebus shrugged and let his arm fall to his side. Then he started to walk along the pavement, moving further and further from the scene. The ambulance moved past him. Someone slapped him on the back and offered a hand. From a distance, the young detective was watching him retreat.

'Away to hell,' said Rebus quietly, not sure for whom the message was intended.

The Gentlemen's Club

It was the most elegant of all Edinburgh's elegant Georgian circuses, a perfect circle in design and construction, the houses themselves as yet untouched by the private contractors who might one day renovate and remove, producing a dozen tiny flats from each.

A perfect circle surrounding some private gardens, the gardens a wash of colour despite the January chill: violet, pink, red, green and orange. A tasteful display, though. No flower was allowed to be too vibrant, too bright, too inelegant.

The gate to the gardens was locked, of course. The keyholders paid a substantial fee each year for the privilege of that lock. Everyone else could look, could peer through the railings as he was doing now, but entrance was forbidden. Well, that was Edinburgh for you, a closed circle within a closed circle.

He stood there, enjoying the subtle smells in the air now that the flurry of snowflakes had stopped. Then he shifted his attention to the houses, huge three- and four-storey statements of the architect's confidence. He found himself staring at one particular house, the one outside which the white police Sierra was parked. It was too ripe a day to be spoiled, but duty was duty. Taking a final deep breath, he turned from the garden railings and walked towards number 16, with its heavy closed curtains but its front door ajar.

Once inside, having introduced himself, John Rebus had to

climb three large flights of stairs to 'the children's floor', as his guide termed it. She was slender and middle-aged and dressed from head to toe in grey. The house was quiet, only one or two shafts of sunlight penetrating its gloom. The woman walked near-silently and quickly, while Rebus tugged on the bannister, breathing hard. It wasn't that he was unfit, but somehow all the oxygen seemed to have been pumped out of the house.

Arriving at last at the third floor, the woman passed three firmly closed doors before stopping at a fourth. This one was open, and inside Rebus could make out the gleaming tiles of a large bathroom and the shuffling, insect-like figures of Detective Constable Brian Holmes and the police pathologist, not the lugubrious Dr Curt but the one everybody called – though not to his face, never to his face – Doctor Crippen. He turned to his guide.

'Thank you, Mrs McKenzie.' But she had already averted her eyes and was making back for the safety of the stairs. She was a brave one though, to bring him all the way up here in the first place. And now there was nothing for it but to enter the room. 'Hello, Doctor.'

'Inspector Rebus, good morning. Not a pretty sight, is it?'

Rebus forced himself to look. There was not much water in the bath, and what water there was had been dyed a rich ruby colour by the girl's blood. She was undressed and as white as a statue. She had been very young, sixteen or seventeen, her body not yet quite fully formed. A late developer.

Her arms lay peacefully by her sides, wrists turned upwards to reveal the clean incisions. Holmes used a pair of tweezers to hold up a single razor blade for Rebus's inspection. Rebus winced and shook his head.

'What a waste,' he said. He had a daughter himself, not much older than this girl. His wife had taken their daughter with her when she left him. Years ago now. He'd lost touch, the way you do sometimes with family, though you keep in contact with friends.

He was moving around the bath, committing the scene to memory. The air seemed to glow, but the glow was already fading.

'Yes,' said Holmes. 'It's a sin.'

'Suicide, of course,' Rebus commented after a silence. The pathologist nodded, but did not speak. They were not usually so awkward around a corpse, these three men. Each thought he had seen the worst, the most brutal, the most callous. Each had anecdotes to relate which would make strangers shudder and screw shut their eyes. But this, this was different. Something had been taken quietly, deliberately and ruinously from the world.

'The question,' Rebus said, for the sake of filling the void, 'is why.'

Why indeed. Here he was, standing in a bathroom bigger than his own living-room, surrounded by powders and scents, thick towels, soaps and sponges. But here was this gruesome and unnecessary death. There had to be a reason for it. Silly, stupid child. What had she been playing at? Mute anger turned to frustration, and he almost staggered as he made his way out to the landing.

There had to be a reason. And he was just in the mood now to track it down.

'I've told you already,' said Thomas McKenzie irritably, 'she was the happiest girl in Christendom. No, we didn't spoil her, and no, we never forbade her seeing anyone. There is no reason in the world, Inspector, why Suzanne should have done what she did. It just doesn't make sense.'

McKenzie broke down again, burying his face in his hands. Rebus loathed himself, yet the questions had to be asked.

'Did she,' he began, 'did she have a boyfriend, Mr McKenzie?'

McKenzie got up from his chair, walked to the sideboard and poured himself another whisky. He motioned to Rebus who, still cradling a crystal inch of the stuff, shook his head. Mrs McKenzie was upstairs resting. She had been given a sedative by her doctor, an old friend of the family who had seemed in need of similar treatment himself.

But Thomas McKenzie had not needed anything. He was sticking to the old remedies, sloshing a fresh measure of malt into his glass.

'No,' he said, 'no boyfriends. They've never really been Suzanne's style.'

Though he would not be travelling to his office today, McKenzie had still dressed himself in a dark blue suit and tie. The drawing-room in which Rebus sat had about it the air of a commercial office, not at all homely or lived-in. He couldn't imagine growing up in such a place.

'What about school?' he asked.

'What do you mean?'

'I mean, was she happy there?'

'Very.' McKenzie sat down with his drink. 'She gets good reports, good grades. She ... she *was* going to the University in October.'

Rebus watched him gulp at the whisky. Thomas McKenzie was a tough man, tough enough to make his million young and then canny enough not to lose it. He was forty-four now, but looked younger. Rebus had no idea how many shops McKenzie now owned, how many company directorships he held along with all his other holdings and interests. He was new money trying to look like old money, making his home in Stockbridge, convenient for Princes Street, rather than further out in bungalow land.

'What was she going to study?' Rebus stared past McKenzie towards where a family portrait sat on a long, polished sideboard. No family snapshot, but posed, a sitting for a professional photographer. Daughter gleaming in the centre, sandwiched by grinning parents. A mock-up cloudscape behind them, the clouds pearl-coloured, the sky blue.

'Law,' said McKenzie. 'She had a head on her shoulders.'

Yes, a head of mousy-brown hair. And her father had found her early in the morning, already cold. McKenzie hadn't panicked. He'd made the phone calls before waking his wife and telling her. He always rose first, always went straight to the bathroom. He had remained calm, most probably from shock. But there was a stiffness to McKenzie, too, Rebus noticed. He wondered what it would take really to rouse the man.

Something niggled. Suzanne had gone to the bathroom, run some water into the bath, lain down in it, and slashed her wrists. Fine, Rebus could accept that. Maybe she had expected to be found and rescued. Most failed suicides were cries for help, weren't they? If you *really* wanted to kill yourself, you went somewhere quiet and secret, where you couldn't possibly be found in time. Suzanne hadn't done that. She had almost certainly expected her father to find her in time. Her timing had been a little awry.

Moreover, she must have known her father always rose before her mother, and therefore that he would be the first to find her. This notion interested Rebus, though no one around him seemed curious about it.

'What about friends at school,' Rebus went on. 'Did Suzanne have many friends?'

'Oh yes, lots.'

'Anyone in particular?'

McKenzie was about to answer when the door opened and his wife walked in, pale from her drugged sleep.

'What time is it?' she asked, shuffling forwards.

'It's eleven, Shona,' her husband said, rising to meet her. 'You've only been asleep half an hour.' They embraced one another, her arms tight around his body. Rebus felt like an intruder on their grief, but the questions still had to be asked.

'You were about to tell me about Suzanne's friends, Mr McKenzie.'

Husband and wife sat down together on the sofa, hands clasped.

'Well,' said McKenzie, 'there were lots of them, weren't there, Shona?'

'Yes,' said his wife. She really was an attractive woman. Her face had the same smooth sheen as her daughter's. She was the sort of woman men would instinctively feel protective towards, whether protection was needed or not. 'But I always liked Hazel best,' she went on.

McKenzie turned to Rebus and explained. 'Hazel Frazer, daughter of Sir Jimmy Frazer, the banker. A peach of a girl. A real peach.' He paused, staring at his wife, and then began, softly, with dignity, to cry. She rested his head against her shoulder and stroked his hair, talking softly to him. Rebus averted his eyes and drank his whisky. Then bit his bottom lip, deep in thought. In matters of suicide, just who was the victim, who the culprit?

Suzanne's room was a cold and comfortless affair. No posters on the walls, no teenage clutter or signs of an independent mind. There was a writing-pad on the dressing table, but it was blank. A crumpled ball of paper sat in the bottom of an otherwise empty bin beside the wardrobe. Rebus carefully unfolded the sheet. Written on it, in a fairly steady hand, was a message: 'Told you I would.'

Rebus studied the sentence. Told whom? Her parents seemed to have no inkling their daughter was suicidal, yet the note had been meant for someone. And having written it, why had she discarded it? He turned it over. The other side, though blank was slightly tacky. Rebus sniffed the paper, but could find no smell to identify the stickiness. He carefully folded the paper and slipped it into his pocket.

In the top drawer of the dressing-table was a leather-bound diary. But Suzanne had been no diarist. Instead of the expected teenage outpourings, Rebus found only one-line reminders, every Tuesday for the past six months or so, 'The Gentlemen's Club – 4.00'. Curiouser and curiouser. The last entry was for the previous week, with nothing in the rest of the diary save blank pages.

The Gentlemen's Club – what on earth could she have meant? Rebus knew of several clubs in Edinburgh, dowdy remnants of a former age, but none was called simply The Gentlemen's Club. The diary went into his pocket along with the note.

Thomas McKenzie saw him to the door. The tie around his neck was hanging loosely now and his voice was sweet with whisky.

'Just two last questions before I go,' Rebus said.

'Yes?' said McKenzie, sighing.

'Do you belong to a club?'

McKenzie seemed taken aback, but shrugged. 'Several, actually. The Strathspey Health Club. The Forth Golf Club. And Finlay's as was.'

'Finlay's Gentlemen's Club?'

'Yes, that's right. But it's called Thomson's now.'

Rebus nodded. 'Final question,' he said. 'What did Suzanne do on Tuesdays at four?'

'Nothing special. I think she had some drama group at school.'

'Thank you, Mr McKenzie. Sorry to have troubled you. Goodbye.'

'Goodbye, Inspector.'

Rebus stood on the top step, breathing in lungfuls of fresh air. Too much of a good thing could be stifling. He wondered if Suzanne McKenzie had felt stifled. He still wondered why she had died. And, knowing her father would be the first to find her, why had she lain down *naked* in the bath? Rebus had seen suicides before – lots of them – but whether they chose the bathroom or the bedroom, they were always clothed.

'Naked I came,' he thought to himself, remembering the passage from the Book of Job, 'and naked shall return.'

On his way to Hawthornden School for Girls, Rebus received a message from Detective Constable Holmes, who had returned to the station.

'Go ahead,' said Rebus. The radio crackled. The sky overhead was the colour of a bruise, the static in the air playing havoc with the radio's reception.

'I've just run McKenzie's name through the computer,' said Holmes, 'and come up with something you might be interested in.'

Rebus smiled. Holmes was as thorough as any airport sniffer dog. 'Well?' he said. 'Are you going to tell me, or do I have to buy the paperback?'

There was a hurt pause before Holmes began to speak and Rebus remembered how sensitive to criticism the younger man could be. 'It seems,' Holmes said at last, 'that Mr McKenzie was arrested several months back for loitering outside a school.'

'Oh? Which school?'

'Murrayfield Comprehensive. He wasn't charged, but it's on record that he was taken to Murrayfield police station and questioned.'

'That *is* interesting. I'll talk to you later.' Rebus terminated the call. The rain had started to fall in heavy drops. He picked up the radio again and asked to be put through to Murrayfield police station. His luck was in. A colleague there remembered the whole incident.

'We kept it quiet, of course,' the Inspector told Rebus. 'And McKenzie swore he'd just stopped there to call into his office. But the teachers at the school were adamant he'd parked there before, during the lunch-break. It's not the most refined area of town after all, is it? A Daimler does tend to stand out from the crowd around there, especially when there isn't a bride in the back of it.'

'I take your point,' said Rebus, smiling. 'Anything else?'

'Yes, one of the kids told a teacher he'd seen someone get into McKenzie's Daimler once, but we couldn't find any evidence of that.'

'Vivid imaginations, these kids,' Rebus agreed. This was all his colleague could tell him, but it was enough to muddy the water. Had Suzanne discovered her father's secret and, ashamed, killed herself? Or perhaps her schoolfriends had found out and teased her about it? If McKenzie liked kids, there might even be a tang of incest about the whole thing. That would at least go some way towards explaining Suzanne's nudity: she wasn't putting on show anything her father hadn't seen before. But what about The Gentlemen's Club? Where did it fit in? At Hawthornden School, Rebus hoped he might find some answers.

It was the sort of school fathers sent their daughters to so that they might learn the arts of femininity and ruthlessness. The headmistress, as imposing a character as the school building itself, fed Rebus on cakes and tea before leading him to Suzanne's form mistress, a Miss Selkirk, who had prepared more tea for him in her little private room.

Yes, she told him, Suzanne had been a very popular girl and news of her death came as quite a shock. She had run around with Hazel Frazer, the banker's daughter. A very vivacious girl, Hazel, head of school this year, though Suzanne hadn't been far behind in the running. A competitive pair, their marks for maths, English, languages almost identical. Suzanne the better at sciences; Hazel the better at economics and accounts. Splendid girls, the pair of them.

Biting into his fourth or fifth cake, Rebus nodded again.

These women were all so commanding that he had begun to feel like a schoolboy himself. He sat with knees primly together, smiling, asking his questions almost apologetically.

'I don't suppose,' he said, 'the name The Gentlemen's Club means anything to you?'

Miss Selkirk thought hard. 'Is it,' she said at last, 'the name of a discotheque?'

Rebus smiled. 'I don't think so. Why do you ask?'

'Well, it's just that I do seem to recall having heard it before from one of the girls, quite recently, but only in passing.'

Rebus looked disappointed.

'I am sorry, Inspector.' She tapped her skull. 'This old head of mine isn't what it used to be.'

'That's quite all right,' said Rebus quietly. 'One last thing, do you happen to know who takes the school's drama classes?'

'Ah,' said Miss Selkirk, 'that's young Miss Phillips, the English teacher.'

Miss Phillips, who insisted that Rebus call her Jilly, was not only young but also very attractive. Waves of long auburn hair fell over her shoulders and down her back. Her eyes were dark and moist with recently shed tears. Rebus felt more awkward than ever.

'I believe,' he said, 'that you run the school's drama group.'

'That's right.' Her voice was fragile as porcelain.

'And Suzanne was in the group?'

'Yes. She was due to play Celia in our production of *As You Like It*.'

'Oh?'

'That's Shakespeare, you know.'

'Yes,' said Rebus, 'I do know.'

They were talking in the corridor, just outside her classroom, and through the panes of glass in the door,

Rebus could see a class of fairly mature girls, healthy and from well-ordered homes, whispering together and giggling. Odd that, considering they'd just lost a friend.

'Celia,' he said, 'is Duke Frederick's daughter, isn't she?'

'I'm impressed, Inspector.'

'It's not my favourite Shakespeare play,' Rebus explained, 'but I remember seeing it at the Festival a few years back. Celia has a friend, doesn't she?'

'That's right, Rosalind.'

'So who was going to play Rosalind?'

'Hazel Frazer.'

Rebus nodded slowly at this. It made sense. 'Is Hazel in your classroom at the moment?'

'Yes, she's the one with the long black hair. Do you see her?'

Oh yes, Rebus could see her. She sat, calm and imperturbable, at the still centre of a sea of admirers. The other girls giggled and whispered around her, hoping to catch her attention or a few words of praise, while she sat oblivious to it all.

'Yes,' he said, 'I see her.'

'Would you care to speak with her, Inspector?'

He knew Hazel was aware of him, even though she averted her eyes from the door. Indeed, he knew precisely *because* she refused to look, while the other girls glanced towards the corridor from time to time, interested in this interruption to their classwork. Interested and curious. Hazel pretended to be neither, which in itself interested Rebus.

'No,' he said to Jilly Phillips, 'not just now. She's probably upset, and it wouldn't do much good for me to go asking her questions under the circumstances. There was one thing, though.'

'Yes, Inspector?'

'This after-school drama group of yours, the one that

meets on Tuesdays, it doesn't happen to have a nickname, does it?'

'Not that I know of.' Jilly Phillips furrowed her brow. 'But, Inspector?'

'Yes?'

'You're under some kind of misapprehension. The drama group meets on Fridays, not Tuesdays. And we meet before lunch.'

Rebus drove out of the school grounds and parked by the side of the busy main road. The drama group met during school hours, so what had Suzanne done on Tuesdays after school, while her parents thought she was there? At least, McKenzie had said he'd thought that's what she'd done on Tuesdays. Suppose he'd been lying? Then what?

A maroon-coloured bus roared past Rebus's car. A 135, on its way to Princes Street. He started up the car again and followed it along its route, all the time thinking through the details of Suzanne's suicide. Until suddenly, with blinding clarity, he saw the truth of the thing, and bit his bottom lip fiercely, wondering just what on earth he could – should – do about it.

Well, the longer he thought about doing something, the harder it would become to do it. So he called Holmes and asked him for a large favour, before driving over to the house owned by Sir Jimmy Frazer.

Frazer was not just part of the Edinburgh establishment – in many ways he *was* that establishment. Born and educated in the city, he had won hard-earned respect, friendship and awe on his way to the top. The nineteenth-century walled house in which his family made its home was part of his story. It had been about to be bought by a company, an English company, and knocked down to make way for a new apartment block. There were public protests about this act of vandalism and in had stepped Sir Jimmy Frazer, purchasing the house and making it his own.

That had been years ago, but it was a story still heard told by hard men to other hard men in watering holes throughout the city. Rebus examined the house as he drove in through the open gates. It was an ugly near-Gothic invention, mock turrets and spires, hard, cold and uninviting. A maid answered the door. Rebus introduced himself and was ushered into a large drawing-room, where Sir Jimmy's wife, tall and dark haired like her daughter, waited.

'I'm sorry to trouble you, Lady –' Rebus was cut short by an imperious hand, but an open smile.

'Just Deborah, please.' And she motioned for Rebus to sit.

'Thank you,' he said. 'I'm sorry to trouble you, but –'

'Yes, your call *was* intriguing, Inspector. Of course, I'll do what I can. It's a tragedy, poor Suzanne.'

'You knew her then?'

'Of course. Whyever shouldn't we know her? She visited practically every Tuesday.'

'Oh?' Rebus had suspected as much, but was keen to learn more.

'After school,' Lady Deborah continued. 'Hazel and Suzanne and a few other chums would come back here. They didn't stay late.'

'But what exactly did they do?'

She laughed. 'I've no idea. What do girls of that age do? Play records? Talk about boys? Try to defer growing up?' She gave a wry smile, perhaps thinking of her own past. Rebus checked his wristwatch casually. Five to four. He had a few minutes yet.

'Did they,' he asked, 'confine themselves to your daughter's room?'

'More or less. Not her bedroom, of course. There's an old playroom upstairs. Hazel uses that as a kind of den.'

Rebus nodded. 'May I see it?'

217

Lady Deborah seemed puzzled. 'I suppose so, though I can't see —'

'It would help,' Rebus interrupted, 'to give me an overall picture of Suzanne. I'm trying to work out the kind of girl she was.'

'Of course,' said Lady Deborah, though she sounded unconvinced.

Rebus was shown to a small, cluttered room at the end of a long corridor. Inside, the curtains were closed. Lady Deborah switched on the lights.

'Hazel won't allow the maid in here,' Lady Deborah explained, apologising for the untidiness. 'Secrets, I suppose,' she whispered.

Rebus did not doubt it. There were two small sofas, piles of pop and teenage magazines scattered on the floor, an ashtray full of dog-ends (which Lady Deborah pointedly chose to ignore), a stereo against one wall and a desk against another, on which sat a personal computer, its screen switched on but blank.

'She always forgets to turn that thing off,' said Lady Deborah. Rebus could hear the telephone ringing downstairs. The maid answered it and then called up to Lady Deborah.

'Oh dear. Please excuse me, Inspector.'

Rebus smiled and bowed slightly as she left. His watch said four o'clock. As prearranged, it would be Holmes on the phone. Rebus had told him to pretend to be anybody, to say *any*thing, so long as he kept Lady Deborah occupied for five minutes. Holmes had suggested he be a journalist seeking some quotes for a magazine feature. Rebus smiled now. Yes, there was probably vanity enough in Lady Deborah to keep her talking with a reporter for at least five minutes, maybe more.

Still, he couldn't waste time. He had expected to have to do a lot of searching, but the computer seemed the obvious place to start. There were floppy discs stored in a plastic box beside the monitor. He flipped through them until he came to one labelled GC DISC. There could be no doubt. He slipped the disc into the computer and watched as the display came up. He had found the records of The Gentlemen's Club.

He read quickly. Not that there was much to read. Members must attend every week, at four o'clock on Tuesday. Members must wear a tie. (Rebus looked quickly in a drawer of the desk and found five ties. He recognised them as belonging to various clubs in the city: the Strathspey, the Forth Golf Club, Finlay's Club. Stolen from the girls' fathers of course, and worn to meetings of a secret little clique, itself a parody of the clubs their fathers frequented.)

In a file named 'Exploits of the Gentlemen's Club', Rebus found lists of petty thefts, acts of so-called daring, and lies. Members had stolen from city centre shops, had carried out practical jokes against teachers and pupils alike, had been, in short, malicious.

There were many exploits attributed to Suzanne, including lying to her parents about what she did on Tuesday after school. Twenty-eight exploits in all. Hazel Frazer's list totalled thirty at the bottom, yet Rebus could count only twenty-nine entries on the screen. And in a separate file, the agenda for a meeting yet to be held, was a single item, recorded as 'New Business: can suicide be termed an exploit of the Gentlemen's Club?'

Rebus heard steps behind him. He turned, but it was not Lady Deborah. It was Hazel Frazer. Her eyes looked past him to the screen, firstly in fear and disbelief, then in scorn.

'Hello, Hazel.'

'You're the policeman,' she said in a level tone. 'I saw you at the school.'

'That's right.' Rebus studied her as she came into the room. She was a cool one, all right. That was Hawthornden

219

for you, breeding strong, cold women, each one her father's daughter. 'Are you jealous of her?'

'Of whom? Suzanne?' Hazel smiled cruelly. 'Why should I be?'

'Because,' answered Rebus, 'Suzanne's is the ultimate exploit. For once, she beat you.'

'You think that's why she did it?' Hazel sounded smug. When Rebus shook his head, a little of her confidence seeped away.

'I know why she did it, Hazel. She did it because she found out about you and her father. She found out because you told her. I notice it's too much of a secret for you to put on your computer, but you've added it to the list, haven't you? As an exploit. I expect you were having an argument, bragging, being competitive. And it just slipped out. You told Suzanne you were her father's lover.'

Her cheeks were becoming a deep strawberry red, while her lips drained of colour. But she wasn't about to speak, so Rebus went on at her.

'You met him at lunchtime. You couldn't meet near Hawthornden. That would be too risky. So you'd take a bus to Murrayfield. It's only ten minutes ride away. He'd be waiting in his car. You told Suzanne and she couldn't bear to know. So she killed herself.' Rebus was becoming angry. 'And all you can be bothered to do is write about her on your files and wonder whether suicide is an "exploit".' His voice had risen and he hardly registered the fact that Lady Deborah was standing in the doorway, looking on in disbelief.

'No!' yelled Hazel. 'She did it first! She slept with Daddy months ago! So I did it back to her. *That's* what she couldn't live with! That's why she −'

Then it happened. Hazel's shoulders fell forward and, eyes closed, she began to cry, silently at first, but then loudly. Her mother ran to comfort her and told Rebus to leave. Couldn't he see what the girl was going through?

He'd pay, she told him. He'd pay for upsetting her daughter. But she was crying too, crying like Hazel, mother and child. Rebus could think of nothing to say, so he left.

Descending the stairs, he tried not to think about what he had just unleashed. Two families broken now instead of one, and to what end? Merely to prove, as he had always known anyway, that a pretty face was no mirror of the soul and that the spirit of competition still flourished in Scotland's well-respected education system. He dug his hands deep into his jacket pockets, felt something there and drew out Suzanne's note. The crumpled note, found discarded in her bin, sticky on one side. He stopped halfway down the stairs, staring at the note without really seeing it. He was visualising something else, something almost too horrible, too unbelievable.

Yet he believed it.

Thomas McKenzie was surprised to see him. Mrs McKenzie had, he said, gone to stay with a sister on the other side of the city. The body had been taken away, of course, and the bathroom cleaned. McKenzie was without jacket and tie and had rolled up his shirt-sleeves. He wore half-moon glasses and carried a pen with him as he opened the door to Rebus.

In the drawing-room, there were signs that McKenzie had been working. Papers were strewn across a writing desk, a briefcase open on the floor. A calculator sat on the chair, as did a telephone.

'I'm sorry to disturb you again, sir,' Rebus said, taking in the scene. McKenzie had sobered up since the morning. He looked like a businessman rather than a grieving father.

McKenzie seemed to realise that the scene before Rebus created a strange impression.

'Keeping busy,' he said. 'Keeping the mind occupied, you know. Life can't stop because ...' He fell silent.

'Quite, sir,' Rebus said, seating himself on the sofa. He

reached into his pocket. 'I thought you might like this.' He held the paper towards McKenzie, who took it from him and glanced at it. Rebus stared hard at him, and McKenzie twitched, attempting to hand back the note.

'No, sir,' said Rebus, 'you keep it.'

'Why?'

'It will always remind you,' said Rebus, his voice cold and level, 'that you could have saved your daughter.'

McKenzie was aghast. 'What do you mean?'

'I mean,' said Rebus, his voice still lacking emotion, 'that Suzanne wasn't intending to kill herself, not really. It was just something to attract your attention, to shock you into … I don't know, action I suppose, a *re*action of some kind.'

McKenzie positioned himself slowly so that he rested on the armrest of one of the upholstered chairs.

'Yes,' Rebus went on, 'a reaction. That's as good a way of putting it as any. Suzanne knew what time you got up every morning. She wasn't stupid. She timed the slashing of her wrists so that you would find her while there was still time to save her. She also had a sense of the dramatic, didn't she? So she stuck her little note to the bathroom door. You saw the note and you went into the bathroom. And she wasn't dead, was she?'

McKenzie had screwed shut his eyes. His mouth was open, the teeth gritted in remembrance.

'She wasn't dead,' Rebus continued, 'not quite. And you knew damned well why she'd done it. Because she'd warned you she would. She had told you she would. Unless you stopped seeing Hazel, unless you owned up to her mother. Perhaps she had a lot of demands, Mr McKenzie. You never really got on with her anyway, did you? You didn't know what to do. Help her, or leave her to die? You hesitated. You waited.'

Rebus had risen from his seat now. His voice had risen, too. The tears were streaming down McKenzie's face, his whole body shuddering. But Rebus was relentless.

'You walked around a bit, you walked into her room. You threw her note into the waste-bin. And eventually, *eventually* you reached for a telephone and made the calls.'

'It was already too late,' McKenzie bawled. 'Nobody could have saved her.'

'They could have tried!' Rebus was yelling now, yelling close to McKenzie's own twisted face. '*You* could have tried, but you didn't. You wanted to keep your secret. Well by God your secret's out.' The last words were hissed and with them Rebus felt his fury ebb. He turned and started to walk away.

'What are you going to do?' McKenzie moaned.

'What can I do?' Rebus answered quietly. 'I'm not going to do anything, Mr McKenzie. I'm just going to leave you to get on with the rest of your life.' He paused. 'Enjoy it,' he said, closing the doors of the drawing-room behind him.

He stood on the steps of the house, trembling, his heart pounding. In a suicide, who was to blame, who the victim? He still couldn't answer the question. He doubted he ever would. His watch told him it was five minutes to five. He knew the pub near the circus, a quiet bar frequented by thinkers and amateur philosophers, a place where nothing happened and the measures were generous. He felt like having one drink, maybe two at most. He would raise his glass and make a silent toast: to the lassies.

Monstrous Trumpet

John Rebus went down onto his knees.

'I'm begging you,' he said, 'don't do this to me, please.'

But Chief Inspector Lauderdale just laughed, thinking Rebus was clowning about as per usual. 'Come on, John,' he said. 'It'll be just like Interpol.'

Rebus got back to his feet. 'No it won't,' he said. 'It'll be like a bloody escort service. Besides, I can't speak French.'

'Apparently he speaks perfect English, this Monsieur ...' Lauderdale made a show of consulting the letter in front of him on his desk.

'Don't say it again, sir, please.'

'Monsieur Cluzeau.' Rebus winced. 'Yes,' Lauderdale continued, enjoying Rebus's discomfort, 'Monsieur Cluzeau. A fine name for a member of the *gendarmerie*, don't you think?'

'It's a stunt,' Rebus pleaded. 'It's got to be. DC Holmes or one of the other lads ...'

But Lauderdale would not budge. 'It's been verified by the Chief Super,' he said. 'I'm sorry about this, John, but I thought you'd be pleased.'

'*Pleased?*'

'Yes. Pleased. You know, showing a bit of Scots hospitality.'

'Since when did the CID job description encompass "tourist guide"?'

Lauderdale had had enough of this: Rebus had even stopped calling him 'sir'. 'Since, Inspector, I ordered you to do it.'

'But why *me*?'

Lauderdale shrugged. 'Why not you?' He sighed, opened a drawer of his desk and dropped the letter into it. 'Look, it's only a day, two at most. Just do it, eh? Now if you don't mind, Inspector, I've got rather a lot to do.'

But the fight had gone out of Rebus anyway. His voice was calm, resigned. 'When does he get here?'

Again, there was a pause while that missing 'sir' hung motionless in the air between them. Well, thought Lauderdale, the sod deserves this. 'He's already here.'

'What?'

'I mean, he's in Edinburgh. The letter took a bit of a time to get here.'

'You mean it sat in someone's office for a bit of time.'

'Well, whatever the delay, he's here. And he's coming to the station this afternoon.'

Rebus glanced at his watch. It was eleven-fifty. He groaned.

'*Late* afternoon, I'd imagine,' said Lauderdale, trying to soften the blow now that Rebus was heading for the canvas. This had been a bit of a mess all round. He'd only just received final confirmation himself that Monsieur Cluzeau was on his way. 'I mean,' he said, 'the French like to take a long lunch, don't they? Notorious for it. So I don't suppose he'll be here till after three.'

'Fine, he can take us as he finds us. What am I supposed to do with him anyway?'

Lauderdale tried to retain his composure: *just say it once, damn you! Just once so I know that you recognise me for what I am!* He cleared his throat. 'He wants to see how we work. So show him. As long as he can report back to his own people that we're courteous, efficient, diligent, scrupulous, and that we always get our man, well, I'll be happy.'

'Right you are, sir,' said Rebus, opening the door, making ready to leave Lauderdale's newly refurbished office. Lauderdale sat in a daze: *he'd said it! Rebus had actually ended a sentence with 'sir'!*

'That should be easy enough,' he was saying now. 'Oh, and I might as well track down Lord Lucan and catch the Loch Ness monster while I'm at it. I'm sure to have a spare five minutes.'

Rebus closed the door after him with such ferocity that Lauderdale feared for the glass-framed paintings on his walls. But glass was more resilient than it looked. And so was John Rebus.

Cluzeau had to be an arse-licker, hell-bent on promotion. What other reason could there be? The story was that he was coming over for the Scotland-France encounter at Murrayfield. Fair enough, Edinburgh filled with Frenchmen once every two years for a weekend in February, well-behaved if boisterous rugby fans whose main pleasure seemed to be dancing in saloon bars with ice-buckets on their heads.

Nothing out of the ordinary there. But imagine a Frenchman who, having decided to take a large chunk of his annual leave so as to coincide with the international season, then has another idea: while in Scotland he'll invite himself to spend a day with the local police force. His letter to his own chief requesting an introduction so impresses the chief that *he* writes to the Chief Constable. By now, the damage is done, and the boulder starts to bounce down the hillside – Chief Constable to Chief Super, Chief Super to Super, Super to Chief Inspector – and Chief Inspector to Mr Muggins, aka John Rebus.

Thank you and *bonne nuit*. Ha! There, he did remember a bit of French after all. Rhona, his wife, had done one of those teach-yourself French courses, all tapes and repeating phrases. It had driven Rebus bonkers, but some of it had stuck. And all of it in preparation for a long weekend in Paris, a weekend which hadn't come off because Rebus had been drawn into a murder inquiry. Little wonder she'd left him in the end.

Bonne nuit. Bonjour. That was another word. *Bonsoir.* What about *Bon accord*? Was that French, too? Bo'ness sounded French. Hadn't Bonnie Prince Charlie been French? And dear God, what was he going to do with the Frenchman?

There was only one answer: get busy. The busier he was, the less time there would be for small-talk, xenophobia and falling-out. With the brain and the body occupied, there would be less temptation to mention Onion Johnnies, frogs'-legs, the war, French letters, French kissing and French & Saunders. Oh dear God, what had he done to deserve this?

His phone buzzed.

'*Oui?*' said Rebus, smirking now because he remembered how often he'd managed to get away with not calling Lauderdale 'sir'.

'Eh?'

'Just practising, Bob.'

'You must be bloody psychic then. There's a French gentleman down here says he's got an appointment.'

'What? Already?' Rebus checked his watch again. It was two minutes past twelve. Christ, like sitting in a dentist's waiting-room and being called ahead of your turn. Would he really look like Peter Sellers? What if he didn't speak English?

'John?'

'Sorry, Bob, what?'

'What do you want me to tell him?'

'Tell him I'll be right down.' Right down in the dumps, he thought to himself, letting the receiver drop like a stone.

There was only one person in the large, dingy reception. He wore a biker's leather jacket and had a spider's-web tattoo creeping up out of his soiled T-shirt and across his throat. Rebus stopped in his tracks. But then he saw another figure, over to his left against the wall. This man was studying various Wanted and Missing posters. He was tall, thin, and wore an immaculate dark blue suit with a tightly-knotted red silk tie. His shoes looked brand new, as did his haircut.

Their eyes met, forcing Rebus into a smile. He was suddenly aware of his own rumpled chain-store suit, his scuffed brogues, the shirt with a button missing on one cuff.

'Inspector Rebus?' The man was coming forward, hand held out.

'That's right.' They shook. He was wearing after-shave too, not too strong but certainly noticeable. He had the bearing of someone much further up the ladder, yet Rebus had been told they were of similar ranks. Having said which, there was no way Rebus was going to say 'Inspector Cluzeau' out loud. It would be too ... too ...

'For you.'

Rebus saw that he was being handed a plastic carrier-bag. He looked inside. A litre of duty-free malt, a box of chocolates and a small tin of something. He lifted out the chocolates.

'Escargots,' Cluzeau explained. 'But made from chocolate.'

Rebus studied the picture on the box. Yes, chocolates in the shape of snails. And as for the tin ...

'Foie gras. It is a pâté made from fatted goose liver. A local delicacy. You spread it on your toast.'

'Sounds delicious,' Rebus said, with just a trace of irony. In fact, he was overwhelmed. None of this stuff looked as though it came cheap, meat paste or no. 'Thank you.'

The Frenchman shrugged. He had the kind of face which, shaved twice a day, still sported a five o'clock shadow. Hirsute: that was the word. What was that joke again, the one that ended with someone asking 'Hirsute?' and the guy replying 'No, the suit's mine, but the knickers are hers'? Hairy wrists, too, on one of which sat a thin gold wristwatch. He was tapping this with his finger.

'I am not too early, I hope.'

'What?' It was Rebus's curse to remember the endings of jokes but never their beginnings. 'No, no. You're all right. I was just, er, hold on a second, will you?'

'Sure.'

Rebus walked over to the reception desk, behind which stood the omnipresent Bob Leach. Bob nodded towards the bag.

'Not a bad haul,' he said.

Rebus kept his voice low, but not so low, he hoped, as to arouse Cluzeau's suspicions. 'Thing is, Bob, I wasn't expecting him for a few hours yet. What the hell am I going to do with him? I don't suppose you've got any calls?'

'Nothing you'd be interested in, John.' Leach examined the pad in front of him. 'Couple of car smashes. Couple of break-ins. Oh, and the art gallery.'

'Art gallery?'

'I think young Brian's on that one. Some exhibition down the High Street. One of the pieces seems to have walked.'

Well, it wasn't too far away, and it *was* a tourist spot. St Giles. John Knox's House. Holyrood.

'The very dab,' said Rebus. 'That'll do us nicely. Give me the address, will you?'

Leach scribbled onto a pad of paper and tore off the sheet, handing it across the counter.

'Thanks, Bob.'

Leach was nodding towards the bag. Not only omnipresent, thought Rebus, but omniscrounging too. 'What else did you get apart from the whisky?'

Rebus bent towards him and hissed: 'Meat paste and snails!'

Bob Leach looked disheartened. 'Bloody French,' he said. 'You'd think he'd bring you something decent.'

* * *

Rebus didn't bother with back-street shortcuts as they drove towards the Royal Mile. He gave Cluzeau the full tour. But the French policeman seemed more interested in Rebus than in the streets of his city.

'I was here before,' he explained. 'Two years ago, for the rugby.'

'Do they play a lot of rugby down your way then?'

'Oh yes. It is not so much a game, more a love affair.'

Rebus assumed Cluzeau would be Parisian. He was not. Parisians, he said, were – his phrase – 'cold fish'. And in any case the city was not representative of the real France. The countryside – that was the real France, and especially the countryside of the south-west. Cluzeau was from Périgueux. He had been born there and now lived and worked there. He was married, with four children. And yes, he carried a family photo in his wallet. The wallet itself he carried inside a black leather pouch, almost like a clutch-purse. The pouch also contained identity documents, passport, chequebook, diary, a small English-French dictionary. No wonder he looked good in a suit: no bulges in the pockets, no wear on the material.

Rebus handed back the photograph.

'Very nice,' he said.

'And you, Inspector?'

So it was Rebus's turn to tell his tale. Born in Fife. Out of school and into the Army. Paras eventually and from there to the SAS. Breakdown and recovery. Then the police. Wife, now ex-wife, and one daughter living with her mother in London. Cluzeau, Rebus realised, had a canny way of asking questions, making them sound more like statements. So that instead of answering, you were merely acknowledging what he already seemed to know. He'd remember that for future use.

'And now we are going where?'

'The High Street. You might know it better as the Royal Mile.'

'I've walked along it, yes. You say separated, not divorced?'

'That's right.'

'Then there is a chance …?'

'What? Of us getting back together? No, no chance of that.'

This elicited another huge shrug from Cluzeau. 'It was another man …?'

'No, just *this* man.'

'Ah. In my part of France we have many crimes of passion. And here in Edinburgh?'

Rebus gave a wry grin. 'Where there's no passion …'

The Frenchman seemed to make hard work of understanding this.

'French policemen carry guns, don't they?' Rebus asked, filling the silence.

'Not on vacation.'

'I'm glad to hear it.'

'Yes, we have guns. But it is not like in America. We have respect for guns. They are a way of life in the country. Every Frenchman is a hunter at heart.'

Rebus signalled, and drew in to the roadside. 'Scotsmen, too,' he said, opening his door. 'And right now I'm going to hunt down a sandwich. This cafe does the best boiled ham in Edinburgh.'

Cluzeau looked dubious. 'The famous Scottish cuisine,' he murmured, unfastening his seatbelt.

They ate as they drove – ham for Rebus, salami for Cluzeau – and soon enough arrived outside the Heggarty Gallery. In fact, they arrived outside a wools and knitwear shop, which occupied the street-level. The gallery itself was up a winding stairwell, the steps worn and treacherous. They walked in through an unprepossessing door and found themselves in the midst of an argument. Fifteen or so women were crowded around Detective Constable Brian Holmes.

'You can't keep us here, you know!'

'Look, ladies –'

'Patronising pig.'

'Look, I need to get names and addresses first.'

'Well, go on then, what are you waiting for?'

'Bloody cheek, like we're criminals or something.'

'Maybe he wants to strip-search us.'

'Chance would be a fine thing.' There was some laughter at this.

Holmes had caught sight of Rebus and the look of relief on his face told Rebus all he needed to know. On a trellis table against one wall stood a couple of dozen wine bottles, mostly empty, and jugs of orange juice and water, mostly still full. Cluzeau lifted a bottle and wrinkled his nose. He sniffed the neck and the nose wrinkled even further.

The poster on the gallery door had announced an exhibition of paintings and sculpture by Serena Davies. The exhibition was entitled 'Hard Knox' and today was its opening. By the look of the drinks table, a preview had been taking place. Free wine all round, glasses replenished. And now a squabble, which might be about to turn ugly.

Rebus filled his lungs. 'Excuse me!' he cried. The faces turned from Brian Holmes and settled on him. 'I'm Inspector Rebus. Now, with a bit of luck we'll have you all out of here in five minutes. Please bear with us until then. I notice there's still some drink left. If you'll fill your glasses and maybe have a last look round, by the time you finish you should be able to leave. Now, I just need a word with my colleague.'

Gratefully, Holmes squeezed his way out of the scrum and came towards Rebus.

'You've got thirty seconds to fill me in,' Rebus said.

Holmes took a couple of deep breaths. 'A sculpture in bronze, male figure. It was sitting in the middle of one of the rooms. Preview opens. Somebody starts yelling that it's disappeared. The artist goes up the wall. She won't let anybody in or out, because if somebody's nicked it, that somebody's still in the gallery.'

'And that's the state of play? Nobody in or out since it went missing?'

Holmes nodded. 'Of course, as I tried telling her, they could have high-tailed it *before* she barricaded everyone else in.' Holmes was looking at the man who had come to stand beside Rebus. 'Can we help you, sir?'

'Oh,' said Rebus. 'You haven't been introduced. This is …' But no, he still couldn't make himself say the name. Instead, he nodded towards Holmes. 'This is Detective Constable Holmes.' Then, as Cluzeau shook hands with Holmes: 'The inspector here has come over from France to see how we do things in Edinburgh.' Rebus turned to Cluzeau. 'Did you catch what Brian was saying? Only I know his accent's a bit thick.'

'I understood perfectly.' He turned to Holmes. 'Inspector Rebus forgot to say, but my name is Cluzeau.' Somehow it didn't sound so funny when spoken by a native. 'How big is the statue? Do we know what it looks like?'

'There's a picture of it in the catalogue.' Holmes took the small glossy booklet from his pocket and handed it to Cluzeau. 'That's it at the top of the page.'

While Cluzeau studied this, Holmes caught Rebus's eye, then nodded down to the Frenchman's pouch.

'Nice handbag.'

Rebus gave him a warning look, then glanced at the catalogue. His eyes opened wide. 'Good Christ!'

Cluzeau read from the catalogue. ' "Monstrous Trumpet. Bronze and multi-media. Sixteen −" what do these marks mean?'

'Inches.'

'Thank you. "Sixteen inches. Three thousand five hundred pounds." *C'est cher*. It's expensive.'

'I'll say,' said Rebus. 'You could buy a car for that.' Well, he thought, you could certainly buy *my* car for that.

'It is an interesting piece, don't you think?'

'Interesting?' Rebus studied the small photograph of the statue called 'Monstrous Trumpet'. A nude male, his face exaggeratedly spiteful, was sticking out his tongue, except that it wasn't a tongue, it was a penis. And where that particular organ should have been, there was what looked like a piece of sticking-plaster. Because of the angle of the photo, it was just possible to discern something protruding from the statue's backside. Rebus guessed it was meant to be a tongue.

'Yes,' said Cluzeau, 'I should very much like to meet the artist.'

'Doesn't look as though you've got any choice,' said Holmes, seeming to retreat though in fact he didn't move. 'Here she comes.'

She had just come into the room, of that Rebus was certain. If she'd been there before, he'd have noticed her. And even if he hadn't Cluzeau certainly would have. She was just over six feet tall, dressed in long flowing white skirt, black boots, puffy white blouse and a red satin waistcoat. Her eye-makeup was jet black, matching her long straight hair, and her wrists fairly jangled with bangles and bracelets. She addressed Holmes.

'No sign of it. I've had a thorough look.' She turned towards Rebus and Cluzeau. Holmes started making the introductions.

'This is Inspector Rebus, and Inspector Cl ...' he stumbled to a halt. Yes, thought Rebus, it's a problem, isn't it, Brian? But Cluzeau appeared not to have noticed. He was squeezing Serena Davies' hand.

'Pleased to meet you.'

She looked him up and down without embarrassment, gave a cool smile, and passed to Rebus. 'Well, thank goodness the grown-ups are here at last.' Brian Holmes reddened furiously. 'I hope we didn't interrupt your lunch, Inspector. Come on, I'll show you where the piece was.'

And with that she turned and left. Some of the women offered either condolences over her loss, or else praise for what works remained, and Serena Davies gave a weak smile, a smile which said: I'm coping, but don't ask me how.

Rebus touched Holmes' shoulder. 'Get the names and addresses, eh, Brian?' He made to follow the artist, but couldn't resist a parting shot. 'You've got your crayons with you, have you?'

'And my marbles,' Holmes retorted. By God, thought Rebus, he's learning fast. But then, he had a good teacher, hadn't he?

'Magnificent creature,' Cluzeau hissed into his ear as they passed through the room. A few of the women glanced towards the Frenchman. I'm making him look too good, Rebus thought. Pity I had to be wearing this old suit today.

The small galleries through which they passed comprised a maze, an artful configuration of angles and doorways which made more of the space than there actually was. As to the works on display, well, Rebus couldn't be sure, of course, but there seemed an awful lot of violence in them, violence acted out upon a particular part of the masculine anatomy. Even the Frenchman was quiet as they passed red splashes of colour, twisted statues, great dollops of paint. There was one apparent calm centre, an extremely large and detailed drawing of the vulva. Cluzeau paused for a moment.

'I like this,' he said. Rebus nodded towards a red circular sticker attached to the wall beside the portrait.

'Already sold.'

Cluzeau tapped the relevant page of the catalogue. 'Yes, for one thousand five hundred pounds.'

'In here!' the artist's voice commanded. 'When you've stopped gawping.' She was in the next room of the gallery, standing by the now empty pedestal. The sign beneath it showed no red blob. No sale. 'It was right here.' The room was about fifteen feet by ten, in the corner of the gallery: only one doorway and no windows. Rebus looked up at the ceiling, but saw only strip lighting. No trapdoors.

'And there were people in here when it happened?'

Serena Davies nodded. 'Three or four of the guests. Ginny Elyot, Margaret Grieve, Helena Mitchison and I think Lesley Jameson.'

'Jameson?' Rebus knew two Jamesons in Edinburgh, one a doctor and the other ...

'Tom Jameson's daughter,' the artist concluded.

The other a newspaper editor called Tom Jameson. 'And who was it raised the alarm?' Rebus asked.

'That was Ginny. She came out of the room shouting that the statue had vanished. We all rushed into the room. Sure enough.' She slapped a hand down on the pedestal.

'Time, then,' Rebus mused, 'for someone to sneak away while everyone else was occupied?'

But the artist shook her mane of hair. 'I've already told you, there's nobody missing. Everyone who was here *is* here. In fact, I think there are a couple more bodies now than there were at the time.'

'Oh?'

'Moira Fowler was late. As usual. She arrived a couple of minutes after I'd barred the door.'

'You let her in?'

'Of course. I wasn't worried about letting people *in*.'

'You said "a couple of bodies"?'

'That's right. Maureen Beck was in the loo. Bladder trouble, poor thing. Maybe I should have hung a couple of paintings in there.'

Cluzeau frowned at this. Rebus decided to help him. 'The toilets being where exactly?'

'Next flight up. A complete pain really. The gallery

shares them with the shop downstairs. Crammed full of cardboard boxes and knitting patterns.'

Rebus nodded. The Frenchman coughed, preparing to speak. 'So,' he said, 'you have to leave the gallery actually to use the ... loo?'

Serena Davies nodded. 'You're French,' she stated. Cluzeau gave a little bow. 'I should have guessed from the *pochette*. You'd never find a Scotsman carrying one of those.'

Cluzeau seemed prepared for this point. 'But the sporran serves the same purpose.'

'I suppose it does,' the artist admitted, 'but its primary function is as a signifier.' She looked to both men. Both men looked puzzled. 'It's hairy and it hangs around your groin,' she explained.

Rebus stayed silent, but pursed his lips. Cluzeau nodded to himself, frowning.

'Maybe,' said Rebus, 'you could explain your exhibition to us, *Ms* Davies?'

'Well, it's a comment on Knox of course.'

'Knocks?' asked Cluzeau.

'John Knox,' Rebus explained. 'We passed by his old house a little way back.'

'John Knox,' she went on, principally for the Frenchman's benefit, but perhaps too, she thought, for that of the Scotsman, 'was a Scottish preacher, a follower of Calvin. He was also a misogynist, hence the title of one of his works – *The First Blast of the Trumpet Against the Monstrous Regiment of Women*.'

'He didn't mean all women,' Rebus felt obliged to add. Serena Davies straightened her spine like a snake rising up before its kill.

'But he did,' she said, 'by association. And, also by association, these works are a comment on *all* Scotsmen. And all men.'

Cluzeau could feel an argument beginning. Arguments,

to his knowledge, were always counter-productive even when enjoyable. 'I think I see,' he said. 'And your exhibition responds to this man's work. Yes.' He tapped the catalogue. ' "Monstrous Trumpet" is a pun then?'

Serena Davies shrugged, but seemed pacified. 'You could call it that. I'm saying that Knox talked with one part of his anatomy – *not* his brain.'

'And,' added Rebus, 'that at the same time he talked out of his arse?'

'Yes,' she said.

Cluzeau was chuckling. He was still chuckling when he asked: 'And who could have reason for stealing your work?'

The mane rippled again. 'I've absolutely no idea.'

'But you suspect one of your guests,' Cluzeau continued. 'Of course you do: you have already stated that there was no one else here. You were among friends, yet one of them is the Janus figure, yes?'

She nodded slowly. 'Much as I hate to admit it.'

Rebus had taken the catalogue from Cluzeau and seemed to be studying it. But he'd listened to every word. He tapped the missing statue's photo.

'Do you work from life?'

'Mostly, yes, but not for "Monstrous Trumpet".'

'It's a sort of … ideal figure then?'

She smiled at this. 'Hardly ideal, Inspector. But in that it comes from up here –' she tapped her head, 'from an idea rather than from life, yes, I suppose it is.'

'Does that go for the face, too?' Rebus persisted. 'It seems so lifelike.'

She accepted the compliment, studying the photo with him. 'It's not any one man's face,' she said. 'At most it's a composite of men I know.' Then she shrugged. 'Maybe.'

Rebus handed the catalogue to Cluzeau. 'Did you search anyone?' he asked the artist.

'I asked them to open their bags. Not very subtle of me, but I was – *am* – distraught.'

'And did they?'

'Oh yes. Pointless really, there were only two or three bags big enough to hide the statue in.'

'But they were empty?'

She sighed, pinching the bridge of her nose between two fingers. The bracelets were shunted from wrist to elbow. 'Utterly empty,' she said. 'Just as I feel.'

'Was the piece insured?'

She shook her head again, her forehead lowered. A portrait of dejection, Rebus thought. Lifelike, yet not quite real. He noticed too that, now her eyes were averted, the Frenchman was appraising her. He caught Rebus watching him and raised his eyebrows, then shrugged, then made a gesture with his hands. Yes, thought Rebus, I know what you mean. Only don't let *her* catch you thinking what I know you're thinking.

And, he supposed, what he was thinking too.

'I think we'd better go through,' he said. 'The other women will be getting impatient.'

'Let them!' she cried.

'Actually,' said Rebus, 'perhaps you could go ahead of us? Warn them that we may be keeping them a bit longer than we thought.'

She brightened at the news, then sneered. 'You mean you want me to do your dirty work for you?'

Rebus shrugged innocently. 'I just wanted a moment to discuss the case with my colleague.'

'Oh,' she said. Then nodded: 'Yes, of course. Discuss away. I'll tell them they've to stay put.'

'Thank you,' said Rebus, but she'd already left the room.

Cluzeau whistled silently. 'What a creature!'

It was meant as praise, of course, and Rebus nodded assent. 'So what do you think?'

'Think?'

'About the theft.'

'Ah.' Cluzeau scraped at his chin with his fingers. 'A crime of passion,' he said at last and with confidence.

'How do you work that out?'

Cluzeau gave another of his shrugs. 'The process of elimination. We eliminate money: there are more expensive pieces here and besides, a common thief would burgle the premises when they were empty, no?'

Rebus nodded, enjoying this, so like his own train of thought was it. 'Go on.'

'I do not think this piece is so precious that a collector would have it stolen. It is not insured, so there is no reason for the artist herself to have it stolen. It seems logical that someone invited to the exhibition stole it. So we come to the figure of the Janus. Someone the artist herself knows. Why should such a person – a supposed friend – steal this work?' He paused before answering his own question. 'Jealousy. Revenge, *et voilà*, the crime of passion.'

Rebus applauded silently. 'Bravo. But there are thirty-odd suspects out there and no sign of the statue.'

'Ah, I did not say I could solve the crime; all I offer is the "why".'

'Then follow me,' Rebus said, 'and we'll encounter the "who" and the "how" together.'

In the main gallery, Serena Davies was in furious conversation with one knot of women. Brian Holmes was trying to take names and addresses from another group. A third group stood, bored and disconsolate, by the drinks table, and a fourth group stood beside a bright red gash of a painting, glancing at it from time to time and talking among themselves.

Most of the women in the room either carried clutch-purses tucked safely under their arms, or else let neat shoulder-bags swing effortlessly by their sides. But there were a few larger bags and these had been left in a group of their own between the drinks table and another smaller table on which sat a small pile of catalogues and a visitors' book. Rebus walked across to this spot and studied the bags. There was one large straw shopping-bag, apparently containing only a cashmere cardigan and a folded copy of the *Guardian*. There was one department store plastic carrier-bag, containing an umbrella, a bunch of bananas, a fat paperback and a copy of the *Guardian*. There was one canvas shopping-bag, containing an empty crisp packet, a copy of the *Scotsman* and a copy of the *Guardian*.

All this Rebus could see just by standing over the bags. He reached down and picked up the carrier-bag.

'Can I ask whose bag this is?' he said loudly.

'It's mine.'

A young woman stepped forward from the drinks table, starting to blush furiously.

'Follow me, please,' said Rebus, walking off to the next room along. Cluzeau followed and so, seconds later, did the owner of the bag, her eyes terrified.

'Just a couple of questions, that's all,' Rebus said, trying to put her at ease. The main gallery was hushed; he knew people would be straining to hear the conversation. Brian Holmes was repeating an address to himself as he jotted it down.

Rebus felt a little bit like an executioner, walking up to the bags, picking them up in turn and wandering off with the owner towards the awaiting guillotine. The owner of the carrier-bag was Trish Poole, wife of a psychology lecturer at the university. Rebus had met Dr Poole before, and told her so, trying to help her relax a little. It turned out that a lot of the women present today were either academics in their own right, or else were the wives of academics. This latter group included not only Trish Poole, but also Rebecca Eiser, wife of the distinguished Professor of English Literature. Listening to Trish Poole tell him this, Rebus shivered and could feel his face turn pale. But that had been a long time ago.

After Trish Poole had returned for a whispered confab

with her group, Rebus tried the canvas bag. This belonged to Margaret Grieve, a writer and, as she said herself, 'one of Serena's closest friends'. Rebus didn't doubt this, and asked if she was married. No, she was not, but she did have a 'significant other'. She smiled broadly as she said this. Rebus smiled back. She'd been in the room with the statue when it was noticed to be missing? Yes, she had. Not that she'd seen anything. She'd been intent on the paintings. So much so that she couldn't be sure whether the statue had been in the room when she'd entered, or whether it had already gone. She thought perhaps it had already gone.

Dismissed by Rebus, she returned to her group in front of the red gash and they too began whispering. An elegant older woman came forward from the same group.

'The last bag is mine,' she said haughtily, her vowels pure Morningside. Perhaps she'd been Jean Brodie's elocution mistress; but no, she wasn't even quite Maggie Smith's age, though to Rebus there were similarities enough between the two women.

Cluzeau seemed quietly cowed by this grand example of Scottish womanhood. He stood at a distance, giving her vowels the necessary room in which to perform. And, Rebus noticed, he clutched his pouch close to his groin, as though it were a lucky charm. Maybe that's what sporrans were?

'I'm Maureen Beck,' she informed them loudly. There would be no hiding *this* conversation from the waggling ears.

Maureen Beck told Rebus that she was married to the architect Robert Beck and seemed surprised when this name meant nothing to the policeman. She decided then that she disliked Rebus and turned to Cluzeau, answering to his smiling countenance every time Rebus asked her a question. She was in the loo at the time, yes, and returned to pandemonium. She'd only been out of the room a couple of minutes, and hadn't seen anyone …

'Not even *Ms* Fowler?' Rebus asked. 'I believe she was late to arrive?'

'Yes, but that was a minute or two *after* I came back in.'

Rebus nodded thoughtfully. There was a teasing piece of ham wedged between two of his back teeth and he pushed it with his tongue. A woman put her head around the partition.

'Look, Inspector, some of us have got appointments this afternoon. Isn't there at least a telephone we can use?'

It was a good point. Who was in charge of the gallery itself? The gallery director, it turned out, was a timid little woman who had burrowed into the quietest of the groups. She was only running the place for the real owner, who was on a well-deserved holiday in Paris. (Cluzeau rolled his eyes at this. 'No one,' he said with a shudder, 'deserves such torture.') There was a cramped office, and in it an old bakelite telephone. If the women could leave twenty pence for each call. A line started to form outside the office. ('Ah, how you love queuing!') Mrs Beck, meantime, had returned to her group. Rebus followed her, and was introduced to Ginny Elyot, who had raised the alarm, and to Moira Fowler the latecomer.

Ginny Elyot kept patting her short auburn hair as though searching it for misplaced artworks. A nervous habit, Rebus reasoned. Cluzeau quickly became the centre of attention, with even the distant and unpunctual Moira becoming involved in the interrogation. Rebus sidled away and touched Brian Holmes' arm.

'That's all the addresses noted, sir.'

'Well done, Brian. Look, slip upstairs, will you? Give the loo a recce.'

'What am I looking for exactly – suspiciously shaped bundles of four-ply?'

Rebus actually laughed. 'We should be so lucky. But yes, you never know what you might find. And check any windows, too. There might be a drainpipe.'

'Okay.'

As Holmes left, a small hand touched Rebus's arm. A girl in her late-teens, eyes gleaming behind studious spectacles, jerked her head towards the gallery's first partitioned room. Rebus followed her. She was so small, and spoke so quietly, he actually had to grasp hands to knees and bend forward to listen.

'I want the story.'

'Pardon?'

'I want the story for my dad's paper.'

Rebus looked at her. His voice too was a dramatic whisper. 'You're Lesley Jameson?'

She nodded.

'I see. Well, as far as I'm concerned the story's yours. But we haven't *got* a story yet.'

She looked around her, then dropped her voice even lower. 'You've seen her.'

'Who?'

'Serena, of course. She's ravishing, isn't she?' Rebus tried to look non-committal. 'She's terribly attractive to men.' This time he attempted a Gallic shrug. He wondered if it looked as stupid as it felt. Her voice died away almost completely, reducing Rebus to lip-reading. 'She has loads of men after her. Including Margaret's.'

'Ah,' said Rebus, 'right.' He nodded, too. So Margaret Grieve's boyfriend was ...

The lips made more movements: 'He's Serena's lover.'

Yes, well, now things began to make more sense. Maybe the Frenchman was right: a crime of passion. The one thing missing thus far had been the passion itself; but no longer. And it was curious, when he came to think of it, how Margaret Grieve had said she couldn't recall whether the statue had been in the room or not. It wasn't the sort of thing you could miss, was it? Not for a bunch of samey paintings of pink bulges and grey curving masses. The newspapers in her bag would have concealed the statue quite nicely, too. There was just one problem.

Cluzeau's head appeared around the partition. 'Ah! Here you are. I'm sorry if I interrupt –'

But Lesley Jameson was already making for the main room. Cluzeau watched her go, then turned to Rebus.

'Charming women.' He sighed. 'But all of them either married or else with lovers. And one of them, of course, is the thief.'

'Oh?' Rebus sounded surprised. 'You mean one of the women you've just been talking with?'

'Of course.' Now he, too, lowered his voice. 'The statue left the gallery in a bag. You could not simply hide it under your dress, could you? But I don't think a plastic bag would have been strong enough for this task. So, we have a choice between Madame Beck and Mademoiselle Grieve.'

'Grieve's boyfriend has been carrying on with our artist.'

Cluzeau digested this. But he too knew there was a problem. 'She did not leave the gallery. She was shut in with the others.'

Rebus nodded. 'So there has to have been an accomplice. I think I'd better have another word with Lesley Jameson.'

But Brian Holmes had appeared. He exhaled noisily. 'Thank Christ for that,' he said. 'For a minute there I thought you'd buggered off and left me.'

Rebus grinned. 'That might not have been such bad idea. How was the loo?'

'Well, I didn't find any solid evidence,' Holmes replied with a straight face. 'No skeins of wool tied to the plumbing and hanging out of the windows for a burglar to shimmy down.'

'But there is a window?'

'A small one in the cubicle itself. I stood on the seat and had a squint out. A two-storey drop to a sort of back yard, nothing in it but a rusting Renault Five and a skip full of cardboard boxes.'

'Go down and take a look at that skip.'

'I thought you might say that.'

'And take a look at the Renault,' ordered Cluzeau, his face set. 'I cannot believe a French car would rust. Perhaps you are mistaken and it is a Mini Cooper, no?'

Holmes, who prided himself on knowing a bit about cars, was ready to argue, then saw the smile spread across the Frenchman's face. He smiled, too.

'Just as well you've got a sense of humour,' he said. 'You'll need it after the match on Saturday.'

'And you will need your Scottish stoicism.'

'Save it for the half-time entertainment, eh?' said Rebus, but with good enough humour. 'The sooner we get this wrapped up, the more time we'll have left for sightseeing.'

Cluzeau seemed about to argue, but Rebus held up a hand. 'Believe me,' he said, 'you'll want to see these sights. Only the locals know the *very* best pubs in Edinburgh.'

Holmes went to investigate the skip and Rebus spoke in whispers with Lesley Jameson – when he wasn't fending off demands from the detainees. What had seemed to most of them something unusual and thrilling at first, a story to be repeated across the dining-table, had now become merely tiresome. Though they had asked to make phone calls, Rebus couldn't help overhearing some of those conversations. They weren't warning of a late arrival or cancelling an appointment: they were spreading the news.

'Look, Inspector, I'm really tired of being kept here.'

Rebus turned from Lesley Jameson to the talker. His voice lacked emotion. 'You're not being kept here.'

'What?'

'Who said you were? Only *Ms* Davies as I understand. You're free to leave whenever you want.'

There was hesitation at this. To leave and taste freedom again? Or to stay, so as not to miss anything? Muttered dialogues took place and eventually one or two of the guests did leave. They simply walked out, closing the door behind them.

'Does that mean we can go?'

Rebus nodded. Another woman left, then another, then a couple.

'I hope you're not thinking of kicking me out,' Lesley Jameson warned. She wanted desperately to be a journalist, and to do it the hard way, *sans* nepotism. Rebus shook his head.

'Just keep talking,' he said.

Cluzeau was in conversation with Serena Davies. When Rebus approached them, she was studying the Frenchman's strong-looking hands. Rebus waved his own nail-bitten paw around the gallery.

'Do you,' he asked, 'have any trouble getting people to pose for all these paintings?'

She shook her head. 'No, not really. It's funny you should ask, Monsieur Cluzeau was just saying –'

'Yes, I'll bet he was. But Monsieur Cluzeau –' testing the words, not finding them risible any more, 'has a wife and family.'

Serena Davies laughed; a deep growl which seemed to run all the way up and down the Frenchman's spine. At last, she let go his hand. 'I thought we were talking about modelling, Inspector.'

'We were,' said Rebus drily, 'but I'm not sure Mrs Cluzeau would see it like that …'

'Inspector …?' It was Maureen Beck. 'Everyone seems to be leaving. Do I take it we're free to go?'

Rebus was suddenly businesslike. 'No,' he said. 'I'd like you to stay behind a little longer.' He glanced towards the group – Ginny Elyot, Moira Fowler, Margaret Grieve –'all of you, please. This won't take long.'

'That's what my husband says,' commented Moira Fowler, raising a glass of water to her lips. She placed a tablet on her tongue and washed it down.

Rebus looked to Lesley Jameson, then winked. 'Fasten your seatbelt,' he told her. 'It's going to be a bumpy ride.'

The gallery was now fast emptying and Holmes, having battled against the tide on the stairwell, entered the room on unsteady legs, his eyes seeking out Rebus.

'Jeez!' he cried. 'I thought you'd decided to bugger off after all. What's up? Where's everyone going?'

'Anything in the skip?' But Holmes shrugged: nothing. 'I've sent everyone home,' Rebus explained.

'Everyone except us,' Maureen Beck said sniffily.

'Well,' said Rebus, facing the four women, 'that's because nobody but *you* knows anything about the statue.'

The women themselves said nothing at this, but Cluzeau gave a small gasp – perhaps to save them the trouble. Serena Davies, however, had replaced her growl with a lump of ice.

'You mean one of *them* stole my work?'

Rebus shook his head. 'No, that's not what I mean. One person couldn't have done it. There had to be an accomplice.' He nodded towards Moira Fowler. '*Ms* Fowler, why don't you take DC Holmes down to your car? He can carry the statue back upstairs.'

'Moira!' Another change of tone, this time from ice to fire. For a second, Rebus thought Serena Davies might be about to make a lunge at the thief. Perhaps Moira Fowler thought so too, for she moved without further prompting towards the door.

'Okay,' she said, 'if you like.'

Holmes watched her pass him on her way to the stairwell.

'Go on then, Brian,' ordered Rebus. Holmes seemed undecided. He knew he was going to miss the story. What's more, he didn't fancy lugging the bloody thing up a flight of stairs.

'*Vite!*' cried Rebus, another word of French suddenly coming back to him. Holmes moved on tired legs towards the door. Up the stairs, down the stairs, up the stairs. It would, he couldn't help thinking, make good training for the Scottish pack.

Serena Davies had put her hand to her brow. Clank-a-clank-clank went the bracelets. 'I can't believe it of Moira. Such treachery.'

'Hah!' This from Ginny Elyot, her eyes burning. 'Treachery? You're a good one to speak. Getting Jim to "model" for you. Neither of you telling her about it. What the hell do you think she thought when she found out?'

Jim being, as Rebus knew from Lesley, Moira Fowler's husband. He kept his eyes on Ginny.

'And you, too, *Ms* Elyot. How did you feel when you found out about ... David, is it?'

She nodded. Her hand went towards her hair again, but she caught herself, and gripped one hand in the other. 'Yes, David,' she said quietly. 'That statue's got David's eyes, his hair.' She wasn't looking at Rebus. He didn't feel she was even replying to his question.

She was remembering.

'And Gerry's nose and jawline. I'd recognise them anywhere.' This from Margaret Grieve, she of the significant other. 'But Gerry can't keep secrets, not from me.'

Maureen Beck, who had been nodding throughout, never taking her moist eyes off the artist, was next. Her husband too, Robert, the architect, had modelled for Serena Davies. On the quiet, of course. It had to be on the quiet: no knowing what passions might be aroused otherwise. Even in a city like Edinburgh, even in women as seemingly self-possessed and cool-headed as these. Perhaps it had all been very innocent. Perhaps.

'He's got Robert's figure,' Maureen Beck was saying. 'Down to the scar on his chest from that riding accident.'

A crime of passion, just as Cluzeau had predicted. And after Rebus telling him that there was no such thing as passion in the city. But there was; and there were secrets too. Locked within these paintings, fine so long as they were abstract, so long as they weren't modelled from life. But for all that 'Monstrous Trumpet' was, in Serena Davies' words, a 'composite', its creation still cut deep. For each of the four women, there was something recognisable there, something modelled from life, from husband or lover. Something which burned and humiliated.

Unable to stand the thought of public display, of visitors walking into the gallery and saying 'Good God, doesn't that statue look like ...?' Unable to face the thought of this, and of the ridicule (the detailed penis, the tongue, and that sticking-plaster) they had come together with a plan. A clumsy, almost unworkable plan, but the only plan they had.

The statue had gone into Margaret Grieve's roomy bag, at which point Ginny Elyot had raised the alarm – hysterically so, attracting all the guests towards that one room, unaware as they pressed forwards that they were passing Margaret Grieve discreetly moving the other way. The bag had been passed to Maureen Beck, who had then slipped upstairs to the toilet. She had opened the window and dropped the statue down into the skip, from where Moira Fowler had retrieved it, carrying it out to her own car. Beck had returned, to find Serena Davies stopping people from leaving; a minute or two later, Moira Fowler had arrived.

She now walked in, followed by a red-faced Holmes, the statue cradled in his arms. Serena Davies, however, appeared not to notice. She had her eyes trained on the parquet floor and, again, she was being studied by Cluzeau. 'What a creature,' he had said of her. What a creature indeed. The four thieves would certainly be in accord in calling her 'creature'.

Who knows, thought Rebus, they might even be in *bon accord*.

* * *

251

The artist was neither temperamental nor stupid enough to insist on pressing charges and she bent to Rebus's suggestion that the piece be withdrawn from the show. The pressure thereafter was on Lesley Jameson not to release the story to her father's paper. Female solidarity won in the end, but it was a narrow victory.

Not much female solidarity elsewhere, thought Rebus. He made up a few mock headlines, the sort that would have pleased Doctor Curt. Feminist Artist's Roll Models; Serena's Harem of Husbands; The Anti-Knox Knocking Shop. All as he sat squeezed into a corner of the Sutherland Bar. Somewhere along the route, Cluzeau – now insisting that Rebus call him Jean-Pierre – had found half a dozen French fans, in town for the rugby and already in their cups. Then a couple of the Scottish fans had tagged along too and now there were about a dozen of them, standing at the bar and singing French rugby songs. Any minute now someone would tip an ice-bucket onto their head. He prayed it wouldn't be Brian Holmes, who, shirt-tail out and tie hanging loose, was singing as lustily as anyone, despite the language barrier – or even, perhaps, because of it.

Childish, of course. But then that was men for you. Simple pleasures and simple crimes. Male revenge was simple almost to the point of being infantile: you went up to the bastard and you stuck your fist into his face or kneed him in the nuts. But the revenge of the female. Ah, that was recondite stuff. He wondered if it was finished now, or would Serena Davies face more plots, plots more subtle, or better executed, or more savage? He didn't really want to think about it. Didn't want to think about the hate in the four women's voices, or the gleam in their eyes. He drank to forget. That was why men joined the Foreign Legion too, wasn't it? To forget. Or was it?

He was buggered if he could remember. But something else niggled too. The women had laid claim to a lover's jawline, a husband's figure. But whose, he couldn't help wondering, was the penis?

Someone was tugging at his arm, pulling him up. The glasses flew from the table and suddenly he was being hugged by Jean-Pierre.

'John, my friend, John, tell me who this man Peter Zealous is that everyone is talking to me about?'

'It's Sellars,' Rebus corrected. To tell or not to tell? He opened his mouth. There was the machine-gun sound of things spilling onto the bar behind him. Small, solid things. Next thing he knew, it was dark and his head was very cold and very wet.

'I'll get you for this, Brian,' he said, removing the ice-bucket from his head. 'So help me I will.'

AUTHOR'S NOTE

There *are* Cluzeaus in and around Périgueux. Lots of them, and all spelt like that. You can find them in the Dordogne phone book. I did.

I.R.

If you've enjoyed

A GOOD HANGING

here's a taster of the first Inspector Rebus novel.

KNOTS & CROSSES

Available in Orion paperback
ISBN: 0 75280 942 3
Price: £6.99

Prologue

1

The girl screamed once, only the once.

Even that, however, was a minor slip on his part. That might have been the end of everything, almost before it had begun. Neighbours inquisitive, the police called in to investigate. No, that would not do at all. Next time he would tie the gag a little tighter, just a little tighter, just that little bit more secure.

Afterwards, he went to the drawer and took from it a ball of string. He used a pair of sharp nail-scissors, the kind girls always seem to use, to snip off a length of about six inches, then he put the ball of string and the scissors back into the drawer. A car revved up outside, and he went to the window, upsetting a pile of books on the floor as he did so. The car, however, had vanished, and he smiled to himself. He tied a knot in the string, not any special kind of knot, just a knot. There was an envelope lying ready on the sideboard.

2

It was 28th April. Wet, naturally, the grass percolating water as John Rebus walked to the grave of his father, dead five years to the day. He placed a wreath so that it lay, yellow and red, the colours of remembrance, against the still shining marble. He paused for a moment, trying to think of things to say, but there seemed nothing to say, nothing to think. He had been a good enough father and that was that. The old man wouldn't have wanted him to waste his words in any case. So he stood there, hands respectfully behind his back, crows laughing on the walls around him, until the water seeping into his shoes told him that there was a warm car waiting for him at the cemetery gates.

He drove quietly, hating to be back here in Fife, back where the old days had never been 'good old days,' where ghosts rustled in the shells of empty houses and the shutters went up every evening on a handful of desultory shops, those metal shutters that gave the vandals somewhere to write their names. How Rebus hated it all, this singular lack of an environment. It stank the way it had always done: of misuse, of disuse, of the sheer wastage of life.

He drove the eight miles towards the open sea, to where his brother Michael still lived. The rain eased off as he approached the skull-grey coast, the car throwing up splashings of water from a thousand crevasses in the road. Why was it, he wondered, that they never seemed to fix the roads here, while in Edinburgh they worked on the surfaces so often that things were made even worse? And why, above all, had he made the maniacal decision to come all the way through to Fife, just because it was the anniversary of the old man's death? He tried to focus his mind on something else, and found himself fantasising about his next cigarette.

Through the rain, falling as drizzle now, Rebus saw a girl about his daughter's age walking along the grass verge. He slowed the car, examined her in his mirror as he passed her, and stopped. He motioned for her to come to his window.

Her short breaths were visible in the cool, still air, and her dark hair fell in rats-tails down her forehead. She looked at him apprehensively.

'Where are you going, love?'

'Kirkcaldy.'

'Do you want a lift?'

She shook her head, drops of water flying from her coiled hair.

'My mum said I should never accept lifts from strangers.'

'Well,' said Rebus, smiling, 'your mum is quite right. I've got a daughter about your age and I tell her the same thing. But it is raining, and I *am* a policeman, so you can trust me. You've still got a fair way to go, you know.'

She looked up and down the silent road, then shook her head again.

'Okay,' said Rebus, 'but take care. Your mum was quite right.'

He wound his window up again and drove off, watching her in his mirror as she watched him. Clever kid. It was good to know that parents still had a little sense of responsibility left. If only the same could be said of his ex-wife. The way she had brought up their daughter was a disgrace. Michael, too, had given his daughter too long a leash. Who was to blame?

Rebus's brother owned a respectable house. He had

4

followed in the old man's footsteps and become a stage hypnotist. He seemed to be quite good at it, too, from all accounts. Rebus had never asked Michael how it was done, just as he had never shown any interest or curiosity in the old man's act. He had observed that this still puzzled Michael, who would drop hints and red herrings as to the authenticity of his own stage act for him to chase up if he so wished.

But then John Rebus had too many things to chase up, and that had been the position during all of his fifteen years on the force. Fifteen years, and all he had to show were an amount of self-pity and a busted marriage with an innocent daughter hanging between them. It was more disgusting than sad. And meantime Michael was happily married with two kids and a larger house than Rebus could ever afford. He headlined at hotels, clubs, and even theatres as far away as Newcastle and Wick. Occasionally he would make six-hundred quid from a single show. Outrageous. He drove an expensive car, wore good clothes, and would never have been caught dead standing in the pissing rain in a graveyard in Fife on the dullest April day for many a year. No, Michael was too clever for that. And too stupid.

'John! Christ, what's up? I mean, it's great to see you. Why didn't you phone to warn me you were coming? Come on inside.'

It was the welcome Rebus had expected: embarrassed surprise, as though it were painful to be reminded that one still had some family left alive. And Rebus had noted the use of the word 'warn' where 'tell' would have sufficed. He was a policeman. He noticed such things.

Michael Rebus bounded through to the living-room and turned down the wailing stereo.

'Come on in, John,' he called. 'Do you want a drink? Coffee perhaps? Or something stronger? What brings you here?'

Rebus sat down as though he were in a stranger's house, his back straight and professional. He examined the panelled walls of the room – a new feature – and the framed photographs of his niece and nephew.

'I was just in the neighbourhood,' he said.

Michael, turning from the drinks cabinet with the glasses ready, suddenly remembered, or did a good impersonation of just having remembered.

'Oh, John, I forgot all about it. Why didn't you tell me? Shit, I hate forgetting about Dad.'

'Just as well you're a hypnotist then and not Mickey the Memory Man, isn't it? Give me that drink, or are you two getting engaged?'

Michael, smiling, absolved, handed over the glass of whisky.

'Is that your car outside?' asked Rebus, taking the glass. 'I mean the big BMW?'

Michael, still smiling, nodded.

'Christ,' said Rebus. 'You treat yourself well.'

'As well as I treat Chrissie and the kids. We're building an extension onto the back of the house. Somewhere to put a jacuzzi or a sauna. They're the in thing just now, and Chrissie's desperate to keep ahead of the field.'

Rebus took a swallow of whisky. It turned out to be a malt. Nothing in the room was cheap, but none of it was exactly desirable either. Glass ornaments, a crystal decanter on a silver salver, the TV and video, the inscrutably miniature hi-fi system, the onyx lamp. Rebus felt a little guilty about that lamp. Rhona and he had given it to Michael and Chrissie as a wedding present. Chrissie no longer spoke to him. Who could blame her?

'Where is Chrissie, by the way?'

'Oh, she's out doing some shopping. She has her own car

6

now. The kids will still be at school. She'll pick them up on the way home. Are you staying for something to eat?'

Rebus shrugged his shoulders.

'You'd be welcome to stay,' said Michael, meaning that Rebus wouldn't. 'So how's the cop-shop? Still muddling along?'

'We lose a few, but they don't get the publicity. We catch a few, and they do. It's the same as always, I suppose.'

The room, Rebus was noticing, smelled of toffee-apples, of penny arcades.

Michael was speaking:

'This is a terrible business about those girls being kidnapped.'

Rebus nodded.

'Yes,' he said, 'yes, it is. But we can't strictly call it kidnapping, not yet. There hasn't been a demand note or anything. It's more likely to be a straightforward case of sexual assault.'

Michael started up from his chair.

'Straightforward? What's straightforward about that?'

'It's just the terminology we use, Mickey, that's all.' Rebus shrugged again and finished his drink.

'Well, John,' said Michael, sitting, 'I mean, we've both got daughters, too. You're so casual about the whole thing. I mean, it's frightening to think of it.' He shook his head slowly in the world-wide expression of shared grief, and relief, too, that the horror was someone else's for the moment. 'It's frightening,' he repeated. 'And in Edinburgh of all places. I mean, you never think of that sort of thing happening in Edinburgh, do you?'

'There's more happening in Edinburgh than anyone knows.'

'Yes.' Michael paused. 'I was across there just last week playing at one of the hotels.'

7

'You didn't tell me.'

It was Michael's turn to shrug his shoulders.

'Would you have been interested?' he said.

'Maybe not,' said Rebus, smiling, 'but I would have come along anyway.'

Michael laughed. It was the laughter of birthdays, of money found in an old pocket.

'Another whisky, sir?' he said.

'I thought you were never going to ask.'

Rebus returned to his study of the room while Michael went to the cabinet.

'How's the act going?' he asked. 'And I really *am* interested.'

'It's going fine,' said Michael. 'In fact, it's going very well indeed. There's talk of a television spot, but I'll believe that when I see it.'

'Great.'

Another drink reached Rebus's willing hand.

'Yes, and I'm working on a new slot. It's a bit scary though.' An inch of gold flashed on Michael's wrist as he tipped the glass to his lips. The watch was expensive: it had no numbers on its face. It seemed to Rebus that the more expensive something was, the less of it there always seemed to be: tiny little hi-fi systems, watches without numbers, the translucent Dior ankle-socks on Michael's feet.

'Tell me about it,' he said, taking his brother's bait.

'Well,' said Michael, sitting forward in his chair, 'I take members of the audience back into their past lives.'

'Past lives?'

Rebus was staring at the floor as if admiring the design of the dark and light green carpet.

'Yes,' Michael continued, 'Reincarnation, born again, that sort of thing. Well, I shouldn't have to spell it out to you, John. After all, *you're* the Christian.'

'Christians don't believe in past lives, Mickey. Only future ones.'

Michael stared at Rebus, demanding silence.

'Sorry,' said Rebus.

'As I was saying, I tried the act out in public for the first time last week, though I've been practising it for a while with my private consultees.'

'Private consultees?'

'Yes. They pay me money for private hypnotherapy. I stop them smoking, or make them more confident, or stop them from wetting the bed. Some are convinced that they have past lives, and they ask me to put them under so that they can prove it. Don't worry though. Financially, it's all above board. The tax-man gets his cut.'

'And do you prove it? Do they have past lives?'

Michael rubbed a finger around the rim of his glass, now empty.

'You'd be surprised,' he said.

'Give me an example.'

Rebus was following the lines of the carpet with his eyes. Past lives, he thought to himself. Now there was a thing. There was plenty of life in *his* past.

'Well,' said Michael, 'remember I told you about my show in Edinburgh last week? Well,' he leaned further forward in his chair, 'I got this woman up from the audience. She was a small woman, middle-aged. She'd come in with an office-party. She went under pretty easily, probably because she hadn't been drinking as heavily as her friends. Once she was under, I told her that we were going to take a trip into her past, way, way back before she was born. I told her to think back to the earliest memory she had . . .'

Michael's voice had taken on a professional but easy mellifluence. He spread his hands before him as if playing to an audience. Rebus, nursing his glass, felt himself relax a

9

little. He thought back to a childhood episode, a game of football, one brother pitted against the other. The warm mud of a July shower, and their mother, her sleeves rolled up, stripping them both and putting them, giggling knots of arms and legs, into the bath . . .

'. . . well,' Michael was saying, 'she started to speak, and in a voice not quite her own. It was weird, John. I wish you *had* been there to see it. The audience were silent, and I was feeling all cold and then hot and then cold again, and it had nothing to do with the hotel's heating-system by the way. I'd done it, you see. I'd taken that woman into a past life. She was a nun. Do you believe that? A *nun*. And she said that she was alone in her cell. She described the convent and everything, and then she started to recite something in Latin, and some people in the audience actually *crossed* themselves. I was bloody well petrified. My hair was probably standing on end. I brought her out of it as quickly as I could, and there was a long pause before the crowd started to applaud. Then, maybe out of sheer relief, her friends started to cheer and laugh, and that broke the ice. At the end of the show, I found out that this woman was a staunch Protestant, a Rangers supporter no less, and she swore blind that she knew no Latin at all. Well, *somebody* inside her did. I'll tell you that.'

Rebus was smiling.

'It's a nice story, Mickey,' he said.

'It's the truth.' Michael opened his arms wide in supplication. 'Don't you believe me?'

'Maybe.'

Michael shook his head.

'You must make a pretty bad copper, John. I had around a hundred and fifty witnesses. Iron-clad.'

Rebus could not pull his attention away from the design in the carpet.

'Plenty of people believe in past lives, John.'

10

Past lives ... Yes, he believed in some things ... In God, certainly ... But past lives ... Without warning, a face screamed up at him from the carpet, trapped in its cell.

He dropped his glass.

'John? Is anything wrong? Christ, you look as if you've seen ...'

'No, no, nothing's the matter.' Rebus retrieved the glass and stood up. 'I just ... I'm fine. It's just that,' he checked his watch, a watch with numbers, 'well, I'd better be going. I'm on duty this evening.'

Michael was smiling weakly, glad that his brother was not going to stay, but embarrassed at his relief.

'We'll have to meet again soon,' he said, 'on neutral territory.'

'Yes,' said Rebus, tasting once again the tang of toffee-apples. He felt a little pale, a little shaky, as though he were too far out of his territory. 'Let's do that.'

Once or twice or three times a year, at weddings, funerals, or over the telephone at Christmas, they promised themselves this get-together. The mere promise now was a ritual in itself, and so could be safely proffered and just as safely ignored.

'Let's do that.'

Rebus shook hands with Michael at the door. Escaping past the BMW to his own car, he wondered how alike they were, his brother and him. Uncles and aunts in their funeral-cold rooms occasionally commented, 'Ah, you're both the spitting image of your mother.' That was as far as it went. John Rebus knew that his own hair was a shade of brown lighter than Michael's, and that his eyes were a shade of green darker. He knew also, however, that the differences between them were such that any similarities were made to look unutterably superficial. They were brothers without any sense of brother-hood. Brotherhood belonged to the past.

11

He waved once from the car and was gone. He would be back in Edinburgh within the hour, and on duty another half-hour after that. He knew that the reason he could never feel comfortable in Michael's house was Chrissie's hatred of him, her unshakeable belief that he alone had been responsible for the break-up of his marriage. Maybe she was right at that. He tried ticking off in his mind the definite chores of the next seven or eight hours. He had to tidy up a case of burglary and serious assault. A nasty one that. The CID was undermanned as it was, and now these abductions would stretch them even more. Those two young girls, girls his own daughter's age. It was best not to think about it. By now they would be dead, or would wish that they were dead. God have mercy on them. In Edinburgh of all places, in his own dear city.

A maniac was on the loose.

People were staying in their homes.

And a screaming in his memory.

Rebus shrugged, feeling a slight sensation of attrition in one of his shoulders. It was not his business after all. Not yet.

Back in his living-room, Michael Rebus poured himself another whisky. He went to the stereo and turned it all the way up, then reached underneath his chair and, after a little fumbling, pulled out an ashtray that was hidden there.

All Orion/Phoenix titles are available at your local bookshop or from the following address:

Mail Order Department
Littlehampton Book Services
FREEPOST BR535
Worthing, West Sussex, BN13 3BR
telephone 01903 828503, *facsimile* 01903 828802
e-mail MailOrders@lbsltd.co.uk
(Please ensure that you include full postal address details)

Payment can be made either by credit/debit card (Visa, Mastercard, Access and Switch accepted) or by sending a £ Sterling cheque or postal order made payable to *Littlehampton Book Services.*
DO NOT SEND CASH OR CURRENCY.

Please add the following to cover postage and packing

UK and BFPO:
£1.50 for the first book, and 50p for each additional book to a maximum of £3.50

Overseas and Eire:
£2.50 for the first book plus £1.00 for the second book and 50p for each additional book ordered

---

BLOCK CAPITALS PLEASE

name of cardholder _____

address of cardholder _____

delivery address
(if different from cardholder)
_____
_____
_____
_____

postcode _____   *postcode* _____

☐ I enclose my remittance for £_____

☐ please debit my Mastercard/Visa/Access/Switch (delete as appropriate)

card number ⬚⬚⬚⬚⬚⬚⬚⬚⬚⬚⬚⬚⬚⬚⬚⬚⬚⬚

expiry date ⬚⬚⬚⬚   Switch issue no. ⬚⬚

signature _____

prices and availability are subject to change without notice